# Gayle Greeno

# The Farthest Seeking

## Ghattens' Gambit #2

Will their
Seekers' quest
see them
caught in the
...struction
that has been
loosed in
Marchmont?

DAW
No. 1153

DAW
No. 1153

$7.99 U.S.
$10.99 CAN.

And don't miss *THE GHATTI'S TALE:*
Book One: FINDERS-SEEKERS
Book Two: MINDSPEAKERS' CALL
Book Three: EXILES' RETURN

Be sure to read
SUNDERLIES SEEKING,
the first novel in GAYLE
GREENO'S wonderful
new Ghatti series,
GHATTENS' GAMBIT.

ISBN 0-88677-897-2

9 780886 778972

50799

S EAN

## "YOU AREN'T *HIDING* SOMETHING DOWN HERE, ARE YOU?"

Somehow they all gave way before Romain-Laurent Charpentier's enthusiasm, parting to let him pass and view the trunk. "As I live and breathe! It's brushed al-alu-mini-um! I do believe it is! Remarkable! Those were the days! Don't see much of it now. What's within?" And suiting his actions to his words, Romain-Laurent heaved up the trunk lid without waiting for permission.

Ezequiel brusquely stoppered a cry of protest. Any sense of ceremony, anticipation had been destroyed. Hru'rul growled a low warning, forcing himself between Eadwin and the open trunk.

Wads of old paper greeted their eyes, while the aroma of oily rags assaulted their noses. Atop the paper and rags lay a note, a checklist of some sort.

While the others perused the list, Romain-Laurent rooted through the packing litter, giving a shout of triumph as he hauled forth a cylinder. "Five or six more, down deeper," he announced. "I can feel them, a souvenir for each of us."

"Charpentier, enough!" Eadwin frowned. "As near as I can make out, this handwritten scrawl at the bottom says, 'Detonate out of range immediately. Highly unstable!' "

# The Farthest Seeking

## BOOK TWO OF
## GHATTEN'S GAMBIT

# Gayle Greeno

# DAW BOOKS, INC.

**DONALD A. WOLLHEIM, FOUNDER**

375 Hudson Street, New York, NY 10014

**ELIZABETH R. WOLLHEIM**
**SHEILA E. GILBERT**
**PUBLISHERS**

www.dawbooks.com

First Printing, June 2000
2  3 .4  5  6  7  8  9

# PROLOGUE

With a sated groan Jenret Wycherley licked each finger, his tongue seeking out every last smear of chocolate icing. It made him look more the greedy little boy than the full-grown man, a man on the cusp of middle age, Doyce decided as she licked her own fingers somewhat more sedately. A final sucking sound, followed by a satisfied "Ah," made the two nearby ghatti momentarily lift sleepy heads.

**"The males of any species take such delight in small pleasures,"** noted Khar, wrinkling her muzzle and bunching her whiskers as she broke into a wide, pink yawn and resettled herself more comfortably against Rawn. Her tone indicated a certain indulgence, rather than condemnation, and Doyce tended to agree with her Bond's assessment. This whole haliday had been a delightful—and long overdue—indulgence. Not to mention a well-deserved one!

An errant lock of dark hair flopping onto his forehead, Jenret sighed pleasurably, a guilty grin stealing across his face. "Bless you, darling, for not lecturing about table manners. I *do* manage to exhibit them at most meals. It's just that . . ." A languid wave of his hand took in their surroundings: a sun-warmed dell like a dimple amongst low, rolling hills that gradually merged into sandy beaches, the smooth sand kissed and lapped by the gulf's waters. Tiny seabirds with long beaks and even longer legs skittered in and out of the foam, left pencil-lead tracks higher on the beach.

"I know. It's beautiful. And so peaceful. Utterly deserted except for the plovers and us." Doyce unknotted her sash and pulled off her sheepskin tabard, bunching it behind her as a pillow before leaning back, the crown of her head brushing Jenret's hip. His hand reached to cradle her face, a finger tracing her jawline as she rolled back her cuffs and unbuttoned the neck of her shirt, basking in the sun and in his nearness.

"See why I wanted to remove all traces of chocolate so thoroughly?"

Rawn, totally coal-black except for a faint white streak atop his head, half-rolled on his back, eyes slitted. **"It's a shame you humans never discovered the joys of mutual grooming."** As if to prove his point, he stretched until his nose touched the underside of Khar's jaw, his tongue flicking quickly. **"Ah . . . I knew it! A smudge of nutter-butter marring that tasty white perfection."** Khar broke into a contented purr.

"Blessed Lady, that's an idea!" Intent on retrieving a disregarded plate that held a lone eclair, Jenret strained backward, then surged up, prize in hand. "Want to try it?"

Despite the warning pinch at his thigh, Jenret brought the eclair closer, its chocolate runny, melting in the unseasonably-warm late afternoon sun. "If you don't want me to smear your face with chocolate and then lick it off, you'd best bribe me. A suitable bribe, one with commensurate value," he warned, brandishing the eclair.

Doyce began to crow with laughter, halfheartedly fending off the threatening eclair. And the more she thought about it, about her indecorous behavior, unseemly, even childish for a matron of fifty-six—wife, mother, and ex-Seeker General—the harder she laughed. It felt so utterly right to revel in such total release, as if she'd been transformed into a new person, all worries thrown aside these last blessed days.

But then, the little town of Haarls on the Gulf of Oord had begun to work its magic on her as soon as they'd arrived, as had the secluded inn run by Dolf Sartorius, a retired Seeker. After their voyage to the Sunderlies, she and Jenret had truly needed to get away, be alone together, except that it taken nearly a full year to accomplish the feat. Responsibilities—they both bore them in equal measure—and after their protracted absence in the Sunderlies, there had been pressing obligations to fulfill. As far as their obligations to each other, they'd stolen moments, occasional days here and there, but a protracted trip had been impossible until now. Not to mention that Khar had required a long recuperation to heal her grievous wounds. If

Rawn and Jenret hadn't rescued them, minds and bodies alike, certainly Khar—and mayhap herself, as well—would have died. Even the mere recollection of that brush with death left her numb inside, the sun no longer able to warm her.

Trying to cast aside the chill that had overwhelmed her, Doyce became all too aware of the eclair's intended trajectory and she grabbed for it, only to find her fingers sliding across the sticky icing as Jenret jerked his hand clear just in time. Pretending to pout, she stroked Khar's striped flank. Even in the midst of such happiness and peace, the fear seized her at unexpected moments—the pressing need to reassure herself that Khar still resided amongst the living. Both Khar and Rawn were so very old, fast-approaching the end of the ghatti's life span. How could they all have grown so old? And with such seeming suddenness. So many of her dear friends amongst the ghatti had seen the years catch up with them: Chak, Koom, Mem'now, P'wa, M'wa—all gone now. Saam and Parm were of an age with Rawn and Khar, even T'ss and Per'la were no longer young. Still, newer generations of ghatti had joined the ranks: Khim, offspring of Khar and Saam, and P'roul, offspring of Khar and Rawn. Not to mention those rascals Kwee and Pw'eek, who'd Bonded with the twins.

"**A bit selfish to want the past, the present, and the future all safely rolled into one. And if you smear chocolate in my fur, I shall not be pleased,**" Khar warned.

But Rawn perked up, eyes shrewdly tracking the hovering eclair. "**Shouldn't mind the custard, though. Would we, Khar? Jenret, old friend, squeeze the middle just a bit more till the custard oozes out.**"

Charmed and distracted by his Bondmate's plea, Jenret didn't notice Doyce's lightning-fast attack, belatedly realizing as her teeth snapped dangerously near his fingers and half the eclair vanished. "Damn! That was a little too close, sweetheart!"

Cheeks bulging as she chewed rapidly, Doyce attempted to radiate contrition as she mindspoke him. *"So much for childish pranks. Grow up, husband, dear. I much prefer my men to be mature and experienced, not callow youths."* Balancing on her elbow, she pulled his head down and planted a kiss on his lips.

*"Ooh, custard!"* he exclaimed as their lips met, momentarily distracted, eyeing the eclair's remains, its rich yellow filling hanging thick at the pastry's ragged edge.

*"Jenret!"* With a final, longing look, he passed it to Rawn, and the ghatt snagged the trophy with his claws to position it between him and Khar. *"It doesn't bode well for romance when the love of one's life suddenly prefers pastry to me!"*

"Oh, hush, woman!" he whispered against her lips, cradling her against his chest as he stared out to sea, at peace with himself and with her. "We've today and tomorrow left for romance. Or had you forgotten?" Letting his cheek rest against the top of her head, he sighed with mock-regret. "Besides, you're so bashful that you're convinced a whole army of clam diggers, fisherfolk, and beach walkers are poised to invade our privacy." He toyed with a button on her shirt. "I shan't embarrass you. Of course, mayhap we should pack our picnic things, return to the inn posthaste? I have a terrible urge for a nap . . . with the right partner."

It sounded tempting but required exertion, and she felt deliciously lazy, relishing the anticipation as much as the act of love itself. "It's just that I love the sun so much at this time of year. We'll see less and less of it as winter sets in in earnest. Bless the Lady for making it so unseasonably warm and sunny near the gulf! It's a reprieve of sorts, Jenner. More than perfect fall weather, autumn mingling with those final, glorious days of summer . . ." And then, without warning, her happiness fled, leaving her feeling like a traitor as anxiety welled in its stead, coldness overtaking her despite the nearness of her husband, her Bondmate. A cloud seemed to have blocked the sun that had shone in her mind. Leaning against his chest until she could study his face, Doyce hesitantly added, "Jenner . . . about those two days we have left. . . . Would you . . . could we start home tomorrow morning, instead?"

"Why?" He'd packed a wealth of queries into his one-word rejoinder, but she could sense him attuning himself to her mood, seriously considering her plea while he searched through the amorphous worries niggling at her brain. Nothing concrete, just a faint edginess, misgivings so insubstantial they were almost embarrassing. But he didn't laugh or attempt to cajole her as he might have done once, make her admit how flimsy her fears were. No, not now when she let him roam her mind without reservation, just as she did his.

"I . . . know." His gentian-blue eyes again gazed into the distance as if to pierce it, make it reveal what it hid. "I don't know what, but something's brewing, isn't it?"

**"You mean other than the snowstorm that's threatening up north?"** The remains of the eclair forgotten, Rawn sat alertly, craning his head skyward as if he could see or hear things that they could not. And indeed, he and Khar could. **"We *have* been keeping up on things, Khar and I, while you silly humans rolled up your pantaloon legs and went wading! Too cold for me!"**

"And what have you two been keeping track of, if I may ask?" Suddenly Doyce didn't feel in the mood for more ambiguities.

Khar looked faintly guilty. **"Other than the weather signs?"** Amber eyes downcast, she groomed a white fore-foot. **"A major snowstorm's brewing north of us. Storms always mean trouble."**

Trying not to hold her breath, Doyce asked carefully, "Nothing to do with the twins, I hope? Yours or ours." If Jenneth and Diccon had landed in trouble while she and Jenret were away, she didn't know what she'd do. They might be adjudged adults in the eyes of most of the world, but to her they were—and would always be—her babies.

Although he listened closely, Jenret continued staring off to sea. "I don't know if it's trouble, Doyce. But somehow it's . . . it's . . ." he groped for the words, the feelings, "sadness, loss, I think. Not danger so much as that." Running both hands through his hair as if it might liberate his brain, he added, "Is that what you're sensing?"

"I . . . I . . ." And now she was angry with herself for having overreacted, allowing her phantom fears to win, to destroy the last few days of their hard-won vacation together. "Don't mind my twitchiness, darling!" Catching him by surprise, she kissed him hard on the lips, letting a reck-less happiness blossom forth, surprising the man as he'd so often surprised her in the past. "We can stay even longer if we want! After all, we didn't guarantee exactly when we'd return. Gave them a date with the proviso 'Weather permitting,' didn't we?"

"Or 'Whether we feel like returning right then'?" Her new mood contagious, Jenret kissed her back, though she noted the faint puzzlement lingering in his blue eyes. Reluctantly she broke from his embrace, began neatly packing plates and bottles and cutlery into the willow-weave basket. "Dark still falls too early these days, Jenner. Now about that nap you mentioned . . . ?"

Gathering and shaking the blanket, he began to fold it into a precise square. "Definitely! And we should hurry while Dolf's still stocking the bar for the evening trade, too busy to chat. You know how lonely it is for him since Ph'raux passed away—having Seekers around makes him happy. Best he remember, though, how much people our age need our rest!"

# PART ONE

The winter wind blustered, whooping down the chimney, startling the fading fire, flames rising and dancing. The frantic, snapping brightness and the storm's gusting protest brought Mahafny Annendahl back to herself, and she slumped clear of the oil lamp's golden halo, more weary than she'd realized. Either it was far later than she'd anticipated, or she'd have to admit that the years had caught up with her. Was Harrap still up? Pottering around downstairs in his study, or saying his prayers?

An abiding satisfaction in that, that Harrap, Shepherd and Seeker both, had become a part of her life, sharing this snug cottage with her. Not that the sharing had come easily, not given her certitude that her ways were always superior, the product of the stringent logic of an incisive mind, but she'd gradually learned to yield on occasion, sometimes grudgingly, sometimes graciously. Neither she nor Harrap were young in years, though she was the elder of the two. Though she'd been loath to admit it, they needed each other's companionship and assistance. For too long now her hands had been near-useless, fingers twisted and deformed as the arthritis implacably claimed each knuckle and joint. It had effectively destroyed her career as a practicing eumedico, unable to manage the hands-on skills her patients needed. Oh, she'd had her teaching to fall back on, training budding eumedicos, but it wasn't the same. Even that had lost its savor, and she did less and less of it, retreating to her cottage and Harrap's company, attempting to lose herself in her genealogical research.

Another gust of wind shook the cottage, and the chimney shrieked as if in dire fear of the storm. This time sparks flew up from the fireplace, drifting beyond the fieldstone apron to settle on the carpet, and Mahafny hastily aban-

doned her desk to stamp them out. How much longer
would she work tonight? Long enough to make it worthwhile to rebuild the fire? Debating with herself, she fumbled in the woodbox, locating some smaller pieces of pine
and a good, solid piece of oak. The heavy chunk of oak
was nearly too much for her crippled hands, and she just
missed dropping it on her toe, grunting with effort and with
pain. Squatting in front of the fire, she bathed her mis-
shapen fingers in its warmth, watching the wash of color
the flames added to her pale skin, rejoicing in the warmth
on her face, on her aching knees. Finally, using the poker
as a cane, she rose and dragged the screen in front of the
fireplace to foil any further errant sparks.

Well, she could either muse the rest of the night away
or work some more. Strange how her body required less
sleep, the older she grew. Occasional catnaps during the
day sufficed to replace much of an evening's missed sleep.
Catnaps—the word amused her, and with good reason as
she gave a fond look at the large, steel-blue cat napping
on an easy chair pulled beside her cherrywood desk. Except
that Saam was no cat, but one of the ghatti, large catlike
beasts with the ability to read the truth in human minds.
To have tenuously Bonded with him after the loss of his
true Bondmate so many years past had been like stepping
off a cliff, forcing herself to formally acknowledge the intelligence and ability of a mere beast who boasted the vaunted
mindpowers that eumedicos no longer possessed, had never
truly possessed here in Canderis despite the mystique they
so assiduously cultivated. And without Saam, would she
have been able to accept the reality of Resonants and their
ability to speak mind-to-mind? No longer shrouded by se-
crecy, by their need for survival, some of the younger ones
were now training as eumedicos, bringing their history full
circle, the fables now fact, just as it had been in the beginning when their ancestors had arrived on this planet.

Poor Saam felt his years as severely as she felt her own.
So unfair when the mind remained so agile, to have the
body falter and fail! Freeing the afghan draped over the
back of Saam's chair, she tented it over the sleeping ghatt,
tucking the edges around him. The old dear felt the cold
more than ever these days, and Harrap had crocheted the
afghan precisely for this purpose. His whiskers twitched as

she fumbled at his neck, then he slumbered more deeply. Dear, dear old ghatt! His chain of days had so few remaining links left—she could feel it though she'd stubbornly refused to admit it. As if not acknowledging it would hold it in abeyance, make it vanish! Eumedicos knew better than to harbor such wistful illusions! she scolded herself. 'Twas a rare human who understood or accepted the truth with the grace of the ghatti.

Aching with an anticipatory sense of loss, Mahafny steadied herself against the top of her desk, blinking away unbidden tears until she again could read the large chart paper with its signs and symbols, its carefully inked names—bless Harrap for that, since her hands were too untrustworthy with pen and ink—and gave the genealogy chart a look of disgust. Did it matter? Did any of it matter when her objective eumedico mind told her Saam's days were numbered? Charting ghatti ancestry with the goal of determining whether any had interbred with the common house cats brought by her spacer ancestors to their new home on the planet Methuen might offer her a puzzle, a project on which to concentrate, but the ghatti could care less! Saam had informed her of that with his usual grave courtesy when she'd nagged at him to help. Still, he always exhibited a mannerly interest in her work, presenting her with occasional tidbits of information he'd stored away. It had rankled more than she cared to admit to have someone she cared about not show an equally zealous interest in her work.

It was less the genealogy that interested her than the genetics of it all, the breeding, which traits were dominant, which recessive. Which traits might prove inextricably tied to the male or female chromosomes. Proving that house cats did or did not interbreed with the ghatti still did nothing to explain ghatti mindpowers, their ability to communicate mentally, their amazing ability to read the truth in human minds. Indeed, why bother at all? Any breeding between the species apparently hadn't enhanced the house cat one iota, though that was unfair, given her prejudice against cats in general—and against ghatti for so many years before Saam had joined her.

*"Saam, why am I doing this? If you don't see any point, why should I?"* Mahafny mindspoke, somehow unwilling to

disturb the cottage's quiet security, a palpable sanctuary against the storm without and the storm within her mind. So attuned to her mindvoice was he, Saam would undoubtedly awake from his doze and comfort her, give her a good talking-to. So he always had and so he always would. Along with Harrap's gentle presence, it was one of the few certainties of her circumscribed life these days. Oh, circumscribed because she chose it to be, eschewing contact with the eumedico world as much as possible, ashamed at being seen at less than her best.

Except that this time, to her increasing dismay, Saam seemed only to half-rouse, a sense of bewilderment clouding his yellow eyes. A nervous yawn and he covertly studied her face as if he didn't really recognize her, was hesitant as to who she was. The essential Saam no longer existed behind those yellow eyes, and the ghatt inhabited his own private world. *"Saam! Saam, dear one!"* Gnarled hand on his head, she let her wrist rest there, as if her pulse might bring him to himself. *"Saam, dear, come back to me, please!"*

Another prodigious yawn and awareness gradually returned, the dulled eyes growing lambent once again. **" 'S late."** His mindspeech came slurred and slow, as if each word were being grudgingly pulled from some secret repository he'd lost the skill to tap. **"Ought to be . . . in bed."** A definitely hopeful look went with his declaration. **"Bed . . ."** he murmured again and settled his chin on his paws and slept.

Bereft, as if an essential part of her had been ripped out, the sharing sundered, she stumbled toward the window and stared unseeing at the snowstorm outside, a shiver vibrating along her spine each time the windowpanes shook and rattled with the blizzard's fury. Pulling the shawl collar of her heavy sweater up to her ears, she ran quaking hands over her silvery-white chignon, its restrained shape an indicator that the rest of her remained in control as well. The plan had been rebelliously shaping itself in the depths of her mind for the past two octants, each detail falling into place as Saam had faltered with each passing autumn day.

A hope, a slim chance that mayhap she could defeat old age and death—not for herself, but for her beloved ghatt. Or, if not entirely defeat, at least somehow hold it at bay a while longer. Now winter had set its teeth, ready to shake the life out of the world, only a day before the High Holidays and the turn of the year. If only it were summer—or at least spring! But Saam wouldn't live until then, that she was sure of when she was rigorously honest with herself. Her hands flashed in the sign of the Lady's eight-pointed star, almost a mockery, a parody of it, given her twisted fingers. Unbeliever she was, but she'd try anything and everything before admitting defeat. She'd distract Death with sleight of hand, parlor tricks if she were able!

Could she? Did she dare? She could do it, but not without help. The question was: Who? At first she missed the hesitant rapping on her door, too lost in worry to hear it. A second flurry of raps and she lifted her head high and proud, straightening bowed shoulders as best she might, still missing the white eumedico coat that added such presence. "Harrap? Come in." Of course it would be Harrap, who else would it be?

Harrap's head—tonsured now by baldness as much as by Shepherd protocol—peered around the door. "Heard you pacing. Well, not so much the pacing as the floor creaking. Too regular to be the storm."

The door slipped from Harrap's fingers as a blocky calico ghatt shouldered it open. Lumbering toward Saam's sleeping form, Parm reared on his hind legs and delicately greet-sniffed Saam's muzzle. **"Dear old boy! Such adventures we've had together!"** His crazy-quilt-marked body, splotches of vivid orange and black and white, seemed almost to deflate as he suddenly collapsed onto his haunches. **"Oh my, oh me . . . gone away! So very far!"** he lamented.

"By the Lady! Is he . . . has he?" One hand clutching his Lady's Medal, Harrap hurried to Saam's side. Almost holding his breath, he eased back the gaily-colored afghan, his hands shaking with relief once he viewed the rise and fall of Saam's side with each slow, labored breath. "Mahafny," he chided, still intent on Saam. "You, of all people, a false alarm?"

"No, not a false alarm, a warning, Harrap. Parm heard it as well." Possessively she fumbled the afghan close around Saam's chin. "I can't ignore any more warnings or it *will* be too late." Her gray eyes froze him with a chilling glare, defying him to contradict her. "Saam and I must start for Marchmont—tomorrow, before it's too late."

Genial mouth now tight with worry and consternation, Harrap eased himself between her and Saam's chair, almost as if he'd barricade the ghatt from her. It made her angry, unreasonably so. "Don't balk me, Harrap! I'd hoped for your help, yours and Parm's, but if you can't see your way clear to aid two old and dear friends . . ." She let the rest of the sentence hover poignantly, exacerbating the guilt she'd purposely sought to induce.

"You can't invest him with eternal life, Mahafny!" His face had grown stern, so unlike the guileless, sunny-visaged Harrap whom everyone adored. "Only the Lady can do that. You can't grant him eternal life—and neither can Nakum!"

For once her hands burned with heat, not their usual icy cold as she laid them on the arm Harrap had defensively thrown across his chest. "I'm a eumedico—I *know* that! And you know what I think of your religion as well!" They'd invested enough time and breath in barrages of arguments about it, so he *should* know her views. No need to tell him how she'd just cast the Lady's sign, and to no avail. "I won't try to halt the inevitable, Harrap," she pleaded, "but mayhap I can slow its pace. Nakum can do that—he *can*, I know he can! He *must*, if only for the love that he and Saam once shared!"

"But we're too old to try this by ourselves in the dead of winter," he protested. "Those days are long gone! I've come to terms with that, even if you haven't."

Stretching against Harrap's leg, Parm worked his claws to attract his Bond's attention. **"Adventure? Ooh! We're not too old for another adventure! Not if it might help Saam!"** A look of startlement, and then the ghatt shook his head. **"Oh, and by the way . . ."** he drifted off, casting an obvious side-glance at Mahafny. Parm's conversations seldom followed a straight path, and Mahafny had no time to listen to his digressions.

"Harrap, we could 'borrow' the twins. Jenneth and Diccon would help Saam in an instant, as would Pw'eek and Kwee." She'd shame Harrap into helping if she had to; her pride no longer mattered. He might try to defy her, but she doubted he'd deny Parm.

"Out of the frying pan, into the fire!" Harrap groaned. "Doyce and Jenret will *not* take it kindly if you inveigle the twins into joining us. Not without their permission!"

"And the twins will have been of age for a full year tomorrow, on their Naming Day—if you'll remember. They've completed nearly half of their training as Seekers Veritas," and she continued demolishing his objections one by one, concealing her triumph as his expression began to waver.

❖

Easing along the narrow row between his seedling flats, the Erakwan Nakum stopped now and then to rub the soil between his fingers, critically noting its moisture, its composition. The seedling arborfer, his "babies," were faring exceptionally well here in this sheltered greenhouse high in Marchmont's rugged Stratocum Range. He crooned to the soil as well as to his seedlings, a feather-light pat of praise here and there, a gentle caress along the new growth, tiny needles a sharp green at each branch tip, older needles darker on top with an almost dusty green underside. At this stage the needles prickled no more than peach fuzz might. Each slender trunk looked no more substantial than twine, and so flexible that it never ceased to fill him with awe at how such delicate things would ultimately grow so thick and tall, unbending.

A sigh of satisfaction, contentment—to be here, here with his little ones, some of whom he'd be privileged to witness grow to towering size long years hence. For these, these trees—offspring of the legendary Hatachawa, favored by the Great Spirit—formed an integral part of his Erakwan heritage, a part near-obliterated not so long ago by the Newcomers to his world, Outlanders who indulged in overcutting, intent on fulfilling their immediate wants and needs, not realizing or uncaring of how long the arborfers required to reach maturity, to reproduce.

Only three of his flats required a judicious watering to make up for the differences in his test soils. It pained him to think he might be stunting some of the infant arborfer, but Nakum desperately needed to test firsthand which con-

ditions fostered superior growth. And superior did not necessarily suggest the speediest, although if he could alter
that, he'd not be displeased. What he'd discovered thus far
was that too-rapid growth tended to produce spindly, weak
trees, all too likely to fall prey to pests or storms. Still, with
care and the Great Spirit's blessing, he'd have saplings
ready to transplant into Eadwin's and Roland's main tree
nursery soon. At least "soon" in the way that he measured
the passage of time.

Absently rubbing his fingers against his leather vest to
remove the last vestiges of soil, he stood at the glass-
covered wall facing east. Bless Eadwin for ordering the
glass to be transported most of the way up here during fine
weather! Easy enough, then, for him to carry each pane
the rest of the way, set them into the frames. Amusing,
too, to gaze through the panes at the stars, the unchanging,
ever-full moon and her eight circling children, soon to
wane, vanish with the turn of the new year, returning one
by one each octad. At this altitude the moons and the stars
hung just above his head, close enough for him to touch if
he but stretched out his arms. Aye! He hardly boasted
brave, loyal Hatachawa's splendid height!

And down below—far, far below—the faint glow of Sidonie, Marchmont's capital, not near so bright and beckoning
as the sky's stars. Oh, he'd been down there often enough,
would partake of their hospitality yet again—enjoy it,
even—on those rare days when his solitary existence became too lonely. After all, he was three-quarters Erakwa,
native to this land, this planet, yet also one-quarter Outlander. Out-spacer, more accurately, a descendant of one
of the intrusive settlers on his people's land, who'd hurtled
who knew how far across space from another world to arrive at this destination. Not only was he a descendant of
these original spacers, but a royal one at that—the blood
of Marchmont's rulers flowing through his veins—and
cousin to the current king, Eadwin, who revered the
arborfer almost as much as he did. Holding up his hand,
he examined it front and back as if to look inside, judge
which blood was Erakwa, which was not. Funny, it mingled
more easily than his people did with the Newcomers.

With a whispered good night to his charges he stepped
through the greenhouse door and into his snow-crowned

world to scan the stars again with naught to separate him from them except the crystalline air itself. As he'd sensed even within the greenhouse's confines, a snowstorm pounded Canderis, south of Marchmont's borders, the stars hazed in that direction. Clad in only his leather vest, a loincloth, and fringed leggings laced on the side, his body drank in the cold, impervious to it, his smooth, coppery skin unmarred by gooseflesh. At rare moments he stewed with impatience, his powers growing as slowly as his precious arborfer, and perhaps they did, but it was just as well, he had time, years upon years of time to grow in wisdom and strength, time to listen to the very earth beneath his moccasins as it whispered its secrets to him.

For seventeen years he'd called this mountain his home, which meant . . . he did the calculations in his head . . . that he was in his mid-thirties now. Oh, any Outlander could effortlessly recite his or her precise age, but Nakum never bothered keeping track with the same rigor he devoted to his arborfer records. His grandmother, Addawanna, undoubtedly remembered his age, though again this would be couched in Erakwa terms, a tale tied to every passing season. With any luck, she'd come visit soon, because he'd promised her more wool to card and spin. The mountain sheep and goats were generous in their sharing. And from the finished yarn he'd do his knitting to pass the long winter nights. Was it only last year at this time that he'd knitted high hiking socks for Jenneth and Diccon? Or had more time spun by than he'd realized?

As for Callis, she came when she came; it did little good to anticipate it or yearn for her visits. But she appeared less and less now, allowing her years—well over two hundred of them (ah, his Outlander blood was telling!)—to gradually catch up with her, leaving her more at one with the land than its people, her Erakwa. And someday, so would he be, but not for many years.

The snow squeaked as he shuffled his moccasins back and forth, sharp little sounds that brought him back to himself, sent a shiver through him that had nothing to do with the cold. Something twinged at him, felt faintly wrong, had felt that way for a lengthening time, though the sensation was elusive, only temporarily captured from the corners of his eyes, the "corners" of his other senses, so to speak.

Each time he concentrated on it, it fled without farewell, made him wonder if he were imagining things, but the things that he, Nakum, could imagine were beyond the ken of most humans. Well, as far as he could judge, it wasn't hurting anything or anyone. A shrug of resignation set his long braids swaying across his back. Ignore it and it might venture closer, like a wild animal too shy and skittish to eat from one's hand until one sat rock-still and patient, unconcerned yet utterly attuned to its emotions. Mayhap he'd tame it enough to identify it; if not, mayhap Callis could explain when next she came.

But there was something else—something beyond that elusive, eldritch sensation—that gnawed at him. Without quite realizing what he was doing, he let his glance swing southward again, hazel eyes, his grandfather, Prince Ludo's heritage, squinting as if he could pierce the overcast skies that hung to the south. "Ah, Saam! Oh, no, is it really time?" He'd tried not to think about the aloof yet lonely steel-gray ghatt who'd temporarily shared his thoughts with him for a brief but special time when he'd needed it so badly, desperately attempting to comprehend the Outlanders and their foreign ways. His human Bondmate dead, Saam had reluctantly sought another to at least partially ease the loss. Much as he'd wanted it to be, Nakum knew he was not the one that Saam sought, had finally convinced the ghatt to focus on Mahafny Annendahl. A task had been assigned him, a task for his people, and he'd been forced to acknowledge how unfair it would be to immure the ghatt in his mountain solitude, unable to 'speak even his own kind, since the mountains trapped and distorted mind-speech. It had been one of the most painful things he'd ever done, redirecting that tentative love, the steady, supportive regard, the sharing of minds toward someone else, though Mahafny had been in need of it far more than he'd been. Still, the loss, the pain, had helped him grow, and he owed Saam for that . . . and so much more.

All things died—some sooner, some later. In all honesty, most of the ghatti that he knew well were very old, at the farthest age span for their species. Even Hru'rul, his cousin King Eadwin's Bond, was what? . . . eighteen . . . and a most splendid beast! As if attuned to his thoughts, even at such a distance, he could swear he heard the wind lofting

Hru'rul's mindvoice his way. **"'Course I magnificent Bond . . . fit for royalty!"** followed by a yawn and a smacking sound as Hru'rul drifted deeper into sleep. Ah, he was fanciful tonight—but not about Saam's fate.

It hurt to think he might not be able to bid Saam farewell, but if he left his mountain fastness to journey to Saam's side in Canderis, time would flow differently, perhaps flee from Saam even faster than it did now. Time passed differently up here in these mountains, stretching long and slow and sweet like maple syrup taffy. Should he need further evidence, all he had to do was look into his cousin Eadwin's eyes, or the eyes of some other Outlander friend who'd known him for years. The momentary shock they exhibited on seeing him during one of his rare appearances was as clear as if he stared into a mirror. He still appeared little older than his teens; not a touch of gray in his hair, skin unwrinkled by age or the elements. He changed within, yet not without. Or if so, he did it so slowly that most unobservant souls never quite noticed the minute alterations to his face and form.

"Goodnight, Saam, dear friend." A straight-armed salute to the south. "With your passing, so passes a piece of my youth. Go well, dear friend." And at that moment an uncanny giggle, hardly human and certainly not ghatti, made the hairs on the back of his neck quiver. Yet even as he spun around, he knew that he'd see nothing, no tracks in the snow, not a flake out of place. Damn it all, whatever that thing was, it was mocking him! Worse yet, mocking the love and respect he felt for Saam. Whatever that "thing" was, it required a lesson in manners!

❖

"Diccon!" Invasive and startling, the touch on the back of her neck sent Jenneth Wycherley slithering across the sofa cushions, desperate to elude her twin's icicle fingers. Her frantic withdrawal panicked a chubby ghatta who'd been curled beside her, napping in blissful peace.

"Raow!" the ghatta screeched in mounting fright, burying her bulk behind the throw pillows until only a broad gray bottom patched with butterscotch and white revealed

her whereabouts amongst the broidered cushions. Extravagant white whiskers ventured beyond a pillow ruffle, followed by a quivering nose, half-gray and half-tan. Light as
a snowflake a second ghatta, her richly mottled pewter-and-
copper coat dusted with ice particles, sprang on the sofa
and applied a cold nose to her sib's backside in as intimate
a location as possible. "RAAOW!" sang out the calico and
exploded from amongst the pillows to hurtle over the sofa's
back. Some might think it a retreat, but it was hardly that.

**"I'll whack you, Sissy-Poo!"** she sobbed, dashing beneath
the sofa and back on it with a speed that belied her size.
Before the smaller ghatta could spin to defend herself,
Pw'eek was on her, white paws buffeting her sister-twin's
head. As her anger gradually faded, she began grooming
Kwee's ears, pink tongue digging deep inside, then rasping
along each delicate ear, thin as a shell. **"So cold,"** she murmured. **"A wonder they didn't freeze, break off!"**

**"And you'll wear them off if you keep licking like that!"**
Kwee muttered, twisting to escape her sister's maternal instincts. **"Let them warm slowly, Sissy!"** Flopping on her
side, she planted all four chilly feet on Pw'eek's ample
white stomach, giving just the tiniest of ghatti smiles as her
sib flinched. **"Ooh! That feels soo good!"**

Stamping his feet as he unwrapped his long red scarf,
Diccon shook his head, minute ice fragments flying from
his damply waving hair, the reddish highlights temporarily
lost amongst the brown shadings. His marvelously blue eyes
still teared from the cold outdoors, and his nose glowed
pink, leaking in the sudden warmth. "Ho, can't believe I
caught you out like that, Jen!" he crowed. "Wish I could
concentrate as deeply when I study!" Slinging his sheepskin
jacket over the back of a nearby chair, he rubbed his hands
together as he marched toward the fireplace.

"Here—give me your dress tabard before you ruin it,"
she instructed, snapping her fingers to quicken him. "Lost
your gloves again?" Hiking the collar of her tatty, much
worn wool robe around her neck, she tightened its belt and
pushed up the sleeves. The robe was a muted navy-and-
deep-green plaid, her father's, and she'd had no qualms
about liberating it from her parents' bedroom while they
were away. Relieving Diccon of his tabard and sash before
he could drag one or the other through the ashes, she

folded them and placed them on an end table out of harm's way—or Diccon's way—one and the same, she supposed.

**"Didn't lose his gloves—" "Barnaby must have snatched them!"** Pw'eek and Kwee cried, as if reciting the punch line of an old, familiar joke.

"Ha! If you'd known Barnaby, you'd be searching for a higher perch right now, as far away from his tongue as you could get! He'd have happily washed your ears and," she stared pointedly at each ghatta's hindquarters, "anything else that needed cleaning." It still took her aback at how familiar Pw'eek and Kwee were with the past memories that she and Diccon held in common. The ghattas had never met Barnaby, the little white-and-tan terrier who'd shared her childhood and Diccon's, but as Bondmates, Pw'eek and Kwee were privy to the memories and thoughts of their Bonds, both past and present. Sometimes she forgot that Pw'eek hadn't been with her forever, and the same for Kwee's relationship with Diccon. So, some good had come from Papa's decision to visit the Sunderlies last year—if they hadn't stopped over at Windle Port, they'd never have found Pw'eek and Kwee.

**"Would too have found you,"** Pw'eek whispered in her mind. **"Would have tracked you anywhere until you were mine, and I yours. I followed you when you wouldn't remember me, when you cast my love from your mind, didn't I?"**

*"Oh, you were so brave! Utterly courageous and determined!"* Jenneth meant every word of it, even as she winked at her twin, confident his awareness of her thoughts and moods let him follow her private converse with Pw'eek without eavesdropping in her mind. He knew as well as she how Pw'eek always craved extra reassurance that she'd outgrown her scaredy-ghatt tendencies. The praise she'd lavished on Pw'eek applied equally to Diccon, for he also had let nothing stop him as he'd searched both sea and land for her.

"So, how was your evening out?" She strove to sound deliberately casual—no sense letting him get a swelled head about how much he meant to her—as she straightened the throw pillows and retrieved her notebook from under the sofa.

A look of mock incredulity greeted her query. "You

mean you weren't with me every step of the way? Safe and
snug here but tagging along in my mind?" Twins they were
and twins they would always be; no need to vocalize a
thought when the other already sensed it, minds intertwined even in the womb, such was the unique ability of
their Resonant mindpowers.

Except . . . as they attained adulthood, certain subjects
became off-limits, cried for a touch of circumspection, a
conscious decision to share rather than a constant and unconscious commingling of minds. Exhibiting more than a
passing interest in the opposite sex was a prime example:
as if she *really* wanted to know *exactly* what Diccon had
been up to this evening with Maeve Fuller! (**"Oh, but you
do, desperately!"** Pw'eek chided. Blast the ghatti for always
making one admit the truth!)

Maeve was two years older and at least two centimeters
shorter than her dear brother—still grumpy about his short
stature—and she didn't need Pw'eek to read Maeve's
thoughts to know what steamily bubbled through them!
Maeve might be blonde and innocent-looking, blessed with
a curvaceous body capable of luring too many impressionable young men, but she cared naught for anyone but herself and her pleasures. If half the stories she'd heard were
true . . . ! Jen burned with indignation. What transpired in
Diccon's mind on glimpsing, even daydreaming of Maeve
Fuller, was explicit enough to make Jenneth extremely hot
and bothered, seizing her with an overwhelming desire to
dunk her twin in the nearest horse trough until his lust
abated!

Warring with herself over whether or not to inquire how
he'd fared with the fair Maeve this night, Jenneth continued
straightening, picking up Diccon's discarded jacket and
hanging it, all the while refusing to meet his eyes. With a
smirk of pure self-satisfaction—at what, she'd love to
know!—Diccon exited the living room, calling over his
shoulder as he went, "I'm absolutely *starving* to death, Jen.
Let me see what's in the kitchen, and then we'll talk.
Want anything?"

Catching Pw'eek's distinctly hopeful expression, she
shouted after Diccon, "Oh, mayhap a bit of whatever
you're having, if you would." With their parents gone, food
was sparse in the pantry, neither she nor Diccon that used

to shopping, planning ahead. Her dinner tonight had consisted of carrot sticks from some rather limp carrots, a handful of raisins, and a toasted heel of bread with nutter-butter. Until a few days past, the lack of food hadn't mattered; she and Diccon had been taking their meals at Headquarters, sleeping there as well. No choice in the matter, what with being Novies, Seekers Veritas-in-training, obligated to spend their time in drills, perfecting their Seeker skills through study and practice, despite the nearness of their home on Seeker grounds. Now, with the halidays, only a bare minimum of Seekers, mostly semiretired, staffed Headquarters, everyone else on leave to celebrate the new year. But no matter how empty and echoing Headquarters might now be, it was even more so here at home without Jenret and Doyce. For the first time in their lives, their Naming Day festivities had been postponed, and Jenneth had felt downright abandoned—especially when Diccon had blithesomely announced he was meeting Maeve this evening.

But before she could dwell on that hurt too deeply, Diccon bounded back with two mugs of cocoa clutched in one hand and an overstacked plate in the other, sandwiches ready to tumble. Rescuing the plate, she regarded the sandwiches's construction with a certain awe. Never in her life had she encountered such slabs, jagged around their edges, thick in some spots and nearly tissue-thin in others. "Where'd you find the bread? And what did you cut these with, Dic? An ax?" Ham and cheese spilled raggedly beyond the crusts, further evidence of an overenthusiastic but inexpert job. A nibble at the cheese told her it was fine, but the ham's gray-green tinge was a bit unnerving—precisely why she'd avoided it for dinner. Oh, well, might as well be sick together! Mama always swore that Diccon and Papa'd eat anything that didn't have mold on it—or at least not too much mold.

Kwee busily scrambled after falling scraps of meat and cheese, determined to have her share before her sister beat her to them. **"We were in need of sustenance,"** she explained, not stopping her search for tidbits. **"Didn't notice you offering to make neat sandwiches, fussy little dainties with trimmed crusts."** An agile leap took her to a new sprinkling of scraps ahead of her sister-sib until Pw'eek shouldered her aside to gain her share.

" 'S true, Jen." Diccon mumbled through a mouthful of sandwich and automatically switched to mindspeech. *"A little kindness never hurt. I was almost too weak to make these."* His eyebrows rose suggestively as he shared that thought with her.

Remaking a sandwich half as neatly as possible, Jen took a bite, chewing thoroughly, allowing the silence to lengthen—not a stray thought or word. Allow him ample time and he'd rush to fill the void, as impetuous as Papa, despite having Mama's looks. And since she possessed Mama's patience in abundance, she let him mentally writhe on the hook of his own desire to blurt out his tale of this evening's eventful happenings with Maeve. Still smugly silent, she licked her fingers to remove leaking mustard and offered Pw'eek a final morsel of cheese before thoroughly brushing her robe free of crumbs.

"All right, Jen," Diccon blurted. "You've wormed it out of me! Can't keep a secret from you, can I?" Slouched in an easy chair, stockinged feet on a hassock, he rested his sandwich on his chest. "I'm older and wiser, tonight, Jen. More a man because of this. Without Maeve to teach me this lesson, I'd still be a mere boy." His features aligned in a solemn mien, his eyes—those intensely blue eyes with their long, dark lashes that all the ladies loved—had gone all dreamy and distant with remembrance.

Did she—or didn't she—want to hear this? And given their closeness, why couldn't Diccon see how uncomfortable this subject always made her? Of course she shared personal things with him, but there were also things that were Strictly Personal, not to mention Utterly Private and Intimate! Even the fact that her beloved Pw'eek knew these things was distressing enough. Shame still coursed through her at how she'd inadvertently turned herself into a spectacle there in the Sunderlies, self-control momentarily overridden by Tadj Pomerol's horrific machine, created to reveal Resonants and to temporarily disable their vaunted mindpowers by sending a surge of near-electric sexual excitement coursing through their bodies. Had near turned herself into a rutting bitch in heat, lusting after Pommy like that! Worst of all, her brazen, shameless display had driven

Bard to berserkerdom and death to protect her and her honor. And all this in front of her own brother, not to mention Davvy McNaught!

No wonder she couldn't look at Davvy without blushing, mortified beyond belief! True, he was Lindy's now, but ah, how infatuated she'd once been with him! Now, when she dreamed of the Sunderlies, a burgeoning eroticism accompanied those dreams, a sexuality that she continually had to struggle to control. Mayhap she was no better than Maeve, deep down inside! She didn't dare come close to any of the young male Seekers they trained with, not unless Diccon were near. The last time they'd dined with Aunt Jacobia, she'd writhed, wanted to hide at the easy way her aunt had flirted with some of the men gathered at Myllard's! No, their Sunderlies adventure, as Diccon called it, had brought no pleasure, only pain. That was what sex did.

But if Diccon truly wanted, needed, to share this evening's experiences, she had to ready herself to listen, that was what their bond of twinship was for, was meant to be. Planting herself in the corner of the sofa, knees drawn to her chest, she wrapped the old robe protectively tight around her. With an interrogative chirp Pw'eek settled herself across her feet, perturbed that she was perturbed, and faintly miffed that Jenneth's lap was barricaded. To appease her beloved, she stroked along the demarcation line that divided Pw'eek's face, butterscotch on the right, gray on the left, except for an orangish daub above and below the eye, and as the ghatta purred, she marginally relaxed. "So?" Even to her it sounded pallid and quavery, and she forced herself to strengthen it, make her interest clear. "So, what happened tonight with the beauteous Maeve? You look as self-satisfied as one of the ghatti!"

Dragging Kwee onto his lap and rolling her over to tickle her tummy spots, Diccon suddenly went bashful, almost blushing. Damn—if he were a girl, she'd have sworn he was playing coy! At last he looked up, blue eyes meeting her hazel ones, his smile distinctly cockeyed. "An ice-cold bath of reality, Jen. Or more accurately, an ice-cold, miserable storm!" Despite himself he began to chuckle. "Any idea how much I spent on dinner tonight for dear Maeve? She ordered every course Myllard's offered!"

Diccon was such a pinchpenny—unless it involved lavishing money on one of his own passing enthusiasms. Still, she'd regarded Maeve as exactly that—his latest enthusiasm. "Purse a great deal lighter?"

"Ah, yes, sad to say. And me with half my haliday gifts still unbought!" A theatrical groan. "And all for naught! Naught, I tell you!" He looked down, belatedly realizing that Kwee was gnawing on his wrist, all four legs tight against his forearm, poised to "disembowel" her prey. "Ouch! Kwee, my little speckle-tummy trout, enough! You treat me worse than Maeve did in my time of burning need!" Slipping a finger inside the hoop on her left ear, he gave a warning tug.

**"Stop dawdling and spit it out! Bad enough I suffered through kissy-faces and soppy-talk once tonight—don't drag it out any worse in the retelling."**

"Oh, you're jealous, my sweedling! Convinced any kissy-faces and soppy-talk should be exclusively directed to you!" Kwee wriggled with ecstasy as Diccon began to scratch her chin, and he finally met his sister's eyes again.

"Well, the long and the short of it, Jen, is that *nothing* happened tonight, *absolutely* nothing!" Having finally forced himself to admit it, he laid a string of noisy kisses along Kwee's neck. "Mind you, when I walked Maeve home, I took every back street and alleyway I could to encourage some privacy—not that it mattered. What with the storm, we could have marched down the middle of Hight Street and been the only two there! Discovered that no matter my many charms, it's well-nigh impossible to penetrate a girl's cloak—let alone any deeper—in the midst of the storm. My ardor wasn't enough to keep her warm—imagine that!"

Limp with relief, Jen collapsed and swung her legs over the sofa's arm, waving her feet in the air. "The Lady have mercy on you, Diccon! Kwee, why didn't you tell him to think with his head, not with his—"

A percussive pounding at the front door finally made itself heard over the wind's rattling at windows and plucking at shingles. Springing up, she exchanged a frightened glance with Diccon, their cozy, confessional little world abruptly being breached by outsiders, interlopers. No sanctuary, not here, not anywhere—not even in her mind. **"Others need sanctuary from this storm, too,"** Pw'eek reminded her, her expression somber in some way that Jen couldn't identify. **"Besides, it's hardly barbarians at the gate—Parm would be soo cross to think you viewed Harrap as that."**

"Dic, it's Harrap and Parm," she informed her twin, who responded, "I know. But why . . . ?" as he untangled himself from Kwee. As usual, she was faster than her brother as they both hurried toward the entrance hall, where they heard the front door open and close. Impatient, Harrap was already inside, stamping his feet, slapping his hands against his arms. "Harrap," Diccon called ahead, "what's the matter? Is Aunt Mahafny ill?"

Hand over her mouth, Jenneth struggled to suppress a moan as the truth flooded her mind. "It's not Aunt Mahafny, Diccon. It's Saam, I just know it! Can't you sense it?" Somehow she'd read it in Pw'eek's and Kwee's expressions, just hadn't allowed herself to immediately grasp the idea.

With a sharp nod, his teeth chattering too much to say more, Harrap let him unpeel him from his blanket coat and multitude of scarves, icy pellets of sleet rattling against the floor and walls. Somehow Harrap looked bulkier than usual, even when they'd divested him of his coat, leaving her momentarily puzzled until Parm's head poked out from a pouch slung across Harrap's chest. Harrap's Lady's Medal rested atop Parm's head and he gave an impatient shake to dislodge it. **"Phew, stuffy!"** Parm took a deep breath. **"Not that *that* matters, though. Oh, woe! Oh, me, oh, my! Don't want to go to Marchmont, but we have to save Saam . . ."** he trailed off with a sniff of misery.

Hustling a protesting Harrap and Parm into the living room by the fire, Jen saw Harrap's normally benign, cheerful countenance suffused with an incredible sorrow. "Saam's not just failing, he's fading—fast, too fast for Mahafny's liking." He sniffled, daubing at his eyes, face wet with snow and tears. "She's so blasted stubborn sometimes! You know how impossible she can be!"

"And?" Could she survive another loss, even one due to natural causes? Saam had been a loyal friend forever; had been charged to watch over Doyce when his first Bondmate, Oriel Faltran, had died, and had continued to watch over her and the twins as well, once they were born. Not only did she love the old ghatt, she revered the dedication that had linked them for so very long. But Saam appeared so drawn and wan of late, as if he longed for a respite from life. "Is he dying? Now? What can we do? Is there anything . . . ?"

Diccon looked sickly pale, mirroring her own look, she supposed. Harrap cleared his throat, determination welling up within him. "Your aunt has a favor to ask of you. She wants to travel to Marchmont tomorrow morning, today, actually, I'd guess."

A low whistle broke from Diccon's lips. "Nakum? That's it, isn't it? If anyone can help Saam, it has to be Nakum!" He was bouncing from foot to foot now, oblivious of the puddles of water surrounding Harrap. "Jen, we must help Saam and Aunt Mahafny! We must! Whatever the risks may be, transporting Saam to the mountains in the midst of winter, this is an undertaking we can't refuse—can we, Jen?"

A sick, sinking sensation seized Jen. "Say what you mean, Dic! You see it as another adventure, don't you? Well, it's not! Not to Saam, not to Aunt Mahafny. To them, it's life or death, not a game!" Much as she loved Saam, she didn't crave another adventure, not after the Sunderlies. Mayhap it was selfish, disloyal to a dear friend, but she didn't know if she could handle it. "Plus, we've obligations now as Novice Seekers Veritas. We can't just leave without permission, Dic!"

"Of course we can! We're on haliday-leave, aren't we? Don't need to ask the Seeker General's permission. No need for Mama and Papa to give permission, either—we're adults now, remember? In fact, no need for them to even *know*—right, Jen?"

A warning in that final statement, despite a glance filled with both supplication and empathy. *"Don't be afraid, Jen. You're so much stronger than you think. Besides, do you want to stay safe and warm, Jen? All safe and warm while Saam dies—all because we wouldn't help? I'll go, even if you won't. Sometimes all we have in life is a chance, Jen, and we have to take it, for good or ill. Like with Maeve tonight—I had to try. Yes, I failed, but at least I tried!"*

She knew Harrap was keenly watching the interplay of their expressions, aware they conversed in mindspeech, patiently awaiting their answer, even—mayhap—hoping they'd deny Mahafny's wishes. *"Sometimes I hate you, Diccon!"* And at that moment she truly did. How dare he equate Saam's life with his attempted dalliance with Maeve!

*"For being right?"*

*"No, for being you, for feeling things differently than I do despite the fact we're so close."* Turning to Harrap, she tossed back her dark hair, strove to steady her chin. "We'll go, Harrap. Tell Aunt Mahafny we'll be ready."

❖

The cobweb caught him unaware, veiling his face, strands snagging on his eyelashes, draping against his ear. Ezequiel Dunay exhaled explosively to momentarily lift it from his lips and vigorously swatted at the web. Damn spiders, anyway! But then, what had he expected to find down here—other than spiderwebs and generations of dust and decay? That and the relics of past lives—royalty and commoner alike, who'd made the castle their home, eight generations' worth of trunks and crates, baskets and bales, chock-full of objects too good to discard, or too outworn or out of style to be of service. Only the Lady knew the last time anyone had ventured this far into the labyrinth of subbasements and passages beneath the castle, including old escape routes tunneling under the city's streets and beyond the castle walls. Other than to fuss over having the castle water system inspected, its cisterns and pipings checked for leaks, his grandfather certainly hadn't been down in recent years, too frail to inspect his territory himself or even bother to direct underlings to do so.

That was why Ezequiel Dunay now found himself far below ground, doing what his late grandfather, Ignacio Lauzon, royal chamberlain, had done in his prime: investigating the castle for which he was responsible, checking where repairs were required, determining what might possibly be thrown out to make room for the latest generation's cast-offs. And in the process, learning every nook and cranny, the secrets purposely built into it and the secrets that happened by default from forgetfulness, the neglect of previous generations. Some of those secrets—forgotten tunnels and passageways—had helped Eadwin elude his stepfather's machinations, had given him and his allies time to rally the populace to his cause.

Ah, how he missed the grandfather who'd raised him! With Ignacio gone, the position of royal chamberlain, responsible to and for King Eadwin of Marchmont, had devolved on him, not simply because he was Ignacio's grandson, but because of his lifelong apprenticeship. So, in spite of his other pressing duties, the thousand-and-one big and small tasks necessary to keep a castle running smoothly, Ezequiel made time to learn the whereabouts of locales his grandfather hadn't taught him. It was his responsibility, his *duty,* to know, and exploring these out-of-the-way places where his grandfather's feet had once trod strengthened his connection to the old man. Despite the numerous souls surrounding him daily—underservants, Domain and Ministration Lords, nobility, tradespeople— Ezequiel often felt very alone and lonely. No time to truly make friends, conscious that his position discouraged intimacy with those he supervised, he'd made do with casual acquaintances. With Ignacio gone, he had no one to turn to, no one with whom he could relax, chat about the day's events, his worries, his happiness.

But becoming chamberlain wasn't the only thing about his life that had recently altered: Romain-Laurent Charpentier was fast becoming a royal pain, not just to him, but to Eadwin as well, though the king strove to be fair, saying that things that never changed ofttimes stagnated. Well, Romain-Laurent certainly loved change, new notions, not to mention details! Why, the man practically counted beans! Blessing the fact that he *was* alone, Ezequiel allowed himself to fume righteously at the injustice, the insanity of it all. Finally a sheepish smile forced its way onto his lips.

No, he wasn't being fair—Charpentier didn't actually count beans, he weighed them! Except it wasn't as straightforward as "Yes, this is five kilos of beans," or "No, this bag is over- or underweight." He insisted on doing it the hard way, determining that a #6-sized bag of beans of a certain variety, harvested at a certain time from a certain region (and dried for no more or less than an octant) should weigh exactly five kilos. With this conclusively settled, he trotted around weighing every bag of beans in the pantries and storerooms, and the new bags currently being delivered. No sir, no supplier would shortchange them with Romain-Laurent on the job! Should next year prove wetter or drier, he'd undoubtedly have to recalculate his findings. Dear Lady, if some supplier cheated by adding stones to his beans, the cook informed Ezequiel and never another order did that person receive. And the man *always* insisted on being called Romain-Laurent, never simply Romain or Laurent!

In all honesty, the man perplexed him, puzzled him. It wasn't that Romain-Laurent lacked reasonable ideas for bringing about change, modernizing and organizing things, but he was so utterly intense and humorless about it. Anyone and everyone he encountered received a tedious lecture about the "new, improved" sort of Marchmontian the kingdom needed to depend on today—and tomorrow— someone (Romain-Laurent being the perfect exemplar of all he preached) not mired by outmoded ideas, ready and eager to look change in the eye, make sure it marched to his beat, neither too fast nor too slow, but precisely plotted to transform the future. Blast Eadwin's kind nature, offering Romain-Laurent the opportunity to put his theories to the test here in the castle, a well-meaning gesture aimed at making things *easier* for Ezequiel as he shouldered the responsibilities of his elevated position!

That and the king's desire to calm Terrail Leclerc, the Internal Affairs Lord, who stood more than ready to pop Romain-Laurent into a cask and ship him somewhere, anywhere, preferably to the Sunderlies! Leclerc had strongly urged that Romain-Laurent's passion for reorganization be practiced on a smaller sphere—castle life—before Eadwin allowed him to impose it on reorganizing Marchmont as a whole! Apparently the rioting pensioners had been the last straw for poor Terrail. In fact, Ezequiel had received a very nice bottle of brandy from the Internal Affairs Lord, along with an apologetic but unrepentant note. Mayhap seasoning, a heavy dose of reality, *would* show Charpentier how to meld theory with practical necessities, make him truly useful. Hmm, mayhap while he was down here, he should check for an empty cask, one that didn't bear the king's crest—just in case. For a moment Ezequiel allowed himself to thoroughly relish the thought.

Even worse than listening to Romain-Laurent propound

his theories about "new, improved" citizens, Ezequiel decided more sourly, was having his ear worn off listening to him pontificate about costs versus benefits—how many souls might benefit from a certain change at a certain cost. Did the benefit match the cost, or was the cost too high or low for what it accomplished? Except Charpentier never seemed to grasp that the citizenry he talked off, that he measured and assessed, were hardly faceless or nameless, had needs and thoughts and dreams that might not match the valuation Romain-Laurent so coolly assigned them.

Anything or anyone above or below his rigorously charted norm annoyed the young man, their deviance an insult. Let him glimpse an Erakwan on Sidonie's streets and he tsk-tsked about useless, unproductive creatures who had somehow gained the privilege of roaming across far more land than their numbers required. After all, hadn't he witnessed it firsthand this past summer while hiking in the Stratocums? Romain-Laurent at one with nature and the land had been such an improbable combination that Ezequiel couldn't envision it, try as he might.

Faintly ashamed at how he'd been maundering, Ezequiel held his lantern higher, avoiding other hanging sheets of cobwebs, careful not to scuffle and raise dust. He was definitely in a better mood now, and mayhap he'd be able at last to concentrate on why he'd come down here. After all, Romain-Laurent was unlikely to find him and deliver his latest lecture. With any luck, by the time Ezequiel finished, Romain-Laurent would be sleeping the blameless sleep of the innocent, assured that his down pillow held neither too many nor too few feathers!

An itchiness overtook him, a sensation of something crawling up his calf, investigating his leg, and he rubbed his foot against the back of his leg to quell the itching. Thank goodness he'd had the foresight to wear old trousers, rather than the knee breeches and stockings that made up part of his ceremonial uniform. Scratch like that when he was wearing hose and they'd be ruckling down round his ankles in no time! If Romain-Laurent craved a revolutionary change, he should study the first order Ezequiel had issued to his staff: No more ballooning breeches truncated at mid-thigh, no more long, high-gartered hosen! Grandfather may have insisted on the traditional, though highly-outdated livery, but Ezequiel had hated them with a passion, his thin legs not made for the long hose. One of the minor embarrassments of his life, Ezequiel of the sagging, bagging hosen!

Phew! He must have mashed that spider. Leaning inside a narrow doorway, Ezequiel swung his lantern to see what this forgotten room had stored inside. Almost empty, except—ha!—that was an old'un! A small trunk was the room's sole possession, still faintly shiny and new-looking under octads of dust. Never had he encountered its like, and his imagination ran wild. Mayhap it was something left over from the original spacers who'd landed on Methuen. Why, mayhap Constant himself had brought it with him on the Resonants' trek from Canderis to what was now Marchmont!

An old footlocker, that's what the soldiers called it, but whatever it was made of had certainly stood the test of time. Kneeling in front of it, Ezequiel pushed two centimeters of dense, powdery dust aside and tapped the surface with a fingernail. Metal of some sort, so it sounded, but not iron or steel. Drawing a fingertip across the bare spot revealed a faint surface pitting, but it didn't seem like corrosion.

Open it or not? Could he? The two snap hasps might unlatch, but what of the round center lock with a tonguelike plate over it? Holding the lantern close, he took careful note of the type of lock, the shape of its keyhole, wondering if he should check upstairs in the key room, see if anything looked to be a match, though some keys were lost, gone forever. One of the certitudes of life that Romain-Laurent would never take into account: Keys that survived the ages never matched a single lock, and vice versa. Breaking it, obliterating a piece of the past went against both instinct and training, even though Romain-Laurent might sneer at such sentimentality. Still, the idea made him feel like a vandal, not to mention a thief, to break into the king's property.

Well, it *was* late, much too late this evening to investigate. Mornings at the castle started far earlier than most supposed, but then, they weren't the ones entrusted with ensuring that any possible need could be fulfilled at a finger's snap! Still, he'd ventured this far, accomplished this much by checking off this room and its contents on his list. A shame to return another evening to finish it off. Squatting, Ezequiel gave the lock a decisive swipe with a cloth from his pocket. Daintiness, a finicky flick, and the dust would rise and float. Nothing wrong with attempting to open the footlocker. If he couldn't, he'd return another night—mayhap with a key or two that might fit, and an oilcan.

The snap locks gave, unhinging themselves stiffly, but the center lock held firm. Hm, what if he slid that button there? Nothing. Either it was locked or thoroughly dust-crammed. Faintly relieved, though he couldn't judge why, Ezequiel left it alone. There was always tomorrow, and what he wanted right now was bed.

♣

Harrap wiped his wrist across his brow, sending his wispy-gray tonsure fringe into spikes. Considering, he studied the piles of supplies he'd hurriedly gathered and absently pulled his wheaten robe away from his chest, flapping it to cool himself. Ironic in the midst of a blizzard to be so overheated from exertion, but then he hadn't truly stopped since he'd set out to plead Mahafny's case to the twins and then hurried home to collect necessities for their trip.

A sniffing at his toes brought him back to himself. **"Should have changed your socks first thing on getting back."** Parm peered up at him worriedly, twining himself around Harrap's ankles. **"By the way,"** he paused to nip at a spot on his lower spine, distracted as usual, **"I think you're coming down with a cold."** Raising his head suddenly, he sneezed. **"Or mayhap *I* am."** Another sneeze, more delicate this time. **"Poor old Saam!"** he wailed, swishing his tail to convey his disheartenment.

Lady bless and keep him going, he had so much to do! But it was never a waste of time to share one's love, and Harrap caressed Parm's head, toying with the ghatt's earrings, the hoop in one ear, the gold ball in the other. He still felt his own set were faintly unseemly for a Shepherd. The fine, dense fur behind Parm's ears felt so soft against his seeking fingers. How blessed he'd been by the Lady to be Chosen as both Shepherd and Seeker, though truth be told, he feared it made him a dabbler at both vocations, endowed with enough faith and hope for one, but not for both. How he loved Parm, would adore him to distraction if it weren't for his bond to the Lady taking precedence, the spiritual above the mundane. A burden of the truth all Seekers sought, and a burden to the Lady's higher truth, and now the burden of Mahafny's unreasoning stubbornness weighted him as well!

*"You needn't go, Parm, not if you've a cold,"* he reassured the ghatt, still as entranced by Parm's crazy-quilt coloration as he'd been on the day they'd Bonded, right on the steps of the Bethel, much to the All-Shepherd Nichlaus's sniffing disdain. If that hadn't been shock enough— oh, a transforming shock and near the fright of his life— he'd met Mahafny Annendahl and Doyce Marbon. Come to think of it, meeting Mahafny had been almost as frightening as his unexpected Bonding, the woman so elegant, so self-assured that she automatically assumed no one would ever have the temerity to cross her, even question her judgment.

Sitting heavily on the bench, Harrap pulled off his wet socks, wincing as his bare feet touched the kitchen's flagstone floor. Lucky for him he'd already stacked clean, dry socks on one of the piles he'd gathered for their leather packs. Instead of putting on the fresh socks, he flapped them against his knee, mind furtively scurrying toward a forbidden elsewhere until he forced himself to concentrate on practical things, not what he craved so badly right now to fight his fears, calm his anguish.

**"Of course I have to go!"** Parm leaped on the kitchen table, resting his chin on the Shepherd's shoulder, purring in his ear. **"If you go, I go. Cold or no cold."**

*"I know. Oh, how I wish . . ."* Why finish the thought? Bad enough he'd even begun it, let it seed itself so treacherously and seductively in his mind. At least Parm never scolded the way Mahafny sometimes did, snapping, "Mind over matter, Harrap! Control it, conquer it!" Let her try it, see how easy it was! It was on nights like these, with worries and responsibilities piling high, poised to topple and crush him, that every fiber of his being suddenly insisted on reliving the overpowering craving for the drug

Hyland Crailford had secretly addicted him to, rendering him oblivious to her mad plan to destroy all Resonants and save the world. The addiction had ravaged his body and mind—been on the verge of stealing his soul—vestiges of the craving still lurking within him, a constant reminder of how fragile and obsessional humankind could be, becoming so utterly dependent on something so unnatural.

**"Just as Mahafny's dependent upon Saam—not that he's unnatural, mind you. It's just that her dependency goes beyond most,"** Parm offered with surprising insight. No, why should it surprise him? Just because Parm could be so easily enraptured, constantly distracted by life's manifold joys, it hardly made him insensitive or foolish. Not a one of the ghatti was. **"And that's why we have to go, like it or not."**

Bewildered, Harrap shook his head, missing the jump in logic that Parm had made so easily while he faltered and stumbled. "Wha . . . ?" Oh, to be lost in the full-throated invocation of the Lady's blessed Mystery Chants, serene and secure, instead of scrambling to keep pace with the agile mind of a ghatt!

**"Because you're dependent on Mahafny, silly. You've two women in your life now—the Lady, and the lady."** Restless, Parm jumped off the table, began nosing at the various piles of supplies Harrap had laid out. **"Is my vest here?"**

*"And I must be true to them both . . ."* A rueful smile lit Harrap's face. *"It would be easier if I could introduce them to each other. Mayhap the Blessed Lady could convince Mahafny to see the truth."* Finally pulling a dry sock over his bare toes, Harrap blessed the fact that the older he became, the less sleep he needed. Heavy wool 'round his ankle now, he paused, puzzled. *"But why doesn't Saam explain to her that it's time for him to go . . ."* biting his lip, he forced himself to utter the truth, *". . . to die?"*

**"Because Saam already half-resides with the Elders, yearning to fully join them, but though his physical life seems increasingly petty and distant, he can't bear to hurt Mahafny."** Contemplating hurts large and small, Harrap hurried to divest Parm of the woolen smallclothes that had abruptly tumbled from the stack on top of his head, scandalizing Harrap no end.

❖

With more forbearance than he'd expected of himself—he *was* growing up, after all—Diccon reined in the horses and applied the brake to the sleigh's runners, testing the response, whether the sleigh veered right or left. It had almost broken his heart, but he'd removed the sleigh bells from the grays' harness. Time enough to put them on later in the day, once they'd traveled well beyond the outskirts of Gaernett. Then he'd let their silvery jangle ring out for the world to hear, like a metaphoric snub of the nose at anyone who questioned their endeavor. Phew—"metaphoric"—where'd he delved up a word like that? Mayhap he didn't need to be so stealthy, but it *was* still early, barely light. Not that it had mattered; he'd scarce slept a wink once Harrap and Parm had left last night.

Kwee was still inspecting the sleigh's interior, burrowing under the heavy lap robes he'd jumbled in the back, along with the horses' blankets. Grain, too, he'd not forgotten that, nor the horses' nose bags. Bucket, ax, a flat shovel, some spare canvas, and plenty of rope. Never could tell when an extra length might prove handy. Should've packed everything away neat and tidy, but he'd do it later. As Kwee slithered beneath his lap robe from behind, a gust of wind buffeted him, left him cringing and tucking his chin tight into his scarf. Bless the sheepskin Seeker's tabard atop his already bulky shearling jacket! Tentatively poking her head from under the plaid lap robe to avoid the wind trying to tug off her whiskers, Kwee ducked back under with a mew of relief. **"Thought sure your arms would be sticking straight out from your sides! You're so thickly bundled they shouldn't be able to reach forward!"**

"It's not easy!" Not when controlling the reins exposed his wrists to the elements, sent the wind swooping up his sleeves like sharp-toothed ferrets down a rathole. Need to set Harrap to knitting wristlets for him, he would! And if the Lady were smiling on him, it might actually indicate his sleeves were too short, that he'd grown a bit more! Laying that thought aside to concentrate on guiding the sleigh, he kept the horses at an easy pace through the knee-deep snow; too many windows along the way already revealing

candlelight and lamplight. A new day begun for some of
Gaernett's earliest risers.

The team and sleigh he'd rented at Myllard's Inn with
its fanciful gables and gingerbread trim, its riot of colors.
Couldn't say that he really remembered Myllard that much;
the innkeep had died when he and Jen had been about . . .
oh, five, he guessed. But they'd known Myllard's daughter
Claire, her husband Wyatt, and their two boys forever.
Wyatt, though, hadn't been well-pleased at being roused
before dawn to let him have the sleigh and team, despite
Claire's cheery wave from their bedroom window. Couldn't
blame him, and Diccon couldn't blame the stableboy he'd
waked in the barn for not letting him have what he'd
wanted without first checking with Wyatt.

With Kwee draped over his thighs and the lap robe
snugged around his waist, he felt almost warm as he worked
his way through Gaernett's winding streets toward Seeker
Headquarters and home. **"Bricks won't stay warm forever,"**
Kwee warned sleepily. But the pink of her claws through
his worsted wool trews and long drawers warned him that
she wasn't as dozy as he'd assumed. **"Adventures are fine
things . . ."** and then she paused to gather her thoughts.
**"But is this right—what we're doing? Stealing off for
Marchmont almost like common thieves?"**

His quick pinch through the robe made her startle. "Uncommon thieves is more like it—an uncommon and highly
unlikely crew of scoundrels! A Shepherd-Seeker, a retired
though still highly respected eumedico, two Novie Seekers,
and four of the most splendiferous examples of ghattidom!
And one of the largest—when you take your sib into account." Except their fledgling endeavor didn't seem nearly
as rousing or thrilling now that he forced himself to think
about it with cool dispassion, not that anyone'd believe him
capable of such a thing! Jen *had* been upset over Mahafny's
request, and he'd ragged at her, shamed her into going.
What if she had the right of it? Didn't he always allow
himself to be swept along by the idea of adventure, the
chance to *do* something, not idly, passively waiting for
events to happen? Though the snow-blocked streets were
empty, he slipped into mindspeech, needing the private solace of Kwee's thoughts. *"Shouldn't we be doing this? Are
we wrong to help Aunt Mahafny and Saam?"*

"What do you think?" No matter how often the ghatta turned the tables and the question back on him, Diccon bristled. Seeking the truth was jolly good fun—except when it forced you to seek it within yourself. Admit any ulterior motives you might have, not allow yourself to draw conclusions based on cherished and deeply entrenched misconceptions, or when crucial information was lacking. No way to simply suppose or hope something, thrashing out the details as you went along. Far more satisfying and fun to engage in the skilled duet between Seeker and ghatta that winkled the truth out of a witness, the poor soul's honesty stripped bare as a newborn babe. So, his precious speckled trout *had* been attending to their lessons more than he'd been!

"Pw'eek and I are just over a year old, and in that time we've faced starvation, even death. We've seen death first-hand—little deaths of creatures whose bodies sustained us, and the larger deaths in the cause of grand endeavors. The coins you carry in your pocket, hoard so zealously," Diccon winced at being labeled stingy, "have two sides, do they not? So does every living thing. One side is life, the other death. Mahafny's seeking to hoard Saam's coin too long. M'wa and Bard would not have approved."

His eyes began leaking at that. Blast the wind, the stinging bits of snow it whirled at him, practically needle-sharp, they were! That crazy Pommy charging at Bard with a machete, striking, and severing Bard's head just as he drove his broken sword into Pommy's heart! Somehow Bard had sought out that death, finally at peace in his ancestral land, the Sunderlies. M'wa, refusing to be separated from his beloved Bondmate, choosing the strange half-life of his kind, of this world and yet not quite, as he'd followed the funeral procession to the heart of that strange, sometimes savage land. Of course Bard and M'wa were as one, just as he and Jenneth were inseparable in their minds, or he and Kwee, and Jenneth and Pw'eek.

But Kwee squirmed, peevish, as if he'd stopped short of grasping an essential truth, so he set himself to think it through again, not allow himself to be sidetracked. *"Do you think Aunt Mahafny means to die with Saam?"* The very idea made his teeth rattle, his jaw ache with the effort of clenching it to stop the chattering as he pushed himself beyond that unpalatable supposition. *"Well, whether she*

*does or doesn't, she's ignoring Saam's right to have his life
end, as all lives must. And ignoring that somehow . . ."* he
struggled with the concept, the word he wanted, *"belittles
it, the necessity of his passing and his right to pass on,
doesn't it?"*

But as he swung the sleigh into the drive that led behind
their home, he couldn't contain himself any longer, letting
it all burst out. "But how can I *not* help, Kwee? She's my
great-aunt, and I love her! I don't want Saam to die, but I
know he must! Not all ghatti have a dear companion as
loyal and as stubborn as Rawn, willing to beard your Elders, question their wisdom, delay a death, as he did for
Khar!"

Letting the horses halt of their own accord, Diccon
dropped the reins and buried his face in the chill, damp
sleeve of his coat, crying soundlessly, unsure what to do,
what was right, not wanting to hurt or lose anyone. Helping
Auntie would hurt Saam; helping Saam would hurt his
aunt. Was there a right or a wrong to things when both
possibilities hurt so very much? "Oh, how I wish Rawn and
Khar were here! They'd know what to do—so would Mama
and Papa!" And he couldn't—*wouldn't*—ask their help, not
through Kwee and Pw'eek, nor through his own Resonant
abilities. That was part of the pledge, the pact. He and Jen,
Kwee and Pw'eek, would just have to figure things out on
their own.

**"Go with her, help her."** Kwee tangled in his scarf as
she scrambled to reach his tear-stained face. **"But helping
her might mean convincing her to accept that Saam must
die, to admit what she refuses to acknowledge. It's hard.
No matter how many times Pw'eek explains, Jenneth still
won't fully accept the essential logic behind Bard's death.
She hears the truth, but it slides right over her."**

With a final gasping sob, Diccon sat upright, hugging
Kwee. "I will help Auntie, I shall!" He rubbed his stinging
eyes with his gloved hands, the damp wool making his eyes
itch even more. "But this trip may resemble a funeral procession more than an adventure." Conquering the quaver
in his voice, he added, "No wonder I need you and Jen
both to make me more perceptive—though it's a losing battle sometimes. And when, my sweedling, did you become
so wise?"

"**M'wa taught me some of it. And having Pw'eek as a sib helps.**" The pale buff outlining her eyes made her look so gentle and wise, his jaunty, blithesome ghatta—wise!

"Then we must share a solemn vow never to let Pw'eek and Jen guess how much we rely on them! They'll become insufferable—well, more insufferable than they already are! Now come on, let's load the sleigh and pick up the others. It's going to start snowing again—just look at the sky!"

♣

Thigh joggling companionably against her twin's, Jenneth unfisted her hand, examining the geometric snowflake pattern in red against the heather-gray mitten. Exactly the same pattern it had been earlier when she'd examined it, and before that and before that. At least it provided color, sawtoothed lines and diamonds, instead of the white mounds looming every which way she looked, with no relief in sight. Even the evergreens were blanketed and mounded with snow, branches slump-shouldered beneath their load. For the most part the road leading out of Gaernett was pillowed with snow, their sleigh tracks the first to mar the pristine landscape, and even they looked hesitant, transitory, ready to vanish at the first breeze that swept more snow across them. And of course it was snowing again! This wasn't how she'd seen herself celebrating the new year, not to mention the eve of her and Diccon's Naming Day!

Twice at around noon—not that she'd really seen much of the sun—they'd passed Transitor road crews dragging plows behind teams of horses, villagers busy with shovels before the next team dragged the heavy, cylindrical roller through to pack the remaining snow. A relief to see them, their breaths white in the air, their horses steaming, the deep blues and greens and browns of heavy jackets, barked instructions cracking in the air. But it could easily be days before most of the roads were touched, especially with the snow continuing to fall.

What had unnerved her most thus far was the silence. Not just the slumberous silence of the snow-cushioned world around her, but the silence emanating from behind her in the sleigh. She'd expected Aunt Mahafny to take

charge, automatically and autocratically take control of this
expedition to Marchmont and to Nakum, but her aunt had
been stone-silent since their first greeting on picking up
Harrap and Mahafny, Parm and the ailing Saam. Even
when they paused to rest the horses and have a brief snack,
her aunt walked around the sleigh, stretching her legs,
munching a biscuit, nodding or shaking her head if it were
absolutely required. All her concentration, all her energy
seemed to be directed to the blanket-wrapped bundle she
cradled on her lap. Did Saam know they were on the move,
heading toward Marchmont? Did he care?

Diccon's silence was equally unsettling. What had turned
her twin so taciturn? Was he brooding over last night's tiff?
Diccon—moody? Lady knew they'd had worse disagreements in childhood, but then, she'd never before said she'd
hated him. The thought near-choked her—oh, why hadn't
the words lodged in her throat! He ought to be bubbling
over with plans and schemes, the quickest route, how to
avoid detection should someone attempt to reason with
Mahafny, try to convince them to turn back. But with
Mama and Papa away, who'd even realize they were gone?
Especially since they weren't required to show up at Headquarters during the High Halidays. Besides, confounding
Aunt Mahafny's wants was tantamount to telling the tide
not to roll in! A futile expenditure of breath and effort.

**"Well, at least we don't have any nasty tides here. Or
waves or water, endless drifting across the sea! And . . .
and separation!"** Pw'eek's 'voice touched a shivering chord
of memory at how the two of them had been swept overboard in the midst of a howling storm, of that endless,
aimless floating under a scorching sun with no land in sight.
And then . . . then their spar had broken, dear Pw'eek
drifting away from her during the night. . . .

The ghatta had snuggled herself under the lap robes and
as near the heated bricks as possible, having announced
that she'd seen enough snow, it all looked alike, and she
had better things in mind, such as napping. *"No, love, we
won't let anything separate us on this trip."* She would *not*
say adventure, not even think the word! *"But I suppose we
should avoid ice floes or icebergs. They could split in half,
separate us, too."* Why she felt compelled to mention that,

she didn't know—borrowing trouble was more like it! Not to mention borrowing an entire arctic ocean!

"Ice floes? Icebergs!" The ghatta pressed her considerable bulk against Jenneth's feet and shins, the beast almost rigid with fear. "Parm *swore* that icebergs have . . . calves! Are they frozen cows? What are they?"

A momentary glow of superiority, a desire to giggle at the ghatta's naïveté, but it didn't last long. How often did she work herself into a fright over nothing, her imagination running wild. More often than she liked to admit, unless Diccon cozened her out of it. *"You shouldn't believe everything Parm tells you, you know."*

But now Pw'eek sounded even more upset—and at her, no less! "But ghatti *can't* lie. We tell the truth! Are you saying Parm lied to me?" Sputtering ghatti indignation from under the lap robes at last alerted Diccon that something was up.

*"No, Parm doesn't lie, beloved."* Best tread carefully; Pw'eek and Kwee were still young and unsophisticated in certain ways, still tended to take things too literally; no matter how thoroughly they'd explored their Bondmates' minds, seemingly simple things could cause them to nearly turn themselves inside out when it came to deciphering humans. Not that human Bonds did much better with their ghatti! *"But Parm's never been adverse to embellishing the truth just a bit, telling tall tales to credulous ghatten. After all, he's never altered a word of one of your Major Tales, has he? Icebergs aren't alive, they consist of ice—huge chunks of it. For some silly reason, we humans say that they're 'calving' when a small chunk breaks off and floats along beside it. It's a colorful description but not an accurate one."*

"Ooh." With a sigh of relief that she'd apparently mollified the ghatta, Jenneth realized that mayhap she'd congratulated herself too soon as a ghatti snicker tickled her mind, Diccon side-glancing her, the corner of his mouth aching to break into a grin.

"Silly Sissy!" Kwee taunted, "Silly baby Sissy! Scared of an old iceberg! Just a big hunk of ice!"

"Am not, Sissy-Poo! Don't go rushing into things like you! I ask first, learn. You, you scatty-brained Sissy-Poo, you'd . . . you'd . . ."

*"Enough!"* Jenneth interjected. Pw'eek and Kwee behaved worse than she and Diccon when it came to gibing at each other! Sissy and Sissy-Poo were their intimate ghatten names for each other, names they'd employed before attaining their True Names on Bonding. If she didn't halt them now, like as not they'd engage in a full-scale battle under the robes, thumping each other and wrestling away. *"Don't even think about it, Diccon! And don't egg them on, or I swear I'll pitch you into a snowdrift!"* Surprisingly, she realized she sounded faintly hysterical.

*"Calm down, ladies, calm down,"* Diccon chided, all humor fading from his voice as he eyed his sister, cast a significant half-glance over his shoulder. *"Besides, it's probably what you should have done to me last night. I was hateful."* She snuggling his arm with hers again to show that she'd accepted his attempt at an apology, secure that he'd accepted her unspoken one, as well. *"Jen, what route do you think we should take? What's likely to be fastest?"*

The need for speed was clear, but the journey to Marchmont took several days, dependent upon weather and mode of transportation. Chewing her lip, she reckoned the possibilities. Straight up to Islebridge, then west to Sidonie—except that they'd have to go through Sidonie or bypass it to reach the Stratocum Mountains and Nakum's private aerie. Don't even think about The Shrouds, where an old trade route led behind a shimmering, high waterfall as the Spray River tumbled down from the mountains. Smaller border crossings abounded, now that Marchmont and Canderis were completely at ease with one another, most tariffs and taxes removed, border patrols and checkpoints existing primarily to aid travelers, not turn them away.

*"How far north do you think the storm struck? All the way across the border?"* It made a difference; winter might be here, but this was the first major storm, either a fluke or a harbinger of a miserable winter. Mayhap Marchmont hadn't had any snow yet.

*"You mean, how long do we play at dashing through the snow?"* Diccon chirped at the grays to pick up their pace where the wind had partially cleared the roadway. *"Or is there a chance we can settle for secondary roads, now that frost's set the ground? Sort of edge ourselves northwest to*

*trim some of the distance? I don't know, Jen."* Pursing his lips, he gave a tuneless whistle and pondered their choices. *"Think Aunt Mahafny or Harrap might hazard a guess? They've traveled back and forth to the Research Hospice in all seasons. It's not that far from the border, except for being in the blasted Tetonords! Couldn't pay me enough to winter there—those mountains are brutal!"*

For whatever reason, the southern end of the Stratocum Range was referred to in Canderis as the Tetonords, as if at one point in history they'd insisted on their own personal name for them. Think of the Stratocums as a high boot, then the foot became the Tetonords as it thrust across the border between the two countries. No sense reminding Diccon. Jenneth turned diffidently, unsure what she'd find behind her, whether Aunt Mahafny had deigned to notice their route so far, or whether Harrap had been petitioning the Lady for a safe journey for them all. She flinched as the assessing gray eyes under the rolapin fur cap met hers, the rest of Aunt Mahafny's face pale and smooth as ice, and as hard. "Aunt Mahafny?" The gray eyes blinked acknowledgment, an indication, Jen fervently hoped, to continue, preferably not about something mundane. "Which highways should we take? Where can we make the best time? We'd best plan ahead, decide now where we'll spend the night. It's too cold to take chances, and we can't risk one of the horses breaking a leg—us either."

"I don't know . . . where . . . Ah!" One hand rubbed her brow as if she were attempting to loosen some nagging memory lodged deep within. "Old acquaintance . . . retired up this way . . . should be able to . . . find it. We'll pass a night there." She blinked once in emphasis.

Reining in the horses, Diccon halted the sleigh in its tracks, aggrieved as he strained around to face his aunt. "You've no idea where it is, do you? You've just pulled something out of thin air and expect us to believe you. Look! It's starting to snow again! We can't aimlessly search for your old acquaintance. Have you *any* idea—any firm idea—where that person lives? These roads are treacherous at night!"

"I said we'd reach my friend's house, and we will, Diccon. Don't ever doubt me." Unpiling the mounded robes covering her and Harrap, she tenderly slid the wrapped

bundle that was Saam off her lap until it rested snug beside
Harrap, glaring at Parm until he settled beside his old
friend. Not looking at her, Harrap began to draw the robes
back in place. "You're not as adventuresome as you pretend, Diccon. Give over the reins, and I'll show you how
to make this sleigh fly over the snow."

She'd prayed for her aunt to take charge, hadn't she?
Heart sinking, Jenneth nudged Diccon to vacate his seat as
she tumbled off the driver's box and scurried to the back
of the sleigh. Harrap had known what was coming, and she
should have as well! Hadn't Aunt Mahafny been notorious
in her prime for her deft handling of the high, two-wheeled
gigs that eumedicos often used to visit patients? And with
patients, speed was usually of the essence. *"We've done it
now, Dic! We knew better and we gave her the opening!
Make sure your hat's securely tied under your chin, because
if it flies off, I guarantee we aren't stopping to go back for
it!"*

❦

Stifling a yawn, Doyce leaned close to Jenret's ear, "These
afternoon naps have been more tiring than I realized." Despite his years, he still blushed like a boy, his pale complexion suddenly suffused with rosiness. Luckily the far end of
the counter where they sat in Dolf's taproom was secluded
and dim, the rest of the room extravagantly decked for the
halidays. A multitude of candles glowed behind pinked-tin
shields, each candle base piled round with evergreen
boughs, running pine, and white and green ribbons.
Wreaths and swags of pine and fir on all available wall
space made the place smell foresty and fresh.

Tonight they celebrated the winter solstice, the start of
a new year, and Dolf's inn was crowded, mostly with regu-
lars, locals from Haarls and the surrounding seacoast vil-
lages, complete with their families, from the tiniest of babes
to the most elderly of grandparents and great-grandparents.
Each time the door opened it carried in a hint of mist along
with the latest arrivals or leave-takers, the taproom abuzz
with laughter and good cheer, toasts serious and humorous.
Behind the counter Dolf darted from one end to the

other, pouring mulled cider and pulling drafts from various ale kegs. Dolf's niece and nephew, about twelve and fourteen, and serious with adult responsibility, carried empty and full trays, wiped spills, passed haliday cookies and cake. Sometimes an occasional remark sent one or the other into a flurry of giggles, endangering glassware and threatening guests with a baptism of liquid haliday cheer.

Nigh onto midnight now, and for a moment the sight of the two youngsters set up an ache of loneliness in Doyce for Diccon and Jenneth. Surely someone had invited them to dinner for tonight, would make some minor festivity for their Naming Day! They'd tarried, pushed back their day of departure again and again, and Doyce had reveled in feeling so reckless. Now, when they should have been halfway home, she was wondering what had possessed her! Thigh pressed comfortably against hers, Jenret reminded her, "Not often we can celebrate the same High Haliday twice. We'll be back soon enough." A pause, long enough to make her turn, convinced he had more to add, though she couldn't guess what. "In fact, I can think of a whole range of ways to celebrate this one . . ."

Despite herself Doyce yawned again. "As long as it doesn't involve another nap!" Khar, stretched on the bar beside her—after all, as an ex-Seeker, Dolf never objected to where any ghatti might want to lounge—yawned, too.

**"Contagious,"** she confessed and fixed her attention on Rawn as he investigated a bowl of salted peanuts, daintily scooping out one nut at a time onto the counter where he batted it before crunching it down. **"But it had better not be** *that* **contagious."**

**"What? Oh . . ."** Rawn tucked his chin tight to his chest, pensive as he licked salt from his paw. **"Was only thinking how odd it is that grinding up these little nuts makes nutter-butter. No . . . not odd, really . . . just that . . ."**

"Hush, Rawn. The more you attempt to proclaim innocence, the worse off you'll be." Jenret slid the peanut dish aside. "And I doubt these are very good for your digestion." Unconcerned that his Bondmate's paw had been fishing through the dish, he took a handful of peanuts, eating one and popping another into Doyce's mouth.

Eyeing the crowd to see who required refills but discovering his services weren't called for at the moment, Dolf

made his way to their end of the counter, bending to retrieve something from beneath it. He brought up three delicate crystal glasses, so thin they had but the merest hint of
substance to them. In his other hand he held a bottle of
celvassy. Leaning forward to read the label, Jenret gave a
low, appreciative whistle.

"Dolf, my good man—you've been holding out on us,
haven't you? Saving the best for yourself."

Although only in his late forties, Dolf Satorious boasted
a head of snowy hair that led people to overestimate his
age until they examined the more youthful features below
it. "No, not in the least!" he protested, pouring reverently,
then letting his hand drift the length of Rawn's spine before
knuckling Khar's chin and ears. With an appreciative purr
Khar craned her neck to ensure Dolf rubbed as many different sensitive spots as possible. "Saving it to share with
friends, fellow Seekers. Always on this night I drink a toast
to Ph'raux."

As he reverently uttered the name of his late ghatt,
Doyce laid a gentle hand on his wrist. He'd spoken
Ph'raux's name with such an intense longing that he'd
looked twice as old and twice as forlorn, and it sent a pang
through her heart.

"Naught wrong and everything right with saluting past
comrades and present company." Gruff, as if he needed to
clear his throat and blow his nose, Jenret exchanged a private glance with Rawn. Drink to the past, drink to the
present, but Doyce dared not drink to the future, a future
that inexorably crept nearer with each new dawn. Would
they have Rawn and Khar by their sides when the next
High Haliday came?

"**As the Elders will it.**" Khar's expression was hidden
as she butted Dolf's shoulder, purring and rubbing against
his neck.

*"When did you turn so pious, love?"* Khar had sounded
almost fatalistic. And, if Doyce acknowledged it, too realis-
tic to make her comfortable with her thoughts. *"You and
Rawn are both stubborn enough to argue it out with the
Elders. After all, I'm planning on celebrating many more
new years with both of you."*

But as she'd 'spoken Khar, she'd realized that Dolf, too,
was speaking, leaning close with an eager conspiratoriality.

"Do you remember Ruxandra Veenstra and P'aer? Retired long before our time, though you must have *heard* of them?"

At his cocked-eyebrow inquiry, she began to rummage through her memories, all the research she'd done on the Seekers Veritas for the Bicentennial History she'd written, indeed, finished just before Swan's death. And hadn't some woman from Neu Bremen gone and "borrowed" half the information, inventing flash and dash and derring-do for the rest when truth was sufficient? *Lives of the Seekers Veritas* had seen five printings, been responsible for influencing countless impressionable young minds, most of them determined to search high and low to find a ghatten with which to Bond! Ah, well, they'd outgrow it as life led them down other paths—all except for a few, a very lucky few who'd be blessed beyond dreams.

"I . . . remember . . . the name." And she did, though that was about all. "Khar? Nothing sticks in my mind as being outstanding or extraordinary about that Bond-pair. Other than," she quickly added, "how extraordinary all Bond-pairs are." Dolf chuckled, but his impatient gaze shifted from one to the other, as if consciously willing her and Khar to remember in depth, remember more clearly. Not exactly a comfortable sensation, pinned by his desire for her to dredge up specific details or facts about Ruxandra Veenstra and P'aer.

Dolf hunched closer, almost ready to pounce, but finally took pity on her as he burst out, "But *that* was precisely what was so extraordinary about them, how they managed to blend, meld, appear totally unremarkable. Exactly as if they wished to escape notice." A hand rubbed at his brow, then blindered his eyes as if to sharpen his mental image, bring it into focus. "Not that I ever knew P'aer—they joined the Elders far before my time with Ph'raux as a Seeker. Though I've heard—"

Jenret rattled the peanut dish to capture Dolf's attention, make him relinquish the celvassy he'd poured but forgotten to pass. "And I take it she lives down here? Tell us their story, Dolf. Give us a tale to start the new year."

But now Dolf fidgeted uneasily, sorry that he'd ever raised the subject, and began polishing the counter with quick, circling strokes, all the time glancing around to see who required refills. "I can't . . . I won't . . ." he swallowed hard, "say much more. Not for me to say, you know?" He seemed to be equally beseeching Khar and Rawn. "She's very old, though she carries her age well. Rumor here-abouts is that she has Erakwa blood in her veins, though none here hold it against her—not after the look she gives them. Strangest thing, though, is that sometimes I swear P'aer is with her, can almost see not just the shadow but the substance. Like what I wish about Ph'raux when I'm feeling lonely. And I *know* I'm seeing true!" he insisted.

"If Ruxie comes tonight, you'll hear—"

The door opened, wintry damp mist swirling inside. A woman stepped from within the enveloping mist, closing the door and leaning against it. "Ruxie came," she announced in a low, croaking voice, and everyone began to joyously blow on noisemakers, tap on toy drums, rattle clapper-sticks. A new year had arrived with Ruxie.

♣

Ruxie seemed to be everywhere at once in her one-room cabin, rebuilding the fire, hauling blankets from beautifully-crafted storage cupboards cleverly hung high near the ceiling, plumping pillows, exiting briefly to shake a throw rug. All the tasks an anxious hostess frantically performs to ready things for unexpected guests. Except . . . Ruxie didn't bustle or act flustered, simply moved with efficient swiftness, never darting but suddenly "there" wherever Doyce chose to look. It was disconcerting enough to make her suspect the older woman glided on casters!

"I tell you, that blasted ghatta hair gets all over everything," Ruxie lamented as she returned inside. "As if you'd need telling, like." A quick smile revealed still-strong, white teeth against a darkish complexion, the legacy of a life spent in the out-of-doors. Her long hair, still more dark than silver, hung down her back in a single thick braid, and her figure was thin and amazingly upright, clad in dark-dyed doeskin trousers topped by a red plaid tunic belted at the waist. Over that hung a shapeless gray-green sweater vest, pockets bulging as if they'd been stuffed with rocks. Just looking at her made Doyce feel twice as cold as she'd been brief moments ago.

Still huddled in her cloak by the fire, Doyce shivered and smiled in return, unsure what in the world they'd gotten themselves into. Standing just behind her, Jenret laid a reassuring hand on her shoulder, and she buried her face in his jacket, steadied by his scent mingled with that of the wool, both heightened by the penetrating mists they'd walked through. Nights along the coast here by the Gulf of Oord turned cold, the rising mist possessed of a knife-sharp chill that cut to the bone. No wonder Khar curled on her lap beneath the cloak, purring loudly enough to wake the dead, while Rawn leaned against the fireplace tiles, soaking up their warmth.

What had possessed them? Agreeing to go off like this with someone they scarcely knew, going they knew not where! At least not through this murky, indistinct netherland of a night, the eight Disciple moons already fading to denote the new year, though the Lady Moon still shone high above. It reflected off the moisture in the air, creating a haze of overarching lightness that never illuminated deeply enough to let them see their feet or the trails they stumbled along, branches dripping on heads and shoulders, the scent of salt marsh and tidal flats sharp in their nostrils.

But Ruxie had downed one small, celebratory drink with Dolf, chatting a little while he hung on her every word, while she, in turn, kept watch near her feet, intent on ensuring that no one trod too close, accidentally stepped on something that was no longer there. Sad, the way old habits died hard; any Seeker would recognize that vigilance, the concern that a beloved Bond's toes or tail weren't pinched beneath an unwary boot.

And when Ruxie'd finished her drink, saluting Dolf with her glass, she'd walked straight to their sides, shrugging off polite, respectful greetings with a brusque nod, though she'd full-stopped once to lean and whisper thanks in a child's ear for the abandoned bird's nest he'd gifted her with. Like the gentleman he was, Jenret had risen off his stool, Doyce as well, sensing that respect—and more—was due, even if for reasons she wasn't privy to. "Don't get down this way much, do ye?" Her voice was rawly husky, though occasionally it cracked, shot high like an adolescent boy's. "Being as you're down," she'd hooked her thumbs in her belt and inspected them frankly from head to toe, "best you come visit me. Now. Mayn't be around next you're down this way. 'Sides, this is a night for tale-telling, and tellers need listeners."

Casually she'd laid a hand on the counter, palm up and open, almost in supplication—not to her and Jenret—but to Khar and Rawn. Or, Doyce had belatedly wondered, had it been a command, a beckoning for them to come, follow after her? Whatever it had been, they'd acquiesced, Jenret hurrying upstairs to their room to fetch cloaks and a small bag with fresh shirts and small clothes. *"What, are we planning on spending the night?"* Foresight? Or something more? After all, Jenret didn't readily yield his creature comforts—and the big featherbed at Dolf's inn ranked high as one of those comforts!

*"Everything's a bit, oh . . . uncanny, isn't it? Bound to be safe, though, love."* Jenret massaged her shoulder and, despite the solace he offered, she sensed exhilaration flowing faster through him, his very glance almost electric with interest. Dear Lady, the man was treating it as another adventure! *"Dolf wouldn't have let us go off with an ax-murderer, you know. Fact is, he seemed a touch jealous at not being included."*

Fine! No former Seeker was likely to have turned to ax-murderer as a way to pass the time after retirement. *"It's just that it's all so unreal, almost surreal."* True, a number of locals at Dolf's taproom had stood them drinks, but she'd learned long ago to take one sip in thanks and surreptitiously dispose of the rest, especially with Dolf's adroit help. *"How much did you have to drink?"* Suspicions aroused, she looked up at him; his eyes were brilliant, sparkling with excitement, but his face lacked that telltale alcoholic flush.

Rawn, bless his heart, came to Jenret's defense. **"Impossible to become inebriated by mere proximity to the fumes,"** he rumbled, straining to lick a spot on his spine that no longer was in easy reach. And then his eyes widened, nostrils sniffing enthusiastically, **"Oh! I smell, I smell . . . aah . . . Ah-WAH-CHOO!"**

"Ah, your handsome beast smells the ghatti weed, he does." While far from grotesque, Ruxie's laugh was disconcerting, rather like gravel being shaken in a rusty canister, but that made it sound more abrasive than it was. It *did* sound disused. Mayhap Ruxie lacked many reasons to laugh—or at least laugh aloud. "P'aer loves the ghatti weed, she does, so I hang it high in the rafters or she'd gobble it all, greedy thing."

*"Jenner, the poor woman thinks P'aer's still alive, still living with her."* Clearly Ruxie had lost touch with reality—at least regarding her Bondmate—yet Doyce couldn't find it in her heart to blame her, or think her mad. Lose Khar and she'd pretend as hard as she could, lose herself in that pretend world until someone rapped on the door and forcibly made her exit into the real world.

Working her head free of the cloak, Khar gazed at her surroundings with amber eyes that sought not just the surface but the depths. **"Don't suppose you've taken a good look in the shadows in the corner over there."** A fractional lift of her head indicated which corner she meant. **"With that ratty, worn sheepskin laid over the big pillow on the floor."**

In truth, the pillow *did* boast a center dent, the concave shape typically impressed by a ghatta's body. And . . . if she squinted . . . then let her eyes float slightly out of focus . . . yes! The slumberous mound of a ghatta, head side-turned to rest on a front leg, hind feet tucked by her head. Almost . . . almost . . . a plaintive, whispery sigh as the ghatta half-roused, then contently settled into sleep again. *"Jenret!"* she 'spoke more urgently than she'd intended, fighting not to tug the bottom of his jacket like an importuning child, desperate for him to notice, reassure her.

*"I know, love . . . I see . . . it."* His hand curled around her neck now, flesh touching flesh in reassurance that she, too, was real. *"It can't be, but I see it, too. Rawn? Khar?"*

Both there and yet not there, a shadow ghatta, a ghost ghatta, somehow more solid than the striped afterimage she'd once glimpsed in the cemetery, past blending with the present at that moment in her quest to understand the first Bondmates of them all, Matty Vandersma and Kharm. And this—real, not real? The strangeness of the evening, the swirling, filmy mists, obscuring so many things, yet highlighting others, departed haliday spirits conniving to create a figment of her imagination? No, not merely her imagination, but Jenret's, as well. Let Khar and Rawn determine the truth of it all, just as they always did, separating the falsehoods, the wantings, the seemings, from reality, the here and now. What would they say? How would they answer?

Stiffly descending from her lap, Khar stepped forward, Rawn at her shoulder, both confidently padding toward the corner, where they bow-stretched in greeting in front of the sheepskin-draped pillow. Dear Lady! That must be the remains of Ruxie's tabard! Why hadn't she recognized it before? Paws dimpling the cushion, Rawn and Khar gingerly climbed aboard, concerned not to jounce the ghatta nestled at the center, who languorously raised a head to greet-sniff them. As they settled around her, the ghost ghatta began to assume a greater solidity, still not completely tangible, yet far more visible, a substance to the shadow, a being inhabiting it, though it hovered on the verge of not-being, one misplaced step enough to carry it beyond.

"Mayhap Dolf mentioned I'm part Erakwa?" Obscurely guilty, as if they'd spied on something they weren't meant to see, they both snapped to attention as Ruxie spoke. With a negligent flick of a hand she directed Jenret to the other chair by the fire, and he obeyed, though Doyce was loath to be separated from him even by that little distance. "Best part of me is, anyway." Ruxie'd claimed a straight-backed chair and turned it round, straddling it, chin propped on her hands where they lightly held the curved top piece.

"Meaning the worst parts of you are Outlander?" Jenret strove to keep his question light, faintly jocular, though he sat stiffly, prepared to leap up and investigate anything else that appeared the slightest bit out of place or time in the small cabin. "Addawanna's teased us about that time and again."

"Didn't say the worst part of me was Outlander." Time had etched a crescent groove on each side of her mouth, deltas of lines radiating from the corners of her eyes, the nose strong and probably more pronounced than it had been in her younger days, or so Doyce guessed. Ears and noses seemed to "grow" as people aged—or was it that the rest of the face shrank, withdrew in on itself? And speaking of ears, yes, Ruxie still wore her earrings, hadn't put them aside on P'aer's death . . or ostensible death. Still, that was merely a tradition, not a hard and fast rule. "Plenty of good in Outlanders, though of a different sort. Not always compatible-like. Nor can you fence off the different parts of you as you can feuding neighbors!" A cough disguised Jenret's crow of delight.

"Thought you might like to hear some Erakwa stories, legends, filtered through Outlander blood. Less ye think they'd be too Outlandish?" Now Jenret laughed aloud, halfway toward being charmed, poised to charm in return, as automatic as breathing when he met any woman who piqued his interest and, most of all, his curiosity.

But Ruxie cast the sign of the Lady's eight-pointed star— almost the last thing Doyce'd anticipated her doing—as she continued, all seriousness now. "And I thank the Lady every sunrise and sunset for my Erakwa blood because it's all that allowed me to keep P'aer this near my side so long."

Whatever happened tonight, whatever they heard, or even surmised, it would be an evening to remember, the mist they'd struggled through a transformative veil now lifting to reveal the varied realities of life. . . .

♣

Steeling herself in advance against the din, aware it might be the final straw that shattered her fragile veneer of composure, Mahafny nodded at Diccon to pound on the door. What with her warped, swollen knuckles perilously close to exploding like roasting chestnuts too near the fire, the pain all-encompassing, she'd have kicked at the door. Not that she'd willingly confess her weakness to the others, or what her efforts guiding the team through the black, snowy night had cost her. Easier, marginally, to bolster Saam against her chest, pretend that holding him made it impossible to knock. Diccon's fist drubbed away, settling into a rhythm— du-du-DUH, du-du-DUH—that set her knuckles, not to mention her very brain, throbbing in concert with each blow.

Blast Trude Voss for sleeping like the dead! Off-shift at the hospice, Trude would return to the house they'd once shared in Gaernett and fall into deep, effortless sleep, com-

plete with a ratcheting rise and catch to each snore that
made listeners wonder when—if ever—her next breath
might be drawn. And sometimes, while Trude slept, that
wretched cat of hers, Peterkin, would wander the house,
scratching at doors, rowling and making an absolute nuisance of himself, hoping someone, either Mahafny or the
housekeeper, would take pity, stagger from a warm bed,
and let him out. Undoubtedly he wanted to escape the
noise as badly as everyone else did!

Even with the door's thickness, the drifting snow packed
against the cottage's foundation and mounded like loaves
of raw bread dough on the window boxes, she swore she
could hear Trude's snores. Nothing could mute them. Swaying, barely able to keep upright, she listened, reassuring
herself that Trude was inside. Again she reeled and
blinked, concentrating on Diccon's fist, rising and falling,
to anchor her, make the world stop spinning. When Diccon
had roused her this afternoon from her reveries, she'd been
expected to take charge, gather her wits, and make decisions. She'd not counted on being forced into that position
yet, had assumed it unnecessary until they reached
Marchmont.

Silence enveloped her, and had been for how many
heartbeats? "Knock again," she snapped, "and keep at it.
With Trude it's like waking a hibernating bear." Wearily
Diccon set up a new, more percussive rhythm with both
fists, an ominous drubbing that made the very snowflakes
shudder, jerk sideways in the night air. She could just make
out the contrast of the pale powder against Saam's dark
wrappings as it piled up in sheltered ridges on the blanket.

How she'd resurrected the trivial fact that Trude Voss
had retired to this out-of-the-way thatched cottage, she
couldn't fathom, but somehow the inconsequential detail
had lodged in her brain, efficiently filed away. Hadn't
seen the woman for what?—a good ten years or more. Hadn't
particularly minded either way; Trude'd been a competent
eumedico and an adequate housemate, barring the snoring.
Liked mindless chitchat too much for Mahafny's tastes, she
who seldom indulged in idle converse. Of course, her steely
silences might have explained why Trude ceaselessly babbled at Peterkin.

If Trude's uncurtained windows hadn't given off a diffuse

glow once dark had fallen, only Harrap's Blessed Lady could have revealed the cottage's location, the night and their surroundings seemingly so empty and enormous. She'd fixed her eyes on that soft, beckoning brightness, her heart and soul as well, and be damned to anything or anyone else, the horses straining to stay ahead of her whip. Mostly they needn't have worried. Reins wrapped around her wrists, she'd set Harrap to cracking the whip and, softhearted soul that he was, he'd enthusiastically flogged the sleigh's side. When Trude's lights had vanished, one by one at bedtime, she'd wanted to cry, unsure if she could locate the cottage in the night, in the snow. No! Things mustn't fall apart this soon! She couldn't, mustn't be doomed from the start! And somehow, drawing from a depleted reservoir of inner resources, she'd blindly navigated them to Trude's yard. Mayhap Harrap had the right of it: the Lady *did* watch out for feckless fools after all, even arrogant ones.

"Yes, yes! I'm coming!" called a voice, querulous mews of various pitches almost obscuring the words. Stretching her length against the door, Kwee mewed back cajolingly, and even Saam restlessly stirred in Mahafny's arms, faintly aware of his distant cousins' vocalizing. "Has Alberda's baby come early? First child of the new year, eh? What?" A lighted lantern in her hand, a scarf already half-furled around her neck, Trude Voss filled her doorway, still trying to cram one bare foot into her boot. Three cats immediately dashed out, unchecked, springing through the snow to circle Pw'eek and Parm and Kwee. Lamplight reflected off more eyes inside, iridescent disks of green, red, and amber like suspended jewels in the cottage's dark interior.

"Trude, it's me, Mahafny Annendahl." To her surprise and everlasting mortification Mahafny staggered, half falling into Trude's ample bosom as the shorter, broader woman stepped forward, agile as one of her cats. "Could we beg a night's lodging with you?" Mahafny mumbled through the torpor that had seized her without warning just as Trude's meaty arm snagged her waist and drew her all the way inside.

For the next while even simple observation proved to be an effort, the details of Trude's cottage refusing to register. Instead, she concentrated on staring back at each cat that stared at her. Just when she'd thought she'd outstared them all, another would appear and sniff at her stockinged feet, then edge closer to sniff at Saam's still form, asleep in a basket by the fire. She thought she'd noticed Trude and Jenneth emptying out three kittens and a resisting mother cat to make space for Saam. So many cats . . . so many inconsequential cats . . . when only one, one ghatt, truly mattered . . . but how could Trude possibly know, even guess . . . ?

Catching her attention as she placed a platter of bacon on the table, Trude smiled with unfeigned pleasure and began pointing at various cats. "Serena, Cyrus, and Jinx, top to bottom on the loft steps. Pleasure's the one keeping her eye on the kittens." True enough, a white cat with one blue eye and one yellow anxiously monitored her kittens as Kwee and Pw'eek rumpused with them. "Smiter's the all-black one over there on my easy chair—hunter par excellence—and Solly and Peterkin are toasting by the fire."

Peterkin? No, impossible! That white cat with patches of black on his hips, hind legs, and tail, as well as a black cap on his head, couldn't be the same Peterkin whose annoyances she'd endured so long ago. "Peterkin?" Would it be an omen if it were, that a mere house cat could survive so many years? A hint of ghatti in him?—hm, might explain his longer life span.

"No, Mahafny, great-grandson of the one you knew— and so thoroughly disliked back then." More food appeared on the table as Trude trotted back and forth without ceasing. From the smell of it, breakfast at near midnight—why not? Not that food held much appeal at this moment. "Here, drink it down, it'll ease the aches and pains," Trude commanded with rough kindness as she wrapped Mahafny's recalcitrant fingers around a mug. "Ever notice we old eu-medicos never completely retire? Always some emergency waiting to happen till we come by." A more astute comment than she'd given Trude credit for, but the woman still chattered just for the sake of chattering.

Somehow she forced herself to eat, lacking the strength to move to the table but accepting a bowl, a plate of whatever Trude or Harrap forced on her, noting as she mechanically chewed that everything had already been cut or broken into manageable pieces. All she had to do was clutch the spoon or fork in her fist like a toddler learning to feed itself and shovel in the food. And at length, she *did* feel marginally better, exhaustion and pain receding enough to clear her head.

Again, somehow without her aid, the table was cleared, the twins sent to the sleeping loft, while Harrap and Parm claimed a pallet in front of the kitchen fire, both asleep almost instantly from their soft breathing. Naturally Mahafny found herself wide awake and alert, which was just as well from the shrewd expression on Trude's wide, bland face.

Leaning back in her chair, fingers laced comfortably across her expansive belly, Trude unashamedly scrutinized her, sherry-brown eyes raking over Mahafny from head to toe. The black cat on her lap languidly extended himself from Trude's hips to beyond her knees—Smiter, Trude'd called him—but examined her with equal thoroughness. Nothing for her to do but to endure it; she had been guilty of equally frank, downright rude assessments of patients.

"Well?" Trude finally asked. "Doubt you simply decided to drop in, pass the time of day, Mahafny. What brings you and your friends here anyway?" A pause as she massaged the black cat's shoulders, and he writhed with ecstasy. "Assuming it's any of my business."

It *wasn't* any of her business, that was the rub, and Mahafny longed to inform her of that in no uncertain terms. Never before had she seen fit to share her innermost thoughts with Trude; no reason to start now. But Trude certainly deserved some answer, some piece of the truth for being roused in the middle of the night, having her home invaded by exhausted, ravenous souls, three of whom she'd never met. Not to mention four ghatti! However, trust Trude to take their presence in stride, and with better grace than she had Mahafny's inexplicable intrusion.

Attempting to avoid the inevitable, she let her eyes roam around the cottage, amusement rising as this time the decor registered: cats here, cats there, cats everywhere—if not live ones, then cat figurines, cat candlesticks, cat carvings, cat sketches, and paintings. "Yes, and if you look more closely at the hooked rug by your feet, you'd see it's cat-shaped. They give me pleasure, Mahafny." Another shrewd look. "And what affords you pleasure these days? Learning what displeased you was always simple enough."

"I. . . . He gives me pleasure." And so much more, she wanted to add, but hoped that echoing Trude's words would suffice to explain. Without volition her hand wandered to stroke Saam's side, but her smile felt brittle, ready to crack into a wail at the unfairness, the injustice of losing a dear companion. "Did we ever consider ailurophilia as a contagious disease, Trude? How long must it incubate, do you think? After all, you were probably the carrier, infecting me, lo those many years ago. A variant strain, a ghatti strain, of course." A superior strain, naturally, though she'd do her best not to rub Trude's nose in the fact. After all, this was the first thing they'd ever had in common, beyond their profession.

"Of course, it's always my fault." Despite her self-mockery, a complacent certainty radiated from her, though that gradually receded as she dragged Smiter's protesting length off her lap. "Would you allow me to take a look at him? I've treated more cats and dogs, horses and cattle than people since I retired, and much prefer the animals, I might add. More grateful and gracious than most human patients." At Mahafny's reluctant assent, she knelt by Saam's basket, peeling back one eyelid and then the other, checking his gums, pressing her ear against his chest.

"Don't want to prod him for any growths or tumors, don't think that's the point. A severe case of old age, I suspect. He's been with you near twenty years, hasn't he? And you weren't his first Bond." With a final stroke the length of Saam's spine, Trude raised her considerable bulk and resettled herself in her chair, absently dusting her hands together, a clump of loose fur sailing free. "Old age must be contagious as well, Mahafny. We're both suffering from it."

"Yes, I'm aware."

"But why in the Lady's name are you hauling the old boy thither and yon on sleigh rides in the middle of snowstorms? Spend the time left to you together by a cozy fire!"

Tell? Not tell? How much to tell? "Don't believe in magic. Don't much believe in prayer, though some do, and it does quite well by some souls." Her raised eyebrow indicated Harrap's bulk, just visible through the kitchen door. "Always believed in hard facts, in knowledge, the diligent application of that knowledge to cure the world's ills—"

"Except sometimes it doesn't work," finished Trude as Peterkin IV sprang atop her chairback, his eyes wide and glowing in the firelight. "Sometimes we can cheat death—under the right circumstances—but never avert it."

"Only because we've not yet found the right knowledge," Mahafny protested. "You *have* to have suspected that sometimes. I know I have."

With a grunt, Trude again dislodged herself from her chair to rummage for an ornately molded bottle and two thin-sided, almost-spherical glasses. "Not celvassy, never could abide the drink. Mayhap you can retain your naturally stiff upper lip on swallowing a shot, but I can't. Just brandy, been sitting there aging—along with me and you. And your dear one, there. Want some?"

The glass was smaller, more fragile than Mahafny liked, but she took it, holding it in both hands as Trude collapsed against the cushions with relief, burying her nose in her glass and inhaling.

"Suspect I shan't get any more out of you tonight except the runaround, eh? And I can't bear to hear you spout mystical mumbo jumbo any more than you can bear saying it. So, you're planning on distracting me with some discussion of bygone eumedico practices, and hope I forget what I asked you." A sip of brandy, then another small one. "Well, I haven't—and I won't—but I'll let it ride. Not easy being a besotted fool, especially when you won't acknowledge it." She flicked a hand in Mahafny's direction to deflect Mahafny's hot denial, and she forced her anger to subside. "Will ask one thing, though. Do *you* need anything else of me?"

How like Trude, forever chary of probing deeply enough at questions or patients; at the first sign of discomfort or pain, she invariably backed off, not wishing to cause further hurt. Mahafny did, however, have something she urgently wanted to ask for, its lack preying at her mind the longer she'd forced them all onward, her strength and determination leaching from her. Why she'd not thought to pack some, she didn't know. Had believed she'd rigorously prepared for every contingency, but this was an oversight of a major magnitude. She matched Trude a sip of brandy. "Have you any . . . *thebaneseng*?" Don't sound eager—or needy—keep it casual. "Should have put some in my kit, but didn't think. Never a bad idea to carry some."

*"Thebie?"* Trude's feet swept off the hassock and landed on the floor with a thud, Peterkin leaping and hissing at the disturbance, glaring reproach at the stranger who'd perturbed his human. "Mahafny!" and her voice went husky, heavy with trepidation. "What the hells do you want with *thebie*?" Her plump face screwed up in distaste and dismay at the mere mention of the drug.

"Didn't ask you to approve, Trude. Don't plan to use it unless I must. It's serious enough for that. Wouldn't ask, otherwise." No, she'd not beg or plead or hector Trude into submission as she'd been wont to do in the past. Either Trude had some and would voluntarily give it over, or she'd . . .

"Search my kit, my herb room for it, wouldn't you?" Trude finished for her. "And I won't have you messing things there, especially since that's not where I store it. Don't have much, only two packets, I think, that I've had forever and then some. Now go to bed, Mahafny." She pointed to a back bedroom. "Get some sleep. Or at least some rest. Take the ghatt with you, if you like, or leave him by the fire with me. I've some thinking to do. Let you know in the morning."

"We need to leave at first light."

"Fine, don't sleep as much as I used to, so let that be a warning to you."

Finishing her brandy in two neat swallows, Mahafny rose and leaned against the table, setting the glass in its center. "Fire in the bedroom?"

"No, I've found that seven cats keep you warm."

"Fine, then I'll leave Saam with you, at least till I've warmed the bed." Saam would stand surety for her honorable intentions, and Trude was the last person in the world to harm a beast, be it cat or ghatt. Best to get to bed before she began to gloat, because for a certainty come morning, Trude would slip her the *thebaneseng* packets. Otherwise, she'd have denied her outright. Cautious, she let a tremulous hand stroke Peterkin's ears, his head. Would have done the same to Trude, but human affection didn't come that easily to her.

❧

Taking a deep breath, Jacobia Wycherley lunged for the crest of the snowbank, unsure if the newly piled snow would support her weight or sink her thigh-deep. With that would follow the inexorable trickle of snow inside her boots. Uneasily balanced atop the bank—so, she hadn't sunk after all—she jumped as far forward as she could, landing evenly on both feet. The heather knit band covering her ears and keeping her luxuriant, dark hair free of her face complemented the color of her eyes, the violet of shy spring flowers hidden amongst the moss. Before she waded up the unshoveled path she pulled off her leather gloves and blew on her fingers. She'd started out from the Saffron Mercantile just outside of town at first light, but given the roads, the easy trip had taken far longer than usual. With the distance the sun had now risen, she'd expected to see some signs of life at the house. Mayhap the twins had considered the indignity of two days of near-constant snow ample reason to hibernate!

"Lazy sluggards!" she sneered, practicing the supercilious tone with which she planned to greet her nephew and niece. They should have had the walkway shoveled by now, or at least begun it. Come to think of it, it didn't look as if they'd lifted a shovel yesterday either. Some of the retired Seekers on the grounds crew had already make a quick pass at shoveling the walkways on Headquarters property. They'd willingly have shoveled right to the front door if her sister-in-law Doyce had been there, still served as Seeker General, but now it was understood that any work done on the grounds around the stone cottage would be the inhabitants' responsibility. Not such a bad bargain to keep the house once Doyce had retired last year, especially when she and Jenret boasted two hardy offspring to shovel paths! Ah, well, let the children enjoy their haliday, sleep late. Seeker training didn't allow the luxury of snuggling in bed until noon.

Plowing along the path, Jacobia realized it already boasted indentations, though they'd turned into shallow dimples, almost erased by falling snow. Mayhap Diccon's intimate dinner with Maeve the other night had been such a resounding success that it had called for a repeat performance! Her nephew was turning into a veritable lady's man, just as his father had been before marrying Doyce— not that that had stopped Jenret from keeping his eyes in practice! Shaking her head, she bounded to the door, trying to knock the snow from her boots but failing miserably. A rap on the door, a brisk tattoo, made her wince, fearing her chilled knuckles might shatter. Nothing. "Come on, my sleeping beauties! Time to rise! Your shovels await!" she shouted up at the windows while giving the door an additional thumping with the heel of her hand. Irritation prickled at her, as did her wool scarf, sticking against her neck from her exertions. Damnation, she'd counted on a good, hot mug of cha before she suffered through the first Mercantiler's Meeting of the year. Assuming it hadn't been canceled because of the weather—then she'd *truly* be irritated—a long, cold ride and a cold belly, and all for naught.

Pw'eek and Kwee *ought* to have heard her, must be waking their drowsy humans even as she stood here, cooling her heels, and the rest of her as well. Now in her mid-thirties, a good fifteen years younger than her half brother, Jenret, Jacobia Wycherley often found herself in sympathy with the twins. Part of it, she supposed, was because she still relished kicking over the traces on occasion, more than willing to play or party when the demanding work of running the mercantile was done. That happened less often than she'd like, what with managing not only her birth father's mercantile, but also overseeing most of the long-term planning for the Wycherley Mercantile—not to mention their new joint outpost in the Sunderlies, ably run by Ozer Oordbeck, or Oh-Oh as some called him. For the most part she loved bending her mind to the problems of running a successful and profitable mercantile. Still, a touch of devyltry wouldn't be amiss right now, and that was why she'd made this detour to see the twins, ostensibly to check on their behavior, but also to see if they'd join her for dinner and darts tonight at Myllard's. Wasn't she due a respite during the halidays?

As her wait lengthened, a nagging restiveness made her shiver despite the layers of sweaters under her fur jacket. A premonition? The ghatti *ought* to have heard, come bounding to the door, working at the knob with their clever paws while the twins straggled out of their beds. Nothing. And now she began hammering at the door with both fists, uncaring how the cold wood bruised her hands. "Diccon! Jenneth! Jennie, Dic? Pw'eek, Kwee, somebody!" Her breathing rushed fast and furious as if she'd run a race, her voice beginning to crack with anxiety.

The explosive slam of a hard-packed snowball between her shoulder blades nearly plastered her against the door. "Dammit, Diccon, I don't know where you've been, but if you've been out all night, rutting like a tomcat, I'll . . ." she spun around in righteous anger. Oh, she'd rip him up one side and down the other, she would! But instead of her nephew, Davvy McNaught peered around the corner of the house, an absurd tasseled stocking cap atop his head, not to mention a wide grin that threatened to split his face.

"Caught you out, didn't I, Jacobia? Fair and square!" His gleeful taunting was designed to distract her from the fact that his gloved hands were rapidly fashioning a second missile. Normally she'd have started molding her own ammunition, ready to return fire, but she was *not* in the mood for it this morning.

Jacobia raised her hands in surrender. "Davvy, any sign of the twins out back by the stable?" With a certain dejection he tossed the snowball over his shoulder and began plodding through the drifts piled at the corner of the house. His stocking cap, inexpertly knitted in every color of the rainbow and some the Lady'd never envisioned, lofted out behind him like a banner in the breeze. So that was why little Byrlie had been begging scraps from yarn bags, then suddenly hushing if Davvy came anywhere near. A stranger would certainly never believe Davvy was a rising Resonant-eumedico, would more likely take him for a street muggins and throw coins at his feet. "Well, did you? Any sign of life out back?"

"Sleigh tracks. You can see where the runners swung in and around, then headed out again. But they aren't fresh—you can barely make them out." Tripping over something buried in the snow, Davvy flailed before swan diving into the drift, only to rise, spitting snow and looking less than amused. "Back door was locked. Is the front?" Upright, he slapped at himself to dislodge the clinging snow. "Damn! Swore I was twelve again—till that pratfall! Ah, such dignity, such grace!" Ignoring his chatter, she worked at the doorknob, not sure if the lock were frozen or her hands too cold to firmly turn it.

"Here," his warm breath grazed her cheek as he reached round her and placed his hands over hers, nearly crushing her fingers as he gripped hard and twisted the knob. "Locked as well. At least the twins remembered one of Doyce's instructions." He sighed. "I hope you realize this means leftovers for me tonight. Lindy promised to cook whatever I wanted for dinner if the twins would join us. Chaperones, you know—not that Byrlie doesn't admirably serve that purpose," he added confidentially. Although she'd been but a child herself, Lindy had been the twins' first nursemaid before her marriage to Bard, and she still took her responsibilities seriously. "I think Lindy also wanted me to check that Jen and Diccon hadn't burned down the house or been indulging in wild, wanton revelries on their Naming Day."

"And without inviting either of us?" Jacobia teased.

"One would hope they had more exciting plans than celebrating with doddering ancients. Wouldn't you have had at that age?" Patting at his pockets, more out of habit than expectation of finding what he sought, Davvy asked, "Got a key? Should've brought Lindy's, but didn't think I'd need it."

Her heart and breathing returned to normal, Jacobia still twinged with apprehensiveness as she mentally practiced giving the twins a stern lecture. About what, she wasn't sure, but she was bound to find some reason—if not, she'd ask Lindy for one. One of the delights of being an aunt was the camaraderie between her and the twins, but she'd also discovered herself turning maternal in the blink of an eye, lecturing more sternly than Doyce or Jenret might. What was it Jenret had ruefully moaned one night when the twins had refused to go to bed? "Standards slip when you have children. They wear you down."

Hoisting her jacket to free her pockets, she fumbled inside for her key ring, fingering the keys until she found the one she wanted. "I suppose we can leave them a note, both of us ask them to dinner, let them decide." A faint disappointment at the idea, but fair was fair. "Can't blame them for deciding this was perfect weather for a sleigh ride!"

"Jacobia," Davvy's brown eyes turned serious under the bangs flattened across his forehead by his jester's cap. "I'm beginning to wonder if this isn't . . ."

Handing him the key, she let him unlock the door, shouldering it to crack the ice that had frozen around the bottom. "Isn't what, Davvy?"

Stamping his boots, belatedly trying to shake some of the packed snow loose, Davvy's words came out muffled. "Mayhap . . . nothing. Let's check if they've left a note for us or anyone else."

Once he'd cleared the entryway, she followed tight behind, not bothering with the niceties of boot scraping. "What do you know that I don't, Davvy McNaught? And do you know something for a certainty—or just suspect it?" Find out the facts—analyze both hard data and intuition—plot out the options, make a decision, and act on it. That was how the head of a mercantile responded to problems, and rarely had it failed her. Competitors had learned the hard way not to judge her only by her looks.

Davvy didn't slow as he headed toward the kitchen, but he did add a major piece to the puzzle of the twins' apparent absence. "Jen and Diccon aren't the first people I've missed seeing this morning. I stopped at Mahafny's and Harrap's first—she'd promised to loan me her notes on upper respiratory problems. The cottage was empty. Ah!" Spying a piece of paper ghostly pale on the table, he braced a hand on either side of it to peruse it in the semidarkness.

Setting a lucifer to one of the oil lamps on the table, Jacobia shoved at Davvy with shoulder and hip, determined to claim her space, not wait until Davvy'd finished digesting the note's contents. Jenneth's neat, nervous script marched across the paper.

*Dear ones all,*

*To whomever may read this, relative or friend, Dic and I and the ghatti are escorting Aunt Mahafny and Harrap to Marchmont. Aunt M. is sure Saam will die if she doesn't bring him to Nakum in time. We don't know if this will do any good, but you know there's no arguing with Auntie when she's convinced about something.*

*Please don't worry—we'll be back soon as we can. Also, please remember we all took a solemn oath not to worry Mama and Papa while they're away. And yes, tell GrammaDama we packed extra stockings!*

    *Love to all,*
     *Jen and Diccon (who had a less-than-fulfilling evening with Maeve—ha, ha!)*

"Convinced about something! When isn't Mahafny convinced she's right?" Almost sputtering, Davvy gave the table an openhanded slap. "Poor Saam, and poor Mahafny . . . I've suspected of late that she'd been dwelling on what life would hold for her without Saam—not that she'd talk to me about it—but I didn't realize she'd take such an extreme action." Without warning he began to drum his fingers, the beat quickening. "And the timing is *so* convenient! What got into us after Doyce's and Jenret's going away party? Pledging that not a whisper of a worry or woe should come their way—not from the ghatti or from us Resonants. I swear, Jacobia, I'll never drink celvassy again!"

But Jacobia now stood looking north out the kitchen window and beyond, sorrow and anger warring within her. "Fools, absolute fools! I could *almost* forgive Diccon, he's so tenderhearted he'd do anything in the world for someone he loved and hang the cost to him! But Jenneth always looks before she leaps—she's equally caring, but she always weighs the consequences, worries—"

"And gallantly attempts a lost cause, regardless," Davvy finished for her. "Damnation! And in this weather—frostbite, broken legs, hypothermia. . . ."

Leaving the window to plow methodically through kitchen drawers, Jacobia found a pad of paper and a pencil. "Making a list always helps, I've found." Licking the pencil, she poised it over the paper, began scribbling.

Hands twisting the tail of his stocking cap, Davvy gave her a faintly bewildered look. What? Did he think she'd go hysterical on him because the twins had taken off on a mad mission of mercy? Had at least a day's head start? Reading her list certainly wouldn't put his mind at ease, though the mere writing of the words helped her immensely.

#1) Whip their bottoms.
#2) Do so after whipping Mahafny's.

The sheet of paper separated from the pad with a satisfying rip, and she waved it under his nose, eliciting the smile she'd hoped for. Now for some detailed lists, some necessary notes. "Play messenger-boy for me, Davvy. I can't waste the time delivering these notes." Such hubris, to assume that her wants and needs outstripped his own! He was a Resonant-eumedico, after all, and hospice patients depended on him, on his touch, his skill. But with Doyce and Jenret gone, *she* bore responsibility for the twins' well-being. "Jen's right, Davvy. We're *not* going to inform Doyce and Jenret, are we?" Already he looked guilty in anticipation of the act. "*Are* we, Davvy?" Her demand circled, slipping back to score a direct hit on her own guilt. Of course Jenret and Doyce should be informed! Struggling with herself, she conquered the thought, the guilt. The twins weren't in danger yet—and the sooner she caught up with them, the less chance they'd have to be in danger.

"I . . . Of course, Jacobia." Lady bless him for his sweet nature, his refusal to argue. Now if only Lindy would bless him for it in equal measure, give in to her heart, cease mourning Bard and marry Davvy. Byrlie needed a father as much as Lindy needed Davvy as her husband.

"I'm going after them, Davvy. I don't know where I'll catch up with them, but I'm going to stop them. Haul them all right back home where they belong. Saam's a darling, but he's so old and ill. . . . You know that, I know that." Hurtful to be so coolly rational over Saam's impending demise, to almost shrug it off. Ever since her youth she'd been so closely associated with the ghatti that it seemed perfectly natural to consider them as members of the family. If it were Rawn, Jenret's Bond, her heart would break nearly as badly as Jenret's would when that day came. "But I refuse to let Mahafny's arrogance dictate this madness, thinking she can outwit death—not when it puts the twins at risk."

❖

Rays of afternoon sun struggled to cut through the overcast, and Jacobia considered the use of subterfuge instead
of brute strength. Simply seek out a likely crack in the
cloud cover and slip through, that's what the sunlight
should do. How fanciful—like the start of an old tale, an
Erakwa legend that Addawanna or Nakum might have re-
counted on one of their visits. Sometimes those legends
held nuggets of wisdom, and now she wished she had
thought on them more deeply. Where was the old notebook
where she'd impulsively jotted bits of tales, intent on preserving the stories, yet unable to do justice to their telling.
A lack of writing skill? Or a lack of understanding?

Already it was later than she'd like, and she sat her
mount with rising impatience, fully ready to depart, her
pack beast loaded but at ease, his weight shifted clear of
one hindquarter as he eyed his surroundings with curiosity,
before swinging his head her way. Roads should be pass-
able now, enough time elapsed for Transitor crews to clear
at least one lane, dig pull-overs into the steep, heaped
banks so one team or another could give way to wagons
or sleighs passing in the opposite direction.

Why not leave and be done with it, not fritter away the
remaining daylight? Her own mount shifted restively as if
in full agreement, the pack beast bobbing its head. Because
she'd promised not to depart until she'd spoken with Davvy
again. But waiting guaranteed that when Davvy returned,
he'd be prepared to accompany her, and that she didn't
want. Her saddle creaked with the cold as she twisted uncomfortably, checking that her snowshoes were firmly
lashed behind her. Davvy had obligations here, not only to
his patients, but to Lindy and Byrlie as well. No matter his
emotional attachment to Doyce and the twins, he couldn't
constantly jeopardize his own livelihood—his own life—
each time they landed in trouble. Though Davvy'd been
tight-lipped about Bard's Sunderlies death, she'd winkled
the details out of Diccon: how Tadj Pomerol's rage had
been stoked at recognizing Davvy; only Bard's intervention
had saved the Resonant-eumedico from death.

Frankly, she didn't need any distractions on this chase.
She wanted to set her own pace, set herself to thinking like

the twins. In maturity she'd tamed her own headstrong urges, a hard-won effort, to say the least, but their shared impetuosity offered her a window into Diccon's mind. The only window she had, since she possessed no Resonant ability, couldn't send her mindvoice through space to chastise Diccon and Jenneth for their mad dash toward disaster. Jenneth's insecurities she understood equally well, a wince of remembrance at the anguish of that awkward age, unsure, insecure, listening too deeply and passionately to her own inner fears, the confusions of a blossoming sexuality leaving her dangling between the havens and hells.

It struck her then—Lady bless, this was too eerily similar, uncannily so—the memory of a headstrong seventeen-year-old running away from home, intent on catching up with Doyce and Jenret as they and their party rode to Marchmont to determine what was causing Canderis's inexplicable trade problems. And running away from the growing realization that her true birth father was Syndar Saffron, mercantile competitor and neighbor, not Jadrian Wycherley, his mind swept clean of coherent thought long years past by his elder son, Jared, with his childish, untrained Resonant abilities. Nothing would have stopped her then; and nothing would stop the twins. Syndar Saffron had stormed off after her, too, just as she planned to ride to the twins' rescue. Did family history tend to repeat itself? But the deeper question was what—if anything—had she learned from her previous escapade?

A rush of tears burned hot behind her eyelids, and she blinked them away, furious that they'd caught her unaware. Ah, Chak—courtly gentleman-ghatt, and so very old and ill. When Chak had died on the journey, his Bondmate, the special envoy Rolf Cardamon, had jumped to his own death off the cliffs leading to The Shroud, his beloved Bondmate in his arms. Damn, damn, damn, don't think about it, don't even think of it! It will *not* come to pass the same way this time—could not!

The stable yard at the rear of Myllard's hummed with activity; many travelers had been savvy enough to read the weather signs, had possessed common sense enough to delay their departures home. Locals now poured into Myllard's, eager for hot cha or mulled cider after nearly a full day of shoveling, primed with tales about the blizzard. And she couldn't sit like an equestrian statue any longer or she'd freeze to death! If she stood just inside the inn's doors, she'd escape the wind, decide how much longer to postpone her departure. Blast Davvy for being so late!

As she kicked a stirrup free to swing down, renewed "hallos" filled the yard, and she guiltily glanced over her shoulder. That's what came from brooding over her past escapades! If her message had arrived at the mercantile too soon, she'd have Syndar and Damaris to cope with, convince she could handle the problem. Considering that the twins were Damaris's grandchildren, it might prove easier to convince her mother than it would the man that she'd only learned to call "Father" when she was the twins' age. Syndar Saffron had taken to parenting with a vengeance after so many years of having to deny paternity to protect her mother's reputation. But with so many lost years to make up, he sometimes attempted to cover ground that had already been covered as she'd grown up. Yes, he'd given over the day-to-day running of his mercantile to her, prideful of her acumen, and then he'd turn around and attempt to forbid her some perfectly reasonable adult activity, like staying out late. Mostly he gave a guilty smile and acquiesced when she or her mother pointed out his contradictory attitude, but Jacobia still had visions of being sent to bed without supper! Parents! Still, Papa Syndar was a dear!

But as Jacobia finally saw who'd entered the yard, she tightened her lips and shook her head, almost wishing it were Syndar bulling his way through the throng. Davvy McNaught came trotting toward her, tilting precariously under the weight of a large pack, his madly-hued stocking cap creeping down over his forehead. Finally! And that pack—so, she'd been right! Except behind him—above the pack, to be more precise—Byrlie perched on someone's shoulders, already waving at her. Did that mean she'd have to face Lindy and the sad resignation in her eyes at having Davvy venture off without her? Worse—what if Lindy had been seized by one of her foreseeings, her ability to faintly glimpse the future? Did she truly want to know how the twins fared—especially if disaster had already struck? Clenching her own eyes shut, she swallowed hard. Lady bless—they didn't *all* propose to accompany her, did they?

"Sorry I took so long!" Panting, Davvy heaved the pack

onto the ground and waved for one of the bundled stable lads, Claire and Wyatt's youngest, she thought. "Had a hard time convincing Feather she was due some haliday-leave to visit her people. Entirely too conscientious, works way too hard and never plays!" Who? Davvy winked at her. "Of course, I tried to conscript Maeve first. Figured she'd scent out Diccon wherever he was!"

Under less strained circumstances she'd have laughed, but now what was uppermost in her mind was getting rid of this unknown, unwanted person. Bad enough to be saddled with Davvy, but far worse to ride with a total stranger! Stepping close, she snapped, "What do you think you're doing?" and moved past him before he could answer, ready to scathingly reject this potential travelmate. But the woman—Feather—had squatted to unload Byrlie and now remained sheltered behind her, arms around her waist, as if shielding herself with the child.

"Unfortunately Davvy didn't have the foresight to consult with me first. I've absolutely no need of—" Despite her best intentions, irritation and condescension turned each word thorny, guaranteed to rankle. She was just warming up to the tongue-lashing she'd meant for Davvy, her frustration at her continued delay stripping away her self-control.

But before she could continue—mayhap qualify her rudeness—a young woman rose from behind Byrlie. "Very well, Miz Wycherley, I understand."

Only then did Jacobia fully take in the stranger's face and figure, startled beyond measure. A young Erakwan woman, surely! The faintly coppery complexion, the wide cheekbones, the straight nose, her lean but solid body all cried out her identity as an offspring of the planet's original inhabitants, the Erakwa, reclusive folk who preferred their woods and wilderness to the structures and strictures of "civilized" life. While most Canderisian citizens had few or no dealings with the Erakwa, the Wycherleys counted at least two as loyal friends, almost extended family—Adda-wanna and her grandson, Nakum.

Feather's response haunted Jacobia, that weary half-turn she'd made on hearing her bluster, the way her shoulders had slumped before she'd consciously squared them, the careful, impassive expression that revealed nothing. Feather assumed she'd been slighted because of her heritage! It happened, more than Jacobia would have liked. When Erakwa *did* venture into towns for market days or such-like, someone always contrived to taunt and tease them, fingers pointed denigratingly at the special few who wore pouches containing their earth-bonds. Hard to convince the Erakwa that those who taunted them were usually themselves ridiculed, scorned for laziness, drunkenness, and other ill-mannered, boorish habits. And with the mild-mannered Erakwa they'd at last found someone seemingly more deserving of opprobrium than their own sorry selves.

"Feather, wait!" Oh, well done! That had sounded more patronizing than she'd planned, and the young woman reacted like a long-suffering beast, halting with weary obedience, though she didn't turn. A minor jolt of controlled, contained power, an almost imperceptible tingling raced through her as Jacobia impetuously placed a hand on the young woman's sweater-clad arm, Feather shrugging it off with studied nonchalance.

"Oughta apologize, Jacobia! Feather's my friend!" Byrlie stood in front of her, red mittens on her hips, wisps of blonde hair creeping from under her red cap. Even worse, the toe of her small boot was tapping up a storm. Byrlie might be only eight, but she was a serious eight, and absolutely relentless in protecting those she loved.

Jacobia managed a mild rejoinder. "And that's exactly what I'd planned to do—if you hadn't interrupted."

"Oh." Byrlie didn't sound exactly repentant and still stood her ground. "So . . . ?" Then the child relented. "Feather, Jacobia's kinda upset 'cause Jenneth and Diccon took Eumedico Mahafny and Shepherd Harrap off to Marchmont. Saam and Parm, too, 'cause Saam's going to die—remember how I told you what Mama told me? I don't know if he's gonna 'die' dead, or if he's going to live with the Elders, like M'wa did, though."

Kissing her fingertip, Feather touched Byrlie's nose. "You've had much on your mind, Miz Wycherley. And naturally you don't wish to be hindered by anyone in your search, even such a one as I." Her voice was musical and low, like a faint breeze rustling the undergrowth, whispering secrets to the earth.

"Yes, exactly!" Jacobia agreed, wry with relief. "I'm worried about the twins, and the last thing I want is a distraction. Nor did I have the slightest notion Davvy planned to—"

"Saddle you with a stranger, let alone an Erakwa," Feather finished for her. "Yes, I *do* understand, better than you might think. After all, you Canderisians are superior in so many things and in so many ways."

"No, that's *not* what I meant at all! You're making too much of my refusal, refusing to understand how you've inadvertently complicated things!" Blast it, couldn't the woman see how she'd been taken by surprise by the whole thing? Was she looking for slights? Expecting mistreatment, insults? Impossible to put things right now, impossible to convince someone so sullen, with such a chip on her shoulder. An apology wouldn't help, nor would she make one that didn't sound genuine! And why wasn't Davvy jumping in, interceding, explaining, smoothing things over? Surely *he* was the one fully deserving of both her wrath and Feather's!

Rolling her eyes and glaring at Davvy, still standing in quizzical dismay, Jacobia muttered, "*You* smooth things over—you're at fault for springing this on me, for letting her think. . . . Oh, never mind!" Gaining her horse, she mounted in a rush and jerked on the rein to bring it around. Wonderful! Apparently she and Feather had been the center of attention from the looks being cast her way. "Davvy, Byrlic—I'm off now! Let's hope I can find them soon!"

♣

Since Parm's frantic alert to Sh'ar early yesterday morning, the skies above Gaernett had come alive with mindvoices spreading northward across Canderis, sometimes buffeted and misdirected by the weather, but gradually reaching farther and farther, alerting more and more ghatti. Ears pricked with interest and sorrow at the message: **"Seek for the Wycherley twins, the Eumedico Annendahl, the Shepherd-Seeker Harrap, and their Bondmates. Report their locale and condition immediately on sighting. Offer any and all help needed—if so required."** Whether barely out of ghattenhood, in their prime, or in venerable old age, ghatti strove to twine their mindvoices to create a mindnet, capable of lofting farther than a lone voice. And as the message swooped from mind to mind, hot debate ensued as to the rightness of it all, sometimes shared with Bond-mates, active and retired Seekers, and sometimes not. Never was it easy to let a legend die, if die it must. . . . But then Bondmates, Seekers and ghatti alike, tended to be fiercely protective of their own—which explained why not a word, not the least hint of mindspeech drifted south-ward toward Rawn and Khar.

Not a one of the ghatti would let their beloved Saam come to harm, nor their ebullient friend Parm, nor the younglings, Pw'eek and Kwee. Held in equally high esteem were Jenneth and Diccon, offspring of their ex-Seeker General Doyce Marbon and Seeker-Resonant Jenret Wycherley. Harrap and Mahafny held a special place in ghatti hearts as well, though any ghatti mentioning Mahafny generally managed to insert a supercilious little sniff, nose in the air as if purposely ignoring something faintly distasteful. Thus had Mahafny haughtily looked down on them before she'd finally gained the courage to esteem and love Saam. Though they'd never do it to her face, the ghatti couldn't resist twitting her just a touch.

**"Search high. Search low. See how our beloved friends fare, succor them if needed."** Not one ghatti or human Bond alerted to the news begrudged the extra work their assignment might entail, already stretched thin as they were on haliday duty. And those Seeker-pairs celebrating the halidays made extra efforts to remain accessible, ready to ride in an instant if needed. . . .

♣

Nor would the ghatti be the only concerned souls lofting messages through the wintery air both day and night. Resonants now did their share, reminding their brethren of their debt to Doyce Marbon and Jenret Wycherley: the opportunity to at last stride forth from the shadows, to take their places as full citizens, respected for their differences, not feared.

Davvy McNaught had started Resonants spreading the

word as soon as he'd begun delivering Jacobia's notes, had
sent word heading north before he'd even seen Jacobia off.
It afforded him at least a minor relief, and he'd honestly
believed he'd resolved another facet of the mounting problem by cajoling Feather into joining Jacobia. But the near-
instant misunderstanding, the antagonism between Feather
and Jacobia had caught him utterly by surprise, he who
prided himself on deftly reading the nuances beneath the
surface. More than anything, he'd been stunned by Feather's reaction, the rising eumedico trainee no longer impassive, polite. Had her hurts been simmering all this time and
him not seeing, not feeling her pain? Easier to believe it
the sort of instant dislike that two competitive, competent
women sometimes cultivate without rhyme or reason. Well,
Lindy would disabuse him of that benighted notion tonight,
mayhap have the insights he'd so sorely lacked. Lady help
him—those two had practically hackled at each other with
barely a word spoken! And now Byrlie was glaring at him
as well!

Morning rounds were long over—might as well be late
for afternoon hospice rounds as well. No choice. One task
still remained as he climbed the snowbank behind Myllard's
stable yard and slipped and slithered down, nearly falling
as he hit the pounded, slick snow over the cobbles. Now if
he could make his way through the streets and back to
Seeker Veritas Headquarters—and if only Berne Terborgh
and Sh'ar were still there. Damn it all, he didn't care what
silly pledge they'd all made over celvassy that night! Surely
Berne would back him!

As he turned onto the grounds, the rose-tinted granite
cupola atop Headquarters resembled a festive haliday cake,
frosted with snow. Near the sunken plaza Seekers with their
sheepskin tabards edged and sashed in different colors went
calmly and efficiently about their business, although a few
indulged in snowball fights, ambushing fellow Seekers,
human and ghatti alike. Funny how a snowfall could
reignite the youth in even the most mature of Seekers
and ghatti.

The bronze statue of Matty Vandersma and his ghatta
Kharm had been dusted free of snow, and he stopped to
admire it, smiling as always at the private humor that
seemed to animate each still face, wishing he could share

in it. Though he wasn't a Seeker, surely he could stroke the bronze ghatta head, Matty's elbow, and pray the luck would be transferred to his wandering Seeker friends. Surely the first Seekers of them all wouldn't object.

But before he could stride forward, a ghatt in his prime threw himself from behind a snowbank, powerful forelegs wrapping around Davvy's ankles. Anyone unexpectedly tackled by twenty kilos of muscular ghatt tended to topple, and Davvy was no exception, desperately twisting and thrusting out his arms to break his fall.

In truth his fall was broken by the snowbank he plowed into headfirst, arms sinking into it as if it were a cloud, his face burrowing into the cold, compacted crystals. Sputtering, he rolled onto his back to cast a baleful look at Sh'ar. Glaring was hardly successful when his eyelashes and eyebrows were coated with snow; he could barely see the tiger ghatt whose legs, belly, chest, and muzzle appeared to have been dipped in white paint.

*"I take it that Berne's still here, then?"* Although Davvy had been around ghatti since his boyhood, many considering him a close enough friend to 'speak him, he always tried to make it a point to give them formal permission. *"Mindwalk, if ye will. And you'd best do so, because I expect an apology!"*

**"Ah, McNaught, always *so* conscientious—and *so* utterly tempting! Your bootlace was dangling and dancing, crying out to be played with, so I obliged."** He sounded hugely unrepentant, and his quick paw-swipe couldn't begin to erase the ghatti smirk on his face. Davvy didn't begrudge him his fun, all too aware of the heavy duties the ghatt and his Bond, Berne, routinely shouldered. If Sh'ar felt secure enough to venture out and roister for a bit, it indicated that Berne Terborgh at last felt at ease as Seeker General after roughly a year on the job as Doyce's successor.

To demonstrate at least a modicum of contrition, Sh'ar stomped across Davvy's chest and delicately groomed snow particles from Davvy's eyebrows. **"Magnificent cap—the tassel on the end almost distracted me from your bootlace."** Sneaking a quick lick at the tip of Davvy's nose, he continued, **"What brings you here today? None of our humans sick, I hope? The last thing Berne needs is to find another**

**replacement to ride circuit—not that anyone's going to get
very far in this snow."**

Removing the ghatt from his chest, Davvy clambered to
his feet and began dusting himself off, unaware that his
dark blue jacket presented a perfect target. The snowball
hit high on his chest, exploding into loose powder that
dusted his face. "I send him in advance to waylay our vic-
tims, then I deliver the *coup de grace*!" Berne Terborgh,
expansive with haliday goodwill and cheer, at least a drop
of it of the liquid variety, bounded over to shake Davvy's
hand.

For a moment the tall, sandy-haired man looked his true
age, thirty-six, a multitude of responsibilities briefly lifted
from his broad shoulders, his beaming face relaxed and
ruddy with the cold, boyish and exhilarated. But growing
concern replaced that as Davvy explained his problem.
"Lady bless and save them all, but I hope it's not our time
to lose Saam!" Genuine pain clouded the Seeker General's
eyes. "I'd have sworn Mahafny Annendahl to be one of
the most levelheaded people I've ever met, not prone to
impulsive gestures, especially a gesture bound to fail. It's
pitiful, in a way, to force a fellow-creature to cling to a life
he's ready to leave." He and Sh'ar shared a look of sympathy, a depth of feeling that subtly excluded Davvy.

Then Berne's eyes widened as he slapped his forehead.
"How could I forget? Doyce and Jenret, Khar and Rawn
aren't due back for . . . what? . . . another five days?"
Davvy nodded. Bless Berne that he felt the same—not letting himself be bound by that silly pledge! Better to do it
by mindspeech or in person? "Well, trust Sh'ar to get the
word out—I assume that's what you want? Have Seekers
keep an eye out for them?" He'd not thought of that, had
been too concerned about notifying Jenret and Doyce.
Leave it to Berne to think of something so practical!

Uneasily rising on his toes as if his paws were suddenly
too icy, Sh'ar mumbled, **"Did that already. A human Bondmate has to rise pretty early in the morning to get ahead
of an enterprising ghatt."** Then, as if fearing he'd overstepped his bounds, Sh'ar craned his head, ostensibly studying a chattering, scolding sparrow that wanted to light on
the statue's head. **"Um, Parm 'spoke me the morning they
departed. I guess . . ."** his head shifted farther and farther

away from Berne, eyes intent on the sparrow, **"I never did mention it, what with the press of things . . ."**

Davvy had no idea what Berne might have said on the strictly intimate mode the two of them shared, but Sh'ar seemed to shrink in size, hanging his head like a scolded ghatten. To save his ghatt friend further embarrassment, Davvy added, "I'm glad as many Seekers as possible are already on the lookout. We all know the twins are clever, resourceful, but they're not full-fledged Seekers. I'm afraid Mahafny can twist them around her little finger, convince them and Harrap to do whatever she wants." He wouldn't say, couldn't say how he feared for Jenneth, of what a fresh death might do to her, even though the circumstances were so different. She hadn't yet fully grieved over Bard's passing, had walled it off within herself, even as Lindy and Byrlie had learned to cope with it, accept it. Lindy had tried to talk with her, but to no avail, Jenneth sitting silent, twisting her Seeker's earrings, her pair and her twin's earrings that had once graced Bard and Byrta, M'wa and P'wa. Let something happen to another loved one, part of her special circle, and it might unleash a grief so profoundly great and crippling that she'd be unable to cope.

But now Sh'ar and Berne exchanged a look, so close to being complicitous that it was almost comical, if Davvy had been in a mood to laugh. "Just because word's gone out, Davvy, don't think that Doyce and Jenret are going to hear about this. And don't you Resonant 'em, either—you hear!" Sh'ar's fierce stare outdid Berne's, especially the way the ghatt's lip's retracted just enough to show his fangs. "They can't do a thing from where they are except worry themselves to death. Time enough for that when they're back." But then Berne minimally relented. "You *do* know who's in Marchmont right now? Decided to spend their haliday there?"

"I'm *not* in the mood for guessing games! Who?" Had Jacobia's churlishness with Feather rubbed off? His feet were wet, his hands like ice, and snow had managed to work its way down his waistband, thanks to Sh'ar. Wouldn't his patients appreciate it when he finally arrived to touch their fevered brows! Rebelliousness seized him—no Resonant-eumedico was going to be ordered around by a mere Seeker! He'd do what he chose, what was best!

"**Holly and P'roul, Theo and Khim,**" Sh'ar offered by way of apology. "**They're in Sidonie, in Marchmont!**"

But Sh'ar didn't need to elaborate on his point. Saam had sired Khim. And Holly's pragmatic practicality combined with Theo's sympathy might just be the remedy Mahafny needed to allow her to think things through again. The next best thing to having Doyce and Jenret there, or so Davvy tried to convince himself. Breaking an oath— even one sworn under the influence of celvassy—wasn't his way.

❧

Etelka Rundgren punched the pillow into a suitably supportive shape while her bare feet fished beneath the covers to draw the flannel-wrapped brick closer to the bed's center where she curled her feet when she sat up at night reading. Bedclothes hitched high under her chin, she pushed her spectacles up her nose and licked her index finger, tingling with anticipation at turning another page of her precious book. Her puddle-brown eyes, already enlarged by her spectacles, grew even larger. Ah, no—utterly unfair! The chapter'd ended without warning!

Twisting a lock of hair the unflattering shade of broom-straw, she contemplated her options. The conclusion of each chapter always provoked a delicious decision, a tantalizing quandary: Close the book now, reserve the dwindling remainder for another night, as many nights as possible, so that it would practically never end? Or speed on, allow herself to be swept into another world by the glorious words, a silent, supportive partner to the diverse characters springing to life on each page? And springing to death sometimes, too. Two nights ago hadn't she practically soaked her pillow with tears as Rolf Cardamon made his noble and irrevocable decision to follow after his beloved Bond—the gentlemanly gray ghatt Chak—in death, just as Chak had so loyally stayed at Rolf's side in life?

Closing her finger in the book—**Lives of the Seekers Veritas**—she gave a shivery sigh and eyed the lantern, wondering how much oil remained in its tarnished tin base. She also wished for the thousandth time that she possessed a graceful, globed oil lamp with a transparent, cut-glass base. Her reflective grin acknowledged how woefully out of place it would look, given the rest of her less-than-elegant decor. Still undecided whether to greedily read on or exhibit self-control and halt for tonight, she let her eyes roam around her bedroom. Mightn't seem much to some, but to her it was *everything*—hers alone, all hers! A real door to shut out the rest of the world, the rest of her family. Her very own bed—true, one leg was propped on a brick—that she shared with no one unless she chose to do so. Sheets and blankets scented with lavender that didn't have to be wrestled for each and every night. Course, if she'd thought of dousing the blankets with lavender before, it might have chased her brothers out of their shared bed, groaning and pinching their noses!

So what if patches of frost grew crystal patterns on her rudely-planed walls? That the shelving surrounding her bed at its head and along and above its right side was coarse and gray with age? Or that the roof slanted so low over her bed there was barely room to sit up straight on the right side? The nightstand her lantern "graced" was brand-new, sparkling-white; her favorite brother, Levi, had made it himself, just for her! And the other boys had chipped in for the almost new, rose-decorated chamber pot 'neath the bed. The lantern's dim light just reached the shelves at the foot of her bed, jars and jars of preserves, pickled beets, carrots, beans, and corn relish; peaches and pears and cherries in their thick syrup, reflecting a medley of rich, ripe colors, like the stained glass in the king's castle at Sidonie. Back when she was just older than Etelka, Mam had actually gone to Sidonie, had taken the tour—oh, not the private quarters, of course, but the public rooms. What Mam remembered best were the windows, plus exclaiming how they managed to keep their carpets so clean, what with all the traffic! Smiling at that, she let herself slip down farther into the bed, rolling her eyes at the shadows cast by the smoked hams and bacon slabs hanging from the rafters.

Well, so what if her own personal, private bedroom had been carved out of a corner of their old storeroom, a rackety extension minimally attached to the house itself? 'Twas still hers, hers alone! With seven older brothers, any shred of peace and privacy should be cherished, never taken for granted. Space was scarce in the small farmhouse; Etelka sensed it at the table where flying elbows threatened her spectacles, not to mention her ribs. Felt it seeing the choicest cuts of meat, the ripest pieces of fruit, the biggest slices of cakes disappearing down her strapping brothers' throats, while she took the odd-cut scraps, the blemished fruit, the broken cookies. Ah, she didn't begrudge the boys their fierce appetites, what with them laboring hard sunrise to sunset and beyond in the fields or barns with Da, but didn't she work hard, contribute, too?

Aye, she worked hard, as did Mam! Cooking, cleaning, scrubbing endless tubs of clothes stained with the soil and the life of the farm. And her not much thicker around than the handle of her wash-paddle; for all that she was twelve, she had the size and look of a runty ten-year-old. But turning twelve had earned her this room of her own, for—her father had whispered confidentially to her mother—she was fast reaching puberty. She'd not heard the word before, had had to sneak 'round late and look it up, her face growing warm and red as she scanned the definition. That? She'd heard words enough for it before, though never that one, but her Da was an educated man, boasting far more book-learning than a farmer needed. (Too much, sometimes, the neighbors whispered when something went wrong at the Rundgren place, another of Da's experiments in growing or grazing gone kerflooey.) Wasn't even worth peeping under the bedclothes to check again—no pubes, and certainly no boobs. Not that she much wanted them, but 'spected she'd sprout them at some future point. What she *had*, would *always* have—more precious than boobies that might or might not blossom this spring, mayhap the next—were her precious books. Five that were all her own!

Etelka also possessed something else, something she was desperately concealing from Mam and Da. No one else knew, 'cept Levi, and he wouldn't tell. He was true to her, and she was true to him, for all the eight-year difference in their ages. Just as she wouldn't breathe a word to any of the other boys how Levi was courting the young widow two farms over, 'cause Levi loved her even more than the land she'd inherited. That morsel of gossip would send the rest of the boys into a torrent of taunts and rowdiness, boisterous, rude comments, shoulder-butts, the smoochy-kissing of hands whenever Levi walked by.

Cautious, she reached beneath the covers to find her very own secret—an orange-tiger kitten, female. An interrogatory "mwph?" was followed by a muffled, breathy purr, and the kitten resettled herself behind Etelka's knees. A prodigious big kitten, she was, way the biggest of the litter, though Sheba, their barn cat, was herself a massive beast, the sort that struck terror in rats or mice. Late in the season for Sheba to be having a litter, but then, puberty had struck Sheba years ago. Da'd been pestering the boys, ordering first one, then another to drown those kittens, and Etelka'd anguished over his decision, already passionately attached to the orange-tiger who followed her around the barn. Not wanting to circumvent Da but not wanting to lose the kitten, she'd smuggled her into her bedroom, stolen kitchen scraps for her, and the kitten had thrived. Didn't know how long she'd get away with being so softhearted, but she'd needed something of her own to love, something that loved her back without any complicated demands. Didn't dare name her, no, that could bring down bad luck on her, guarantee Da'd discover her. Just called her Baby. Her little gem of a baby.

"Telka? You still reading in there?" her Da called. "Put down the book, turn down the lantern. Words won't rearrange themselves or vanish overnight, you know. They'll be there waiting for you in the morning. That's why they're so wonderful, coming alive when our eyes touch them."

"I know, Da. But it's just such a splendid book. I wish it would go on forever'n'ever!"

Her Da laughed, knowing too well what it was like to be so joyously ensnared in a web of words. "I suppose it almost does go on forever. Or at least go on. The Seekers Veritas are a vital part of Canderisian society to this very day, not just past lore or legend. Mayhap you'll see a Seeker-pair someday here in Marchmont. 'Course, if you're ever lucky enough to meet King Eadwin, you might meet his Bondmate. They're true-Bonded, folk say, though he's hardly had time for Seeker training."

"Goo'night, Da," she whispered back and slid beneath the covers, shifting the balled-up kitten to nestle against her stomach, its little form so warm and sweetly breathing, and far preferable to a flannel-wrapped brick. Except what she couldn't figure out was why cats always yawned a fishy smell, even when they hadn't been eating fish. "Ghatti don't do that, I reckon. Leastwise the book hasn't mentioned it." Still, she'd take the kitten's fishy little yawns any day, any way, since she'd likely never see one of the ghatti.

❖

The inn about twenty kilometers north of Gaernett had been crowded when Jacobia had arrived well after dark that night, even its stables packed with humans as well as horses, weary travelers relieved to find a dry and reasonably warm place in the loft. By morning Jacobia had heartily wished she'd opted for the loft, instead of accepting the innkeep's invitation to sleep in the tavern room itself, all the inn's beds already occupied by three or four souls. Hay and straw had to be softer than the inn's plank floor. Nor had she ever fully appreciated until now the sheer quantity of spilled drinks a tavern floor could absorb—wine and whiskey, celvassy, ginever with its juniper-scent and a mule's kick. Made fiery celvassy seem civilized by comparison. Why even bother to calculate the tankards of beer and ale, not to mention other liquids or semi-liquids best left unnamed, which had also baptized the floor countless times?

Feeling almost vicariously drunk from the fumes, she'd saddled up before first light, anxious for fresh air and open space. No more strangers snoring in her ear, unwitting elbows in her eye or ribs. Two or three of those errant limbs had strayed and stroked with less than innocent intent, propelled by someone wide awake and fervently hoping that she wasn't. Well, "someone" would have some explaining to do about her tooth marks in his thumb—she'd seen to that! Another slimy soul now nursed a dagger slash across his palm, deep enough to ensure that wielding a snow shovel would provoke painful reminders of his coarse, vulgar intent.

Her wrath at such indignities and her worry had lashed her along on this, her first full day of searching, cantering when she could along still messy roads, stopping occasionally to rest the beasts, alternating the load from one horse to the other, pack beast becoming mount, and back again. As the day wore on, she'd come to prefer Frost, her original packhorse, to Blaze; Frost boasted the better personality, inquisitive and a good listener, his silence eloquent as she aired her vexations aloud.

"Excuse me, has anyone seen a sleigh carrying two Novie Seekers, a Shepherd, and an elderly woman with a regally elegant bearing?" she asked at each village she passed through, shouting the same question at travelers coming south on the road. "They've four ghatti with them"—that should have made their passing more memorable! But so far Jacobia'd encountered but two sightings, and those both close to Gaernett. They seemed to have vanished after that, and her consternation waxed as the negative responses mounted. "Neither luck nor the Lady is riding with us today," she grumbled to Frost, who bobbed his head in agreement.

When not fretting over the twins' whereabouts, Jacobia flagellated herself for having offended the Erakwan Feather so badly. "Tactless and stupid! And you needn't agree!" she cautioned Frost. But wrong as she might have been, Feather'd been wrong as well, finding slights where none had been intended. "Should've vented my aggravation on Davvy instead of on Feather. Don't tell me I'm becoming as stubborn and stiff-necked as Jenret!" Capable of annoying people—or worse—with her arrogant ways? Surely merchanters had experience at smoothing over disagreements, convincing a wary seller to accept a lesser price, blandishing a buyer to pay just a few coppers more. If she'd lost her touch, kept on like this, then no one would sell her wool for spinning and weaving, no one would buy the mercantile's finished cloth! "Rack and ruin awaits!" she declaimed to the skies, oblivious to the fact that she'd loosed the reins, given the handsome but stolid Blaze his head.

His dawdling pace finally distracting her from her soliloquy, Jacobia realized they approached a crossroad. Tiredly rubbing her eyes, she studied the signpost, rising in her stirrups for a better look. Icy snow coated the sign, obscuring the words, and as she glanced 'round to get her bearings, she had to admit she no idea where they were; two days of snow had inexorably altered once-familiar land-scapes into an indistinguishable mass of uniform whiteness.

"And not a soul in sight to ask!" A slap of the reins against the palm of her gloved hand emphasized her quan-dary. "Let's see . . . the last village was . . . Verduin?" Or had that been the one before? She'd fully expected to have run her wayward crew to ground by now, smugly sure the sleigh would break a runner, a horse cast a shoe, some small, delaying problem to give her ample time to catch up. The whole scenario had played itself so perfectly in her head: reprimands on her part, apologies on theirs, and they'd all turn round, return home. Except that Aunt Ma-hafny was unlikely to prove meek as a lamb! Neither she nor Harrap were foolish or careless when it came to organi-zation and planning; neither, for that matter, were the twins. Diccon and Jen were hardly little children running away from home, propelled by dreams of fame and glory; they were adults—oh, young ones, to be sure—but adults all the same, and she'd best not let rosy memories obscure that reality. If their goal was reaching Marchmont and Nakum, they had a fair chance of succeeding, weather willing. The one thing they lacked, however, was time—and that was working against her as well.

Continuing to slap the reins against her palm, Jacobia contemplated reality, not make-believe. So, how to catch them, catch up with them? How many logical routes to Marchmont, and which would they have chosen? Or was there some shortcut she could take, be there (wherever "there" was along the way) waiting to greet them? Frost gently butted her thigh, greedily nosing at the pocket that held the sugar lumps. "Not right now, Frost," and rubbed his forehead to console him.

Matching the collective canniness of those four minds—not to mention the ghatti—was no easy endeavor. Some of the routes leading to the Stratocums also led first to Sido-nie—and into the loving embrace of Aunt Francie, Doyce's sister, who'd clap her niece and nephew in King Eadwin's dungeons if she had to, to halt their mad scheme. So, that meant they'd avoid Sidonie if they possibly could, aim right for the mountains. Still, they'd need supplies along the way, wouldn't they? Their team would burn a prodigious amount of energy in weather like this. Eyes narrowed, she stared

down the track that the uninformative ice-coated sign
pointed to—clearly a secondary road, not a main thorough-
fare like the one she'd been traveling—that had barely
been plowed. Of course, she was sure now. Stare hard and
she could just discern the track of runners, the pocked
marks of hooves. And not fresh-edged, either. Yes, she
knew precisely where she was now and, better yet, suspected where they'd stop along the way. A major sheep-
steading out there, the family called . . . called . . . "Doesn't
matter what they're called," she informed Frost.

With more faith than facts at her disposal, Jacobia turned
Blaze's head toward the track, wishing the Transitor crews
had managed more than a quick pass at the junction. Still,
hardly unexpected, given that it wasn't a main artery. Frost
momentarily balked, hooves set, refusing to budge, and she
could scarcely blame the beast; it was late, the sun rapidly
sinking, night approaching. "This time you get the tavern,
Frost. I'll sleep in the stable." All the more reason to move
faster, then, to reach the steading. "Come on, old thing,"
she cajoled, digging a sugar nugget out of her pocket and
waving it in front of Frost's nose. Perking up, he began
following, jaws comically crunching. Seeing his obvious
pleasure, she fished out a second lump and popped it into
her own mouth, grateful for its sweetness as Blaze gave an
indignant snort at being ignored.

♣

The farther along the track Jacobia ventured, the narrower
it became, winding between snow-laden evergreens that
bowed over her. Darker, too, as she urged the horses along,
the route discernible because it seemed to lie a little lower
than the land on either side, the snow's surface now completely untouched, pristine, except for the flurried prints
of bounding rolapin. The sleigh's runner tracks had grown
fainter, then improbably veered apart as if the sleigh had
been ripped in half not far back.

"Not a sleigh, cross-country schussers! That's what we've
been following!" Branches, windblown from the storm or
snapped from the snow's weight, littered the path, making
unreadable runes on the snow. All in all, she didn't much

like it, the woods' stillness, as if holding its breath at their intrusion. Even the horses took edgy strides, tired and twitchy, longing for a stable, a pail of mash followed by a nose bag of oats.

Turn back, take the clearer, better-traveled road? The thought hung temptingly in the back of her mind, but she pushed it away. After all, she'd found a shortcut, could gain on the twins. Slipping down from Blaze, she distributed sugar nuggets to both horses, cosseting them, checking their shoes for lumps of ice and packed snow. Finally, another nugget for each, along with a brief hug. Whether it bolstered their spirits, Jacobia couldn't judge, but it helped her, reminding her that she had companionship, uncommunicative as they might be. Retrieving the snowshoes from behind her saddle, she laced them on, shuffling and stamping experimentally. Bless Claire's Wyatt for unearthing an old pair; inns always had a closet of oddities people had left behind. Not that she'd had reason to think she'd need them—except mayhap for some fun once she'd found the twins. She stopped short, staring back at the diamond lattice-pattern imprinted in her wake; Nakum had taught her to use snowshoes on one of his visits. How he'd skimmed the snow on his—not that he'd had real need of them, given his light-footedness—while she'd trodden on her own tails, or snagged the webbing in the crowns of shrubs barely visible above the snow. Nakum. . . .

With a contemplative sigh, she knotted Frost's lead to Blaze's saddle and began walking, tamping down a path as best she could, letting the beasts follow single file behind her to spare them for a bit. "Don't know how far ahead the steading is. It may not even be on this track," she warned the horses. "What we need now is a place to camp. A nice fire, blankets over both of you. Two blankets over me." Alternating puffing and panting with cajolery, she continued along, watching her feet and taking exaggerated steps, afraid she'd trip herself. Not exactly the best way to spy out a good spot to camp, spend the night. A clump of snow weightily dropped from a branch behind her, and she startled, planting one snowshoe atop the other, and down she went. That, in turn, panicked a rolapin, its long white ears streaming bannerlike behind it as it sprang across the snow, its densely furred feet the animal equivalent of her snowshoes. It took longer than she liked for her heart to stop racing from her scare.

Full dark now, from her glimpse of the sky as she'd lain there, untangling herself, the Lady's Moon still low, barely visible, more a pale, faded white shadow than gold. Mayhap even the moon wondered whether it was worthwhile to rise higher. After all, anyone sensible (unlike herself at the moment) would already be at home, thinking of bed. "Fine, even the Lady's forgotten about lost lambs tonight," she snapped. Damn—she'd actually acknowledged she might be lost! "I am *not* lost!" she informed the horses, in case they had any doubts. "I've merely misplaced the way!"

Trees had inconsiderately rooted themselves wherever she turned, no reasonable-sized clearing to be had for a camp, let alone some sort of minimal windbreak for the horses, for her tent. And the muscles in her legs were growing tight, burning and cramping from her exertions. So much for the natural resiliency of youth; except she wasn't a youth any longer, even if she didn't always feel very adult, despite her business acumen. How unfair!—as if life had bypassed her when she hadn't been looking, too intent on making a contribution to the mercantile, not allocating sufficient time to enjoy herself. Each passing year came but once, and had to be savored then, or not at all. Did she think to vicariously relive her youth through the twins?

Halting so abruptly that Blaze gave her an impatient nudge, almost capsizing her, Jacobia sniffed, sniffed again with growing appreciation. Clearly both horses had noticed the wafting scent as well—woodsmoke, a fire! Some trapper had set up a nearby camp for the night, would know exactly where they were! Just follow her nose!

But haste engendered additional obstacles, tree limbs snapping in her face, snagging on saddle and packs. Not enough moonlight reached down to highlight the rise and fall of the land, gray-white and lacking definition, small dips and rises more prone to catch unwary feet than were their larger, less subtle fellows. Picking herself up after tripping over something determined to extract a passage-toll from her, she shook snow out of her cuffs, rolling her eyes in dismay at her impetuosity. "There!" she whispered, almost superstitious about scaring away the momentary glimpse of light up and away to her right, located at a level about twice her height. Yes!—the reflected glow of a campfire, hints of dancing, golden light. A big campfire, it must be to reflect so clearly. Oh, let whoever it was continue being so profligate with wood, have dry wood in plenty, because she planned to bask in its warmth, not huddle over a miserable little economizing fire!

Aim toward the beckoning light. No need to sing out for guidance, at least not yet. Except . . . how to ascend to that level? A more tangible darkness ahead, as if they approached a rise, a spot where the earth had sheered apart ages past, though her faint path followed the segment that hadn't risen. Wonderful, strap the snowshoes to her arms and flap them like wings, fly up! One of the horses snorted—Frost, she was sure—at her silliness. With a more determined snort Frost shouldered by Blaze and past her to take the lead, leaving Jacobia momentarily tangled in reins and lead lines, fumbling to sort them and praying neither horse would plant a hoof on her snowshoes. Another sharp sniff explained his rising enthusiasm: the odor of warm mash being mixed, the clang of a spoon or stick against the side of a kettle or bucket. No wonder Frost had taken matters in hand!

Off they went, winding through more firs and spruce, hemlock, cedar with its fans of needles like chains of crewel-stitch. And yes, their way gradually sloped upward, the horses shifting to find the best footing, but definitely climbing. Now the fire blossomed straight ahead, welcoming her, obscuring its surroundings with its well-tended, beckoning blaze.

"I'm tired, I'm hungry, and I'm cold!" she announced with all the agreeableness she could muster to greet this stranger. "And I'll willingly sample some of the horses' mash—if they and you can spare any!"

Ducking from beneath a slant of lopped evergreen boughs planted against the back of the rise where yet another fault angled into a second stone escarpment, someone stepped toward the fire, blocking it from Jacobia's sight. "I don't remember inviting you to join me." Light gilded her outline but obscured Feather's face. "After all, this is *my* abode, temporary as it may be. Why must your people always crave what isn't yours? Demand it as their due?" Gaping at Feather's hostility and the utter unfairness of it all, Jacobia couldn't find any words to defend herself, explain her need. "Oh, I shan't let the beasts suffer. But you can pitch your own tent anywhere you like—as long as it's out of my sight."

❧

Humbled, yes, that was only right, only fair. Made to recognize that she was *not* the center of the universe, that the world balked at always revolving around *her* wants, *her* needs! Feather savored the sensation: she'd bested Jacobia Wycherley, put her in her place! Let her learn how pride stuck in one's craw, hard to swallow as a boulder. Let her learn firsthand how it burned to throttle one's self-respect, behave with meek submission, constantly and uneasily aware at the shimmering edge of every sense that people denigrated you and yours, if not always with condescending words, at least with unconscious, condescending expectations.

What *they* expected! Feather had *never* fit their expectations, never would! But for that matter she'd never quite matched her own people's expectations. Chilled in a way no fire could warm, she hunched closer, staring at the flames, through them, marginally aware her fire was dying. Should tighten it, shift the coals inward, feed it just enough fuel to keep it steadily burning. Patiently tended, the fire would last the night without wasting wood. From beyond the rise floated the muffled sounds of swearing, Jacobia's grunts and groans as she struggled to pitch her silly tent. That, too, those sounds of dismay and irritation, provided Feather with sufficient fuel to keep her own anger stoked, but not burning bright as before.

Why was she returning home for the High Halidays? This time of artificially constructed revelry and mirth overshadowed the winter solstice itself, and for that day and its turning her people reverenced the Great Spirit, gave their thanks, but never indulged in major festivities. Instead, it was a time to contemplate the past, retell old legends, search out their patterns in the present. . . . Ah, how she'd ached to hear them as a child, but she was far too old for them now, dissatisfied by their simplistic explanations when far better, more comprehensive answers existed.

Better to have remained at the hospice, used the time that others so frivolously wasted to learn more, study harder, serve extra ward shifts. Examine patients—even from a painfully calculated, polite remove, for some refused to be touched, treated by an Erakwan. Couldn't they realize that eumedico knowledge transcended its bearer, the human vessel that contained such learning?

Ah, well, some still refused to permit Resonant-eumedicos anywhere near, naming them by their old name, "Gleaners," still fearful of their shadowed past. Generally the Resonant-eumedicos in training treated her better than most Canderisians, aware of their own too recent and painful past history. They had been ostracized, reviled, knew what that did to one's soul to be forever outcast, a rejection engendered by unreasoning ignorance and prejudice. Now, almost a full generation later, they still felt that they must work harder, be more intense and focused, able to best eumedicos at ordinary medical techniques unaffected by mindpower. They might sympathize with the slights—large and small—that comprised Feather's daily portion, but they had little time to fight her battles for her.

It was knowledge that touched patients, helped and healed them. And, if she were rigorously honest with herself, would not her own people prove equally wary, loath to have this new and foreign medicine practiced on them? Her ultimate goal involved melding the very best of the old, traditional ways of her people with the best aspects of her eumedico training. She'd learned much at the hospice, some of which she willingly embraced, and some she scarcely approved of, while the eumedicos had grudgingly accepted some of the basic tenets of Erakwa healing, herbs and simples that they'd forgotten about or ignored. Her dual role as teacher and student left her uneasily teetering between two worlds, despite Davvy's encouragement and enthusiasm, but the tenuous balance he offered gave her the courage to continue.

All her life she'd hungered to know more, learn more, discover the why and how of nature's ways, most especially nature's creatures. Her people were an integral part of nature, attuned to the earth and the skies, the mountains, the rivers and streams, and from this the most responsive—a special, chosen few—drew a quiet power. Slipping her hand inside her quilted jacket with its ridiculous calico print—diffidently purchased from a sneering shopkeeper in the hope the garment would allow her to blend in with the citizenry of Gaernett—she wrapped her fingers around the leather pouch that protected her earth-bond. As always, it comforted her, offering renewed fortitude. And with it arose a distinct damping of her wrath at Jacobia Wycherley and what she represented.

Shaking her head—ah, was she becoming an easy mark, too quick to temporize, excuse?—she added more dried meat to the pot, checked to see if she'd brewed sufficient cha. Hospitality. It was important to her people, an obligation to treat strangers courteously if they chanced upon an Erakwa settlement, especially during this hallowed time of seasonal change. Food and rest, shelter and reserved friendship freely given to all, unless or until they proved unworthy. This was her encampment, her "home" for this night, and she'd turned away Jacobia Wycherley with angry, spiteful words, ignoring the woman's worn appearance, her obvious need. Jacobia might well prove unworthy, fulfill Feather's critical view of her and her kind, but so far all the woman had done was to exhibit an astounding ability to rub her emotions the wrong way. Now Feather must pay a price for judging too quickly, make some gesture of conciliation. If Jacobia spurned it, then she'd have done her best, could sleep with a reasonably easy heart and mind.

Rising, she shed the ridiculous quilted coat and stuffed it in her pack, then checked on the two horses as she made her way along the path Jacobia had imprinted in the snow. It staggered and meandered, the woman so exhausted she'd been unable to track a straight line without stumbling. The horses whickered and nuzzled her, greedy for attention and more food, little clouds of vapor puffing from their broad nostrils. The black one with a dusting of white like hoarfrost along its forehead and withers was especially flirtatious, and Feather laughed at its long eyelashes, amazingly like Jacobia Wycherley's. How would the woman react to such a comparison? Relishing the thought, she followed the wavering track.

"So." Arms snugged across her chest, Feather fought to drop her defensive stance, self-consciously watching Jacobia Wycherley's struggles with the tent. She'd almost raised it, backing to stretch one of the guy lines, though it remained stubbornly and fractionally short of her goal, the tree trunk beyond reach. As the wind picked up, vigorously snapping the canvas, Jacobia shied in surprise, rearing backward on the guy line, both feet flying out from under her. Adamantly ignoring Feather's presence, Jacobia picked herself up and began edging tentward, winding the rope around her arm to maintain its tension as she fumbled for a bag of tent stakes.

"I spoke in haste, should not have turned you away with harsh words." Even to her own ear she didn't sound overgracious, the words squeezed out with an obvious reluctance despite her best intentions. Worse, helpless laughter began bubbling inside her as Jacobia pawed with one leg, desperate to snag the bag closer but determined not to ask for assistance. "Please . . . join me for the night. Dinner is almost ready, and I ask you to share it with me."

"No, no." Intent on her task Jacobia didn't meet Feather's eyes, one booted foot still fumbling after the bag. "This is fine, will do. No need for me to intrude." Two quick strides and Feather jerked the small bag clear, teasingly shaking it just beyond Jacobia's reach. In the dark the sting of anger in those violet eyes didn't lash as badly as it had in the stable yard. "Give me the stakes, if you please."

With a sigh Feather brought the bag within reach but refused to release it as Jacobia's hand claimed it. "Haven't we aggravated each other enough? And for no real reason, except our pride? Can we not start afresh?" and she released her grip.

Mouth as tight as her hold on the bag, Jacobia finally quirked one corner of her mouth in a lopsided, unwilling smile. "It depends," she paused, and Feather gave her her full attention, "on whether you're a better cook than I."

A challenge? Some sort of contest? What could she say to ensure temporary peace—that she was an excellent cook, a terrible cook? Did this indicate that the Wycherley woman would not eat Erakwa cooking, disdained it? Stymied by the possibilities, uneasy and unsure whether further insult was intended, Feather opened her mouth and, to her consternation, not one word issued forth. To her profound relief, Jacobia amplified her question, face still grave, expression faintly severe. "Best understand I won't eat anything with lumps larger than a copper!"

Canderis's largest but least valuable coin. "Any lumps you may find are meant to be there—dried berries. But each is smaller than a gold piece, much smaller," Feather emphasized as she relieved Jacobia of the guy rope and let the tent fold in on itself. "If we strike your tent, spread the canvas over my evergreen windbreak, it will be even warmer inside." A grateful nod and Jacobia scurried to release the other lines.

♣

Writhing within the blankets' smothering confines, Saam managed to poke his head clear, the blessed freshness of the air sleeking along his muzzle, teasing at the hairs of his inner ears. Fresh air, the joggle and jounce of riding . . . another circuit, more truths to be sought, new adventures! It *had* to mean that—that was what it always meant—and he spread his whiskers wide and seeking. Oh, to stretch, set every lax muscle into play, flexing and contracting . . . a blue-gray body bursting with contained power and self-control, ready to explode into action at need . . . ! Once it had all been his to command, and the whisper of the past made him feel almost alive again.

Now even cracking open his bleary eyes required too much effort, but his deep memories harbored no doubt about how alive he was, would always be. The sleigh's swaying rhythm soothed, so like his old pommel platform's easy roll when dear Oriel loosed the reins for a bit, simply let the gelding amble along, dipping its head to investigate a clump of grass, nibble some sweet purple clover blossoms. Purple clover blossoms . . . bees buzzing . . . sun warm on his fur . . . his platform rocking . . .

Yes, Oriel *had* returned for him, after so many years of loss and yearning! He had but to lick himself and he'd taste his beloved Oriel's touch on his fur. Why, oh why, couldn't he turn his head to lick his flank? What bound him so tightly—his dream? But this was no dream, he knew it, not with Oriel's burgeoning chuckle in his mind at how he fussed himself. Inhabit this constricting by-world a bit longer and surely Oriel would 'speak him, tell him what a brave and true Bond he was!

No? Well, if Oriel chose to play games, tease his dear Saam, he'd seek for Doyce, because wherever Oriel was, Doyce was sure to be near. Garnet earrings . . . everlasting roses for their everlasting loves. Wouldn't Doyce and Khar be surprised? Rault should have the earrings ready, soon. Or mayhap he'd seek out Bard and M'wa, Byrta and P'wa—as if you'd ever find *them* separated! So much easier not to strain his ears, let his nose do the work, scenting out Doyce. Mouth ajar, he inhaled hugely, let the air and its scent fragments flow through his nostrils, drift across his palate.

Strange, a scent of like-Doyce, but not-Doyce . . . and more male, at that. Odd, very odd. And a feminine one who bore an odor similar to what that arrogant Jenret Wycherley always exuded, he who was always dressed in black, almost foppishly handsome, though his Bondmate Rawn was rock-steady! Rawn? Khar? **"Dear Khar! Come to me, please! Why is Oriel teasing me so, refusing to 'speak me?"** Khar would explain, smooth his wounded pride. She and Doyce excelled at that. **"Khar?"** He rowled aloud in his mind, only to be distracted by a weak, fretful mewl. What poor, pitiful beast was making that racket?

At last another accustomed scent tweaked his nose, followed by a lick across his cheek, crimping his whiskers. The burred tongue was real, no doubt of that! Ouch, mind the eye, Parm! **"Hullo, old chap. Whimpering in your sleep, you've been."** Parm, silly old Parm, sounded stodgy, very serious—why? Parm, the gayest ghatti of them all, destined to play the eternal jester and jokester, often at his own expense. Ah, give old Parm a taste of his own medicine, he would, for acting stodgy like that!

**" 'Ware, Parm! Don't tackle that rattlesnake! I'll handle it!"**

**"Snake? Where? What snake?"** A satisfying shriek from Parm, but a frenzied and heavy hind foot planted itself in Saam's belly as Parm scrambled over him. **"Can't let it hurt Mahafny!"**

Ah, he could see that cairn of sun-baked boulders, all mossy gray with pinprick sparkles in that clearing in the Tetonords where they'd halted for a rest . . . because . . .

because they were hunting the men who'd *killed* his beloved Oriel, had attempted to kill him! That menacing,
muzzle-twisting scent engulfing Oriel as they dragged him
off his horse, rending, splintering sounds as they cracked
open Oriel's head, while yet another foul one hunted him,
prepared to finish off the wounded ghatt. He knew what
that scent was now—formaldehyde! They were preserving
Oriel's brain! Wanted his, too, for comparison, transparent
little slivers mounted on glass where they could seek the
elusive "connections" that formed their Seeker Bond! Fight
them! Claw and gouge them, slash at their eyes, bite and
rend their evil, grasping fingers and hands! Ah, how his
head hurt—resounded with the silence—his link to Oriel
completely severed, severed unto death!

Compassionate hands, he felt the difference immediately,
made no effort to bite, tucked another blanket over him,
loosely hooding his head but still leaving his eyes and muzzle clear. A finger chucked his chin, rubbed along the jawline and he gave a sputtering purr. Must present a silly
sight—like a babe in swaddling clothes, probably wearing
some baby bonnet as well. Probably looked more clownish
than dear old Parm! Another sputtering purr at that
thought.

None of the ghatti would be caught dead wearing baby
bonnets . . . though Barnaby wore them with amazing good
grace. Little ruffly socks, too. But then, what could one
expect of a mere dog, a diminutive terrier, good-hearted
but a trifle dense. His doggy humor had never struck Saam
as particularly funny, though Parm would roll and rollick
on the floor, overcome by Barnaby's doggerel. The children, the twins, had dressed up Barnaby when they were
little . . .

Ah . . . *that* explained the almost-Doyce scent and the
almost-Jenret scent: their twin offspring, Diccon and Jenneth, must be near. But they were too little to partake in
his adventures, barely out of toddlerhood . . . should be
chasing after Khim and P'roul. *His* handsome blue-gray coloring underlay Khim's magnificent stripes. Of course he
was a proud papa, proudest perowmepurr around, though
he willingly shared the title with Rawn, P'roul's sire.

No . . . couldn't be either set of twins, human or ghatten,
here with him now. But he'd not mind finding Barnaby by

his side. Dogs were loyal and, after all, Parm swore by him. **"Parm, has Barnaby come with us? Wherever it is that we're going, that is?"** Not very elegantly phrased, but then Parm could winkle out his meaning. Start one straightforward conversation with Parm and you'd soon find yourself nattering about seventy-nine other things. With luck—and persistence—you might even coax Parm to spiral back round and answer your original question.

**"Oh, Barnaby!"** Parm wailed, his breath gusting warm in Saam's ear, annoying worse than an exploring insect. **"Ah . . . oh . . . I meant to tell you, Saam . . . Barnaby ran into Mem'now yesterday . . . or was it the day before? No, it couldn't have been, 'cause Mem always stops by . . . you remember, Saam, how he does linger if there's custard baking in the oven. But Barnaby's tongue is so much longer that he never . . ."** Parm rolled on with his tale, inexorable as the tide, and fully as likely to wear one down over time. . . .

The intrusive new blanket tucked 'round his head and ears bore the rich aroma of the out-of-doors: pitch and pine needles, leaf mold, campfire smoke, the sweat of strenuous exertion and good, fresh earth. If Oriel were otherwise engaged, then Nakum must be near—the blanket wouldn't lie. Well, generally they did lie on something, but it wasn't the sort of lie where a clever ghatt could seek out the truth, just wool fibers. By the Elders, he was turning Parmish!

Dear Nakum, the Erakwan lad, coming into his manhood, his skin and long braids forever awash with the scents of rendered fat, dried berries, smoked meat laced with fat and, most of all—cedar bark. A certain peace touched his lonely soul just from Nakum's quiet presence, comfort of sorts. Distinctly *not* Oriel, but good, an utter rightness to him all his own. Yes he could share his mind with this lad, for the resilience, the power of the very earth they walked upon flowed through the boy, reaching out to Saam himself. Beside Nakum, Saam ran like the wind, because while he sprang at his side, old age and infirmities would never dare touch him! If only Rolf and Chak had been able to eternally run at Nakum's side . . . !

But Nakum had *denied* him, gently thrust him away, set him in a different path. For Nakum had undertaken a crucial endeavor for the good of his people . . . and Saam had

been superfluous, loved and respected, but unneeded. . . .
Those mountains with their high, thin air, their perpetual
snow, were so *very* cold . . . and Mahafny *had* presented a
challenge no self-respecting ghatt could deny! This way he
needn't stray far from his dear Khar'pern and Doyce—he'd
given Oriel his solemn vow on that. Without Saam near,
who would guard them, watch over them and love them
until Oriel returned? And in turn, Mahafny discovered how
to let her heart love, and he strove to love her back . . .
an easier task than he'd anticipated.

His gut knotted in protest, and he fought an urge to
retch, his stomach utterly empty except for the bile that
threatened to rise. A convulsive swallow, and he absently
licked his chops. So thirsty his tongue wanted to stick to
the roof of his mouth. *"I am fading away,"* he cried deep
within himself. *"How did this, when did this . . . happen?"*
But only the breeze heard as it scattered bits of his essence,
depleting him even more. *"Please, beloved,"* ah . . . so many
beloveds had deserted him, no longer came at his call, *"Beloved, succor me, love me—for love is what quenches the
hungers of death that claw at my vitals!"*

Even with his eyes screwed tight, glittering stardust spangled and obscured the faces of his beloved humans, his
ghatti friends, stardust that etched the glimmering, spiraled
way that led to the Elders. He hovered, so light, so insubstantial that he could effortlessly float through the eight
spirals of knowledge and growth that led to the Elders.
Soon he'd be able to properly greet them. Their not-so-
distant voices called and crooned seductively, cajoling him,
urging him toward the final choice that would allow him to
freely soar within their space. Should he? Often of late he'd
bent his thoughts inward, contemplating what he would
become . . . and when . . . While all ghatti died, each
became an indissoluble part, a fragment of the firmament
that upheld the collective ghatti mind, a piece of the whole.
Ah, to see Kharm, Mother-of-Them-All again, to bow-
stretch at her feet in homage. . . .

Hands! Horrible, vile-smelling hands roughly snatching
at him, jarring his fragile body, wrenching him up and out
and away! That smell! Ah, he recognized that death smell
that clung to hands and clothes! Snarling, Saam fought
against the enshrouding blankets, kicking, arching his back,

flailing to slither free. Fight! Fight! That wretched, nauseating aroma, so antiseptic and clean that burned his nasal passages. A cloying stink of formaldehyde as well—someone positively reeking of it! Wrenching his eyes open, clear yellow rims encircling dilated pupils—torchlight and lantern light searing his brain—he glared and fought, scoring his foes with claw and fang, rejoicing in the shouts of shock and pain that greeted each successful strike. Slash them! This time he'd win, save Oriel! No, he'd not let him die again, not see his brain endlessly dissected, disgraced like that!

**"Help me, Parm!"** he yowled, **"Get Khar and Rawn, Barnaby! M'wa and P'wa, too! Don't let the foul ones snatch you—I'll hold them at bay till you break free! We *must* save Oriel, do you understand?"**

Swinging her cloak from her shoulders, Mahafny enveloped Saam within it, drawing up its folds beneath him as if tightening the drawstring in a sack. *"Beloved Saam, dear, beautiful Saam. It's me—Mahafny. Oh, please, don't squander your strength like this. We've reached the Research Hospice, will spend the night here. Don't you remember? I've told you time and again, but you don't seem to listen to me anymore."* "No, that's perfectly all right, fine. I can manage him. My apologies to those who got in the way of his teeth or claws. Make sure you have any wounds properly disinfected and bandaged."

"I think we're aware of the procedures," came a dry response. "We *are* eumedicos, you know."

Eumedicos? Research Hospice? Mahafny? Had he hurt her, she who needed and depended upon him so much?

Misshapen, swollen-jointed fingers eased a path through the obstructing cloak like diffident mice, stroking him, attempting to lift him clear, but her hands were suddenly too weak to support his chest, lift his hindquarters. Mahafny! Oh, only let her hold him in her arms and he would come to himself, *be* himself. Except . . . except . . . who was he these days? Saam Past? Saam Present? Saam Future? Not another Bond to sever, please!

❖

Whistling for the sheer joy of hearing the notes cascade through the air, Nakum surveyed the new day, his skin judging the force, the composition of the winds that always played across his mountaintop. A fine day, but too early yet to crank open the glass panels, let the infant arborfer trees directly bask in the sun and brisk air. Best let the sun rise a little higher first. What he most emphatically did not want was sickly hothouse trees, unable to stand through the tumultuous thunderstorms of summer, the fierce gales of winter. Strength yet flexibility, enough to bend yet not break, show their respect yet never obsequiously bow to the elements. Just as his people, the Erakwa, had bowed yet never had broken, though it seemed they had ofttimes bent beyond natural resiliency in their generations of dealings with the newcomers to their land, their planet.

Sometimes he wished his people had pushed back, would push back a little harder, stand firmly rooted and let the new world part to either side. Too many things dwindled, withered without a modicum of assertiveness. New world ways were like the heavy, relentless march of imperceptive feet that crushed, destroyed all things dependent upon their bonds to the earth. Sometimes the unthinking tread came through ignorance or innocence, and sometimes with intentional, premeditated malice. Still, what was, was, but the future could be, would be different. Did not the legends say so, how the world changed through the ripening of time? But how to know when the ripening came?

After many years even the newcomers had finally grasped how precious arborfer was, how difficult and slow to grow and flourish. Treated properly after the giant, straight trees were cut, the wood ultimately turned hard as steel, boasting a multitude of uses, from knives to water pipes, all as durable and enduring as the ages. Why rip the land's bones and body asunder to mine its ores, foul the skies and rivers with refining it?

And he, Nakum, would ensure the arborfer were restored throughout the wilderness, their numbers increasing in relation to the demand for them. All in good time, all in good time, and with the help and support of his dear cousin Eadwin, the king, and other like-minded souls. They'd reforest Marchmont with grove upon grove of arborfer, see if they didn't! And the children, Erakwa and newcomer offspring alike, would gaze up in awe and gratitude at the trees' willing sacrifice, aware that their own offspring would flourish as well.

But his whistling shriveled, dying away to a forlorn whisper as he reached his greenhouse nursery. Something dark and noxious had been smeared on the windowpanes, splashes of it corrupting the pristine snow that endured from one winter to the next, and the next. Even his neatly carved paths had been violated, their crisp edges gouged and pocked, chunks of snow broken free and strewn like rubble. And across the fresh dusting of night snow, scuffs that looked almost like footprints and yet did not. At least not the prints of any living creature he knew, human or otherwise.

Scraping a nail against the dark excrescence on the glass, he tried to gauge what it was, how easy it might be to remove. His babies needed their sunlight; worse, the newly opaque glass might trap more heat inside than the seedlings could stand, delicate needles turning brown and brittle, their tiny root tendrils gasping for moisture. Whatever substance defaced the glass was hard to his touch, and as he drew the point of his knife across it with the utmost caution, a hairline crack appeared, the edges beginning to flake off. Gathering a few dark flakes on his fingers, he sniffed but couldn't immediately name the pungent odor. Continue scraping or go for a bucket of warm water and cloths? Either way the leavings of such filth would further befoul his perfect whiteness with black, sootlike residue or dark-stained trails of wash water.

His indecision nearly hobbled him, left him unsure, full of misgivings. Who or what had done this? What must he do to right it? Ensure it never happened again? Instinctively his hand sought out the pouch that hung around his neck, the bond to the earth that he'd claimed as a child, still unaware of his mixed ancestry, his bond an amalgam of two different worlds. If Addawanna were here, she'd briskly cuff his head, scold him for not thinking hard enough, deep enough, tasting and testing the flavor and texture of each message the earth whispered.

Yet of late the messages had been conflicting, downright contradictory at times. Strange, when so much of the world slumbered, hibernating deep during the wintertime. Any messages should be short, perfunctory, downright sleepy.

Instead, too many things were on the move, the touch of odd happenings in distant places, unexpected people and events irresistibly pointing toward his mountain-fastness as if it were some new lodestar in the night skies. He'd ignored the indistinct murmurs and mumblings for the most part, convincing himself it represented nothing more than the grumpy restlessness that often plagued a world caught between waking and sleep, or sleep and waking. So autumn had turned into winter, so winter would turn into spring soon, as the pattern repeated itself every year.

Now he concentrated, intent as if he were rooted in the earth, partaking of each particle stirring deep beneath the mantling blanket of snow and frost. Yes, Mahafny still struggled toward him with Saam. And what would he do about that? Was that sort of hope, help, his to grant? The root-branch that indicated Mahafny and Harrap and Doyce's twins also had a forking that ran toward someone else he knew. No, thinking of branches and forks wasn't right—from him to them his "roots" branched out; but from them to him those intersections would be convergences, connections. The connections and convergences to Mahafny and Saam, and ultimately back to Nakum, ached and grumbled at each node, as if distinctly unhappy, rancorous. He'd label himself over-fanciful except that after long effort he finally unsnarled some of the conflicting emotions. Oh ho! No wonder there were problems!

Not a doubt about it. Though he'd not set eyes on her in recent years, Nakum thrilled to Jacobia Wycherley's sonorous vibrations, still tinged with faintly self-centered, self-righteous overtones. Ah, how lovesick he and Aelbert had acted over her when they'd all been as young and foolish as the springtime! But his cousin Aelbert had been imprudent about many things, and faithless till the very end, redeeming himself only by sacrificing himself and N'oor to save the others. Aelbert had perceived, too late, that wanting something too badly, no matter how well-deserved, destroyed the soul. The thought of seeing Jacobia again, on his terms, his lands—not as a guest at her brother's house—left him weak-kneed. So, the old emotions hadn't died, he'd not outgrown them. Interesting . . .

But the person with her—obdurately straining in one direction while Jacobia tugged the other way with equal stubbornness—was . . . Feather? Feather! One of his own people! More like him in a way—with her mixed blood—than most of his peers, except she had heeded the call of her Outlander side. Addawanna had had no quarrel with that—had scolded *him* often enough that he should, as well—but she'd been sorely wounded at Feather's slighting of Erakwa ways. When and why had her destiny intertwined itself with Jacobia's? This convergence would require watching, more than a little unraveling before it was concluded!

All this transpired to the south, although it was inexorably moving closer, like a shifting glacier creeping along a slope. But what to make of the sensation of mounting dread practically on his own "doorstep" just to the east? Something had begun to stir within the castle's depths, his cousin's castle, and Eadwin knew naught of it as yet. Something just barely awakened, something old and potentially dangerous, and due to be unloosed by utter innocence. Could it be tamed? Licking suddenly dry lips, Nakum confessed his own ignorance. If taming failed, who or what could disable it, conquer its prodigious powers that no longer docilely followed the precise patterns minutely etched within its being?

This was danger beyond his ken, beyond the wisdom of the Erakwa, a danger that had already once harried his people into the depths of the woods and the heights of the mountains as the newcomers had scattered and fled, sought out more land. Safe land, land that wouldn't abruptly explode under their feet . . . Had his people, had the newcomers, not lived up to the world they'd created? Were they doomed to see it destroyed beneath their very feet. Yet again his people would be hurt, mayhap through no fault of their own! Think! Think! Did not catastrophe portend the end of one stage, the beginning of another—mayhap a newer, better world? So said some of the legends and tales of his people. But what was the matter with *this* world, *his* world?

The sound washed over him—a cross between the mocking cry of a distant bird and the high-pitched shriek of an overexcited child—set him shivering not with cold, but with a new fear and a growing respect for the unknown. "Na-na-na-Na-na-NAA!" Then a giggle that gradually faded

away. He ached to draw his knife, spin round and confront
whoever—whatever—it was, but he controlled himself. Had
to or be shamed, because Nakum sensed beyond doubt that
there was no one there except him.

❖

"Well, thank you again for your hospitality." Morning had
augmented all the discomfort Jacobia had previously suffered in Feather's presence, worsened, somehow, by the
new and niggling sensation that *she* was an interloper, an
intruder on Erakwa lands. Besides, they couldn't continue
on together, could they? Here she was, mounted on Blaze
and ready to ride, her packhorse patient behind her, while
Feather had just shouldered a pack larger and weightier
than the one Frost carried! Without a mount, she couldn't
possibly match Jacobia's pace. Besides, most likely they
planned to travel in different directions, each toward her
own goal.

"Mmm." A noncommittal response if ever she'd heard
one! Feather adjusted the tumpline around her forehead,
then shifted and tightened the straps across her shoulders,
bouncing once to settle her pack in place.

"Mayhap when you've returned to Gaernett, you'd join
me for dinner one night. . . ." Why did that sound so dreadfully haughty, as if she'd deigned to accept Feather as a
provisional equal? Lady bless, she owed the woman a good
dinner—and more! Frost gave a friendly snuffle, nosing at
Feather's arm, prodding her in the hope that she'd produce
more warm mash. It struck Jacobia then: why had Feather
burdened herself with mash when she had no horse?
"Mash?" she blurted, "Why are you lugging mash around
with you?"

Feather's eyes—the same hazel as Nakum's, Jacobia noticed, wondering if that indicated she, too, was of mixed
blood?—blandly met hers, her expression humble. A tiny,
fleeting smile showed a bare hint of white teeth flashing
against her coppery skin, and it reminded Jacobia of an
animal quickly baring its teeth in warning. "Why, it's a
known delicacy amongst my people. A special haliday
treat."

"Bosh!" and fought her tongue into submission before she uttered worse. The Lady grant her patience in dealing with this prickly, oversensitive woman! "I may not be a Seeker, lack one of the ghatti at my side to test your words, but I don't find that a very credible answer!"

"And why is it me—my people—who are forever in the wrong? Are you and yours never mistaken, never in error? So superior that you can tell us go here, go there, do this, do that? We are *not* children for you to order around! Answer your own lackwitted question—if you've intelligence enough to do so!" Feather's very stance had assumed a stubborn set, anger simmering, ready to boil over.

Her unease growing, Jacobia impulsively clutched the saddle pommel, convinced Feather felt an overwhelming urge to pull her off her horse and administer a thrashing. Nakum had sometimes borne a similar expression when he was younger; unlike his grandmother, Addawanna, he hadn't always succeeded in shrugging off the interlopers' overbearing ways. And being mounted, literally looking down on Feather, rather than looking her square in the eye, conferred another unfair advantage on Jacobia.

"You've the right of it. As questions go, that wasn't a very clever one. I'm sorry." Warily Jacobia dismounted. "I suppose you packed the mash when Davvy first asked you to accompany me. Then, after our . . . misunderstanding, you were angry and probably set off without unpacking it."

A reluctant nod from Feather, her lips compressed tightly, until one corner of her mouth betrayed her, flickering in a reluctant grin, a dimple revealing itself. "We're both very headstrong people."

"Ah, then you've not met my brother, Jenret!"

"Isn't meeting Mahafny Annendahl enough?"

Now Jacobia's laughter rang out, unfettered, but it quickly faded away. The twins! She *had* to catch up with them, convince them, as well as Mahafny and Harrap, to abandon their mock-heroics before someone took hurt. "I wish we could travel together!" she blurted before she could stop herself. "But you have relatives to visit. And you couldn't keep up, anyway, not without a horse." Could she split Frost's burden? Neither she nor Feather were very heavy; each horse should be able to carry one trim rider and a fair amount of gear. Except that Feather's pack looked heavy enough to flatten her to the ground!

Shifting her feet, kicking sticky snow this way and that, Feather studied the ground. "Have you decided which route you'll take? How to make the best speed?"

"You mean once I figure out where I am?" It stung to admit that, but it was the truth. "Bear northwest, I guess, south of Roermond, until I hit the Spray River. The roads are reasonably good up that way, and the rolling hills are easier than forging through the Tetonords. *That* I don't fancy in the least!"

"Then what are we waiting for?" With an "umph," Feather gave her pack a final hitch and broke into a trot, not bothering to glance behind her.

"But wait!" Mounting in clumsy haste, Jacobia swung her gelding's head northwest, Frost following obediently at the tug on his line. "It's not that I wouldn't appreciate your company, your knowledge of the woods, but you can't keep up!" she shouted ahead, only to belatedly realize that all she could see of Feather was a string of tracks. Could *she* keep up?

♣

While the Research Hospice would never be deemed a warm, intimate edifice, Harrap felt at peace within its uncompromising, hygienic confines, had instinctively felt so ever since the first day he'd set foot within this isolated place of hope and healing nearly twenty years past. Comfort came, he reflected, from knowing he was needed here, that his Lady was needed—Her wonders and Her works— despite what most agnostic eumedicos might argue. There was always room for another hand, divine or human, capable of healing souls as well as bodies. And some of the souls in greatest need during those dire times had been the eumedicos. That was why he and Mahafny had made such a good team, she administering to the running of the Research Hospice, relentlessly guiding it back to its original lofty goals, while he served as her spiritual counterweight, shepherding eumedico and patient alike, guiding them to revere the Lady's gift of their immortal souls.

Mahafny had been instrumental in analyzing the range of Resonant abilities, attempting to uncover a scientific rationale for their telepathic skills. In truth, she strove to demystify their gift, make it as natural as left-handedness—a genetic quirk, no more or less—to diminish the unreasoning terror most Canderisians held for the unjustly demonized Gleaners or Resonants. Her unstinting labor had also offered a way to expiate the sins of her daughter, Evelien, and Doyce's stepson Vesey, who'd intended to warp Resonant abilities to bolster their own mad, vainglorious plans for power.

But most of all, Harrap was relieved to be back at the Hospice because of their mad sleigh ride here from Trude Voss's thatched cottage. A day, a night, and another full day of unrelenting, unremitting hell! Shivering, he drew his shawl higher around his shoulders as he walked, less briskly than he liked, toward the common room. Surely some old acquaintance would be off-shift, eager to hear the latest doings in Gaernett, as well as suggest who, if anyone, might let him have just a bit of red yarn, because he was running short.

*"You* do *fancy the red trim, don't you, Parm?"* Standing square on his own two feet was a blessing; if he never saw that sleigh again, it would be too soon! Even in his dreams last night the bed had careened like the sleigh! Refusing sleep, resisting practically any food, Mahafny had handled the team like a woman possessed, yielding to nothing and no one. A part of him was suffused with admiration for her unflagging determination, but the more rational part of him had been scared witless by her obsessive resolve to reach the Research Hospice in the scant amount of time she'd allotted for the journey. Weather and road conditions be damned! Mayhap the Lady had performed one of Her minor miracles, considering Mahafny's astonishingly quick recovery after their exhausted arrival at Trude's. He'd prided himself on knowing her better than most, but even he now detected new facets to her, not all of them as benign as he might have wished.

Better by far to contemplate his knitting, not the unknowable human mind. *"I think the red's just the thing."* Yes, focus on his knitting, the complex duet of yarn and needles, loop here, interweave there, up and over and around! Knit two, purl two . . .

Whiskers wide, Parm reveled in the astringently clean smells that cut the omnipresent steaminess of the air—courtesy of the massive boiler that unceasingly provided sterilized water—as he padded at Harrap's side, the wheaten robe brushing the ghatt's flank now and then. **"Don't care about the red trim, or the green, don't really want . . ."**

Stopping short, Harrap shook a finger at Parm. *"Of course you do, of course you want it. It'll be even colder where we're going, and the last thing I need is for you to take sick on me!"* Unconsciously attempting to form the Lady's eight-pointed star to ward off danger, his hands plucked and twisted his knitting around the needles until it bore little resemblance to the ghatt-sized cap it was meant to be. *"If anything were to happen to you, Parm . . ."* Helpless, he couldn't finish the thought, as if even his faith had turned insubstantial, full of flaws. "Ah, Lady, forgive me!" he whispered, eyes closed in anguished prayer. Selfish of him, given how much anguish dwelt in this world, anguish at the many things humanity suffered but could never change. "If not in this life, mayhap in another," was the Lady's credo, but at this moment it sounded more like a threat.

Settling his rump on the cold marble, Parm tilted his head and set a hind foot scratching beneath his orange chin, mouth grimacing as he angled his head more and more, his foot digging away. **"You'd what?"** Vigorously shaking his head, he proceeded to groom the hind claws on that foot, rather like a person cleaning a comb. **"Act as pigheaded as Mahafny? Try to cheat your Lady, our Elders, of a ghatti soul?"** His uncompromising directness shocked Harrap. **"What she endured to deliver us here wasn't natural, Harrap. Think on it."**

"I acknowledge that she—"

**"Hush! Mindspeech, remember!"** Parm reminded as he stole an edgy look to each side. **"And don't drift either. Resonant-eumedicos go rushing by when you least expect them. You're so flighty sometimes, it's practically like shouting in their ears. Can't blame them for not being minddeaf, overhearing you, then."**

To have Parm, his darling crazy-quilt ghatt, turn snappish

on him like this! Too much, entirely too much, and so unde-
served—first Mahafny, and now Parm. And what did he
do? He meekly accepted it as if it were his due, too soft,
too good-natured to stand up for himself, too prone to turn
the other cheek. It made him doubly resentful, at himself
and at them. Lady help him, Mahafny had treated him and
the twins like . . . like excess baggage during their trip
here! She'd shown no respect or compassion for anyone or
anything other than her own needs, and little enough for
those! How she'd brutalized the horses had been criminal,
goading them, sending them floundering through drifts, the
sleigh scarcely touching the snow, one runner or another
making an occasional, jolting contact as they sailed along.
Then she'd abruptly order one or another of them, Jen or
Diccon or him, to find a fresh team—beg, barter, or steal
it, for all she cared! Humiliating! Even more humiliating to
beg her to stop to answer a call of nature, and poor Diccon
had borne her wrath time and again for that. Mayhap the
jouncing had upset the young man's kidneys—he knew his
own still felt as if they'd turned to jelly. Her concern had
been exclusively reserved for Saam, not that he could bring
himself to begrudge Saam that.

Oh, Lady help him! What had he done to his knitting?
Totally mangled it, turned it into a nightmare of knots and
slipped stitches! Could he unravel it, start anew? At this,
at least? *"Now look what you've made me do! It's all your
fault!"* Never had a Shepherd of the Lady sounded so petulant over a dropped stitch.

So vividly, vitally orange-and-black mottled against the
unrelieved white of utilitarian floors and walls, Parm regarded him with infinite patience and love. **" 'Tisn't me
you're upset with, though you're taking it out on me and
your knitting. I thank your Lady you're not knotting me
like that!"** His eloquent green eyes locked on Harrap's. **"I
will not leave our world without warning, if you promise
not to hold me beyond my time. And should you die first,
your Lady will hardly notice me—that's how quickly I'll
slip through the door at your side. Even a goddess can't
keep one of us out if we truly want in, you know."**

A woman in a long white coat came striding down the
hall, smiling at them both, and Harrap spun to greet her,
flustered at being unable to recall her name, achingly clue-

less at who she might be. Must know her, the way she beamed at him and quickly stroked Parm's head, though her stride never slowed. "Harrap, my favorite Shepherd! If you're hunting for Mahafny, she's just down the hall at the apothecaire's. Will you be leading the services tonight?"

"Ah . . . ah . . . of course," he babbled, hastily tucking his knitting behind his back. "Directly before dinner. Don't be late . . . ah, my dear Pilar!" Thank you, Lady, her name had leapfrogged to the front of his scattered wits just in time!

**"Well, she *does* work on those frog experiments, those tadpole thingies,"** Parm reminded him.

*"Do we want Mahafny, or do we want yarn?"* he asked, breaking into a trot after Parm, who'd already sleeked his way down the corridor, ears alert. For his own peace of mind, better not to see Mahafny for a bit longer, at least until he'd ordered his thoughts, recovered the charitable, nonjudgmental attitude required of his faith. *"Common room's around the corner. Parm?"* His sandals slippity-slapped against the marble as he hurried after the ghatt, intent on heading him off. Have to tighten the straps and now, before he killed himself. Had loosened them too much to make room for his double-layer of wool stockings. *"Parm, wait!"* he called, more urgently now, down on one knee, working the recalcitrant buckle.

"No, Ruud, I'm *well* aware of the proper dosage, how often it can be safely taken—with or without your most recent research on the subject." The carrying tone and its rising inflection on certain words were all too familiar. "I realize it's irregular to request such a quantity of . . ." What? Harrap couldn't make out the word, wished he were closer or that she hadn't chosen that moment to drop her voice.

"Consider, please, that there are four of us in my party . . ." and then all he could make out was a querulous rumble of admonitions and cautions that ran on like a low growl of distant thunder before finally fading. "Of *course* you have certain responsibilities, Ruud, as do I. I can't order you, and I won't order you. I no longer head the Hospice, but whatever consideration you can offer for old times' sake, I'd appreciate. And it would save you from asking Van Grunsven, now, wouldn't it? I know how *annoying* it was when I was chief to be constantly inter-rupted for petty bureaucratic details by some *insecure* soul unable to assume responsibility for his own job."

*"What did she ask for? I missed it."* Sandal now too-tightly crimped, Harrap limped nearer, listening as hard as he could. Surely there was no harm asking Parm to fill him in on what he'd missed? It wasn't like asking him to read someone's mind without that person's permission. After all, his hearing wasn't as keen as it once had been.

But Parm's fur was hackling along his spine, his tail be-ginning to fluff. At the sound of the door latch, he whirled and fled back down the corridor, leaving an astounded Har-rap in his wake. **"Scoot, scoot, scoot as if your life depends on it!"** Not an overexaggeration, considering Mahafny's re-cent vile temperament. Yarn streamers trailing, Harrap frantically limped along, intent on retreat while it still lay safely open ahead of him. Now the grating of door hinges came faintly to his straining ears. If he could just hobble around the corner—yes!

*"But what did she ask for, Parm? I'm curious—thought she'd stowed everything she considered crucial in her kit. She always does!"* Ah, refuge at last—the common room, the last place Mahafny'd be likely to venture into, even if she felt the unlikely need for companionship. And as long as they were here, he'd not mind a cup of cha. And a chance to check about his red yarn. Parm would explain later, or he'd find some excuse for asking Mahafny. After all, hadn't Pilar said she was there? Nothing simpler—just bide his time until her mood turned less foul. Possibly the spring of this coming year . . . or the next.

♣

Chin propped in hand, Jenneth sat alone at the long trestle table, digging her spoon into her leftover oatmeal, sculpting mountains and valleys, waiting until the milk she'd dammed finally spilled over and coursed into a miniature valley. Long, narrow windows cast bars of midmorning sunlight across the table's pine planks, making her squint as she examined the results of her handiwork. Efficiently clearing dirty plateware and mugs from previously occupied spots along the table, the kitchen assistant ignored her, leaving her alone with the remains of her breakfast and her thoughts. The solitude suited her mood, though she hadn't gotten very far in grappling with her worries. Conquering them wasn't a likely option, more like learning to live with them, like having a nettlesome neighbor move next door . . . or a prickly aunt.

She yawned and stretched, spoon still in one hand. Ought to rouse herself, help with the cleanup; usually did so without even thinking about it. Or mayhap she shouldn't; she was a guest of sorts, shouldn't intrude on their routine. After all, Novie Seekers were trained to do scut work, but much as help might be appreciated, this wasn't Headquarters, wasn't her "place," and good intentions often caused more work in the long run. Besides, she needed all her energy for her moody thoughts. Being gloomy required more energy than most people realized.

**"So finish your porridge, stoke up your energy."** Pw'eek had rolled to expose her white belly to the shafts of sunlight, and now gave her a sly, begging look from the corner of an eye.

She tested the porridge with her spoon to be sure. *"It's rather cold and sticky now. But if you want it . . ."* While Pw'eek always had her welfare in mind, the calico ghatta was never adverse to considering the welfare of her own ample stomach, and now Jenneth wished she'd given her darling a bowl of fresh, fragrant porridge, the cream warming as it floated on top. *"There is just a touch of cream left in the pitcher, beloved. I'm sure Cook wouldn't begrudge it."*

**"But Diccon might!"** Kwee meandered beneath the table's full length before springing onto the bench, rubbing her chin against Jenneth in a good-morning greeting. That accomplished, she promptly jumped down and gave her sister's forehead a perfunctory wash. Kwee often seized the initiative on these morning ablutions, preferring to be "washer," rather than "washee," in the vain hope that Pw'eek might relax and doze, forget that Kwee's own ears demanded a rough-tongued cleansing. Pw'eek tended to be too methodical and overly thorough as far as her sib was concerned.

Shorn of his usual exuberance Diccon moved with an uncharacteristically rigid carriage as he entered the dining hall, and Jenneth could sense the physical discomfort radiating from him. *"Diccon, what's the matter? You look stiff as a board!"*

*"As long as you don't say 'stiff as a corpse,'"* Diccon retorted, wincing as he swung one leg, then the other, over the bench, a stifled moan escaping as he gingerly sat. "I'm convinced the human body was *not* meant to spend two days and a night on an unpadded sleigh bench, said sleigh jolting and bolting over rough terrain while being driven by a maniac whom we affectionately call 'Auntie'! Give it over, Jen." He lunged to capture her leftover porridge and abruptly thought better of it, wincing, so she generously slid the bowl in his direction. Poor Pw'eek would have to make do with some other tidbit. "I'm starving! I'll start on leftovers till Cook brings out something hot." The over-brightness of his eyes, and the faint flush to his skin made her suspect he ran a low fever.

"Everything's on the sideboard, piping hot in chafing dishes. That way the eumedicos can have a bite whenever they can steal a moment." Gesturing toward the sideboard, she spun round on the bench, poised to rise. "What do you want to eat, Diccon? I'll get it." The unfeigned gratitude that poured through her mind revealed his real relief at not having to stiffly clamber over the bench.

"A little of everything," he suggested, scraping the bowl with his spoon. "Actually, a large portion of everything." Well, whatever ailed him hadn't affected his appetite, that much was clear. Still, if Diccon were sickening with something, the Research Hospice was the place to be; surely they boasted enough eumedicos to cure anything! Of course Research Hospice eumedicos tended to be involved in pure research, and patients here were the exception, rather than the rule. How these eumedicos would react to a real, live patient complaining of an untidy collection of symptoms that didn't fit some abstract hypothesis of disease remained to be seen. And if they were anything like Aunt Mahafny, their bedside manner might be sorely lacking!

Loading a plate with scrambled eggs, bacon, sausage, and two pancakes that she topped with cinnamon applesauce, she brought Diccon his light breakfast and stole back a sausage to share out between Kwee and Pw'eek. Wiping her fingers, she poured fresh mugs of cha. "Not sure if I should have this," he confessed as he took a guilty sip.

"Why ever not?" How she'd missed cha the last few days, what with Aunt Mahafny refusing to linger long enough at a rest break to even boil water!

"Lady bless, Jen!" Torn between embarrassment and laughter, he rolled his eyes. "Didn't you count how many times I was in and out of the sleigh? I swear my kidneys have been battered to death and my bladder's sprung a leak! And that's what I've been doing, time and again, ever since we left Trude's!"

"That's what all those mad dashes from the sleigh were all about?" So, some sort of bladder infection. Adding two lumps of sugar to her cha, a momentary wickedness seized her. "Diccon, naturally I assumed you were marking trail for us in case we became lost!"

"That, too, I suppose. Except it didn't feel very funny, Jen."

**"And never once did he make the least effort to scratch over what he'd done!"** Kwee sounded faintly disapproving, yet proud. **"Just think! If any wild ghatti live in the Tetonords, they'll be positive the biggest ghatt of all has arrived to mark off his domain!"**

"I could ask Aunt Mahafny, Dic, but I think some flax tea might help." Eager for her twin to feel better, she rushed for the door to the kitchen. Surely Cook would have some dried flax seeds somewhere or, if not, she could ask one of the eumedicos for some. Distracted, concerned, she registered her Aunt Mahafny's silent entrance too late and ran smack into her. Her aunt's shrunken and worn appearance, even after a night's restorative sleep, took Jen aback, despite her simmering ire at her aunt's high-handed travel methods. Equally surprising was her untidiness, as if she'd only minimally bathed, had scanted tending to both hair and clothes. If the journey here had been hard on Diccon, it must have almost completely depleted the older woman. Tenderness and sympathy overrode her anger.

Mahafny had always refused to allow pain to deter her, but how she'd sustained her mental and physical strength, Jenneth couldn't begin to imagine. Come to think on it, Mahafny hadn't allowed Diccon's pain, or Harrap's tiredness, or Jenneth's own fears to deter her, and that daunted her more than she cared to admit.

"How's Saam faring this morning?" His frenzy the night before, on their arrival, had torn at her heart. For Saam's benefit she'd forgive her aunt almost anything—except for allowing Diccon's problem to continue unabated, not noticing and questioning it, offering a 'script to make him better.

"Resting comfortably, sleeping a little now, true sleep, I'd say," her tone noncommittal, exactly what Jenneth expected of a eumedico. Offer the barest of details, be neither overly positive nor overly negative. How she prayed that Mahafny at least confided in Harrap! "Now, what's wrong with Diccon?" As if unable to control herself, one hand kept brushing at a bulge in her pocket.

"Nothing, Auntie!" Diccon hastily interjected, casting a cautionary glance at his sister. *"Don't you dare tell her!"*

But Mahafny didn't need Saam to read the truth in her grandniece's and grandnephew's minds, not when Diccon's face revealed every emotion. Might as well hang a slate round his neck with his joys and woes writ large for all to see!

"So, excessive urination, eh? Burning and stinging when you void? Any discharge?"

Physically shrinking until he looked like a little boy caught out, he muttered, "Yes to the first, as well you know. Yes again, and no." Not exactly a seemly breakfast conversation, but hardly an unusual one, given their mother's early eumedico background, and the fact that Davvy and Aunt Mahafny visited so frequently. She and Diccon'd heard worse over meals, things that had made Diccon positively squeamish! Still, she pitied her brother, now the focus of Mahafny's cogent regard.

"And just *how* far have we progressed with the fair Maeve?" A certain grimly amused forbearance in her aunt's query.

"Aunt Mahafny!" Diccon roared, shushing her with his hand, eyes refusing to meet either of them. "It's not . . . I mean . . . Oh, please, I've endured Papa's lecture on sex! Don't *you* start on me!"

Mahafny sniffed. "I'd say a little therapeutic intervention is called for, as well as a more detailed discussion at some other time. Ask Davvy if you're too embarrassed to ask your father. Intercourse isn't the *only* way you can catch an infection of that sort." Furiously mulling that statement over in her mind, Jenneth discovered herself blushing more hotly than Diccon. "The flax tea is fine, Jenneth," Mahafny continued, ignoring their cowed expressions. "And ask the apothecaire for some tallywhacker tea for your brother." For a moment her face brightened with secret amusement. "That should keep Ruud guessing! At any rate, he'll know what you need, Jenneth." And with that she stalked out of the room, swiping a biscuit from the chafing dish as she passed.

"But I couldn't . . . I didn't . . ." Diccon moaned ceilingward.

**"Didn't but did,"** Kwee corrected. **"And you were ecstatic at the time. Would have done it again if Maeve hadn't been put off by the blizzard!"**

Staring off over his head so she wouldn't fluster him any further, Jenneth ineffectually patted her brother's shoulder in consolation. "Oh, dear! At least Aunt Mahafny didn't *actually* catch you in the same compromising position as she did Papa that time!" And then exploded with laughter.

"I know! But it still feels as if she's applied her boot to my backside!"

♣

. . . Time . . . before there was time . . . when mountains walked and trees sang songs to the skies . . . Time . . . before there was time . . . when summer was a beautiful young maiden with a warm, sweet breath, radiant skin, and sunbeamed eyes, who left her father's hut, her People's village to seek . . . Time stretched and contracted, formed its own private patterns . . . tales told, sometimes retold, touching heart and mind . . . Ruxie's hoarse voice rising and falling, a voice like ripping brocade that then turned silky sleek for long periods, as if the tale itself had power to heal, return things to an earlier state of being and becoming . . .

Doyce distinctly remembered eating and drinking at times, even sleeping—or so she thought. Soon the cramped, one-room cabin merged with memories of Callis's egg-shaped dwelling beneath the earth's surface atop her mountain. That same sense of perfect containment, the security of the womb for at least a brief period, both Callis's dwelling and Ruxie's adrift in time's stream, either timeless or capable of having time pass it by . . . Time conjured its own patterns here . . .

"Once, long, long ago, long before time was time as we know it, the Great Spirit foretold that the earth would be peopled by Erakwa and Outlander alike. That these new people would descend from the skies, people unlike the People in the color of their skin and hair, dissimilar in their thoughts and deeds, but still formed of earth flesh." Ruxie now paced the cabin's confines as if to outrun or evade the tale she told.

"And that time came to pass exactly as the Great Spirit had predicted—like shooting stars, like flaming arrows from the skyways, the strange Outlander ships rained down upon the earth." **"Plunging down like a plummeting osprey striking the surface of the lake for a fish,"** interjected P'aer from her pillow, and Ruxie paused to stroke the ghatta's aristocratic, narrow head with its over-large ears and lambent eyes. Her profile, when glimpsed, was nearly straight from brow to nosetip, only the slightest dip at the bridge of her nose. Her ghostly fur was a pale, frosty gray that took on a lavender, almost pinkish hue toward her extremities.

"Yes, dear," Ruxie crooned, "but that's *your* version, not ours. Stubborn creature, aren't you?" and winked at Doyce and Jenret. "Still, no one enjoys hearing a tale told differently, even though it still tells a truth." A mock frown. "You wouldn't credit how long we argued once over whether to use 'Newcomer' or 'Outlander' to describe these beings!" and she slipped back into her story again without a missed beat.

"Now, the Great Spirit had informed the People, the Erakwa, that it would be their duty to guide and aid these Outlanders, for they were like unto little children in this new place. And little children is right!" Ruxie's thick braid swung as she tossed her hands skyward in an age-old gesture of dismissive dismay, the equivalent of a worn-out parent muttering, "I give up! I can do nothing more!"

"Like little children, they lacked training, possessed terrible tempers, happily destroyed things. Worst of all, we beheld how they smashed at and destroyed the earth, their Outlander objects gouging raw wounds in its flanks, toppling trees, shattering rocky bones, ripping the earth apart. To us it was like striking one's mother, but we tried to be forbearing, for they were young, still innocent of reason. And, in truth, we were more than a little afraid, fearful of these strange, temperamental beings so lacking in respect for the earth. Ignoring the Great Spirit, we withdrew, left these childish beings to their own devices, and prayed the land was large and forgiving enough to contain both us and them. The Great Spirit warned us that we must mend our ways, not avoid our duty, but most of us did not listen." For a moment Ruxie returned to the here-and-now, hoarse as a crow, gulping down a mug of water in two swallows. "Doncallis listened and obeyed, though she was one of the few."

Greatly daring, since Ruxie seemed to be present and listening, Doyce framed a query that had been nagging at her. "You cast yourself, your people, as the beholders, watching, observing us, yet rarely interacting. Yet somehow you seem to think that we are the beholden, owing you in some obscure way—at least according to your lights."

The undisguised distaste in Ruxie's eyes flared so briefly that Doyce was unsure she'd seen it, though her face burned. A shrug, almost apologetic, and Ruxie took hold of herself. "Ah, worse even than our dislike of the Outlanders was our growing dislike of ourselves, our failure to aid them, teach them to hear how the earth sobbed at being ripped apart, mangled for no just cause. We could not teach them to listen, learn. Never is it pleasant to confront one's own flaws or failures." Not an easy confession to make, no confession was. "But always the circle turns, comes 'round to its starting point yet again, just as season follows season. And at that time, mayhap, we Erakwa will become beholden, given a second chance to save ourselves, the earth, and the Outlanders from themselves. At least that is what we hope, if the Great Spirit is merciful . . ."

. . . Tales upon tales, legends that lurked and leaped in Doyce's mind, taking root, blending with her past, her people's past heritage, for good or for ill. Tales of kindness and tales of outright treachery by jostling, jealous demigods and humans alike, tales that inspired and instructed, if one

took the advice to heart . . . Dawns and sunsets came and
went, but she lacked proof here in this cabin, safe-woven
within it by a protective tapestry of tales . . . until P'aer
acerbically informed her Bond, **"Enough. You'll wear off
their ears, my love. Though no doubt you've a story for
that, as well, how humans once boasted long, pointed ears
that were worn down by constant lectures!"**

"Have I been *that* bad?" Given Ruxie's downcast eyes
and reluctant chuckle, P'aer's warning had hit home. "So,
you should return now to Dolf's. But I am pleased we had
the opportunity to meet. . . ."

. . . Unclear how it happened, though her legs were tired
from walking, Doyce again found herself ensconced at the
counter in Dolf's taproom, Jenret beside her, paler than
usual and sporting a dark stubble that indicated he'd gone
several days without shaving. Cautious, she touched his
cheek to reassure herself the stubble was real. "Jenret, how
long were we gone?"

Shaking his head to clear it, he concentrated on her question, glancing at Rawn for the answer, but Dolf beat him
to it, their old friend's expression anxious and yet almost
covetous, as if his curiosity loomed greater than any worry
over their prolonged absence. "Three days and nights that
I've held your room for you, though it's gone empty."

"I'm sorry," Jenret interjected automatically. "Of course
we'll pay for those nights."

"No need. No one needed the room, so it would have
gone unused regardless." He leaned to top the brandy snif-
ters she and Jenret held, though they'd taken but the barest
sip, his eyes red-rimmed, boring into them, silently pleading
for them to share what had transpired during their absence.

"Three days? Three nights?" Doyce looked around her
with wonderment. "Khar? Is it true? Why didn't you say
anything, let us know?"

**"Why? What would have changed? There were tales to
be told, tales to be heard."**

"But, but—" almost sputtering now, still unable to wrap
her mind around the fact that three days had evaporated
in the blink of an eye. "Jenret! We're overdue! We should
have started back two days ago—sooner, except for my
dawdling."

But Dolf wasn't to be put off. A singular yearning constricting his features, he thrust himself forward across the counter. "Is P'aer still . . . there? Still—" Though his lips didn't speak the word "alive," it hung in the air. She let the barest of nods confirm it, incapable of explaining to Dolf or to herself how the shadowy form existed, timeless and eternal, yet no longer truly of this world. Dolf crumpled, began to quietly cry. "Why, oh *why* couldn't Ruxie have shared her secret with Ph'raux? Then I wouldn't have to be so eternally alone!" Head pillowed on the counter, he let the sobs of longing shake his body until Jenret slid his arms around his shoulders to comfort him.

"Jenret, we leave at first light," Doyce murmured as she sipped at her brandy. With each sip reality intruded.

# PART
# TWO

"W–well, w–what do you th–think?" List in one hand and trinket in the other, Theo held his prize aloft to catch the light. It was, without a doubt, the most tacky bauble Holly had ever seen, even worse with the light glinting off it. Random bits of brightly colored glass joined by leading depicted Sidonie's royal castle—or mayhap it was a mis-shapen cat or ghatt, she couldn't be sure. Then again, it needn't represent a thing as long as it captured a gullible visitor's eye and loosened his purse strings.

"Mmm," Holly offered, schooling her face to indicate noncommittal interest. What she wanted to do was glare at the pipsqueak shopkeeper—a dapper little mole in shades of rich brown velvet, temptingly strokable, if only to rub the pile in the wrong direction—inform him how tawdry his wares were, how outrageous his prices. "Depends on whom it's for, Theo," hoping it might make him think a bit harder, consider both the person and the present. Theo adored poking through shops in strange places, gleefully pouncing on tasteless objects and engaging shopkeepers in endless small talk about how and where the objects were made. Some of the things he'd bought in Samranth's bazaar on their Sunderlies trip were appallingly garish, blatantly ugly, but Theo thrilled over each one like a child with a precious new toy. He'd have burdened himself with even more tasteless gimcracks if his Bondmate Khim hadn't managed to talk him out of some or find a suitable distraction.

**"He wants to send Dannae a remembrance,"** Khim confided, and her sister-sib, P'roul, Holly's own Bond, let her eyes droop, her head loll, sappy with adoration. Casting an anxious look at both ghattas, the shopkeeper almost seemed to sense their interior dialogue, and Holly wondered if he were a Resonant, able to read people's thoughts, even converse with the ghatti if necessary. Here in Marchmont Holly had discovered that about one in ten people were full-blown Rosonants, while others exhibited shadings of the ability: able to receive mindspeech, or occasionally project it. And what a shock it had been in her early teens to discover that Canderis's dreaded Gleaners were in reality closeted Resonants. Now she thought nothing of it—how times had changed, how liberal and open-minded she'd grown!

**"Of course Seekers are far superior to mere Resonants,"** P'roul murmured, giving a demurely slant-eyed look at her beloved.

*"Now, now, pride goeth before a fall."* Seeing that that old adage didn't dissuade P'roul, much as Holly might secretly approve of the ghatta's sentiments, she changed it to something more likely to hit home. *"Pride goeth before a ghatta attempts to climb down a tree!"* And was rewarded by a dismayed ear-swivel.

Lady help her! Best pay attention to Theo, not gossip with the ghattas, or Theo might already have purchased the trashy shop's entire inventory! Late afternoon and they'd been wandering from shop to shop in Sidonie's old quarter since before lunch. Or lunchtime, she amended, since they'd never eaten lunch. "Theo, who's it meant for?" Try again, Theo still rapturously contemplating the clashing colors of the glass. Force him to articulate, and he might see the person—and the clashing gift—with greater clarity.

"I . . . I w–wanted to s–send s–s–something to D–Dannae," he sputtered, a wave of crimson flooding his ears. "I t–truly es–steem her, Holly." A patronizing smirk dimpled the shopkeeper's face at Theo's stammered reply, and she considered shaking the pomaded little popinjay, informing him that Theo's stammer was emphatically not a clue to her cousin's mental capacities. The man should realize that, given that he full well knew he entertained two Canderisian Seekers Veritas in his shop.

Exuding a patently false innocence, Holly stepped nearer the shopkeeper, ostensibly to more closely examine Theo's treasure. Hardly a small woman, tall and solidly, even broadly built, Holly constantly obsessed about her weight and her shape. Well, time to put that weight and shape to

good use! Gripping her wrists, she casually applied outward
pressure, biceps and pectorals clearly flexing and shifting,
even under the boiled wool jacket she wore. A reminder
to the little man that she wasn't above a tad of intimidation,
could easily pick him up and snap him in half. So much for
friendly relations between Canderis and Marchmont!

Ah, yes, that was more like it—he appeared absolutely
cowed! Yes, give the man a modest smile, a hint of demure,
downcast eyes! Only then did Holly realize that P'roul and
Khim were each astride a foot, heads back-tilted as they
inscrutably examined his paling face. "A real . . . truly a
wonderful bargain," he babbled, the price suddenly half
what he'd quoted before. Roughly twenty kilos of ghatta
on each foot plus those assessing amber eyes tended to win
bargains galore for Theo. Or if not a bargain, at least an
honest price, instead of the inflated ones that so many
greedy souls charged the gullible.

Now she was enjoying herself, lunch almost forgotten as
the shopkeeper stood immobile, except for his wringing
hands. "Well, I'm not entirely sure, Theo. First, I'm not
sure it's precisely right for Dannae. And second," she let
the pause lengthen, "I'm still not convinced that's the best
price we can get. I think we ought to ask Arras Muscadeine, Lord of the Nord and Defense Lord—I'll remind you
to ask him over dinner tonight."

The little man was fish-belly pale now, tongue nervously
darting to remove a fine beading of sweat from his upper
lip. "We can always come back another day. Besides, let's
take another look at that arborfer pendant we saw two
shops over, the one shaped like our Lady's eight-pointed
star." Now that had been exquisite, the price more than
reasonable from the very first time they'd asked. "Why
don't we stop for a bite to eat and think it over?"

**"At César's? Cheese sticks and cha, mayhap some sau-
sages?"** Khim suggested, enthusiastically rubbing against
any available shin, and Theo beamed at his beloved Bondmate from his great height.

"Y–you're r–right," he conceded, "b–both of you," and
hinged like a folding pocket rule to caress Khim. Relinquishing the gewgaw with a certain reluctance, Theo turned
to leave, only to triumphantly snatch up an equally dreadful
leaded-glass cylinder that he thrust in front of Holly's nose.

"P–perfect for the Seeker General! C–can't you s–see it on his d–desk, filled with p–pencils?"

She could—just barely—but the vision made her eyes water. Theo on one of his haliday gift-giving sprees was incorrigible. Best let him have his way sometimes; besides, the Seeker General couldn't fire Theo for exhibiting terrible taste, could he? And the price was fair—couldn't be fairer unless the shopkeeper paid them to take it away. Almost dancing with impatience as Theo hunted through his waist pouch for exact change, Holly began tugging him clear as soon as the wrapped parcel was tucked under his arm. If she could slip a pair of blinders on him, she might be able to extricate him from the shop.

"Come on. A snack first, and we *do* have to decide what to get the twins—even if we're a bit late delivering the presents. Mayhap Khim and P'roul have some ideas, because I'm fresh out at the moment."

Having shared their ghattenhood with the infant twins, Khim and P'roul still accorded them honorary littermate status. Their Bonding had—for better or for worse—inducted Theo and Holly into the extended Wycherley-Marbon family as well; hence their invitation to stay with Arras Muscadeine and his wife, Francie, Doyce's sister, and their son Harry. Somehow all the relationships had sorted themselves out, even during Doyce's tenure as Seeker General when she'd become Holly's and Theo's superior officer.

The ghattas had already scampered into the square before Theo could gather his paper-wrapped parcels and distribute a share to Holly. Well, Khim and P'roul would claim a table for them—undoubtedly outside so they could watch and be watched, the vain things!—at César's, since the ghattas adored what Arras called saucissons. The memory of their cheese sticks made her mouth water, not to mention the enticing recollection of the three-tiered chocolate cake she'd spotted in the window earlier, each dense layer separated by a luscious slathering of raspberry preserves! Pray to the Lady the luncheon crowd hadn't devoured it all! Then, with a sigh, she thrust the temptation out of her mind; she *had* slimmed down during their stay in the Sunderlies—wonder of wonders—and she'd managed not to regain most of the weight. Eat the cake; pad her middle with a roll of fat!

As if reading her mind Theo cast a commiserating look her way as he hurried out. "A l–little p–piece wouldn't hurt. We've been w–walking and w–walking."

Her stomach concurred, but her brain didn't; always too kindhearted for his own good, Theo was woefully lacking her own essential pragmatism. His long stride, though awkward-looking, ate up the ground, and she hurried to catch up. Theo could devour the whole cake and not gain a gram; she'd gain it simply by watching him eat it. Again he seemed to read her mind. "I know, l–life's unfair s–sometimes. But it's n–not f–fair," his final words shot out with vehemence and without a trace of a stutter, "to always deny yourself, be so masochistic. Small pleasures are nice, too."

Adjusting her sober gray scarf around her neck, she nodded, linking her arm to Theo's, snugging him close in silent thanks. "Turning Resonant to me, are you?"

"No–no. But I s–saw that look in your eyes. K–know you t–too well." In spite of herself, she watched the Marchmont faces watching them, curious about the two Seekers marching along their streets, faint smiles at Theo's cadaverous appearance, his gangling limbs. Hearing giggles behind them, she turned to catch sight of three little boys trailing after them, mocking Theo's walk, flapping their elbows and wrists and knees as loosely as they could. A scowl sent them scurrying away.

"H–here we are!" Satisfaction plain, Theo heaped his parcels on a marble-topped table the ghattas had claimed, each perched on a chair, while a waiter in a thick, quilted vest and a red apron stood a few paces away, ostensibly looking bored but craning his neck their way whenever he could. What fascination outdoor dining held for the natives in weather like this Holly couldn't imagine. Best not to dwell on the cold, but she still winced as her bottom touched the cold wrought-iron chair.

**"No, we didn't order,"** Khim and P'roul 'spoke in unison, and then P'roul continued, **"No point in petrifying the waiter. We really ought to send more Seeker pairs up here so they'd stop staring at us as if we each had two heads."**

"Mayhap after accepting such a dazzling specimen as Hru'rul as the norm, they're shocked to see such scrawny beasts," Holly teased back. Both ghattas had flirted outrageously with King Eadwin's Hru'rul, and Holly made a

mental note to check when they'd last taken their contraceptive 'scripts. Here she was, the one doling them out to
P'roul, at least, and she couldn't remember for the life of
her, and doubted that Theo would either. Flirtations were
one thing, pregnancy another, unless a ghatta truly desired
it. So, too, must the ghatt involved, since all males took a
related medication that quelled their urge to seek and fight
over available mates.

Distinctly miffed at the idea Hru'rul might outshine their
dramatically striped beauty, they stared up and away, ignoring her, as did Theo, busily whispering with the waiter.
"Y–you know," Theo sounded downright mournful as he
wiped his cold-reddened nose with a handkerchief, "I
m–miss having J–Jen and D–d–diccon around. First t–time
w–we'll have missed the H–high Hali–d–days with them."
An answering bleakness chimed in her own soul but receded as the waiter arrived with steaming mugs of cha redo-
lent with honey and spices and—she sniffed—brandy! So
that's what Theo'd been discussing with the waiter. Her
mood further brightened as Theo hastily repiled his parcels
so that the waiter could set down the basket of cheese
sticks, each long, soft stick of bread laced with cheese,
sprinkled with coarse salt and caraway. Finally, saucers of
warm milk for each ghatta, as well as what looked like
small plates of pâté. Theo had splurged again, not to mention indulging the beasts. A sausage apiece would have
been more economical, but his darling Khim loved the tiny
cornichons used to garnish the pâté.

"Well, we'll be back in time to help celebrate. It's 'offi-
cially delayed' this year until Doyce and Jenret return. If
the Gulf doesn't toss storms their way, they should be having a blissful, worry-free time. We vowed that they would,
and by the Lady, they will!"

Without warning Khim began to choke on a tiny pickle,
her face contorting as she hacked and coughed. Straining
toward her sib, her tail lashing, P'roul muttered what
sounded like *"I say 'Tell'!"* as Khim sputtered back, **"And
I say 'Not'!"** before lapsing into falanese, their own secretive ghatti language, to continue their argument. Still anxiously stroking Khim, Theo began energetically waving with
his free hand. Or almost-free hand—it looked as if Theo
were directing an invisible band with his cheese-stick baton!

Curious what had caused such animation, Holly glimpsed Ezequiel Dunay, the Head Chamberlain, approaching, his sky-blue cloak swirling around his thin calves in their silken hosen, the breeze tousling his auburn hair, and Holly's heart beat a little faster. In her own mind she recostumed him in a shimmering forest green cloak to complement his vivid hair, the official sky-blue livery too pallid, too insipid for her taste.

"D–don't tell m–me you've es–scaped the c–castle!" Theo jovially offered Ezequiel a cheese stick. "L–let you out of your d–dungeon!" The two had hit it off on being introduced some days back, while Holly found herself either rapt with admiration or afflicted with Theo's stammer—so severely that she wondered if it were contagious—whenever she attempted to converse with the handsome, sometimes harried, man who bore the responsibility of running the castle.

Stroking the stripes on each sleek head with his fingertips, he murmured at Khim, "Your sire, Saam, was a good friend to me, once long ago." Still flustered from her coughing fit, Khim's muzzle crimped comically, making her look more guilty than pleased. Done admiring the ghattas, Ezequiel hungrily snatched a cheese stick from the basket. It vanished in three quick bites. "Mind you, I oversee breakfasts, luncheons, dinners, and banquets for a whole castle, but I never seem to find any time to eat."

"S–so t–that's how you s–stay s–so . . ." Clenching her lips, Holly vertically gestured with her hands bare centimeters apart. Why risk further humiliation by attempting to sputter "trim," "slim," "slender," or anything else fraught with such betraying sounds!

"Scrawny?" Ezequiel finished for her as he gave his stomach a regretful pat. "Truth be told, weight settles around my middle now that I'm older. Did the same thing with my poor grandfather. But never a bit of it would migrate to our spindly shanks—might as well stuff my hose with these cheese sticks!"

Trying not to gawp at his admission, she nodded with true fellow-feeling. When no words followed her violent nodding, Ezequiel gave a faint shrug and graciously changed the subject. "Speaking of dungeons, Theo, mayhap you'd both like to see the ones at the castle. Oh, not really dungeons," he hastily added, "but the underground passageways. The ones Doyce and Jenret and Parse traveled during our troubles some years back. Doyce and Constant and Callis spirited the king through them so he could rally the people."

Eyes as excited as if someone had offered him the keys to the king's treasury, Theo burst out, "C–can you s–spare the t–time? W–we wouldn't be in–t–truding?"

"No, not in the least." Raising an eyebrow in query, Ezequiel took another cheese stick at her hasty nod. "King Eadwin wouldn't mind in the least, might even join us. Has to be fairly late, though, because we've both so much to do. A few nights hence? I'll send word when I know exactly. Come after dinner and we'll indulge you with some special desserts to build up your fortitude for venturing into the depths."

Desserts? Was the man mocking her, tantalizing her? Never, she vowed, would a crumb, a morsel, a sliver of those special desserts pass her lips!

"C–can't w–wait, can we, H–Holly?"

❖

Strange, passing strange, and "passing" was the operative word. Romain-Laurent blew on chill fingers, still counting passersby under his breath. A certain satisfaction to it: four vertical lines with a hatchmark through them. No, don't dwell on the neat completion of a set of five because—quick!—two more vertical lines must stand separate, waiting to expand into another unit of five. He'd been hard at this survey since the Bethel bells' noon cascade of chimes, and at their third chiming after noon he'd select another likely survey site. Most likely with a different density and a different, more straightforward layout.

He tapped his pencil. No planning, no forethought! Cobbled streets came winding higgledy-piggledy into this pocket-sized square, rather like spider legs. Inefficient, too, since most of the twisting streets lacked any junctions to join them. About the only way to navigate from Lane A to Street B was to hunt out a shop boasting a private drive, cut through it to the back alley between lane and street, and hope for another private drive leading onto the street. And people did so with appalling regularity, their muddy boots told him that. Think of the wasted space in those alleyways waiting to be transformed into prime frontage for new establishments if someone had had the wit to properly connect these wandering streets!

And why, *why* didn't it occur to people that they could easily walk from the west side directly to the square's north side instead of walking from west to south to east to north? Of course, that would mean they'd be struggling against all the other obedient passersby, rather like salmon fighting their way upstream to spawn, but that could be resolved by having the outermost perimeter of the square flow one way and an inner lane flow in the other direction. But then, how to allow for openings or gaps in the pedestrian traffic so that contrary traffic could cross over into the shops? Possible, possible, but it called for a regimented solution, easily devised later when he had time. But how to master changing people's mind-sets?

Preconceived notions! Practically every soul in Marchmont suffered from them! Always done it that way, and always will do it that way, now and forever. Change—now that was a Goddess he could worship, believe in wholeheartedly! Methodize, Prioritize, Alter, and Modify would serve as the handmaidens for his Goddess of Change. A sheepish grin as he scored another flurry of pedestrians on his notepad. Hadn't the professors at the Collegium in Montpéllier warned that attempting to change, improve daily life held more peril than promoting a new religion? People were so *entrenched* in their ways that he and his fellow graduates had a *duty* to literally raise people's consciousness, let them glimpse the horizon of change beyond the dull ditch they'd dug themselves into. Well, a miracle or two of his own devising should do it—a miracle of modern management— reveal the benefits to them, the savings in labor and money, and he'd gain his converts.

Word had it that Alex and Lily were progressing with their plan in Bertillon to reorganize the wharves for optimum efficiency. Whether it ever became more than a plan on paper, actuality, remained to be seen. He'd sent them suggestions for improvements and modifications that would increase their chances at success, and they were obviously so busy implementing them that they hadn't had a chance to respond, to thank him. And Florimel was chipping away in Marsan with her milling project, though if she'd not inherited that mill, she'd still be seeking a site to implement it. No, unfair to sneer just because opportunity had fallen into her lap! Padric's meticulous agricultural surveys were all well and good, but he'd yet to convince many Massif farmers to pay attention to long-term supply and demand patterns and grow with the trend, not after the fact.

Oh, he wished them well, truly he did, but they still exemplified small minds engaged in small plans. Had a one of *them* or the ten others in their class managed a posting to Sidonie after graduation? He'd purposely chosen the *real* challenge: to alter an entrenched bureaucracy at its highest levels. Oh, it would take time to modify their views, create a receptive climate for change, then tantalize them with a varied menu of the possibilities within their grasp—if they'd but extend their reach! Different choices, though not too many, that was hardly wise. Too many and they'd choose none; that had been proved time and again. Either/Or served best. At most, an Either/Or followed by a totally unpalatable third option. The problems in Internal Affairs had been unfortunate, a shame that he'd tried to move so fast. Oh, it had stung, but he was over it now, and thankful for the free time in between one position and the other. Otherwise he'd have been entirely too busy to hike the Stratocums as he had, gain firsthand knowledge of what could be accomplished there. An absolute revelation—in more ways than one!

Until that night, deep in the woods, high up in the mountains, he'd rued every step of the way in this rough, untidy world. Nature really *ought* to be curried, groomed into submission, so untidy and wasteful! Hadn't he had to pay his Erakwa guide far more than the going rate just to have him accompany him? Worth it though, to have a firsthand chance to study one, formally establish that his previous notions were absolutely accurate. But that night! That night of starshine, the moons brilliant and beckoning, he'd learned something more!

The splintering green light had zoomed down from the skies, and he'd sat up, breathless, while his Erakwan guide had merely grunted and rolled over, gone back to sleep.

The light began to pulsate, throb in fast and slow bursts. Trying to communicate with him! No doubt about it! He, Romain-Laurent, *chosen* above all others, to record the first words from space in over two hundred years! The code was old, had been near-archaic when his ancestors had landed, but he knew it, the dit-dit-dot, dot-dit-dit, each pattern representing a letter, spelling out a word. Most of the message he'd missed, not yet adept with the code, but he'd snatched a stick, feverishly digging at the ground to mark it down, transcribe it in his notebook come first light. What else could it have been? Some silly will-o'-the-wisp? Hardly! And then the green light had compressed itself into a tight sphere and whizzed off back into the skies—almost a little forlornly, he'd thought.

Even the mere memory of that moment stimulated him, reminded him he was not alone, set his creative juices flowing. Sad to waste them on such petty things as this, but his time would come. Now think, think! What did he see in front of his nose? What did he know? Analyze the weak points, the old-school ways of thinking, better it, improve on it . . . ! He licked his lips as his gaze flicked from shop to shop.

Why, *why* did people insist on opening so many small shops, each selling one or two types of wares? Hardly cost-effective when they could invest their capital in a range of goods or products everyone required on a daily basis. How much easier, more convenient to construct one large shop with a wide array of merchandise, let wine be purchased alongside meat. As it was, someone undoubtedly purchased red wine at the vintner's, only to discover at the butcher's that the beef didn't look nearly as fresh and appetizing as the chicken. And that was but a throwaway idea off the top of his head!

Excitement building as the ideas began to flow, Romain-Laurent fumbled in his pocket. Clothing! Why had it never crossed his mind before? Inside his pocket he located the beetle he'd found on the walkway, probably swept out of a shop. Tapping it ruminatively, he puffed warm air on its belly and watched the legs begin to wriggle and writhe. One visited a tailor or seamstress, had a jacket or gown made to order. Oh, a certain amount of ready-made clothing existed for those too poor or frugal for fine work, or

those in a tearing hurry. Absently he plucked off a leg,
rolling the brittle limb between his fingers. Had anyone
conducted a scientific study of sizing? Might there—he
snapped another leg—might there not be physical differences, different body builds between city dwellers and
country farmers, depending on the amount of physical labor
done? Interesting point . . . make a note. Etienne was
floundering for a decent project, always short on original
ideas but ideal when it came to a detailed statistical analysis. Do him a kindness, it would, though he'd keep the idea
of Sunderlies production for ready-made clothes to himself.

Kicking frantically with its remaining legs, the beetle distracted him, so he held it more firmly between thumb and
middle finger, digging his nail into the separation between
shell and head. Now there was an odd couple there, just
emerging from that gimcrack store. Both in their early to
mid-thirties, he'd guess. She was tall and athletically built,
solid-looking, with a pleasant, open face devoid of artifice,
a sensitive mouth—not what he'd expected. The man at her
side was built like a lightning rod—and tall enough to attract lightning, too! Loose joints that probably clacked and
clattered when he walked . . . Oh ho! Those *had* to be
ghatti! Nothing like La'ow or Hru'rul, of a certainty, but if
there existed a ghatti prototype, these fit it. ("Ask Cinzia
re: ghatti proto," he scribbled.) Handsome stripes.

So, those were the two Canderisian Seekers visiting Lord
and Lady Muscadeine. Cinzia had casually mentioned a haliday visit, but this was the first time he'd seen the strangers.
Not that he'd been invited to many haliday parties or dinners. Just as well, meant fewer gifts to buy, and he had a
devilish time selecting gifts for other people, could never
bother to attend to their likes or dislikes.

Late for lunch, but they were heading—oh, bless them!—
they were heading straight across the square to César's, confidently striding *across,* not detouring west to south to east to
north! Mayhap there was hope after all. Would Canderis be
more amenable to his grand plans and strategies for improvement? Something to consider. Now, mayhap if he could speak
with them. If only he were better at ingratiating himself with
people, but an easy bonhomie just wasn't his style. Starting
to rise, he noticed the beetle's remains still clamped between
his fingers, the beetle headless now, his wing case crushed.

Flicking it away with a little shiver of disgust, he sucked his fingers, wiped them on his jacket lining.

On second thought, no, he'd not speak with them today. While he'd hesitated, who else but Ezequiel Dunay had come confidently striding by, disarranging yet another of his plans. Fine, stand and chitchat about nothing while he nearly burst, questions surging through his brain! Filching their cheese sticks. Oh, Ezequiel, your stockings are bagging and sagging! Really, a clever fellow like you should put your mind to the problem, devise a solution. Haven't you ever wondered how *I* manage to look so tidy with thigh-high hosen and you can't even hold knee-hose in place. *His* stockings never drooped, not with them securely fastened to his thigh-bands with buttons and loops. A discreet tug at one's waist and the effect was transmitted down, snugging the stockings. No garters for him!

And thinking of hosen made him realize how chilled he'd grown, posterior frozen from sitting on this granite mounting block for Lady Change knew how long! Enough! Find another time, another place to question the Canderisians. He needed to calculate the average number of people passing through the Rue Boiserie at quitting time. Amazing, really, the sheer number of cabinetmakers, furniture makers, joiners and crafters, the mosaicists who applied the inlay on tabletops and desks. Big shops and workshops, smaller ones jammed on second or third stories, specializing in particular pieces of furniture. Marchmont was justly famed for such pieces. But each and every establishment opened and closed at the exact same time; now, if they staggered work shifts, it would improve everything, including being able to buy a cup of cha and a croissant or a glass of wine without being elbow to elbow with everyone else struggling for a quick breakfast or after-work refreshment. Again, just a simple way to even the flow of humanity, regularize it. And wouldn't a host of harried café and tavern owners thank him!

❖

Canderisians and ghatti, the coded green light from the stars, Erakwa, change, change, Change! How it all mingled, simmering in his mind, ideas shouting out to him, so many he could scarce keep track! Alive with ideas, creativity practically sparking from his fingertips! The green messenger light—Carrick, he'd called it, in honor of King Constant's twin brother, who'd fled back to the stars on the repaired spaceships—hadn't been able to penetrate, reach him here in Sidonie, but he'd found a way to contact Carrick. Twins separated, unable to communicate, the name so fitting. And he had so *much* to tell Carrick, if he but found the time.

Hurrying along—he always hurried, who knew what might be missed if he dawdled—Romain-Laurent made a sharp right at the carriage drive between the boulangerie's and the leather-goods shop, curious how efficiently he could reach his goal by these confounded back alleyways. To his consternation, he ran smack into a group of Erakwa, traipsing along in a tight cluster, gawping at everything in sight, from laundry on the line to some discarded, rusty bread pans. Probably be scavenging before he could blink, would clank wherever they went. Well, at least the back alleys were more suitable for them than finding them in the middle of the square, calmly taking up residence and starting a cooking fire. Rarely did they purchase much of consequence, though sometimes they offered trinkets for sale—arborfer. Ridiculous to allow a precious, highly limited commodity to be controlled by unsophisticated folk like that! Amazing how they seemed to consider every place their feet touched as their own, utterly at home here, they were. He sniffed. Honestly, they meandered around Sidonie as if they had every right to be there!

Still, he did feel a certain fascination toward them, a desire to know them more thoroughly, a chance to assess them. Mayhap his guide, the boy Glashtok, hadn't been a fair sample of the Erakwa, what with his giggling shyness, though he doubted it. Still, never ignore a chance to learn more, not when it was directly under his nose! Biology was not his bailiwick, but he couldn't help being curious. Children were generally malleable, were they not? And he hardly planned to hurt one.

Smiling until all his teeth showed, he held out his pencil toward a little boy, mayhap four, who shoved his lower lip above his upper one and stared at the pencil. The child wore nothing but moccasins, a leather breechcloth, and a fringed leather vest that looked too small for him, and Romain-Laurent shivered. Again he held the pencil enticingly closer, but the child intently stared at his full balloon trunks and suddenly jabbed his finger between thigh-hose and trunk, hooking a button loop and pulling. No choice but to move with the brat or have his clothing ripped.

"No!" he commanded, shaking his head and frowning in a way that even a mere dog could comprehend. "Bad! No!" But the child continued tugging, so he snapped his pencil hard against the child's knuckles. Did so again, this time on the child's forearm, to see if the blow would leave a momentary white streak against the coppery skin. How satisfying when it did! But now a stocky Erakwan male lifted the child clear and stood facing Romain-Laurent. Nothing to worry about, the man was considerably shorter than he—besides, everyone knew the Erakwa were cowards, drifted away or outright ran from confrontation. Just remain calm, self-assured, exude an aura, not of arrogance but of natural superiority.

At least this Erakwan was adequately dressed against the weather, or more so than the child. Buckskin leggings extended beyond the breechcloth, and he wore high moccasins with an intricate beadwork design, and a red-plaid shirt, obviously not from a tailor's shop. Hm—another market for clothing, though what would they pay with? Mayhap an arborfer trinket like the one depending from the man's ear beside the long, thick braid.

Romain-Laurent shifted slightly from foot to foot, already tiring of this waiting. As if equally bored, the Erakwan removed the pencil from his hand, reaching up and rapping him on the nose with it. Stung, stepping backward rapidly, he watched as the Erakwan snapped the pencil in two and followed, holding a piece in each fist. It couldn't be! He could swear the Erakwan planned to plant them in his ears! So, he'd *hurt* this Erakwan, he would! Rip the earring from his earlobe, and then—

"Romain-Laurent! Whatever you're planning, don't!" What was Ezequiel doing in these back alleys? But a sense of relief, of kinship swept over him, his legs shaking ever-so-slightly in their trim hosen. With words he couldn't understand, Ezequiel spoke with the group, squatting to tease the children, pass out a few treats from his basket. "Have you another pencil on you?" and Ezequiel held up his hand without even looking, and Romain-Laurent ungraciously dug into an inner pocket and placed one in the chamberlain's hand. Waste of a good pencil! Holding it ceremoniously across both palms, Ezequiel presented it to the little boy. A part of him wished he'd had another beetle instead of a spare pencil, could have put that in Ezequiel's hand. Let him give that to the brat!

At length, Ezequiel rose, uttering pleasant farewells and head-bobs of respect. "Just go ahead of me and don't look back," Ezequiel told him. "And don't let me ever catch you doing something like that again. Or better yet, pray that I catch you—because if I'm not there, you may regret it."

"I can take care of myself." Found himself tugging at his waistband. "You don't understand that in the collection of data, it may prove necessary to put oneself at minor risk. The knowledge gained can be worthwhile." Did Ezequiel expect him to follow after like a leashed puppy? As soon as he decently could, Romain-Laurent broke free, went his own way with stiff good-byes and minimal thanks. Damn it to the hells! How could he concentrate on counting the outpouring of workers on the Rue Boiserie at quitting time when all he wanted to do was to play over in his mind those special moments that Ezequiel had stolen from him. Ezequiel couldn't even begin to imagine what he was capable of! But now he'd have to find something better than the beetle to lighten his mood. He wanted so badly to pass along his ideas to Carrick, but he needed to be composed for that.

♣

"Etelka?" "Tel–ka!" "E–tel–ka!" Etelka Rundgren could hear her parents and her brothers calling all over for her, hear the rising note of worry and concern in their voices. Now, if all worked right, one or another of the boys, Levi, most likely, would notice the bit of red wool she'd laboriously unraveled from an inner seam of her jacket and artistically snagged on a fence post earlier in the day. Once they spotted it, they'd think they knew which direction she'd taken, while she'd have quick-footed the other way. Her nose was suspiciously runny—from the cold, she told herself—and her eyes a bit blurry as she hefted her burlap bag in one hand and shoved her spectacles into place with the other.

The front of her red-and-black block-check jacket rippled and bulged, straining at its buttons, giving her the silhouette of a woman great with child. "Y'ew?" came a muffled inquiry from beneath the heaving fabric. "Y'ew? Mew?" The kitten's squeaky voice made her smile, as did the pink nose now poking between two buttons. How she loved the little orange freckles on that pink nose! And with that thought she began to walk even quicker, determined to ignore the pleading in Mam's and Da's voices, her brothers' goodwilled whoops that usually convinced her to hastily abandon whatever private hiding place she'd found before they discovered it.

"We *have* to reach Sidonie, Baby," she told the orange-tiger kitten, sleek and warm against her stomach. "Da said it again at lunch, and this time he'll not brook any of the boys ignoring his orders. Tomorrow Rosten's to drown the kittens. And that means you, too."

"Y'ew?" Somehow Telka could hear an equal worry in the kitten's voice, as well as a note of thanksgiving at being saved.

Take it in easy stages, she counseled herself. Bit by bit. Can't get far tonight, not with dark coming on. And with the dark came a drop in temperature; already it felt colder, colder and more lonely and empty. "I wish I had a sheepskin tabard so you could ride on my shoulders, Baby, my precious gem." She'd wished for any number of things in her young life, but mostly had been contented—had made herself be contented—with what she had, what she was given. Wishing for a tabard was simply a way to pass the time as she walked, keeping to spots where the lane was hard-frozen so that her tracks in the powdery snow wouldn't show. But this, this kitten, this gleeful, fleasome kitten was *hers,* and no one could make her relinquish it, even if it meant abandoning her folk, the home where she was loved, and her glorious, new, oh-so-private bedroom.

Settling her rolapin-fur cap lower on her forehead, she

snugged the chin strap to pull the earflaps firmly in place. 'Twasn't easy wearing two pair of mitts, wool inside leather outer mitts. Couldn't feel anything much outside, just her fingers inside. Just to make sure, she slipped her thumb into the palm of her hand, rubbing it. Could curl all her fingers into a fist inside these mitts, there was so much room! The mitts, like her jacket, had been Baptiste's last winter. Absently flapping the temporarily empty mitten-tip against her leg, she hurried along.

Tonight they'd stay in the ramshackle old outbuilding on the Widow Rochelin's land. Poor, sweet lady was so ancient, her hearing and sight so bad, she'd not likely notice—or attempt to visit the building. 'Twasn't even a path shoveled to it, so she'd best hope the back window still opened like Levi'd showed her two summers ago when they'd borrowed a scythe and a whetstone. "Ssme–oo? Y'ew?"

It took her aback, as if the kitten were reading her thoughts. "Smoke?" Doubtfully, she considered it. "Yes, we can manage a wee fire, still bits of charcoal scattered around the old forge. But I don't think she'll smell the smoke—do you?" It had been nagging at the back of her mind. Open a jar of damson preserves or elderberry wine behind Widow Rochelin's back and her nostrils would dilate, begin to flex, her whiskery lips working in delight. Age had robbed the Widow of many things, but a keen sense of smell wasn't one of them. Hadn't she whacked Rosten once when they'd been visiting, and he'd slipped out to the kitchen to open the nutter-butter crock Mam had sent over? Yanked his finger out and jammed hers in first, she had. Moved spry, she did, when it came to food.

"I wish I knew how far it is to Sidonie, Baby." A long way, that she knew. But if King Eadwin loved ghatti, then surely he'd like a cat, especially a lovely one like this, so big and beautifully orange-striped. And such gorgeous golden eyes, pale gold on the outer edges, deep amber around the pupil. 'Twould take, oh . . . she calculated again on her fingers, eyes squinted with concentration and the deepening dusk. 'Least five days, mayhap six, given the length of her legs, but that might be too optimistic. Depended on if the weather held, for sure. Would she dare hitch a ride on a passing wagon?

"Naa–ow! Hh'ride! Rh'ur, hhhrmmm." The kitten's vo-

calization subsided into a purr, but Etelka wondered. Silly
to pretend the cat 'spoke her, 'twas just a cat, not one of
the ghatti. Patting the lump in her coat, she hurried on.
Mayhap she had a Resonant cat—this was Marchmont,
after all! Hh'ride? Funny how it sounded like ride, except
for that "h" sound the kitten kept emphasizing before she'd
drifted asleep. Hh'ride . . . hh'ride. Running her tongue
over a cold lip, she played with the word, the sounds. Hide?
Was that what she'd meant? Hide in a wagon so the driver
didn't know she was there? Small paws worked at her
sweater, pushing and kneading, then subsided. It might
work, it might just work!

And drays *did* stop at the Widow's, for she allowed them
to water their teams, rest the beasts. Some were kind
enough to pause a spell, gossip with the Widow, toast their
feet at her fire at this time of year. Just wait her chance
and slip aboard! She'd reach Sidonie even faster!

A breeze whipped snow at her legs, flung hoar-frosted
fallen leaves at her face, flapping at her like bats. Didn't
matter that she knew they were leaves; didn't matter that
she liked bats with their delicate fur and long, soft, supple
wings. It made her feel lonesome already, half-wishing she
dared turn around, go home. But no, if she did that, Baby's
life would be forfeit—drowned in a barrel or bucket
tomorrow—and she'd be alone again. No one to share her
thoughts and dreams.

♣

Diccon stood midway along the ferryboat, compulsively
gripping the rail, his fingernails pressure-whitened except
for the blue tinge from the cold. His gloves were in his
pocket, but he didn't want to relinquish the rail to dig them
out. The bobbing pieces of dull white ice, flat segments
large and small, but all with jagged, knifelike edges, unnerved him, and he couldn't tear his eyes away, secretly
convinced they'd slice through the ferry's hull without his
continued vigilance. So, it had turned colder farther north,
cold enough to freeze slower-moving water along the riv-
erbanks, but the ice hadn't managed to expand its hold
across the river. Instead, the currents, the winds, probably

the ferry itself had fragmented it, sent it floating along, pieces colliding, heaving and rearing back, then settling with a flat, sullen plop. Some pieces cast ominous shadows in the setting sun, while others refracted it, turning a sullen, red-orange light the color of a heated iron bar.

Broad and wide and swift, the Spray River had further swelled with autumn's heavy rains and the excess water pouring down from the Balaenas, lakes large enough to be considered inland seas. As water shot from the "mouth" of the smallest of the three Balaenas—Pettibal, the littlest whale-shaped lake—it poured over the falls at the Shroud, sent the current rushing and racing ever faster as it commenced its long journey to the Frisian Sea. More water poured into the Spray just below the falls as the Riviere LaPierre joined it slightly south of Sidonie. LaPierre could hardly be classified as a placid tributary, its westward branch, the Petit Pierre, ambled along the Stratocums's foothills, but its eastern branch, Grand Pierre, cascaded from the heights of the Cumulonim Range itself. He'd seen some of the cataracts, been heartily thankful Uncle Arras wouldn't permit any canoeing.

Paws on the rail, her head level with his elbow, Kwee's gaze darted from one bobbing piece of ice to another, ready to give chase, if need be. **"They're not as bad as the icebergs Parm told Pw'eek about. These aren't icebergs, are they?"**

He shook his head to indicate they weren't. With Kwee on the alert he felt secure enough to look across the Spray to Marchmont on the farther shore, indistinct in this light, but indisputably land. He'd taken the ferry many times before, so what ailed him? He always came through whole, if a bit pale. Still, from first light until late this afternoon they'd engaged in a mad dash from the Research Hospice to the ferry crossing, and he'd already had a bellyful of jouncing. But somehow the ferry's jouncing was even more unpredictable than the sleigh's, his stomach always in the process of rising or falling. Besides, any time they'd journeyed to Marchmont before, he'd been excited about going, not filled with second thoughts that lay in his stomach like lead.

Once, his parents and Auntie Mahafny and Harrap had taken a primitive, bucking ferry across the Greenvald

River. That had been another journey, a different quest. Now he and Jenneth and the ghatten had assumed their parents' places, were now participating adults, sharing in danger, hoping against hope for answers. His parents' quest had been to track a killer, while this new quest required them to elude death, find answers that would heal, or at least halt time in its flight. . . . But oh, Lady, please! Don't halt time's flight on this blasted ferry, condemn him to spending the rest of his life aboard it! At least, though, he wouldn't be humiliated by asking them to stop if he had to pee!

A convulsive swallow, his mouth flooding with saliva, a raging river's worth. **"You aren't seasick, are you? Can you get seasick on something that's not the sea?"** Kwee nudged his hand, her markings indistinct except for the delicate shadings of cream and buff that highlighted her toes and inner legs, her underchin. **"Remember the *Vruchtensla* during the storm? Are you going to . . . well, you know."** Her muzzle crimped drolly at the thought of such disgrace.

"I hope not!" If fervent prayers were in order, he'd recite them. Humiliating not to be able to control his stomach, almost unmanly. Especially while Jenneth calmly sat on one of the benches, all drowsy beside Pw'eek. If she could take it in stride, couldn't he conquer a little queasiness?

**"Mayhap it's not the bouncing that's making you queasy. Could be other things . . ."** she paused to give him time to probe within himself, acknowledge what discomfited him so. Not that he had to dig deep—he already *knew*, had known from the beginning, should have listened to Jen's cautions. None of them should be here—aiding and abetting Aunt Mahafny wasn't going to help anything or anyone! On, he'd *tried* to broach the subject to his aunt! And each time he screwed his courage to the sticking point, had begun to remonstrate with her, her ice-gray glare and quelling retort had left him flayed. Painful as those experiences had been, at least she'd acknowledged his existence, that he held a differing opinion; other attempts had been infinitely more painful: she simply stared through him, didn't speak, her eyes wide and glazed. Who was she then? Where was she?

*"I know, sweedling. You don't have to prod me. But couldn't we call it seasickness—for lack of a better term?*

*We have to continue—at least finish crossing the Spray. I don't think ferryboats turn round in mid-river all that easily."* Leaning forward, he nuzzled her forehead, and she bumped against his nose, scraping her jowl along his cheek so hard her teeth grazed him. What could he do—would he do—once they landed in Marchmont?

An unexpected grip on his shoulder and he started, involuntarily lurching against the rail, the pressure forcing a cough from him, threatening to dislodge whatever lunch still remained in his stomach. Harrap hovered beside him, looking even more wretchedly ill at ease than Diccon felt. Harrap did *not* relish water sports, couldn't even swim. His dash across the gangplank at loading time had resembled a man steeling himself to rush into a burning building.

The sailmaster bellowed to trim the large, triangular sail, and the sweeps on each side pulled harder, the ferry shooting ahead and settling into the chop with a rhythmic bob. If it kept up the rhythm, he could bear it. A covert glance revealed fewer pieces of ice floating out here at the center of the river, all of them matching the ferry's bounce, keeping their distance.

"What next?" Harrap's desperate grip had told Diccon all he needed to know about how the Shepherd fared. "We aren't taking any more boats or ferries, are we? I'd do anything in the world for Mahafny, but I can't abide . . ." Trailing off, he stared down, shamed by his outburst. "I've prayed and prayed to the Lady, but it doesn't do any good."

Sensing how urgently his Bond needed consolation, Parm came scooting to his side, and Diccon looked—then looked again, harder—convinced his eyes were betraying him . . . or his mind. No, the calico ghatt sported a knit vest and a little cap with ties under his chin. Lips involuntarily atwitch, Diccon swallowed his laughter.

**"Well, I think it's fetching,"** Kwee informed him. **"But it takes a ghatt like Parm to carry it off."** The cap was a deep green with a red pom-pom and red ties, the vest charcoal gray with green and red edging.

Was that how Harrap had occupied himself at the Research Hospice during their stay? Knitting? Not daring to contemplate Parm's outfit any longer, Diccon stared into Harrap's worried face, wisps of tonsure floating free like dandelion down. "Why ask me what's next, Harrap? Best ask Aunt Mahafny."

"But, Diccon, you and Jenneth are my only hope! I asked Mahafny and she snapped at me, told me to ask you! I know my way around the Tetonords near the Research Hospice well enough, but nothing about the land hereabouts!" An angry slap at the rail with a pair of mittens—charcoal gray with the same red-and-green trim as Parm's outfit, then Harrap murmured for his Lady's forgiveness. "I can't get her to listen, think things through, do anything other than worry and fret over Saam! Dear Lady, someone had best take charge, or I don't know what I'll do!"

If Harrap's faith in himself and his own resourcefulness had already frayed, then things were even worse than Diccon had imagined. *"Jen, sister-sweet, wake up, I need you!"*

*"Well, of course you do,"* she 'spoke him sleepily. *"Your brain's been twittering away, absolutely annoying, like gnats. Couldn't help overhearing half of it. And no, you won't be seasick, because I won't allow it."* Yawning and stretching with unconscious grace as she rose from the bench, she swung wide around one of the sweep-handlers who gave her a frankly appreciative, assessing stare as she made her way to them, knuckling sleep from her eyes. The way the man's eyes lingered made Diccon consider thrashing him, but that would doubly upset Jenneth. When someone eyed her like that, she almost shriveled, and the fact that he'd witnessed it would make it twice as bad. No sense calling it to her attention, then. The funny thing about Jenneth was that she was drop-dead gorgeous, even for a sister, but half the time she never realized it, tried to minimize it whenever she could.

Linking arms with them, Jenneth gave a final yawn before slowly declaring, "So it's more serious than we realized." She'd pitched her voice low, aware of Mahafny sitting stiffly, almost alertly, on a passenger bench, Saam bundled in her arms. "I suspected as much, but I kept hoping." A sigh, and she nibbled at the end of a long, dark lock that had blown across her face. Disentangling it, Diccon tucked it behind her ear. Just like little Byrlie nibbling on her braid!

"How long before we can link to Uncle Arras?" That hope had already whispered at the back of his mind, but he'd discarded it; Uncle Arras boasted powerful Resonant skills, but he could be anywhere in Marchmont, what with his responsibilities. Still, it *was* the halidays; he might well be at home in Sidonie.

"We could try. Or try for Harry, he's grown enough that his powers should have stabilized." Adolescence sometimes caused havoc in Resonants who'd shown promise from infancy, once crystal-clear sendings and receivings becoming as unruly as the growing bodies imperfectly containing them. "For that matter, we could send out a general plea for help. Someone should respond."

"But what good will it do to contact Arras Muscadeine?" Harrap wanted to know. And then he paled to the shade of his much-washed, wheaten-colored robe. Diccon hoped it was a play of the dimming light, but no, Harrap looked ready to faint. "You wouldn't have Arras *stop* her, would you?" and his eyes filled with reproachful tears.

"Isn't that what you want, what we *all* want?" Muttering under her breath, Jenneth looked puzzled, even incredulous at Harrap's response, and Diccon couldn't blame her.

**"But you mustn't stop her!"** Slipping behind Jenneth, Pw'eek leaned her considerable bulk into the back of her knee, buckling it, and Diccon clung to his sister to keep her upright. **"We've started and it's too late to stop, go back. No matter what happens, nothing will ever be the same again—but if we give up, go home, things will be even worse! Mahafny will have failed, and you'll have failed her. Saam may find peace, but you three won't!"**

Parm, eyes wide under his knit cap, added, **"Let the cycle happen. Let Mahafny try. If you don't, we'll lose both her *and* Saam!"** Too easy to forget that Parm boasted more wisdom in his tailtip than he and Jenneth, Kwee and Pw'eek could muster combined. **"After all,"** Parm continued, **"Harrap and I've lived with her for many years, know more about her, mayhap, than you do, what drives her on, what has the power to unmake her world."**

"Couldn't we at least ask Uncle Arras to help us reach Nakum? And King Eadwin would help, too, I know he would!" Brightening, Jenneth shared a look of relief with Diccon.

Hating himself, knowing he had to do it, he countered, "Jen, think! That's what you do best—not me! Uncle Arras will be sympathetic but totally unyielding. Not matter how much he respects the ghatti, he isn't a Seeker, isn't a Bondmate. Can only dimly envision what the loss of a Bond is like." The mere thought of losing Kwee made him more nauseous than the ferry's jouncing. "At the very least he'll have us both under lock and key—"

"Which means," Harrap finished, "that Mahafny and Parm and I would be condemned to go on alone." Straightening his bowed shoulders and taking a deep breath, he forced himself straight and tall, Parm, too, miraculously looking younger and more alert, more courageous despite his ridiculous outfit. "And if we must, we shall." A valiant effort, except that Harrap's final words quavered as he clutched at his Lady's Medal, holding on to the one fragile lifeline left to him. Adults suddenly dependent upon *him*, upon Jenneth? Their responsibility loomed larger, more daunting.

**"That's what being a Seeker Veritas means. Doing the hard things, finding the truth, the deep truth, even when it causes pain. Knowledge deepens with pain and sorrow,"** Kwee reminded.

He met Jenneth's eyes, brilliant blue staring into hazel, the amber-and-green highlights more pronounced as her anxiety, her apprehensions grew, outpacing his own. Not that his own weren't plenty enough! *"Shall we see it through to the end—whatever the end may be, sister-dear?"*

*"Of course, brother-mine, meddlesome twin."* But her chin quivered almost as badly as Harrap's had, her eyes suspiciously bright. *"We do what we must, as best we can,"* and held out her hand to shake on her promise. Turning from him, she stood on tiptoe to kiss Harrap's cheek. "Don't worry. We won't desert you and Mahafny, won't let anyone pry us away from you."

❧

"No, it's a lovely beast," Jenneth said with a certain regret, "but we need something sturdier, stronger." The stabler rolled his eyes at her dismissal and grudgingly led away a nicely-made roan gelding about ten years old. Lanneau's Stables had better stock than the other two they'd visited, but Jenneth refused to be easily satisfied. Ordinarily she'd have jumped at the chance to hire a handsome beast like the roan, but those long, thin legs made her wary. The beast had too much of the racehorse in him, bred for the flatlands.

"Was that wise, my dear?" Slumped on a bale of hay, Harrap worked one hand against the other, his knuckles cracking. "This is the third stable we've visited, and nothing's satisfied you. It's late. Can't we start fresh in the morning, choose our mounts then?"

His plaintiveness, plus the dark circles under his eyes, only increased her self-doubts, left her wishing Diccon were here after all to lend moral support. Dear Harrap looked as if he might fall asleep then and there, stubbornly refuse to wake until spring, and the thought that she was failing him, failing everyone, hurt. But before she could further fret herself, the stabler returned alone, no horse following on a lead. Casting dark looks at her and longing looks at his tin plate of rapidly cooling dinner, he launched into a spate of complaints she could barely follow, his gesticulations equally eloquent and far more comprehensible. Wasted time . . . dinner going cold . . . silly women who couldn't explain. . . .

Trundling after the stabler, her round sides rolling as she hurried toward her haven, her Jenneth, Pw'eek gave an anxious mew at the woebegone figure Jen knew she projected. **"This might call for some demure tact."** As if she'd been absent a hundred years, she rubbed frantically against Jenneth's shins. **"After all, that's why everyone agreed you and Harrap should come, not Diccon. Oh,"** craning her head to stare at Jenneth, she added, *"do* **ask about the lovely, stocky little beasts out back in the yard. A bit bigger than a pony, but broad and solid. And explain again— slowly and clearly—exactly what you want.** *He,"* she gave a little sniff, **"can't read your mind, you know."**

It stung. Even her beloved Pw'eek was losing patience, rebuking her! But it had made so much sense at the time: Dic'd take Aunt Mahafny to an inn, so she and Saam could rest, while she and Harrap scouted some decent horses for their journey. Of course Diccon had balked, scoffed that she wouldn't be taken seriously, would be cheated. And having a less-than-worldly Shepherd at her side would hardly encourage any sharp dealers to strike a decent bargain!

"You're forgetting who I am—who you are, Diccon." Even Harrap had clapped a hand over his mouth to smother a chuckle. "Who Harrap is—for that matter!" Parm gave an ecstatic bounce that sent his cap askew, dangling off one ear. And Diccon had stood there on the roadway just above the ferry docking and steamed, literally and figuratively. Cross and confused, he'd huffed and his breath condensed in a steamy, swirling cloud in front of him, hazing the street lantern's glow.

Of course Kwee had spoiled the joke, just as Jenneth had known she would, the ghatta's love for Diccon too strong to allow him to be bested, even by sisterly teasing. "Just because we're Seekers, you mean?" he huffed again. "We *are* in Marchmont, Jen. Seekers don't carry all that much weight here."

But before an argument could erupt in earnest, Harrap had jumped in to support her and convince Diccon of his error. "We're only just across the river from Canderis, so no doubt the inhabitants here have seen more than their share of Seekers. Any lost souls who even *think* of cheating us will be terrified that Parm or Pw'eek will read the truth in their minds."

But now, on yet another tedious, unproductive visit to a stable, her conviction about her ability was fading. Mayhap it would've been easier to stay with Aunt Mahafny and Saam, though she'd dreaded the duty. And mayhap she was just being overconscientious, too choosy, balking at setting the next leg of their journey in motion.

**"Being indecisive won't let us turn round and go home, you know. But you *are* right to hold out for suitable mounts."**

Squatting to stroke Pw'eek, the ghatta's expanding purr of pleasure enveloped and reassured her, reminding her of how much they needed each other. Together they had resourcefulness and courage to spare—didn't they? With a deep, resolute breath she rose, squaring her shoulders and ostentatiously tugging her sheepskin tabard into place. With any luck, the stabler wouldn't recognize the pale green trim and sash as the designation for a Novice, a Seeker still in training. "I'm sorry if I've acted overly critical, or didn't seem to recognize decent horses when I see them. Every mount you've shown me has been excellent—good, well-cared-for beasts. I can see how much you care about your horses, your stable." An imploring hand on Lanneau's forearm. "But we need horses suitable for riding and capable of pulling a carriage or sleigh." That had been another aspect of her disagreement with Diccon; she wanted to leave their options open. After all, they didn't yet have a firm idea of what it would take to reach their goal, their route and the weather still in question.

An affirmative rumble came from deep in Lanneau's chest at such praise, superceded by another burst of speech, more closely interrogatory. Marchmontian speech was basically the same as Canderisian, but it *did* possess a lilting roll to it, an over-quick rhythm that made it difficult to understand unless the listener concentrated. Even Uncle Arras could turn temporarily unintelligible if overexcited or extremely angry. As Aunt Francie had once put it, "At that point I just smile attentively and wait till he runs down."

"En zo des beasts can! Ze bes' beasts, aimable en staidy. Pool ze carriage or ze sleigh, aussi!" Perplexed, wanting to please, he deferentially removed his knit chook from his head and began twisting it in his hands, studying her intently. "Zere more you should expliqué? Z'en I fin' you parfect mounts! Me, Lanneau," he struck his chest, "Gif zatisfaction. Specially to splendide jeune filly . . ." he tapered off, making the sign of the Lady's eight-pointed star as Harrap glowered and started to rise. Grinning widely as if he'd never even momentarily entertained any impure thoughts, he emended, "Tell Oncle Lanneau! Zen 'e aidé you bes'e can!"

"I know I'm asking so much of you," Jenneth implored and—at Pw'eek's suggestion—cast her eyes downward demurely. "But I can see you're a man who can understand, fully appreciate, such complex needs." Ooh, this was nauseatingly coy, worse than Maeve when she coaxed a new young man to her side! Well, then, what did Maeve do next when she'd reeled one in, giddy with anticipation? Hating herself, hating the way it made her feel—almost dirty, degraded, she stepped even closer to Lanneau, intimately tucking an arm through his.

What made it even worse was that he wasn't an unattractive man, a bit stubbly, dark blond hair in need of a trim, not young but definitely not old. If he weren't . . . if she weren't . . . would she? How could she even think of such things at a time like this? No wonder Pommy had thought her a slut! Breathless, head spinning, she rushed on, "You see, we're riding up into the mountains. I know it's not the best time of year, but my aunt insists . . ." *"Now what?"* she 'spoke Pw'eek in rising panic, fearful she'd revealed too much, too caught up in other wants. *"I can't tell him exactly where we're going. Someone might ask later."*

"Zay no more!" Theatrically striking his forehead, Lanneau beamed at her, his smile genuine, relishing her flirtatious nearness and equally pleased at having deciphered her needs. "Zose nize ponies I keep ou'back, yes? Zurefooted, strong, already zay boast zere winter coats! It be late for ze tour of ze king's arborfer nurseries, but not zat late! Always people come and wan' to zee! Me, Oncle Lanneau," again he struck his chest, puffed with pride, "take my broder's infants, ze l'il ones twice so ze learn zere heritage!"

"Yes," her knees wobbled, weak with relief, "the arborfer nurseries." Bless Oncle Lanneau for leaping in, making his own astute assumptions, especially when she hadn't even remembered Pw'eek's suggestion about the ponies! If anyone *were* following them, searching acres of arborfer nurseries under Roland d'Arnot's supervision would distract them long enough for their final sprint toward Nakum's lonely peak higher in the Stratocums. "Now, how many ponies can you let us have?"

Nothing to be proud of, using her feminine wiles like that. Mama wouldn't ever have done such a thing, nor Aunt Mahafny either. But they knew how to command, create an atmosphere where people sprang to obey, eager to help. Mama's friend Sarrett, with her gilded hair and beguiling face and figure, had fought long and hard to have pleabringers and defendants see only a competent, composed Seeker, when she and T'ss rode circuit. Still, Sarrett was frankly gorgeous, even in middle age, and she couldn't come close to matching Sarrett's looks. And Aunt Jacobia certainly didn't run the mercantile by flirting or appearing helpless! *"Pw'eek, why didn't you stop me?"*

But before Pw'eek could respond, Parm gave Jen a
cheeky ghatti smile. **"Because, my dear, there's nothing
wrong with working with what's at hand, as long as you
understand how and why you use it, and don't let it use
you. Just as I let people think I can't focus on a single
thought without straying to seventeen other subjects. But
that's our little secret, you know."** Slowly and deliberately
he delivered a ghatti kiss her way, both eyes squeezing shut,
then springing wide open.

❖

Spend the night? Press on in the dark? Distinctly less snow
here, so the roads should be clear; continuing by the light
of the Lady's Moon was a distinct possibility. Could she
still ride? And for how long? Mahafny wasn't sure, didn't
want to think about the answers she'd have to give to be
scrupulously honest with herself. Ofttimes evasive, noncommittal responses gave patients more hope—and more life—
than brutal honesty, clear, uncompromising answers. Do
what she had to do, then worry about the consequences to
her aging body. She'd always worked that way, her life
secondary to her patient's needs. No reason to change now,
not if it would benefit Saam.

The inn here in Bertillon boasted a parlor, and they'd
paid extra for its privacy, the innkeeper scratching his head,
put off by their standoffish request. But then, they were
Canderisian, and everyone knew they were a bit odd, different from Marchmont citizens. Ignoring her protests, Harrap had removed her boots, forced her down on the parlor's
leather settee before leaving with Jenneth. Wasn't quite
long enough to stretch out on, so she lay on her back, knees
raised, contemplating the pressed tin ceiling, too tired to
nap. The grids formed squares, a star—mayhap a snowflake—centered in every other one. Its regularity, its consistency, appealed. Examine it and one knew exactly what to
expect, no surprises. Generally, if there were no surprises
in store, it also indicated one wouldn't be subjected to any
disappointments. This time she wasn't so sure.

A pungent smell gradually intruded on her nostrils, and
she sniffed once, hard, her lips tightening. "Ah, Saam, you

didn't!" she whispered and swung herself off the lumpy settee, padding across the floor in her stocking feet. She'd settled the ghatt in an easy chair, confident its thick arms and padded back would protect him from falling now that he was no longer restrained by his wrappings. Luckily she'd left most of the towels and shawls around and under him. Mayhap the chair hadn't sustained any great damage, though a faint residual odor might be detected on damp-ish days.

Smacking his mouth, Saam swiveled his head, blindly searching for her as her voice slowly registered in his brain. As if with a monumental effort he opened his yellow eyes and blinked: this time the fogginess that usually inhabited them had dissipated. Working as tenderly and efficiently as she could with her ruined hands, she stripped away soaked bedding and slipped dry ones beneath him. "Why didn't you tell me you had to go?" she grumbled, more to make conversation than to accuse him.

"Forgot it . . . till I had." Straining his head, he gave her hand a passing lick. "Sometimes I'm . . . elsewhere . . . and when I'm elsewhere. . . ." Leaving the thought unfinished, he gave her a pleading look.

*"But when you reside in that . . ."* she hesitated, as if saying it might give it added credence in Saam's mind, *"that body, it doesn't need to urinate, doesn't need food or water, or any of the things we living beings take for granted."* Stroking his back, she winced at how thin he'd grown, his beautiful blue-gray fur coarse and matted, almost sticky to her touch from lack of grooming. No matter how hard she'd worked to keep him clean, her ministrations couldn't approach the scrupulous efficiency of his own tongue. *"What am I going to do with you?"* Always they mock-scolded, teasing about each other's supposed frailties or intractable habits.

"Oh! Let me go! Let me go!" Saam screamed in her mind, his frantic yowling counterpointing his mental plea. Now he was struggling, his emaciated body writhing beneath her hands, his unexpected strength confounding her, leaving her hard-pressed to keep him pinned in the chair as he fought to flee, claws shredding the fabric, clinging for dear life as she pulled him back. "Where? Where are they? Must find Doyce and Khar! Promised Oriel I'd . . ."

Clinging for dear life. . . . Ah, if only he'd cling to life—just a little longer—that was all she asked. Wasn't she asking less of Saam than Oriel had done at his death? Give her a chance, time to find some way to save him! Again Saam twisted and writhed, desperate to turn his claws against her—her—and her aching fingers could no longer hold him tight. Hating herself for exposing their dual weaknesses, she shouted for Diccon, praying her nephew was near. So unfair, unjust to involve someone else, employ brute force to control the ghatt, but until she could separate herself, get to her eumedico 'scripts, she had no choice.

"Aunt Mahafny, what's—" Bursting through the parlor door, Kwee fractionally ahead of him, Diccon left his query uncompleted, the problem all too evident. "Still feisty when he chooses to be, isn't he?" Dodging Saam's flailing claws, he flinched when the ghatt hissed his hatred and fear in his face.

"Isn't you he's hissing at," she tried to explain. Diccon nodded as he slipped a shawl across Saam's chest and between his front legs, bringing the tail up snug behind a foreleg, and tightening his hold on both ends. Once he discovered the trick, Saam would slip his bonds in an instant, but for the moment he kept making ineffectual lunges, the shawl harnessing him in place. Praying he could contain Saam long enough, she scrambled for her bag, frantically searching for the 'script she'd measured out so scrupulously before they'd left, each packet labeled, sealed with a drop of wax. Part of her methodical preparations, because she'd known that once on the road, she wouldn't be able to trust her hands, any remaining deftness fled. Now even the wax seemed too daunting for her warped fingers to peel, but at last she pried open the packet. Damn! The ewer held water, she'd checked on entering the parlor, but she should have poured it, had it in readiness. Pouring took both hands these days. Set the packet down so she could pour, and she'd never pick it up without spilling the powder. Let the Lady have mercy on her! Had she become half-witted as well as half-crippled?

But Kwee stood on the settee, so young and vital, her pewter with coppery-shaded fur fluffed and fresh. Gingerly the ghatta nipped the packet from Mahafny and neatly held it by a corner. Still reverberating with Saam's yowls of pain, fear, and confusion, Mahafny aimed the ewer at an empty glass and poured, water overflowing before she could halt, sluicing off the table onto the settee. The ghatta's fur rippled with dismay as the water pooled on the leather, puddling around her paws.

*"I'm sorry, but I've got to calm him before he hurts himself or someone else."* She didn't relish 'speaking any of the ghatta except for Saam, her old friend, and Parm, on occasion. Wasn't her way, never had been. Never a Seeker, merely a surrogate, but she *was* a eumedico, and that was sufficient, one ghatt companion more than enough, a world encompassing just the two of them.

**"Stay calm and you'll stay steadier. Diccon and I are here, don't rush."** Kwee stood almost on tiptoe, an expression of deep unhappiness marring her face, already screwed from clenching the packet between her teeth. **"It hurts Diccon to see his dear Saam like this."**

So ensnared had she been with Saam, her nightmarish battle to keep him alive, that Mahafny'd not considered how his decline, his impending death might affect anyone else. Diccon and Jenneth had grown up with Saam and Rawn and Khar around them all the time, furry substitute parents. And Diccon was a softhearted boy—man, she corrected herself—as subject to strong, intense emotions as his father.

Quickest way to lower the level of water from the glass—drink it. And Mahafny did so, gulping so rapidly she nearly choked, water pouring down her vest. Now, the packet. But Kwee had already tilted her head over the glass, so all Mahafny need do was relieve her of the packet. To her surprise, Kwee's jaws suddenly captured her wrist, teeth indenting but not breaking the skin, her grip freezing Mahafny's hand in place as the powder flowed out. **"Didn't want my toes dusted, too."**

Now! Stir the mixture with the pipette, the glass rod chattering against the side of the glass. "Diccon, you'd best dose him, my hand's not steady enough. I'll hold him." That she could manage, she hoped, wrapping the shawl's tails around each palm. "Keep your finger firmly over the end of the pipette until the tip's in the corner of Saam's mouth—that's right, use your other hand to part his lips.

Now remove your finger from the top. Two doses should suffice."

But Diccon's deft hands had outraced her instructions, and already a second dose flowed into Saam's grimacing mouth. A tear had formed in each magnificently blue eye, but Diccon's hands never trembled, his touch gentle. At this stage she'd likely have broken the slim glass rod between Saam's teeth. "Impossible not to be around eumedicos in *our* family, Auntie. It rubs off." A hint of a grin as he blinked away the tears. "As long as it's not blood, I'm fine. I leave that to Jen. I don't even like going into butchers' shops!"

As Saam's body slowly relaxed, Diccon unwrapped the shawl and slid it clear of the ghatt, making him comfortable. "Go, get your things put away, Auntie. I'll sit with him a bit longer to make sure the 'script took."

Gratefully, she sopped at the mess she'd made, frustrated and embarrassed at having had an audience for it. Blot the water she'd spilled on the table, the leather settee, hope the inn's servants would trade her some clean, dry rags for the sodden, urine-soaked towels she'd taken from beneath Saam. Set the glass aside until it could be properly cleaned, neaten her 'script case, have it in order for the next emergency. A comfort in being orderly, methodical in her tasks, the rhythm familiar and soothing to her ragged worries.

Looking into her case, she strove to ignore the siren song emanating from the compartment holding the eight remaining packets with their black seals, cracked and dry with age. The drug eumedicos carried in case of dire personal need, the drug she'd sworn she wouldn't take until she was at her last extremity. Already she'd used two of the precious packets. It restored flagging energy and strength, conferring the ability to continue long after body and brain begged for rest. Had Harrap seen it there, he'd have snatched it from her, thrown it into the nearest fire. Even after all these years it had retained its potency. Most prudent eumedicos generally kept a few doses on hand in case some major crisis—a raging epidemic, a natural disaster, a war—required them to work for days and nights without surcease, selflessly caring for a multitude of patients.

Against her own better judgment she palmed a packet and made a fist around it, shoved the fist hard into her pocket. Best to have it on hand. In doing that, wasn't she admitting that she'd require another dose, and sooner than she might have liked? How much longer? Four days, five, six before they reached Nakum? Could she continue without the stimulant? Drive herself on and on without faltering or failing? Had to, must, if she would save Saam. A small shrug, a bitter grimace—why deny it? She'd take it again when the need—or the urge—became too overpowering to ignore, pay the cost later. The farther they traveled, the more treacherous the terrain—and very likely the weather—would be. Yes, a small dose was enough—just enough—right now to keep her going, ensure she burdened no one else. Later, a larger dose would be required to sustain the same effect. And only eight packets remained!

The mere thought of the drug sent a jolt of energy racing through her, almost as good as ingesting it. A flush of color burning her cheeks, her shoulders straightening, her hands uncramping, mind and body mimicking the effect, crying out to taste it again. Before these last few days it had been almost eighteen years since she'd touched it—and then but one small dose—in the aftermath of the abortive war between Canderis and Marchmont. Too many wounded, including her dear cousin, Swan, too few skilled hands available. Her hands had lost their skill, even back then, but her brain hadn't, and she'd ceaselessly moved from bed to bed, to and from the makeshift operating arenas, advising less skilled eumedicos, seeking ways to save as many as possible. All eumedicos-in-training were given a scrupulously monitored dose to learn firsthand what the drug could offer, how it altered their actions and reactions, their response to exhaustion and pain. As the drug wore off, some of the young eumedicos always broke down, crying, begging for more to halt the long, painful slide back to normality. Now she remembered why they'd cried.

When should she take it again, how long before she'd need it? And the more she thought on it—arguing and compromising with herself—the more she craved it. Just let her taste it again and she'd fly up the mountain with Saam in her arms, free him from this cruel facsimile of death that had entrapped him! Yes, a few moments alone, no one looking on, asking what she was taking. . . . A smile at the easing it would offer, her body reacting as if she were thirty again. Giving herself a mental shake, she snapped her case shut, looking around guiltily, only to encounter Kwee, her soft green eyes fear-bright. *"You won't tell Diccon. You mustn't tell anyone. Do I make myself clear?"*

Did silence denote assent? It wasn't as if she were lying to the ghatta—she'd shut the case, wrestled against her longing and won, hadn't she? Would Kwee respect her wishes or not? The ghatti always kept their own counsel. Without saying either yes or no, Kwee deliberately slid her gaze from Mahafny and paced to Diccon's side, her swishing tail a silent accusation.

♣

Always he'd loved to roam at night, wander from room to deserted room, along endless, echoing corridors and up and down empty staircases, for this was when some of his most original ideas visited him, companions on these nightly walks, assuming flesh and blood and substance simply by being at his side. At times he argued with them in a hoarse whisper, debating their points, arms gesticulating, waving as if batting away night moths that yearned to gather round the incandescent ideas—more brilliant than the sun's rays— that radiated from him. Ah, hard during the day to keep his light under a bushel, but he tried, had learned long ago to obscure himself behind an earnest, overzealous façade, off-putting to all but the most determined, the most masochistic, or to the rare kindred spirit whose flame, alas, never burned as brightly as his. Disappointing, that, but he refused to lower his standards, limit his goals.

Other nights, his boon companions deserted him, and he faltered through the emptiness by himself, insubstantial as a ghost, sure his physical presence cast no shadow, left no impression wherever he trod. Naught to do but accept it. He'd done something wrong, thought something wrong, and the glorious horde no longer clamored to stride at his side. Mayhap they were jealous of Carrick, of his coded messages into deep space? Mayhap they believed he'd abandoned them?

Asking, wondering why, *why* did no good; the wrongness would gradually dissipate and he'd be gifted by their company once more. From these extremes he'd learned that commonplace solitude had its small pleasures—neither importuned by genius nor totally bereft of existence.

Of course, wherever he walked about the castle, just before dawn or in the depths of night, someone, some few souls were generally stirring, because a castle was never empty and still. Tasks to be done, from high strategy and political compromise that flourished privately behind closed doors to the mundane business of mopping and polishing floors heavily trafficked during the day. Occasionally he glimpsed these people, let them glimpse him, if the mood struck. Smile, scribble furiously in his notebook, stride purposefully—that was all that was required to claim his own private sphere, the protective bubble that let him float unmolested and unimpeded through the castle universe. Should he and his horde not care for company, tapestries offered refuge behind their heavy drapings, the half-landings of stairs, anterooms where one could flatten oneself against the wall, scarcely breathing until the menace of discovery bypassed him, ignorant—as usual—of his fleeting, furtive presence. Best they remain ignorant, for their own sake, of him and his horde. The horde didn't relish company other than his own, as choosily selective as Romain-Laurent himself.

For a brief span each night he made it a point to sleep in his room, inhabit it and scatter about some of the artifacts of daily existence that lesser mortals expected to see: a shaving kit, comb and brush, a jar of hair pomade, circulars collected on the street and emptied from pockets at the end of the day, loose change, whatever he could contrive to make him appear normal, that confirmed his existence. Clothes neatly hung or folded, mayhap a soiled stocking dangling from the footboard of the bed, a dirty tunic half-slithering off a chair. He'd chosen this room with care; three more spacious ones with superior views had been offered him, all on the orders of the king, naïf that he was!

No neighbors inhabited the rooms on either side, nor across the hall. No one above or below him either. Oh, someone might spend a night or two a few times each year, but luckily Eadwin rarely indulged in elaborate balls or major festivities and entertainment. Minor functionaries from a trade or agricultural delegation, visiting relatives of

castle servants, were spared the expense of lodging, thanks
to the king's kindness. Solitude was important. Here, Romain-
Laurent could be himself, draw meticulous diagrams and
organizational charts, compile detailed lists, work out the
hundreds of details that the horde implanted in his brain.
The more innocuous or incomprehensible charts he crook-
edly hung on the walls to give the cleaning staff something
to gossip over. Others, more precisely labeled, he maliciously mounted to stir up things, see what would happen,
who might look at him askance after hearing that their jobs
were charted several rungs lower and at a dead end for
advancement. He might lack power, but even the potential
of power could shake people's complacency. Soon enough
they'd learn to worship the Goddess of Change!

And sometimes, when he was alone, just his neutral self
in solitary residence, he opened the triple-locked trunk at
the foot of his bed and regarded the treasures he'd collected, stolen, or "liberated" through the years and put to
ingenious use. His grandfather had had an equal passion
for things and ideas, preferring them to most people. He'd
plant Romain-Laurent on his lap and show him how things
worked, how they connected to perform a certain specified
task. Patiently he let the little fingers fumble at the gears
and cogs, the springs and levers, reconstructing what had
been taken apart. A major effort for a small child, an effort
even today for him, lacking his grandfather's easy dexterity.
Still, he learned, came to appreciate, even love the orderliness, the concentrated effort required to activate this mechanical terrain. Even better was devising new uses for old
things, or basing some new device on old principles. Often
he could envision it, but couldn't make it function.

At home he was mostly ignored, overlooked as if he
weren't there, because to acknowledge his existence was to
acknowledge imperfect goods, that Romain-Laurent was
but half of a whole—one twin born alive, the other dead.
Two older sets of twins, a pair of boys and a pair of girls,
saw no need to include an odd sibling in their doings, his
mere presence unbalancing their unity. What had he done
wrong, except be born alive?

Worse were the mind-to-mind conversations that sparkled
and spangled over his head, yet rarely a word addressed
aloud to him, other than, "More bread, Romain-Laurent?"

Even his name was only half his—the other half belonging to his stillborn brother! Whatever he did wasn't important to them—this child so woefully lacking in Resonant ability—so he did what he chose for the most part. Their brief flurry of interest surrounded him in his late teens when he admitted that voices talked to him, instructed him to do things. Alas, though, it wasn't Resonant ability, just some quirk. Or an attempt to show off, beg for attention, his parents believed. Mayhap the Collegium at Montpéllier could shape him into something—and there he'd learned a passion for organization, for subtly-built constructs of ideas that had the power to *change* things.

His grandfather had collected odd bits of mechanisms like a jackdaw, even paid high sums for antique pieces belonging to the original spacers who'd inhabited the planet, and it had literally been child's play to pocket pieces for his own burgeoning collection while he was growing up, matching the parts against drawings in old books, curious which pieces would best serve his purposes—once he knew what his purpose was. Later, at the Collegium, he'd stumbled on the "Verboten" Room and how to bypass its security, a rite of passage of sorts. There, he learned more, yearned more for what was . . . what *could* be yet again! Oh, the technical ability, the facility, would never be his, but he could dream the dreams that lesser mortals, engineers, construction experts, would follow, create from the images cramming his mind. And one day, when teachers and students had scoffed at one of his ideas, he'd vowed that he'd do whatever it took—contact other worlds in space, even—to find those who could reveal how to implement his ideas. Normal minds were too constrained, Resonant minds as well—just look at his family! Even some of the voices in his head had jeered at the grandiosity of such a plan, though he'd gradually won some over.

No, it hadn't happened right away, nor had he expected it would. The object hidden in his trunk at the castle had required years of effort and revision as he secured better parts, though it was still crude, primitive, utterly basic. The solar condensers had been a fiasco, so he'd fallen back on a battery-powered radio-telegraphy drive. Oscillators, transmitters, frequency and wavelength, carrier signals and waves, amplification . . . all like a foreign language yet so seductive in its promise. And he'd accomplished it on his own! He—usually so quick with ideas, improvements, eager to point out where a fellow student had gone astray—had zealously guarded his secret because it was so far superior, primitive though it was, to any future they'd ever contemplated on a wine-drenched night of fantasy and formulation. The flashing green lights he'd witnessed in the Stratocums had been an answer to a promise he'd made to himself. Even the voices within him had temporarily gone silent, whether in awe or anger, he couldn't judge, but they'd be forced to acknowledge his brilliance, return to meld their own inspired thoughts to his. . . .

Once during every eight-day oct, he sent out his code, praying his contact had time to listen to it amongst all the meaningless babble and staticky emissions that must fill outer space, winnow it out, find time to respond. And when he did, as he had a few times in the past, Romain-Laurent would nearly fall off his chair in ecstasy at the contact, communion with a like-minded soul! Music of the spheres being sung to him, he, Romain-Laurent Charpentier, the only one who'd listened, who'd tried to hear—had heard! The daily laughter, the snide remarks, the outright rudeness, the moments of being ignored as if he had no existence—at home, at the castle, sometimes even at school—all became tolerable.

First he would run his antenna out the window, hooking it into brackets implanted amongst the ivy. Twice now he'd made it higher in the three octants he'd been in residence, since the Internal Affairs Lord unceremoniously had "promoted" him to the castle. The castle guards had had to rescue him the last time, found him hanging from the ivy after he'd lost his footing. He'd pretended to have an assignation with an unnamed young woman to explain what he'd been doing. Lovely, lovely illegal technology, so simple, yet so clever!

Then came the music of the spheres, that lovely staccato dit-dit-dot. Child's play to memorize the old dots and dashes code, but transmitting them with anxious fingers that stuttered and stammered out too-long dashes and over-short dots was something else again. Practice, practice, practice! It worked best when he let his mind float free, almost as if something, someone else directed his fingers. Listen, listen to this new voice that now inhabited his brain, so far superior to his hordes, to himself, even!

*Continue toiling,* the voice advised, and he could almost feel a kind hand on his shoulder, patting his back. *Someday they will understand, appreciate how you struggle to lift them from their ignorant depths, show them a superior world. They are infants, and no infant truly wishes to be born, secure in the insularity of its mother's womb. Only later, much later, does it realize what new horizons have unfolded before it. You are the key, Romain-Laurent, the key that will unlock the blessings of a technological future beyond even the one that we envisioned.*

The dots and dashes of the message came crisp and precise, without hesitation, falling so rapidly that it wasn't easy to transcribe it. Indeed, he didn't dare consider what the message contained until the transmission was completed, otherwise he'd miss letters, whole words or phrases.

Ah . . . how had he gotten here? Wandering, wondering, wandering. This open door—the first time he'd ever seen it unlocked, ajar behind the serviceable baize curtain. Rumor had it that Ezequiel, the Chamberlain, retired into the subbasements and cellars on certain evenings. Did he, too, seek solace in exploring alone? Cataloging and organizing his finds, mapping plans in his head? Didn't he realize how similar they were? Though, of course, Ezequiel would never have his vision, forever chained to castle routine. And Carrick would never bother even attempting to contact Ezequiel, not while he had Romain-Laurent as his acolyte of Change.

Go down, join Ezequiel? No, he had a presentation due soon, one that could alter not just his life but the lives of so many others, soon to be grateful for his abilities, though they didn't yet realize that. Back to his bedroom, prepare, anticipate objections. Yes, another chart should clarify things so that even the dullest soul could see it plain and simple! Copies to be made. Speaking at a joint meeting of the Domain Lords and the Ministration Lords, what a coup! A chance for change at the highest levels!

♣

Nothing like the close of an old year and the beginning of a new to make you realize how many problems still remain to be resolved! Eadwin resignedly fingered his list yet again. And this, mind, was but the first joint meeting of the Domain Lords and the Ministration Lords this year. Another seven to look forward to, one each octant. At least he wasn't expected to attend the individual Domain or Ministration meetings; he merely had to endure both a verbal and a written report on each one.

Not for the first time he wondered if he'd ever be able to wean his Lords from meeting in the throne room, a grand hall that left much to be desired, for smaller, more intimate meetings. Moderate voices disappeared, probably clung like bats to the high-arched beams of the ceiling. Louder, more aggressive voices reverberated and boomed, especially if one were familiar with the hall's acoustical tricks. Still, it was a far more inviting place than it had been when Constant Minor had served as Steward, or during Wilhelmina's long reign. New carpeting, fresh paint, and polish made the hall more airy, less darkly imposing, moth-eaten tapestries and tattered, dusty banners gone, along with a large selection of antique armaments and the bellicose statement they made. Habit, that's all it was, unlikely much had been changed since Constant I! But he'd be damned if he'd sit on the throne, preside over this meeting from there. Instead, a chair and table on a platform marginally raised him above the others. One couldn't flout tradition too much, though he'd tried at first; now it offered a certain comfort, a cushion to fall back on, and that in itself was troubling.

To his left sat the four Domain Lords, each actively responsible for governing a quadrant of Marchmont, their titles hereditary, the holders blood kin to Marchmont's rulers, though that wasn't strictly true any longer. Prosper Napier, Lord of the Ouest, and his line had been ejected for Napier's support of Prince Maurice eighteen years ago. Replacing the Napiers was the Beaumarchais line, old, respected but less-than-royal, according to the records. But he'd known Guillaume Beaumarchais at the Agricultural Collegium, trusted him for his solid instincts and instinctual love for the land, and he'd appointed Gilly—who'd wasted no time producing five sons and two granddaughters (thus far!) to succeed him. The Ouest Domain prospered and multiplied as enthusiastically as the Beaumarchais clan.

Technically, Arras Muscadeine wasn't of the blood royale either, though he *was* related to Eadwin's mother, Fabienne. Certainly his appointment had been less traumatic to hidebound conformity than Gilly's. How could it not be, given Arras's unswerving devotion to serving justice, refusing to allow Maurice to inherit the throne through chicanery and treachery? Ah, how he depended on Arras, both as Lord of the Nord and Defense Lord, the same positions Eadwin's putative father had held. And may Maurice be looking down and gnashing his teeth!

Eugenie Vannevar, daughter of the late Auguste Vannevar, had succeeded her father as Lord of the Levant, assuming the position with all the zest and sweet-natured intelligence her father had exhibited before he'd been cowed by his ailing wife's dependence on one of Maurice's prime associates, Jules Jampolis, Public Weal Lord at the time. He'd served until ten years ago, but had truly never been the same, so Eugenie's presence was refreshing, though sometimes a little too rectitudinous for Eadwin's taste.

And finally, outlasting all predictions and many people far younger than she, the Lord of the Sud, Quaintance Mercilot, assisted by her great-granddaughter, Monique. Her age had to be ninety-plus, though his mother could undoubtedly figure it with greater accuracy. An even hundred wouldn't surprise him! Deaf as a post now, but her eyes still shone bright and merry and shrewd. Poor dear had shrunk, the once mountainous bosom and full-moon face whittled away by time. Actually, she and Maurice had been first cousins and, strictly speaking, she stood closer to the throne than Eadwin himself. Woe to any soul who presumed to address her as Lady of the Sud rather than Lord! As Quaintance had declaimed time and again, "Being a lady isn't what it takes" to be a good Domain Lord, and Eugenie Vannevar had taken her cue from Quaintance in her mode of address.

So, the four on his left were present and accounted for. Now for the Ministration Lords to his right at a long table with seven seats, though currently only four were occupied. One empty seat he immediately discounted: since Arras Muscadeine held dual titles, Lord of the Nord and Defense Lord, he generally sat with the other Domain Lords. Carn

and Terrail weren't late yet, but they were pushing it—and
his patience—very close, especially as the other Lords sat
there, relaxed, commenting amongst themselves, yet attentive to any gesture or throat clearing that indicated his
readiness to start.

Discreetly stretching his leg beneath the table, he prodded Hru'rul with his toe, stroking the ghatt's hip until a
satisfied purr rumbled forth. *"Hru'rul, ask La'ow if he or
Cinzia can remember the saying Doyce concocted to remember the Ministration Lords."*

Ha! Who said change never occurred? Permitting Cinzia
Treblicote and her Bondmate La'ow's predecessors to attend these joint meetings had been met with incredulity
and incendiary howls verging on the insurrectionary—with
the exception of Arras's knowing smirk, modestly filtered
by his mustache. Finally, his Lords had grudgingly accepted
that it could foster trust between king and lords—he a complete novice to royal rule, untrained in the governance of
a kingdom. After Maurice's rebellion, he had to *trust* those
he'd appointed or inherited, or that he and the Domain
Lords elected to Ministration posts. Originally Hru'rul had
served his purpose, but the ghatt had never been fully
trained in Seeker methods and protocol, becoming fidgety
and frustrated during long, involved arguments. Once he'd
grimly padded forth from his temporary lair beneath the
table and buffeted Tinian Salaverry with a massive paw!
Hru'rul had termed it "dithering," while Tinian saw his
actions as a "waiting game." Allowing the Seeker-Bond
liaison from Canderis to serve in the role of truth-arbitrator—
if required—meant Hru'rul could wander when he chose,
better able to indulge his restlessness than Eadwin was.

Now what was the Doyce-ism? 'Twasn't an insult, more
of a tribute to Doyce Marbon. When she'd once confessed
the mnemonic device she'd employed to keep track of the
seven Ministration Lords, he'd been both charmed and
even more impressed by her devotion to duty.

La'ow 'spoke him, though his yellow eyes remained fixed
on Cinzia. **"Between the two of us, we think we've nailed
it."** His mindspeech turned absolutely stentorian and Eadwin half expected him to commence with a dramatic throat
clearing. **"In All Everyday Affairs, Embark Dynamically,
Proceed Wisely, Conclude Joyously."** Hardly a bad motto

to live by, come to think of it, and an excellent way to run a meeting, if he only could. *In All Everyday Affairs* (Internal Affairs, External Affairs), *Embark Dynamically* (Exchequer and Defense), *Proceed Wisely* (Public Weal), *Conclude Joyously* (Commerce and Justice).

**"Being joyouser when done,"** grumbled Hru'rul, **"even joyouser not beginning."** Clearly Hru'rul's patience had worn thin before he'd even called them to order.

*"Doesn't work that way, and you know it. Don't you think I'd rather be somewhere else? Like at the arborfer nurseries? Being a ruler means you have to rule—or at least guide."* That was his preference—guide, direct, influence and mold opinion, not issue edicts or decrees.

Resettling across Eadwin's foot—and the ghatt knew very well that would cause it to fall asleep—Hru'rul had the last word. **"Terrorize 'em. Meeting finish faster."**

Damnation! Where were Terrail Leclerc, his Internal Affairs Lord, and Carn Camphuysen, his so-new Public Weal Lord that the fellow was still distinctly damp behind the ears? If the poor fellow didn't learn to leaven his spirits, approach his job joyously, he'd wear himself out before he even started. Tinian Salaverry, External Affairs, was present, of course, and that's whom he would have expected to be closeted with Terrail Leclerc, cards flying for a final hand of Tally-Ho. They were teased about the pairing of their names often enough—"Tinian-Terrail"—sounded like some sort of ratta-ta-tat drum roll.

Gabriella Falieri, Justice Lord, met his eyes for an instant before demurely lowering hers to study the brief in front of her, then smiled at something Lysenko Boersma, Commerce Lord, whispered in her ear. Without any flirtation at all she caused men's hearts to beat faster, his own included. Lysenko he'd inherited and been glad of it, hated to hear the old man talk about retirement. Still fit, though small as a banty rooster, Lysenko possessed a sneaky left that had tricked many a boxer in his day and had caught Gilly out when he'd been foolish enough to challenge him to demonstrate. Urban Gamelyn, Exchequer Lord, still compiled data, adding and subtracting, modifying figures on other pages of his report. The old year might be done, but it would take time for Urban to devise a full accounting of how the country's economy had fared this past year. That answer, of course, determined much of what the other Ministration Lords, even the Domain Lords, could do this year. Controlling the purse strings was no easy task, but Urban was scrupulously equitable when reductions in spending were required, favoring no one Domain or Ministration office over another.

Bothersome that Gilly and Urban could barely be civil on even a surface level, and that Terrail and Tinian always became too obviously "hearty" and masculine in his presence. Urban's sexual persuasion was what it was, perhaps announcing itself a little too obviously in the light, breathy voice, the fastidious attention to fashionable fit and attractive objects, but never had he witnessed the man act rashly on his private desires. His sexuality was kept strictly separate and private, despite the fact that he rented a palace suite. Quaintance, however, adored him, playing the coquette around him, declaiming at the top of her lungs that at last she'd found a man her charms couldn't sway! And he had also heard Quaintance administering a thorough dressing-down to staff members who mocked Urban, both to his face and behind his back. "Lady bless!" she'd trumpeted. "If *I* wouldn't be caught in bed with the likes of you, then why should a man of Urban's taste and discretion desire you!"

Ah, good, good, Terrail and Carn, at last—the younger man distinctly ill at ease as all eyes scrutinized their tardy entrance. Mouthing "Sorry" at Eadwin, Terrail's eyebrows drolly rose to where his hairline had once begun as he threw up his hands in a "What could I do?" gesture. Carn must be disturbed, fretting over something, had sought out Terrail for advice. If Terrail had assuaged some of Carn's concerns, provided some background, the meeting might progress more smoothly—mayhap faster, if they needn't bring Carn up to speed on every issue. As Public Weal Lord, Carn oversaw the general health and well-being of the citizenry, and he tended to see people, individuals, rather than issues. A narrow focus, mayhap, but good for the people.

"Ladies and Gentlemen, good morning and a good new year to us and our nation. Shall we begin?"

♣

Sandwich plates and soup mugs unobtrusively vanishing under Ezequiel's watchful eye, Eadwin sleight-of-handed his final sandwich quarter to Hru'rul. Baked ham and brie, no less, and Hru'rul licked his fingers in case the least flavor of cheese should cling to them. **"No soup?"** he prodded Eadwin. **"Nice, slurpy soup?"**

*"You hate lapping soup from a mug,"* Eadwin reminded him. *"And secondly, Ezequiel distinctly whispered under the tablecloth that it was cream of broccoli—weren't you listening? You dislike cream of broccoli almost as much as I do!"* The difference was that the ghatt could pick and choose, while *he* maintained a decorous composure, wouldn't dream of grimacing. Someday he really *should* instruct Ezequiel to inform the cook that he intensely disliked cream of broccoli soup. Off with her head if she ever served it again! For all he knew, the cook may well have thought he adored it—always finished it, didn't he?

"Dunay, if you'd escort Romain-Laurent Charpentier inside, I'd appreciate it. We're just about ready for his report." Glancing 'round, Eadwin decided they had time for two quick votes—lunch should have given everyone time to digest the facts along with their meals.

First, a stiffening of the penalties for tax evasion, jointly proposed by Urban and Gabriella. "This is not entirely punitive," he emphasized to the assembled Lords. "We're allowing a grace period to pay, with no penalties attached, no questions asked. Further, Urban has structured a payment plan that won't bankrupt those who wish to pay but simply cannot at this time. Certainly the last thing we want to do is to seize property or possessions, unless there's no recourse." Amazingly, all agreed, even Carn. No need himself to vote unless a tie-breaker was required. And if he strongly objected to a proposed law, he could always veto it.

The next bill was at his own instigation, though he had moments when he wasn't entirely sure of the wisdom of it. Terrail had felt much the same, but as Internal Affairs Lord had sponsored it since it involved education. Simply stated, mandate that the teaching of science include more hands-on experimentation, not just pure theory, but some Lords were bent on stretching the idea to a not-necessarily logical conclusion, traveling roads they hadn't even reached.

Wasn't *doing* something, actually *experiencing* what happened and why, better than rote memorization? Lady bless!—they weren't going to allow mere children to dabble in illegal technology! Surprisingly, Gilly and Eugenie voted against it, as did Tinian Salaverry and Lysenko. Still, it passed, but Eadwin felt troubled, couldn't quite decide why. Disagreement, opposing opinions, he understood, also the way traditions came into play. If Quaintance had voted negatively, it wouldn't have been unexpected. But Gilly, someone with a degree from a higher institution of learning—if only about agriculture—surely he should be able to see the benefits of the idea. No sense brooding, the vote was over and done.

From the corner of his eye he glimpsed Romain-Laurent, slicked-back hair gleaming, hosen taut, as he clutched his papers, a thick sheaf. Thorough lad, prepared to drown them in a sea of paper! The crisscrossed stack indicated Romain-Laurent had made copies for everyone. What the young man planned to present, Eadwin hadn't a clue, just faith that he sincerely hoped was not misplaced. Had purposely given him leeway to devise a project that fit Marchmont's needs, would improve things through innovative methods. Charpentier was young enough to see things with fresh eyes, try new ways—even invent them. Eadwin admired such openness. Surely there had to be uncharted ways to improve life—no matter how good it might be, life could always do with a touch of improvement, originality. Not . . . oh, he didn't know . . . different for the sake of being different, like a new fashion craze . . . but . . . and here he always bogged down, unable to articulate it any further. Unfair, mayhap, to pin such hopes on someone untried, untested, but that was his prerogative as king.

**"Don't like him."** Hru'rul's unexpected pronouncement left Eadwin gaping in disbelief at an uncontroversial comment of Urban's, and he made a mental note to apologize later. **"Maims creatures, rips and tears. Saw him. Eyes so bright, smile so happy."**

*"Hru'rul, nonsense, you must have misunderstood. He told me about finding that bird with the broken wing—is that what you're referring to?"* Romain-Lauren had put it out of its misery; it had sickened him to do so, but he had— or so he'd explained it.

"Wing broke *after* he find bird. Ask La'ow. We sit, watch, then leave, too sick-making."

Ask La'ow. The ghatti do not lie. Thus, asking La'ow for confirmation was tantamount to disbelieving Hru'rul. Mentally reeling under the implications—which grew by the moment—he concentrated on aligning the paperwork in front of him. *"Later, Hru'rul. We must talk later, I promise you. I need to know more."* The frog in his throat worsened as he introduced Romain-Laurent, as if even his body protested what he'd heard. Talk to Cinzia and La'ow as well. Had they sensed any other aberrant behavior he'd not noticed?

"Ladies and gentlemen, I believe most of you have met— at least informally—Romain-Laurent Charpentier, a recent graduate of our Collegium in Montpéllier." Knowing looks and raised brows at that, and Gilly, half in jest, made the sign of the eight-pointed star for protection. Montpéllier boasted a certain avant-garde reputation, too much so for many tastes, who muttered that the institution didn't merely press for change, it fomented it. Eadwin experienced a strong desire to kick himself—how could he have invited Romain-Laurent to speak just after the vote on hands-on science teaching in the schools? Nothing to do but forge ahead. "In fact, some of you have already had the unique experience of working with him."

Terrail Leclerc, Internal Affairs Lord, snorted derisively and rolled his eyes. What had gone wrong there? He'd thought Terrail the perfect person to mentor Romain-Laurent. Look at the way he'd soothed Carn before the meeting; young people gravitated to him for advice, hints on how to advance, not to be left behind as others around them rose through the ranks. He could polish rough edges, instill confidence in limp, submissive personalities until they could stand up for their views. Surely he realized all new, untested ideas required time to mature, a refining hand with detail.

"His area of expertise is—in many ways—new to us: to take received notions and turn them on their collective ears, examine if this is the best, the only way, to do things. Some of us have a knack for this, at least on occasion, but we do so by instinct, not training. Charpentier is one of a special new breed, young men and women educated in the most current methods of management and organization, areas we take for granted, handle as best we may without seriously analyzing them." True enough. Mayhap he was one of the few who'd ever spent sleepless nights wondering how to govern. No small blessing that he'd had Arras by his side, his mother Fabienne, and others, but his crown hadn't come complete with a guidebook.

"What I've asked Charpentier to do is to devise not merely the outline, but the details to alter our ways of thinking, develop a project that only his specialized expertise can make viable. Whether we accept and attempt his proposal is entirely up to us. Equally, it's our responsibility to determine where he may have erred, or be right yet have overlooked significant aspects that only we are uniquely qualified to know. Our long experience is both our strongest and our weakest points. Romain-Laurent's strong point is his knowledge of regulating, organizing, manipulating . . ."—ah, why had he used that particular word?—"to effect quantifiable change to benefit our nation." At some point during his introduction his hands had begun shaking, so much so that his water goblet sloshed as he raised it to parched lips. "Romain-Laurent?"

A nice-looking young man, he thought again irrelevantly, not overly handsome by any means, but neatly slick, as if a cat had groomed him into shape. Dark hair and large, dark eyes, still a touch clumsy in movement, brain more agile than his limbs. The clothing he'd taken to wearing, though, privately amused him. Those old-fashioned thigh-length trunks with the long hosen, the ones that Ezequiel had always abhorred! Had Charpentier chosen them to rile Ezequiel, or was it a homage to the past to make the future—his ideas—more palatable, indicate he was equally at home in both worlds? Come to think of it, though he'd had many a conversation with Romain-Laurent, little or nothing of it had verged on the personal. Instead, at odd moments—sometimes the oddest ones—he'd pop out of nowhere, those brown eyes so entreating that he'd made time to listen, suggest, argue, and advocate. Had been refreshed at hearing novel—even faintly radical—ideas, untried as they might be.

What had he missed? "On page three you'll see that . . ." With a frantic look at the title page—"A Major Highway to Connect Gavotte with Sidonie: Prospects, Potentialities, and Problems"—he flipped to the proper page.

But after a moment he couldn't follow the written text. Amazing! He'd had no idea the young man was such a proficient speaker! Lovely tone and delivery, proper emphasis at exactly the right spots, even hints of drollery as needed. But it was more than that: face, form, and voice exuded a passion, a belief in what he proposed, an almost . . . Eadwin shook his head, gripped his water goblet and tried to think, momentarily block the voice from his ears. An almost messianic passion that swept his listeners along with him on his invisible road, his highway to the future. Despite their initial dismay, the faces in front of him registered their conversion to a cause.

Chin on his fist, Gilly looked more attentive than he'd ever been during lectures at the Collegium, while Gabriella Falieri was poised on the brink of rapture, lips parted, breathing quick, the pupils of her eyes vastly enlarged. Come to think on it, Eugenie Vannevar bore an almost identical expression. Tinian and Terrail both frowned as Romain-Laurent mentioned a possible stumbling block, only to eagerly nod in relief when the problem was neatly demolished. Even Arras gave more than polite attention, fingering his mustache. A covert look showed that the only two not seemingly impressed were Urban Gamelyn, jotting copious marginal notes and savagely underlining parts of them, and Quaintance Mercilot, too hard-of-hearing to truly appreciate Charpentier's deft delivery. Instead, magnifying glass out, she perused Romain-Laurent's prospectus, occasionally swatting at her great-granddaughter Monique's wrist to make her turn the page, Monique attending more to Charpentier and his handsome legs than to her granddame.

So why, why, was it that Romain-Laurent's presentation made no more impression on him than water on a duck's back? Not a detail lodged in his brain; he might as well have been listening to a lecture in an ancient foreign language that he'd never heard of, let alone studied! And above all, his buttocks ached abominably from sitting so long on this hard wooden chair. Mayhap he'd have to approve cushions, after all, though he'd long-ago told Ezequiel to remove them at meetings. Minor discomfort made for quicker decisions, he'd discovered early on.

And . . . and . . . something was pricking his left calf
fiercely, making it itch.

*"Hru'rul? What . . . ? Are you responsible for this . . .
my . . ."*

Hru'rul pinked him again with his long upper and lower
incisors. **"Damn straight Hru'rul doing something! Man be-
spelling you. Not Resonant, exactly, that sure. But everyone glassy-eyed with word-massage. Like when you pet me
too much and I go sappy."**

Not possible. Oh, a superlative speaker could sway a
crowd, especially if the listeners already shared at least
some of the same beliefs, or were predisposed to consider
them. The larger the group, the less likely the speaker
would depend on rational arguments and logic beyond a
few bare points. What caused the speech to soar beyond
those few points was the voice, the emotion, the enthusiasm, the ability to expand that belief, make ideas tangible,
accessible to the audience. Rude though it was, Eadwin
raised both hands to his beard and vigorously scratched, as
if to dig below the surface, uncover what was missing. In
some indefinable way Romain-Laurent was not in control,
appeared more a conduit, minutely different voices, each
with its own inflection, pouring forth.

At precisely that moment of insight, Romain-Laurent
halted his presentation, tailored to be mercifully brief and
precise, and now stood ready to answer questions, amplify
on the details. Like dreamers, his audience awoke, came
back to life, faintly regretful at abandoning the dream
world so vividly evoked in their minds. Expressions went
flacid, then tightened, faces growing reserved, regaining individual details.

"Questions, anyone?" Palely radiant, tremulous with exhaustion, Romain-Laurent held himself lightly on the balls
of his feet to hide his faint swaying, prepared to pivot
toward anyone who spoke.

"It's not that a new, wider highway between Gavotte
and Sidonie isn't an interesting idea," reflected Lysenko
Boersma. "Opens up more trade with western Canderis,
most obviously, but . . ." and drifted off, perplexed. Pinching the bridge off his nose, the Commerce Lord struggled
to recapture a transient thought. "Mountains," he finally
uttered. "That's the problem we have now with the roads,

climbing through those mountains like that in the winter, they're closed a goodly part of the year from snow. Terrail could tell you more." Of course Lysenko was getting on in years, but Eadwin had never heard him sound so dazed. Mountains!

True enough. Marchmont's westernmost city, Gavotte was situated where the Merebal tucked against the Pettibal's "tail," a port city on the isthmus between two inland seas. It, along with Sidonie, Pont d'Isle or Islebridge, and Mirabelle had been the only four cities originally allowed direct trade with Canderis during the long times when relations between the two nations had been strained. Goods from Gavotte had to be either sailed along the Pettibal coastline, then unloaded and carried by wagon to Sidonie, or reloaded onto another ship once they'd passed The Shrouds on the overland route and sailed along the Spray River. That, at least, was generally faster than the current overland route, since the Stratocum mountain range rolled down to touch Pettibal and the Spray before rearing up again on the other side, turning into Canderis's Tetonord range. The overland route was aptly referred to as the Ups-and-Downs, up a mountain, down the other side, up the next mountain and so forth.

"It took generations to lay the road we have. Generations come and go, but mountains remain. How do you plan to overcome them?" Terrail Leclerc had regained just a touch of asperity, a tone that reminded idle dreamers to stuff their dreams in their pipes and smoke them before overlooking something so obvious right away. Help young staff members, he would, but he wouldn't put up with arrant stupidity, a case of ignoring the obvious. And he had suffered a healthy dose of Romain-Laurent before.

"But that's the beauty of this plan." Still earnestly eager but a bit put out, Romain-Laurent swept his hand flat in front of him. "We rid ourselves of the problems they cause by cutting *through* the mountains. See page four. Preliminary surveys show that by utilizing segments of the current roadway where it runs through the divides and connecting these segments to tunnels that run as straight and level as possible, we can cut kilometers off the route. Might I remind you that snow doesn't fall in tunnels! Note the preliminary figures—both optimal and minimal acceptable gains, depending on the chosen route.''

"Cut *through* the mountains? *Bore through their hearts?*" Arras traced across the map so thoughtfully included in the Appendix. "How, precisely, do you propose to do that?" and Terrail chimed in, "Do you realize how many laborers that would require, the number of days, the time span involved?"

But Romain-Laurent shook his report. "Engineering colleagues assure me it's possible to create digging screws to bore through the mountains, that controlled explosives—"

"Verboten! You and your sort have taken over the Verboten Room at Montpéllier, haven't you?" shouted Eugenie Vannevar, almost as puce as her dress. "Explosives are forbidden! And how do you propose to power your digging screws? Dispose of the tons of rubble created?"

"You see, that's exactly your problem," Romain-Laurent snapped back, rolling his report into a cylinder and smacking the palm of his hand hard enough that Eugenie started, even Quaintance looking up at the sharp sound that had pierced her silent world. "Please, Lady Vannevar—"

"*Lord* Vannevar!"

"Lord Vannevar. We constantly accept and do not question. You are obviously thinking of illegal technology, and I can understand, fully appreciate your fears. How wise of you to air your concerns here and now. But my colleagues at the Collegium have made strides in reconfiguring various machine plans.

"Further, isn't it time we rethought our position on 'illegal technology'? Cautiously use what was known to our ancestors, replicate it, and improve it to suit our needs?" Impatiently forestalling Eugenie's simmering response, he continued, "Always the word is 'No!' No this, no that, on perfectly utilitarian devices that our ancestors conquered and controlled, made to do their biding. Don't dismiss this out of hand, I beg you! At least think long and hard about it—the consequences of our antiquated beliefs, the benefits of more open attitudes. Don't decide now, mull it over during odd moments, read some of the latest writings on the subject. I've copies if you'd—"

Quaintance Mercilot vigorously waved her lace-trimmed hankie in the air as Tinian Salaverry raised his hand for acknowledgment. Wordlessly they looked at each other and then, together, exclaimed, "Erakwa!"

"Defer to the External Affairs Lord," Quaintance whispered in a papery-thin voice, though her eyes snapped.

As External Affairs Lord, the Erakwa came under Tinian's purview for the selfsame reason that dealings with Canderis and the Sunderlies did. Despite the fact that the Erakwa freely roamed Marchmont and Canderis with no truly fixed abode, boasted no homeland with discernible—even if disputed—boundaries, the Erakwa held the status of a "foreign nation." Eadwin had seen to that because of his cousin Nakum and his people.

"Quaintance is correct, Charpentier. What do you propose to do about the Erakwa who live in those mountains that you propose to core like so many apples?" Treated with respect, Tinian was a foreigner's best friend, though never to Marchmont's detriment. "Will they be given advance warning? Moved? Recompensed? In fact, legally—Gabriella, what do you think?—the land should be considered as much theirs as ours. Must we obtain permission first?"

His sky-blue suit at last showing the effects of perspiration, Romain-Laurant fixed Tinian with an incredulous stare, his mouth downturned as if he'd tasted something sour in Tinian's queries, but all petulance vanished as he smiled sweetly at Gabriella. "Our courts have espoused the concept of eminent domain in the past, have they not?" Gabriella gave a wary nod. "Yes, we are dealing with the *concept* of a sovereign nation, one that may not be subject to our laws of eminent domain, but is that status justified? The Erakwa are naught but nomadic wanderers, can find other mountains to wander. *Really,* if you've ever had the misfortune to deal directly with these people, you know what I mean!" Not content with stopping there, he strove for humor. "With most of them such questions would be equivalent to asking an elk what it might prefer. It doesn't know, doesn't care, as long as it has plentiful grazing, limited predators, and numerous lady elk available."

"About what we all want out of life!" Deep within Eadwin, something snapped, self-control crumbling. "In its most basic form, of course!" Fury coursed through his veins, set his temples athrob. How had the lad developed

such a blind prejudice? A concept of lesser human beings?
Was that what was being taught at various collegiums nowadays? If so, he'd best remind himself to have Urban check
on Montpéllier's funding. Lady grant him strength!

"What I think most sensible is this, Charpentier. It's been
a long day for us all, alas, you've come last. Mayhap not
the most opportune moment to cram fresh ways of thinking
into our heads, especially when your own objectivity seems
flawed." Control, keep control. No need to lash out at the
chap in front of everyone. "Let's all read Romain-Laurent's
report carefully, note comments pro and con—and, my
friends, think broadly, widely, differently—and give them
to—" he cast a helpless, pleading glance at Eugenie Vannevar, hoping she'd be spending a few octs in the city before returning to her quadrant. "Eugenie to create a
synopsis. And Romain-Laurent, feel free to rethink your
proposal, given what you've already heard, prepare objections to arguments that you know will arise.

"Meeting adjourned!" He spit out the closing so fast that
no one could object, nor would any have dared, he suspected. For once in his life he was suffused with kingly
wrath that he mustn't allow to pour forth. Lady save him,
what now?

**"What now is we leave. Cinzia and La'ow stay, yes? Lis-
ten quiet, not sneaky quiet but quiet."**

*"Admirable idea, Hru'rul. Ask them, beg them, order
them—I don't care."* Rising with such intensity that both
chair and table were shoved clear, his chair teetering on
the edge of the dais, he spun on his heel and left. The chair
made a resounding, thoroughly satisfying crash as it fell to
the floor. For two coppers he'd flee and join Nakum in his
mountain fastness, or at least visit Roland and the arborfer
nurseries! A very long visit! In fact, if he could guarantee
heavy weather, he might be snowed in for the winter. Joy,
solitude! Fabienne would govern as regent in his absence,
and would countenance far fewer shenanigans than he did!

❖

Her conscience quaking, Telka cast a wild look behind her
as she fumbled with the ropes that stretched the canvas
taut over the load, the kitten reaching between her coat

buttons to snag a piece of fraying hemp. Her claws were quicker, more dextrous than Telka's nervous fingers, and she wished the kitten could undo the knots. Where Master Suggs had gained his knotcraft, she couldn't guess, but he apparently took pride in creating the most complicated ones she'd ever encountered. Nor would it do to cut the rope with her pocketknife—the tampering would be too obvious.

A shaky breath and another surreptitious look at the Widow's side door, just to be sure the wagoner wasn't about to leave, and she took herself in hand, concentrating. There! Back it off, loosen the next twist, gain some slack. How to retie it once she and the kitten took shelter beneath the canvas, she didn't know, but she'd figure out something. Wait! Splinter-thin as she was, she could eel her way under the loose flap—let Suggs think he hadn't knotted this corner as tightly as the others. 'Twasn't the same as breaking and entering, nor stealing—just a matter of borrowing a bit of a ride, staying reasonably warm and safe from the wind. But if you had to struggle to justify your actions, Da always said, then you probably were doing something borderline wrong to begin with. Didn't care, she told herself fiercely, she'd not let them drown the kitten, her little orange-gold darling! Da also said that sometimes folk had to take a stand, fight for what they believed in, but she was too little, too young for her voice to heard or she'd have stayed, stood up for herself and the kitten. Mayhap this'd show them how serious this was, that she was no longer a mere child to be overruled and overridden by any and everyone!

Almost set now. Feed the slack through the eyelet, work the canvas free just a bit more. Lower lip tight between her teeth, spectacles sliding down her nose, she tugged as hard as she could, easing the canvas clear. "You go first, little one," she coaxed the kitten, prodding it with a free hand while she flapped the canvas invitingly. "Kitties love to explore. Find a spot for us to hide, that's my baby."

Giving her a quizzical look, it blinked its amber eyes and stretched a paw to pat her cheek, pleased at being talked to. A quick paw lick and another pat, followed by a "Y'ew?" Hind feet catching and tangling in the sweater Telka wore under her red-and-black jacket, the kitten wriggled out farther between the buttons, then hesitated. "Mwa? M'murst?"

"Yes, dear. You first, then me." One of the horses stamped, his bridle clanking, and Telka nearly leaped clear of the wagon, guilt growing. Ordinarily she'd have spoken to the horses, stroked their foreheads and velvety noses, made sure their blankets were snugged tight against the chill. Master Suggs always had the nicest horses. You could tell a great deal about a man by the way he took care of his team. In fact, each time he returned to them, they always gave him a rising whicker of greeting, straining against their worn collars to nuzzle him.

An eager whicker rang out, and Telka heard the heavy side door opening, the smell of cinnamon and brown sugar floating over the wintery air. Oh, Lady help her! Had he refused a third piece of pie? "Hurry!" she whispered as the kitten's head swung round at the noise, and she hooked her under the forelegs and shoved her forward. Scrawny tail quirked, the kitten balanced on the tailgate, fastidiously sniffing her way along before diving into the dim, enclosed space, Telka tight on her tail, boots thrashing in the air until she found purchase for a knee and shoved herself deeper within the wagon.

Room, but not much to spare, and she wormed around until she could yank the canvas into place, darkness completely engulfing them. Hand clamped over her mouth to muffle her labored breathing, she heard Master Suggs's footsteps travel the wagon's length, his deep voice rumbling a final thanks to the Widow for the respite, not to mention the apple pie. Barely a breath later, Suggs had efficiently stripped and stowed the horses' blankets, the wagon groaning as Suggs swung himself up and gave his team an encouraging chirrup. A lurch and tilt as they swung across the frozen ruts to clear the yard, and then the dray settled into an even, rocking motion.

"Mr'aow?" The kitten's nose began exploring her ear, but when Telka tried to stroke her, the kitten skittered away, only to dash and tag her. Tucking her spectacles in her breast pocket—she couldn't see much in the dark with or without them—she grimly wriggled after the rascal to pin her down. Games were hardly appropriate, not if they didn't want Master Suggs to discover his stowaways. Feeling like a mole, she let her hands do her seeing. Burlap sacks, some lumpy, some solid yet marginally yielding if she worked at it. Tighter-woven cotton sacks for fine-milled flour and cornmeal. A half-wheel of cheese, cut side freshly waxed, and she fought the urge to peel it away like a little mouse, steal a nibble. Smoked bacon slabs encased in rough mesh. Firkins of butter, or so she guessed; onions in net bags, their papery skins rustling, their green tops smelling tenderly fresh; the earthy scent of potatoes. A whole load of victuals for Master Suggs.

But not one furry kitten had her searching fingers encountered, and she entertained a heart-stopping vision of the baby's head popping out from under Master Suggs's unsuspecting elbow! Her whole body tensed, anticipating his shriek of surprise. But at last the kitten hauled itself over her hip, her claws pinpricking, and curled up against Etelka's stomach, the kitten's purr so loudly pleased with itself that surely Master Suggs would hear it, would wonder if he'd taken on a hive of bees instead of the honey he carried! Nestled atop a tangle of empty sacks, Baby protested as Telka shifted her, working with her elbows tightly pinned at her sides as she spread the sacks over them both. Her feet still complained of the cold, but she didn't dare try to strip off her boots, burrow her stockinged toes in the sacks. Shoulder blades and spine poked by potatoes, she dimpled a cornmeal sack to pillow her head, then cuddled the kitten close.

"You'll like King Eadwin," she barely breathed the words, thought them as hard as she could, the way a Seeker might. Safer to be silent, despite Master Suggs's tuneless singing floating down to them like a lullaby. "And just wait till you meet the mighty Hru'rul!"

❧

Hands clasped behind his back, Harry Muscadeine trudged after his parents, wrestling with his impatience. Of course Mama always walked slowly, her arm firmly locked in his father's, supporting her weight, checking her balance should she waver. And Mama enjoyed being freed of her cane or crutch for a short while. Mostly she accepted the cane as

another appendage, an extra leg, and Harry admired her
for not fussing over her dependence on it. As a small child
he'd been frankly surprised to discover other mothers
didn't have canes—not when they could be so much fun to
play with. How many times had he hooked things off
shelves supposedly beyond his reach? Dispatched ferocious
beasts with his newfound sword?

It was just that it was so confounded *slow*! They'd sailed
down the LaPierre to Bertillon this morning, and *that* had
been quicker than walking from the landing dock up the
street to the central square! Wouldn't mind it half as much
if he stood at his mother's side, arm in arm, his head bent
to hers, sharing her little jokes about passersby or the shop
window displays. With him bringing up the rear, all he
could catch were wisps of conversation, tantalizing as the
scent of food to a starving man. Mama wasn't a gossip, but
her acute hazel eyes—so like his own, Auntie Doyce's, and
Jenneth's—and her questing intelligence meant that she
noted anything pertinent. And anything impertinent, for
that matter! Most of all, he enjoyed discussing things with
her.

Being an only child meant that his parents mostly talked
to him as if he were an adult, let him listen in on, even
take part in conversations that a child probably shouldn't
overhear. Sometimes, of course, he didn't understand—
missed the allusions, didn't catch the joke—but that happened less and less as he grew older. Hearing so many
adult conversations gave him a different, oh, weightier view
of life and its seriousness. Much weightier. In fact, he knew
precisely why his father had taken a day away from the
castle and King Eadwin: after the Domain and Ministration
Lords' joint meeting yesterday, he needed it.

"Eadwin's been edgy of late," Arras had confessed on
the boat, grinning as guiltily as a schoolboy skipping school.
"Hru'rul, as well. And talk about a foul mood after the
meeting—not that I blame them." He'd nodded, expression
serious to show he understood how unusual that was, even
though Papa was addressing Mama. "I swear there's something in the air, something almost tangible, yet I can't get
a whiff of what's troubling them, meeting aside. It *is* the
High Halidays, after all!" As if *they* should automatically
hold trouble and worry at bay, Harry had thought to him-

self. Troubles always happened when they *chose* to happen, not when you'd expect them to happen!

"Arras," his mother had said reasonably from her blanketed deck chair, her eyes sparkling so bright and her cheeks pinked from the breeze, "you know what happens when he's busy like this." And Papa had looked puzzled, almost grumpy at being informed of a logical explanation practically under his nose. Should he explain, or let Papa work it out himself? 'Twas plain as the aristocratic nose on his face! He supposed he could cheat a bit, 'speak Papa, give him a hint, but his mother took pity on his father. "You know perfectly well where he longs to go when he's mewed up in the castle, buried under work!"

"To Roland's arborfer nurseries!" Papa had exclaimed, his mustache bristling. "I've been so snowed under myself that it clean wiped it from my mind! Of course, I needn't run to the nurseries when I have you and Harry awaiting me each night!" Harry'd dodged just in time to avoid his father's openhanded cuff of affection.

Hadn't King Eadwin told him how he'd wanted—practically from the time he'd been Harry's age—more than anything to be forester, to work with his arborfer trees, happily pruning them, studying their growth cycles, discovering what made them thrive? And what he wanted most of all— now that he was king—was to ensure that a carefully controlled harvesting system would guarantee the planting and nurturing of new trees to replace any old ones cut down. Plant enough new baby trees, in fact, to make up for the wanton despoliation of whole arborfer forests by earlier generations. People hadn't known better, hadn't realized how slowly the trees grew, how rarely they reproduced— that's what came from not listening to the Erakwa, then or now, like that man in yesterday's meeting. No wonder Eadwin felt such kinship with Nakum, not simply because of shared blood, but because of their shared interests! Only let Eadwin steal away to the nurseries for a few days, work outdoors with Roland D'Arnot and his crew . . . have Nakum join them from his mountain . . . why, the king'd be cheerful in no time at all! And if Eadwin cheered up, so would Hru'rul!

Oh, bosh! He'd nearly collided with his parents, hadn't noticed them halting to greet someone. That was the problem with being out with Papa, whether in Sidonie or here in Bertillon, or anywhere else. People were always eager to catch Arras Muscadeine's ear, ask his advice, beg favors large and small from King Eadwin's right-hand man, the Defense Lord and Lord of the Nord. Now Papa was fingering his mustache, politely listening to some plaint or other, promising to look into it more fully on their return to Sidonie. Dancing from one foot to the other, Harry stopped himself before his mother could catch him, cast a remonstrative glance his way. He was old enough now not to suffer fidget-fits, but he was having one all the same. Blast it all, he still had shopping to do for the halidays—the twins' gifts to buy!

Somehow celebrating the halidays a bit late this year had given him an excuse to delay his shopping, hope for some late bargains. His pocket money didn't seem to stretch very far these days. Besides, after seeing some of the atrocities Theo had lugged home, what if Theo's exuberant lack of taste had rubbed off? He still hadn't a clue what to give the twins, especially now that they were adults—somehow the four-year gap in age seemed insurmountable in a way it hadn't just a few years ago. *They* were training to be Seekers, had all sorts of very adult things to master, while he was still just a boy.

Just a boy, what an expression! Sometimes being thirteen was downright miserable, though he was doing the best he could to grow out of it. Fact was, he was already as tall as Diccon, and planned on being plenty taller! Hadn't he gotten his copen-blue jacket this autumn—he stretched an arm out in front of him—and weren't his wrists already protruding too far? At least his Resonant skills were recovering; he could receive *and* send with greater clarity and greater assurance. Last year in the Sunderlies, he'd been downright hopeless. Another year and he'd be as good, even better than he'd been as a child. If he'd remastered such skills, didn't that prove he was well on his way to manhood?

Would the man *never* stop complaining? Hands behind his back again, fiddling with his cuff buttons and silently whistling, Harry sauntered in a half-circle that brought him to where he could see the goings on. His father wore his serious face, but Harry could glimpse a mischievous twinkle in his eye, could read his mother's impatience and growing tiredness in her stance. Shifting until he caught her attention, he cocked an eyebrow back toward the bridge spanning the LaPierre, indicating his intention to wander back, admire its architecture. He sniffed once, his nose a bit runny in the cold, but also because he wanted to check again. Yes, it definitely felt like snow! The heavy, wet kind that carpeted the earth, packed perfectly for building forts and snowmen, incited snowball fights. He supposed the twins were too old for that now. Then so was he.

Going back to the bridge was always nice. He loved its three high arches, how they let you *see*, almost *feel* how the curves bore the weight, distributing it evenly to the sunken pilings. How did builders ever learn what worked, what didn't? The arches allowed all but the tallest-masted vessels to pass beneath it even when the river was running high, and the graceful archways permitted fast-moving chunks of ice to float through and enter the Spray, not collide with the pilings, pounding and gnawing at them, ultimately dislodging them and sweeping the whole bridge away! Large and small piers punctuated both sides of the river, the royal sloop tied up at one of them. Not many boats this late in the season, and he missed their presence, the perpetual bustle surrounding them. Still, he scanned the banks as thoroughly as he could, checking to see which ships and boats had docked, which might soon set sail. Ah, looked as if Gaetan Boucher and his barge planned one more trip upstream, probably a final load of grain, even some special soil samples so that Roland and the king could test their different qualities. Ho, take some of that lush, rich Sunderlies soil, and the arborfer would sprout fast and furious, grow taller than the castle itself!

At last! His parents were free of the importuning man, moving again! As he hurried to catch up, a lance of familiar mindspeech pierced Harry's brain. Totally familiar but totally out of place! What was—? Still intently listening as he rushed along, new boots slick-soled against the thin layer of snow covering the cobbles, he caught a toe in a seam, found himself falling full-length into a cold, dirty puddle while the voice went on inexorably inside his head. Sputtering, he raised himself on his elbows as he heard the message's conclusion. Oh, no! Angry, scared, he pounded one fist in the puddle, dirty water mingling with his tears.

The next thing he knew his father had grabbed his collar to hoist him onto his feet, mud and slush dripping down the front of his once-neat jacket. "Are you all right, Harry?" His father demanded, roughly wiping his face with his handkerchief, then attempting to determine where to wipe next. The handkerchief wasn't up to the job, but it hardly mattered now. Not after what he'd just heard.

Chin trembling, he tried to answer, reassure both parents that he was fine. But the words came hard, and he knew he sounded more shaken than he should have from a simple, though undignified fall. "F–fine, Papa. Sorry about the mess, Mama." Oh, damnation, don't let him cry anymore, show his worry, or he'd give away everything! And he couldn't—he'd promised! He was an adult, wasn't he? And most of all, he couldn't, *mustn't,* look back at the bridge or down by the walkways connecting the docks!

❧

"Down! Down!" Diccon whispered harshly, seizing his aunt's shoulders and practically folding her in half around Saam as he thrust her behind a barrel. Jenneth had reacted with equal alacrity on spying Harry standing by the upper wall near the bridge, hand shading his eyes as he scanned the anchored crafts. Luckily for her, Harrap had responded with the instincts of a hunted animal, diving for the wall's sheltered overhang, Jenneth crowding after him.

*"I think it's worse than mayhap Harry spying us,"* Jenneth 'spoke him from her hiding place. *"Check the moorings, Dic. I can't see them now from here, but I swear I spied a sloop with the royal pennant! You know the king lets Uncle Arras borrow it whenever he likes! It just didn't register when I noticed it before."*

*"Only you could choose a stable this near the river!"* Diccon grumbled. *"I suppose you were determined to hire horses able to swim as well! Sail, even, if the need arose!"*

Beside him Kwee craned her neck, wistful for another glimpse of Harry, and he could see half of Pw'eek's face— the butterscotch side—peering out from where the stone wall angled. Both Kwee and Pw'eek considered Harry a jolly playmate, taking turns pouncing on each other from behind the furniture or exploding up and over concealing shrubs. Mama had not been pleased about the state of the flower beds after Harry's visit this past summer. Neither he nor Jenneth had brought the vegetable garden's tattered condition to her attention, had just sighed and set to work straightening it as much as possible, restaking plants, clipping broken, limp branches, and gathering up green tomatoes and beans strewing the row-paths.

*"No, you mayn't go play!"* Cross at Kwee's intent crouch, body poised to spring up the stairs and attack an unsuspecting Harry, he reminded her of her duty, their duty on this expedition. *"Remind your Sissy as well—tell her that reminder comes from me—double whatever Jenneth told her!"* By the Lady, how much longer would they have to huddle here? He'd left Mahafny seated on the cold stone path, pressed between the barrel and the damp, unyielding wall, and already she was shivering. Near as thin as Saam was, and that was worrisome. Not much flesh on her bones to keep her warm, just sheer determination to persevere. While he grasped the utter importance of his own Bond with Kwee— appreciating it more with each passing day— he couldn't quite fathom the curious linkage between his aunt and the elderly ghatt, not to mention the bond between his aunt and Harrap. The unwavering intensity and devotion of it perplexed him when he tried to reason it through, but then, the more he pondered his own Bonding, the less he understood it. Well, this was hardly the moment for pondering; he lacked the patience for it and besides, Jenneth was an accomplished ponderer, far better than he.

*"I don't care whether you like it or not, Diccon. I'm going to 'speak Harry. Warn him we're here, why we're here."* Her mindspeech showed she'd been pondering, all right, though not in a direction Diccon approved. Now what was he going to do with her? Why couldn't she leave well enough alone sometimes? If she 'spoke Harry, they were in for it now! *"He won't tell, I'm sure of it, but someone should know where we are—or at least that we've made it this far. If anything goes wrong . . ."* He shrugged helplessly, looking back at his aunt, a lock of silvery hair floating loose on her cheek, her other cheek pressed against Saam's head. Her eyes were closed, and somehow that was a relief. Would it help Mahafny and Saam if Harry knew what they planned?

*"Diccon, sometimes I'm not sure she's even with us, except in body. It's not like her, and you know it. Harrap's scared half out of his wits, though he won't say so. You'll just have to live with the fact that Harry will know."*

He felt anger at her having decided the matter on her own, without him, but there was nothing he could do about it—not here, not now. She had no right to make that decision, not with everything riding on their success! **"But *you* have the right to decide? Who decided you're the leader? Did we vote on it? Are you more or less qualified than Jenneth?"**

*"It's always a pleasure to be appreciated by one's Bond!"*

**"Appreciated and adored, as well you know."** The softest of purrs, for his ears alone. **"But faulty thinking won't be tolerated. Besides,"** a sidelong, significant glance in Jenneth's direction, **"if I don't cure your wrongheadedness, Jenneth will—and that's likely to be more painful."**

Insofar as he could judge, she hadn't yet 'spoken Harry, just said that she planned to do so. Not wise, sister-mine, to reveal your hand like that, not with Diccon the Determined at the ready! Remember our lessons: any warning, any threat gives the recipient valuable time to prepare against it. Expend your effort on the action, not the warning.

Mayhap if he and Jen were physically together, he could convince her not to 'speak Harry. Not much of a chance, but a chance to out-argue her, plus he'd feel better with them together, their closeness a comfort. 'Speak Jen, ask her to slip over here with Harrap and their ghatti? After all, they had better cover than he, would be less likely to attract Harry's attention. No, she was clever enough to know he'd use his physical presence to intimidate her. And somehow he relished the whole process of hiding, escaping detection, until he suddenly popped up at her side.

Couldn't she see? Despite the fact that Harry was "family," he posed a danger. Uncle Arras and Aunt Francie would winkle any secrets out of him in a trice! Peering out, guardedly glancing around, especially at the steps leading down from the upper riverwalk—Harry'd come tearing down them if he spotted them—he bent low, head down, and dashed toward Jenneth's hiding place.

Just as he straightened and ran like blazes to cover the

final few meters in the open, he heard Pw'eek shriek
**" 'Ware! Look out!"** followed by Kwee's equally anxious
cry of warning. Damn! Harry must've spotted him! Starting
to pivot in mid-stride, ready to run full-out back to his
original hiding spot and dive to safety, Diccon collided with
a slim but solid body that sent him staggering toward the
lip of the low retaining wall that formed the outer edge of
the walkway. Whoa—he'd be in for an icy bath unless he
could right himself!

Mouth wide in panicky shock at what she'd precipitated,
Jenneth raced after him as he reeled, the backs of his thighs
slamming against the top of the wall, upper body bending
backward, all-too-aware of gravity's designs on him. *"Jen!*
*Watch where you grab—* " But his plea came too late, Jenneth beside him now, snatching at his flailing arm as her
other hand locked on his sash to drag him forward. Just
as he'd feared, her recklessness put *her* in equal peril of
overbalancing, which she realized too late, causing a look
of sheer terror at the river below. If someone has to fall
in, let it be me! he prayed to the Lady as he tried to twist
from her well-meaning grip. Jenneth was near-phobic about
falling into water, any water—had been since being swept
overboard from the *Vruchtensla*'s decks in the midst of a
storm. Not that he blamed her!

Her yank on his sash, already slung too low on his hips,
nearly jerked his feet clean out from under him, his upper
torso leaning outward even more to compensate, leaving
him precariously perched on the retaining ledge, feet finally
losing contact with the ground, scrabbling for purchase in
thin air. *"Jen! Let's go! I don't mind the water!"* But if they
went, he realized, this time they were going together. Might
as well get it over with, end this infernal seesawing. Head
thrown back to stare skyward, he let himself sag, preparing
for the immersion. Brr! Didn't the water look all scummy-
brown and miserably cold!

A hand knotted in his sheepskin tabard at the neckline
and Diccon discovered himself flying up and forward before
he could even begin to square his feet under him. He
landed hard on his bottom. "Ow!" he complained as the
hand released him, letting him flop, crack the back of his
head against the wall. The river had to be softer! Despite

the unexpected pain from the blow he watched Jenneth as she too was hauled clear of the edge.

"Now what be ye doing dancing an' daunting around on the brink like that? Couldn't find a tightrope?" With a protesting yelp at the unfairness of the accusation, Diccon sat up to confront a spare, elderly man, arms easily folded across his chest, and with a stance that seemed to naturally dominate the whole walkway. Otherwise, he wasn't much to look at, Diccon decided as he rubbed the back of his head, probing for a lump. He wore a faded black flat cap, its leather brim settled low on his forehead, and a navy double-breasted jacket that appeared he'd been born in, so ancient did it look. Weather and wind had seamed his face, and white squint lines like a cat's whiskers radiated from the outer corner of each brown eye. A short pipe, thankfully unlit—its cold aroma already bad enough to make Diccon screw up his nose—protruded from between darkened teeth exposed in a generous smile. If that weren't enough, Pw'eek and Kwee were making utter fools of themselves by rubbing against the man's knees and shins, even rearing up to rub their shoulders against him!

"See ye got a Shepherd one back there," a thumb cocked over his shoulder in Harrap's direction. "Must be a naughty one, a be 'iding so. Prolly for consorting with that ghatt. Mind ye, I doan mind ghatti, but that wee cap and vest be downright 'umorous."

Clutching the icy hand Jenneth belatedly thrust at him, Diccon let her help him to his feet. "You two, being baby Seekers an all, should be too old fer 'ide-n-seek. The Shepherd's too old for it, too, not to mention that nice older lady I spied as I come down the stairs. Though she's so wraithlike t'would be easy fer her to 'ide." He emphatically pounded the bowl of his pipe against the palm of his hand, cocking his head from one to another, patiently awaiting an answer. Except, Diccon realized, he hadn't asked them any questions! He looked something like a hawk, a small, spare one, but deceptively fast and strong.

Jenneth cast an uneasy, artificial smile his way. "Just going to Lanneau's stables for some horses we've hired." He nodded, kept nodding as if urging her to keep speaking. "And we . . . we did so want to see the bridge up close.

Didn't we, Diccon?" She gripped his hand so hard that he had to fight not to wince, retain his calm.

"Aye, 'tis a 'andsome sight. Even folk that see it often, come to look at it again—like 'Arry Muscadeine, him as is the son of Arras Muscadeine and that nice Canderisan lady. Funny, 'ow your eyes are mighty like 'is." He beamed wider, tucking his pipe in the corner of his mouth and making a contented sucking sound. "Bits an pieces of other family resemblances, too. By the by, I'm Gaetan Boucher, master of the *Papillon,* that barge o'er there." His pipe was pressed into duty as a pointer. "Been running the LaPierre for, oh, thirty years now. All over afore that."

❖

Calf muscles stinging, Jacobia strove to pick up her pace as Feather forged ahead, nearly beyond her view. But haste gave her recalcitrant feet the moment they'd been waiting for, her wobbly ankle promptly planting her left snowshoe across the right, as if she'd turned pigeon-toed. If she'd not been so tired, she could have regained her balance with a series of strenuous gyrations, but as it was, she simply toppled forward in a heap. Tempting to just lie there until spring thaw—or beyond. It would take that long, at least, to regain her wind, let her muscles unknot.

Traveling with Feather was not for the faint of heart. In fact, they traveled together only in the strictest sense of the term; to Jacobia's mind it was more reminiscent of the children's game of "Follow the Leader." Keeping a certain distance between them ensured that they didn't annoy each other too much and allowed Feather enough freedom without Jacobia too obviously retarding her normal pace. The suggestion had been Feather's when Jacobia had caught up with her that first day. Having easily outpaced the horses, Feather had sat waiting, passing the time by carving a piece of wood into a toy for Byrlie. "Ah, so we *are* going the same way, after all," she'd mildly noted before swinging her pack back in place and lithely speeding off. "See you at camp tonight. It's *your* turn to cook dinner."

And it was her turn again, tonight, to fix dinner. "Bah!" Jacobia yelled into the snow before lifting her head. Natu-

rally Feather was now completely out of sight. "Bah! Brr-
ah!" With effort she bent her knees and lofted her feet
into the air, her snowshoes still tangled, and concentrated
on uncrossing them, waggling them this way and that. Well,
at least Feather wasn't here to see and offer smug suggestions. Only the Lady knew what she looked like were anyone to view her from above—undoubtedly something
similar to a beetle stranded on its back, waving its legs,
though she lay belly-side down. The snowshoe's wooden
frame smacked against something, and Frost gave a startled
snort. The beast had ventured too close, curious at her
antics, and she'd whacked his tender nose. He was far better natured than Feather and boasted nearly as much endurance. Probably boasted more common sense—and
significantly less conceit—than Feather and she combined!

As the horse nuzzled her body, making little whoofling
sounds and nibbling here and there, she waited till his bridle came within reach of her gloved hand. "Ho! Back, boy!
Back, Frost!" Obediently the gelding began to back, straining at her weight, his head and neck gradually rising as she
swung onto her bottom, then onto her knees. "Steady, now.
Steady, boy!" Best check that her snowshoes were still clear
of each other. Grunting, she swung one leg wide from the
hip to bring it forward and stoically planted it in the snow.
Now for an upward thrust and lunge, and she'd be up,
the other leg straightening as she rose. "Eee-oomph!" she
encouraged herself and embraced Frost's neck.

After their first day "together," Feather had pointedly
suggested that the horses would hamper them on the snowy
trails Feather planned to traverse. If, of course—she'd
noted with a studied offhandedness—Jacobia was utterly
determined to catch up with her quarry, and was fit enough
to walk some distance, a challenge if ever she'd heard one!
A fenced field dotted with shaggy-coated cattle had offered
a likely spot to abandon the horses and know they'd be
left in the caring hands of some pleasantly surprised farmer.
Blaze had been delighted, increasingly fussy at winding
through the heavily wooded trails Feather chose across the
rolling hills and dales, but Frost had refused to meekly
remain behind. Backing off, he'd jumped the fence, floundering in the drift on the other side before breaking free

and trotting after them, enthusiastically neighing as if it were a game.

Feather'd given the beast a long, lingering rub up his forehead and behind his ears, the gelding lowering its head so she could reach. "I guess he can stay with us a bit." Despite herself she'd experienced a jealous twinge at Frost turning his affections to Feather, but since then, he'd seemed content to keep pace with her.

Given the givens, Feather might have been better off leaving *her* with the farmer and retaining Frost as her travel companion. *He* rarely made a misstep, seldom complained, and acted gratified by their companionship—more than she was usually capable of at the close of a strenuous day.

Damnall! Now where had Feather gotten to? How was she supposed to tell? The sun was angled so that it reflected off every bank and drift, every knoll until her eyes blurred, tearing at the uncompromising brilliance. A few spots in the landscape revealed a green like dark jade, firs and pines that had divested themselves of clinging snow, thanks to the sun's warmth and a freshening breeze that now scattered frozen spangles. The icy flakes swooped and boiled around her, stinging her face and making her squint even more. An abrupt thud broke the snowy silence, and she and Frost startled, bumping into each other, each huddling closer to the other, momentarily spooked. Yet another clump of snow dropping free, not some human nearby, much as she wished it.

Tilting her head back so far her hood fell off, she bellowed, "Feather!" but heard only fragments of her own voice bouncing back at her, and no answering cry. Fine, she needed a point on which to orient herself, but even the spot where she'd so recently fallen full-length was difficult to locate, its edges already soft and blurred, its hollows filling with blowing snow. Any marks Feather might have left were long gone; the way her feet skimmed over the surface, her tracks looked like the brushing of moth wings. Strange how the glare seemed more diffuse, as if the blowing snow had diluted the brightness to make it spread further. It wasn't snowing again, but it might as well have been with the scintillating particles lofted by the breeze.

Still, if she concentrated, she could get her bearings. Keep angling northwest and she'd be fine, would find

Feather up ahead, stolidly waiting. In fact, the Erakwan
woman seemed to derive a certain enjoyment from it. Now
to select the best path, the easiest way. And if she were
lucky, Feather might even call a halt for lunch! "You
know," she confided to Frost as she leaned forward on her
toes and picked up first one snowshoe and then the other,
"what I hate about all this?" Ear cocked as if to listen,
Frost walked at her side. "For all Feather's wilderness
savvy, even *she* doesn't know precisely where the twins are!
We're aiming at a 'goal' that's highly mobile, not to mention unpredictable. How's that for tilting the odds in their
favor? But whenever I want to give up, go home, I just
think about Mahafny. And that makes me so mad it gives
me stamina—not to mention making me toasty-warm!"

Skim each snowshoe across the surface, don't waste energy lifting the foot high. Just shuffle forward. Trot, trot,
trot, shush, shush, shush. Veering leftward might help,
down that little incline. They'd be sheltered from the worst
of the wind, and it looked invitingly level each time she
glimpsed it. As if to mock her, the wind gusted and whirled,
little funnels of snow spinning by like dust devils.

That decided her. "Come on, Frost, let's drop down over
the lip, get out of the wind." Scanning her surroundings,
she aimed toward a break in a hedge of funny, stalklike
things, all wildly tilted every which way—probably sunflower stalks or raspberry canes. Mantling snow made the
most obvious things assume different forms, appear brand
new and exotic. Like those giant mushroom shapes. No,
more like overturned wicker baskets coated with snow.
"Ah, willows!" and felt pleased to have solved one puzzle.

Downward into the dip and through the break, leaning
her weight back to keep from pitching forward. Mind the
snowshoes, don't let them snag on the canes or stalks. Yes!
Just up ahead—a good packed stretch, flat and smooth,
practically swept clear of drifted snow. Easy going, a way
to make up lost time, though it wasn't straight, tended to
meander a bit along the edges. The occasional hummocks
would be easy to avoid. She'd catch up with Feather in
no time!

Unaware of what lay beneath the snow, Jacobia stamped
her snowshoes and ventured farther into the frozen marsh,
Frost following more circumspectly, sniffing the air, head

swiveling as he examined his surroundings, but Jacobia paid no heed. If he wanted to be curious, fine.

The last few days hadn't been a competition, not really. The important thing was to find Jen and Diccon before they got into any further trouble. Whether Feather could outlast her or she could match Feather's endurance was *not* the issue. Except there wasn't a Wycherley alive who enjoyed being bested. Or a Saffron, either, for that matter! Grinning, she shuffled on her way.

♣

Yes, this was more like it! Smooth and firm underfoot, just a faint ripple to the snow, rather like waves carved by the winds. After a few strides under such ideal conditions, Jacobia knelt and untied her snowshoe bindings. Why blunder along with them when the snow was so firm, capable of supporting her? A newfound sense of freedom made her want to run and caper. Must be an outlying field or meadow blanketed by snow, scarcely a bush or shrub marring this perfect white expanse, like a painter's canvas awaiting the first brushstroke. Tying her snowshoes together, she slung them over her shoulder, hooking the lacings to one of the loops on her pack.

She danced the next few liberating steps, the snow squeaking but yielding just enough to give her purchase. Let's see—the gap in the canes behind would serve as one landmark, but best select a significant feature up ahead, something immediately recognizable to let her stay on course. Checking over her shoulder to make sure the gap was where she thought it was, she was chagrined that Frost hadn't followed her. Should have noticed it immediately, if she'd not been so charmed by the chorus made by her own squeaking boots! "Frost! Come on! Easy going, no wading through drifts!" But no matter how she coaxed and whistled, the horse continued picking his own path, forcing his way along the wavering boundary of snow-bent cane. It hurt that he wouldn't obey—were they about to part company at last?

Still bent on making up lost time, she began walking briskly, swinging her arms, clapping her gloved hands for warmth. Perfect—as if someone had carved out this nice, broad swath for her pleasure. Ha—she'd discovered an easier route than Feather's—even if it had been by accident! The only thing missing was the sun. Oh, it was there, somewhere up above, but all she could see was pearly light, no one spot showing a more golden glow than the rest. Well, best be satisfied with what she had.

As if it had searched her out, the wind swooped down on her again, driving snow granules into her face, intent on flapping her hood. Left, right, left, right, steal a glance after every second verse of her heartening marching song, her eyebrows and eyelashes thickening with caked snow, nostrils tickling from tiny pinpricks of ice. Phew! That gust had whooped out of nowhere, had threatened to sail her back to her starting point! "Need some bricks in my pockets!" she shouted into the wind to encourage herself, missing the solace of Frost's silent but encouraging presence. Not to mention the fact that his bulk helped block the wind.

Damn! Was he still pickily edging along the fringe of the meadow, or had the whipping wind made him give up, seek out some sheltered spot, even a dry, warm barn not that far distant that he could sense and she couldn't? Must be one nearby to go with the meadow. Gloved hands shielding her eyes, she strained to pick out his dark bulk against the whiteness. Nothing, and her exasperation sharpened, making her stamp her foot at discovering she'd veered off course, had drifted too far toward the opposite side of the canebrake. The snow felt deader, softer here, each booted foot settling a little deeper. And no squeaking accompaniment, more of an occasional crunch with soggy squelches. Strange, she couldn't exactly hear it but could just sense a rilling, a nearby liquid warble.

What on earth? Another stamp of her foot, more experimental this time, her senses straining to capture and identify the elusive sensation. Staring down, she realized that the snow around her feet had grown more translucent, less obviously white, especially when she kicked the top layer aside. Slush! How long had she been marching through slush? The skein of footprints immediately behind her resembled miniature mirrors as moisture oozed into them, gleaming in the diffuse light.

Not exactly frightened but increasing wary, she stepped

sideways, only to find each step settling into even wetter slush. Again the liquid warble of trickling water sang in her ears, followed by the faster gurgle of flowing water. A dull "crump" and the ice under her left boot cracked and began to tilt, pitching her off-balance, her left leg plunging knee-deep into dark, icy water filled with bits of rotting vegetation and a rank, dank smell that wafted through the cold air. As her other leg buckled, that knee slammed down to break the lip of the ice around the sinkhole she'd broached, enlarging it.

Dear, Blessed Lady! She wasn't blithely tripping across some meadow or field; she'd gone brainlessly marching across a marsh, a bog! What she'd ignorantly identified as snow-bent sunflower stalks or raspberry canes were reeds! Wouldn't Feather be amused! She'd interpreted things to match her expectations, couldn't even identify a marsh when she stumbled into the middle of it! And where she stood—or desperately tried to stand now—was undoubtedly a slough, one of the streams that slowly drained excess water from the swamp, the faster, more active water not as solidly frozen as the rest!

Her boots dragged at her, feet already icy, the water wicking its way higher up her pantaloons as she settled deeper, more chunks of grayish, honeycombed ice dislodging themselves, angling upward. Nothing underfoot that she could feel, no bottom—it might be only another six centimeters deeper or it might be a meter. Either way, it was enough in which to drown! Reaching behind her with both hands, she groped for solid ice and leaned back, intent on distributing her weight over as much surface ice as possible, rather than boosting herself onto the tenuous lip of the opening. Her pack hindered each effort and the snowshoes presented an even worse obstacle, dragging and catching each time she tried to slide clear.

Could she roll over? Easier to belly-crawl, worm her way along. As she started a cautious roll, the ice creaked ominously at her shoulder. Fine! Stay on her back, sweep one arm as far as she could until it sank in the slush, pull herself clear just a bit. Then the other arm, almost like backstroking. The bent reeds weren't *that* distant, and if she could grasp a handful, she could anchor herself, ease the rest of her to solid, if soggy, land. Even then she wasn't sure if she'd dare stand, would rather sprawl full-length until terra firma truly lived up to its name! Her teeth gave a momentary, betraying chattering, reminding her how cold she was, how the frigid water burned her skin, the pain rawly sharp and shocking as it flowed into her jacket sleeves at each wrist, runnels trickling down the neck of her jacket, weighing down her hood.

And again—sweep that arm back! Pray her foot could shove against some temporarily solid spot, slide along slow and smooth and . . . Damn! Now she was pinned in place, couldn't budge, feebly waving her arms and legs. Something had snagged one of her snowshoes, probably a branch lodged in the ice, one end free to hook the snowshoe lacings. Could she break free, continue her backward creep? Or was it better to undo the chest straps on the pack, slide out of it? Feverishly fumbling at the leather ties with her sodden gloves was impossible, so she shoved a gloved hand into her mouth, bit down and yanked her hand free. There, that was better! She needed her hands bare to really feel what she was doing. No, idiot, that was a button, not a knot!

As the ice grumbled and flexed around her, she felt herself gradually settling deeper, as if sinking into a feather bed, but this sensation was far from pleasant. Struggling to keep her wits about her, not panic any more than she already had, Jacobia set herself to grimly assessing how to reach dry land, her fingers picking away at the knot. She'd do it, dammit! Take it one excruciating step at a time, one soggy, icy-drenched centimeter at a time. Oh . . . wouldn't it be nice to take a real step, not wriggle on her back! She was *not* going to drown in the dead of winter—it was unseemly, downright ridiculous in winter! Not to mention that she couldn't safely see the twins home if she were to drown! And so what if that was an icicle forming on her nose! Let Feather make any snide remarks, and she'd cut her dead, never speak to her again, go her own way without her!

❧

"You won't tell them?" Mahafny kept her head bowed, as if she were assiduously studying the deck's planks or the toes of her boots. A breeze plucked at a tendril of dangling silvery hair. No, it was Gaetan Boucher, delicately lifting it back in place. "Won't stay, you know," she whispered, wondering if the rosy pinkness of her scalp were visible. Hadn't believed she could blush from shame at her age, had thought it a trait long gone, vanished with so many other aspects of her youth. "Please," she implored. "Don't tell." Raising her clenched fist, she extended it over the gunwale as a pledge. "I'll toss it overboard if you promise not to tell. My word on it."

A roughened knuckle wedged itself beneath her chin to lift her bent head. Silly, since Gaetan wasn't as tall as she, but she knew he wanted the light to scrutinize her eyes. Both for truth and to assess how far gone she was. Though it pained her, she uncomplainingly left her arm outstretched, hoping she could unclench her fingers when the time came. Wouldn't do to fumble, reveal what it really was. Saam was ensconced belowdecks, and in her mind she sensed his slumbering, finally free from the throes of the dream that had set his sides heaving, his breathing coming fast and shallow. A relief to unswaddle him, cover him with but a light blanket, but such freedom came with a price: freeing his limbs freed something in his brain, urging him to flee. As if he dimly realized such freedom was shortlived. What she feared most was that he'd flee toward death.

The team of draft horses, big, broad bays, tramped steadily along the towpath, an occasional clank of chain, the squeak of leather harness sharp in the cold air. A shod hoof rang as it clipped a stone, sent it spinning into the river with a splash. The LaPierre had been dredged and evened along its westerly bank, a towpath cut and graded, allowing barges like Gaetan Boucher's *Papillon* to uneventfully travel upriver against the currents, unload at Sidonie or beyond. How far beyond, she wasn't sure, but however far Gaetan could take them meant that much less riding, effort. So why, then, should she crave the drug so badly now, when she'd gained a respite, didn't need to drive her body onward? Because she'd summoned the willpower to abstain last night?

"Well?" His knuckle prodded her chin higher, to the point of discomfort. Yet still she couldn't bring herself to meet Gaetan's dark eyes, flecked with copper near the pupil, so she concentrated on staring at his stubbled chin, his mouth calmly shifting his stubby pipe from side to side as if he had all the time in the world. "When did tha last take it?"

"At first light yesterday morn, when we set out from the Research Hospice for the ferry. And I've lasted till now." Except her night had been sleepless, every muscle in her body twanging, begging rest but refusing to relax. Lifting her chin clear of his intrusive knuckle, she stared over his head, exasperated; finally she capitulated and met his eyes. "I know what I'm doing, what the proper dosage is. How dare you question my judgment!"

"And just a few breaths ago it was, 'Please, don't tell! I'll toss it overboard, I promise!' " The foul-smelling pipe stem jabbed at her. "Crotchety old eumedico, ain' you? Crotchety and prideful. Not to mention disdainful of h'any advice fra an outsider." A skein of geese passed overhead, their mournful calls fading in the distance until they sounded like a pack of dogs. Late to be heading south. Where would they spend the night? At least they boasted intelligence enough to fly south, not north as she struggled to do! "Go on, then," he urged, the pipe stem now pointing toward the river. "Drop it o'er the side like tha promised."

Not daring to openly show her relief, she strove to project a sorrowful obedience as she labored to unfold her fist. "Course it woan matter muchit, will it?" Gaetan continued, contemptuously spitting over the side. "Since tha really hid it in the t'other 'and."

With the little dignity left to her, she folded her outstretched arm against her chest, cradling it with the other. "How could you *possibly* know!" Her vexation encompassed a multitude of concerns. "How did you know I was a eumedico? That I'd been dosing myself on *thebaneseng*? That I'd switched hands?" Harder and harder to keep this up, her willpower faltering, failing, craving the release, the newfound energy, the insensitivity to pain that the drug offered. If she didn't have it soon, she'd, she'd . . . What? Jump overboard into the LaPierre? Grovel at the man's feet? Go mad? Any or all of the choices were equally likely.

"Come, sit down." He'd taken her elbow now, leading

her like a docile child over to a storage bin that served as a bench. "I'll stand guard while tha takes it, if tha must. Pretend like we're still convarsing, so's you woan be interrupted."

Hands tremulous, she worked to break the wax seal and unfold the packet, bringing it at last to her lips and touching the bitter dosage with her tongue. So bitter, yet so welcome that she licked the paper for every last grain, like a starving dog lapping at the butcher's wrappings for any hint of meat or blood. Release swept over her like a tidal wave, threatening to suck her under, immerse her in delirious oblivion, but she laboriously conquered the sensation, controlled it. As long as one took precautions, possessed an iron will, *thebaneseng* could be mastered—at least for a time. "Thank you." Pinching the bridge of her nose, her eyes squinted shut as the rushing impact abated "Ah!" Now that she could concentrate, she'd discover how this elderly riverman possessed such knowledge about the drug, about her. "What gave me away? Most people don't recognize the withdrawal symptoms. And how did you know I'm a eumedico?"

Momentarily shushing him with a raised hand as he started to answer, she craned her neck to stare at the cabin where Saam lay. No, he still slept; he'd simply struggled to roll over, change position. Mayhap Harrap had forgotten to shift him from one side to the other. Sad to say, she and Harrap stacked him this way and that, almost as if the poor thing were a parcel, but they varied his position out of love and concern: sores might develop, fluid settle in his lungs.

Perching beside her, Gaetan Boucher clasped one knee, his free hand delving deep into a pocket on his double-breasted jacket. Returning her full attention to him, she nodded. "Beast sleeping well? 'Ere. All fresh, if tha want it?" A new clay pipe lay stark white against his brown hand. "Baccy 'as its own consolations, as well."

For a moment the lines and planes of self-righteous reproof formed on her face, etched there for all to read. Then she began to smile. Blessed Lady, how dare she be judgmental when she abused her own body thusly! What gave her the right to feel superior? Somehow, the thought of holding the pipe, stroking its smooth curves, tucking it in her mouth sounded soothing. After all, she needn't light it unless she wanted to actually smoke it.

Unconsciously mimicking the riverman, she gingerly set the pipe in the corner of her mouth, teeth clenching the stem. Yes—much the same effect as giving a baby a pacifier. Raising her silvery brows in query, she looked at him, giving him time, wondering who and what he truly was. Didn't sound like a native Marchmonter, that was for certain.

" 'Ow did I ken tha was a eumedico? 'Twas no tha hard. Most, *most*," he emphasized, "but not all, wear an air of superiority like a cloak. Doan think they even realize in most cases. But the training's hard and burdensome, I 'spect, and fra all that larning, one's a right ta feel proud. But there's more. . . ." He'd cocked the brim of his cap low and shawled his collar higher against the coolness of the falling night. Rising, he puttered with the bow lantern for a moment, rehanging it to his satisfaction before returning to resettle himself, though his eyes narrowed, fixing on the sky.

"Snow dusting during the night, I 'spect," he murmured, as much to himself as to her. "Pretty come morning. 'Twill storm harder higher up in the mountains." A constricted smile briefly split his face as he swung toward her. "Wasn't pretty in that tent 'ospice that time 'bout eighteen years ago, was it? That's 'ow I knew you was eumedico."

The admission jolted her, resurrecting a jumble of grim images she'd put out of mind for so many years. The horror of war—a war that had inadvertently begun between Marchmont and Canderis, and then transformed itself into an internecine battle within Marchmont—the usurping Prince Maurice's forces against his putative son Eadwin's hastily assembled, untried supporters for possession of the late Queen Wilhelmina's throne. Once Canderis had thrown its support behind Eadwin, things had sorted themselves out—a tidy euphemism to describe messy, brutal fighting at close quarters, eumedicos feverishly working to save as many wounded as possible. She herself had hurried from cot to cot in the makeshift hospice tents, advising less senior eumedicos, Canderisian and Marchmontian alike, how best to staunch those gaping sword wounds, save limbs. And when tenacity and expertise failed, taught them to surrender, consign the poor soul into the Lady's hands.

Ah, how she'd fought for her cousin, Swan Maclough. Seeker General. She'd fought for time, and at least she'd gained Swan that, let her die later on her own terms. On Swan's terms? Or on *her own* terms, stubbornly refusing to release the Seeker General from the living? Had she? Had she caused needless, additional suffering? Was that what she was subjecting Saam to, as well? No! No on both counts: had Swan died there on the field of battle, Doyce might well not have been named Seeker General. And Saam, how could he want to part from her?

Despite her training, a lingering moisture clouded her eyes, and now she owed it to Gaetan to hear his tale. "Were you one of the soldiers, one of the townspeople who rallied to Eadwin's cause? Were you wounded?"

Gaetan again spat at the water. "Nay, was upriver at the beginning. But my eldest, Germain, fought for Eadwin's cause. Wouldn't 'ave him now at all if it 'adn't been for you. I was at the 'ead of 'is cot, 'olding 'is 'ands tight, while you was at the foot, barking orders. Weren't fra you and the others, 'e'd 'ave lost that leg in a blink of the Lady's eye." He absently knocked the bowl of his pipe against the rail, a trail of tobacco sparkling like falling stars as it tumbled free. "Leg 'e kept ain' real strong—begging tha pardon—but it's far better than none at all."

If she saw him—Gaetan's son, Germain—would he stir the faintest of recollections in her, this once-young man now limping toward middle age? Except how often did one "see" a patient? Note any personal details or desires beyond the wound or disease?

"As for the *thebie* tha're taking, I kenned that at the tent 'ospice as well. Learnt the signs, saw them amongst some of the older, better eumedicos—the ones who worked without pause, healing, guiding the younger eumedicos, never resting, never sleeping. Asked the Bannerjee twins later, since they've known me and my kin a passel of years. More an one Boucher boasts the broidery of their stitches!"

It made her laugh, the first genuine laugh she'd indulged in in some time. "I'm afraid my stitches were always serviceable, but very utilitarian. No patience for fancywork."

"And that's clear, too. No patience. Or, given the givens, tha doan 'ave time for patience, just 'aste. Am I right?"

A nod at his perspicuity . . . about so many things.

"And is it worth it? Doing this to thaself? To the others? If it is, I'll shutter my mouth, keep mum, but I think your Shepherd man kens something's wrong. Would'na make a good spy, always looking too embarrassed. When 'e isn't turning green each time 'e steps clear a the cubby."

"It's worth it. Life always outweighs death in value, and I'll fight for it anyhow and any way I can. Oh, there's a price to pay, but I've never been niggardly about paying what's due." A hand on his shoulder now. "What price do you want?"

A muted roar, his pipe slamming the rail. Lady bless, she'd insulted him—now she'd done it!

"My price? Tha'd *bribe* Gaetan Boucher?" Though he pitched his voice not to carry, his emotion, his affronted outrage communicated itself to the team of bays, their ears pricking up, their gait increasing, as if they'd outpace it if they could. "My price is that tha all come back safe'n sound! Moderation, woman! Tha knows that better than an old riverman. Nor do I want to tell that Muscadeine lad that Gaetan Boucher helped his cousins, his friends along the road to death—do tha ken that!"

"Understood, sir." It struck her that again she clutched something in her hand—the pipe, forgotten for a time. "And one final favor, if you would? Might I keep the pipe? And have a pouch of tobacco to go with it?"

"One addiction or another, eh?"

♣

The slush cushioned, jiggled her like a hard-boiled egg in aspic; each time she stretched out her arms they bobbed, their weight dissipated, fled. Even the cold didn't matter anymore—strange how she'd fought it so hard at first, then gradually acquiesced, chills diminishing, muscles unknotting. Muscles unknotting . . . but the knots wouldn't unknot. . . . A relief . . . a release from the burden of fighting, and Jacobia smiled dreamily. But her smile brought her back to herself, an unpleasant sensation, her face was cracking—no, not her face—a thin sheet of ice coating like a second skin, compounded of tears, perspiration, and snow crystals.

Not going to be found like this! A fly in amber. Or like some woebegone maiden who'd thrown herself and her cares into the bosom of the water, believing drowning offered surcease from all pain. Fight! she commanded herself. You're not an icicle—yet! By slow degrees her brain stuttered, then fired with anger at her body's sloth, at its abject willingness to capitulate, give in and give up. The anger warmed her enough to crack open her eyes, roll her head. Unfinished business, by the Lady! Think of Mahafny— she'd not given in, given up! Think of Mahafny . . . that should make her toasty-warm! Ah, poor Mahafny! Without Saam, what did she have left? And if Jacobia couldn't rescue the twins from their own misguided efforts, what would *she* have left?

Oh, her mother Damaris would still love her, as would Syndar. But with each of her mother's compassionate looks she'd suspect she was being held obscurely accountable for the twins' deaths. Had tried, but been found grievously wanting. Jenret and Doyce? Impossible to face such heartache, such sorrow, and expect any sympathy for her well-intentioned failure. Were their positions reversed, she'd not be able to muster any How did people decide to give in, give up? Was it a conscious choice, or one that emanated from the very depths of a flagging heart and soul? Not cowardice, exactly, but an abdication of spirit. Did acknowledging it make one a lesser person—or merely a realist? And Harrap would comfort with the age-old litany of his Lady: "If not in this life, mayhap in another . . ." But surely that didn't mean a second chance couldn't exist in *this* life?

Her thoughts were too complicated for her brain, still stuttering along in fits and starts, beginning again to register the cold and complain, throbbing aches in parts of her anatomy still with sensation. Bending her right arm across her chest, she commanded her left hand to find it, push it over her head, wincing as she smacked herself in the eye, unaware how low her hand had drifted until the stiff fingers poked. Better than a sharp stick in the eye? Barely, or so she judged. And where the hells was Feather? Sitting snug and smug by some nice campfire, drying her boots, boiling

water for cha, drowsily wondering when that stubborn, arrogant Outlander would catch up?

And where, come to think on it, was Frost? Where had
he wandered off to? At least he'd had the horse sense not
to follow her out onto the ice, or they'd have broken
through even sooner, very possibly in deeper water.
"Fr–fra! F–fr–frost!" Interesting . . . her voice sounded as
if it had been hibernating. Not that she expected him to
gallop to her rescue, break a path through the ice and drag
her to safety . . . but it *would* be nice to know she wasn't
alone, completely unregarded. And deep in his horsey
heart, Frost would mourn her loss. . . . Stop that! Stop
thinking like that!

Somehow she raised her head to stare blearily across the
expanse of snowy ice and, while her head was raised, her
wandering hand slipped from her face to drop next to one
ear. Oh, oh, watch that! A delicate shell of ice, her ear was
brittle, ready to snap off at the slightest touch. Touch—yes.
Snowshoe? Probably, since she'd never extricated herself
from her pack-turtle-on-its-back-pack. Her sense of touch
was circumscribed, but she seemed to have thrust several
fingers through holes. Had to be holes, 'cause holes had
edges—yes? Otherwise they were just emptiness, acres and
acres of emptiness. . . . So this was good, downright excellent! Oh, yes . . . she'd been calling, should keep calling,
just in case. . . . "Fr–frost!"

Could be that lumbering black shape in the distance, one
of many lumbering black shapes. No, more likely the reeds,
their burden of snow finally dropped so they could sway in
the wind. Then again, might not be. No sense worrying,
wondering. Now, about those holes her fingers had found.
Oh, my . . . that one had something poking through it . . .
a . . . a not-finger! A protruding thing—more like a coat
hook than a finger—nice to be tidy, had hung up her
snowshoes. . . . Ah, that branch that had snagged her snowshoes, halted her progress! Well done! Still, she'd already
determined that—hadn't she? Fine, since she was back
where she'd started, she could close her eyes and sleep
again, wrap the coldness around her like a comforter, let it
block out any further chill or pain.

Except now anger churned through her, not just anger
at the offending branch, but at the snowshoes as well, nasty

things, hanging her up like that! With a low, guttural growl she fumbled at the branch hook, wanting to break or bend it, tear it from its icy mooring. No, wait! An absolutely ludicrous idea, an invitation to complete disaster, but . . . squinting, she licked her lips, trying to visualize, to *see* behind her. Lift the frame free, skid her body away from safety, venture closer to the open water where her lower legs bobbed. Then struggle through the whole farce once more. Well, why not? Was better than just lying there, her legs sinking deeper.

Except her fingers refused to close on anything, didn't want to flex. When had they stopped being nice, obedient fingers? Probably about the time she'd stopped being a nice, obedient child. The thought made her giggle, negligently wave her hand in the air.

Except now she couldn't lift her wrist, her whole arm immobilized. Ho! No doubt her hand had frozen solid in the slush. "Will you stop waggling your hand and just hold still!" The voice, Feather's, came out of nowhere and—surprisingly—sounded breathless and frightened, rather than acerbic. "Can you help me, help yourself at all? I can't risk coming much closer or we're both going to be soaked through."

" 'S cold," Jacobia acknowledged, her mood airy, almost cheerfully dismissive of a minor discomfort. "But y–you'll g–get used to it." Funny, even her teeth felt cold, the way they had when she'd been small and eaten boiled sap poured on pristine snow. She'd been greedy, overeager for her share, would scoop up a handful of snow with the congealed sap atop it instead of peeling it off when it cooled. Ah, sweet stickiness and a crunch of snow, her tongue, her palate turning deliciously numb, then gradually warming to savor the sweetness as the snow melted. Sometimes she gobbled so fast her head began to ache, cold exploding above her nose and between her eyes.

"Your clothes and boots are totally waterlogged." Feather's voice sounded near, but not near enough. "I've spread my weight as best as I can, but I don't dare slide out much farther. Why didn't you call for help, you impossible Outlander?"

Something was wrapping itself around her wrist, she sensed the hovering busyness of Feather's fingers, though not much else. "Wanted to call!" She slapped at Feather with her free hand, unable to see if her blow had landed anywhere near. "Didn't want you to th–think I was a b–baby! Can . . . t–take care of myself!"

"Of course you can, if you know the land, listen to the earth." Feather sounded conciliatory. "You have to be one with it for season upon season, have seen it, listened to it in all its guises. Its looks, its desires and needs, alter with each season. When it's cloaked with snow, it can harbor surprises for the unwary."

But now Jacobia was sliding backward, a steady hauling that stretched and wrenched every muscle from wrist to hip. "Ouch!" she protested, her clothes crackling where the folds had frozen.

"Back, Frost! Back!" So, Frost was with her after all. Good Frost! He was dragging her clear of the slough. Yes, horsey had hooked a big fish. "D–did Fr–frost go get you?" It sounded like some children's tale, the brave horse risking all to save its human, the kind of tale that had always brought a tear to her eye when she'd been a child. Now, if the horse had been one of the ghatti, *that* would have made even more sense!

"No, but he stood guard—stamping and whinnying." Squeaks and crunches as Jacobia's body slithered onto solid ground, reeds snapping and popping as Frost trampled them down. "I forgot to listen. The earth told me your footsteps—Frost's, as well—had ceased, but I labeled you lazy, a laggard. Once the emptiness whispered loudly enough, I began to backtrack, looking for you both."

❖

Wielding his twig broom as if it were a weapon rather than a cleaning implement, Nakum viciously attacked the ashes and clinkers strewn round the brazier that warmed his underground dwelling. Naturally, the harder he swept, the higher the ashes flew, floating and settling on even more of his belongings, marring the neatness of his snug ovoid home. Finally, after an exasperated "Feh" and a string of choice expletives, he calmed enough to sweep slowly and thoroughly, and not stir things even more. Finished except for dusting the diaphanous membrane at the ceiling's highest curve, he threw himself on his bed, grumbling, unable to relax on the piled furs that covered the wall ledge where he slept.

He was exhausted. Oh, not the sort of physical exhaustion, even mental fatigue that his earth-bond could readily alleviate, but an exhaustion that stemmed from utter frustration. No matter what he did, how hard he cogitated on who or what was responsible for all these minor disruptions in his life, he was no closer to grasping the truth. Always a step behind, never a step ahead! And he was not amused! How had the . . . the *whatever* . . . managed to broach the sanctity of his home, accessible only through a circular door that expanded and contracted like the iris of an eye at his or Callis's touch? Only a very special few had ever entered his egg-shaped home, formed by a giant gas bubble in ages past when the earth had writhed and heaved to escape the heat below as the Great Spirit had hatched the world, but left this perfect ovoid fullness unbroken, as if it held a promise within it.

Finally, sitting on the edge of his bed, he let his hands dangle between his knees, staring down at the lush pelts he'd tumbled onto the floor. More mess, but this one was his fault, tumbling everything in his search for the miscreant. Mayhap some cha would relax him, let him temporarily forget how he was being constantly bested. Except he didn't even know for a certainty what game they played—if game it was!

Puttering around, he set the cha to steeping and tried to think on the tasks he'd set himself for the morrow. Except how could he possibly know until he learned precisely what pranks that . . . that *thing* would play during the night! Two mornings ago he'd discovered his sacred tree desecrated— no, be honest, decorated—with unlikely bits of yarn in bright shades. Yarn would round and about, up and down, strands of it fluttering and dancing in the breeze. Half the day it had taken him to unwind it, salvage what he could of his yarn, ensure that bits and pieces didn't float off in the wind. Who knew how far the winds could carry them? Whether they might prove hazardous to some small creature on the lower slopes if its feet became entangled in it?

Every time he turned around, little things were wrong,

out of place! Actually, some of the things weren't so little, required major time and effort to rectify, but—he had to reluctantly admit—nothing had been severely damaged. Other than his pride! He was at his wit's end keeping up, setting things right. A litter of mischievous ghatten playing and prowling around his domain would cause fewer problems! At least with ghatten, he could discipline them, teach them respect for another's belongings.

Peering inside the pot, he judged his cha had brewed enough and poured the liquid into his mug, reaching blindly toward the shelf with a free hand to retrieve his honey jar. His questing fingers encountered stickiness, and he glanced up, pouring cha on his hand, his worry growing. Yes, someone, some *thing,* had liberally smeared the outside of the jar with honey, a small pool of it surrounding the container. Such waste dismayed him, as did the messiness. Blast that creature! Determined to remain calm, enjoy his cha, he left the jar as it was, simply stretched on his toes to reach the honey-twister. Clean it later, it would wait. Savor the cha while it was warm, inhale the fragrant sweetness released by the clover honey mixed with it. Ah, yes. . . .

At least his arborfer seedlings had yet to be toyed with; the creature apparently possessed some respect or discretion. Oh, various tags and labels had been rearranged, pots shifted, his records muddled, but nothing to physically harm them. Indeed, they flourished, growing even more vigorous, as if they were thriving on this squabble, deriving nourishment from it in some indefinable way. Mulling it over, he carried his mug back to his bed and dropped down—only to rise with a shout and a curse, hot cha spilling down his pant leg, making him do a little dance of frustration as he grabbed at the bedding, stripping it back. A cluster of pinecones had been lurking under the covers, waiting to prod his posterior. They *had* to have been collected on the lower slopes—malice aforethought, not some momentary whim!

One by one he removed the cones, arranging them in a neat ring on his birch table. "I don't know who or what you are," he sputtered, scanning the smooth curves of his home as if something might materialize through them, be discernible to his naked eye, "but I'm going to find you, flush you out if it's the last thing I do!" Despite his resolve to remain calm, he shook his fist.

This was insane! Here he was, cursing, threatening—what? Ah, didn't he wish he knew! Because if he knew what he faced, then he could best this malicious creature, make it choose a new home, find a new being to annoy and frustrate. What had he done to become the butt of such capricious antics? He waited, every sense pitched, wondering if he might again hear that high, thready giggle. Sometimes he swore he heard it, other times not. Or was his mind playing tricks on him?

A shuddering sigh as he sipped what little cha remained in his mug. Ah, well, time to clean the honey jar, sop up the spilled cha. At least up here on his frozen mountain he needn't worry about ants making a path to the jar! Addawanna'd be proud of him for discovering one small—very small—blessing.

♣

Each finger, each toe pulsed and burned with the torment of fire, the pain seething along her arms and legs to commingle with the other hurts that Jacobia remembered at odd moments, because pain was something one was unlikely to forget, as if it left scars that should be visible to the naked eye. Did every real physical scar have an invisible but matching mate, a counterpart? She considered that as she flew across the landscape. Well, not flew, exactly—but floated, mayhap that was a better word. Definitely wasn't walking—her feet would have protested the outrage. The movement, the floating, left her slightly nauseous, so she closed her eyes to avoid the world whirling by. Did a cloud think the sky whirled around it—or did the sky believe the cloud floated within its confines? Now a butterfly could both fly and float. . . .

After that came the fever and the racking chills that left her quaking like an aspen, sure she'd shake off her leaves to form a golden cloud. At least the chills distracted her from the hollow, raling cough that monotonously issued from some nearby soul, made her almost gasp for breath in sympathy. No, that was *her* making those horrid noises;

a relief, almost, when the relentless cacophony of hacks turned deep and sticky, roiling within her.

A damp cloth brushed hair off her temples, and a hand touched her forehead, rested there. When it finally removed itself, she noted the skin was coppery, the hand square, gnarled at the knuckles. Not Feather's hand; she boasted thin-fingered hands smaller than Jacobia's own. But the hand had the familiarity of an old friend . . . except it was so hard to think, what with the steam curling around her, the shocking hiss of cold water spattering on hot rocks. Scents in the steam, aromatic and penetrating, making everything in her lungs loosen, rise to clot her throat. No holding it back or she'd choke; it disgusted her, but she flung her head aside, spat copiously. Revolting! Hands on her back, cupped hands, the outer edges pounding a rhythmic beat, flesh thumping against sticky, damp flesh. Other hands rubbing her feet, working at each toe until she was sure they'd snap off one by one. What would she do with her toes then? Carry them in a little leather bag until she could find someone to sew them on? String them like beads? Still, she could manage without one toe—look at dear Pw'eek, a sort of scallop on her right front paw, where the absent toe belonged.

"So!" The voice behind her was richly choleric but muted, and the hands never stopped their beat against her back, jarring her body and brain, making it hard to listen. "She your prob'em to set right, Feather. 'Cept mebbe you bite off more'n you kin chew, eh? So high'n mighty now, dat what you t'ink, t'ink rules for eve'ybody 'cept you! You *'bove* rules, Feather? Dis one not, no t'anks to you! You 'sponsible for her life—mebbe it remind you Outlanders value life jes like Erakwa."

The fingers working her toes halted, a hand clasping the arch of her foot so tightly it pained her. "I *know* that, old woman! Don't tell me my duty! I let my bitterness cloud my judgment, ignored a human life hanging in the balance. I'm doing all I can!" But Feather couldn't seem to leave well enough alone. "With what I've learned of *their* medicine *and* ours, she'll survive, despite being unversed in wilderness ways."

"Doan call me, 'old woman,' you legend-lost child. So prideful of Outlander ways you no longer lis'en to our world. Or worse, lis'en but ignore the message—when your earth-bond not wort lis'ening to? Why you bother keep it? I, Addawanna, once was proud to gift you wid it, teach you all I know of healing lore."

Addawanna! Nakum's grandmother—that's who Feather was arguing with. So they'd located Feather's people—or been found by them. It hurt too much to think, determine a sequence of events. Another cough racketed through her, left her gulping for air. Stopping would be a joy. But she needed to ask Addawanna a question, if she could only remember what. What she was . . . looking for . . . no, *who* she was looking for! " 'Wanna!" The hands paused in their steady beat, suspended but ready to resume. "Addawanna!" Amazing how much breath was required to speak her name, but she sorely needed that breath for other purposes, like living. "Jenneth and Diccon, ghattens! H–have you seen . . . ? Heard any . . . ? Mahafny and Harrap are . . . with them. Saam's dying." Now her pain was more than purely physical as she hugged herself and rocked back and forth.

"Ah-ah-ah!" A cup of liquid at her lips, the hot fluid trickling down, cutting at the revolting mess clogging her throat. So smooth, sweetly cleansing! "An dey journey toward Nakum—yes?"

A nod was all she had strength for, and she wearily rested her head on a hand, hating the damp, sweaty feel of her hair. Fighting the spasm, keeping the next cough at bay, she sputtered, "Can he . . . ? Are they . . . will they be . . . all right . . . ?"

"Too soon to say. To say a t'ing does not mean it comes true. Your ghatti know this. Now rest, liddle one." Hands eased her shoulders against a bed of furs and fir boughs, her head and chest propped on crude pillows. "We dry you, inside an out. See what tomorrow bring. Nakum must heed many calls. Mebbe he need his ol' granmutter sort dem out."

She wanted a definitive answer, an answer that reassured her that none of her efforts had been in vain, but since Addawanna was being insistently tight-lipped, Jacobia slept.

❧

Feather shrugged the furs higher, tried to stuff them in her ears to block Addawanna's droning. Bad enough she remained immured in this sweat lodge, listening to Jacobia's coughing, her clogged breathing, but must she listen to Addawanna rattle on and on as well? True, the sound of her voice, the rhythms of the old tales, soothed Jacobia, eased her feverish tossing, but to Feather the incessant yammer whittled at her nerves. All she wanted was some undisturbed sleep! Sweat tickled down her cheek where she'd snugged the fur, the air too warmly moist to require any covering, and she reluctantly shrugged it off. Concentrate on something, *anything* to block out the old woman's nattering—she could do that, couldn't she? Just as she shrugged off Outlanders' snide comments, refused to hear them, give their rudeness validity by reacting to it. Being subjected to this outworn cant, refuge of the credulous, the unworldly, was even worse, made her fume with the unfairness of it all! Even amongst her own kind she lacked a say, the right to choose to hear such folderol!

Rolling onto her other side, she presented her back to Addawanna in mute but eloquent commentary on what she was being forced to endure. She gritted her teeth, listed eumedico procedures in her head, dredged up the most unlikely medical conditions she could think of. But Addawanna's words still drifted through her mind, pervasive as woodsmoke. . . . "Kulshanala . . ." Feather thought she said and went rigid. How many years since she'd heard that name, been called by her "true" name? How many years since she'd answered to it? By ten she'd insisted on being called by the Outlander translation of her name, "Feather," would "hear" no other.

Ah . . . no . . . not Kulshanala . . . Kulshana! The Tale of Kulshana and Shanakul, that's what Addawanna now regaled Jacobia with. Easy enough to commence any Erakwa legend or tale with the words that started them all, set the listeners ready and waiting. "Once, long, long ago, long before time was time as we know it. . . ." Long before time was time . . . yet it seemed she forever lacked time enough! Look at the time she was wasting here! Why had Davvy McNaught been so insistent she take time off, enjoy the halidays? Did he think her in danger of wearing herself out, turning careless through overwork? No, the harder, the longer she worked, the sharper, more precise she became!

Jacobia's cough rattled, and Addawanna never paused in her telling, so Feather unwillingly hoisted herself up and slipped an arm under her shoulders, brought the wooden cup to her lips and let her sip before lowering her again. Casting herself down cross-legged, she threw a rancorous look in Addawanna's direction and sighed. Not that it did much good! Tired, wanting desperately to sleep, she planted an elbow on each knee and rested her head in her hands. Worse than being trapped in here with a whining, buzzing mosquito!

"So!" Addawanna lightly smacked her hands against her thighs. "You no like list'nin' me, den *you* tell tale! If you still 'member it, not crowded out of head by ev'ryt'ing else you cram inside, like bear gorging self for winter sleep!" A taunting smile greeted Feather when she wearily lifted her head. Did the old woman truly think she'd fall for one of the oldest tricks in the world, challenging her like that? The old woman planned on showing her up, throwing her "ignorance" in her face as she faltered and stumbled through the tale.

Well, easy enough to prove her wrong! No, she'd not thought on this tale or so many others in a long time, but she *would* remember it, force it out of the dark recesses of her mind, just as she remembered those obscure eumedico facts so needful on rare occasion.

Again resting her head in her hands to focus her concentration, Feather began, counting on the formulaic beginning to sweep her along into the tale proper . . . she hoped! Damn! What had she gotten herself into?

"Once, long, long ago, long before time was time as we know it . . . twin girl children were born to an Erakwan woman. They were like as like could be, except that Kulshana was dark, while Shanakul was pale, which was as it should be, since Kulshana's father was an Erakwa brave, but Shanakul's father was one of the Star People. Indeed, the twins' mother had no idea she had lain with one of the Star People, for he had wreathed himself in starlight and moonbeams, and the girls' mother innocently believed she but basked in the shot-silver light of the night skies.

"At first Kulshana and Shanakul were close as close

could be, like an egg with twin yolks. Yet for all their closeness, they were very different. Kulshana was forever asking
why, why? Or how, how? Why do Maple's seeds wing down
like that? How does Rainbow paint his colors across the
sky? Why does Beaver build? Why—when she observed
her reflection in a stream or pond—did she view Shanakul's
pale reflection instead of her own? She probed forever
deeper when the answers didn't satisfy her, even though
the selfsame answers had forever guided her people, given
their lives shape and meaning. So she would take the answers and busily remold, reshape them with her hands until
they suited her. Yet she could never understand why she
so needed Shanakul's quiet presence, always harking to her
soothing voice effortlessly reciting the very tales that never
seemed answer enough to Kulshana.

"Much as she'd loved her sister, she gradually began to
despise Shanakul and the musty old tales that grew within
her, springing to life from her lips. Wanting to be different,
singular, she strove to cast out the Erakwan beliefs that
hampered her, but her sister kindly took them within her,
fostering them so they grew and flourished, her tales flour-
ishing as well. Shanakul's earth-bond now glowed with both
star-silver and earth hues, while Kulshana's bond looked
ever more dull and dim.

"Again and again Kulshana stared into ponds and lakes
and streams, wandering wide to find new ones, hoping that
the reflection she saw would reveal her, Kulshana, not
Shanakul."

Feather faltered, shook her head. . . . Looking down into
the icy slush, Jacobia's pale, cold face staring back at
her . . . so easy to have taken a stick . . . pushed her
under. . . . The thought had crossed her mind, stark as a
lightning bolt against a storm-dark sky, but she'd conquered
it. Eumedicos do not kill; they cure . . . even those they
hate. . . . Coincidence, just coincidence! Firming her voice,
she slowly picked up her pace as she continued, her shaking
hands tucked in her lap, hands that could heal, remold broken bodies, hands that could. . . .

"One day Kulshana invited her twin for a walk and
brought her to the mossy bank of a deep pond she'd found.
'Come, Sister—look! Do you see me or yourself when you
stare in the water?' Curious, Shanakul knelt, stretching far-

ther over the bank until she could see the reflection of a face amidst the concentric circles the feeding minnows and water bugs made. But before Shanakul could decide, let alone answer, Kulshana pushed her head down with all her might and held her beneath the water's surface until she breathed no more. Slipping her sister's starry-silver earth-bond free from her neck, she hung it around her throat where it collided with her own lusterless earth-bond, then toppled her sister's body into the pond's depths amongst the water weeds and willow roots. 'Now I have what my sister had as well as what I have! All the answers are within me, are mine!'

"But these new parts crowded out the last bits of Kulshana that had made her what she was, a daughter of the Erakwa, and these pieces roamed homeless and alone, no one to shelter them as Shanakul had once before. As the seasons changed, Kulshana slowly recognized her loss, the right answers no longer enough, no longer nourishing her. Worse yet, the stolen starry-silver earth-bond turned the stagnant shades of pond scum and mold, and her own became black and hard and shrunken. Her heart and spirit felt full unto bursting yet strangely empty, crying out to recover what she had cast aside.

"Hurrying back to the pond, she reached deep, deep down below the water's surface for her sister's hand, holding her breath to bursting yet crying piteously inside—not for herself and her loss, but for her sister, the twinned half of her that she had discarded as worthless, her half alone of value. At last their fingers intertwined, Kulshana heaving with all her might until Shanakul's pale form broke the surface of the pond.

" 'Sister, why do you weep?' asked Shanakul as the water streamed from her to mingle with Kulshana's tears. Pale she might be, but from within her emanated a radiance, a rightness of spirit that awed her sister.

" 'I sorrow for what I lost, for what I did not cherish,'' wailed Kulshana, beating her hands against her breast, throwing herself on the earth to weep. 'You and the ways of our people, the right answers that I so heedlessly cast aside. I believed I did not need them because I could not encompass them within my heart. Ah, forgive me! Please, please return them to me!

"Her sister looked on in sorrow as well. 'I cannot, my sister. Some are forever lost to you, will never find their way home to your heart. Other parts I nurtured, and they now are a part of me, just as they once were a part of you. No longer can they be separated, divided, or they will wither and die. Yet, mayhap someday, when you behold yourself as worthy, you shall be worthy, no longer be beholden to me, our spirits intermingling as one once more, with no thought of mine or yours.'

"And with that Kulshana had to be satisfied as she removed both her earth-bond and her sister's and returned them to Shanakul. And Kulshana still ceaselessly seeks for an answer, the truth as to her worth, and that answer will reunite her and her sister."

. . . a hand rocking her, shaking her shoulder, harder now, and Feather sat up, lost, confused, until Jacobia's racking cough brought everything back to her. "I be sittin' up half dis night," Addawanna complained, stretching. "You do yer share, now. S'eepin' like stone, you were, neber budging, no hearing me when I speak, jes selfish, selfish s'eep."

"Did I . . . did I finish . . . ? Did I tell it rightly?" She wanted, needed proof, approval, a way to assess her worth.

"Tell what right? You always tellin' me dis, tellin' me dat, tellin' me how right you always be. What you t'ink you tole me now? T'ink I fergit? No fergit if neber tole it! Kulshanala, sometime I wonder 'bout you! 'Cept I *neber* yet find right answers! Mebbe someday. . . ."

Crouching to push more stones into the fire to heat, Feather stared at nothing . . . and at everything. Had she dreamed it? Surely Addawanna had dared her to join in the tale-telling—or had she? And why that particular tale? Did the old woman think she'd lesson her, make her see the parallels between Kulshana and Shanakul, between Feather and Jacobia? Ha! Tenuous at best! Those ancient tales were crammed with such absurdities!

♣

Meditatively working his jaw from side to side, Harrap craned his neck back until he feared his vertebrae might pop, despite the cushioning collar and scarves swathed round his neck. Yet no matter how high he gazed, the mountain range lacked a visible top, and it troubled him, left him awash in nervous sweat at the immensity, the unendingness of it all. And *that* was what Mahafny proposed climbing, one way or another! The Blessed Lady's havens were more accessible!

**"You can't see the top because it's shrouded in mist, you know. Not to mention that you're standing too close, right at the base like this."** It didn't feel close to Harrap—anything but close. But what he did know was that he didn't want to be any nearer—even if it meant Gaetan's barge again as well as the ferry! He'd dance with joy on their decks! Awed despite himself, Parm's eyes were darkly wide as he balanced against Harrap for a better look. The red pompom on Parm's hat bobbled, and Harrap absently toyed with it, shamefacedly wondering what had possessed him to gaud the ghatt like that. Warm was one thing, decorative flourishes something else again, given Parm's exquisitely muddled coloring. Except Parm seemed to relish the knit vest and cap, not to mention the additional stares and whispers it engendered. **"And the higher we climb, the closer we'll come to your Lady."**

*"Not close enough, I fear."* And fear Harrap did. He harbored no doubt the Lady's will would be done, but it didn't necessarily mean that he'd like the outcome. What would his quotidian life be like without Saam's presence, possibly without Mahafny's? No one chafing at him, no one needing calming, and ofttimes it worked the other way 'round: him requiring a dose of Mahafny's bracing, nononsense attitude to make him see the light. He was too old, too set in his ways to alter what he was—part-Seeker, part-Shepherd, ever-devoted companion—and one role without the others would no longer sustain him.

Would any Bethel have him back full-time? Endless prayers, the Mystery Chants sung for the Lady's greater glory—those he could accomplish in his sleep. Had done so recently, unless he'd missed his guess. Never did he burden others to pray with him unless they freely chose to do so; reluctant prayers had little worth to the Lady. On rare occasions Mahafny might stiffly kneel behind him, not exactly participating, but taking it under advisement. And keeping tabs on Mahafny and Saam this trip, not to mention the twins and their Bonds, had left him with scant time for his Lady or himself, not to mention Parm.

**"We are Bonded, each unto the other,"** Parm reminded him. **"What touches you touches me, your joys and troubles doubly mine, but we each must serve at what we do best. Mahafny needs you more right now, just as Saam needs me."**

Nodding his gratitude, he licked his lips, nerves still overwhelming him, and wished he hadn't. Already his face was chapped raw from the wind, the scouring cold of winter. Gotten soft, he had, in more ways than one. Not daring to tackle Mahafny directly, ask what she'd requisitioned from the apothecaire, was one indication—especially since he now strongly suspected what she'd dosed herself with on the barge. Had had the evidence in front of his nose after they'd left Trude's, but had refused to see. Except Mahafny's hellish bargain with her body might be the way—the only way—she'd have a crack at winning this daunting game of life and death. One could never outwit the Lady, but mayhap he could convince Her new rules pertained, request some special dispensation. But drugs! How could he stand idly by and let Mahafny abuse herself like that?—not after what he'd suffered through.

Finally tearing his eyes from the mountain wall looming in front of them, Harrap cast a glance at the river, Gaetan and the barge slowly working their way upstream. Now the barge looked ridiculously small, a child's version of a boat on a string, tugged along a bare trickle of a stream. His previous fears of boats seemed ridiculous, almost petty, against this newly risen one. "But I am *not* small or insignificant in the Lady's eyes," he reminded himself and formed the eight-pointed star of his faith. "She sees all, knows all, cares for all." Didn't she? Now was not the time to question, to discover his faith had faltered. No, hardly his faith, just its unworthy vessel.

To his rear Diccon and Jenneth loaded the ponies, checking the pack balance on the sides of each saddle. Only four ponies, each round and sturdy-legged, two chestnuts, one black, one gray. Maude and Mignon, Jester and Willy, according to Jen. Riding would be mostly out of the question, asking too much of the beasts on steep stretches of winding trail. But they'd carry their gear and supplies, carry a weary soul a ways, pull flagging walkers along beside them. He resolved to walk as much as he could—more than he could—to ensure that Mahafny rode, because if she conserved her energy, she might not consume as much of the drug. And Parm could ride, no sense wearing those dear paw pads any thinner!

Ah, how he'd matched Hylan Crailford pace for pace, pulling her little goat-cart, debating and discussing life's meaning with her, hoping to instill the Lady's saving grace in her bitterly confused heart without revealing he'd been sent to spy on her actions. Wrong, mayhap, in the larger order of things, but absolutely crucial at the time. Someone had to track where and how her misguided views found fertile ground, the number of equally deluded followers flocking after her, espousing her apocalyptic theory that the "end" could only be averted by the ritual sacrifice of all Resonants.

However, Hylan's canny innocence, her instinct for self-preservation, had outwitted him, and to carry on her plans she'd addicted him and Parm to some obscure hallucinatory herbal mix that he still craved at times, the craving striking out of the blue, even when he believed himself happy and content. Never did he dare let down his guard, but sometimes Mahafny would read the naked need in his eyes, every fiber of his being lusting for it, just a touch, a taste, and she'd set him a distracting, strenuous task, or talk with him and walk with him, pace through the night until dawn broke and the urge lessened. Or, if not lessened, had been fought under control, another skirmish won, though the war within him would continue. Little wonder that if someone ordered him to portray his Lady, his crude drawing would unwittingly mirror Mahafny's severely elegant face, the two becoming one at times.

How many too-brief days did they have to accomplish this task? How much longer could Saam cling to the thin thread of life that animated his body, if not always his mind? How fast could they climb? Daunting equations with too many variables and unknowns. What little he remembered of his math was that whatever was done to one side of the equation must also be done to the other to maintain equality, make them balance. Did that mean sacrificing a hale and healthy life to balance Saam's? No! Mathematics might require that sort of exacting parity, but not the Lady! But he shivered despite his affirmatory conclusion. Diccon? Jenneth? Pw'eek or Kwee? He'd humbly offer himself for whatever good it might do.

**"And make me chase you all the way to your Lady's hearth—or beyond?"** Parm obviously didn't find his random musings very inspiring. **"If you wish to climb the Spirals with me, and visit the Elders, fine. I'd love to hear you arguing theology with Kharm, Mother-of-Us-All! Together, we'd confound her so badly she'd bite her own tail in frustration!"**

Brightening at Parm's vision, he swept off his cap to cool his feverish thoughts, when he sensed her presence. How many years had he been at her side, almost before she, herself, had realized her need? "If you're ready, you and Parm," she tucked a hand in his elbow, learning against his arm, "the twins and I want to start. Once their natural exuberance wears off, I suspect we'll fall into a steady but more seemly pace. The kind that gets the job done."

For a moment she sounded almost like her old self, but Harrap couldn't meet her eyes, those cool gray eyes that would expose her secret, reveal whether she'd had her ration of drugs for the day. Better to pretend, sometimes. Not to fool himself or to mislead her about what he knew, but simply to ensure that things progressed smoothly for as long as possible. That was his immediate goal.

Cumbrously propping his foot on an outcrop to retie his boot, Harrap then methodically did the same with the other boot, his wheaten robe swinging scandalously high above his knees to reveal shockingly purple pantaloons underneath. "Remember them? They still fit. Fit better than before, in fact! A bit faded from being folded and put away for so long."

A twitch at the corner of her mouth. "I'd not thought of them for years! And the green jacket with the red lapels— the booty from a nice bit of wagering, was it not? The pantaloons, though—outright thievery. Robbery! You sat on the poor man and stripped them off him, apologizing all the while."

"Because it was needful, if you recall." He was pleased she remembered. "I knew the Lady would turn a blind eye, condone a lesser evil for a greater good—that we follow after Doyce and Jenret, help them extirpate the evil that had entered all our lives." Why had be brought it up? Brought up the memory of her daughter, Evelien, and that cursed Vesey, Doyce's stepson?

Saam's legs churned in his wrappings, as if he, too, recollected those days, those needs. "Well, I certainly hope the Lady *did* turn a blind eye," Mahafny added, toying with the edge of Saam's blanket. "After all, that man had the ugliest, scrawniest shanks I've ever witnessed!"

❖

Assuming the lead, Jenneth cautiously studied the winding track ahead, sun-drenched and wide at this level, her feet biting firmly into the snow base just beneath last night's powder. No slipping or sliding, and that meant less wasted energy, less wasted time. If she allowed her mind to wander to pleasanter days, this could almost be fun, a brisk hike on a clear winter's morn, secure in the knowledge there'd be hot chocolate and sandwiches, warm beds awaiting them at the end of the day. Behind her the gray pony followed at the end of its lead, Pw'eek balanced atop the load. Pw'eek and Willy had struck up a friendship, and every so often when she half-turned to check Willy, Pw'eek would be stretched along his shaggy neck, seemingly whispering to him. But of course, who wouldn't want to be Pw'eek's friend, much as her dearheart sometimes found that hard to believe.

Saam's ceaseless mewling relentlessly followed in her wake—if only she could speed her pace, escape the sound. Wasn't his throat raw from wailing? It hurt her ears, pierced her brain. He'd commenced his incessant plaint as soon as the ponies had started upslope. Either the motion frightened or hurt him, or it resurrected dim, confused memories of past rides, and asking would do no good, might mire his mind even more deeply in some other world. Push his pitiful wail out of her mind, don't think about it, let it float away, or tears would flow. Don't do it, don't sink into sorrow, don't succumb! A vehement kick at the snow. Sorrow was a luxury she couldn't afford, not if she were to help Mahafny and Saam reach their goal.

Sorrow . . . Saam. Sorrow . . . Bard and M'wa. Bard was dead, and she dared not sorrow. No, keep her wits sharp, note the landscape, gauge the path ahead, determine where problems might arise. The trail was good thus far, worn and packed enough by occasional traffic on the lower slopes to make walking easy. The fresh powder scattered in front of her feet. This was, she suspected, a secondary route to Roland d'Arnot's arborfer nursery and, with luck, they'd ascend to the higher slopes before anyone intercepted them. No way to become lost, their way obvious, edged by mounded berry bushes, a few frail twigs making dark maze patterns against the snow. Overhead, an occasional birch tilted across the track, always high enough so she needn't duck. Firs and spruce dotted the shoulder of the trail, some young, but most thick-trunked yet not over-tall from their constant battle against the winds. Their dense clusters served as windbreaks, and the higher they climbed, the worse the winds would blow. What those higher stretches of trail were like she couldn't guess, but the scent of snow in the air taunted her. Gaetan had been right about last night's weather, the barge lightly dusted early this morning, but a good five centimeters here. More on the way? Likely the peaks snagged the clouds, shook loose the snow they contained!

*"Pw'eek? Does anyone miss us yet? Has anyone realized we're gone?"* Despite Pw'eek's and Diccon's presence—and that was near enough to make her feel reasonably whole and secure—an obscure loneliness burdened her. Mayhap it came from not glimpsing a soul ahead of her, the powder pristine except for occasional chains of small animal tracks. And unless she purposely looked back, it didn't seem anyone toiled behind her. Emptiness resounded in her ears, Saam's wailing had ceased. A good sign or bad? *"I hope Mama and Papa aren't too upset when they find out. Or GrammaDama and Aunt Jacobia."*

Pw'eek's face appeared, framed between the pony's ears, her lovely round face with its split coloration above the white mustache. Ah, those limpid eyes, always swimming with apprehension—no wonder that two delicate shadings of green were needed to express the enormity of such woes. **"Beloved, haven't you been listening? You or Diccon?"**

*"Listening to what? To whom?"* What was the ghatta

talking about? Lady above, she hadn't even heard a peep out of Harry since she'd 'spoken him, well-aware what that must be costing him. He was a loyal cousin. It felt good that at least someone—two someones, in fact—kenned their whereabouts. She shouldn't discount Gaetan, after all.

With an agile leap, Pw'eek sprang clear of the pony and landed on the packed track, galloping ahead so Willy wouldn't be forced to halt. **"The very air's been buzzing with word of our absence—haven't you been listening? Resonants and ghatti call back and forth, inquiring as to our whereabouts. Isn't it nice they all care so much about us?"** Overwhelmed, she licked her white ruff.

*"You haven't answered, have you?"* For a moment her stomach gave a quesy flutter. *"Have Diccon or Kwee been listening? Responded?"* Bless the Lady neither Auntie Mahafny nor Harrap were Resonants, couldn't catch a breath of mindspeech unless it were directed right at them. But Parm? Oh, dear, he'd launch into a monologue with any soul who 'spoke him! Have a high time chatting away about this or that, inadvertently revealing their location!

Pw'eek determinedly plopped herself in the center of the path, her mouth prim. **" 'Course he hasn't! Shame on you! He loves Saam, realizes how crucial this journey is!"**

An abrupt tap-tap-tap, tappity-tap cut the stillness, and Jenneth twitched, jerking the pony's lead. Ah, there! Black with a crest touched with white and red, its thick ivory bill hammered against the battered scaliness of a pine's red-brown bark—a tipper-tapper drilling for insects.

"But has anyone discovered where we are? Why we're here?"

**"Well . . . nooo."** But the beast sounded distinctly miserable. She wasn't telling an untruth, but something obviously bothered the ghatta. Too short and clipped a "no" made Jen nervous, as did Pw'eek's equally drawn-out answer, as if the dear wanted time to decide on precisely what to say.

Stripping off a glove, she stroked Pw'eek's head, tickling the orange patch over her right eye, delivering a tantalizing scratch behind each earring to remind her of the further delights awaiting a loving Bond. *"Hurry and tell me before your bottom freezes."*

**"It's just that we can't always keep Saam quiet."** With a touch of coyness, she thrust her ear against Jenneth's hand, sliding her head back and forth when Jenneth's fingers remained still. **"Parm's doing his best to tamp down on his mindcries, but it isn't easy. Some of the older, wiser ghatti may have put together the bits and pieces, may suspect, but they've been very restrained about sharing those suspicions with their Bonds."** She stared fixedly at her white paws as she finished. No wonder the ghatta radiated embarrassment; she and Pw'eek had had it drummed into them, as did all Novie Seekers, that such selective sharing was improper, likely to undermine their Bond. **"They want to give Saam time and space to reach his own decision. Mahafny's efforts may or may not be right, but they're unwilling to pass judgment."**

That was the way of it: Seekers determined the truth, but they never passed judgment. A reminder that she, too, had no right to judge Mahafny. Making her see the truth was another matter. Straightening, she pulled on her glove, listening as the others closed the gap. Might as well stop here, have a cold lunch. *"I know. None of us are sure—except Aunt Mahafny."* Grabbing a piece of snow crust that her boot had cracked free, she side-armed it up the trail, and as it skittered and jumped, Pw'eek sprang after it as if possessed. Uncle Parse always swore that the easiest way to cheer up a gloomy ghatta was to give it something to chase after, be it truth or a crumpled piece of paper. Except best be careful when they caught it—and they always did, sooner or later. Then one had to deal with the consequences.

✤

# PART
# THREE

✤

Theo drummed his long fingers against his stomach, both out of contentment at the four utterly delectable desserts he'd packed away, and—though he'd not consciously admitted it—from nerves at venturing so deep beneath the castle in these narrow, dim passageways. It was all so much more *enclosed,* confining than he'd envisioned, the raw smell of the stone at his side and overhead. Even the man-made passages offered little solace since they'd not been made to his measure. Come to think of it, he'd have to order a specially-made coffin—or more likely, Holly'd have that task—because otherwise his feet would overhang the end! He didn't fancy being buried in two pieces.

As the tallest he followed last, praying the others would point out any obstacles, but still found himself whanging his head on some looming projection or beam the lantern light never quite illuminated. Or, more honestly, because he was constantly staring at where he planted his feet, afraid of falling headlong. A muffled snort erupted as another cobweb languorously drooped across his cheek, its strands tickling his neck. "Argh!" and the hair on the back of his neck prickled at its ghost-light touch.

**"Come on, let's catch up!"** Even Khim didn't sound overly sympathetic, more bent on exploring, indulging her curiosity.

*"Easy for you to say. You can see in the dark."* He wasn't lost, he wasn't lost! There—just ahead—dull spheres of lantern light, murmurous voices, mostly soft, but sometimes echoing and carrying. Now what antique trash or treasure had they uncovered?

Exploring beneath the old castle with Ezequiel had sounded mysterious and inviting at the time, but he'd had no inkling he'd react like this, convinced he'd been en-

tombed, planted down here in a space far too small for
him. Seemingly solid walls leaned inward, ceilings that had
stood the test of ages hunkered lower in the blink of an
eye, the castle prepared to crush him like a bug! Ridiculous! Arras Muscadeine negotiated the passageways uncon-
cernedly, and while he lacked Theo's lofty stature, the man
was tall, and boasted a far broader build. So, too, did Holly,
for that matter. **"I heard that! I'm going to tell, I'm going
to tell!"** P'roul chanted ahead of him. Her taunting offered
a moment of delicious indecision for his own Bondmate—
should she or should she not join in teasing him?

*"Please,"* he 'spoke, willing to cravenly beg, *"just . . .
just don't!"* How unbearable if both ghattas began to rag at
him. Worst of all, Holly might catch wind of his cowardice,
discover his increasing anxiety and insist on going back.
He'd be the laughingstock of this late-night excursion. Oh,
Ezequiel, Arras, Harry, and King Eadwin were mannerly,
kind souls, all of them, but they'd be hard-pressed not to
relish a laugh at his expense.

"F–found s–something g–good?" he called, hoping his
voice sounded steady and sincere in its interest. And at
least it alerted them that he loitered back here—loath to
advance, loath to retreat—should anyone wonder, happen
to care. If he died down here, they'd have a mighty difficult
time threading his corpse through all the bends and curves,
up and down the narrow passages, especially once rigor
mortis set in.

**"It's all right, beloved. Stop being so gloomy! I promise
I'll thrash P'roul later, make her pay for her teasing.
Though you *do* present a tempting, though narrow target
at times."** Ah, so Khim hadn't deserted him after all! **"Of
course not! I'm right with you. If you take a quick step
forward, you'll tread on my tail. So please don't."**

Palm sliding down the wall for balance, he knelt beside
Khim, her presence making him marginally calmer. Yes, if
he could remain folded in half, the ceiling was very nearly
high enough, not threatening at all. Rummaging in his
pocket for the candle stub he'd been issued, he scraped a
lucifer against the rough-hewn wall. He'd not dared attempt
it before, afraid his shaking hand would extinguish the lucifer before the flame even grazed the wick. And if he *had*
managed to light it, the candle's jittering dance would have

revealed his nerves. There! Now that he could gaze at Khim, see more than a shadowy form, he'd survive this special treat!

Raucous whistling bounced off the walls, sour notes battering his ears as it came closer, but an indication that someone was moving down the passageway toward him. The off-tune whistler was bound to be Harry, and Theo held the candle higher to signal his position. Wasn't very tuneful, wasn't even a whistle sometimes, more a whoffle of air. Still, it was good of Harry to alert him that he'd turned back. The boy was lucky to whistle at all, what with the scrapes on his chin, that split lip from his fall in Bertillon yesterday. Theo winced, recollecting the numerous times in his own youth when his lanky, spindly limbs had betrayed him, tripping and tangling him until he sorted them out—and always under the eyes of someone he'd yearned to impress. Amazingly enough, he was coordinated now, though casual bystanders rarely believed it. By dint of painful practice at simple, and then increasingly complex exercises, he'd learned to manage his limbs. The trick was to begin any action a half-beat ahead of normally-sized people so that the messages from his brain had time to reach his extremities!

Candle steadied on his knee, Theo watched Harry's shadow-shape advance, features becoming more distinct, a gleam of belt buckle, buttons flaring like miniature suns. And at his side padded Hru'rul, King Eadwin's Bondmate, an imposing ghatt with a thick, luxuriant ruff and large, tufted ears. But, alas, no tail—a bird of prey's meager trophy had been snatched from Hru'rul in ghattenhood, his eyes barely open.

With a disconsolate sigh Harry slumped cross-legged in the passageway, lolling against the wall while Hru'rul piled on his lap, vigorously shaking each paw to dislodge the dust. Rolling his eyes at Theo, Harry gave a smile that faded before it could fully form. Sitting on his heels, Theo leaned closer in silent camaraderie. "W–what's the m–matter? No m–magnificent d–discoveries? N–no gold, no g–gems? No arti–facts of the d–distant past?" The boy's attitude puzzled him. Harry'd been gung ho to explore down here when he'd first heard what Ezequiel had planned for Theo and Holly, had begged the king to come

along. Now he acted like a world-weary traveler who'd seen
the sights a million times, could find no new excitement
under the sun.

"What?" Harry jerked as if leaving a trance, and Hru'rul
resettled himself with a long-suffering expression, his hindquarters safe on the floor. "Oh . . . no. No gold and gems,
that is." Slipping a hand in a pocket, he drew out something
whitish brown and displayed it on his palm. "This, so far.
An old penknife, see? It's got the royal crest on it. King
Eadwin said 'twas mine to keep." Trading the candle for
the knife, Theo examined it, working at opening the blade.

"N–needs s–some oil. N–not rusty, exactly, b–but old, s–
stiff." No matter how he tried, it wouldn't budge when he
sank his nail into the groove that gave purchase for unhinging the blade.

"Oil," Harry repeated, as if the word, the very concept,
were foreign, his own fingers busy peeling melted wax from
the candle, working it between his fingers, molding it over
a knuckle. "Theo, what . . ." Head still bent, he strove to
sound indifferent, more engrossed in pinching at the candle.
"What do you do when you've learned a . . . well, a secret,
let's say. . . . Well, not exactly a secret," he amended, attempting to disguise the obvious, "well, something no one
else knows. When, mayhap, someone else should?"

"Sh–should know?" Theo balanced the closed penknife
between thumb and middle finger, turning it on its axis with
his other hand. "A–are you honor–b–bound to k–keep the
se–secret? W–will it h–harm s–someone if you don't re–reveal it?" Confusion and woe shrouded Harry's face as he
silently nodded. This wasn't the sort of conversation he'd
expected from Harry; the lad possessed a good, logical head
on his shoulders, wasn't prone to chase off on mindless
schemes the way so many lads were—as he'd been at that
age. How many times had Holly drummed reality into his
head—and anywhere else she could pummel him? Besides,
how many deep, dark secrets could Harry possibly be
privy to?

Now Harry prodded the candle with the lucifer end he'd
salvaged from the floor, puncturing the wax, seemingly intent on placing each puncture precisely so. "I mean, you
and Holly and I and the rest kept it secret from Papa,

from Auntie Doyce, and Uncle Jenret about the exploding custables, didn't we?"

"Y–yes, well, we d–did," Theo agreed. And he and Holly had been doubly vigilant after that episode, unsure if it had been an accident or an outright attack. "B–but the ex–plosion had already h–happened. If t–telling m–meant *n–not* having an ex–plosion, th–that w–would have been another s–story. One th–that we'd h–have t–told to s–save people from p–pain and suffering, mayhap even d–death!"

"Yes, but, don't you see, if the 'happening' is inevitable—" Harry's eyes darkened with sad longing as he turned toward Theo, the candle illuminating his face from below. "I gave my solemn *word* that—"

"Come on, you two! We've found it again! That trunk Ezequiel told us about. And he's got a key he thinks might work! Who knows what treasure may be locked inside!" From the sound of his voice, even King Eadwin had yielded to wishful thinking.

"Most likely someone's dirty laundry from ages past!" scoffed Arras Muscadeine, and at the heartening sound of his father's voice, Harry slid Hru'rul off his lap and hurtled toward the comfort of the light and his father's voice. It took Theo somewhat longer to realign his limbs and follow. *"Any idea what that was all about?"* Head down, shoulders protectively hunched, Theo hurried not to be left behind.

**"Mayhap."** Anytime Khim sounded so blandly innocent, Theo took note, sure something was afoot. **"But not everything that happens is *our* business—at least not Seeker business."** Now what was *that* supposed to mean—don't be nosy?

❖

Armed with a rag, Ezequiel knelt and handed his lantern to King Eadwin, who obediently lofted it, paralleling Ezequiel's gestures until the light fully illuminated the lock. From behind came Holly's hushed gasp as the beams reflected off the silvery-gray surface of the flat-topped trunk, mantling it with a luminescent, faintly otherworldly aura that seemed to expand, absorb the storage alcove's remaining space. Clearly that brandy-sauced second dessert had turned him fanciful. A reluctant, admiring "aah!" escaped from Arras Muscadeine, and Eadwin's mouth quirked as he winked at Ezequiel, neither ever expecting to hear the Defense Lord succumb to involuntary rapture.

Although he'd removed some of the dust when he'd first found the trunk, Ezequiel cleaned it more thoroughly, paying special attention to the lock. No sense jamming years of grime into its mechanism. Almost sheepishly he retrieved a feather stashed in his breast pocket and stroked with the tip, then picked delicately with the quill end. Such scrupulous attention might well be for naught, the key not fit, the trunk prove empty. Well, so be it. He'd not guaranteed any surprises, the discovery of unexpected riches, or meaningful mementoes of the past. Over his shoulder he inquired, "Harry, would you do the honors? See if the key fits?"

Easing into the pale circle of light, Harry held out his hand, unsteady with excitement or nerves. Still, let the lad enjoy himself, claim a part in this adventure—an adventure in housekeeping. Or, A Place for Everything, and Everything in Its Place—the problem with the underground storerooms and passageways was recollecting precisely where things had been stashed or stored. Would Ignacio have chuckled at this mock-ceremonious moment, fraught with mystery? The old man might have cleared up the puzzle simply by searching his capacious memory, but that would have denied them the thrill of discovery.

Fumbling with the key, Harry crouched and jabbed it at the lock, missing on his first attempt, the key metallically protesting as it scraped across and away, etching a thin line in its wake. Flushing, lips tightening, Harry side-glanced at him, then stabilized the key with both hands and slid it neatly into the lock. "Fits!" he crowed, but didn't yet attempt to turn it, desirous of prolonging the suspense. Ezequiel couldn't blame him—anticipation was half the joy.

"May not do a thing beyond that," Eadwin admonished, a hand on Harry's shoulder as he brought the lantern nearer. The king's hand wasn't entirely steady either. "May be cut for entirely different tumblers. Looks right, though." Unwilling to shatter the silence, an almost reverential one, yet unable to resist, he mouthed the soft fanfare of imaginary trumpets. "Ta-ta-ta-Ta-ta-TA!" Eyes screwed shut, lips molding some silent plea or wish, Harry turned the key.

Nothing. "Try turning it the other way," Eadwin suggested, unwilling to give up, concede defeat.

The key turned halfway, then met resistance, and Ezequiel laid his hand over Harry's to see if, together, they could turn it farther without snapping it in the lock. With a drawn-out, grating protest that set everyone's teeth on edge, the lock popped open.

Eyes aglitter, body raptly tense, the king was completely caught up in the moment, unself-consciously enjoying himself, and Ezequiel was pleased this impromptu expedition had temporarily banished his worries. Unfeigned enjoyment struck at rare intervals when the weight of a kingdom and its people rode on one's shoulders.

"Mademoiselle Holly, if you please! Let your lily-white hand be the first to lift the lid, and reveal to us . . ." a dramatic pause, "the debris of times past? Dirty laundry that evaded the sentence of the royal washtubs? The grandiose poems of a previous Marchmont ruler, strained of rhyme and racked of rhythm? Even worse, the bathetic verses of a love-besotted fool? Who knows what treasure troves await us?" Ezequiel had equally entered into the spirit of the thing, hadn't realized his own gift for melodrama.

The lantern cast a subtle citrine aura around Holly, transforming her into a more delicate, ethereal being, as if she'd materialized from another time and place, another world. No, hardly their ancestors' world with its brave-hearted, strong women, intellectual equals or superiors to their mates, but from some mythic past of ancient legend, where fragile, diffident females swooned at brave men's feet, utterly dependent on them for safety, security, and love. Safety, security, love—wasn't that what *he* wanted to end his loneliness, the isolation surrounding him despite the ranks of servants at his beck and call? And Eadwin as well, still unmarried and still lacking an heir, other than his cousin, Nakum. Safety, security, and love—to unstintingly give those as one's greatest gift, to be the blessed recipient, in turn. Well, the swooning at his feet part was a bit much, he acknowledged. Better yet to have a partner at one's shoulder!

Would Holly ever consider . . . ? No, best not to even think it. After all, Eadwin appeared attentive as well, and it would never do to purloin the affections of someone the

king had his eye upon as a possible mate. The kingdom
came first, and the kingdom needed heirs. His duty was to
ensure the king's and the kingdom's well-being above and
beyond his own petty wants.

This—and more—flashed through his mind as Holly gingerly took Harry's place before the trunk. But as she placed
a hand on the lid, Hru'rul forced himself between her and
the trunk, the fur along his spine spiking, a growl resonating from deep in his chest. What? Jealousy? Unlikely, since
the two ghattas—Holly's P'roul and Theo's Khim—didn't
react as if Hru'rul were threatening or challenging Holly,
though they both acted ill at ease, bodies tense and tails
atwitch.

"Yoo-hoo! Hello! Is anyone down here?" Lady help
him! Romain-Laurent sounded like a simpering old lady!
A rising wave of aggravation quenched his moody romanti-
cism of moments before. Bad enough Romain-Laurent had
"invaded" the castle with his relentlessly objective ways,
counting and calculating, spouting about systems and meth-
odology, but now he'd invaded Ezequiel's own "private domain," the shadow world of half-remembered corridors,
hidden rooms, and concealed byways that honeycombed
the castle's lower levels. Places that should only be accessed
by a royal chamberlain or work crews. Rising stiffly, consciously investing himself with the pompous superiority that
his job sometimes required to put meddlers in their places,
Ezequiel marched to the alcove entrance, taking Theo's
candle and holding it overhead.

"We're down here, Charpentier! What do you want?"

Fussily neat, as if no dust or cobwebs would ever consider clinging to him, Romain-Laurent bustled along the
passageway, avidly glancing right and left, methodically
compiling a mental inventory, and Ezequiel resented him
for it. "Ho! I'd no idea so much usable space existed down
here! You should have told me earlier, Dunay," playfully
chiding him with an admonitory tap to his shoulder. "This
could prove useful for any number of projects I've had in
the back of my mind." Thrusting a cloth tape into
Ezequiel's hand, he backed off, unreeling the measure,
bending close to check the markings. "Is the king down
here as well?" Cocking his head, he sketched a quick dia-

gram on a scrap of paper, murmuring figures under his breath.

Somehow the others had spilled into the corridor, an audience to his confrontation with Romain-Laurent. He was good-looking in a tightly-buttoned, finicky way, as if every hair on his head been assigned its exact location within the ranks. Not to mention the affectation of those thigh-length hosen that he'd so reluctantly donned as part of his formal chamberlain regalia while Ignacio was alive. Except *his* hosen never ruckled, always tautly covered Romain-Laurent's trim calves with nary a run or catch. "It's a bit late, Charpentier. Couldn't sleep? Lonely?"

"Something like that." Damn the man for always sounding so agreeable; it was impossible to provoke a rise from him, and even insults rolled off him, never riled him. "It was just that I had an interesting idea, truly forward-looking . . . and when I went 'round to see if anyone was awake, would listen to me refine my plan, I couldn't locate either you or the king." He beamed impartially at all of them, apparently unsurprised to find them gathered here. "When an exceptional idea strikes, you shouldn't wait till morning to polish it—you'll have forgotten the details by then."

"So keep pencil and paper by your bedside," Arras growled, tugging at his mustache.

"Oh, I do, I do! I recommend that everyone should—so simple a measure and yet so invaluable!" Now Romain-Laurent was edging into the alcove, brightly expectant despite the lateness of the evening. Actually, early morning now, Ezequiel judged. "I'd heard how you wandered down here at odd times of the night—very impressive not to cut into your work time, very laudable—so I figured I'd take a chance, see what was down here. Who was down here, more exactly. After all, the door was ajar. During the day it's always locked." He smote his forehead. "Oh, foolish me! You aren't *hiding* something down here, are you?" A sudden boyish glee to his tone, rather than one of censure. Mayhap being the boy wonder, the unacknowledged Lord of the unfledged Ministry of Management wasn't all it was cracked up to be. Mayhap Romain-Laurent was lonely, too, worked overlong days to stave off that loneliness—just as he did.

Somehow they gave way before his enthusiasm, parting to let him pass and view the trunk. "As I live and breathe!" Holly rolled her eyes at the quaint phrase. "It's brushed al–alu–mini–um! I do believe, do believe it is! Remarkable! Those were the days!" Bending almost reverentially, Romain-Laurent breathed on the surface, polished the condensation with his sleeve. "Don't see much of it now. What's within?" And suiting his actions to his words, he heaved up the trunk lid without waiting for an answer, let alone permission. Ezequiel brusquely stoppered a cry at such innocently efficient sacrilege. Any sense of ceremony, anticipation had been destroyed. Again Hru'rul growled a low warning, forcing himself between Eadwin and the open trunk.

Wads of old paper greeted their eyes, while the aroma of oily rags assaulted their noses, somehow stronger, more intense than expected, their petroleum-based odor sealed in tomb-tight for all these forgotten years. Atop the crumpled paper and rags lay a note, its top edge ragged where it had been ripped from a pad. A printed form of some kind, the paper yellowed and oil-spotted, the type still discernible, though, as Holly raised it on the palms of her hands and presented it to Eadwin at his nod. Gathering around, no one—Ezequiel included—could make much of it. A checklist of some sort, it contained such categories as **Item** followed by a series of boxes with a name or code number beside each one; **Reason for Return** announced the next header, and its subsequent list made some sense: **Wrong Item; Wrong Size; Defective (Please Explain)**, followed by several blank lines. **Disposition of Item** read the final header, followed by boxes for such choices as **Returned; Repaired; Refitted; Discarded;** and **Destroyed (Please Indicate How/When/Where).**

"Disposition of item? Ill-tempered, do you think?" quipped Eadwin, but while they'd perused the list, Romain-Laurent had been rooting through the packing litter, giving a shout of triumph as he hauled forth a cylinder about half a meter in length and mayhap twenty centimeters in diameter, a bit larger around than a dessert plate.

"Five or six more, down deeper," Romain-Laurent announced. "I can feel them! A souvenir for each of us." It clearly struck him then that he'd overstepped his bounds, trodden in matters not his to decide. "If His Highness agrees, of course. After all, they *are* royal property, not souvenirs."

"Charpentier, enough!" Still engrossed with the list Holly patiently held, Eadwin frowned and brought the lantern closer. "As near as I can make out, this handwritten scrawl at the bottom says," he cleared his throat, " 'Detonate out of range immediately. Highly unstable!' Can't read the signature, but the title looks like Chief Engineer."

Harry, in his eagerness to see what Romain-Laurent had retrieved, had wormed closer; Ezequiel envisioning the two of them battling over the cylinder, two boys each coveting the same new toy. Indeed, Charpentier had wrapped his arms around it, cradling the cylinder against his chest despite its greasy surface, one hand patting it as if it needed soothing, toying with first one button or switch and then another, the way a parent distracts a fractious child by playing with its fingers or toes.

Without warning miniature red and green lights began flashing in a quickening pattern along its length, while another line of green lights turned one by one first to amber and then to strident red, no longer flashing now, but intensely glowing, pulsating deep within. They cast an unearthly glow on Charpentier's hand, outlining each finger in crimson.

Despite Romain-Laurent's protective embrace, Harry squinted at the base, finger tracing a string of letters around the circumference. "Peri-odic Linear Ultra Mensura—"

"Plumb!" Eadwin spat the word with an intensity that sliced like a knife. "Plumb!" he repeated with loathing, just as a tinny, otherworldly voice, neither male nor female, announced with measured emphasis, "Preparing to self-destruct! Detonating in two minutes. Counting: One minute, fifty-nine . . ."

♣

For an instant all was totally still, totally silent as the disembodied voice continued its count, everyone entrapped in a past when Plumbs—originally planted across the land to inventory this new world's resources, pinpoint the locations of ores and specific geological deposits—had turned rogue,

wreaking havoc on this new planet, this new home their
ancestors claimed across space and time. The voice grew
deeper and still the mechanical voice matter-of-factly
counted downward, like a child chosen as "it" for a game
of hide and seek. At the end of the game, Holly remembered, came the warning phrase, "Ready or not, here I
COME!" A shudder rippled through her. This was *not* the
time to passively wait, not while a slim chance remained
that something could be done, something—mayhap someone—salvaged from the disaster unfolding in front of their
disbelieving eyes.

Already P'roul acted upon on her thoughts, transmitting
them to Khim and Theo and Hru'rul, who'd sunk his fangs
into the leg of Eadwin's trousers, tugging the king backward as hard as he could, twenty-five kilos of ghatti straining for all he was worth. It flashed through Holly's mind
that if he didn't succeed, likely Eadwin's body would be
found sans pants, and they wouldn't have been blown off
in the explosion!

According him the respect a tested soldier deserved,
Holly didn't worry about Arras Muscadeine's reaction; already he grimly struggled to wrest the stainless steel cylinder, the Plumb, from Romain-Laurent's convulsive grip, the
two welded together, mayhap coupled for eternity by fate.
Propelling Harry toward the doorway, Ezequiel used his
free hand to snag the king's waistband and join on Hru'rul's
side in the tug-of-war, while Eadwin protested that they get
Harry clear.

And Theo, her dear cousin, already waited, bent and patient at one end of the trunk, ready to lift once she grasped
the opposing handle. Slamming the lid and snapping the
lock, she nodded and they heaved in unison, the trunk rising between them. Lady have mercy, which way should
they run, which route to choose to move the trunk's deadly
cargo as far distant as possible from the detonating Plumb?
If they guessed wrong, they'd have ringside seats for the
chain of explosions that would follow.

But Arras took the decision into his own capable hands,
his fist traversing a compact arc that resoundingly concluded on the point of Romain-Laurent's jaw, both his features and grip slackening as Arras scooped up the Plumb.
"Run right, Holly!" he shouted and began sprinting left-

ward as she and Theo spun right, the direction that Ezequiel, Harry, and Eadwin had taken . . . or so she prayed.

Running full tilt now, the trunk awkwardly banging and bruising hips and thighs. Bent at knees and neck to avoid hitting his head, Theo's cramped posture barely slowed them, though the contorted position must be hell on him. "Move, move, move!" she commanded the shadowy figures racing ahead of her, wanting them as far away as possible, needing a clear path for their burden. If Eadwin stopped, insisted on helping, she promised herself she'd deck him as efficiently as Arras had Romain-Laurent: Two minutes— sixty seconds to a minute. A minute was roughly the length of time the average person could hold his breath and not feel discomfort—or so she'd read. Not exactly something she'd attempt at the moment, wasn't sure if she'd drawn a breath since the countdown began. The unnaturally precise voice sounded fainter, further distant, what was it chanting now, what number short of doom? "Forty-nine, forty-eight . . ."

"Damnation!" Assuming Arras could rid himself of the Plumb and escape, find some place to take shelter, they were all accounted for except for Romain-Laurent. "Theo!" Already she was heaving the trunk upward with both hands and her knee, straining to hoist it on Theo's scrawny back. "Charpentier!" But with a surge of strength, he jerked the trunk onto her own back.

"Can't carry it and stay low enough!" he gasped as he propelled her forward. Impossible to turn, take a farewell glance, but in her mind's eye she could see Khim and Theo sprinting, see those gangling limbs pumping, an arm protectively raised above his head to ward off the low ceiling beams. Well, she'd bet on Theo before and never lost a wager. Please, Lady, let her not lose this one either! Because what she'd lose was a beloved cousin, closer to her heart than her own brothers.

With her next labored breath the earth commenced rocking and pitching, rattling her between the walls like a pea in a dried pod. Dust, dirt clogged the air, shifting and eddying as a roiling, echoing Ka-RUMP and a rush of compressed air crashed down the corridors to meet her. Unprepared, she slammed hard on one knee, the trunk

lurching off its perch. The last painful sensation she felt
was a corner of the trunk hitting like a hammer blow to
her temple.

❖

Chest heaving, brow covered in sweat, Nakum sat bolt upright in bed, grabbing at nothing that was there, convinced
he must rescue something. What? His mind churned
blankly, and gradually he let his arms fall, clutching his
thighs for reassurance. Not a dream, but a nightmare, a
ghastly devastation that had invaded this, his private space,
his sanctuary. First that *thing,* that nasty little trickster
creeping 'round when he least expected it—and now this!
Were the two related? Had one caused the other? The very
earth was crying out its pain, the waters of the world chuckling with glee at their chance to invade new territory. If
the trickster being had contrived *that* simulacrum of his
world, it was *not* amusing.

But as he sat hunched, heart still pounding, picking mind-
lessly at the furred covers, he slowly perceived that he
*hadn't* dreamed, that something horrific *had* been loosed
upon the earth, and he'd been caught napping in more ways
than one. From everywhere and nowhere a muted "tsk-
tsk" filled the ovoid room, just as if his grandmother, Addawanna, or Callis, even, were chiding him, so like did it
sound. Cautious, he trailed a hand to the earthen floor,
only to recoil at what it told him with that fleeting touch.
What was this, what was happening to his world! How
could such disorder and discord find him here?

Steeling himself, he swung his legs clear of the bed, letting his feet brush down, prepared to jerk away if necessary. Mayhap he *was* still trapped in the throes of a dream?
Possible, certainly, except he rarely dreamed—his conscious
and unconscious thoughts one and the same, always attuned
to nature and its ways, to the land, the earth and its doings,
to his precious trees. His trees, his arborfer!—and Nakum
leaped to his feet.

Pain shot through him, catapulting him to his hands and
knees, and he registered an all-encompassing desolation
he'd never before experienced. The earth, the *earth* was

passing a message, crying out for help! Within that he could sense that his infant trees up here on the mountaintop were fine, as were the larger nurseries lower down, though even they murmured and muttered at the baneful sensations coursing through their sensitive roots. Relieved but still shaken, he pressed his hands to his temples, fighting to decipher the full import of the discordant messages battering at his inner being. Each message had a different, urgent plea, but all contained a similar refrain: he must venture forth, hasten from his mountain fastness to succor them. And beyond that, every particle of his soul cried out that Eadwin needed him, and for Eadwin's sake he'd gladly go.

Dressing without lighting the lamp, he hastily gathered a packet of food, his bow and quiver, a few small odds and ends, and checked that his pouch was securely strung around his neck. No, it would never do to be severed from his earth-bond at a time like this. Thankfully he'd slept with it beneath his pillow, or he might not have waked in time!

But as he stood at the entryway, steeling himself for what lay ahead of him, he stopped short, achingly aware of another, conflicting tug. Saam! Saam and Mahafny and the others were approaching, struggling nearer, and time ran short for Saam. Could he, should he desert Saam—even if he was unsure he could do what Mahafny wished? Forcing himself still, he listened with all his heart and mind, knuckles white around his earth-bond, striving to decide which cause was most urgent. Damn, why couldn't Callis be here to at least lend a hand! This was all too immense, too many disruptions jumbling at his feet, tugging at him from all directions! Nakum, to whom the passage of time felt timeless, seamless—days flowing into octs, octs into octants, octants into octads—desperately needed more time!

One thing at a time, but which first? A precious though short span of life remained for Saam, and by normal standards, Mahafny and the others still had much traveling ahead of them. While he, Nakum, could run with the wind, skim across snowy scarps and icy ravines as if they were a grassy, level meadow. Down to Sidonie and Eadwin first, see what tasks awaited him there, decide if he could accom-

plish them or must concede defeat. Then back to his beloved mountain peak . . . and Saam.

If he'd read things aright, Addawanna would be along
soon, and that might buy some additional time. Time! It
fled with every hammering heartbeat! While Addawanna
didn't boast the concentrated powers that he and Callis
commanded—too deeply interested in too many things to
bother with more than mere fragments of power—she still
possessed her own uniquely clear-sighted vision and nimble
abilities. No doubt she'd have his invisible nuisance house-
broken and performing tricks by the time he returned!

Besides, he harbored an intensely selfish, personal reason for reaching Eadwin's side as soon as he could. Were
Eadwin to die, *he,* Nakum, would be crowned King of
Marchmont, the next direct heir to the throne. And he'd
do anything to escape that fate! As would the people of
Marchmont, he was sure! Erakwa and thrones were anti-
thetical, impossible to encompass within the same thought.

"Saam, hold on, old boy! Give me a chance to say good-
bye, if that's what it's to be." And he was out the door
and lightly running down the trail in the moonlight, his
breath vaporous behind him. The thought of Callis's slaithe
was tempting—ah, that sleek birchbark shape with its trim
white arborfer runners—but he bypassed its snow-shrouded
form without a backward glance. No need for it, not when
he could make better time on his own two feet. And when
the twins arrived with Mahafny and Saam and Harrap,
they'd enjoy trying it out—certainly more than Doyce and
Khar had!

♣

At first Mahafny assumed she merely registered the normal,
throbbing ache of an overtaxed body as she lay wakeful
beneath the tarp, the familiar pains of muscles protesting,
each heartbeat echoing and enhancing the hurt. Restlessly
she stirred, wondering if she could rise without disturbing
Saam and Jenneth too much. Saam slept the sleep of the
dead, thanks to the medicine she'd dosed him with, the line
of his mouth lax, but Pw'eek, protectively curled around
him, a foreleg tossed over his shoulder, gave her a fretful

glance, seemingly as twitchy as she felt. Behind her she could hear that the ponies hadn't settled either, chuffing and stamping, halters creaking as they bobbed their heads. Propping herself on one hand, she scanned their pitifully simple night camp, checking for the cause of the ponies' wakefulness, but saw nothing out of the ordinary. Two tarps hung from evergreens, their edges pinned down with chunks of snow and, midway between them, a small fire burned, reflecting what heat it might inside. More the pretense of heat than the actuality, and she shivered. Well, whatever ailed the beasts came from within, just as her own worries and aches did.

No! There it was again! It wasn't her aging body's protests that had wakened her—whatever it was came from without, not within. Vibrations rolling up through her arm, her hip, invading her body. *"What is it? Do you know?"* Whether Pw'eek would answer, she wasn't sure, the calico too bashful, too self-conscious about revealing her woes to the world. Much as she loved her niece, Jenneth's Bond was a tiresome little beast, constantly craving reassurance.

**"Don't know!"** Fur prickling, Pw'eek's head was in constant motion, twisting to locate the danger. **"Don't like it, hateful feeling—going to wake Jenneth!"** On her feet now, straddling Saam, Pw'eek looked ready to bolt, but Mahafny doubted she'd willingly be separated from Jenneth's side, brave beyond all bounds when courage was called for.

*"No, don't. Let her sleep. I'll get up, check around. Might as well anyway, the way I feel."* And that was a fact; her own secret drug enabled her to do without rest, in fact, made it well-nigh impossible to sleep in more than brief catnaps when her body finally cried for respite. If she continued futilely twitching and tossing under the blankets, she'd undoubtedly wake Jenneth—and Saam. Besides, the vibrations were curious—was there some logical reason for them?

Clumsily easing from under the blankets, she conscientiously tucked them tight to conserve the warmth she'd abandoned. Lucky for her she'd not stripped off her boots tonight to let them dry, let her feet breathe, but her hands weren't strong enough, and Harrap had been preoccupied, had forgotten to help her. Still keenly aware of the strange vibrations—almost undulating now, an ebb and flow to

248                    *Gayle Greeno*

them, first stronger, then weaker—she folded one leg in front of her, learning heavily on her knee as she rose. At least her knee didn't hurt any more than the rest of her.

Curious if the vibrations were confined to one spot, she paced away from the fire, but the rumbling still tickled deep in her bones, like standing next to a frozen road trafficked by an incessant stream of quarry drays. Now what had made her think of that? Staring at the murky sky that blanketed them, she wondered how long she'd dozed, whether it was nearer morn or midnight. It had warmed during the night, the snow releasing a misty, milky cloud that occluded the sky, the stars, even the Lady Moon. Sometimes, when she looked just right, a twisting tendril fingered its way through the air, and she exhaled gently through her mouth until a miniature plume climbed in its wake.

Ah, the tremors had faded! Well, while she was up, she might as well toss some wood on the fire, watch to make sure it caught. Then she'd decide if she could sleep anymore. But as she limped toward the fire, a grinding, rumbling wave of motion swarmed through the earth beneath her feet, and she swayed drunkenly, the world around her improbably flexing, rising and falling, evergreens swaying, creaking. Earthquake? Now a shift, a loud crack sundered the air, followed by growling sounds as one wall of her world began to collapse, pieces of it tumbling at her! A pony screamed, high and thin, and she joined her voice with the beast's. Dear Lady, an avalanche?

"Up! Up!" she screamed, grabbing a tarp and jerking it clear, praying the onslaught of cold air would rouse Diccon and Harrap. As she spun to dash toward the tarp sheltering Jenneth, Pw'eek, and Saam, desperate to scoop up Saam, a chunk of snow big as a washtub bounced crazily at her and bowled her off her feet. More pieces, mostly smaller, bounded and tumbled, slamming against the tarp, collapsing it over its occupants like a winding sheet to ready Jenneth and the ghatti for a sepulcher of snow.

Crawling, slithering, her hands frantically clawing a path, Mahafny fought her way toward the tarp, faintly aware of Diccon's shouts behind her and Harrap's answering cry. A few final snow chunks pelted her, most no larger than her head or hand, mixed with a powdery slide of snow and crushed ice, as if a giant flume poured its contents on their camp.

Emerging like a sphere popping from underwater, Pw'eek burst into view, vigorously shaking herself before shooting toward the other tarp, intent on checking that her sib Kwee was unharmed. "Don't worry, Aunt Mahafny! I've got Saam! Everything's fine!" The tarp rippled like a live thing as Jenneth burrowed toward its edge, and finally Mahafny spotted her dark head against the white snow. Hampered by her bundle, Jenneth clambered upright and turned back the blanket to peer inside, just as a young mother lovingly regards her child. "All he did was wake enough to yawn full in my face—then he drifted right back to sleep!" Leaning closer, she pressed a kiss on Saam's forehead. "Oh, to be so nonchalant! Pw'eek and I were scared stiff!"

Still on her knees, arms supplicantly raised to receive her precious burden, a weary relief washed over Mahafny, coupled with a compelling desire to give in, give up, sleep forever and ever, now and for all the ages hence. Yes, to slumber alongside Saam. Why was everything so blurred? It shouldn't be, now that the earth had regained its equilibrium, stood firm as it was meant to. But this unexpected accident, death beckoning so close, set off a quaking confusion within her.

❖

Standing just beyond the striated birchbark wall of the sweat lodge, Addawanna rejoiced as the night air caressed her moist, overheated skin and absently lifted her braid to let her neck dry. By the second day the scented steam had fully worked its way into Jacobia's lungs, loosening the strictures and obstructions, just as it should. An old way, but the right way. Above her the stars shaped themselves into forms to illustrate her people's legends and myths. That trailing nebulosity of light over there?—why, what else but the smoke from the Great Spirit's campfire? Which had come first? The legends, or the stars' configurations? Intriguing—someday she would ask Callis. If, tonight, she descried a new shape in the stars, would it herald the com-

mencement of a new tale? After all, did not all legends
have a basis in fact before assuming lives of their own?

What had summoned this wanderlust at this turning point
in the seasons when she and the others should be at home,
celebrating the change, the eternal promise that darkness
would again yield to the light? Was she seeking something,
someone? Something that had been lost . . . or something
that needed to be found, discovered for the first time or
discovered anew? Or was it simply the restlessness of advancing age? Pursing her lips, she made a face at her
own fancifulness.

As she studied the skeins of stars, idly seeking a new
pattern, a new design, a fresh way of envisioning what she'd
always seen, Lennap and Glashtok came to stand on either
side of her, their birchen buckets deposited beside the door
flap. Soon enough she'd forsake the night and its stars, the
breeze, the glistening snow to return within, ladle cold
water on heated rocks until clouds of steam enveloped the
three women, made them indistinguishable. "Curious, is it
not," asked Lennap, "that Feather should return to us now,
and with an Outlander, no less." Odd it might be, but Lennap accepted it, not uncritically but speculatively, confident
the incident had a place, a meaning he wasn't yet privy to.
Knowing Lennap he'd peck away at the incident like a
raucous blue-crest with an acorn until he broke through to
the kernel within.

"Mayhap the unscrolling of a new pattern," added Glashtok with the brash enthusiasm of youth.

"My thoughts, exactly." Addawanna pointed a guiding
finger at the stars. "Look, there and there and there. What
do you make of it, you with your youth and keener sight."

"With that dimmer cluster to its right?" Glashtok stroked
the pouch containing his earth-bond, his unlined brow extravagantly furrowed as he set himself to solving the problem. "Wait! A star shoots across! Connects them!"

But Addawanna's vision was torn from the stars as the
earth's tidings made themselves known, tremors welling
through her, body and soul lamenting the sorrowing sum-
mons the earth delivered. Falling upon the earth, she embraced it to calm its woes as best she might, but snow
obscured her healing touch. Lennap, too, had been stricken,
falling to his knees, both hands cupping his earth-bond,

forehead bowed against the earth, even Glashtok had registered the uncanny trembling, though not as severely, since sky and air called more strongly to his heart than earth.

The tremulous vibrations haltingly told of intense pain and desolation far away, the telling a mere shadow of reality. Even this far south the earth suffered, sharing the anguish of its more distant brethren, all connected, a part of the whole. As the swaying and jouncing gradually ceased, Addawanna rose, not with the toilsome efforts of old age, but with a sluggishness engendered by shock, wanting desperately to disbelieve what she'd heard. It could *not* be! It was *not* possible! So, that which had once struck fear in their hearts had been loosed again. Again the earth and the Erakwa would suffer, through no fault of their own! Ah, the legends could not lie quiet, await their retelling around the winter fires, must act on their own!

Lennap impulsively reached for her hands, and she took his willingly, both of them needing a connection, a way to ground their dread. "Was that . . . ?" he swallowed, hard, the fringe on his buckskin vest fluttering above his pounding heart. "I know the tales, you *know* I do, but to couple *this* with tales past . . ."

No easy answer to give him, to relieve his mind. "Mayhap yes, mayhap no," her nails whitening as she gripped Lennap's hands. "Yet why not? Cannot legends come to life?" and heard Glashtok whimper, bewildered by the growing strangeness of this night. "It was a . . . Plumb. We partook of the earth's sorrow, must mourn, as well." Old though she might be, the Plumbs had existed before her time, though her grandmother, Doncallis, had witnessed their awful power firsthand. And this knowledge had been painstakingly passed along to Addawanna and others blessed with the earth-bonding, the tales that corresponded with it. In turn, Addawanna had passed them along to Nakum, to Glashtok and others, a new generation, a new repository for past wisdom. Flesh and blood, bone and sinew, every particle of the earth-bonded *knew,* for past was present was future, all wheeling one into the other. And why not? Had not the earth, the very soil, existed then—just it as did now? Just as it would in the future? If the Plumbs did not wrench it asunder . . .

If so, the Outlanders would unthinkingly alter this world

again, remold it to their petty desires, and the land and its people—her people, the Erakwa—would have no say, kindred and kindred spirits separated, split apart. And but one earth for them all to share—had not the legends predicted the coming of the Outlanders, their spaceships so like Glashtok's falling star? Yet what was once learned was often forgotten . . . except for this wrenching reminder. . . .

Sounding as young, unsure, and untried as Glashtok, Lennap forced himself beyond the experience, analyzing it, trying to draw forth a centrality or core to it. "Is there a . . . connection, a convergence, think you . . . that an Outlander now resides amongst us? Conveyed by none other than Feather, whose path has merged with ours once more?"

Feather. Could she be caught up by forces she no longer understood? Be playing an unwitting role as a messenger between two worlds? But if so, what was the message? Prudence said that messenger and message should not be confused with one another; they were not consistently one and the same. What did this presage? "You may be right." More focused than she at times, Lennap often pressed to the heart of things while she lingered, savoring and sampling everything the earth whispered to her. "As to Feather, at least," she amended. "As to the Outlander, she is called Jacobia in their tongue. I do not know her value as yet, but think it great."

"She is . . . beautiful," sighed Glashtok, obviously smitten after seeing her but once. "Such eyes! Never have I seen the like! Nothing like that fussy, fuming one I brought into the mountains this summer—why I still do not know!" Nor would she enlighten him. Already it appeared that Glashtok had voluntarily relinquished a piece of his heart to Jacobia. Such was the case, sometimes, just as once, long ago, she had given her heart to an Outlander, one with royal blood, though she'd cared naught about that. From that brief union had been born a daughter who commingled both cultures, and from that, Addawanna's grandson, Nakum. Who was to say that the admixture did not have advantages, a slow erosion of their insularity? Feather, as well, had been born of mixed blood.

But was Jacobia Wycherley part of the message? A part of these peculiar happenings, and so conveniently delivered into their hands? "Almost . . . I can see her face in the stars," Glashtok breathed, adrift in his own musings. "See, Wanna? Where you pointed before? Those three stars so very close in line to the others you pointed to? Like a hand to a brow when someone desires to look far into the distance? The dim cluster of light I showed you before becomes the eye."

Was it possible? Was Jacobia Wycherley now meant to be the Beholder? Observer and visionary, witness to all that went awry? And with that, did any previous Beholder become the beholden? Mayhap too great a leap of faith to make right now, but sometimes legends lived and relived themselves in different guises. And right now, she'd best return inside the lodge. Feather's eumedico ways often proved good, but she lacked proportion, her balance precarious. It did not matter that Jacobia was an Outlander, not when she now lived amongst them. She, too, hovered between two worlds, a new one she was just learning to envision, an old one that must be seen afresh.

♣

Forcibly throttling a cry of outrage as Ezequiel drove him along the passageway, Harry grimly set himself to do his duty, and his duty was protecting his king. *That* was what Muscadeines did, no matter the personal cost. Marchmont's ruler must be protected, even at the expense of his life. Ezequiel had immediately recognized that, had done *his* duty; he could offer no less. And Papa—he'd reacted without hesitation, springing into action without a thought for himself . . . or for Harry. Inwardly groaning, Harry shoved the resisting king forward, shadowing his movements, chivying him, pushing at Eadwin's waist, slamming his shoulder into his back to force him ahead. If the king whirled 'round, tried to return and aid the others, he'd trip him, he would! And if he trampled Harry, he'd still have to face down Hru'rul, and that gave Harry some comfort.

"Oh, please, oh, please!" he whispered under his breath. No time to explain to the Lady, tell Her of their plight. His Papa was the bravest, strongest man he knew, and if Papa couldn't succeed, then no one could. Except . . . except . . .

could Papa escape in time, or would he be blown to bits . . . or just crippled . . . blinded? He hiccuped on a sob and pushed harder, momentarily hating Eadwin, hating him for forcing him to choose between his king and his father—which wasn't fair, 'cause Eadwin would've gladly snatched the Plumb, run off with it to protect Arras Muscadeine. Oh, how was he going to explain it all to Mama?

Like some ravenous beast creeping up on them, the explosion seized and shook them, the growling rumble battering them, while the ground beneath their feet shuddered and recoiled as if it were alive, desperate to escape. Octads upon octads of dust swamped the air and he blindly grabbed for Eadwin, felt Ezequiel's arms embracing them both, all three lurching but somehow remaining upright. Bits of stone and brick, old mortar hailed on their heads and shoulders, and in the dark he couldn't tell when a piece of debris would smash him until it was too late. Lady help him, how he'd been scared when those custables had exploded, but that had been mild compared to this eruption of raw power!

"Will . . . will the castle fall on our heads?" he cried, choking on dust, eating it, tasting it, along with a bitter metallic flavor floating heavy in the air. The thought of being buried alive turned his knees watery, his bowels near to bursting. Hru'rul uttered a gargling challenge which degenerated into a shrieking yowl as stones clattered down on him.

"Don't think it's likely." Ezequiel coughed, spat. Finally loosening his grip, he fumbled at Harry, checking for injuries. To his surprise, his shoulder hurt fiercely, as if he'd been punched, and when he swallowed, his ears popped as if he'd been underwater swimming. "We're nearer the castle reservoir system than I'd like, though." Another spasm of coughing doubled him over, so the king completed Ezequiel's train of thought. "When this was built, two streams were channeled under and into the castle to ensure ready access to water. Standard defense tactics for a siege situation—if it had ever proved necessary."

Harry nodded. Wasn't he the Defense Lord's son? He knew that, as well as how succeeding generations had completed more engineering, channels and piping that filled cisterns throughout the castle. Additional cisterns on the rooftops fed rainwater downward. As if he needed a plumbing lesson! And then the irony of the word caught him full force and he let out a wailing giggle that came cascading out of him, harder and faster. Even plastering his hands over his mouth couldn't stop it, until Eadwin shook him and sharply smacked his face.

Ah, ah, ah—NO! Mayhap he shouldn't even have *thought* such a thing! Not with that roaring, racing sound now pounding in his ears, the air precipitously damp and cool as it clung to his sweaty body! A cataractous noise rushed toward them from the direction they'd fled. Oh, Papa! Where *was* he, why hadn't he come?

"Take Harry, press upward as fast as you can. You should be able to climb faster than the water can rise, as long as the stairwells aren't blocked." Eadwin passed Harry into Ezequiel's arms as if he were a parcel. "I'm going back, see if I can help the others. Come, Hru'rul!" One hand trailing against the wall to guide him, Eadwin had already gained a lead as Harry and Ezequiel righted themselves.

"Don't be a fool, Eadwin!" Ezequiel cried after him, and Harry stood stock-still, trying to conquer his trembling. Stay? Or go? Someone should forge ahead, rally search parties, start the servants and castle mechanics on the pumps. "I know these passages and corridors like my own hand!" Ezequiel protested, stumbling after the king. "Can travel them blindfolded!"

Eadwin's wobbly laugh told Harry that the king was fierce scared, too. "And so you do, Ezequiel. I can't match your expertise, no matter how I've studied the old prints and diagrams. Just one thing, though." Now he truly did sound amused, not simply scared. "Ignacio once confided that you'd never learned to swim—spent too much time at your royal duties. Remind me to rectify that when we're clear of this." The king's voice came fainter now, but Harry was sure he'd said *when*, not *if*—the king thought they'd survive! "Swimming lessons, Ezequiel—you'll love them! People learn very quickly in the dead of winter—otherwise they turn into human icicles!"

❧

Wetness lapped along her body, and Holly tossed soaked hair clear of her face and rolled onto one shoulder, convinced it might be wise to raise her aching head above the stream now coursing around her body. What in the name of the Lady was she doing here? Where was she? Where was Theo? Miserably wading against the flowing water that rose higher with liquid chortles of delight, P'roul levered herself under Holly's chin to support her head. *"All right! All right! I'm getting up!"* It wasn't easy or comfortable, but by stages she gained her feet, concentrating on outstaring the darkness, extending her arms until she encountered walls. A dull thrumming in her head, and her fingers cautiously explored until she encountered a lump. "Ouch!"

**"Yes, you've a lovely goose egg. And once we're out, you'll have all the time in the world to admire it, garner sympathy, even."** P'roul didn't sound in the best of moods, but then, Holly didn't feel exactly sanguine either. While she stood here stupidly wondering where she was, the water continued rising, now lapping at her knees. The crushing blackness disoriented her, and for the life of her she couldn't remember why she was here—wherever "here" happened to be.

*"P'roul? What are we . . . ?"* Indistinct crackles and creaks . . . like being surrounded by crickets, but occasional sharper cracks suggested old wood snapping, finally capitulating to forces greater than its endurance. *"Where's Theo and Khim? Have they mislaid themselves again?"* Why was she standing in the middle of a freshening stream in the depths of a moonless night? Where was the blessed Lady Moon that never waxed or waned? And why did every turbid thought have the consistency of cornmeal mush? Oh, dear, what a muddle—and how aggravating!

Something bumped against her thigh, nudging like an impatient old dog awaiting his supper bowl. "Oh, Blessed, Blasted Lady!" The exclamation set her head throbbing, but not as hard as it would if she didn't do something soon with this blasted trunk! With that, it came flooding back— their midnight expedition with Ezequiel and the king beneath the castle, the Plumbs, and Romain-Laurent's bungling. Lady help them all—if she didn't drag these Plumbs clear, get them some place safe, they might blow up the whole castle, half of Sidonie, even! A slim chance that water might damper their explosive power, render them inoperative, but she wasn't about to test that theory. She'd leave that to Romain-Laurent—after she'd put a kilometer's distance between them!

P'roul balanced atop the trunk now as it rocked and prodded against Holly's legs. **"Come on, dear one! Use your wits! Dunk your head to clear it—then we'll find a way out of here!"**

Much as the idea repelled her, she obeyed, rapidly dipping her head underwater before she could change her mind, then shakily righting herself to mop her face. *"Rather like the old adage about fighting fire with fire, I suppose. Water with water."* It did help; her thoughts became less mushlike, more focused.

Clutching the handle at one end of the trunk, she began towing it behind her, stumbling as it bumped and banged against her. Fine—if it was *that* impatient to take the lead, she would happily splash in its wake! Let it search out the obstacles the water obscured, the crevices, the chunks of rock. But it did indicate that the flow was increasing; the water had now risen to her waist, and she was relieved P'roul had hitched a ride. Unlike her sire, Rawn, the ghatta didn't relish wading or swimming if she could avoid it. **"Do you know the way back?**

A good question, a fair one, even. "Think so!" She'd spoken aloud just to hear how voices carried now that the underground chambers and passages were flooding. Talk about a voice being drowned out! And, truth be told, she'd hoped that if she spoke aloud, a familiar voice might answer. "Theo and Khim went for Romain-Laurent, didn't they?" She was fairly confident of that, but wanted to be sure. After all, best to know when to worry and when not to. "Any word?"

Thank the Lady she possessed an excellent sense of direction, an inner compass of sorts, but she'd never tested it in total blackness, a void lacking a single visible reference point. Well, nothing like a little challenge to heighten the senses! Retreating through these winding corridors and ways, up and down stairs, was just a game of blindman's bluff. Come to think of it, the last time she'd played it, they'd ended up in the Sunderlies—this time all she got was the cellars. "Any word from Arras?" Keep her

thoughts, her questions lightly casual, not that it would fool
P'roul, but it might deceive her own fears. With a grunt,
she switched her grip on the handle—a wonder her shoulder hadn't been dragged from its socket—and trudged
along, letting her free hand play along the wall. When the
wall vanished, she'd determine if they'd reached an inter-
section or found a dead end, a storage room.

**"Theo and Khim reached Romain-Laurent, though *I*
think they should have left him, the ninnyhammer!"** Even
in mindspeech, her words fairly crackled and sparked, an
angry ghatta expressing her displeasure over rank stupidity.
**"But . . . neither Khim nor I've heard word from Arras."**

"You don't think . . . ?" She stoppered herself, refusing
to finish the sentence aloud. Harry might still be somewhere ahead, and her voice might carry, the old passages
playing acoustical tricks with human voices. "Do I want to
know how high the water's reached on Theo?" she asked
instead, because that *was* a concern. Put Arras Muscadeine
out of her mind, don't think it, and it won't be true! He was
too strong, too clever, too determined—and he'd willingly
sacrificed himself to protect his king and Harry.

**"Good thing Theo's so tall,"** came P'roul's laconic response, laced with just a touch of understatement. **"I suppose we should hope Romain-Laurent can swim!"** Theo
swam—after a fashion—his legs thrashed, his arms parted
the water, but he sank like a stone; his long, cadaverous
frame boasted so little body fat he could exhaust himself
treading water just to keep his nose above the surface.

She longed to go after Theo with every iota of her being,
but willed herself onward, forward. Damn Muscadeine! She
knew how he must have felt. She, too, had a duty, a responsibility greater than Theo's welfare, because it could irrevo-
cably alter so many lives. Somehow, some way, she'd get
these Plumbs out safely. Then mayhap they could discover
what should be done with them.

♣

" 'Smost remarkable thing I've ever witnessed!" gushed
Romain-Laurent indistinctly, his jaw swollen, beginning to
darken where Arras's fist had landed. He'd bitten the inside

of his cheek as well, gone puffy inside and out. Rotten shame he'd not bitten his tongue and effectively silenced himself, or so Theo judged.

"Um, r–remarkable," he agreed, taking Romain-Laurent's elbow to hustle him along.

"Absolutely Ka-BLAM!" Charpentier tossed his arms wide in giddy exuberance, nearly whanging Theo with the lantern they'd salvaged. The dust still sifting down created bright, twinkling motes that made Theo think of fireflies. "I must, absolutely *must* see how much damage it did, assess its power! How soon until we can venture back?" Scrambling after Theo, he bumbled along, raising the lantern high to examine the sights they passed instead of watching his footing. "I mean—do you realize, man, what this *means*?"

**"Tell him it means I'm shredding his shins, just for starters, if he doesn't stifle himself. Are we heading the right way to find Arras?"** Khim darted ahead, always choosing an upward-sloping corridor, ears constantly aswivel to gauge the ominous gurgle of water they could hear behind them. Theo hunched his shoulders fatalistically; sooner or later it would catch them. For now he and Charpentier were dry and in reasonable condition, more than could probably be said for Muscadeine.

*"Let him babble, Khim. If he has a pet project churning in his mind, he's happy, easier to manage. I don't think it's sunk in precisely what he's done, the damage he's caused."* Giving Romain-Laurent an encouraging nod to keep him moving, he asked, "N–no. W–what d–does it m–mean?" Given their limited acquaintance Theo surmised that Charpentier heard his stammer but didn't see the whole man behind it, had dismissively written him off as a lightweight, wits a bit slow. So let the man lecture; mayhap he'd learn something, mayhap not.

**"Up here, this way!"** Khim encouraged. If luck stayed on their side, Khim's rising path should intersect with the castle storerooms at the first level of the cellars. Where that might lead, Theo had no idea, and envisioned popping through a disused door in the cook's larder, of having her take after them with a skillet. She was a formidable woman, even rounder than his Dannae, but nowhere near as young or as adorable. However, her desserts had won over his stomach, if not his heart. **"Keep going! I'm going to hunt for Arras this way. Not likely, but best make sure."**

*"Take care, love! Hurry back!"* How much had he missed of Romain-Laurent's edifying lecture? Probably not enough. "What it *means,* man, is that if we determine how these things work, possibly replicate them, we could start anew—as if we'd only just arrived on this planet! And at the worst, if we can't, well, we'll have a few left for engineering projects of a magnitude we've never dared contemplate, let alone attempt! Say we want to construct a dam, bring down a cliff face to block a river and reroute it! Ka-BLAM!"

His blissful expression while babbling about such destructive, disruptive forces almost froze Theo in his tracks, his skin crawling and itching, making him yearn to be as far distant as possible from this man. Distasteful as it was, he laid a dirt-stained hand over Romain-Laurent's mouth to silence him, make him listen. "Il–legal t–technology, c–can't try to r–repli–cate it! Mustn't! G–got us into t–trouble in the f–first place! A–and w–we know even l–less about t–tech–nology than our an–ancestors did! W–we'd b–blow ourselves to the L–Lady a–and be–beyond! You'll g–get to m–meet your an–ancestors, all r–right! And th–this t–time th–there won't even be a few s–spaces–ships to s–save s–some of us!"

But Charpentier simply backed clear of Theo's restraining hand and continued his onslaught of logic, his expression deadly earnest. "Why can't you people *ever* look at the broad picture, at all the possibilities, the potentials? Don't you have *dreams,* Theo? *I* do! When people like me try to drag you, kicking and screaming, into a world we *could* inhabit—a *superior* world—it's 'Oh, no, we don't do things that way.' Can't anything *ever* change, improve in this quaint, archaic world?" He'd fixed Theo with the ardent gaze of a true believer, willing others to dare believe along with him. Then, almost peevishly, "And why are my feet getting wet? Where's the water coming from?"

Discarding whatever shards of hard-won patience remained, Theo clasped Romain-Laurent's shoulder, let his powerful, bony fingers close tighter and tighter until Charpentier regarded him with wide, worried eyes. "B–because, you f–fool, w–when you set off th–that," he couldn't bring himself to say the word, get stuck on the "p" sound, "damn th–thing, you broke into the streamb–beds that run be–be–neath the c–castle. Th–that f–feed the cisterns and the water p–p–p . . . you know! L–likely s–some of us may d–drown be–before we g–get clear! W–what if you've k–killed the k–king?"

"Oh!" Charpentier's mouth dropped open. "Oooh! No!"

♣

Once the king announced his intention of returning for Papa and the others, Harry's resolve hardened. Let Ezequiel go for help; *he'd* been charged with a double duty: protecting his king and rescuing his father. Hanging back in the shifting gloom as Ezequiel and Eadwin argued, he waited till the king went splashing away and slithered after him, practically holding his breath, concentrating on match-ing his splashing to Eadwin's. With any luck Ezequiel wouldn't notice his absence until it was too late, would assume he'd scurried ahead. The water swirled around him, unseen things bobbing by, banging him. Though he couldn't really see through the semidarkness, he could imagine the ceiling creeping lower, forcing him deeper into the water. Not just the ceiling, but the whole castle bearing down on him, pressing the air out of his lungs—if the water didn't steal it first!

Don't think on it, don't think on it! Just follow the splashes, the muffled cursing, Eadwin calmly and fluently damning anything and everything involving the castle and its old, hidden ways of access and exit, so far below the earth. Without a doubt now, the water *had* risen, and Harry was half-swimming, half-wading as he shadowed the king. The king was brave to attempt this without regard for his own safety; oh, not as brave as Papa, but Papa'd had years of training as a solider. *He* wouldn't panic in a situation like this, so neither would Harry. Except the wetness, the darkness, the enclosed sensation was all a *little* worse than Harry'd anticipated. Mayhap mud puppies relished it, but he didn't.

Warily, he mindspoke on the strictly intimate mode, the one that only he and Papa shared. No sense alerting Ead-

win how he trailed behind, dogging him. And no doubt
Eadwin was 'speaking Papa as well, trying to fix on his
location. But there was nothing, not even a distant whisper
from Papa's mind, and that was worse than the water, the
closeness, the dark. Nothing—not good, not good at all—
but mayhap Papa had hurt himself, or the solid stone of
the passages had somehow baffled his mindvoice, sent it
ricocheting in another direction. It happened sometimes.
Papa hurt was more of a comfort than the other possibility,
the one he kept trying not to think about. And the more
he tried not to, the more he did. No! Not possible, not
*his* Papa!

Without warning he fell full-length, plunging facedown
in the dark, flowing water—could hear it giggling, laughing,
and bubbling at its release as it swirled around his head—
and came up gasping, coughing. Sputtering, he fought to
regain his breath, to not hear the water's glee at trapping
him. As if still toying with him, the water smashed him
hard against the wall, and he wanted to cry in pain and
frustration. Suddenly a hand gripped the back of his collar,
half-strangling him, but holding him safe, the king pinning
him against his chest so the current couldn't sweep him
under and play with him again. "Cough it up!" he ordered,
Hru'rul on his shoulders, the ghatt's wet, furry face thrust
forward to inquiringly sniff Harry. To his embarrassment,
a mighty sneeze exploded from him, and Hru'rul jerked
back, raising a large paw to vigorously scrub at his muzzle.
As if a few more drops of moisture mattered!

"I *can* swim!" Harry emphasized, in case the king contemplated sending him back. Though how he'd return
alone, he didn't know. "Just drove water up my nose when
I tripped."

"I know. Did the same myself a bit before—Hru'rul was
*not* pleased at the dunking!" Harry could sense, more than
see, Eadwin's rueful smile. "Now let's get going. Keep your
hand on my shoulder or arm, if you can." And with that,
Eadwin began wading again, Harry in his wake, sometimes
finding firm purchase for his feet, sometimes kicking mightily to propel himself ahead.

"Has Hru'rul contacted Khim and P'roul?" Harry asked,
hoping against hope that either good old Theo or Holly
had found Papa, was conducting him to safety. Lady help

him, how would he explain to Mama if Papa were lost, dead? It made him want to 'speak P'roul and Khim, find out for himself, in case Eadwin chose to honey coat the situation.

Breaststroking, gliding along, pulling himself from one rough wall outcropping to the next, Eadwin had little breath to spare, burdened with both Hru'rul and Harry. *"Holly and P'roul are moving the Plumbs. They're almost clear of the cellars, I think."* Pausing, he felt out another handhold, let his feet shove off against the floor to coast ahead. Harry couldn't help being impressed, almost as if the king knew where to find them. *"Khim and Theo are considering doing dire things to Romain-Laurent, but at least they're still mostly dry. They haven't found Arras yet, but they're looking as they go."*

*"Do you think Papa's . . . dead?"* Frightening enough to form the thought in mindspeech, but even worse to utter it aloud—as if the dolorous words made it more final, somehow, snuffing all hope. Was this how Diccon had felt when Jenneth was swept overboard, although *he*, at least, had known she still lived. The major question had been *where*. And now a wave of remorse swamped him at the thought of Jenneth and Diccon—how he'd not told anyone at all what they were doing, where they were going! What if something went wrong? Who'd know where to look? And all because of his stupid pride, his stupid honor: *Can you keep a secret? Don't tell!* Oh, Theo'd been right! Papa very likely dead, and the twins courting it, marching up the mountain with grumpy old Mahafny Annendahl, their aunt, and jolly old Shepherd-Seeker Harrap! And the ghatti, too!

No, he *wasn't* crying! After all, Eadwin could hardly avoid splashing his face. What to do, what to do? Confess to Eadwin—except, well, if Eadwin didn't make it out of this labyrinth, most likely he wouldn't either. Snuffling now, snorting, he crammed the tears behind his lids, felt them leaking whether he wanted it or not.

**"Hush, boy!"** A massive paw rested featherlight on his head, the claws extruding into his sodden scalp just enough to capture his attention. **"Ghatti always knowing, yes? Of course! Not liking what they know, but ghatti ready when time comes to tell—if needed. Is not Saam Khim's sire? Now wiping nose on sleeve, you, yes? And kicking harder,**

**yes? Giving my Eadwin some help, like he helping you and your sire."**

*"Yes, Hru'rul."* And in earnest of his promise, he began to kick more vehemently, easing his grip on Eadwin's shoulder. *"They're safe, then?"*

**"Safe as us."** That was hardly encouraging. **"Safer, even. At least they not swimming!"** It wasn't much comfort, but it was all he had—best be content with it.

♣

Snugged cocoon-tight in the angle where wall met floor, as if his very life depended on it—and it had—Arras Muscadeine lay still, attempting to decide if he were in one piece. His back, from the neck down to his heels, felt riddled with slices and punctures where shrapnel had struck, and his ears rang so badly he could almost believe he'd stuck his head in a Bethel bell and encouraged the village lads to bang on it with sticks. Experimentally opening his eyes, still sheltered by wall and floor, he was shocked to no longer see the glaring blast that had seared with a brilliance beyond the sun's. Had expected it permanently imprinted on his eyes, its glow eternal. Instead, darkness had consumed it.

Now, how to get to his feet? Needed some space, some room to maneuver, he did. Could he do that without rolling on his back? No, too much effort, his limbs ditch-water weak. Setting his jaw he rolled over, hissing as his back hit the floor, and rolled as rapidly onto his stomach as he could. Fine, now he had space to move his arms and legs instead of hugging the wall. Try again—up. Draw up his knees, push with both arms. A surge of red-hot pain shot through his arm, making its presence spectacularly known near his right shoulder. Well, he'd answered his own question: He was in one package, but not exactly in one piece. Right arm and right collarbone, broken. But at least he'd shifted onto his knees. Letting his head loll forward, he cradled his bad arm against his chest, indulging in little panting sounds until the hurt waned.

But that hurt and all the others were as nothing compared to the welfare, the whereabouts of the others—most especially Harry and Eadwin. Had everyone escaped? Even though he'd been the only one directly in the explosion's path, old passages might have crumpled, beams fallen, ceilings collapsed. Too possible, given how Jenret and Parse had wandered lost down here, trapped by an explosion from above. Parse had been buried alive, would have had the castle for his coffin if Jenret hadn't dug him out, breathed life into him.

"Harry? Eadwin?" he called. "Hallo! Anyone?" Odd—couldn't seem to hear himself speaking—he *was* speaking aloud, wasn't he? Clearing his throat, strangely sore and raspy—coated with grit, he supposed—he tried again, his calls abraded into weak, thin cries as they left his lips. Good hand on his vocal cords, he bellowed for all he was worth, emptying his lungs of air. Mayhap he was so muzzy from the explosion he didn't really know what he was doing. Yes—he *was* speaking aloud, shouting, from the way his throat hurt, though he couldn't hear a thing. The blast had deafened him; had it blinded him as well? Was the clinging dark because there was nothing to see, or could his eyes see nothing? No, there! Faint flecks of light behind him, where fragments of the Plumb still glowed, cooling toward darkness.

Somehow that helped with telling "up" from "down," and he lurched to his feet, good shoulder propped against the wall as he strained to see ahead along the passageway, longing for some familiar, dear shape to materialize from the darkness. Not that he'd hear anyone coming. Ah, Francie'd die of grief if anything had happened to Harry! Could he mindspeak? Contact Harry or Eadwin, even one of the ghatti? Concentrating, he let his mind reach out, unsure if he'd succeeded or whether his thoughts merely whirled within his head, unable to find an outlet. Not a pleasant feeling, too reminiscent of Maurice having him locked within an iron casque, mindspeech effectively dampered. Funny, he'd known deaf Resonants before, perfectly capable of conversing in mindspeech but aurally unable to hear a hammer smash against an anvil, even if they stood beside it. Well, then, damn it! He'd find his king and his son with or without his hearing! Which way? For a moment the logic almost escaped him, still more muddled than he'd realized. Away from the Plumb, idiot! That had been the whole point, hadn't it? He'd dashed this way, sent the others dashing in the opposite direction, as far from him and the cursed Plumb as their legs could carry them. Removing his waist sash, he fashioned a crude sling for his arm. Then, whistling a jaunty tune, though he couldn't hear a note, Arras limped on his way. At least whistling would alert anyone still down here to his presence, let them know he was coming.

Ha! Farther than he'd thought—he *had* managed a good sprint! Let Francie indulge in any more jests about his waistline and he'd set her straight! Scuffing ahead, blindly feeling for obstacles, chunks of stone and masonry, he accidentally bypassed the alcove where the Plumbs had been stored, his good hand temporarily occupied with adjusting his sling. Still, it couldn't be *that* much farther, he consoled himself as his footsteps wavered, his whole body slightly listing. Still whistling, stopping to give an occasional shout, he misjudged the distance he'd sprinted in the dark, veering into a secondary passage off the main corridor, cautiously pleased at managing so well, still confident he'd locate someone—even that damned fool Romain-Laurent! Thoughts of getting his hands on Romain-Laurent energized him, made the time pass, set him into a shambling trot. No common sense, none whatsoever! Attempting to reorganize everyone else's life when he couldn't even take care of his own! Ha!

Stopping, he sniffed warily. Odd, that. Smelled like water, a dampness wafting toward him. A tickling vibration against the soles of his feet, as if something rushed along the corridor at him. Temporarily deaf, still half-blinded, Arras Muscadeine started violently as the racing water slammed against his shins, making him fight for his balance. Water? Now he knew precisely what he'd do to Romain-Laurent! Drown him! The bloody fool and his meddling had cracked the castle's water system, mayhap even given an underground stream a new, easy venue to explore!

Lady bless, the water felt cold! And given his exhaustion, its chilly touch leached the last of his strength from him as it inexorably climbed higher and higher—to mid-thigh, to his waist, now chest-deep. So easy to just lie back, float, let it carry him where it would. Ah, how the water soothed the burns and stings on his back, blessedly numbed his arm and shoulder! Coward! Surging upward like a breaching whale, spurting water, shouting, he urged himself on. He was a soldier, damn it! Fight! Find a way out! Or, a little voice in his head told him, at least find Harry so they could die together. . . . Even Eadwin would do in a pinch—the younger man as dear to him as a brother. No! Pure selfishness, that . . . hadn't he sacrificed so much to ensure Eadwin attained the throne . . . ?

Past mingling with present, Arras plowed through the water, stumbling, swimming with one-armed strokes in deeper channels, always fighting, always seeking higher ground. But as he approached another intersecting corridor, a new confluence of water poured into his own stream, sweeping him away, drifting and sinking, only to rise and bang his head on the ceiling. "Harry, I'm coming!" he screamed at the top of his lungs. It wasn't a lie, it couldn't be—didn't need one of the ghatti to tell him that—not if he believed it with all his heart and soul. Somehow he and Harry and Eadwin would be reunited.

**"Hru'rul, too? Being as how I am most puissant ghatt of all!"** Hru'rul? Well, why not? He loved Eadwin as well or better than Arras did. Naturally Hru'rul was welcome to join them!

*"Of course, you overgrown, nub-tailed, fleasome ghatt!"* he jovially responded within his mind, already creating his own scenario for the end. Ah, to have Francie here as well, though he'd not wish that on her . . . though, since it was *his* imagination, *his* end, he could people it with whomever he chose, with no hurt or pain accruing to them, couldn't he?

♣

Hands patting at the final submerged steps, Ezequiel shook himself like a dog as he emerged from the water. Never had basement stairs, *dry* basement stairs, seemed so comforting, or the lighted lamps along the way so beautifully bright, heralding an entrance into another world—an orderly world that obeyed his least command. Now he ran, water streaming from him in rivulets, bursting through the doorway and parting the curtain, grabbing at the first servant who sped by. The man looked aghast, eyes wide with shock, momentarily not recognizing the sodden figure abruptly confronting him. "The castle guards, bring them!" he shouted full in the man's face, reinforcing his verbal order with a touch of mind-coercion, fully aware it was wrong, but wrong be damned!

Then, steeling himself, he sent his mindvoice resonating through the castle, sounding an alarm, stirring anyone, awake or asleep, who possessed even the most minimal Resonant skill. He, like his grandfather before him, boasted lackluster ability, indifferently skilled at best, more proficient at sending than receiving. Given this, they'd chosen as castle servants those receptive to hearing mindvoices, able to take instruction without him voicing the orders aloud. Thus the castle staff always moved swiftly and silently about their business, not a raised voice to be heard.

Yet it appeared his needs had been anticipated, the castle already alive, swarming with people intent on tasks, not aimlessly milling, awaiting direction. Who could possibly have . . . ? Most, he realized, were fully dressed, though a few of the busiest still wore night shifts hastily shoved into trousers, bedroom slippers, even. Urban Gamelyn, flapping along in brocaded turquoise slippers, never gave Ezequiel a second glance as he strode by with another man, urgently gesturing, shaping plans with his hands. Momentarily he wondered if his experiences underground had rendered him invisible, but no, he was simply in the way, and flattened himself against a wall as a work crew laden with planking and tools swept by.

Exhaustion left him rooted in place, uncaring if the curtain got wet. For the life of him, he couldn't move, couldn't even think anymore as a tremor ran through him, even his jaw quivering. Only then did his weary eyes begin to take in the damage surrounding him—some of it subtle, some blatantly crying out to be rectified. There, a major heave and buckle to the floor like a wave, parquetry pieces popped loose, ready to snag an unwary toe. And there, two windowpanes completely gone, letting in wintry air and a hint of dawn. Other panes were webbed with cracks. Water dripped from the ceiling, creating an expanding puddle, and it hurt his very soul to glimpse *his* castle in such disorder, such disarray that he buried his face in his hands and groaned.

A tap-tap-tap caught his ear, its regularity cutting through the controlled activity as the sound came closer, and he wished he could fade into the curtain, be camouflaged by it. Peering between his fingers he caught sight of Arras Muscadeine's wife, Francie, with Fabienne, the king's elderly mother, on her arm. Hair untidily braided, both were garbed in hastily belted dressing gowns over night shifts, their hair loose and disorderly, but both looked wide awake, anxious but in utter command of themselves.

Shame suffused him at having let Harry slip away, chase after the king. And he . . . he'd had no choice but to hurry on, someone had to sound the alarm, summon help. Those parts of the city directly surrounding the castle had to be alerted that very soon—if not already—they'd be knee-deep in water, cellars flooding, water seeping under doors. And if those blasted storm drains hadn't been properly cleared of snow, worse could happen. For all he knew, parts of the city might have already sustained major damage from the explosion, or the ensuing rise and settle of the land.

"Something exploded, has it not?" asked Tante Fabienne without preamble. "Woke some of us, though others of us couldn't sleep until our adventurers had returned to tell their tales." She paused, waiting for an answer that Ezequiel couldn't bring himself to speak. Bad enough to have to deal with Tante Fabienne, as she was affectionately known, but it had totally slipped his mind that he'd assigned Arras, his family, and their Canderisian visitors suites for the night, since they'd be up late prowling. Facing Francie Muscadeine's reproach *now,* sooner than he'd anticipated, was more than he could bear.

He nodded, miserable and weary beyond belief. "Yes, an explosion." The word "Plumb" stayed locked inside, its utterance beyond him. "It caused considerable . . . damage . . . down below . . ." and he couldn't continue.

Fabienne fingered an escaping lock of white hair. "Yes, the best we can judge so far is that it tore the piping free from two of the roof cisterns. Early reports also suggest the dam on one of the underground streams gave way. We're draining the two cisterns now, before they cause more damage, but we still need a full assessment from

down below. Have the damage checked on-site." He goggled stupidly. "Runners are bringing back damage reports
as fast as they can, and we've one master engineer here,
others arriving shortly with workers and supplies."

"The king's down there, correct?" Fabienne hadn't even
alluded to her son, but the Lady Francie wasn't about to
mince any words. "And Harry and Arras? The others, too?
You're the first to surface, as far as we can tell." Her hazel
eyes had turned pensive as she reckoned what needed to
be done, problems as critical as her husband and son vanishing. "Cinzia Treblicote and La'ow have volunteered to
venture below with one of the master plumbers and an
apprentice, see if they can sense anything of Hru'rul or the
two ghattas. Also three standard search parties are combing
whatever passages they can . . ." she hesitated, "pass
through, I suppose one should say. At least they've got
swimming bladders. Still, I doubt they can get very far.
Hoses are being laid, the pumps set up, but it all takes
time. No easy way to pump out the water without flooding
something else nearby. Diverting it could be equally
dangerous."

"I couldn't . . . I can't . . . swim," he admitted, wretched
as a dog who'd failed his master. Did she judge him a
coward? Believe he'd taken to his heels, abandoning
them all?

"We know, Ezequiel." Fabienne patted his arm, touched
his cheek and he kissed her hand, unable to bow without
falling. One was elderly, the other infirm, yet both exhibited
the cool control and skill of natural-born tacticians, capable
of shrewd assessments and pragmatic orders, even with
loved ones lives at stake. "Can't keep pumping forever and
a day, Ezequiel, not with the stream still flowing free. Go,
now, unfold your plans, young man. Spread them out—
old and new—and trace your path for the engineers, the
mechanics. Show them where and how you went, the routes
the others would likely attempt. Then mayhap we can determine where to look, what to repair first, divert or dam
if we must."

A tired but triumphant cry floated up the stairs behind
him—Holly's voice! "Ladies, continue taking charge—
please! Everyone will obey you two without question."

Already he'd turned, slithering behind the curtain and

bounding down the stairs, not sure what he hoped for, what he'd do if his wishes were answered. No, why wish for a vaporous, delicate female when he had wonderful, competent Holly to count on! Now to get hold of himself, no use if he couldn't be calm and collected, do his share and more. Ignacio would've taken this in his stride, and so must he! His work had only begun, for all the rest of this night—or early morn, whatever it was—and beyond. Rescuing Eadwin and the others was crucial, but finding a secure place for what he prayed Holly had recovered—the trunk containing the mates of that infernal Plumb—was of paramount importance!

♣

As the false dawn made a pretense of limning the horizon, the chaos greeting Nakum as he drifted smoke-silent into Sidonie only confirmed that some dreadful nightmare had been unwittingly loosed on the land. Water soaked the streets, flowing like veritable rivers, geysering from drains and catch basins. The only way this profusion of water could have been liberated was if the very land had been rent asunder, allowing subterranean streams to escape their beds, awakening them to cavort and flow free. No wonder they sounded so gleeful, babbling and chortling and trilling as they investigated their new territory, liquidly fingering beneath doors, warbling as they plunged into basements!

Worse than children on a forbidden escapade, relishing their freedom, naughtily rushing and rollicking where they shouldn't, destroying things in their wake! How they chortled at sweeping their cousin Snow's feet from beneath him, dissolving him and sluicing him along with them, willy-nilly. Water had always firmly believed the Snow and Ice cousins were chilled and snobbish, looked askance on them as Common Water, blandly toiling in river and streambeds, in humble ditches—lacking ambition, initiative, forever seeking the lowest point! But of course they reluctantly admired the Sea Water branch of the family for its ability to splash and roar, cast up towering waves that smacked down with a force capable of capsizing or crushing anything in their path. Now Water was making mock of Nakum, relishing taking him down a peg, showing him it didn't enjoy being taken for granted. But surely any slights had been unintentional on his part, *had* to have been when he had so much to listen to and decipher.

Willing himself to a stillness that rendered him as insubstantial as mist to the average eye—forever insisting on looking for things it recognized—Nakum glided through the city and toward the castle, barely dampening his moccasins. No question that his cousin Eadwin's city was afflicted by a major catastrophe, but Eadwin's immediate troubles as he navigated the flooded passageways didn't concern Nakum as much as the other trouble that Eadwin would soon face. He had faith in his cousin's ability to extricate himself from his immediate problem, though he sincerely hoped he wouldn't come down with a cold—or worse. His cousin, done in by a racking cough and fever, and Nakum unwillingly propelled to the throne! If anyone was solicitous of Eadwin's health, Nakum certainly was! Too bad he hadn't brought along Addawanna's version of a mustard plaster!

As he passed some of the arborfer-fronted houses, built nearly two hundred years past, he reached to stroke them, revering them for their sacrifice, and repeated the gesture at shops or houses with arborfer trim around doors or windows, the decorated edgings that capped their corners. It gladdened his heart to see it as strong and lovely as it had been when first carved, some—no doubt—by Callis's contemporaries who'd aided Constant and the first Outsiders who'd settled Marchmont. Instinct told him that any piping or plumbing that had given way beneath the earth was not the arborfer's fault. Their trunks, bored hollow for use as water conduits, had not rotted from age or split under the pressure. What had happened, he surmised, was that their man-made couplings and connective joints had failed to withstand the strain, as had the later iron piping. Arborfer withstood the ages, the onslaught of time.

Now . . . how to enter the castle unobtrusively? Bad enough when he was expected, had been formally invited. There were still some, more than a few, who viewed his appearance as if he were some sort of carrion bird, hovering near, anxious for his cousin's death. Ridiculous! Didn't they realize how constrained, how confined a castle was? Even poor Eadwin suffered, though he bore it with more patient resignation than Nakum could ever hope to muster. As if he harbored the least desire to rule this land they insisted on calling Marchmont! He didn't even rule over his own domain—or what he referred to as his "domain," his aerie high in the mountains—regarded himself as its caretaker, serving at the wish and will of the Great Spirit above. How else could he be so much a part of things, privy to the gossip of the earth and water (well, apparently not the water of late) and air, the soughing of trees, the songs of birds, the death throes of creatures serving their purpose as prey? While painful, it was an integral part of the greater circle of life and death.

And with that, guilt turned him melancholy, left him pondering how Saam fared. How could he have deserted an old, trusted friend in a time of dire extremity? How high had they climbed thus far? Damnation! His brain had been whirling with too many worries, and he'd not thought to warn the mountains and its creatures that these were friendly intruders, not intruders at all, in fact. Well, mayhap the earth would sense their benign intent, not deal with them too harshly.

Just beyond the castle walls he located the remains of the old potting shed that served as his usual secret entrance. Even less of it remained than he remembered, planks rotting, roof caved in, the whole thing settling. It offered a back entrance to the castle through its upper cellars. Given the water down below, mayhap he should choose another way inside. Indecisive, he stood, one hand tapping distractedly against a board, his mind not immediately catching on a better alternative route. Only belated did he notice an elderly but hearty man who'd stopped short, a shovel over his shoulder, to fixedly stare at exactly where Nakum stood. Indecision had made him inadvertently shrug off his veiled presence, become discernible even to those intent on other matters. Well, let the old man wonder.

That decided him, and with a brief, polite wave of acknowledgment he walked unhurriedly into the remains of the garden shed. A little water never hurt anyone. With luck he might be able to skirt the worst flooding, stay dry, and not antagonize the water any further. A polite greeting

was one thing, but he wasn't about to propitiate them until
he was sure what had precipitated their release.

None too happy, he headed deeper into the tunnel, hating the musty, dusty odors, the rotting ripeness of dead
creatures and household waste that some slothful, shiftless
soul had dropped down the opening, instead of properly
disposing of it. He should speak to Ezequiel about neatening the tunnel—this was a disgrace! Ezequiel would be mortified. Too bad the errant waters hadn't been diverted *here,*
cleansing with their passage. Never when he entered within
the heart of his own mountains did he feel like this, a
moody oppression stealing over him by degrees, weighting
his shoulders, his feet. That world was natural, the land's
creation its own; this was not. Clutching his earth-bond and
breathing through his mouth until he accustomed himself
to the stench, Nakum pressed on, trying not to think how
much he missed his baby arborfers.

❧

Closing her eyes, Cinzia Treblicote shook both arms so vigorously that wrists and fingers flapped like drying laundry.
Already she'd started scanting her breathing, shallow inha-
lations meant to conserve air, not a good sign. How she
abhorred being enclosed, confined, unreasoning panic seizing her at the mere thought of it, just because her stepmother'd once locked her in a closet when she was only six.
Of course her boots had been mucky! She'd been helping in
the barn when her stepmother'd called her in, her city-bred
nose giving one horrified sniff before making Cinzia strip
off the offending boots and dragging her by the ear to the
closet. The grate of the key turning in the lock. Winter
cloaks and jackets dragging their woolly sleeves and hems
across her mouth and nostrils, enveloping her with each
breath. Scraping her neck and her chin, clinging and crackling against her hair, making it rise of its own accord. Worst
of all was the way the garments loomed above her on their
hangers and hooks—only a matter of time till they swooped
down to smother her!

La'ow sat, his plumed tail carving slow, wide arcs across
the stone floor, down here, down here wherever it was that
they were. Not the closet, no, the first sublevel, where the

plumbers stored their gear. **"Love, let me chase away the bad memories, hunt them down and slay them,"** he begged, considerately not fixing her with his appraising stare. Instead, he began sleeking the fringes on a foreleg, tugging at snarls with his teeth, then eyeing the results.

*"Which reminds me—you need a thorough brushing, and soon. I don't know why you shed so late in the season, but it's the bane of my existence! The housekeeping staff's as well. Three complained to Ezequiel just yesterday."* Long white eye whiskers wriggled as he snaked a look to see if she were serious. *"And thank you, fur-heart, but I have to conquer my fears on my own. Best purge them from my system now, not after I'm down below."*

"Seeker Treblicote?" The plumber's apprentice, Theoni, tugged at her sleeve, and Cinzia forced her eyes open, twitched her lips into a sickly smile. "Master Xavier says ye don't *have* to go below with us. Not if you're so afeered." Theoni was a delicate slip of a thing, not exactly what Cinzia had expected as a plumber's 'prentice, not with her wispy build and her pale-complected face topped by tiny ringlets of blonde hair.

**"On the other hand—or arm—so to speak,"** La'ow neutralized his expression behind an exceptionally furry paw, **"note those triceps and biceps. A few more years and she'll bend pipes into pretzels."**

Master Xavier's shrewd eyes rested on her as he resettled a knit cap on his balding head, finically rolling it above his ears. "No sin in admitting yer limitations, miss. We all 'as some." Battered thumbs hooked his waistband and heaved, though his knee-length pants still hung amazingly low on his hips beneath the broad belly. Given the crammed tool belt around his waist, his trousers defied the laws of gravity. "Me, I hate working on the rooftop cisterns—too high for me, even though the edges are walled. Take one look and I go all wambly." **"Make sure you follow behind Theoni, not Master Xavier,"** La'ow advised. **"Otherwise the view will be . . . broadening. Mayhap even light-reflective."**

Still absorbed by her own fears, La'ow's allusion laboriously worked its way through her brain and then, without warning, she fought to smother a rising giggle. Apparently Master Xavier was subject to rising-moon syndrome, buttocks peeping, then creeping above his trouser-top horizon

as he bent and stretched about his work. Without a doubt
his heavy tool belt aided and abetted the tendency.

Aware that Theoni and Master Xavier still studied her,
clearly concerned, she walked to the trapdoor and swung
onto the ladder as nonchalantly as she could, not looking
below her. Let her feet find the first rung. "Missy, no! Wait
up." Xavier's strong arms, covered with an unmown
meadow's-worth of grizzled hair, retrieved her and the ladder until she forced herself to unlock her death grip.

"First things first," he chided. "Ye ain't prepared, like!
That allus causes mishaps." A whistle brought two younger
apprentices on the run, one still industriously plying a needle with such concentration that he stumbled twice yet kept
stitching. "Know the kitty-ghatt'll ride on yer shoulders if
it turns wet below and we 'ave to wade. Yer dress tabard's
flimsy-like, an I doan want you trekking back for that
sheepskin one you wear outa doors. Get that wet and you'll
be dragged under fer sure." The coats, the cloaks . . . enveloping her . . . bearing her down. . . . No, no more!

Hovering at her side with an odd piece of shaped canvas,
the dark-haired 'prentice diffidently proffered it, though she
couldn't determine how to don it, assuming one was *supposed* to don it. He flapped it invitingly, and when that
failed, chewed at his lip, suddenly brightening as he slipped
a hand through an opening. Fixing her with an expectant
gaze, he rose on tiptoe, arm in the air, the canvas ruckling
around it. Belatedly deducing what he wanted, she bowed
her head and allowed him to slip it on, then busy himself
with the ties under each arm and around each upper arm.
Though she couldn't exactly see herself, it seemed some
sort of half-shirt with abbreviated sleeves, the bottom ending just below her bust, where more ties snugged it firm.

"Double sailcloth," Xavier pointed out with satisfaction.
"Rudely stitched in the rush, but the best we could do.
Domie's idea," a pleased nod at his apprentice, who
flushed, then squeaked in surprise as La'ow rubbed against
his ankles.

**"Very clever! Thank him for both of us,"** he instructed,
and so she did, profusely, as the second apprentice strapped
a leather tool belt around her waist. A part of her felt
cheated on discovering her belt wasn't as encumbered with
assorted devices and tools as Xavier's and Theoni's. Sheer

silliness—as if she'd know what to do with half of them! Let's see—candle loops holding six candles, a waterproof lucifer box, a ball peen hammer, a wrench, a coil of light rope, and strips of white cloth, each some thirty centimeters long. Bandages? For people or for plumbing?

"Markers," the second 'prentice explained, jerking one free and knotting it around his dark-haired mate's wrist. "Ye tie 'em 'round to mark where ye been, so ye can tell yer way coming back." Now that was a brilliant idea! Especially the "coming back" part! "They're lumi . . . lumni . . ." he struggled through his own version of the word, "luminosimuss-like, we soak'em in a solution of glow powder from the Sunderlies."

"How brilliant!" she assured him, and wondered why he giggled. Oh.

"Now yer boots," Theoni instructed, readying herself to straddle Cinzia's leg as she obediently raised it. Off came one boot and then its mate. In their place Theoni helped slip on thick knit booties complete with flexible rubber soling of gutta-percha, another Sunderlies bounty. The diamond pattern incised on each sole would prevent slipping—she fervently hoped.

"*Now* you're ready!" Xavier beamed his approval as he slammed a hard, domed leather helmet on her head which immediately sank to mash the bridge of her nose. Darkness, closeness, trapped again! "Oops!" Removing her helmet, he fiddled with the liner, packing in felt strips, then resettled it atop her head where it rested without obscuring her vision. "I'll head down first, you next, and Theoni last." The darkness swallowed him, his tool belt clinking and chinking, the comforting sounds growing more distant and muffled.

This was the moment she'd dreaded, abandoning the light, descending into blank blackness, La'ow draped across her shoulders until they touched bottom, however far down that might be.

" 'Tis a brave thing ye be doing, Seeker, aiding us in locating our king and the others," the master plumber bawled up at her as he steadied the ladder. "Twice as brave sin' you doan much care for being dark and snug like this. Me, it's a second home, all cozy-like."

The final rung didn't exist, and she toppled backward,

La'ow's weight dragging at her until he could spring free. Xavier caught her and tilted her upright as Theoni descended with all the graceful cheekiness of a romping squirrel, despite the lanterns hanging from her belt and a thick coil of rope over her shoulder.

She didn't feel very brave, far from it. And with Theoni between her and the ladder, she couldn't even run like a coward. Might as well be brave, then. "My Seeker Veritas duty is to serve the king in any way I can, as well as serve as liaison with Canderis. If there's a chance La'ow can contact Hru'rul . . ." Not just Hru'rul, but Khim and P'roul as well. The whereabouts of her two Seeker colleagues truly concerned her, as did the loss of Harry and Arras Muscadeine, especially Harry, who helped at odd tasks and entertained La'ow. His intelligence, curiosity, and delight in all things related to the ghatti had made him a pleasure to be around.

Theoni lit lanterns and handed them out, their yellow glow chasing away some of the hobgoblins cluttering her mind, threatening to immobilize her with childhood fears. "But they could have sent Resonants," Master Xavier persisted, "the king, Lord Muscadeine, and his son are all powerful Resonants."

That was true, and the Lady knew how she'd wanted to temporize, grasp at any straw to avoid agreeing to descend into the darkness. But the ghatti employed all their senses as well as their mindspeaking abilities, their sight and hearing far keener than humans, their whiskers and fur attuned to the slightest air current. Besides, confess her fears, reveal her weaknesses to someone with Lady Francie's mettle? Seekers learned the truth about themselves; their Bonds saw to that, and La'ow had worked long and hard with her to overcome her problems. After all, any available body could bolster falling walls or clear debris, but few others in this land were capable of doing what she and La'ow were so capable of.

**"And it's hardly wise to refuse the sister of our former Seeker General, the esteemed Doyce Marbon and that striped beauty, Khar'pern,"** La'ow teased, but told a truth. **"Ah, I know where Khim and P'roul inherited their good looks!"**

*"We'd not have refused anyone aid—Seeker General or ditch digger—you flirt! Stop pretending otherwise!"*

"So come along, then." At Xavier's instruction she followed, praying the corridors would continue to be reasonably wide and high and unobstructed. And dry! Please, Lady, let her not have to wade through water—not without a blue sky above her. Oh, dear, here she was right behind Master Xavier—and La'ow had warned her not to! Something more to pray to the Lady to deliver her from, especially if highlighted by her lantern!

Time ceased to hold any meaning in these passages that constricted into tunnels with kilometers of pipe laid along the center, allowing just enough space for a body to scrape by sideways, upper body curled around the pipe. Each time she forgot and raised her helmeted head, a dull clunk reminded her. Most tunnels appeared neither overclean nor too dirty, though on occasion Xavier scowled and grumbled, plucking up a discarded tool or fitting and either hooking it to his belt or placing it where it could be retrieved by the next crew.

Sometimes he halted without warning, rapping on the pipe with a wrench, then tilting an ear to listen, hoping, mayhap, that someone out of sight might rap back, signal their location. "Arborfer," he amplified once, his tap more respectful, and the pipe resonated with a lovely, harmonious note. "Can withstand most anything, they can—'cept us and our carelessness. And they overlook a muckle of that, forgiving our ham-handed ways. Ah, I wish I'd been alive in those days when they were laid. Went once to the king's tree nurseries, an some Erakwa men showed me how they worked with it. Mayhap, if things go well, someday we'll have enough arborfer for more pipes! Beautiful, beyew-ti-ful." A wistful sigh seemed to float up from the bottom of his rubber-soled slippers. "Almost criminal, sacrilege to think some was tore loose in that explosion!"

Onward they went, hunched, then crawling on hands and knees for a few short rods, Cinzia stifling a scream when Xavier's lantern went pitch-black. She did scream—more a short "eek"—as La'ow's tail accidentally brushed the base of her neck.

**"Sorry."** Twisting back, he slipped his head beneath the brim of her helmet, his nose cool against her temple. **"I'm**

**proud of you—of course, I always am. You're doing fine."**
The long fur in his ears, as well as his muzzle stood out
stark white in the light, while the rest of him blended with
the walls, almost as if he'd dematerialized, his face floating
in nothingness. **"Interesting down here, absolutely fascinat-
ing hidey-holes and shortcuts. Definitely worth a roam. Perfect ghatti territory!"**

*"Mayhap if life with me ever proves too boring, you can
'prentice with Master Xavier."*

A complacent chuckle tickled her mind. **"Never, lovey-
heart! But when we retire . . ."** Purposely leaving his
thought unfinished, he continued prowling ahead.

Ahead of her the sound of an untrammeled flow of
water, splashing, streaming free, iced her soul and made
her cringe. Earlier, Xavier had shown her how a hand on
a pipe could sense the flow of water, its confined, directed
movement tickling her palm. Put an ear on the pipe and a
faint rilling could be overheard, as if the water quietly chatted with itself. He'd made her listen at empty pipes as well,
ones abruptly drained by the explosion, their source cut
off. A disconsolate drip or two might cause a faint ping,
but that was all. Sometimes the timbre of distant voices
carried along empty pipes as other workers toiled to repair
a segment farther along. Thrice she'd noticed a shadowy
figure out of the corner of her eye, crouched or standing
contemplatively against the wall, cheek pressed to it or
hands smoothing it. After the first time, when both Xavier
and Theoni had looked at her askance, she'd not mentioned
the figure again.

But this new onslaught of water heightened her uneasi-
ness, her body lagging, the tunnel too narrow to turn and
retreat from the sound. "Come on, come on," Theoni
urged, her small hand firm against Cinzia's hip, both calming her and inexorably pushing her ahead. "Another rod
and you can stand up again. There, you'll see. Master Xavier's got a new lantern lit."

Feeling like a moth drawn to the light, she scurried
toward its brightness on sore hands and knees, yearning to
meld her feeble light to it, force the darkness to recede.
Now, through the tunnel's mouth and onto her feet—like
a human being again! The scent of water, fresh, not stagnant, was everywhere, a continuous plashing in her ears.

Worse yet, dampness all around, the walls dripping with condensation or spray, the flooring puddled.

"Take a look," Xavier instructed, almost with awe, and raised his lantern high, Theoni following suit. Even adding her lantern to theirs couldn't completely illuminate the outer limits of the large chamber they'd entered, but at its farthest end she could just make out a sinuous arch of water—shiny black, then separating and widening into a shimmering gray with white or translucently ragged edges—pouring forth from a slot far above. It fanned out before cascading downward into a widening column that crashed and splattered against the flooring, then welled into a grated hole the size of a dinner table. "Storm drain." His shout sounded like a whisper, human vocal cords unable to compete against the water's rush. "That's the overflow from above being drained here."

"Above?" Her lantern waved, semaphoring her distress. "You mean we're *below* water, below the flooded tunnels?" Underground and underwater simultaneously?

"No, just reaching that level. That's water from the roof cisterns up above, 'less they've drained them or shut them off. Rest is overflow from the streets, justifiably returning to us what's ours to dispose of." Helmet jarring hers, he placed his mouth closer to her ear, as if she might be hard of hearing, the pounding water smothering her senses. "Chief engineer'n I disagree. I say they gotta be swept outward, out this way, from where Ezequiel said he was. Can fight the water's force only so long. . . ." He trailed off, nodding sagely but sadly.

Moisture taming his flyaway fur, La'ow began quartering the huge, echoing chamber, leaping onto a maze of pipes and racing along them before springing to higher ones, listening, always listening. She knew without asking that he'd been constantly casting his mindvoice in all directions, alert for any response.

Unexpectedly he loosed a prodigious yowl and came springing down from pipe to pipe, haste and excitement turning his usual flowing grace into a ludicrous scrambling parody. **"Ask the good Master what lies at the drain's other end! Does he know where it flows?"** His eyes were wide, his tail lashing, as he paced in figure-eight patterns by her shins.

But Xavier had apparently divined La'ow's thoughts, tool belt clanging as he ran clumsily toward another ladder that to Cinzia's eyes rose into nothingness. "I knew it! I knew it!" he exulted. "Your big boy heard them, didn't he? Right where I said they might be. We've got to get topside! Think I can trace the streets the drain runs beneath! Hurry—boost him up to me!"

*"Do you mind!"* She cradled La'ow in her arms before passing him up to Xavier. *"You can ride on my shoulders, but it will be slower, I'm afraid."*

**"Away we go!"** La'ow cried, springing from her arms onto the master plumber's broad shoulders, black tail like a mustache beneath Xavier's nose. **"Not done yet! Now we've got to track which drain they'll pop out of!"**

Letting Theoni ahead of her on the ladder, Cinzia wearily dragged herself up, rung by rung, relieved they'd narrowed down the king's location, but all too aware that not everyone had yet been accounted for.

♣

Ceaselessly thrumming in his ears, churning his thoughts, the rushing water's clamor wore at Harry's resolve. Enclosed like this, it was ominously loud, swashing and swishing without respite. The water's force had further sapped Eadwin's dwindling strength, and now they were thralls to its power, swept along by it. Occasionally Eadwin fought back, edging them into new channels or streams as they surged by, somehow gauging their position, shifting their course. Sheer stubbornness to try to outwit the underground stream now that it ran free, unfettered, and Harry dully wondered if there were rhyme or reason to Eadwin's decisions. And most of all, he wished Eadwin would stop pitty-patting at the wall, just swim! But when Eadwin instructed, "Grab!" he did, and each time a handy protrusion or small cavity lurked near the top of the wall, waiting to be clutched. Either a series of minor miracles or . . . his weary mind refused to take it in.

They clung to several of these smooth, small openings now, each just deep enough for a hand to insert itself, while Eadwin swept his free hand higher until he'd located an iron ring. "Rest a bit." He huffed, gave a strangled cough. "Then, when I say 'go,' hang on and kick like hellhounds are nipping at your heels. We've got to fight the flow." The whiteness of the king's hand, doubtlessly as water-wrinkled as his own, limply indicated their future direction. Harry could just make out the whitish blur, which meant that at least a little light crept in from above, or he'd finally learned to see in the dark. Every so often it seemed as if their surroundings brightened, just enough to tantalize him into thinking he could see more clearly, before they swept into darkness yet again.

Plowing splayed fingers through Harry's hair, Eadwin eased it off his forehead, out of his eyes, and Harry blinked his relief. "Yes, you *can* see now, can't you? There are a few vents here and there—didn't you notice before? One over there—see?" By straining, Harry could just make out the slit, detect a delicate tickle of moving air against his wet face. "Didn't you notice before? Air's never completely stale, just a little tired. The vents also let in a little light— must mean dawn's breaking aboveground."

Light—dawn up above, and Harry shivered, slowly realizing how long they'd been searching. Not forever, only until dawn. And that, in turn, left him acutely conscious of the cold, his limbs numb, even the core of his body, his heart, cooling slowly but surely. Rather peaceful, in a way, to lose himself in lethargy. He'd not asked about Papa again, though he'd sent his mindvoice streaming out time and again, listening with all his might both within his mind and with his ears. Once he'd caught a snatch of conversation, only to identify it as Theo and Romain-Laurent, somehow above them now. Good! At least Theo and Khim were safe.

"Why do you think these cavities are here, Harry? Dumb luck, chance, or something more?"

Harry managed a little shrug, pressed his quivering lips tight. How he hated it when grown-ups condescended to children, droning on about trivialities—as if that would distract them, make them stop worrying a problem to death by tricking them into thinking of something else. "C–couldn't reach them if we weren't f–floating. Theo, mayhap, but n–not us. D–did they hold some sort of rafter or b–beam once?" He'd not hurt the king's feelings for the world, so if it meant discussing something silly like this, he'd do it—at least for a while. Better than forcing his legs to kick again, and that he'd be doing soon enough.

"Not a bad guess, Harry. But actually they were designed as handholds." Eadwin tended to be more scholar than king, and Harry recognized the opening notes of a mind-numbing lecture. Dear Lady, he was already numb, and Eadwin apparently planned to talk him into a stupor! "Didn't old Ignacio ever spin you the tale about the horrible flooding that occurred—oh, you'd best ask Ezequiel the precise date—one spring when Constant was constructing this castle? 'Twas the wettest spring on record—a warm front stalled between the mountain ranges, and the winter snows melted in record time. Plus heavy, drenching downpours beyond belief. Well, the ground was already saturated, couldn't absorb any more water, and the lower levels of the castle flooded—drowned fifteen workers one way or another."

Harry listened, not really hearing or caring, more concerned with conquering his chills, the perpetual drag of his limp limbs. "After that disaster Constant had rude directional markers carved up near the ceiling, handholds as well, so that if the passageways ever flooded again, anyone working down here might have a chance to make his or her way clear."

"Clear?" Harry shook his head, wished he hadn't as wet tangles of hair dripped in his eyes. "You mean you actually have *some* idea where we are, where we're headed?" It sounded impossibly rude, doubting the king like this, but he didn't care. "Does Papa know about these markers?" Frustrated beyond belief, he beat and churned at the water, not caring that he splashed Eadwin and Hru'rul. "Are you *saying* that Papa could be following these markings, too?"

"Harry, I just don't know—not for sure." Eadwin's eyes were shadowed, sunken deeply into his head, his beard muskrat-sleek. "It depends on whether Arras paid any attention to those old tales . . . if he even heard them told." His eyes closed, stayed shut for longer than Harry liked. "My . . . mother said . . . that when he was a lad, he worshiped my true father, Maarten. They'd go on nature walks together, but your father was often restless, so active . . . he didn't always listen. My father, I've been told, was more contemplative, like me." Knuckling moisture from his eyes, Eadwin gathered Harry close in a hug, and Harry felt the king's quivering melding with his own. "I've tried to gauge Arras's position, where he'd have swum or floated when the water caught him, if he didn't make it to higher ground like Theo and Charpentier. Hru'rul says they're scarcely wet." A reluctant chuckle. "Hardly seems fair, does it? All these channels ultimately feed into major storm drains—that's where we're heading, that's where your father should be heading."

"Or his body!" It was all too much to bear, the odds too great—all this aching misery, being trapped in this cold, wet darkness, lost despite what Eadwin promised. All for naught! Every bit of his being shouted it, screamed it; he *knew* it, had steeled himself to unflinchingly face the truth. If the Plumb hadn't killed him outright, he'd died soon after. Sometimes, no matter how hard one tried, one failed. But the effort mattered, and he shouldn't, couldn't hate Eadwin and himself because they'd failed. Even so, desolate sobs overtook him, racking his body in counterpoint to his shivers, setting his teeth clattering, jarring them together so hard he bit his tongue, tasted blood.

"And wouldn't the Shepherd Harrap remind you about having faith. Faith has conquered failure time and again!"

"Stop it!" Harry yelped, pummeling Eadwin's chest and shoulders, slapping at Hru'rul and nearly dislodging him, smashing a fist into the wall. "Stop it, stop it, stop it! He's dead!"

"Then explain the mindvoice that Hru'rul just snagged out of thin air!" Harry found himself pinned against the wall, Eadwin's forearm levered across his upper chest, and Harry slowly, almost reluctantly stopped flailing, praying Eadwin would say it again, craving the assurance of repetition. Oh, to hear it repeated—his Papa lived! "He's not aware that he's 'speaking, not directing his mindvoice toward anyone in particular, but Hru'rul distinctly heard it. Said it sounded as if Arras were singing, though it didn't make much sense to Hru'rul. Something like 'mow, mow, mow your oats'!"

**"And 'bout now be kicking like crazy. Papa Arras floating by!"** To reinforce his statement, Hru'rul slipped off Eadwin's shoulders, enthusiastically paddling, ripples V-ing out behind him in a broadening arrowhead pattern.

♣

Wide-eyed and more than a little nonplussed Etelka drank
in her first view of Marchmont's capital, or at least this
segment of Sidonie just beyond the castle walls. It was . . .
she studied the puddle at her foot, only to discover that in
those long moments while she'd looked away in awed appraisal, the puddle had crept closer to her boot . . . *very*
wet here! Meditatively, she rubbed her shoulder blade, then
switched to massaging her lower back, while all around her
men and women of varied ages strode purposefully, some
bandoleered with heavy canvas hoses, others lumbered with
buckets, picks, and shovels. The kitten sat on her feet,
skinny tail wrapped tight, her amber eyes, still tinged with
the blue of babyhood, equally wide and her head aswivel
so as not to miss a single thing.

The second wagon she and the kitten had hitched a ride
on hadn't been near as comfortable as Master Suggs's had
been. In fact, she hadn't appreciated how clean and comfy
it was at all till she'd changed over, more concerned with
her new conveyance's destination than its cargo. Should
have paid more attention! The second wagon had been
chock-full of scrap iron, nasty, clanking, some rust-coated,
some oil-scented; most pieces had been tossed in loose, and
they rattled and shifted at every rut and bump, threatening
to bury her and the kitten. Without a doubt she bore
bruises galore 'neath her clothes, worse than being pinched
and poked by her brothers half the night. And twice she'd
rudely cupped her hand over Baby's mouth as she'd
shrieked her pain at having a toe or tailtip nipped by shifting scrap. The bagged scrap was hardly cuddlesome either.

So . . . this was Sidonie, eh? Taking off her spectacles,
she polished them on her shirt-tail before shoving them
back in place for a closer look. Well, right enough—just
east of the LaPierre River, but this looked more as if the
town floated *in* it. Strange, especially in winter like this.
Snow, yes, but she didn't think it had rained any since
they'd started out, nor had a surprise thaw come to turn
the land mushy with water. The walls rearing up about
houses blocks ahead undoubtedly ringed the castle. Lucky
for her that her vantage point was on a slight rise, things

appeared awfully swampy around the walls. Mayhap it was a moat?

Somehow Sidonie wasn't as impressive as she'd pictured it being, and stood, pinching her lips in disapproval. Not just swampy, but messy, downright untidy, too. Tiles slithering off roofs, cracks in building foundations—and worse—not to mention how cobbles had heaved and humped the streets. Mayhap that amazing fierce explosion that had rocked the scrap wagon just before they'd arrived had something to do with all this. Lady knew, she and Baby had clung together for dear life!

"Now what do we do, Baby?" 'Twould be nice if the kitten would answer, like one of the ghatti, because Telka felt in urgent need of some sage advice. "If all that water's seeped inside the castle, too, the king won't have time for us. He'll be too busy drying carpets, scraping out mud and such like."

Increasingly aware of a creeping dampness, she looked down again to discover that the puddle now lapped at her boot. No wonder Baby hadn't bothered to answer—she'd already darted to higher ground. What to do, what to do? played through her head as she followed the kitten up the limestone steps of a shuttered shop and sat on the topmost step, her back angled into the alcove where the door was set. Couldn't sit here once the shop opened, but it was too early, the wagon having arrived at Sidonie's outskirts at first light. What with all the wagoners gathering round, babbling about the explosion, it had been easy to slip away unobserved. Now, hungry, thirsty, tired, and wishing she had a place to pee—that always happened to her when she saw so much water—she did the best she could, striving to remain cheerful as she opened her sack to remove her remaining apple.

"Yee-ow! Yee-umm!" Baby capered on the steps, tail straight as a lightning rod. "Yee-umm!" she shrieked her entreaty again at the top of her lungs as Telka bit into the apple, teeth excising a hail-bruise so she could spit out the bad spot. Butting at her elbow, rearing to pat a paw against her cheek, her mouth, Baby demanded her share, eyes watchful, expression hopeful.

Etelka still wasn't sure what to make of it, but the kitten adored raw apple, would devour it all if she let her. She

also clamored for raisins and the dried apricot halves
Etelka had brought with her, although she hadn't disdained
such mundane and more typical feline fare as the cheese
and sausage and dried herrings in her sack. How comical
the kitten looked gobbling down raisins, her jaws working
and working, trying to unstick her teeth and then, licking
her lips in satisfaction, she'd beg another! The only problem with mixing fruit and felines, Etelka had discovered,
was that it made the kitten's poopy awful stinky, no matter
how deeply she tried to bury it.

Taking another meditative bite and nipping off a piece
for the kitten, Etelka examined her surroundings more
closely. Oozing water trickled around snowbanks and bored
under them, puddles all over, rivulets, even, in some places.
To her right, shouts and commotion, people backpedaling
as an absolute geyser of water erupted from a street drain.
Wasn't meant to be a fountain, as far as she could tell.
Mouth ajar at the incongruity of it all, she dropped her
guard on the apple, only to discover Baby licking away, her
raspy tongue scraping off the white flesh. Hurriedly salvag-
ing what was left, she bit off a few more tiny pieces for the
kitten and snapped away at the remains herself, thankful
it served as food and almost as drink, Da's apples were
*so* juicy!

"You can have the core when I'm done," she promised,
feeling sorry she didn't have more to offer the kitten, as
well as herself, but they'd eaten everything she'd brought.
Last night in the wagon, rocking and clanging along, she'd
dreamed of claiming a whole chicken leg for her very own,
surrounding it with Mam's mashed potatoes and gravy, buttered turnips and parsnips. As if she'd ever had a whole
chicken leg to herself! Not likely, unless someone figured
out how to cross a centipede with a chicken!

"Well, Baby, mayhap we should find out what's going on
here. Then we'll know what to do. At least we can head
for higher ground." Sounded funny to say that—how Da
would laugh—but 'twas the literal truth. In fact, best head
for higher ground tout suite because, while she'd been
munching her apple, the puddle in front of her had grown
into a small pond, rising to the top of the shop's lowest
step. Well, nothing to do but to wade, much as she hated
wetting her feet. 'Twouldn't do her boots or her feet any

good, not in this weather, not without something dry to change into and a fire to toast her toes. The stockings in her sack were her best ones, had to be saved for when they met the king.

"Come on, Baby!" Gingerly stepping into the water, she coaxed the kitten along behind, praying she'd hurry. But the kitten refused to budge, mewling piteously, striking at the water with one orange paw, then recoiling in dismay. Checking her footing, Telka turned, prepared to scoop her up under one arm. "Ye-ouch!" she yelped, sounding uncannily like the kitten, as an orange body clung to her leg like a burr, clawing its way higher until at last it reached the blessed thickness of her jacket, a clash of orange against the red-and-black block squares. At least then the claws didn't hurt as much. Scrambling onto her shoulder, the kitten surveyed her watery domain with relief, nose-sniffing Etelka's ear, sounding like a whooshing pair of bellows. "I *knew* I shouldn't have read you those sections from the book about how the ghatti ride on their Bondmates' shoulders!" she huffed, wading along as rapidly as she could. "Bondmates have lovely thick sheepskin tabards, and now I certainly know why! Your claws hurt!" Unrepentant, the kitten alternately crooned and nibbled at her ear as Telka hopped and stretched her way to dry land.

♣

Disconsolate, Nakum squatted beside the natural stone of one of the underground walls and studied the wide crack where the rock face had sundered, its wound rawly bright against long-exposed stone. Tracing the crack with a finger, he finally placed his hand over it, palm down. If only he could knit the fracture together, make it whole again. Alas, he could not, and his heart mutely wept for the pain, the unhealable hurt the earth had suffered. So much damage, destruction everywhere he'd trodden, sympathy welling forth at the jagged scars of man-made origin. Everything clamored and cried for his attention, wailing their stories at him, begging for redress, if not repair.

How far had he come? How many passages had he walked, swum where fetid waters had slowly begun to drain, depositing a miasma of misery behind. How foolish, unnecessary it had all been! The hows and whys of this disaster still eluded him, but he sensed the Plumb's detonation had been accidental. Certainly nothing his cousin, Eadwin, would have countenanced. Eadwin revered the earth, the arborfers, far more than most of his kind. And pragmatically, Eadwin would hardly have approved an explosion that could have toppled his castle!

Eadwin's presence and that of the others—friends and acquaintances—permeated these lower depths, but Nakum ignored the distraction, intent on documenting the earth's ills. Yes, they faced danger, and their well-being concerned him, but he had faith that they would surmount it. In fact it had become downright crowded in spots, corridors and passageways swarming with would-be rescuers and workers; more than once he'd flattened himself against a wall, blending with it to avoid discovery. Besides, he had more pressing matters at hand: to soothe the earth, listen to its litany of woes, calm the clangor of subterranean voices barraging him. More damage had occurred in an instant than through centuries of human habitation, or even millennia-worth of nature's shifts and upsurges, compression and furnacelike heat, the interplay of the elements, and violent but spontaneous upheavals. Such hurts presaged transformation, the earth's ongoing metamorphosis, just as limestone compacted to marble over the aeons.

What to do? Ah, to roll back the moment, unmake it! He had power over some things, but very limited power compared to this monstrous rending. A special, though small, ability to stretch time, warp and bend it to curtail its flight or speed it along, though not always that. Ofttimes events progressed too fast for him to grasp, left him helpless to slow their pace as they whizzed by. What could he do?

Hand still in place, commiserating with the pain, he rested his forehead against the stone, his eyes closed. For a moment the squelch of his leather garments distracted him as he shifted. "I give my oath that this will never happen again, that you will never be disturbed in this manner while I have life, have breath to stop it. That is my vow."

Had he offered too little or too much, strayed far beyond his ability's bounds? Increasingly plagued by the cling and drag of wet garments against his skin, he rose, shaking one leg and then the other, smoothing the leather into place. Time to leave these depths, walk the surface of the world, find his cousin Eadwin. If not Eadwin, then Ezequiel as a start, a decent, dedicated man he'd known since they were both young together for a brief time. True, Ezequiel's skills involved material things, objects, that was his training, his bent, but he'd unstintingly help in this time of crisis. Especially since it involved both Eadwin and Marchmont.

♣

As they wandered, circumspectly taking in some of Sidonie's sights, what Telka most noticed were the people thronging the streets: some uniformed and boasting a military bearing and precision; others garbed in elegant sky-blue livery, though much bedraggled by their exertions; and finally, people who appeared everyday folk like her family, mayhap of higher status or lower, but otherwise unremarkable. Yet everyone engaged in feverish, concerted efforts, prying open drain covers, frantically chopping at ice and snow that blocked grates. Sometimes when they broke through, water gushed forth, and soon that street or alleyway was submerged ankle-deep in streaming water. Always she'd been told to beware of strangers, especially strangers with city-bred, city-slick ways, but so far she and the kitten might have been invisible, few—if any—showing interest in her or the kitten.

Once, when she'd dawdled to watch a particularly diligent crew, a stout, middle-aged woman had come bustling out of a bakery, holding a tray of fresh biscuits. "Here, child!" she grumped. "Might as well have a couple. 'Tis the last baking we'll do today."

Hand hovering over the tray as if it possessed a mind of its own, Etelka wondered if she dared accept food from a stranger. Best decide quick, for Baby balanced on her hind legs, ready to climb the woman's canvas apron, determined to sample the biscuits on her own. Should she, shouldn't she? "Thankee, ma'am, but I'm not real hungered." Debating, wanting to appear a woman of the world, she dug deep into her pocket, found one of four coppers and the one silver she'd hoarded for emergencies. "Mayhap I could buy one—for later, you know. If they're not too dear?"

Juggling her tray, the woman pushed frazzled hair back from her forehead with a thick wrist. "Lady bless us, love. Everyone needs strength today, laboring to rescue the king! Take some, eat! When this trayful's gone, there's blessed little more I can bake, way the waters are rising in the cellar. Ovens'll be flooded shortly." Lips tightening, she shook her head at the impending disaster, suddenly looking down as the kitten tested the set of her claws in her apron hem, ready to scale the heights. "Must be the buttermilk in them! Even your kitty wants some! Now take some, afore bigger souls than you gobble'm all down."

Hastily complying, Telka crumpled a piece for the kitten, holding it cupped in her hand since the street was so wet. Tiny whiskers tickled as Baby nosed out every crumb, began industriously licking in the cracks between her fingers. Before she could demand more, Telka wrapped the biscuits in her kerchief. The woman stood, beaming on them both, calling "Fresh biscuits! Fuel yourselves, lads and lasses, then find our king." But most souls were too intent on their business to stop, though two or three snatched at biscuits on the fly, calling their thanks over their shoulders as they rushed onward.

Now might be a good time to ask, since the opportunity had presented itself and Etelka had gained the woman's attention. " 'Scuse me, ma'am." Evincing interest in the toe of her boot, too embarrassed to raise her eyes, Etelka mumbled, "Is there a place nearby where . . . I could . . . ah, relieve myself?"

A roar of laughter greeted her query, the woman chortling till her face turned beet-red, leftover biscuits bouncing on the tray. "My dear child, who's going to notice a bit more water here today?" Frankly, Telka didn't find it very funny. As if she were common enough to simply lower her drawers in the middle of the street! What were these city-people like, to suggest such a thing?

Shamed, she scooped up the kitten, her package of biscuits held tight in the other hand, determined not to lose them. Smelled good as Mam's did, and she could hardly wait to find a secluded spot to eat them. But the eating would definitely have to wait, 'cause she couldn't keep pressing her knees together this hard. Scowling, the internal pressure building the more she thought about it, Etelka minched along, but before she'd gone more than a few steps, the woman called her back. "Child! Don't take on so! Never meant to embarrass you, just teasing-like."

Gesturing toward the bakery, she waved Etelka inside, the girl wiping and wiping her muddy boots before the woman scooted her through the shop and out the back. "Over there, child." The woman pointed at a two-door convenience, and Etelka rushed inside, sighing with relief at the sight of the polished wooden seat and the neat stack of paper squares. Only after she'd fully relieved herself did it occur to her to consider where, precisely, this all went, especially on a day like today.

Not quite sure what to do next, she peeked in the bakery's back door and gave a shouted thanks and a wave as the woman quick-stepped down to the basement ovens. Hmph! Things looked mighty different from back here, behind the buildings, more homey in a strange way—sort of the difference between a "company face" and a "family face"—all sorts of messy things, needful objects essential to normal daily life, things you didn't mind bosom friends seeing, 'cause you'd seen their equally homey things time and again.

Wet back here as well, worse, in fact, because the alleyway consisted of a dirt lane with two parallel tracks worn lower where wagon wheels had rutted the earth. Still, if she kept to the center ridge, she and Baby weren't exactly high and dry, but they were higher and less damp. As she meandered along, unclear where she was headed, she made quick work of the biscuit she'd shared with the kitten, then started on the second one with a more leisurely appreciation of its flaky tenderness. "All right, all right!" she complained, disgruntled at the kitten's bad manners as she leaped and sprang, intent on snagging the biscuit from Telka's hand. "I'll save some, promise! You're my growing baby, aren't you? Want you to grow up big and pretty, don't we? Feed you enough, mayhap you'll be a ghatta when you grow up."

Didn't happen that way, she knew full well, but pretending was fine, so long as you could always admit which was pretend and which was for real. Da said that he pre-

tended, sometimes, when he had a mucky, dirty job to do
and didn't much feel like it. Made it go faster if he pretended the manure he shoveled was jewels or gold when
he mucked out the barn. He'd gaily waved a shovelful in
her direction, inquiring, "May I scatter diamonds at your
feet, my lady?"

So, what had the nice bakery lady been saying? That the
king was missing? That certainly put a crimp in her plans.
How had they misplaced a king, anyway? And why on
earth was everyone digging up drains and sewers? Did they
expect to find him there? Not very logical, not to her way
of thinking. Certainly wasn't the first place *she'd* hunt for
a king! So *where* would *she* search? The question occupied
her so thoroughly that she neglected to give Baby her share
of the biscuit until she heard her anxiously squeaking,
"Y'ew, y'ew, y'ew!" Ofttimes she did it in response to
Telka calling her "Baby," and she felt as if they conversed,
the kitten answering her. Could she teach her to say
"Telka?"

Ha! Another group up ahead, two men braced and
straining against the end of the biggest wrench she'd ever
seen, plus an older man and woman jamming pieces of
board in place to deflect the streaming water as the men
heaved and twisted at a bolt. Didn't look as if water had
been meant to rise out of that grating they were wrestling
with, but it certainly was now. Not wanting to distract them,
she gave them a wide berth, though she had to rush back
to snatch Baby, who was stealthing nearer, oblivious to the
water she waded through, her ears intently aswivel to capture some faraway sound inaudible to human ears. "Not
likely to be a rat, silly," she scolded. "Not in all this water.
And I doubt it's a fish flicker-finning along." Stomach fur
soggy and clumped, the kitten protested with a "Y'ew!
Y'ew!" and, not knowing what else to do with her, Etelka
tucked her inside the front of her jacket.

Detouring puddles, leaping streams, she distanced herself
and Baby from whatever had so intrigued the kitten. Merciful Lady! Up ahead, set in the stonework foundation of a
dilapidated house with loose clapboards, she spotted a
hinged iron door, the sort of trapdoor that gave people
access to a cistern down below. The metal doorplate
creaked and groaned, water spurting round its edges, and

she could swear the door bulged from the mounting pressure behind it. Then, strangely, the trickles ceased, the door settling with a sigh, though horrendous grumblings and gurglings still resounded, as if pressure had shifted to build elsewhere and needed to find release soon. From the shrieks of shock and surprise emanating from the house's inhabitants, she suspected it had—the excess water rising between their floorboards.

Curious and concerned in equal measure, she wondered what to do. She might not be a neighbor, but it seemed unneighborly not to help. Retrieving the kitten from inside her jacket, she plopped her on the back steps of the adjoining house and stashed her sack behind a porch pillar, saying, "Stay, Baby. Watch the sack." Steeling herself, she waded through water and mud to snatch up a rust-encrusted shovel she'd noticed leaning against the fence. Not much, but it was what she had, and with that, she rammed the blade against the trapdoor's latch. Didn't want to pry up, hadn't been opened in ages, less she missed her guess, not to mention how the sudden pressure had further strained and warped it.

Wedging the rolled shoulder of the shovel under the latch tip, she pulled with all her might, then reset her feet and firmed her grip and tried once more, forcing bent legs straight and heaving upward. Next thing she knew, she'd landed hard on her fanny with a terrific splash that soaked both her and the kitten, who'd clearly not stayed put. The shovel's handle had separated from its socket. Stupid old shovel!

Now she was determined to get the trapdoor open—do or die! The why didn't matter so much as feeling she *ought* to be doing her share, doing something to aid the people of Sidonie, caught in this strange, unseasonable flood. Pry the trapdoor open and she'd poke inside with the shovel-handle, mayhap unclog whatever was blocking the water's normal path, make it flow the way it should to drain that poor old house!

Spectacles mud-spattered and askew, she removed them, blinking and squinting as she fumbled to find a pocket. Must be something else around here that she could use. Yes, that big square cobblestone, salvaged for some reason, mayhap for a doorstep or a weight. She was little, but she was mighty—even Da admitted that. Whip-strong she was when she had to be, but being whip-strong wasn't always sufficient. Smart went with strong, and the smarter one thought, the stronger one became. Wasn't the brain a person's strongest muscle?

The kitten now reared against the trapdoor, clawing it with all her might, rowling and crying, as if she were desperate to gain entrance. Amazing how loud and piercing their little voices could be—high-pitched shrieks that could wake the dead! Telka shivered. Mayhap *that* was what blocked the water—a corpse, a bloated, lifeless body! Dragging the kitten clear despite her voluble protests, she rammed the cobblestone as close and tight to the door as she could, stood her full weight on it to make sure it sat stable in the mud. Now, wedge the shovel handle between the latch end and the cobblestone and bear down with all her weight on the handle's length. If it were as old, as rotten and useless as the shovel blade, it'd snap and she'd plop facedown in the puddle of the water and snow chunks.

She pulled down with all her might, but nothing happened, except for her face turning flaming scarlet, what with the exertion. Spitting on her hands, she slid them to the very end of the handle, then jumped as high as she could and landed full-weight on her stomach across it. Oof! There—something had budged, she'd felt it! But not enough. Even if Baby perched on her shoulders she lacked sufficient weight to do any good. Well, try again. If she'd budged it, mayhap she could budge it a bit more. Nothing said she had to succeed all at once. This time she hung from the end, flinging her heels in the air and swinging back and forth, bouncing for all she was worth. The kitten paced and pranced, rowling her frustration.

Where were all those work crews when she needed them? When the capital needed them? As if in answer to her question, a slim, auburn-haired young man dressed in dirty, wet clothes came pell-melling down the alleyway, shouting, "This way! This one—La'ow's tracked him here!" A crew with crowbars, ropes, and shovels overshot the alleyway's entrance, then swung back, following tight behind him. His face was white and worry-twisted, and he scarcely glanced at Etelka as he launched himself at the handle, cruelly pinching her hand when his landed atop it as if hers were invisible. "Ouch!" she protested, but her cry of pain veered into a triumphant yelp as the wooden handle dipped lower. She'd not believed the slim man big enough to make such a difference.

Up popped the latch, the trapdoor flying open and clanging against the foundation. To Etelka's amazement and consternation, a large, sodden cat sprang forth, the biggest she'd ever seen despite his plastered, clinging fur. And behind him, tight on his tail—except a part of her noticed that the cat had no tail, just a stub—came a boy a bit older than she, his face gray and exhausted, lips blue with cold. He came through so fast, had so little control that it looked as if he'd been expelled or ejected from below ground, the drain system practically spitting him out. Landing in a heap at her feet, he painfully turned around and crawled toward the opening, leaning so far inside she feared he'd tumble in again. "Pass Papa up, Eadwin!" he cried, stretching out his arms, his voice so hollow and echoey that Telka went all shivery.

But before the boy could further endanger himself, many hands caught him up and lifted him clear, warm, dry blankets now cocooning him as he was passed along. In his place, the auburn-haired man slithered partway into the opening with a rope, while other folk grasped his waistband, clung to his ankles and legs. "Eadwin! King Eadwin! Arras! Are you there?"

Utterly stunned at this bizarre turn of events and more than a little tired, Etelka planted herself on her fanny on the curbing, near as mucky and wet as the blanket-wrapped boy beside her. He was weeping hard now, as if he'd checked his emotions for so long that once they broke loose, there was no stoppering them. Gasping sobs jolted him and he clung with all his might to the big cat, snugging his blanket around them both. Not to be outdone, Baby scrambled and clung to the heaving mound of blankets, desperate to lick the big cat, but unable to work her way close enough. Embarrassed, Telka pried her away, near snatching the blanket, too, until she guiltily unhooked Baby's claws. The mere sight of her, so sunnily orange, was wondrously warming, and she held her hands on either side of the kitten, practically basking in her body heat.

"King Eadwin?" It struck her now what the auburn-

haired man had cried. "Is the king down there?" She
tugged at the boy's blanket, but he didn't notice, eyes riveted on the dark maw of the opening as a semiconscious
man with dark hair and a drooping dark mustache was
hauled clear. More people crowded the alleyway, more
flooding in, and it was even harder to see between the
growing forest of legs. "Is that the king?"

But the boy had shakily risen, blanket trailing after him,
as he yelled, "Papa! Papa!" and broke into a run. No, that
couldn't be the king, then. But who was that thin man with
the gray streak in his hair? The one coming up next. Had
she found the king after all? Found him—not just for herself—but for all of Marchmont, when she'd scarcely even
realized he'd been lost? Oh, my!

❧

Before she could even think, let alone screw up her courage
to approach the king and beg a boon of him—that Baby
shouldn't be drowned no matter what Da had decreed—
King Eadwin and his companions had been swept away by
the crowd of rescuers. The surrounding streets resounded
with cheers, cries of thanksgiving, but the joyous sounds
rapidly grew more muffled with distance. Gaping in shock
at the speed of it all, the empty alley now strangely forlorn,
Telka wrestled with the unpalatable fact that she and Baby
were again alone, bereft of hope. Never would she find
another chance to approach the king that closely! Oh, it
wasn't fair! It truly *wasn't* fair—not after she and the kitten
had journeyed so far! Face tight and shiny with unshed
tears, Etelka's mouth puckered. Not gonna bawl, 'twon't
do no good!

Worst of all, she was wet and cold and achy, arm and
shoulder muscles strained from all her hard labor. Near-
sightedly searching around, Baby bouncing at her feet,
mewling and darting a few steps in the direction where the
large cat had disappeared with the rest, Etelka finally located her burlap sack, kicked clear off the porch and half-
trampled with muddy, damp footprints. With a sniffle she
retrieved it, not that it held much, now that the last of their
food had been consumed. It still contained what had been

a clean, dry flannel shirt and a sweater, a bit small but in good repair, no ravels or darns to it, and dry stockings. Her hairbrush as well, and a soft little brush she used to groom the kitten, burnishing her coat sunbeam-bright. And, of course, her precious copy of *Lives of the Seekers Veritas*. Oh, please let it not be water-stained!

Another sniffle. That was the problem, one sniffle invariably encouraged more. Oh, for a nice secluded spot to huddle in, hug Baby to her breast for consolation. Oh, how could they—how could everyone—have been so *mean*? So thoughtless! Da and Mam, King Eadwin. Nobody cared if Baby lived or died except her! "Oh, Baby!" she wailed, finally succumbing to all her woes, "They're not very friendly or considerate here, Baby, no, they're not! What are we going to do?" Before there had been hope, now all hope had been dashed, washed away as completely as the king had been swept away from his castle to this mean, empty back alley.

At last she hunted out a private little niche where a rackety, wood-slabbed fence no longer formed a crisp right angle to the house it abutted, its boards loose, some leaning against the wall. Wedging herself into the space, she hunkered on her heels to make herself as small and inconspicuous as possible. Ha—as if it mattered! As if anyone would notice her, anyway! Deciding which side of her sack felt drier, she spread it across her shoulders and coaxed Baby into her lap, folding herself over the protesting kitten and beginning to cry in earnest. "M'wrp?" trilled the kitten as she struggled to break free. "Mmuz'wa? Gr'aan Hru'rul!" The pink, freckled nose softly nudged first one damp eyelid and then the other.

Two pairs of boots flashed by her nook place, moving with a confident assurance that indicated both the boots and their owners had a destination in mind, someplace where they were wanted, expected. The footsteps made her sad, twice as lonely. Then Etelka shook her head, listening harder, abruptly aware she could no longer hear the even tread of feet—whoever it was had stopped dead. A woman spoke, so close that Etelka nearly jumped. "Don't understand how we could have missed her. La'ow? Are you sure?"

A man's voice followed. "Urchins can vanish faster than

you can say 'Scat!' Best keep searching." He spoke oh so very la-de-dah, each vowel richly round and elegant, his nose too high in the air to notice anyone crouched at her level. "And did I mention, dear, that I *love* your tool belt?"

"Well, *I* don't think the child's an urchin." The woman sounded stubborn, faintly defensive to Etelka. "La'ow and I barely glimpsed her in all the commotion, but she looked like a country girl to me. A nice little country girl with her kitty."

By the Lady above! Were they talking about her? Ever-so-cautiously Telka peeked from beneath her sack, one hand clamped over Baby's muzzle. Oh, why hadn't she thought to put her spectacles back on so things wouldn't be so fuzzy and blurry! What could they want with her? Had Da reported her missing, sent her description all the way to Sidonie and beyond? Mayhap all Marchmont knew she was a runaway! And . . . and if they found her, would they take Baby from her, save Da the trouble? Return her home, ashamed, forlorn, alone?

"Takes a country lass to know another, Urban," the woman reproved. "Any luck, La'ow? Ah, I *see*! Fine, but you'd best head back to the castle now, that's a dear. No sense causing any more startlement than necessary." A pause, though Telka couldn't hear the La'ow-person answer. "Handsome is as handsome does, now scoot!" With a rising fear of discovery, Telka hunched the sack over her head, crouching stock-still and pretending to be a stone. Just let Baby behave, not betray them, no matter how innocently the kitten meant it!

Boot toes invaded her space and, without warning, hands locked on her shoulders, kind but firm, not to be balked. "Well, Urban, what have we here?" asked the woman, dragging Etelka clear of her shelter, forcing her into a duckwalk to keep up with the tugging hands. Didn't dare uncurl herself, not and reveal Baby. Etelka stole a glance from under her sacking. Two dimples showed as the woman smiled, a hopeful sign. "You're the child who helped rescue King Eadwin, aren't you?"

Should she admit it? Or would that land her in more trouble? Mayhap common folk weren't supposed to interfere in serious matters involving the king. Mayhap she'd stolen part of the auburn-haired man's glory by finding the king first, trying to rescue him—though she hadn't even known who or what she'd found! She'd been more concerned by that house, the cries of its inhabitants as the water rose through their floorboards!

"No," she desperately insisted, shaking her head to reinforce her disclaimer. "No, not me. Just happened by right afterward. Ought to be going now. Folks'll be worried I'm late!" The lie tasted foul on her tongue, a hateful, specious smile pasted on her face.

"Don't be so modest, child!" The man had a light laugh, frothy as beaten egg whites, that made Telka feel like less than nothing, some paltry amusement for him. "I doubt there are two little girls with your color hair and a nice orange-tiger kitten with them. But mayhap I'm wrong." Betrayed by her broom-straw-colored hair—such an ugly shade that everyone couldn't help but remark on it! He tapped his lip thoughtfully with a finger. "Cinzia, if we bring the wrong child to the castle, King Eadwin will *not* be pleased with us!"

Serious-sounding and worried, the woman chimed in, "Probably forfeit our positions, without a doubt! Oh, dear! Who else'll employ us, then?"

Allowing Baby to slip from her increasingly lax grasp, unclear if fortune might have smiled on them at last, Telka picked at the puzzle in her mind. Baby seemed terribly intent on sniffing the woman's boots, her knees, and the woman bent to tickle her chin, the tools on her belt chinking. Mayhap she'd overreacted, and they didn't mean to chastise her? And if she continued stubbornly denying any involvement, the nice woman would lose her position. Wasn't so sure whether she cared about the man, though. Squinting, she examined one face after the other, looking for contradictory expressions, eyes projecting something mean and hard while the mouth smiled, evidence of a lie. If they were having her on, toying with her, she'd kick their shins and dive between their legs, run like the wind! Baby would follow, outrace her, no doubt about it. "And if I did? Go with you, I mean," she addressed her query to the woman, trusting her more.

"Well, I expect that either way—did or didn't help rescue the king—you'd be given a warm bath and a hot meal and a good bed. At least until Hru'rul, his majesty's Bond, determined the truth of the matter. He'd know right away if you were being opportunistic, claiming someone else's just desserts."

"*That* was Hru'rul? Truly?" Despite her tiredness, she essayed a little skip in place, her face shining beneath the dirt and grime. "Oh, Baby! We've found the Great Hru'rul. You're saved!"

❖

"Trail's blocked for . . . oh . . . twenty meters." Diccon stomped his boots, intent on shaking out the snow that had lodged in trouser folds, formed tiny ice balls on his woolen socks where they rose above his boots and snugged in his pant legs. And paying greater attention to *that* than he was to the import of his news on their aunt. "That overhang already had snow creeping off the edge—too dark to tell when we camped, or I'd have chosen a safer spot. Still, no major harm done. When it cut loose, most of it tumbled down the trail as if it were a chute." Cheeks rosy, he eagerly grabbed the tin mug of cha that Harrap handed him. "Wish I could have seen it! Not slept through it! Whatever that rumbling was last night, it jarred something fierce! Mayhap the mountain had indigestion!"

Equally snowy from accompanying him on his survey, Jenneth gave him a quelling stare and 'spoke him to silence. Leave it to Diccon—everything was an adventure. "*Is not!*" he insisted, but the sparkle in his eyes gave him away. Couldn't he *ever* think ahead, think what this meant? Delay, additional effort and worry, and the very real possibility they might not arrive at Nakum's with Saam in time. Diccon wasn't exactly selfish, but he *did* tend to only consider how things affected him. Right now she wanted to shake him, hard, wake him to the rest of the world's crucial needs.

Seated on one of their saddles, Mahafny toyed with a strand of hair, then began picking at the fabric of her trousers. She acted unaware of her ceaseless activity, never-still fingers an outlet for her nerves. Jenneth watched some more, only to drop her eyes, ashamed at prying where she shouldn't. Mahafny's face was set and pale, almost lifeless-looking, but her eyes were suspiciously bright and darting, flickering, refusing to settle on any one thing or person for any length of time.

"So. Can we hike over it? Around it? We can't waste any more time here, sitting and admiring the view." Something about her brittle implacability, each word dropping flat and dead, made Jenneth lean against Diccon, unsure if she were protecting him or if he were protecting her.

*"Don't worry, Sis. I'll sort it out, make her understand what we're up against."* Hardly a morale-building statement! Would there be enough pieces left of Diccon to pick up and paste together when Mahafny finished with him? Kneeling with easy charm before his aunt, he captured one of her fluttering hands in both of his as he fixed her with a level, guileless look. Jenneth couldn't fail to notice that Kwee had positioned herself well behind Diccon, planning on shielding herself from Mahafny's ire.

"We can't go around, Auntie. That's a sheer wall on one side of the trail, and the woods are too thick on the other side. Not to mention a steep drop-off." A dramatic gestured indicated the slope. "Jenneth and I could probably pick our way through, but I doubt you and Harrap could get very far. Nor the ponies. Mignon caught a hunk of flying ice right on her cannon, and she's pretty sore. The other would suffer similar bruises—or worse—if we try it."

Eyes no longer flickering, Mahafny stared at Diccon, possibly even through him, and her unblinking regard made her look surreal, as if she'd passed far beyond her body's physical self. Ice-gray eyes, cold as ice; was she dead inside? Had she given up? A part of Jenneth thrilled at the thought, selfish though it was, for it meant Mahafny had acknowledged the inevitability of Saam's death. Had Mahafny reluctantly faced reality, come to grips with the fact this was a fool's quest in the dead of winter? But if Mahafny stared reality in the eyes, she still hadn't blinked, and Jenneth's hopes fell once more.

"Twenty meters blocking the trail, eh?" Mahafny's gaze finally broke away from Diccon's to take in first Harrap, then Jenneth, before returning to rest on Diccon with detached interest, as if she'd just noticed his presence. "And how *deep* is it? Head-high? Twice that? What?"

Half-glancing at Jenneth for confirmation, he rubbed his

brow before answering. "Oh, probably about a head-and-a-half high at the worst spots."

"Well, bless the Lady you're short, since we're utilizing you as a measuring rod!" Jenneth sucked in her breath as color flooded Diccon's face as if he'd been slapped. Oh, how Diccon abhorred any reminder of his stature! Not that he was terribly short, she loyally amended, but he still hovered just below average height. In truth, she stood about two centimeters taller, though she'd never admit it to her twin, since it nettled him so. No wonder he'd chased after the diminutive Maeve—he could actually see over the top of her head!

"And most of the snow is in chunks, hunks, am I correct? Not a solid pack?" Miserably, Diccon nodded, lips compressed to avoid snapping back at his aunt. Give Diccon that, he'd turn the other cheek if he possibly could. "Well, boy—what are you waiting for? An engraved invitation?" Resting a hand on each of Diccon's shoulders, Mahafny levered herself to her feet. "Shovel it, lad—shovel it!"

*"I'm sorry, Jen! I can't hold back any more!"* he whispered in her mind, and she opened her mouth, prepared to blurt something, anything, to distract him, but was already too late. "And what do you propose we shovel it *with*, Aunt Mahafny? Our bare hands?" He'd jumped to his feet, looking from Harrap to her and back for support. "Jen and I have done our level best for you, but this is folly! Harrap, as well. How *he's* put up with you all these years, suffering your arrogant, self-centered demands, I'll never know!" Diccon's resentment shrilled through the air. "No wonder Saam's had enough—dying's the only way he can escape! If *he* wants to do what *he* wants to do, he has to *die* to do it! Well, I'm not about to do the same—and I won't let Jenneth either!"

The keen smack of flesh against flesh, and this time Diccon's face crimsoned from a real, openhanded blow, delivered not by Mahafny, but by the Shepherd-Seeker, Harrap. "Do *not*," he emphasized, "do not *ever* speak that way to your aunt again, or to any other soul! Do you understand me? It is unbecoming—uncivil and ill-bred—even more so issuing from a young man of Marbon-Wycherley stock." Aglow with righteousness, Harrap resembled a virtuous knight tender of his lady's honor, but which lady, Jenneth wondered, fighting back tears at Diccon's shaming.

Momentarily fearful her brother would turn on Harrap,

even fight him, Jenneth scrambled to Diccon's side, his conflicted emotions battering at her. Kwee loosed a low, guttural wail of dismay, her tail thrashing, thumping even as she began abruptly washing her face, slanted eyes downcast as she struggled to recover her poise. *"Dic,"* she 'spoke urgently, 'spoke him again, until she'd convinced herself he was truly listening. *"Diccon, love. Easy, love. You let her get your goat, and then Harrap reacted against your overreaction. Let it go, don't take out any more anger on anyone, and don't berate yourself with it. None of us is in a very good mood."*

"Aunt Mahafny, even the ponies would protest if we asked too much of them. Running us ragged, running yourself ragged isn't the way to do it—if you want to succeed." Despite her best intentions she couldn't help scowling at Harrap, had never deemed herself capable of scowling at such a sweet, unworldly man who cherished them so deeply. And who, obviously, loved their aunt even more. Eyes closed, his chest heaved while his lips moved rapidly and soundlessly, praying the Lady's forgiveness for striking someone in the heat of anger, she didn't doubt.

"We *can* clear the trail, but it won't be quick or easy." Could she search out a middle ground, not betray either Diccon or Aunt Mahafny, endorse both sides? "I *wish* we had shovels. Mayhap Dic and I can load snow on the tarps, and you and Harrap can drag them clear and dump them. The ponies, too. But ask yourself, as a rational being, a eumedico—if we attempt it, is it worth the effort? Will Saam still be alive? I'd calculate that it'll take us two days to clear the trail. Two days you'd not counted on losing."

But Harrap now feverishly dug amongst the ponies' gear, finally unearthing a curved wooden rectangle from within a saddlebag and brandishing it aloft. "Didn't anyone listen to the stabler?" Without waiting for an answer he began dumping supplies from another bag to reveal an identical piece. "They've a dual purpose—they frame the pony's barrel and," with rising elation, gleeful as a child producing a surprise, he whooped, "they're shovel blades in a pinch! See?" Scooping at the snow, he tossed it in the air, beaming as it filtered down over his head and shoulders. "All we need are handles—saplings or branches!"

Tucking a frame-cum-shovel under each arm and working his robe from beneath his knees, he rose and diffidently approached Diccon, tenderly touching the cheek that still bore the fading imprint of his palm. "Forgive me, I beg you. We all defend what we hold most dear on this earth, in this life or in another. And I'm not so old and feeble that I can't do my share of digging, or dragging, or anything else. In fact, if I start tonight, mayhap I can even knit some booties for Parm and the others, so they can dig without freezing their little paws."

Embracing Harrap hard, Diccon smothered a manic giggle against the Shepherd's chest, shoulders heaving as Harrap patted his back, crooning endearments and apologies into Diccon's unruly hair. At length Diccon broke free, scrupulously refusing to meet her eyes, not to mention not glancing anywhere near Kwee or Pw'eek. *"Booties!"* he caroled. *"Boo-ties, Jenneth! Oh, dear, oh, my . . ."* and left her quaking with wild, suppressed laughter.

**"The one who deserves to wear them, look foolish, doesn't have to—just his poor, long-suffering Bond,"** sniffed Pw'eek. **"Not to mention her even more innocent sib!"**

"And Saam lives, *will* live as long as I've breath in my body." Mahafny didn't sound entirely mollified, but she attempted an amenability that Jenneth hadn't seen in her aunt for some time. "Mayhap I've been too demanding. But I only demand the best from those whom I believe capable of excellence. You're younger, stronger, more resourceful than I—that's why I've pinned all my hopes on you. Would your mother, your father let Saam die without doing *their* best to prevent it? Please?" she beseeched.

And that was patently unfair, invoking their parents' names in her cause! Of course Aunt Mahafny was manipulating them, as adroitly as ever, and they'd all obediently fall into line, anxious to please. What else was there to do? But the reminder of her parents, most likely now returning from their much-needed haliday, left her nerves ajangle with remorse at prodigally supplying them with a new set of worries, whether they knew it or not.

♣

Spirits lifting, Feather gladdened at the ease with which she'd regained her people's effortless lope, that swift, soft stride that reverently flew across the earth, scarcely brushing the surface yet drawing strength and endurance from it. Let an Outlander glimpse such movement, and the most that might be remarked on would be an occasional puff of snow, a sprinting shadow akin to a swooping hawk's, nothing the untrained eye would focus upon when other, more obvious things were there to see. She'd forgotten the joyousness of such travel, her previous days with Jacobia a crude facsimile of her people's capabilities, laughingly reminiscent of a young child painstakingly copying her mother at her chores, serious yet inept attempts. Just as well, though, or she'd have so far outdistanced Jacobia that she might never have found her again—or not found her in time. Not found her alive. . . .

The admission made Feather stumble, but she lightly regained her footing, more than a little embarrassed by such laxity, her superficial concentration. Too many thoughts clashing through her mind, who and what she was, what part Jacobia played in all this and, most of all, why Addawanna had stepped in? Convenient, that, at least for Jacobia. Despite her best efforts, Feather found it toilsome to truly listen, understand the earth's messages, as if she'd become a stranger, a foreigner in her own land, the old tongue, the old ways stiff and rusty with disuse. Even a certain disdain that rose unbidden when she least expected it, one part of her life rearing up to mock other parts, other times. Not exactly a battle between them but, at the very least, a contest of wills. In the midst of seeking the balance, Addawanna might scowl at her, or shake her head regretfully, then look very thoughtful. No wonder the balance proved elusive.

Addawanna sorted through the earth's messages with an ease that left her envious, as did the other Erakwa in their party, four men and four women, all earth-bonded as well. Two she recollected from their shared childhood, but the others ranged in age from late adolescence to near Addawanna's years, though age sat so very lightly on most of their people. Closemouthed as well, they were, unless she asked outright for aid in interpreting the earth's murmurous messages. The trembler, the dregs of the earthquake they'd experienced a few nights past, was an example she was determined to puzzle out unassisted.

What had it been telling them, grumbling and grinding like that? What did it presage? An unexpected sympathy for the eumedicos-in-training welled within her; now she knew how they'd felt when they'd come to her, anxious about a patient, baffled by questions and conundrums that contradicted their texts. What held mystery to them was rarely mysterious to her. Ha! Mayhap she was an Erakwan-in-training again!

And Jacobia clung to them like a burr, still feverish and dolefully coughing, her feet swollen and blood-blistered, skin sloughing off from their prolonged immersion. Her Erakwa compatriots passed her from one sturdy back to another like a sack of cornmeal when their path narrowed; otherwise they swung her between two of them on a litter, the constant rocking turning the woman pallid, green-tinged with nausea. Downright colorful, what with the rosy tinge of fever! Her illness, her loss of control, as well as her continual worry about her niece and nephew made her a poor companion and an even more frustrating burden. Did Outlanders think they could simply will things their way? Ha! If she longed for free will, the mastery of her fate, let her learn to walk first!

Just as she and Jacobia had, their party traveled northwest, drawing ever closer to The Shrouds where it spanned the Spray River, and shortly they would cross behind its thunderous veil, leaving the artificially named Canderis for Marchmont, also falsely named. As if a name conveyed ownership of a thing no once could own! Marchmont, apparently because they sought Nakum. But why had Addawanna burdened them with Jacobia—good nature or pressing need? True, Jacobia believed her wandering relatives would seek out Nakum, that they had pinned all their tenuous hopes for Saam on finding him. Addawanna, as well, seemed concerned for Nakum, muttering and irritable, arguing with herself or some invisible being, invoking aid. All fussy and fuming, Addawanna was, and most of it directed, deflected onto her! What had *she* done to bring problems raining down on Nakum's head? She'd not seen him for years! He was a full-grown Erakwa, as was she— let him solve his own problems! Or let Addawanna fuss and fume at him instead of her!

Her turn now to transport Jacobia on her back, and she

took the shifted burden in stride, never slowing. "I . . . I'm sorry—" Jacobia fell into a fit of coughing. "Should . . . should have . . . kept Frost for me to ride." Jacobia's humiliation at being carried thusly was palpable to Feather, as if the woman had regressed to infancy, lacking control over things, destined to be swooped up in unfamiliar arms, toted on unfamiliar backs, dependent on the goodwill of lesser beings—Erakwan—to reach her goal. The universe the Outlander woman believed herself the center of had altered, moving her as it so chose.

"Frost is being well taken care of." What? Did Jacobia suspect her people might feast on horsemeat stew? Unfair—why did she perpetually assume Jacobia would think the worst of her, her people? Because others often did? "He couldn't have matched this pace, not on our winter trails."

Her cheek, where it nestled against Feather's neck, burned unnaturally hot. "I suppose not, but he was a good-natured beast, clever, loyal. He couldn't have wanted to be left behind—he didn't before."

"Better-natured than I, you mean," Feather teased.

"More comfortable to ride," Jacobia corrected. "I don't think . . . you take being bridled very kindly. Few of us do." Again the coughing started, Jacobia feebly muffling it by pressing her mouth against her shoulder. "I . . . thank you . . . and your people . . . for your efforts."

It sounded sincere, downright humble. And Feather struggled to think how *she* might feel, what lengths she'd go to, if those she loved—so very few—should venture on a fool's mission that could easily result in death. In turn, would many—any—miss her if she died? Vanished from the face of the earth—and that must seem precisely what she'd done by abandoning her people, seeking eumedico wisdom in Gaernett. It left her thoughtful, considering, even a touch melancholy for what had been hers, still was, if she so desired it. Moccasins skimming the snow, she yearned for the oneness she'd once absorbed from nature, the union with land and sky, with the winds and water, with all of nature's creatures—trees and flowers, animals, birds, fish. Even the wriggling worms that reinvigorated the soil. Think of them anymore, and she'd weep the next time she threaded one on a hook! Outlanders weakened you, made you sentimental—fah!

✣

At the command of Fabienne, the Queen Mother, Eadwin's bedchamber had been transformed into a mini-infirmary, its pleasant but rather spartan furnishings now crammed with two additional beds hastily reassembled by servants, along with feather mattresses and pillows, fine linen sheets, and woolly blankets. The paraphernalia of the sickroom cluttered tabletops and any other available surface: bandages and dressings, salves and ointments, basins and washclothes, spoons, scissors, and more. "It might prove best," Lady Fabienne had informed Francie in a confidential tone, "to keep all three children together. Reassure each that the others are safe and reasonably sound."

Francie had stared, baffled at Fabienne's meaning. The only real child present was Harry; Eadwin was hardly of an age to qualify, even if Fabienne still referred to him as her child. All *three* children? "Ah," she'd finally breathed, understanding dawning. Most any sick man regressed to acting the small child again, whining, complaining, stubbornly refusing what was best for him—a perfect portrait of Arras at this moment. Bless Fabienne's foresight! It allowed her to hover between Harry's and Arras's beds, more worried, in truth, about husband than son, as well as keep a judicious ear and eye on matters of governance now being conducted from the sickroom, even as eumedicos and their assistants came and went.

Flat on his stomach, head laid on his good arm and his bad shoulder padded by pillows, Arras endured the ministrations of two eumedicos, each equipped with an assortment of nasty-looking picks and probes, tweezers and little spoonlike scoopers being busily employed up and down Arras's bare back and upper thighs. For modesty's sake—his, not hers or Fabienne's—she'd spread a towel across her husband's backside. When the eumedicos were ready to probe there for shrapnel, she'd decided it would be wise to beat a hasty retreat, lest Arras's dignity turn as tattered as his bottom!

Buttressed by a half-dozen pillows, Harry sat and took it all in, and the feverish glint in his eyes gave her cause for alarm. He wasn't hot; she'd felt his forehead time and again, a mother knowing better than any eumedico when her child was ailing. Still, that hectic glitter, that forced gaiety, didn't bode well, as if he'd forcibly locked something deep inside him. Mayhap he'd been unable to release the daunting fears that had stalked by his side while he and Eadwin had searched for Arras? Inner terrors often haunted children, and while Harry had outgrown most of them, she had to admit that adults harbored their own unique sets of inner terrors. He'd confessed almost shame-facedly that he'd turned back to protect Eadwin because that's what Papa would have done. And done so more than half-believing his father dead in the explosion. He'd shown a mature presence of mind and bravery, but when the brav-ery had run its course, her child had again appeared. Now to coax him to sleep—or to unburden himself to her.

Grumpily accepting the attentions of three more eumed-icos, Eadwin immediately dispatched the most senior one to Arras's side. An occasional yelp or expletive split the air as one eumedico or the other daubed antiseptic on a scrape, catching Eadwin by surprise as he looked the other way, intent on dictating orders and instructions to various Ministers and staff members. Carn Camphuysen had al-ready come and gone—at a run—concerned about drainage and disease, and now Terrail Leclerc and Urban Gamelyn listened intently at Eadwin's side.

Only Fabienne had been able to cow Eadwin into gulping a dose of some foul-smelling concoction that the eumedicos insisted would counteract any possible waterborne patho-gens. After witnessing that epic battle of wills—king against queen mother—Francie had wisely decided to wait until Arras was too weak to protest, and Harry too sleepy, and then trust to her powers of persuasion plus luck. Already balky, Arras ached to battle someone—like a eumedico ar-rogantly instructing him to down a spoonful of medicine.

"On the matter of security, guarding the Plumbs . . ." Eadwin dictated, enunciating each word distinctly and at a speed designed not to overwhelm his secretary, not allow him to miss a word. "By my command, they shall be guarded, secured at all costs, from any and all interference by any being other than myself and Defense Lord Arras Muscadeine until further notice. . . ."

"What? WHAT DID YOU SAY?" Arras bellowed, his volume increasing with his rising irritation at catching only the echo or hint of a word here and there. "EADWIN, I'LL ASSIGN A ROTA OF MY MOST SENIOR STAFF! IT'S MY RESPON—"

"Darling, don't shout." Positioning herself in front of Arras, Francie cupped his chin in her hand, forcing him to watch her lips move. "Let us shout—you're the one who can't hear, not us." His deafness was understandable but worrisome; he'd been nearest the Plumb when it had detonated. The eumedicos refused to hazard a guess on how permanent the injury might be, not at this early stage. Auricular damage had also temporarily impaired his mind-speech, though this was improving much more quickly than his hearing.

Lips compressed to throttle his frustration, he studied her face and gave a curt nod, intuiting the gist of her message. "Sorry. I want those things utterly secure, safe from prying hands." A cough to hide his emotion. "Could have maimed or killed Harry, Eadwin . . . the others. Collapsed the castle like a pancake!"

Old soldier that he was, his own welfare was secondary, the well-being of those around him paramount—so typical of Arras! Stroking his cheek, she brushed his mustache, tugging it to force a smile out of him. "If anything had happened to Harry—" he interrupted himself to kiss the palm of her hand. "Oh, Francie, I've never been more watery-boweled with terror in my life! I'd gladly go bare-handed against twenty swordsmen than suffer such uncertainty again! Sheer agony!"

"And Eadwin," she nodded in the king's direction to cue Arras to her response.

"And Eadwin," he repeated. "Like a brother . . . Besides, if I'd lost Eadwin, facing Tante Fabienne's ire would be worse than my twenty swordsmen *plus* a cavalry troop in full charge!" Without warning he stiffened, his whole body almost levitating off the bed. "OUCH! WATCH WHERE YOU STICK THAT BLASTED THING!" and the senior eumedico moved to the head of the bed, miming an apology. The metal fragment she displayed on the palm of her hand turned Arras wide-eyed.

Leaving him to the eumedico, Francie retrieved her cane and stumped to Harry's bed. Her tiredness mirrored in her halting gait, the tremors more pronounced than usual, she registered the growing clumsiness in her right arm and hand, marginally useful at best. No point in being impatient with her body, she'd lived thusly most of her life and rarely mourned her diminished ability; others were worse off. Arras, Harry, Eadwin, Holly, Theo—any or all of them could have been crippled for life, paralyzed. . . . Abruptly she shut her mind against the rush of morbid images she'd ruthlessly banished during their long, bitter wait for news. She and Fabienne had had little choice, needing all their wits to organize the rescue efforts, see to the damage inflicted on castle and city.

Rest, and the knowledge that her two men—or boys— were fine, would alleviate that. Well past noon now, and it had been a long night, an even longer, more agonizing morning till they'd been found. Now, during this lull, mayhap she'd have a chance to winkle out what was bothering Harry, so transparent to a mother's eyes.

To her dismay Hru'rul had beaten her to it, ensconced at the foot of Harry's bed, oversized front paws, thick with dense fur around the pads, tucked to his chest. The beast's generally imposing mien had been replaced by bedragglement, his tawny fur still not fully dry, though he'd obviously been rectifying that, aided by a young woman respectfully slicking his coat with a fine wire brush. Though he politely lifted his chin so she could unmat his side chops and ruff, Hru'rul's eyes never wavered from Harry's, the boy distancing himself from the ghatt, nervously picking at his blanket while they engaged in a battle of wills.

"Hru'rul, Harry," she greeted them, and gave Hru'rul a rub behind one ear, her fingers creeping to tweak the tuft at the tip. "Am I interrupting?" Knew very well she was, and wondered whose side to take—Harry's or Hru'rul's? If Harry had mischief in mind, best she know it in advance— such as attempting to enter the subterranean levels of the castle again.

"No, Mama," and he defiantly broke free from Hru'rul's commanding gaze to regard her, all innocence, his smile just a shade false to someone who truly knew him. "Hru'rul and I were having a . . . discussion."

"About?" she prompted. At moments like these, she'd give anything to communicate with the ghatt mind-to-mind. But Hru'rul, for all his rough-hewn ways and limited training as a Bondmate, would never 'speak her unless a genuine emergency necessitated it.

"Oh, things!" A dismissive wave. "What it was like down below, how brave King Eadwin is . . . and Papa."

What could be preying at him so? There was *something,* and the more she worried at it, the more she doubted it involved today's happening. Come to think on it, he'd been a touch furtive, wriggling out of certain conversations, his concentration divided, for several days. Ever since they'd sailed down to Bertillon, and Harry had taken a fall. His subsequent furtiveness had struck her as amusing, some sort of phase: boys his age discovered a hundred-and-one new things to pique their interest daily, things to imagine, romanticize, embellish, or brood over. Interest in the opposite sex being just one of those things—no, mayhap a hundred of those hundred-and-one things! Had Harry developed a crush on someone? Become infatuated with a young serving maid? Someone else?

He always relished tagging along with Cinzia and La'ow, but she'd put it down to his familiarity with and love for the ghatti. Ever since he'd been big enough to puzzle out relationships, he'd viewed Khar and Rawn as an auxiliary aunt and uncle, Khim and P'roul as near-cousins. And now Pw'eek and Kwee, his cousins' Bonds, had joined their extended family. Alas, though, no matter how doting the parent, one couldn't stroll out and purchase a ghatten for a child, and after some bitter long-ago tears, Harry'd accepted that.

"Harry, you'd tell me if something were bothering you, truly worrying you?" Eternal optimists, each and every parent had to say it, had said it too often to count. "Something that's bigger, more serious than you can easily handle? Where someone more experienced might be able to help sort things out?" And anticipated his answer all too well.

"Of course, Mama!" That spurious sincerity, that too-ready smile meant to distract her from the stony hardening of his hazel eyes, implacable and blank. "Absolutely!"

Probe further? Shake him? Lock him in his bedroom for safekeeping? But before she could decide on a course of action, a commotion at the entrance to the king's bedchambers distracted them all. As the door swung back, two guards escorted Nakum inside with insincere deference, their standoffish, rigid posture bespeaking their true feelings regarding the next in line to the throne, King Eadwin's heir and cousin. For a moment Nakum stood immobile, as if their antipathy weighed him down. His deerskin trousers and vest were dirty and scraped, damp in spots, the soft leather sagging, clinging too snugly where it had dried and shrunk.

"Nakum!" Eadwin gave a shout of genuine pleasure. "What brings you down from your mountain retreat? The floods spat me out of a sewer, cousin! As fragrant as I may be, I'm still king, so you'll have to continue biding your time!"

A crow of laughter from Nakum. "Mayhap the sewer spat you out, Eadwin, precisely because you stank so terribly. Even sewers have standards, you know!" But in the next breath he'd turned deathly serious. "Cousin, what have you *done* to the earth, what have you loosed upon it?"

❧

Diccon bent at the waist, mittened hands loosely dangling until they swept the snow. Snow! Chunks and hunks and lumps, large and small, some rock-hard, while others disintegrated when grasped, hands suddenly empty but for a cascade of uncatchable fine powder. Which was worse? Groaning softly he braced his hands on his knees and straightened. All in all, he preferred the chunks; made you feel as if you'd accomplished something when you heaved one aside, an empty space created. Besides, they gave a satisfying thud when thrown. You could sweep and scoop that damned powdery stuff forever and not feel you'd accomplished a thing.

"'Ware below!" bellowed Harrap as he heaved on a stripped tree branch, using it as a pry bar. Heeding the command, Diccon briskly sidestepped; Harrap's enthusiastic attack on the snow mound had sent him dodging more than once as chunks shifted, careened down. Poor Jen! She'd caught one square in the back and been knocked flat. Didn't matter how many times Harrap'd apologized, Jenneth still wore a distinctly sour look and skittered at every sound. Oh, she didn't blame Harrap, not truly, but she didn't relish surprises, testing herself against the unexpected, the way he did.

Heads popping over the top of the mound, Kwee and Pw'eek came scrambling down, skitter-scattering along. By rights, roly-poly Pw'eek ought to be the one to tumble, come bouncing down like a ball, but as he watched, Kwee bounded too quickly and carelessly, lost her footing as a chunk caved into sparkling snow crystals beneath her paws. Landing in an undignified sprawl at the bottom, she lashed her tail, sending more powder flying.

*"Are you all right, sweedling?"* Pride deflated, she gathered herself into a more presentable—and compact form— and pawed at her ears to dislodge snow, then fluffed herself. And all the while Pw'eek neat-footed it down, prissy, mincing steps with those precious little white paws. Halting at the bottom, she bestowed a consoling forehead lick that Kwee suffered with minimal good grace, miffed not only by her clumsiness but also because she'd fallen in full view of everyone.

**"Ooh! Guess what we saw on the other side!"** Pw'eek wreathed around Jenneth's shins, eagerly regarding her Bond, coaxing her to share in the game.

"And what was that, my pretty one?" Jenneth and Mahafny had just returned with the tarp, ready for another load, Mahafny already cuffing and kicking hunks of snow onto the tarp. Not a precious moment wasted with her; Diccon shook his head. At least her cutting anger had been spent, the last of it burned off by nearly a full day's hard labor. Yet still she worked steadily and hard, so hard that it shamed him. Embarrassed to have paused so long, watching more than working, he began digging with renewed zeal, shoveling snow in Jen's and Mahafny's direction. His efforts didn't stop his curiosity from twitching: what had Pw'eek and Kwee seen?

**"Tell them, Sissy-Poo!"** Pw'eek urged. **"You saw it first. If you hadn't hurried so fast on our way down . . ."** Oh, he'd kiss the little chubkin, he would! Pw'eek, generous to a fault, was willing to let her sib bask in the glory of their discovery to erase the memory of her ungainliness.

Shaking herself yet again to dislodge the fine snow glistening against her fur, Kwee perked up, good spirits restored. **"It's soo big, Diccon! You ought to see it! An enormous sheep, a ram, with massive horns that start in a ridge across its forehead. Then each one curls up and all the way around an ear till the tip points out. It's splendiferous . . . and oh . . . such menace in his eyes when he caught us spying on him!"** A demure shoulder lick. **"Of course, I could thrash him—if it were necessary."** A cheeky side-glance in Pw'eek's direction. **"With Sissy's help, of course!"**

**"But why would you want to thrash him?"** Pw'eek's butterscotch eyebrow patches nearly met as she perplexedly scrunched her face. **"He's probably a very nice ram. After all,"** she sounded distinctly huffy now, **"Wartle was a very kind boar, an absolute gentleman, though a bit rough around the edges. The nicest wart hog I've ever met!"**

**"The** *only* **wart hog you've ever met, silly Sissy! If there really was a Wartle!"** Pw'eek swore she'd been befriended by a wart hog while searching the Sunderlies beaches for Jenneth after they'd been separated. But Kwee persisted in deviling her, swearing there'd been no wart hog, that Pw'eek had imagined it, fever dreamed it because of her infected toe. No ghatta enjoyed being doubted, having her veracity questioned.

**"Did, too! Did, too! He fixed my toe! Nipped it right off!"**

But Diccon had had enough. They'd bicker and snipe night and day if someone didn't distract them. Bless the Lady that *he* never teased Jenneth so severely! Belatedly realizing he'd been leaning on his shovel again instead of plying it, he tossed a dusting of snow at them to quell their despute. "Do you think it's still there? That we might catch a glimpse of it?" He spun 'round toward his sister. "What do you say, Jen? It sounds like one of those sheep that lives on the slopes below Nakum's place. The ones he collects the wool from, whatever's caught on twigs, or rubbed off against outcrops. What do you say, Aunt Mahafny? Have we earned a break—just a short one?"

"Isn't that what you've been doing—standing there wool-

gathering without a sheep in sight—while the rest of us
toil?'' Yes! A distinct twinkle in her eye, and exactly the
sort of needling comment he expected from her—and so
often deserved! Her face had regained its color as she
worked, her gray eyes bright, but even now she never
slowed her pace, still busily loading the tarp as she talked.
The way she was working, she'd slave all night if necessary.
Where these surges of energy came from, he couldn't understand, but wasn't it just like her to be so contrary—fresh
when they were exhausted and vice versa? Mayhap she
saved everything up, expending her energy when the need
was greatest, hoarding it otherwise.

"Promise I'll work twice as hard when we're back!'' He
mimed extravagant and exaggerated shoveling motions.
"Dig like a badger if I have to!''

"Or I'll badger you! How about living up to your name
and working like a 'Diccon'?'' But with a negligent wave
of her hand, Mahafny released him and Jen from their ser-
vitude. "Hurry back. There's a chance we can clear the
worst of this by nightfall. We've made better progress than
expected. Then we can start out fresh in the morning.''

Without awaiting a further invitation, Diccon began a
mad scramble up the mound, Jenneth at his heels. The
ghattas already perched atop it shying snow "pebbles'' at
their Bonds with deadly accuracy. "You'd best work twice
as hard, Dic,'' Jenneth warned as they climbed. "Auntie
scares me when she acts like that, never stopping, never
even considering others might need a break. It isn't right,
doesn't make sense. And then you know what she turns
into afterwards, one of the walking dead, there but not
there, a shell without substance.''

"Don't worry about it for now, Jen,'' Diccon soothed as
he tackled the downslope side, leaning back to maintain his
footing. "Deal with it when we return, right? Then we'll
see if we can't make *her* rest. I work better without her
gimlet eyes boring holes between my shoulder blades. Talk
about exactingly rigid standards!''

Giggling, Jenneth skipped down beside him and stared
at the mound from the other side as she stamped her boots
free of snow. "Only a eumedico can be so picky!''

"Or a sister!'' Diccon added as he shot up the trail,
scarcely waiting for the ghatta to take the lead.

❣

They'd abandoned the trail sooner than Jenneth would have liked. Oh, not that she feared they'd lose their way back to camp—after all, she had but two basic directions to worry about: Up and Down. Up was Diccon's choice, convinced that scaling this low ridge would prove a short-cut, faster and easier than hiking the winding trail. Sometimes they hurried along rock ledges swept clear of snow, or jumped from one outcrop to the next, hanging onto each other for balance and clutching at scrub trees if any grew near. The snow base was firm enough to support them so that they didn't have to struggle through it. Acting equally liberated, Pw'eek and Kwee had entered into the spirit of things, spurring each other on, both striving to be first to spy the mountain sheep again.

Still . . . it would be dark soon, and they'd been exploring far longer than she suspected Mahafny's permission encompassed. Again she settled her knit cap more tightly, eased her scarf higher round her ears, the wind colder, more insistent as the sun dropped lower. Gasping as another gust swept between two ridges, she and Diccon found themselves plastered against a rock scarp, unable to move until it died down. Once already she'd asked whether they should turn back, but Diccon had shushed her, impatiently shading his eyes, hoping to pick out tracks. The only thing she'd consider proof positive that mountain sheep lived nearby would be a steaming pile of droppings!

Mayhap she should ask again, make Diccon listen to reason. Yet she was reluctant to deny him his pleasure, so she searched out Pw'eek, quartering back and forth with Kwee. *"Darling, will we find your woolly friend again? And I mean soon—not later!"*

Slightly disgruntled at the distraction, Pw'eek reassured her. **"We'll find him. He's such a distinguished-looking beast, all thick fleecy white! I want to see if I can talk with him."** Then, twisting 'round to regard Jen, Pw'eek surveyed the distance behind them and gave a trill of dismay. **"Ooh! We *have* come an awfully long way, haven't we?"**

*"And not a thing with us to eat,"* Jenneth noted with understated casualness. That little reminder was bound to work wonders on Pw'eek's stomach.

"**You mean you didn't bring any . . .**" even from this distance she could see the ghatta's convulsive swallow, "**Some trail mix? A bit of sausage? Nothing?**" Springing toward her as fast as her legs could fly, she wailed, "*Nothing at all?*" Although still too distant for her to actually hear it, Jenneth swore Pw'eek stomach rumbled. Unless it was another avalanche—and she looked around nervously.

"Jen! Over here! Come on, hurry!" Embracing a twisted spruce to halt himself as he slithered to her side, Diccon gasped, "I'm sure I caught a glimpse of him!" and seized her arm to hurry her along.

Determined to dig in her heels—literally and figuratively—Jenneth did so, and worked to make her tone as severely Mahafny-like as possible. "Diccon, listen to me! I'll go look this final time. but if there's nothing to see, we turn around, go back—do you understand? Back! Shovel!"

With her clinging like an anchor, her feet firmly planted, Diccon could no longer be swept along by his own enthusiasms—she hoped. Finally her urgency filtered through to him and, studying her, studying the way they'd come, he blinked and let out a gusting sigh. "Got carried away again, didn't I? Should have stopped me." He flapped a hand in apology. "I know—stopping me requires applying a plank to my head—repeatedly! Sorry! Heat of the moment. Which I wish we had a little more of," he confessed, dancing in place to stay warm. "Truly, Kwee thinks she's scented it. I'd love to see it—and so would you, don't deny it! Come with me this last time, and then we'll scoot back, do our duty!"

Cuffing him—both because he deserved it and to speed him along—Jenneth released him to scramble ahead, but he waited and linked hands with her to traverse an icy patch. Climbing as silently as possible, they reached the ridgeline and peered over, their breath climbing whitely toward the skies. The landscape below them wasn't at all what Jenneth had expected.

A space like a giant, shallow soup bowl dropped off beyond them, its curved sides littered with ground moraine ranging from small pebbles to smoothed boulders. To the west, against the glare of the declining sun, stood a gully or ravine packed with talus and scree, and toward the northern part of the soup bowl a small tarn glimmered orange-gold, reflecting the sun. Aeons past, a glacier had carved out this cirque, chewed a crevice into a ravine during its stately slow journey down it, churning, working itself wider and wider as it reached the bottom of the crevice, depositing moraine as it continued on its way. Here within the cirque the snow lay thinner, more patchy, the rocks warming in the sun, melting the snow around them.

Shadows fell heavily in spots, long fingers of dimness cast by trees and rocky spurs at the top, dark blotches seemingly as large as a team of oxen and their wagon, though the boulders themselves didn't appear as daunting. The edge of one shadow rippled and moved, and Jenneth held her breath, elbowing Diccon. Yes! Shifting from shadow to sunlight, the mountain sheep lowered its magnificent head and pawed at the ground, scraping the snow crust clear. Now the ram grazed, ripping at dead grass stems, though not for long; almost immediately it raised its head and swung it in their direction. His eyes hesitated on them, then implacably swept leftward and down from the ridgetop, finally fixing there.

*"Oh, damnation, Jen! Look! It's Kwee, sneaky-slithering along!"* Sure enough, hunkered low, Kwee stealthed along, occasionally gathering herself to spring behind a tree trunk or rock, each time decreasing the distance separating her from the ram. The ram pawed the earth again, though this time he didn't bother to check what his hooves had exposed. Instead, it served as his warning to these interlopers on his mountain.

*"Pw'eek! Where are you? What's Kwee up to?"* First and foremost in Jenneth's mind was keeping better track of her precious Bondmate than her twin had done; determining how close *she* stood to the ram. Pw'eek would no more let her sister expose herself to danger without her sib at her side than she would let Diccon.

A medium-sized, weather-stained gray stone with ocher lichen twitched and shifted, revealing itself as Pw'eek, hunkered watchfully to the right and slightly above Kwee's current position. **"Sissy-Poo insists *she's* going to talk to this beast! I've warned her he's grumpy, hasn't had a pleasant day. You can tell—just look at how he pawed the ground."**

Bellying over the ridge, Diccon elbow-crawled toward

the cirque's base. *"She's incorrigible, Jen! Absolutely single-minded. Ignoring me in favor of that mutton-head!"* He continued snaking along, angling to intercept the ghatta. *"I swear I'm going to drag her back—by her tail, if I have to!"*

The ram trotted a few paces back and forth, seemingly impatient for the encounter, and Jenneth wanted to hide her eyes, not have to watch. She suffered the selfsame reaction when Diccon was bent on doing something foolhardy and she couldn't stop him.

Flashing down the last of the slope, Kwee made straight for the ram, springing into the air and shouting, **"Whee!"** as she tagged his fleecy hindquarters. **"See, Pw'eek! Look at me, puissant ghatta, clever and brave! He doesn't want to talk, so I'll tame him, teach him a lesson. Taming wild beasts by the power of my personality!"**

**"But you said something rude to him! You're supposed to 'speak nicely to wild beasts—not try to tame them! You're the one in need of taming,"** Pw'eek admonished.

Back arched, tail high, Kwee pringle-toed around the ram, forcing him to circle uneasily to keep her in sight. Determined to taunt and tantalize him even further, Kwee dashed close to tag the ram's muzzle, and the beast tossed his head and snorted, angrily pawing the ground. Keeping his massive head with its heavily ridged horns low, the ram made minor feints, testing the ghatta. Then, without warning, it lunged cat-fast at Kwee, forcing her to spin and turn tail, still jauntily casting insults over her shoulder as she galloped across the cirque's bottom, daring the ram to chase her.

The ram obliged, rocketing in pursuit with long, springy strides, Kwee only belatedly realizing that she was gaily racing directly into the mouth of the talus-filled gully, a steep, broken upslope with little clear ground for ghatti paws, the setting sun glaring in her eyes. To the ram, though, this was familiar territory, a play area where lambs gamboled and a challenge ground for upstart rams intent on stealing his flock. Many were the skulls he'd butted here, sending competitors tumbling down the rocks.

"Hey, you!" On the cirque floor now, Diccon ran flat-out after the ram, shying chunks of snow in his wake. More misses than hits, and besides, a snowball would hardly inflict much damage on that thick-fleeced rump. "Leave my

Kwee alone, you greasy old mutton-head!" But the ram was bent on finishing what Kwee had so rudely begun.

With a sigh at the inevitability of it all, and more than a little anxious, Jenneth negotiated the downslope on her own rump, unfortunately not as fleecily padded, since her tabard-tail kept riding up. A blur of gray and butterscotch as Pw'eek landed in her lap, the added weight sliding them faster, Jenneth kicking at protruding rocks and trees, envisioning both her and Pw'eek draped over a rock in short order. It gave her an idea, though, along with her growing concern about wearing through the seat of her pantaloons.

*"Dic! Don't annoy him! He's already angry enough!"* A lame exhortation, but anything bordered on understatement as far as Diccon and the ram were concerned. Reaching the bottom with a painful thump, Pw'eek sprang clear and Jenneth regained her feet, shakily starting after Diccon. Fine, now all she had to do was catch up with Diccon *and* the ram! Someday, she fumed, she was going to leave him be, not pull his chestnuts out of the fire for him!

"Jen! Run, run!" His shout echoed off the sides of the cirque, the rocks, the reverberations intensifying the rising fear in his voice. Sprinting for all he was worth, Diccon came retreating back across the cirque floor, dodging stones, the ram in hot pursuit, head lowered and meaning business, his eyes a blazing dark orange that almost threw sparks, as did his pounding hooves. Not a one of the ram's steps was misplaced, misguided, whether his hooves landed on rock or ice or snow.

**"This way!"** Pw'eek urged, suiting her actions to her words as she scooted toward the gentler southern upslope, aiming for a convenient tree. But Kwee—once pursued and now gleefully pursuing—chased after the ram, harrying him by swatting at his thick tail, then zipping between his legs and passing him, passing Diccon and whirling back to savor the chaos she'd created. Except, as she whirled to entice the ram after her, she skidded on an ice slick, chin slamming down hard as all four legs splayed out from under her. Groggily shaking her head, she gingerly attempted to plant her paws under her but found the effort too confusing. Dazed, breath knocked out of her, she simply lay there.

Deciding the fallen ghatta was easier to catch and batter, the ram veered and Diccon let out a frantic shout as the beast pelted past. *"Pw'eek, I suppose we'd better do something, before the ram butts Diccon and Kwee off the mountain."* Dashing in hot pursuit, Jenneth began stripping off her tabard, praying she wouldn't trip or slip as it came over her head. As she darted by, she dragged the tabard across the ram's head, momentarily in a panic as it lodged on a horn, but with a mighty tug she freed it. Snorting, emitting a high-pitched cry of fury, the ram swung after her, intent on cracking heads with any one of these pestiferous interlopers it could reach, as annoying as summer flies. Pw'eek did her share, weaving in and out, forcing the surefooted ram to change course, slow slightly with each diversion.

"Get Kwee and get out!" Jenneth yelled, cutting in front of the ram again and waving her tabard in his face. As he made a befuddled stab at it, she was off again, the tabard dragging in her wake. A skid as the ram made a tight cornering turn to follow and, heart in her mouth, she began picking her way amongst the talus on the cirque's far side, squinting against the sun. Well, if she couldn't see very well, neither could the ram. Dodging between and over rocks, stumbling, nearly tripping time and again, somehow she managed to keep her feet under her, aware of the sharp clatter of the ram's hooves ever closer behind her.

*"How close is he?"* If this were to work, she needed to get her timing exactly right. The ram was no fool, and even faster than she'd imagined. Of course, he'd devoted his whole life to practicing these nimble moves! Already her lungs burned, her legs increasingly rubbery. Scrambling beside her, Pw'eek considered her question and sank back on her haunches to gauge the distance.

**"To your right—now! Straight at it, cut 'round sharp. If you fall, just keep rolling!"**

"Ya!" Jenneth yelled, flailing her tabard behind her, positive she could feel his hot snorts of breath. "Ya, ya! Come on, you ill-tempered brute!" The rock Pw'eek had guided her to loomed from the snow, its tip looking ready to spear her. Praying she possessed the strength and the daring, Jenneth boldly leaped it, draping her tabard behind her to conceal the rock. She landed hard, the talus shifting and slithering beneath her feet, and she pitched to her knees, adamantly refusing to look behind her. A booming, hollow thud resounded through the cirque, mingling with her own wild laughter. Oh, did Diccon owe her for this escapade! A stripe against his Sunderlies seeking for her!

"**Poor thing's going to have a terrible headache,**" Pw'eek noted sadly.

❖

"**Rawn, quick! There it goes! Sailed right by again!**" Khar reared on her haunches like a watchful woodchuck, pink nose sweeping skyward, tracking something elusive. As Rawn belatedly joined her, she placed a white forepaw on his shoulder for balance against the phaeton's jounce, still straining upward with all her might.

"**Think someone's trying to contact us?**" Rawn's brow wrinkled, his white blaze zigzagging like a flash of lightning. "**If so, the mindnet's overshooting us. Can't exactly spring into the air and snag it. Wish I could—I swear it was downright dull at Dolf's, barely a peep out of any of the ghatti. There's always news to pass on, even on the halidays.**"

Settling with murmurous discomfort, Khar curled her front paws against her white bib, head bobbing rhythmically with the phaeton's motion. "**Well,**" she pointed out, more temperately than she felt, "**if anyone *does* want to reach us, we're not exactly where we said we'd be. We're far later than expected—should have been home by now, remember?**"

"**Going to mention anything to Doyce?**" Rawn's tail lashed against the leather seat before he regained control. "**A miss is worse than no message at all. Means there's something to hear that we haven't heard. If the news is big enough, mayhap we'll find out when we stop for the night, bound to be gossip at an inn. Our last haliday night. Should be in Gaernett shortly after noon tomorrow.**" With just a hint of grumpiness, "**As you've already pointed out.**"

In the seat in front Jenret and Doyce aimlessly chatted about minor topics, both gripped with a subtle sense of sadness and loss, the letdown that comes at a haliday's close. Khar sympathized; neither wanted to plunge back into the real world just yet by speculating on what might have transpired during their absence. Why worry the other unduly with formless fears? They now shared in the truest sense, but sometimes the not-sharing was more merciful; picking at something intangible made it worse, gave it an excuse to exist.

**"Wonder what the news is about?"** Hindquarters raised, he stretched forward, vigorously miming sharpening his claws, seized by an urge to vent his frustrations by scoring the leather. **"Well, as Jenret always says, 'Trouble generally lingers long enough for us to catch up with it.' "** At that gloomy thought, good intentions fled as he extruded a single claw and carved a hair-thin line, a private signature to acknowledge his presence. He slanted an eye at Khar to see if she'd noticed, planned a reproof, but she refused to give him the satisfaction. **"Any Seekers due this way? I've lost track of the circuit schedule,"** he confessed. **"They're all such children these days! A wonder they're not assigned ponies instead of horses!"**

A major admission for him—two, in truth—and Khar blinked her surprise. Her dearest Rawn had forgotten which Seeker-Bond pairs were riding circuit and where. And that aside about them all being "children," did that indicate Rawn was feeling elderly and vulnerable—or merely venerable? So much for a restorative, rejuvenating haliday! **"You know Parse and Per'la always take this part of the circuit when they substitute during the halidays."** Come to think on it, she found herself a bit fuzzy on the schedule as well. No reason not to be, she and Doyce no longer assigned the circuits, hadn't for a year now. At times she mourned no longer being so deeply involved—until she remembered the problems that forever accompanied their position. Let Berne and Sh'ar deal with them!

**"I miss Ph'raux. Utterly dependable about passing along word, even after he and Dolf retired,"** Rawn grumbled. But why bring that up now when they were far nearer Gaernett than they were to Haarls? Or was it simply a mention of another of the ghatti to be missed, mourned? But then, Rawn had had the right of it before when he'd said that the world had been passing them by. All the time they'd been there, she'd had an uncanny sensation that truth, though not the whole truth, was being passed along to them. What Doyce always called the "don't worry the invalids" technique.

In mutual silence they watched the countryside, already

bleaker looking, more wintry the farther north they traveled, the Gulf of Oord left far behind. In front, Jenret passed Doyce the reins and slipped an arm around her waist, snugging her close. What were they saying? Ah . . . nothing of import . . . something about Jenret's mother Damaris and his sister Jacobia—she could relax, half-doze.

An almost imperceptible drizzle moistened the land around them, further diminishing the scrim of snow, caked with dirt thrown up by passing traffic, that edged the roadway. Down here the blizzard had been milder, melting away like a memory. The moisture heightened the limited hues of the land as row after row of apple trees slid by the phaeton. Old ones, Khar judged, gnarled trunks with heavy branches oddly forked from frequent pruning, some angling groundward, while others saluted the sky. In her mind she decked them with spring blossoms, how they'd drift and flurry across the roadway in a scented storm of petals, layering a white-lace coverlet across the earth. So fragrant! Would she ever see or smell another spring? Ever bask in that first touch of saturated sunlight, her fur glossy bright?

Why dwell on it? She didn't *know*, and the fact that the truth eluded her perturbed her more than she'd willingly admit. She wanted to know! Yearned to experience so many more springs, revel in them—not vicariously relive them in memory, through the collective minds of the Elders! Already, through Rawn's intervention, she'd been graced with one more spring than she'd expected. Ah, to always lovingly reside in the here and now with Doyce and Rawn and Saam . . . except Saam, her first love, was fading, had admitted he couldn't promise whether he'd be there upon their return. That was his truth, nor could she deny it. How many petals could be plucked from the flower and have it remain the same? The aches she carried were always with her. P'aer had found a way to elude death, avoid abandoning her beloved Ruxie. Wrong or right? No, it was P'aer's truth, admingled with Ruxie's heritage. As if they both inhabited a halfway world, a way station . . .

"Look!" Rawn breathed in her ear as Doyce halted the phaeton, an elderly man bareback on a swaying plow horse thudding toward them between the rows of bare apple trees. Though not exactly trotting, the horse obviously moved at a swift and unaccustomed pace. For the briefest

instant the horse reminded her of Twink, the steady old
gray mare that Faertom had ridden on his Transitor surveys. How long had it been since she'd thought of either
of them? Past was past, and Faertom dead. But what had
become of Twink?

The old man, garbed in russet-and-green-checked trousers and a loose mustard-colored work smock, made a vivid
contrast against the glistening black of the tree trunks and
branches. And he was waving urgently as he clapped
muddy boots to the mare's sides, though not a shout could
she hear.

"Resonant," Rawn murmured, smug at identifying one
before she had. **"Jenret caught his 'speech right away. The
man said we'd intersect about here."** And so they did, Jenret lightly swinging from the phaeton, Doyce delaying long
enough to twist the reins around the hand brake before
joining him.

Bellied against the horse in a slithering dismount, the old
man rushed at Jenret and Doyce, his eyes teary, gripped
by strong emotion, and Khar's fur shivered and rippled in
anticipation of bad news. Except . . . through his tears, the
man smiled broadly, obviously an awestruck admirer. They
popped up in the oddest, most inconvenient places, and
Khar schooled herself to patience.

"Niver, niver did I think I'd see the day," he bawled,
extravagantly pumping Jenret's hand. "Face-to-face with
the great Jenret Wycherley, who's meant so much to us
Resonants!" Rawn cocked his head at Khar, a touch prideful at having his Bond thus praised. But the man had hardly
begun, had no intention of halting. Finally releasing Jenret's hand, he trotted to Doyce, clasping hers in both his
dirt-stained ones as he stiffly dropped to one knee, pressing
his forehead against her hands, his balding pate roseate
with emotion. "And our Lady who came late but true into
her powers. Ah, well I ken the night you sent your power
soaring through the skies like a beacon to strengthen our
resolve, telling us the time had arrived to stand brave and
free, prideful of who and what we are!"

Nonplussed, Doyce reclaimed her hands and, after a
minor struggle, succeeded, tucking them out of harm's way
behind her back. Lifting his teary but cheerful countenance
to hers, he caught sight of his own hands, staring at the

dirt with dawning dismay. "Been mounding over the cabbage and carrots when I got the call," he apologized, and Doyce quickly took his arm, helping him rise. "Niver thought it'd be me chosen to deliver the word, but I'm proud, pleased as punch!" Done scrubbing at his hands with a handkerchief, he blinked owlishly through his tears and honked his nose. "Beno Wellink, at your service! Wife an me own the stead just beyond that rise there. More orchard than farm, cider and apples, that's what Wellink's is known for."

**"Rawn, shall we greet Mr. Wellink?"** If she could but close the distance between herself and this man, sniff at his dirt-stained knees and boots, remind herself of spring and flowering orchards, her dread might recede. And if possible, Khar planned to speed Beno Wellink's recitation, much as she relished hearing her favorite human lauded. What news? What word was he meant to deliver? May fleas nip him!

Without awaiting Rawn's response, she neatly shifted from the seat to the phaeton's floorboards before gingerly jumping to the shoulder of the road. The simplest actions these days required two stages, or her body protested.

Ostentatiously springing from the seat, Rawn caught up with her. **"Better in two stages than not at all,"** he reminded her. **"What's Wellink's news, do you think?"**

**"Neither completely bad nor completely good."** Never expect too much, avoid disappointment. **"Truly bad news he'd have blurted out by now or been struck speechless."** Drawing herself up to display her stripes to their best advantage, she padded toward Wellink, her head alertly cocked, tail held high and quirked in inquiry.

He greeted them both with just the proper amount of friendly reserve, holding a hand down for them to sniff, and Khar's estimation of him rose a notch. Clearly he'd encountered ghatti before, and on friendly terms, but Jenret and Doyce's presence had overwhelmed him. "Won't let me 'speak you, I 'spect. That's why I've been speaking out loud, so you could listen without prying." Fishing in the capacious front pocket of his mustard-yellow smock, he retrieved a paper packet ripe with an alluring aroma. " 'Spoke my daughter Zenie when I caught the hint of your Bonds' mental signatures and went charging to the paddock for Matilda, I did. Told her to rush and meet me with a morsel of that smoked herring we'd bought yesterday."

When Rawn purred, appreciably impressed by such thoughtfulness, Khar administered a disapproving shoulder bump. How could he snack on smoked herring when her beloved and his stood there, straight-backed, hands anxiously clasped, awaiting the man's news? Jenret had assumed his thundercloud look, while Doyce had gone pale and still, as if her merest move might precipitate some catastrophe no one could avert.

With a ribbonlike twist Khar reversed herself to present a rigidly reproving back to Beno Wellink, adamantly shunning him and his proffered package. Then, with deliberation, she canted her head over her shoulder, amber eyes fixed on his watery blue ones as she eloquently inclined her head in Doyce's direction.

"Ah, forgetting myself, I am!" Wellink smote himself on the forehead with the packet, while Doyce said tightly, "Mr. Wellink, you indicated you have news for my husband and me?"

Now his face rearranged itself into a more serious mien. "Aye, ma'am, that I do. Been part of a Resonant rondelet for years, I have, more years than you've lived. Don't have the same pressing need for it as we once did, seventeen years back and before, thanks to you and yours. Now we mostly trade a dollop of gossip or local doings, weather reports, such like—not to warn of danger, the chance of being 'sposed for what we are.

"Maundering, I am!" and again repentant slapped himself with the packet. "Since no one knew 'zactly where ye was, we used the rondelet to cover as much territory as possible, increase the chances of finding you. Efficient, eh?" His chest puffed with pride. "Now, this news is important, I'm sure, but you're not to fesh yourselves o'ermuch by it, though it's been a regular shocker here as the word spreads round. A Plumb 'sploded in Marchmont, in Sidonie—right in the king's castle, no less!" A short moan escaped Doyce's lips, and Khar forcibly restrained herself from shredding Wellink's shins. "Not to worry! The king, Eadwin as he's called, wanted you to know special that he and his are unhurt. And that your sister, the Lady Francie, and her husband and the boy, Harry, are fine."

Doyce visibly sagged with relief, only to stiffen as Wellink warbled on. " 'Course, I reckon Lord Muscadeine won't be sitting pretty for some days, what with the shrapnel pieces plastering his backside."

Voice tight with strain, Jenret interjected, "Where did they find a Plumb? Where did it come from?"

"Out of Ruxie's tales," murmured Doyce, and Khar couldn't help wondering herself.

"Ah . . . ah . . . from an old trunk." Wellink scratched his head as it gradually struck him that there must be a better answer.

"Doyce? The twins? Think they're likely to know anything more?" Between them, they should be able to mindspeak as far as Gaernett, attract the twins' attention. And if the two of them were in a mood to slither free of their parents' hail, Khar'd do more than take them to task when they reached home!

Attentive, mouth ajar, Wellink watched them attempt to reach the twins, knowing enough not to interrupt. "Nothing." Doyce sighed. "And I don't think they've purposely turned minddeaf on us, Jenner. I can feel the emptiness, can't you? They're not there." A new possibility struck her and Jenret simultaneously. "You don't suppose—"

"They've headed for Marchmont?" Jenret finished for her. "It'd be just like them to want to help out. Turn it into an adventure, even." Fist absently pounding his palm, Jenret scowled as he thought it through.

Beaming nervously from Doyce to Jenret and then from Rawn to Khar, Wellink worked to smooth things over. "An isn't that just like children? Aggravating-like, but not serious. Why, if you'd seen some of the things Zenie put the wife an me through afore marriage settled her down, you'd know what it is to be feshed! Why, I recollect the time—"

Stepping forward, Doyce seized Beno Wellink's hand, bringing her voice under control as only a trained Seeker could, intimate, confiding, inviting the listener to pour out his heart. "Anything else, Mr. Wellink? Anything that you've omitted or forgotten—a detail mislaid in the excitement. Mayhap it seems minor to you, but it might not be to us. Think hard, Mr. Wellink, please!" After all, Khar reflected, better for the person being questioned to voluntarily tell what he knew, rather than allow one of the ghatti

to rummage through his mind! And she was about ready
to rummage, with or without Doyce's say-so!

"Well, there's weather, always weather. That got passed
'long with the rondelet, too. Been stormy up round Gaernett, blizzards and such. Their first batch of snow barely
kissed us here, a reminder of what's to come. Weather's
working our way, as well. 'Cept," he added judiciously,
sniffing the air, "it'll rain here, and plenty of it. Trees won't
mind, nothing like a good drink afore the real winter sets
in." Jenret had already edged toward the phaeton, collecting the reins, one foot on the step, though his eyes remained on Wellink.

"Our thanks to you, Mr. Wellink. We truly appreciate
you bringing us the news. Couldn't have a better, more
responsible soul entrusted with it." As she strolled to
Doyce's side, Khar admired her self-control. "I think it be-
hooves us to move along, then." Khar was airborne,
Doyce's arms plucking her up and depositing her in the
phaeton.

"Then you won't be joining my wife and daughter and
me for dinner?" Wellink called forlornly, balancing on his
toes to tilt himself after them. " 'Twould have been such
an honor! Chocolate-applesauce cake for dessert, even!"

Jaw set, his touch gentle as he shook the reins to start
the team, Jenret turned as Doyce hissed at him, "Wave
nicely, dear. Look as if you mean it!" and they both looked
back to bid farewell to Wellink, still on tiptoe, hand up-
raised, fingers bending in a baby wave. Aware again of the
package he clutched in his other hand, Wellink tossed the
smoked herring into the rear of the phaeton.

Already Rawn was working his way under the seats,
snagging the package with his claws to unwrap it. **"Good
old sort, I'd say, even if a touch garrulous."** The paper
rattled. **"Want some, Khar?"**

"You'll get indigestion," she warned, and a part of her
hoped that he would as she listened to the argument gathering force in a front seat.

"You will *not* contact Davvy, and neither will I! Not now,
not during his afternoon rounds, not unless it's a matter of
life or death, Jenret." The phaeton had picked up speed,
Jenret recklessly snapping the reins.

"It *will* be a matter of life or death once I get my hands

on the twins!" Jenret retorted. "And Davvy's not the only Resonant I can contact. Now hold tight, darling. We should be in Gaernett by midnight, earlier, mayhap, even if Rawn and I have to trade places with the team!"

❖

She'd stayed her tongue—near bitten it off at the root to avoid uttering what she'd *wanted* to say—when the twins had come whooping back, faces shiny bright from cold and exhilaration. Diccon's chin boasted a scarlet streamer of blood, while Kwee appeared totally abashed, picking her way along as if her ribs hurt.

"Don't! Don't say it," Harrap had entreated, stepping between her and the twins, pleating and repleating a fold in his robe. "It's done. Let your wrath go. We'll finish in the morning—when we're fresh. It'll go faster, then." Whether he referred to the slim hope she might mellow overnight or the remaining shoveling, she didn't know, didn't ask. Sometimes Harrap had the right of it, she could reluctantly acknowledge that, though not always to his face. Except it *hurt* unbearably to think how she and Harrap, even Parm, had labored like slaveys while the twins and their ghattas went larking around, never a care or concern for those left behind. Mountain sheep, indeed! Did they think she suffered like this to amuse herself? Had found yet another way to prove her superiority, her diligence toward duty? No! Every beat of her heart, every breath she drew was all for Saam!

Supper had been a wordless, withdrawn affair, Jenneth and Diccon seeing to it, equally silent except for an occasional giggle that neither could choke down. Jenneth, she'd immediately noticed, lacked her sheepskin tabard, and that struck Mahafny as highly irregular. Her niece was hardly the sort to misplace or lose things, especially anything as precious as her Seeker's tabard. Not only an outward badge of her status, it also provided a layer of warmth, protection from the elements. As Jenneth shivered and held out her hands to the fire, Mahafny heard Diccon whisper, "I'll fetch it in the morning, once we're through, Jen. My word on it."

"As long as *he's* not wearing it!" With that, the whole

story poured out, Harrap the perfect audience, whole-heartedly joining in the laughter, prone to appropriate gasps of dismay as they reenacted the scene, while she'd sat in sullen, stony silence, Saam cradled on her lap while she spooned broth into his mouth. Eyes averted, concentrating on positioning the spoon's rounded tip in the corner of Saam's mouth—she was too dog-tired to locate the pipette—she found herself adrift in time, half-believing she listened to Jenret and Doyce, not Jenneth and Diccon.

Lady help her, the *thebie* had worn off, and if she didn't lie down soon, she'd fall over. Without a word, a look in their direction, she clasped Saam and haltingly rose, convinced the whole world could hear the sharp reports of her cracking, popping joints, their occasional grating sounds. Diccon—bless him for this small favor, at least—had shaken and reslung the tarps for the night, and she settled beneath one with weary gratitude. She'd purposely chosen the farther tarp, the one that Diccon and Harrap had previously shared. With luck, the twins would take the hint that she'd prefer a different bed-partner, one who hadn't annoyed her, continually tried her patience, or at least not as thoroughly as the twins had. Besides, the twins would relish sleeping together, a throwback to the days when they'd been small, one constantly migrating to the other's bed to nestle together like ghatten, the physical contact as gratifying as their mental bond.

Could her rigorous, rational mind fully encompass what that was like—what they shared? The closest she'd ever come, she supposed, was her relationship with Saam, and that had been discomfiting enough at the beginning, without asking him if it ran as deep, as emotionally all-encompassing as his Bond with Oriel. Or even his brief liaison with Nakum. But the niggardly portion she'd been allowed to taste, to savor, had altered her to the quick. While she remained wakeful, she eased Saam's constraining wrappings—each night, at least for a short while, she freed his limbs so he could flex, not be forever cramped tight, immobilized. Done, she shrugged out of her own jacket and lay down, pulling up the blankets and nestling Saam close. Wrestling her sweater cuff high on her arm, she slipped her bared arm beneath his head. She'd regret that come morning, but she'd deal with that then.

As she'd hoped—though not as she'd expected, at least of late—Saam gave her hand an inquisitive, lingering sniff as he languorously stretched, forming a teardrop shape as all four paws touched. Curling himself tighter, his paw pads sought the bared flesh of her forearm and wrist. Another considering sniff at her hand, and her thumb, stroking along his muzzle, registered his grimace. *"Are you there, Saam?"* Mayhap he'd 'speak her tonight, manage a bit of pillow talk. Just please, please, don't let him call her Oriel! How she cringed inside when he did, not simply because it denied her, but also because she feared he dwelled so far in the past that he'd never again be conscious of the present and her presence.

**"No, I'm not 'there,' I'm 'here.' "** An interrogatory wrist-sniff. **"You smell . . . funny."** Without a doubt she did, even her own dulled senses caught an occasional whiff of the *thebie,* its residue exuded in her sweat, her urine, mayhap in her very breath. Ah, best to sleep with her back to Harrap tonight. His innocence had given her the benefit of the doubt more than once, but he'd recognize the clues soon enough, more attuned than many would be, given his own inadvertent addiction. Innocence? Or a too-keen awareness of how she'd purposely compromised herself— day after day—combined with diffidence at confronting her? He'd let her get away with things before, but even he had his limits. Slapping Diccon's face had forcibly reminded her of that.

*"Could do with a wash, I know. Plenty of snow, but I'm too old for a rubdown with it."*

His chuckle tickled her mind, but then he turned dead-serious. **"How much . . . longer?"** Struggling, he replanted his paws against her, restlessly kneading her flesh. His kneading didn't suggest comfort and contentment as much as a fretful urge to flee, escape his physical hurts. **"This can't go on . . . much longer."**

Two interpretations lay open to her, and she purposely chose the one she wanted in her heart, sought to soothe him with it. *"Another few days, love. We'll reach Nakum in another few days, if the weather's willing."*

Somehow he'd twisted lightning-quick to grip her frail

wrist in his jaws, his teeth pinching, not yet puncturing flesh, but rendingly near. As his jaws inexorably tightened, he demanded, **"Why are you doing this to me? Why are you subjecting me, yourself, the others . . . to this? Cannot we peacefully share these final days? I *know* what you're doing to yourself—Parm told me. As if the very stench of you hasn't revealed how far you've fallen!"**

*"Saam, please . . ."* How dare he confront her like this? Challenge her? When all she wanted was to save, at least prolong, his life!

**"I would . . ."** he sighed, a little coughing sound rumbling in his chest, **"truly cherish the chance to see Nakum once more. But . . ."** And he drifted off—into sleep, into unconsciousness, into another world of his own devising, Mahafny didn't know—or care. Instead, she hugged his final statement to her: Take what you've been told, don't delve too deeply! Her purpose did not lie in searching for the truth, the honest answers he had tried to offer her. Instead, she'd remain content, willingly accept his final thought as evidence that she'd chosen the right path. He *did* yearn to see Nakum again. And wasn't that where she was taking him? Triumphant, she ruthlessly quashed any doubts he'd managed to raise, unable to afford the luxury of doubt. A eumedico *had* to believe that the course of treatment was *right,* would *succeed.* If not, what was the point of it all?

Ah, she'd not even noticed Harrap slipping in; he sat now, removing his boots, his back to her. Laboriously she rolled Saam and herself over and away to present her back to him, let her breath slow and even, concentrated on quelling her pounding heart. Nice to know it could still beat that fast and furious without benefit of the drug!

Oof! Paws deliberately marched across her, compressing the air from her lungs as Parm climbed over—instead of around—her. Sniffing Saam's face, he delicately licked his old friend's closed eyes, his muzzle, before settling down on the other side, Saam crammed between them. Polishing his own paws to his satisfaction, Parm turned his head away from her and curled for sleep. His elaborate efforts to ignore her weighed on her, so used was she to exchanging ritual good nights with him. Ah! He knew about the *thebie*! Had told Saam! Had he told Harrap?

Well, what did it matter if he had or hadn't? She'd made her choice, couldn't back out now. Deal with it come morning, if she must. And now she was sliding down a long chute into sleep, oblivion, or so she hoped. Dreams she couldn't bear.

# PART
# FOUR

"Doyce! Glad you're finally back!" Davvy McNaught fumbled to unwind the long tail of a fantastically varicolored stocking cap from around his neck, where it also served as a scarf. For a long moment Doyce seriously considered strangling him with it, so frustrated did she feel. "Jenret! Welcome! Did you all have a good time? Good weather?"

**"Give him a moment," Khar advised. "He's just rushed over from the hospice. Let him draw a breath or two—and then you can strangle him."** Khar's glare never wavered from Sh'ar, compulsively washing and rewashing his face with first one paw, then the other, adamantly refusing to meet her eyes. **"I'll be occupied ripping off Sh'ar's whiskers—one by one."**

**"Allow me to assist you after that,"** Rawn growled.

Per'la, perched on the arm of the settee beside her Bond Parse, attempted to restore peace with ever-sweet reasonability. **"We did what we thought best at the time." "And with the best intentions in the world,"** interjected T'ss, her boon companion. **"A joint promise,"** Per'la continued smoothly, peridot eyes imploring Doyce, **"to let you enjoy a worry-free haliday, ensure that ghatti and human alike weren't constantly plagued by petty problems that could be handled without involving you."**

**"And you call *this* a petty problem?"** Rawn had been unobtrusively easing toward Sh'ar, prepared to trounce the larger, much younger ghatt within a whisker's-breadth of his life, but the coal-black ghatt now wheeled to glare at two of his oldest friends. If Doyce and Jenret felt betrayed on all sides, it was clear that he and Khar felt equally so.

Unbuttoning Doyce's jacket and stripping her of it as if she were as young and as needful of help as Byrlie, Lindy pursed her mouth sympathetically, her expression hedged by only the faintest hint of repentance. Sympathy was the last thing Doyce wanted, though she wouldn't mind a hint of repentance on Lindy's part, somebody's part! What she wanted was facts! Not half a fact here, another there, two halves that never equaled a whole!

"Doyce, please! We all meant it for the best . . . it . . . well, it sort of grew out of the aftermath of your going-away party." Lindy's eyes were downcast now, but Doyce distrusted the way her mouth quirked, as if her longtime friend, the twins' first nursemaid, found the situation humorous. Clutching Doyce's jacket, Lindy heaved a sigh. "Well, the word spread . . . mushroomed, really . . . and Resonants and Seekers alike thought it was a capital idea. And it was," she insisted, taking the end of Doyce's scarf and tugging to remove it. "Of course, being winter, things had to snowball . . ." Parse gave a crow of delight; his carroty-red hair, full of winter static, floating in a nimbus around his head.

Easy enough for her to remain impassive, not when she couldn't find even a spark of humor in Lindy's comments. They all sat or stood in a shamefaced tableau around Lindy's neat but homey parlor: the Seeker General Berne Terborgh and Sh'ar; Jenret's mother, Damaris Wycherley Saffron and her husband Syndar; Sarrett Bruckner and Parse Rudyard, and their Bonds, T'ss and Per'la; Lindy and Davvy. No doubt other culprits were involved, but these would do for a start, give her and Jenret someone to vent their ire on. But where were Mahafny and Saam, Harrap and Parm? Had one of them been taken ill? No, someone would have mentioned it, just as Syndar had grunted something about Jacobia languishing with a migraine, acting as discomfited as if he'd been forced to discuss a feminine "problem" in public, though Damaris, as always, remained serene.

They'd passed through Gaernett's Ring Wall just before the Bethel tolled midnight, slowing enough to curtly acknowledge the salute of the Guardians on duty and driven the flagging team direct to Lindy's. Oh, to be in her own home, falling into her own bed! Now, hungry, tired, and overwhelmingly angry—at exactly who or what—she couldn't be sure, Doyce stood, waiting to hear precisely what was going on, what they'd missed, happily oblivious to life tying itself into complicated knots while they'd lingered in Haarls. Back against the wall, arms folded hard across his chest, Jenret impartially glared at them all, almost daring anyone to remove his jacket. Even his mother, Damaris, knew better than to interfere, not with that scowl darkening his face.

Although Jenret had contacted friend after Resonant friend in Gaernett, none had been able to add much concrete detail to the happenings, Jenret extravagantly ruing the fact that, unlike ghatti, Resonants couldn't winnow truth from rumor and gossip. Or, Doyce now belatedly realized, they purposely hadn't said much, still honoring their silly pledge. To a Seeker, it was the ultimate blow, to be intentionally denied the truth. Finally, when she'd been sure Davvy would have finished his rounds, she'd 'spoken him, sensed his relief on learning they suspected the twins were in Marchmont, and they'd hastily arranged for this meeting for their arrival.

Khar's and Rawn's search for the truth, 'speaking every ghatti within hailing distance on their harried ride, hadn't been any more successful. Any ghatt or ghatta contacted had pressing business elsewhere, had been laid up with a stubborn hairball, or had turned into a dithering version of Parm. Khar had steadfastly refused to contact Saam, fearful of worrying him, while Parm had been nowhere to be found, though a young and especially cheeky ghatt had implied something about a tryst! Rawn had sniggered at that, and Doyce had feared Khar would box him senseless, though she'd restrained herself to deliver but a single stinging paw slap.

Blowing on still-cold fingers and flexing his hands, Davvy claimed a mug of cha from the tray Lindy now passed, while Sarrett offered sandwiches, whispering a few brief words of commiseration about errant offspring, having five of her own to constantly monitor. Doyce took a mug with gratitude, but waved the sandwiches by, unable to eat despite her hunger pangs. "When did the twins leave for Marchmont?" Convince someone to begin at the beginning, and she'd winkle out the rest.

"**And if you don't, I will,**" Khar promised, now positioned bare centimeters from Sh'ar's face and implacably staring down her nose at him, Rawn acting as rear guard, intently regarding an especially vulnerable spot on Sh'ar's neck.

Looking to Lindy for confirmation, Davvy said, "First day of the new year. So they had a head start on Jacobia, nearly two full days by the time we found out and she left." Well, so much for Jacobia's mysterious migraine!

"And damned if I approve of my daughter traipsing who knows where in the wilderness between here and Marchmont to find the twins and drag them back!" Syndar Saffron bellowed, half-rising from his chair, eyes glinting violet sparks, his bullet head now entirely devoid of hair, though his features still showed how brawlsome he'd once been—and still could be. "Lady knows, I adore your twinnies—thought the two together would exhibit better sense than that batty aunt of yours, Jenret!"

"What do you mean Jacobia—" "How could they possibly have left *then,* when the Plumb didn't ex—" "—and don't ever refer to Mahafny Annendahl as my batty—"

Voices rising, everyone simultaneously expostulating, explaining, or defending themselves, and Doyce struggled to be heard over the din. "Didn't know till well after they'd left—" "—Should have guessed Saam was failing—" **"—All ghatti on the alert, ready to aid them if necessary—"**

" 'S awfully noisy in here!" came a small, sleepy voice that Doyce doubted she'd have heard if it hadn't been for an unexpected tug at her sash. Byrlie, eyes asquint at the parlor's brightness, her blonde hair sticking in all directions, grinned at her, face upturned for a kiss. "Hullo, Auntie Doyce." She rose on tiptoe, waiting until Doyce swiftly dropped a kiss on her forehead. "Why're you all shouting so? So noisy I couldn't sleep, but that's fine, 'cause I wanted to stay awake till you came," she yawned, "but I couldn't."

Gradually the clamor diminished, faltering to a close as the others realized the child was present, and Doyce finally found herself able to hear again. "Would *you* like to tell me what happened, Byrlie? What's going on? The grownups aren't being very helpful, even though they mean to be."

"Can I have a sandwich?" Fisting a yawn that made her blink owlishly, the child riveted her eyes on Jenret's untouched sandwich half. *"Jenner, give it over. It's for a good cause,"* and he immediately passed it over. "They're nicer when they're cut diagonally," Byrlie noted, taking a bite out of the center and thoughtfully chewing. "Ooh, Mama! Horseradish sauce!" Jenret swallowed hard.

"Guess I can 'splain it. Pretty easy, really." She contemplated the sandwich but didn't immediately take another bite. "Awful sad, it is—really. Poor Saam's worse, and Mahafny decided she and Harrap should rush him to Marchmont right away."

It most emphatically was *not* what she'd anticipated hearing, and she looked helplessly at Jenret, hoping he could puzzle out this new piece. "To visit Nakum?" Jenret interjected. "Doyce, Mahafny must believe Nakum possesses some power that will keep him alive, though how, I don't know."

A mouse-sized bite so as not to stuff her mouth. "Uh-huh. And they asked the twins to escort them, so of course they said yes. They love Saam whole bunches and heaps, just like I loved M'wa." She nodded sagely, as if to indicate there'd been no other option. "And then Jacobia decided to ride after them, stop them. It's been an *awful* long time, and we haven't heard anything." Another nibble. "Course *I'm* not worried about Jacobia—even though Mr. Saffron fusses so—'cause Feather was traveling the same way, even though they had an awful squabble. Didn't they, Davvy? But Feather'll help her, if need be, I know she will." As Lindy slipped behind her, Byrlie leaned back into the comfort of her mother's body, head tilting to bestow an upside-down smile on her mother. "Won't she, Mama? And when Feather and Jacobia catch up with everybody else, Feather can help Mahafny, 'cause she's a eumedico, too, plus being an Erakwan. Feather'll fix Saam if Mahafny can't, won't she, Mama?"

"Of course, lovey, she'll try her best. We women stick together, don't we?" Lindy's hands framed the child's face. "But you know what we talked about . . . ? Like M'wa, but not like M'wa?"

"More like what happened to Papa, but not so bloody or bad." A sigh. "I *know,* but I can *wish,* can't I?" She waggled her fingers at Khar and Rawn, blew them each a kiss.

"Then the twins were likely somewhere in Marchmont

when the Plumb exploded? Mahafny and Harrap and the ghatti as well. And I'd guess that Jacobia and Feather haven't yet caught up with them." Jenret sketched in the final details to this newly complex picture, so vastly different from what they'd originally envisioned. Different, more dangerous, and far more prone to failure. Nakum's mountain-fastness in the midst of the Stratocums, in winter, no less!

"Lady help me!" Davvy looked truly stricken, his face ashen. "When you said you knew the twins were in Marchmont, I assumed you'd somehow learned the whole story, not that you'd deduced only a part of it—and wrongly at that! I thought you were taking it awfully well, considering that I'd expected you to flay me alive when we 'spoke earlier. No wonder nothing's been making sense to any of us, we've all been talking at cross-purposes."

Per'la, all fluffy cream-colored fur, nervously circled on the arm of the settee, and Doyce still mourned with her for the loss of that beautiful plumed tail. **"As much as we revere Saam, we ghatti didn't feel it was our place to step in, attempt to alter the pattern of life and death. We just don't know what he wants, aren't sure if he knows himself, but it's his decision."** A graceful jump down and she glided to Khar's side, wreathing herself around her. **"But do remember this—nothing can have gone too terribly wrong thus far, or we ghatti would have known, wouldn't we, Sh'ar? Seekers and Bondmates have been ready to ride, if need be."**

"Resonants, too," Davvy added, now distinctly uncomfortable standing anywhere near Jenret and his glower.

"One last thing, Lindy." Turning to the younger woman, Doyce shifted her outside the parlor for privacy, Byrlie reluctantly remaining behind as her mother released her. "Have you felt anything? Seen even a fragment of what's happening—what *will* happen?" Lindy possessed a strange, almost uncanny "gift," the ability to foresee the future, or envision an event as it transpired kilometers distant. Her "sight" wasn't always entirely accurate, both in what Lindy saw and her interpretation of it, but it *might* offer some bare hint, a possible clue, and Doyce was torn by both wanting and not wanting to know.

"Don't think I haven't tried, left myself as open and receptive as possible." Lindy was close to the twins, should be able to feel, sense how things were going with them, especially if the situation were dire. "Not a thing. Visions never come on command. Though sometimes a feeling of coldness and sadness, futility, sweeps over me when I'm least expecting it. Nothing more definite than that—I'm sorry, Doyce."

"I'll try to take that as good news." She let Lindy encircle her with a hug, leaning into it, hugging back. "No one's to blame."

Releasing her, Lindy sought her hand. "Then let's go back, see what can be done."

"How quickly can you reach Marchmont?—that's the question." Berne broke from his huddle with Parse and Syndar Saffron as Doyce and Lindy reentered the parlor. "And I think Parse has just the thing to speed your trip, Jenret."

Dragging out his crutches, Parse levered himself from the settee. "Broke my artificial leg before I could even ride haliday circuit duty. Slipped on the ice, no less! Poor Sarrett had to ride in my stead, but I had the worst of it, home with the children and me with only one leg to chase them!" Sobering, he gave them a little bow. "But mayhap it's for the best. While I was laid up, I finished my 'mud buggy,' instead of constructing a new leg."

He'd swung to the center of the room, balancing on his crutches, hands sketching the air. "Basically it's a standard buggy, stripped down as light as I can make it and with the springs reinforced. But what you must see are the wheels!" Ever vigilant, Sarrett stationed herself just behind her mate, prepared to tilt him upright if he wavered. "Extra strong rims with treads," interweaving his fingers, he tried to indicate what he meant. "Not just to dig in with, but to cast off the mud—should work the same with snow, shouldn't it, darling?"

A vision of Parse's last major invention, his wheeled chair—two models, no less—and the race in them between Mahafny and Francie swept through Doyce's mind. Well, they *had* worked, not broken or crashed, although Doyce had come out the worse for wear given her proximity to them. "We'll take it, Parse, and with thanks," she assured him before Jenret could protest, insist they ride. No point voicing it aloud, but in addition to her other worries, her most pressing one was whether Khar could withstand such a long, hard ride, and she was deathly afraid the dear ghatta could not.

"And you'll have escorts taking you along the way, riders and either a Seeker or a Resonant driving fresh teams, so you can sleep, or at least rest." Berne looked relieved, but not as relieved as Sh'ar. "That way you can travel day and night."

"I volunteer to drive the first leg of the journey—after all, it seems appropriate, since I only have the one!" Parse mugged a face at her to camouflage his concern as his glance took in both Khar's and Rawn's exhausted stances. "Sarrett will be one outrider. Berne, would you like to do the honors as the other, you and Sh'ar?"

♣

Red-knit chook clasped to her breastbone, Jacobia wavered as the wind whipped her hair around her shoulders, shoved at her. It hurt to stand, her feet unwieldy and sausagelike, but it was worth the pain to depend on her own two feet, free to turn this way, then decide to turn the other way, examine the breathtaking view as sunset approached, gilding the misty haze above The Shrouds, so very far below. As the sun's angle altered, crescent rainbows and brilliant chromatic streamers danced at the edges of the mist and spray rose from the horseshoe-shaped falls below. Beyond the glinting prisms, to her left, the Spray River tumbled, too turbulent to freeze solid except in the most severe, long-term cold. From here she could see, but not hear, the water splash as it riffled down smaller falls until it blended into a gray-green ribbon etched with changeable whiteness as it slammed from rock to rock, the sound of the falls scarcely discernible, a mere memory, though her ears still thrummed and tingled with its roar.

Placing each foot with care she turned her back on the falls to glimpse the curved shape of Pettibal, the smallest of the three large inland lakes, the Balaenas, each uncannily whale-shaped, father, mother, and baby, nose to tail, nose to tail. From the baby's enthusiastic blowhole depended the Spray River, eager to reach The Shrouds, tumbling over it on its way to the sea. Pettibal looked placid at this distance, a broad expanse of deep-blue water, except for its near edge where winter waves ruffled pale lacey patterns as they pounded against the shore.

Never had she viewed these wonders from such a lofty perspective, and the sight brought tears to her eyes at such natural beauty, the simple fact of their existence, changeable yet unchanging. This, this was the land her people had searched for across the skies, had found, so many years past! Even the mountains' rocky formations unflinchingly presented their own harsh beauty, a mélange of hues and shadings within each stone and outcrop. Easy to say offhandedly that they were brown or gray or black, tan or white in some spots, but a closer examination revealed striations of pink and rose, rusty red, greens ranging from spring pale to dark jade, minute sparkles of silver or gold. Solid colors, translucent ones, transparent, geometric shapes, miniature crystalline spires.

At her side Addawanna rocked her weight from heel to toe and back, and Jacobia detected a touch of impatience. And why not? To the Erakwan woman this view was nothing new, merely an old, familiar friend. "I shouldn't have taken so long, I'm sorry." But as she swung toward the older woman, Addawanna stood with her back to her, gazing at the high peaks. "You're worried about Nakum, aren't you?" Despite her illness and injuries, she'd sensed Addawanna's constant preoccupation throughout their days of travel. Addawanna's touch she'd welcomed no matter how miserable she felt, Feather's touch less soothing for its tendency toward brusqueness. But from the older woman's patient hands something had transmitted itself to her, a worry over Nakum strikingly akin to her own concern over Jenneth and Diccon.

Lowering her eyes from the high peaks, Addawanna offered them a half-salute in farewell, seemed to return to herself, her burnished-copper skin basking in the rich, velvet light that should have shadowed and emphasized her age lines, but instead, erased them. A headshake set her graying braids tossing like a young girl's as she smiled. "No, not Nakum, so much. But ev'ryt'ing. I worry fer ev'ryt'ing." Her arm's broad sweep encompassed the sights Jacobia had so greedily drunk in, her other arm rising as if the Erakwan woman would embrace it all if she could, cherish it safe and close to her breast.

"If not Nakum, or not really Nakum—then what, exactly?" Given the literal burden she'd been to Addawanna and her people, Jacobia would gladly share her burden, if she could. Both grandmother and grandson had been loyal friends to her family, and such faithfulness demanded a matching commitment in return. Undoubtedly Addawanna had smiled and frowned in equal measure over her adolescent attraction to Nakum, untested, untried, but intense, the girlish pleasure she'd derived in pitting Aelbert and Nakum against each other to win her affections, unsure where they might truly lie. Not with Aelbert, certainly, now dead and gone. And ultimately not with Nakum, the gulf between them too broad, each stranded on an opposing bank, lacking the confidence to build a bridge between.

Squatting, Addawanna brushed snow aside to touch the frozen earth with a hand, stroking it much the way one gentled an upset animal, soothing it until it came to itself again. "Fer time bein' Nakum an arborfer are fine. But the land is uneasy, no wantin', no likin' change. An at hands of your people—again."

Mystified, even miffed, Jacobia asked, "Why?" with more heat than she'd intended. "What are 'we' doing? What have we done?" Of course the planet Methuen had been transformed into a different world with her ancestors' arrival in their spaceships, but had they changed things so very drastically? Parts of the land, yes, but certainly not the wild beauty she'd just drunk in so thirstily.

"From time 'fore dere was time, the land remakes itself, but is long, slow process. Mountains doan spring up overnight, nor do dey wear 'way in single day. Look at long time it takes arborfer to grow tall. How many gen'rations of your people born, die 'fore one tree reaches up to touch sky?"

Although her tone was impersonal, unemotional, Addawanna's words stung. "Don't some changes happen overnight—or practically so? Floods, volcanoes, earthquakes—like the tremors we felt, oh, how many nights back? Or was that just me quaking with chills?" Either had been possible, the ripples surging through the earth's skin shaping themselves into a swaying counterpoint to her feverish imaginings. And sometimes they hadn't been imaginings, but tales that had floated through her brain until she no longer was sure which was which nor quite who she was now, everything within her in the process of fusing her into a new form.

Addawanna's grudging chuckle blossomed into rolling laughter, tears of amusement squeezing from her eyes, eyes that suddenly looked infinitely sad and old. "Silly chil'ren, you an Feather, fer all your years. T'inkin' you know oh-so-many answers, but learnin' not *knowin'*. Oh-so-busy, way too clever to lis'en 'cept wid ears. Land, the earth wantin' to talk, tell you t'ings. An then you go, 'What, what? I did not know, I did not realize.' "

Feet convinced someone had stuffed live coals in her boots, Jacobia limped to a boulder and warily sat, feeling rather as if she were brooding over a large egg. "What don't I realize? What did Feather and I miss?" On the outcrop below theirs, Feather and the other Erakwa efficiently removed any traces of their halt for a brief supper. If she didn't know better, she'd swear they practically dusted and polished the snow, artfully assuring that it resumed its pristine condition.

"Dat 'earthquake' you say you felt—dat was earth crying its pain, sendin' its cry tru'out de land. Past has taken over present, and your people are its cause. Dat was Plumb 'sploding, its pain quivering tru' de earth, remindin' it of past hurts, destruction!"

"A Plumb?" echoed Jacobia. "That's simply *not* possible! They're all gone by now—corroded, eaten away by the elements! Even if you found one, it couldn't be operable after all this time! There hasn't been an explosion in over two hundred years!"

"I know what land tells me. An dey *not* all gone, inoper-able. Some still exist, have sprung to life, destroyin' yet again."

❖

Cinzia Treblicote entered Urban's sitting room and closed the door, ruefully shaking her head at the effort expended in reassuring Etelka that bathing in the king's palace was *not* an imposition or an intrusion. Commoner or not, a bath was necessary. Other than young Harry Muscadeine, she'd not dealt with an abundance of children of late, so she'd treated the girl as a small adult and things had ultimately worked out.

**"Would've gone better if I'd been there. Think of the confidence that my mere presence—that of an exalted ghatt—would have instilled in her!"** The long-haired black ghatt with white toes and a white bib, a white muzzle and tail tip preened as he 'spoke his Bond. **"And what a ghatt I am!"** One yellow eye winked at Cinzia to indicate he didn't take himself *that* seriously. **"Bet you haven't even told her you're a Seeker, Seeker liaison to the king!"** White whiskers a handspan long and wide flexed. **"A very important—and cushy—position! If truth be told, of course. And I do."**

Exhibiting twinned, impassive smiles at La'ow's obvious flamboyance, P'roul and Khim resumed grooming, La'ow now attempting impartiality as he licked first one, then the other. **"By all rights I should be attending Hru'rul. After his morning swim, he's in dire need. It will require all my considerable skill to make him halfway presentable to his Bond, let alone two stunning ghattas such as yourselves."**

"La'ow, anyone'd think you're more essential to the castle's well-being than Ezequiel, though we know better!" *"You spoiled, insufferable . . . darling,"* she concluded on the intimate mode as she poured ale from the pitcher on the sideboard. "Anyone for a refill?" Holly and Theo shared a lavishly brocaded sofa, one of Theo's long legs dangling over its plumply curved arm, while Urban Gamelyn sat fussily in a velvet winged chair, twirling a crystal wine goblet by its stem. Mostly though, he cast oblique glances at Romain-Laurent, who patiently sorted tinted glass fragments into piles, occasionally matching one piece to another and crowing in triumph when they fit.

"Every glass figurine I cherished, Cinzia. Every last one, shattered, smashed. Only three intact goblets out of a set of twelve." His smooth-shaven chin, marred by a shaving nick—so unlike him to be careless—quivered as he glared at Romain-Laurent's back. "Took me years, years to collect! Irreplaceable!"

"Is that all that was damaged in your suite?" Cinzia inquired with real sympathy, aware of how much Urban cherished his figurines, how he'd skimped and saved during his junior service as an exchequer clerk when money was tight. Two pieces she'd personally selected as giftings for him, she and La'ow critically examining each piece in the glassblower's shops forever and a day, judging the light's play on them, the overall lines, the clarity of the crystal. Urban had no close relatives left, so a gift from a friend was worth all the effort involved in its selection.

"Look up." Morosely Urban indicated the ceiling and she did, noticing the large crack with its smaller, hairline cracks spidering out from it. Oh dear, it ran through the boss as well! "And the bedroom doesn't bear looking at! The wardrobe toppled, smashed against the foot of the bed—both doors cracked in half." He sounded as if he might cry. Urban found comfort from a continuity with objects from the past, his grandfather's wardrobe, his late mother's wine goblets. Even the ceiling boss had a family history, painstakingly moved here from the old family residence.

"It's only furniture," called out Romain-Laurent, bobbing up like a jack-in-the-box from behind the sofa. "Was it old? Well, if it couldn't withstand some thumps, throw it out and buy a new piece. No sense in emotional attachments to rackety old furniture. Downright perverse, I'd say. The latest, most advanced—that's my motto!"

Although they'd both been in silent possession of the sofa, apparently content to be companionable as long as no sustained conversation wasn't called for, Holly stolidly twisted to face Romain-Laurent as Theo held a hot compress in place on her shoulder. A puffy, livid bruise marred her temple. "Charpentier, stop being such a cheerfully insensitive ass, especially about things you don't understand, never bothered to learn. The man *cared,* that's enough. Despite his own personal losses, despite the exchequer work awaiting him, he's been gracious enough to entertain us in his own private rooms. Not leave us alone to brood over what happened."

To her surprise, Cinzia's stein was half empty, she'd apparently been sipping away, more thirsty than she'd realized after what already seemed like a full day of work and worry so precipitously begun when the explosion and its aftershocks roiled castle and city alike. The ale tasted good, smelled better, far better than the dank sewer-water scent that floated everywhere.

**"And invaded your hair and clothes,"** chimed in La'ow, his plumed tail swaying

*"I had a quick wash, changed my clothes! My bathroom isn't functional, let me remind you! Just because you were more surefooted than I, didn't fall in, even Master Xavier said it was bound to happen to one of us—"* Oh, what was the point? La'ow had wanted to get a rise out of her, and he'd succeeded!

Both legs now jutting straight in front of him, his toes practically prodding Urban's chair, Theo studied his intertwined fingers with rapt attention. "What'll b–become of the P–plumbs—the r–remaining ones? A–any ideas?" The dilemma obviously weighed on his mind, weighed on everyone's right now, and his experience with the Plumb had been more immediately personal than most people's. Not to mention that Holly had assumed the risky responsibility of ferrying the remaining Plumbs to safety, achingly aware of the very real chance they might explode!

Cinzia's mind spun on from there, inventing detail upon detail. Lady bless, but she hoped Holly wasn't an imaginative soul—just envisioning that solitary dark journey practically paralyzed her! Shouldn't be overburdened with imagination, given her broad, solid physique, but outer looks seldom revealed a person's full measure. After all, to their ultimate regret, too many had initially discounted Urban, not reckoned with the hardheaded, committed public servant camouflaged by a certain prissy effeteness. When unpleasant decisions had to be made, Urban made them—and lived with the consequences without whining.

Holly shifted in discomfort, and P'roul was at her side in an instant, sniffing her all over for reassurance. "All the time P'roul and I were struggling through the tunnels . . . I kept thinking I heard that flat, disembodied voice . . . inside the trunk . . . counting down." She shook herself, like a dog shaking water. "They've been harmless this long, may well continue to be harmless. As long as no one pushes the wrong buttons again." Neither rancor nor censure tinged her observation, she'd simply stated a fact, and Cinzia doubted if she could have schooled herself not to berate Romain-Laurent for his stupid, thoughtless act. She'd heard a great deal about Holly and Theo through the years, had met them in Canderis but hadn't gotten to know them well, their leaves rarely coinciding. Nor had she expected an opportunity to further their acquaintance, not once she'd been stationed up here.

**"And most of the time it suits us just fine,"** La'ow reminded her. **"I wasn't cut out for riding circuit. My beautiful coat, my glorious fur, whipped and tangled by the elements? Not on your life!"** As if to emphasize the indignities of such a life, he rolled onto one hip and splayed his rear legs, curving forward to groom the long feathery fur on his tail. Purposely he let his pink tongue freeze just outside his mouth, rolling a yellow eye to gauge her reaction. **"I think I've captured Urban's pensive expression rather nicely! You should hear me imitate you—I had the ladies here giggling fit to burst. But I showed restraint, knowing they'd already put in a harrowing day."**

With an understated superiority that females of any species could appreciate, P'roul and Khim claimed Cinzia's attention. **"Yes, we know he fancies himself as adorable—" "He *can* make your whiskers sag with laughter, but basically he's harmless. Now, about the Plumbs?"**

What about the Plumbs? She'd mentally digressed, allowed fantasies of the dark, cloying closeness down below to commingle with her childhood fears, take precedence over the most crucial issue. What *did* one do with something so potentially dangerous? Far better when they'd languished, the trunk unopened, forgotten in the subcellars. What one didn't know about, one didn't worry about . . . or utilize in some horrible act of destruction. . . .

"I suppose," fingers steepled in front of his mouth, Urban spoke through them as if the words themselves required confining, "that we should keep them under lock and key—forever and a day, and a day beyond that. But no matter how zealously we guard them, mistakes happen. A guard's abruptly taken ill on the day a new cleaning maid decides she really *must* dust that room . . ." As Cinzia doubtfully shook her head, he continued more stubbornly, "Stranger, more imbecilic things have happened in life— and will again. If you'd prefer a scenario involving active treachery, guards can be poisoned or overpowered, the Plumbs stolen. For what evil use I don't dare think, but evil inhabits the world around us. Uncaring, unthinking, utterly determined to have its way."

She hated it when Urban turned so downhearted, a bleakness emanating from him, as if he'd intimately experienced such vile betrayals firsthand. Attempt to comfort him at such moments and he'd draw away, both in thought and body, physical contact unbearable. But Theo doggedly brought them back to the problem. His stammer did vanish on occasion, but she'd hardly expected it now, not given his intense frown, the crucial nature of the subject under discussion. "Destroy them!" One hand smacked against the other, and Romain-Laurent jumped, dropping half an aquamarine glass dolphin that shattered into more pieces on the floor.

"Destroy them!" thundered Theo. "Find somewhere safe, figure out how to detonate them from a distance, and then we'll be free of the bloody things!"

"*Can* they be disabled, permanently shut off or shut down?" Urban wanted to know.

"I doubt it." Pouring more ale, Cinzia wished she hadn't and set aside her stein. "If that were possible, our ancestors wouldn't have gotten themselves into the mess they did, would they? Something went wrong with the Plumbs— some technological aspect went awry—and they began exploding at random—remember? If they *could* have fixed them or rendered them harmless, they *would* have. Their brave, beautiful new world, full of natural resources, turned treacherous on them, through their own fault—"

"And some fled, and some stayed and bled, and made our world as we know it now. The end." Romain-Laurent dusted his hands together. "So much for repairing your dolphin, Urban! And so much for gloomy murmurings about the past! This is a golden opportunity, don't you see! We've six left. Used judiciously, we can accomplish projects that would normally require generations of labor, given our old-fashioned, outmoded ways, our distaste for technology." Agog with excitement, anticipation, he hurtled on, "This is our *chance,* a chance to chart a new path, embrace technology, learn from it. Mayhap we can construct our own Plumbs—oh, crude facsimiles at first, I grant you that!" An airy, dismissive wave of his hand. "Think of the mining we could do! A channel dredged!" A joyous little skip carried him to the center of the sitting room, thrilled at being, at long last, the center of their disapproving attention. "Think how efficient they'd be compared to octs or years of labor by hand! I must *think*—think this through. Think bravely, boldly, and beyond our usual constricted thoughts—if you can! *This* is the pivotal moment I've been awaiting all my life!"

Throwing his wine goblet across the room, Urban rose, hands trembling, face pale. "Oh, I *am* thinking bravely, boldly, and beyond my usual outdated thoughts. Been struck by a new vision! Theo, my good man. Do you think you could manage one end of my wardrobe if I lift the other end?"

A hesitant, perplexed nod from Theo as Urban mused, "Mayhap the door panels can be repaired, replaced, but I'd rather sacrifice the whole piece in a noble cause."

"N–noble cause?" Theo echoed.

"Drop it on Charpentier. Crush him flat—before he can hatch any more ill-advised, downright dangerous schemes!"

"You wouldn't!" sputtered Romain-Laurent, eyes darting, desperate for someplace to run, to hide, only belatedly realizing he was surrounded.

"Oh, wouldn't I?" was Urban's rejoinder as he stepped forward.

A childish shriek mingled with high-pitched feline yowls cut through the rising tension enveloping the room.

**"Oh, my. I do believe Etelka's finished her bath. As has Baby. It's wonderful to be clean, well-groomed, but soapsuds in the eyes *do* sting. Hurry along, Cinzia—you're all Etelka has right now."** La'ow marched between Charpentier's cringing form and Urban's wrathful one. **"I suspect the ladies and I can straighten this out, though I confess we approve of Urban's plan. Mash him flat!"** A large paw slapped the carpet for emphasis, as if the ghatt had pinned a bug. **"That's what I adore about Urban—he never ceases to surprise me. So few humans are capable of that."**

Plumbs! Rubbing her temples, Cinzia realized she had a full-blown headache, had had it for some time. *How* had their discussion degenerated into childish threats? And from Urban, no less! None of this boded well; if *their* dis-

cussion had gone awry, undoubtedly future discussions
would founder and flounder, too. People with inflexible
convictions pitted against others with equally strong,
though dissimilar, views? Not a pleasant preview of the
next few days or octs, she decided, as she shot out the door
and down the hallway to Urban's private bath.

**"Make sure they've both washed behind their ears, since
I won't be there to check."**

*"And if you don't stop annoying me, I might be forced
to* trim *that matted spot. Trim it, clip it short as I can. Not
patiently tease it out with a comb. I'll let you and the ghattas
meet Baby when I think Telka's ready. And don't let Urban
do anything foolish, love. We've all enough to be concerned
over without him taking on Charpentier."* Just what she
needed right now, a little hayseed of a child seeking hope,
justice, in a world that had just survived a major—and literal—upheaval!

♣

The tub was large, larger than any Etelka had ever seen or
heard of—long enough to practice the dead man's float
without bumping head or toes on its sleek white surface. It
reminded her of Mam's best cup and saucer, the fine porce-
lain one with gold trim Da'd brought back from the fair
for their anniversary, but that was whisper-thin, the cup's
lip translucent when held to the light. This tub was *solid,*
she couldn't begin to guess how many people it would take
to tip and drain it when she was done! But to finish, she
had to begin, dare to step into it, this lovely but frightening
swan-shaped tub with a spigot-thingy and fourcets. Least
that was what Cinzia had named them when she'd showed
her how they turned on and off, how water gushed from
the swan's beak. Good thing the swan's neck permanently
twisted over his back or he'd have flooded the floor!

And the *suds,* bubbles and bubbles just frothing and
foaming, ready to swallow her up when she climbed in.
With neat economy and more than a little trepidation, she
began removing her wet, dirty clothes, unsure where to pile
them so as not to soil anything else. Like the stack of white
towels with peach stripes, all fluffy soft and smelling so

fresh and clean, one unfurled on top, its end near enough to grab when she finished bathing. Finally, she folded her clothes as small as she could and laid them in the corner where the sea-blue tile was freshly cracked and loose, stood there in her smallclothes, debating. Being here like this in that snooty Gamelyn-man's private ablution chambers unnerved her more than she wanted to admit, out of her depth before she'd even stepped into the tub.

Baby circled the tub again, stopping to sniff a water droplet, then dropping on her stomach to crawl beneath the swan-tub's belly where, confusingly, four clawed feet held it off the floor. Popping out on the other side, the kitten reared, stretching full-length against the tub's side, claws scrabbling as she gave little jumps to peer over the edge. Locking her hands around the kitten's middle, she hoisted her up, letting her view the mounded suds. The kitten energetically struggled to reach them, and Telka held her closer so Baby could touch the bubbles, her toes splayed wide as she pawed at them, only to flinch away when they burst.

"Seems we've already seen enough water for one day, doesn't it, Baby?" And that was the Lady's truth, sure as sure. Fact was, given all the water she'd seen draining *out* of the castle, she couldn't imagine how they'd found enough left to fill her bath here *in* the castle. A shiver at her dumb luck, at Baby's luck, and she hugged the kitten harder. Not only had she helped rescue the king, King Eadwin, and the majestic Hru'rul, but she'd been invited into the very castle itself, was to meet the king!

Or would once he had time from his plumbing problems. She expected that was what Cinzia'd meant, though she'd misspoke and said "plumb problems." Still, whether 'twas "plumb" or "plumbing problems," it sounded like one of those phrases adults used when they didn't want to true-name something, wanted to be mincy-polite. Like "manure" wasn't "manure" or even "dung," but "waste matter" or "night soil." Still smelled the same, whatever they called it.

"Well, Baby, best we both get cleaned up." Depositing the kitten on the pile of towels, she resolutely stripped off her smallclothes and, reluctantly, her glasses—the ultimate nakedness—before mounting the little set of steps beside the swan-tub. Good thing they were there, or she'd have had to give a hop, straddle the edge and ease into the water without landing ker-splash. Phew! Not as deep as she'd feared, must be a thick bottom on it. And oh, didn't the hot water feel scrumptious after all that time crammed in the backs of those drays! This was like a dream after the washtub at home. Poor Levi and the other boys could barely fold themselves into it, only their butts and heels touching, torsos and folded legs poking way above the edge.

Oh, how darling! A wee swan soap dish made of birchwood floated in the tub, an oval of scented, peach-tinted soap, brand-new, awaiting her. And it had—she squinted—the king's seal on it, no less! Oh, dear, had that Gamelynman stolen the king's soap? Well, it was too late for her to care, and with a gentle shove she sent the birch swan majestically gliding across the tub. Too big for toys like that, but she couldn't resist. Hair first, so she dunked and lathered, scrubbing at her scalp, wishing the mirror were low enough to show the towering turban of suds she'd created. Knee to her chest, she began scrubbing with the flannel washcloth, then stretched her leg, toes buoyantly sculpting the bubbles, making them swirl and eddy. Now she raised her leg higher, her toes peeping from the soapsuds, all pink from heat and cleanliness against the pearly white bubbles.

"Baby! No!" Claws skittering, Baby balanced on the tub's sleek edge, amber eyes fixed on the toes playing peekaboo with her. Her long, skinny tail skimmed the water's surface, its tip dipping below, but she paid no heed. "Baby, get down! This instant! Down!"

"Mmwa? Naow Y'ew?" The kitten sounded aggrieved as she cast a look over her shoulder at Etelka, then went slinking along the edge, making a lightning dart at the bubbles with one paw or the other. The end of her tail dripped, looking like a length of orange, sodden yarn, the kitten dividing her gaze between the suds where Telka's toes had appeared and disappeared, and Telka herself.

Smothering a giggle, Telka eased her leg beneath the surface, let it pop up invitingly right by the edge. Startled, Baby almost leaped into the air, then tagged her toe with a wet paw, not a claw out. Rolling onto her side, just managing to keep her head above water as she half-floated,

Telka extended her leg further, readying her toes to appear in a new location. It was then that she saw that the beautiful stack of towels had toppled off the chair, lay strewn on the tiles. "Oh, Baby! You didn't break my spectacles, did you? How could you be so messy?" Her foot shot up despite herself and the kitten stretched to tag it, hind claws screaking as she scrambled to keep her footing.

The next thing Etelka knew, the kitten surfaced, emitting high-pitched wails of terror, suds flying, water splashing and soaking the floor, the tumbled towels. A desperate paw snagged the tub's edge but found no purchase, the kitten kicking and thrashing, sinking and bursting up again, her shrieks interrupted by a violent sneeze. Holding her breath, trying to avoid flailing claws, Telka lunged and grabbed the kitten by the scruff, though hind claws raked her arm. Lifting as quick as she could, she deposited Baby over the edge.

"Oh, Baby! Look what you've done! Look what we've done!" Water, water everywhere, soggy towels, the walls splashed and dripping, water trickling under the door. Suds still drifted as the kitten unsteadily stood and shook herself.

Unbidden, the picture invaded Telka's mind, and she began sobbing. Drowned—this was what Baby would have looked like if Levi had drowned her! The beautiful orange fur plastered flat on the scrawny body, the tiny head all sharp wedges . . . ! And surely they'd throw her out for being so inconsiderate, so messy and untrustworthy, and she'd *never* save Baby from drowning. Surely this was a preview of how it would be, how Baby would suffer and flounder and flail and cry, bubbles rising from the water, until . . . finally . . . they stopped, the thin mewls of terror heard no more!

"Telka? Etelka?" A rap at the door. "It's me, Cinzia. Are you all right? What's wrong, love?" Sinking back into the tub, hiding her face behind the edge, she began to cry in earnest, totally ashamed at having come so close to succeeding, only to fail. And all because of an impossible, impractical bathing tub! Wouldn't . . . couldn't look up as Cinzia entered, tongue clicking tsk-tsk as she surveyed the damage. When she finally raised her eyes, knowing she must, had to face her fate, Cinzia was briskly toweling the kitten, her fur quill-spiked but contentment blazing on her tiny face.

"Thinks I'm her mama, grooming her," and the kitten purred louder, eyes slitted in ecstasy, chin raised for the scrubbing towel. "Are you clean enough? If so, get out before you threaten the water level any more."

"But I . . ." she stretched an arm as far as she could reach, but her fingers missed the towels on the floor, "haven't got anything, not a stitch."

"Well, I wasn't planning to look." Cinzia concentrated on the kitten, scrubbing and rubbing, shifting the towel to find a dry spot. "Try the cupboard over there. Should be some more towels, a fresh robe. You didn't splash *that* far, did you?"

Dripping, adding her own contribution to the water puddling the floor, Etelka pattered to the cupboard and snatched the first robe that came to hand, wrapping it around herself and rubbing at an ear still full of soap bubbles. "I'm so very, very sorry," she used her best small, meek voice, staring down at her bare feet. "I'll clean up, mop it all dry, wash the towels—everything! Anything else you want done, too!" Her nose was drizzling, her voice going all wambly as she wailed, "Just don't, oh, please, don't drown Baby!"

"Merciful Lady, child! Why would we want to do that?" Retrieving a dry towel from the cupboard and expertly rewrapping Baby, Cinzia placed the bundle in Telka's yearning arms. "Not a little beauty like that. Not when there are things you've not even begun to guess about her."

"I love you," Telka whispered at the pink nose with its orange freckles, all of Baby that protruded from her towel wrapping. "You won't let them take Baby away, drown her?"

"My oath on it," Cinzia intoned.

❧

Clutching a protesting Baby with both hands, Etelka trotted with unsteady dignity at Cinzia's side, wishing both that she *had* opted for the third pair of socks and that Cinzia would slow her long-legged pace. Lady bless, they had more halls and corridors in this castle than they had living space at home! Space just going to waste, begging for some good use other than connecting distant rooms. Each and every one of her brothers could claim a corridor for a bedroom and there'd still be plenty left over!

But despite deploring the wasted space, Etelka felt an almost physical pain at witnessing mute reminders of the explosion, a lump in her throat that refused to budge. Some areas remained in pristine condition, but other locations revealed conspicuous damage: splintered oak paneling, crumpled mosaics, broken stonework on the floors, puddles, soaked plaster dropping with messy thuds, once-perfect things mangled and distorted. So much damage 'twas hard to take it in. And what would Da say? "People, Telka! Those are things, can be replaced, repaired, done without. Were people hurt?"

So she asked, diffident but concerned, wondering how she'd allowed herself to be saddened by things that couldn't feel any pain. "Was anyone hurt, Cinzia? Killed?"

Cinzia paused, rubbing her lip, before a barrier that blocked their passage, workers erecting scaffolding all the way to the top of the arched ceiling, stockpiling support beams and repair materials. "What, child? Ah, no, no one killed, by the Lady's grace. Plenty with broken limbs, concussions, bruises, though. She watched out for us."

Addressing a cluster of workers, a handsome man with deep auburn hair (Such hair! Etelka sighed with envy.) and a lovely, sky-blue costume with knee britches and hose (Wrinkled, she noted.) impatiently pointed here and there at the ceiling, emphasizing a spate of instructions that never slowed but finally tapered off. Why—that was the man who'd come rushing at her in the alley, throwing his weight on the pry bar and pinching her hand! Workers nodding, off he went at a jog trot, waving and calling, " 'Lo, Cinzia. Backtrack to the west wing. Daren't let anyone through this way till the ceiling's shored up. Where's La'ow—napping?"

Ha! Cinzia acted as if she'd been caught out at something, cheeks pinking, then made the funniest tugging motion, like straightening a nonexistent garment, before she caught her and Baby watching her. Telka stared hard at the ceiling, letting Cinzia settle herself, sorry she'd been so curious.

"This way, I think," and Cinzia turned on her heel, striding in a new direction, Etelka kite-tailing along, squeezing Baby tight so she couldn't spring free, worse than hugging an eel, it was. "I've been here, oh, six years now," Cinzia muttered, "and I swear I can't always find my way around. At least La'ow has some sense of direction!"

"Oh?" Telka cautiously murmured, unsure if a response were required and wondering yet again who this La'ow-person was. He'd been there in the alley just before Cinzia and the Gamelyn-man had found her, but had left before she could meet him. Most folk seemed to know him, but he'd been absent all day, far as she could judge. Still, sound interested, attentive without being pushy, and she might find out—or at least find out some other interesting thing.

Except . . . how could she be attentive to Cinzia with so many rare sights competing for her interest, crying out to be noticed and admired. Yes, people deserved first consideration, but odds were she'd never see these objects' like again, not a little farm girl such as herself. She wanted—no, needed—to memorize them, impress such wonders deep in her memory so she could replay, review them on those cold winter nights when no one had any time for her, and she had but little time to herself, hands eternally busy but her mind free.

Her outfit, for example—conjured up out of nowhere for her. And wouldn't Mam just hang on every little detail? Soft pantaloons in a deep jade green—velour, Cinzia said it was. An exquisitely simple, plain white shirt topped by a waist-length vest in shades of the fall forest. Even had touches of color that Cinzia swore brought out subtle highlights in her puddle-brown eyes, her broom-straw hair—if such a thing were possible! Though the waist sash of deep gold silk was truly vexing, slithering around her waist, even the knot sliding out in a whispery rush of fabric till Cinzia fixed it. True, the indoor boots of supple leather *were* meant to be grown into—apparently even the castle practiced economies—but two pairs of thick socks helped. With luck, she'd not fall out of them or disgrace herself in some other clod-footed manner.

Ah, now if only Baby didn't disgrace her! Recovered from her immersion in the swan-shaped tub, her orange fur sleek and crackling with excess energy, Baby wanted to explore, sniff things over, pat and bat with her paw, play hide and pounce. Put her down for an instant—as she innocently had earlier—and the kitten cheerfully left a trail of disasters in her wake. The mere memory of it was enough to make her give Baby an admonitory shake, squeeze harder till she squeaked in protest.

Once her paws had hit the floor, Baby had immediately scampered to the nearest worker, a woman reverently retrieving mosaic bits from the buckled floor and sorting them in regimented color order on planking laid across two sawhorses. And hadn't Baby gone zooming atop the impromptu worktable, skidding through row upon row of tiles, batting them right and left to clatter on the floor? Mortified, Etelka had snatched her back, apologizing, temporizing, retreating to the safety of Cinzia's side. Looking as if she wanted to burst into tears, the woman had settled for ripping the kerchief from her head and throwing it on the floor. Then she'd kicked a little tile after them, spiteful like—and who could blame her?

Having slowed at remembering the near-disaster, face again hot with shame, she hurried to catch up with Cinzia, so elegantly casual in midnight-blue pantaloons and a forest green tunic cut by a red waist sash broidered with gold. And so kind to a total stranger, like just now, pulling her close for a quick hug! "Now remember, this is hardly a formal dinner with royalty, but it's about the closest you'll experience right now, with things in such disarray. The kitchens bore the brunt of the damage. But regardless of the informality, I expect you and this scamp to be on your best behavior. Understand?" She stroked Baby's pink nose, and the kitten grabbed her finger, claws curling round it as she dragged it to her mouth and began nibbling.

"I . . . I'll try," Telka stammered. "Be oh so polite, not ask for seconds, use my napkin, not speak till spoken to, everything I can think of." But brutal honesty compelled her to add, "About Baby? I don't know, truly. She's awfully . . ." and found herself groping for a word that wouldn't sound condemnatory in Cinzia's ears and her own.

"Rambunctious?" Cinzia offered, eyes dancing in what was a face so somber and serious that Etelka struggled to match it. "Do your best, child. No one will throw you in the dungeons—they're too wet right now." Mayhap Cinzia

found that funny, but Etelka certainly didn't! 'Twasn't that
she deemed Cinzia a liar, but how could she *possibly* know
for sure?

"B–but would they b–banish her? S–sentence her to
d–die?" Face puckering, she wailed it again, "DI–IE?" on a
rising second note, unnerved by the terror in her own voice.

Convinced her bones had melted as Cinzia shook her,
Telka buried her face in Baby's soap-scented fur, stubbornly mute as Cinzia uptilted her chin. "Of course not,
child! I gave my oath on it, didn't I? Whyever would King
Eadwin do such a thing? I'm Canderisian, a foreigner, and
even *I'd* never think him capable of that. You should know
the king's reputation far better than I."

As if she and her family had ever hobnobbed with royalty! They were simple farmers, subsisting on their crops,
their small house snug but not fancy, their taxes paid on
time! No sense acknowledging the depths of her ignorance
to Cinzia, though, or she might decide even this "casual"
dinner with the king was beyond Telka's abilities!

Blotting a treacherously leaky eye on Baby's head, she
squared her shoulders and began her march toward
greatness . . . or the executioner. "T–tell me again . . .
who'll be there?"

"Well, me for starters, and Urban—you've met him already—and my friend, La'ow. Then, of course, King Eadwin and the Queen Mother, the Lady Fabienne. Arras
Muscadeine, Lord of the Nord, and his wife, Francesca—
Francie, she's called—and their son Harry. You saw the
senior and junior Muscadeines come bursting out of the
sewer opening with the king; you helped save their lives as
well. Possibly a few servants to serve dinner. And, oh, yes!"
She struck her brow, feathering her hair. "Word has it that
the king's cousin, Nakum, is also visiting, though I've not
yet seen him. He's an Erakwa. Ever met one before?"

Somberly shaking her head to acknowledge her innocence, "and . . . and Hru'rul?" His presence mattered more
than any of the Erakwa.

"Naturally! Where else would he be? Though he is prone
to rambling on his own; in fact, he rambled off for four
whole days this fall, and oh, how the king worried. Ghatti
enjoy night rambles, you know. A chance to wander, see
the sights, sniff the evening's scents without their presence

intimidating anyone. Most of us in the castle and the old town just beyond the castle walls are familiar with Hru'rul, but he does make some people nervous. Same thing still happens in Canderis on occasion, despite the fact that Seeker Bond-pairs have traveled the country seeking truth for generations."

Rapt, she drank in Cinzia's words—how wonderful that Cinzia spoke so authoritatively about Seekers and ghatti! Mayhap later she could ask . . . and Etelka never noticed the maid standing on tiptoe before the double doors at the end of the corridor, feather duster softly whishing as she industriously cleaned the ornate door carvings. But Baby certainly noticed, spellbound as the duster flick-flicked back and forth, its feathers rustling. Without a by-your-leave, the kitten squirmed from her arms like quicksilver. Telka squeezed tight too late, then threw herself after Baby, only to be betrayed by her overlarge boots. Down she went, skidding along the polished floor, arms vainly outstretched. Merrily outracing her, the kitten slowed and went into a crouch, stalking the maid from behind, wide amber eyes riveted on the undulating feather duster. Left, right, left again, the small but powerful orange-striped haunches twitched with building momentum, and Baby launched herself at the duster, now swaying so enticingly along the wainscoting.

"Grrr-ROW! ROW, RRR!" screamed the kitten as she sprang and sank her claws into the duster, mouth stuffed with the feathers. The young maid reciprocated with a rising shriek but refused to relinquish the duster's handle, the kitten dangling while muffled growls emanated from the depths of the feathers, only her ears visible.

The maid gave the duster a shake and shrieked anew, unsure what to make of this orange apparition as Telka limped after Baby, one boot on and one boot off. Arms squeezing Baby's middle she tugged with all her strength, but the kitten remained clamped to the duster, adamantly refusing to yield her prey. "Let go!" Etelka commanded in her best grown-up voice and, assuming she was the one being so ordered, the maid dropped the duster, her cheeks, red, her mouth wide with shock.

"Grr-ROWL! Grr! Hrrmmm!" the kitten exulted through the feathers, triumphant at last.

"What's going on out here?" A neat-bearded man clad in a brown-plaid bathrobe, sticking plasters on his forehead and cheek, flung open one double door. "Cinzia, what have you brought us?" Another twist and squirm, hind feet planted in Etelka's protesting stomach, and the kitten ripped free again, dashing for the door, head held high, proudly clutching the duster to show off her "kill."

With great presence of mind the man ripped off the robe's tie and attempted to lasso the kitten, just missing. Now hampered by a flapping bathrobe that revealed a nightshirt beneath, he still made an ineffectual grab for the duster as the kitten darted between his bare ankles. "Hrrmmm! GRRRR!" Baby warned and conveyed her prey to safety.

"Fine!" said the man, gingerly examining the back of his hand. Oh, Lady bless!—Baby had raked the man in passing! "Have it your way! Feather dusters don't taste very good, you little minx!"

His voice did it, those pleasant tones, the way his mouth quirked when he spoke. Slowly she superimposed her image of the half-drowned man with the man now before her, rebelting his robe. The king! King Eadwin! For the first time in her short and previously uneventful life Etelka Rundgren fainted.

❖

Words . . . floating like soap bubbles . . . bursting in her ears . . . "Cinzia?" "Messenger . . . morning . . . let her parents . . ." Bubbling . . . rainbow spheres . . . swan soap dish . . . No, Baby! Don't hurt the . . . swan . . . soapy . . . water sloshing . . . drowning . . . Promised no . . .

"Ginger beer," propounded a voice she didn't recognize. "Ginger beer, don't you think, Fabienne? Settles the stomach, helps that queasy feeling after a faint."

"True enough," agreed a second voice, older and with cultured, elegant diction, "though it made Eadwin burp something fierce when he was a boy. That's half of it, though, I suppose—gives those roiling gases an outlet and lets the stomach settle."

Should she open her eyes, she'd expire on the spot—she

knew it! Or fervently wish she had. Baby—oh, darling, dear little Baby, her joy—had scratched the king! Something tickled her nose—the feather duster? Cracking her eyes open, letting her body remain limp, she strained to see. Oh, dear! Someone had removed her spectacles! Long and tickly, like a feather boa. No, furry—soft, draping fur swishing across and under her nose. Yet a further indignity that they'd toy with her at a moment like this! Suddenly the end of the fur quirked like a raised eyebrow of acknowledgment. It seemed . . . very much like . . . a tail. Tail? A prodigiously furry tail?

The sneeze built and built within her, then, leaving her no option but to rear up and explode, clapping both hands over her mouth, eyes bulging with the force. Now the world swam before her eyes, both head and stomach vastly discomfited by her vertical position. "Lady keep you well," the first voice blessed her, the one who'd mentioned ginger beer. A richly but plainly dressed woman, whose pleasant face had clearly experienced continued physical pain in its time, presented her with a small linen square, exquisite flowers broidered round its edges. "La'ow does relish teasing unsuspecting sleepers and Cinzia, alas, is too soft-hearted to insist he display proper manners."

It was all *too* confusing! Yes, Cinzia had mentioned her friend La'ow several times, but she'd *never* even hinted he was *furry!* Face half-buried in the handkerchief, Etelka discreetly sought Baby's whereabouts, not to mention that of the unknown but fursome La'ow. Yes, that orange blur had to be Baby, deprived of her feather duster, and then her vision miraculously cleared as someone—Cinzia, she supposed—dropped her spectacles into place on her nose, affixing the bows behind her ears.

Well, at least she'd gained clarity of vision, if not of thought! Baby sat motionless, almost mesmerized, amber eyes flickering between two magnificent beasts. Hru'rul she immediately recognized, but the other beast was almost equally as imposing, self-contained and wise-looking, yet utterly different in appearance. When a mug was pressed into an unresisting hand, she raised it to her lips without thought, as entranced by the sight as Baby. A gulp—Lady help her, she was thirsty!—and she sputtered and sipped again. As the liquid landed in her stomach a spectacular but unexpected burp forced its way between her lips. Oh, dear! Was no humiliation to be spared her?

"You see?" the older woman fondly commented. Eyes downcast, convinced she could endure no more humiliation, she stiffened as Cinzia began gently rubbing, patting her back, exactly like a mother burping a baby. She smothered another, more genteel, burp in her handkerchief, vowing never again to drink ginger beer!

"You've not met my special friend, my Bondmate, La'ow," Cinzia whispered from behind. "Handsome brute, isn't he? Though don't tell him so to his face—he already has a swelled head."

Friend? Furry friend? Bondmate? Lady bless and keep all ignorant country bumpkins! "He's a ghatt!" she squeaked, almost accusatorily. "You're a . . . *Seeker*!" Oh, either this was too good to be true, or too true to be good—which she wouldn't hazard a guess on for the life of her. How could she *not* have realized? The colors of Cinzia's outfit tonight, that tug at what had to be the missing tabard . . . If she'd fainted before, she was now near ready to swoon! This was exactly like becoming a part of *Lives of the Seekers Veritas*! But why, oh, why hadn't Cinzia told her, why had she kept it a secret?

All that and more crowded her thoughts as she studied La'ow, whose coat of long, dark fur swirled and shifted like black silk in a gentle breeze. White toes and a white tail tip, white on his muzzle that crept into a point on the bridge of his pink nose. "Those are the *hairiest* ears I've ever seen!" she breathed, awestruck, not minding Cinzia's indulgent laugh. The fine, paler hair of his inner ears was long and luxuriant, almost obscuring the gold stud on the right tip, while the good hoop on the other ear jutted horizontally, unable to hang freely amidst the fur.

But in an entirely different, more majestic way, Hru'rul was even more commanding. He lounged at ease on his side, freckled in tawny browns and buffs, an incredible ruff and side chops enlarging his face to twice its size, and his ears boasted a tuft on each tip. From her protective crouch beside Cinzia, she could make out his poor stub of a tail. And the great, the magnificent Hru'rul observed Baby— *her* Baby—with a benignly lazy yet intent gaze, and Baby stared back, equally fascinated but blessedly silent and still.

Then that Gamelyn-man, Cinzia's friend, gave a soft, haughty chuckle and broke the spell. She'd forgotten his presence in this strange bedchamber, crowded with three beds, almost like home. He moved more gracefully than most men, and she did have to admire that as he came around a table, inspecting dishes and silverware, lifting lids from salvers and chafing dishes, the mingling aromas beckoning to her from across the room. Obviously her stomach had settled!

"Here, let me serve, Eadwin. Everyone sit wherever it's comfortable. Dinner isn't fancy tonight, but it's filling. Lamb stew with a mashed potato crust. Bread pudding with raisins. Sunderlies melon and grapes. Have to eat them tonight—most of the melons are cracked, the grapes bruised." Loading two plates, he passed one to the king, seated cross-legged at the foot of his bed, and the second to a youthful man lounging amongst the pillows behind the king. Telka didn't know whether to be struck more by his amazing long braids and his stained deerskin clothes, or his expression, a study in worry even when he smiled graciously at Urban. Mam'd swear he looked as if he carried the wearying weight of the world on those slim, coppery-colored shoulders.

As Cinzia left to assist Urban, Telka screwed up her courage to boldly survey her surroundings and its inhabitants more thoroughly. Odd, everyone huddling in the bedchamber like this, almost having a picnic—no wonder Cinzia'd warned her this was casual. Mayhap the dining room had been damaged, like the kitchens. And the kitchen help had labored under adverse conditions to produce this sumptuous dinner. The selfish part of her wondered if she might have a whole melon to herself—they looked smallish. Wouldn't that be the height of luxury, not to share with anyone! 'Cept she would, 'cause that was mannerly, and no telling what quick-step troubles a whole melon might provoke come morning.

Dragging a turquoise-striped comforter around his shoulders, much as she'd seen him earlier today, though dry now, the boy piled down beside her and stuck out his hand. "I'm Harry. Harry Muscadeine. Sorry, I was too bushed earlier to think. Thank you for your help. Might still be splashing round that sewer system if you and Ezequiel hadn't gotten

that trapdoor open." A shiver racked him and he drew the
comforter tighter as the middle-aged woman hurried to his
side, Etelka noticing for the first time that she used a cane,
depended on it heavily.

"No, Mama, I'm fine," Harry grumbled, shrugging off
her hand almost irritably. Telka sympathized; being fussed
over like that was for little children. Couldn't give in to
shivery feelings, especially not in front of adults, not if one
wanted to be taken seriously. "No fever, no chills. But just
thinking about being underground again gives me the shivers." His mother tapped gently on his head with her cane,
a private signal of some sort, Telka suspected, and moved
on, allowing him his privacy. Now there was an admirable
mother!

Smiling fondly at his mother's retreating back, Harry
continued as if there'd been no interruption. "You saw my
Papa this morning. He's over there, plate of food on the
mantlepiece. Can't hear much right now, and that makes
him grumpy, but he doesn't mean it. Doesn't much fancy
sitting down or lying on his back right now. Shrapnel, you
know," he whispered confidentially. She wasn't exactly sure
what shrapnel was, but gathered Harry's father's backside
had been peppered with it. As filled plates appeared in
front of them, Harry began to wolf down his food. He
wasn't ill-mannered about his eating, but he certainly was
*fast,* and Etelka forced herself to eat at a more measured
pace. Oh, please, please, don't let me drop anything, smear
gravy on these pillows or drip on these borrowed clothes,
she prayed.

"That's Nakum, the king's cousin and next in line to the
throne." Harry's eyebrows veered leftward alarmingly to
indicate the Erakwan. "He's been underground for the
longest time, surveying the damage below, thanks to the
Plumb."

"Plum?" Scrutinizing her plate, she couldn't spy any
fruit, not even any plum prunes. Shouldn't be in stew anyway, but who was she to say, not here in a castle like this,
ignorant of everything except her own ignorance. "Plum?"
she repeated, only to discover her mind doing a dizzying
little spin and flip-flop as she mentally added the silent "b"
to the end of the word. Impossible! Or was it? What else
could have caused that horrid rumbling, that percussive

boom that she'd heard? The way the earth had shaken? The damage she'd subsequently seen? The carrot speared on her fork wobbled in midair, finally dropping free and leaving a slick of gravy down Harry's comforter.

" 'S all right," he assured her with a full mouth, neatly picking up the straying carrot chunk and shoving it between his lips, his cheeks bulging. A convulsive swallow. "Grannie Inez always *would* protest it was clean, 'just fell on a piece of paper' was her way of putting it."

She nodded numbly. The carrot wasn't important, but the Plumb was. Here she'd run away from her family to save Baby and thrust them both into a new world where ancient history sprang to life again! Oh, if Mam and Da knew, they'd be wild with fear that she'd ventured to Sidonie, let alone that close to a bona fide Plumb! "How do you know it was a Plumb? How do I know you aren't just making that up to . . . to scare . . . me, impress me!" she sputtered.

" 'Cause I was there, read the lettering around its base." More vehemently, a hand locked on her wrist, he stared at her with hazel eyes, tawny-green with fear. "Ask Hru'rul, ask La'ow if I tell the truth. They know!" Staring down at her wrist, he released it, clearly abashed at the red ring he'd created. "I'm sorry, but I *know*! And so does everyone else in this room, all the castle by now! And the news will travel."

As improbable as it seemed, she believed him, had had too much experience reading her brothers, near as good as one of the ghatti, she was. She chewed thoughtfully on a piece of potato. No wonder that Erakwan, Nakum, looked so morose! Da'd always swore the Erakwa had a special kinship to the land, as if they were all part of one large, extended family. Seemed funny to think of having an Auntie Boulder or an Uncle Valley, but she supposed it was possible. 'Twould bear more thinking about later. One thing about visiting Sidonie, your mind got opened real wide to a host of new ideas.

It dawned on her that she'd polished off half her plate of stew and Baby hadn't uttered a word of protest, shown any interest. Usually meals were a battle, Baby ravenously attempting to devour her food, cheerfully consuming anything within tongue's reach, ignoring reproaches and dodg-

ing cuffs and slaps. Normally she'd have pounced on that
piece of mislaid carrot, gulped it down and grabbed for
more, importuning her all the while. Was she sickening or
something? "Baby? Aren't you hungry?" and snapped her
fingers to attract the kitten's attention, hoping the hum of
adult conversation would cover her question.

Dropping two more biscuits on her plate and resettling
himself into the depths of the comforter, Harry followed
her gaze, his own biscuits neatly vanishing except for the
few crumbs he caught on his plate. "I know," he murmured, "but your wee friend has something momentous on
her mind. Hru'rul, too, 'less I miss my guess. He's never
been one to turn down a meal, nor La'ow, either, though
he's skinny as a rail under all that fur! Almost pitiful
looking."

"Well, she's never met any ghatti before. Of course
they've captured her attention."

"Ooh, that should hold me—at least till dessert's
served!" Slumping in temporary satiation, Harry balanced
his plate on his stomach. "Why? She doesn't look all that
different." He'd tracked back to his previous comment,
prodding Telka. "I mean, hasn't she ever caught sight of
herself in a mirror?"

Deciding whether or not she should wrap her biscuits
and save them, in case this turned out to be the sole meal
the castle would provide, Etelka didn't immediately grasp
the import of Harry's words. Finally, slowly, " 'Course she
has—went all spooked, her tail fluffed up. Then she kept
looking behind the mirror to find the other kitten."

Oh, how that little smirk on his face set her cringing,
made her want to slap it! Thinking he was *so* superior!
"What?" Give him a good shake, she would; she was
country-innocent, not ignorant, and what else did he *know*
but wasn't saying? And it had best not have a thing to do
with Plumbs!

But, as if aware of their attention, Baby gave a little
shake and began padding straight toward Hru'rul, the most
yearning expression on her pointed little face. Tension radiated from her, her whole body rigid, prepared to spring
away if he so much as bent a whisker at her the wrong
way. Abandoning his languorous pose, Hru'rul rolled onto
his stomach, his tufted ears cocked forward.

Suddenly the kitten planted her bottom on the floor and swept her ears sideways as she raised her pink nose ceilingward. "Ye-OW? Yee-OWW?" she cried piteously. "Pwa'pwa? Perowmepurr?"

Stretching his massive head forward, Hru'rul touched his leathery nose to the little pink one, then began greet-sniffing one side of her face and then the other. Dutifully, the kitten turned to present her bottom to his inquisitive nose. Again she uttered that pathetic cry, "Perowmepurr?"

"Y'ew?" exclaimed Hru'rul in an inviting squeak. To everyone's shock the kitten threw herself on Hru'rul's back, burrowing her head deep in his ruff hair, gleefully attempting to sever his spinal cord with her needle-sharp baby teeth. No matter that her teeth weren't long enough or sharp enough, or Hru'rul's ruff too thick to penetrate, it was excellent practice.

The king beamed with possessive pride. "You were right, Cinzia! I should have guessed when he went wandering last fall. My Hru'rul's a proud Papa, so that makes me a Grandpapa! Congratulate me, everyone!"

"What?" whispered Telka, though no one noticed. *Her* darling, *her* Baby—one of the ghatti? It couldn't be right, it wasn't possible! Baby's mother was Sheba, a perfectly nice barn cat, a superior mouser, and Baby's father *had* to be one of the other barn cats, mayhap from the next stead over. *Lives of the Seekers Veritas* had never mentioned that any of the ghatti were . . . er, half-ghatti.

Nakum slapped Eadwin's shoulder. "That's what I cherish so about you Marchmontians. What's a little more mixed blood in *this* family, eh Eadwin?"

But it was Urban who politely posed the question now thrumming through Etelka's brain: If Baby were part-ghatti, hypo . . . hypothet—whatever Da called it—would the kitten Bond with her? Could they, mayhap, even become Seekers?

As Cinzia considered, the Lady Fabienne gave her son Eadwin a direct and challenging stare while she ironically applauded. "What joy! At least Hru'rul has sired an heir. That's more than some royals in this room have managed!"

Etelka couldn't understand why the king's laughter sounded rueful, and why everyone rolled their eyes so, finally laughing in spite of themselves. What she wanted was to hold Baby safe in her arms again, run back home and live life just the way she always had, nothing changed, altered—except for Da wanting to drown Baby. Oh, dear, what was she supposed to do now?

♣

One arm embracing the black pony's shaggy neck, Harrap trudged along, half-hypnotized by the rhythmic sway of his robe as first one, then the other boot stepped ahead. If he looked up, really strained to see the tops of the peaks, his heart sagged into his boots. Better to simply hug Jester and plod on—swish, step, swish, step—exchange a pleasant word with Parm, sprawled on the pony's broad back. He'd walked whenever he could, felt foolish precariously mounted on one of the ponies, unsure what to do with his legs. Use the stirrups and his knees bent like a frog's, he'd poke Jester behind the ear. Let them hang loose? They didn't actually drag, it just seemed as if they should. Besides, the beasts had enough to carry without his weight increasing their labors.

Mainly he didn't look upward because at this angle he didn't want to contemplate the peaks. He'd considered them forebodingly high and sheer when he'd attempted the same thing at their base, and the higher they toiled, the higher and sheerer they appeared. That instilled new fears, that they truly weren't progressing, gaining on their goal. Made him superstitious, it did—a haunting dread that mayhap other godheads ought to be propitiated, that he shouldn't cleave solely to his Lady. The utter capriciousness of such a thought made his lips twitch with a smile. Abandon his Lady? Never! Too bad Addawanna wasn't along to regale him with tales of her people's Great Spirit, and their lesser gods. On this trip he might not argue with her as stringently as he had on previous occasions. Somehow her stories revealed new facets when he thought of them told on this mountain, its very cliffs and crags and ledges eagerly listening.

To steady his thoughts, he drew a deep breath—or tried to. The air tasted thinner up here, harder to draw into his lungs, but that was silliness. The sunlight spread itself more thinly, like a Bethel butter ration striving to coat too much bread. A washed-out lemon, but still capable of casting shadows that loomed, his own fears poised to spring at him from the dark.

**"Silly old Harrap!"** Parm, chin sunk on his forepaws, cap creeping over his eyes, still vigilantly tracked Mahafny and Saam astride the pony ahead of them. Jenneth led now, with Diccon in the rear. **"It is colder—or is it just me?"**

*"It's not just you. Colder. Icier, too. Whatever that pitifully weak sunshine melts turns to ice faster than I can snap my fingers."* As if to prove his point, he slipped, grabbing at Jester's mane. Yesterday the footing hadn't been as treacherous, but mayhap that was due to euphoria at having shoveled their way through, the fact that they could now make progress. Thank the Lady this higher trail was reasonably unobstructed, especially given its stomach-sucking narrowness when it ran along a ledge, a sheer drop on one side, a sheer wall on the other. Occasionally both twins scurried ahead, shoveling as they went, kicking snowdrifts off ledges to sift down in a sheer white curtain of sparkling crystals.

Today everything wore a slick coating, the sun pallidly reflecting off patches of ice, ice encrusting barren tree branches, clinging to fir needles. A stark purity to such glinting white and translucent ice, but a dangerous one. **"Saam knows,"** commented Parm, out of the blue. **"Told her he knows . . . and that I know. Don't think Mahafny wanted to hear whether or not you've uncovered her secret."**

*"Does she think that I—or her addiction—will vanish if she doesn't acknowledge it?"* Sometimes dealing with the twins was easier, more straightforward, than constantly tailoring himself to Mahafny's volatile fit. Unreasonably angry, he swiped at a clump of snow with his boot, sent it sailing at Mahafny's pony, stinging its rump and making it skip along faster. *"What am I going to do with her, Parm? Well, not with her—but about her. She'll kill herself dosing herself like that, pushing her body so hard!"*

**"She hasn't told you because she esteems you, doesn't want you to think ill of her. Saam and I have talked. It occupies his mind, and he doesn't thrash as much. Sometimes he makes sense, sometimes not."** A purr fizzled and failed, Parm too gloomy to sustain the effort. **"Right now his mind's latched on how he didn't attend, failed to notice something was wrong when Hylan began drugging us. How he assumed I was being my usual muddleheaded self when I 'spoke him to report where we were. He said we both deserve a dressing-down for ignoring, covering up Mahafny's . . ."** he couldn't say the word.

If anything, Parm's admission further upset Harrap, and he whirled on the ghatt, jerking Jester to a startled halt. *"Then why, by the blessed Lady, has he let Mahafny get away with this insanity?"*

Parm hooked his cap with a paw to resettle it. **"Because he says he's part of a plan he doesn't know the beginning or end of—can barely comprehend the present. He swears it's bigger than his desires, than what he so desperately needs and wants."** Well aware of Harrap's accusatory glower, he tried again. **"Where he's been all this time, I don't know. My senses simply aren't acute enough to follow what he says. . . ."**

*"But it* has *to mean something, Parm! Don't play befuddled now."* But before Harrap could worm any more sense out of Parm, Diccon had dropped Mignon's reins, and was trotting toward them, his brow furrowing with concern.

"Everything all right, Harrap? Need a rest? Time to ride a ways?" A gust of wind swooped down on them, streamering Harrap's scarf and providing an excuse to avoid Parm's eyes, so full of untapped wisdom and sorrow. And bent on being totally obdurate and unhelpful, no answers to give or share. Oh, Parm *knew* the truth, but the ghatt just wasn't about to enlighten him right now. Well, blast and damn Mahafny and her addiction to the deepest pits of the hells! Of course his blessed Lady didn't believe in the concept of hells, gave each soul innumerable chances to live a better life, but right now he'd give his eyeteeth to create a temporary hell. The curse warmed his soul, though it didn't lighten his mood.

"No, fine." He smiled with spurious sincerity. If Parm could do it, so could he! "Everything's fine, dandy! Nothing like a good, brisk hike to make your blood boil—warm your blood, I mean!" Wonderful! There was truth, there were shadings of truth, and here he was feeding the lad a bald-faced lie!

Gloved hand toying with a saddle strap, Diccon sucked in his breath, making a little whistling sound between his teeth. "Sarcasm doesn't become you, Harrap? What's wrong?"

"Mayhap I need a mountain sheep to chase—or to chase me. Take my mind off things." With the tattered dignity still remaining to him, Harrap gathered Jester's reins and marched up the trail. He would *not* look ahead; he would *not* look up! He did *not* care that Mahafny and Saam rode ahead on Daisy; he did *not* care if he could see the peaks or not! Let everyone and everything orbit in their ordained places, because he could *not* change or move them, no matter how hard he tried! Swish, step, swish, step. What mattered now was square beneath his feet, especially if he wanted to stay on them. Pride goeth before a fall, as does ice. Swish, step. . . .

♣

Standing stock-still, Diccon studied Harrap's and Jester's receding forms, Mignon nuzzling and butting his back, silently suggesting they follow. Mignon didn't like being last in line, preferred having a pony ahead of and behind her. Kwee, ribs still stiff from her recent tumble, wincingly stretched to bridge the gap between the pony and Diccon's shoulder. **"No, I don't know, either. Mayhap Pw'eek will know, or can ask Parm. She's better at that sort of thing than I am."**

A major admission for Kwee to voluntarily concede her sib's superiority in any matter, rather like him admitting Jenneth surpassed him in certain areas, and he gave Kwee a wink. Oh, it was fine when she was as good as he—but no better—and there were other things, girl-type things—where he didn't mind if she excelled. But some things he took for granted as "his" alone—and for her to best him at those *did* hurt. He expected her to be more "sensitive," didn't he? Oh, he could be equally sensitive if he worked at it, but often it came at the expense of something more important, like enthusiasm or single-mindedness of purpose, the ability to function, precisely because he *didn't* let squishy oversensitivities bog him down! Talk about wading knee-deep in emotion and apperception, slatherings of sympathy and empathy!

But it *did* have a place—Jenneth would have winkled out what ailed Harrap before he could even confess. Since it wasn't Kwee's forte any more than his own, mayhap they both should practice—as long as nothing more pressing required his attention. Ah—luckily something did! The sun now looked like a pale blob of candle wax, nearly invisible against the sky, no longer blue but hazy and diffuse. Another gust plucked at him, intent on blowing up the back of his jacket. At least his tabard sash prevented it from creeping any higher. The wind, the atmosphere, the sky oppressed his senses, and he wrapped an arm around Kwee, anxious a harder gust might sweep her off Mignon's back. "Storm, I think. Don't know how bad, but mayhap we should halt early, soon as we can find a place for the night." The wind swept up his words, tossed them at the soughing firs, their shadows scourging the snow as the wind shook them.

*"Jen? Noticed any spot to pull off the trail, any sort of shelter ahead? A niche, an overhang? If not, keep looking—sharp! I swear we're in for more snow, or at least some nasty weather."* If anyone could spot a suitable shelter, Jenneth could. Girls always found homey, comfortable spots to nest in, just like that private bower Maeve'd showed him. Jenneth'd probably find a cave, and if she didn't, well, he'd take his ax and hew one, damned if he wouldn't! Ah, wonderful! Brute strength versus brains. He had a brain, he merely had to use it, look at things as Jenneth would, see beyond the seeming. Mayhap even notice something she'd overlooked, and then how he'd crow.

Mignon needed no further encouragement, and he scrambled to keep pace and still scan their surroundings. Damn! Something had better turn up soon! Now the wind was positively wailing, whipping the tree branches into a frenzy. Sometimes he could almost swear it harbored a sort of high-pitched, naughty giggle. And more fool he for thinking he heard it! See what came of trying to be so sensitive!

❖

**"I don't like it in here!"** Kwee moved wraithlike along one wall of the cave, her fur wanting to hackle along her spine.

"It's . . . it's . . ." she grasped for a word, even an image to share with her sib, but it eluded her, made her want to sink her claws into it and pin it down, grab it by the neck and shake the stuffing out of it. **"Can't you feel it?"** Ready to explode with frustration, she whirled on Pw'eek, standing patiently at her flank, and fought to deflect a lashing paw. Hadn't even realized she'd raised it. How could she cuff Sissy for no good reason, other than that she was scared spitless—and probably hissless as well. And when she was scared, the quickest way to conquer it was to thrash Sissy. Then she generally felt brave enough to take on the world.

Abruptly dropping on her haunches and drawing her head tight to her shoulders, Pw'eek licked at her white ruff, then tentatively stretched to lick her sister's face but halted, pink tongue protruding, as Kwee grumbled a warning. She was *not* in any mood to be placated, have her formless fears scrubbed away. **"Oh—how could Diccon choose this cave! Rather be outside—even if it snows all over me!"** she wailed and vehemently licked her shoulder, then fell into a spate of nervous grooming, twitching here and there, licking and biting at herself, but her hackles wouldn't lie flat.

**"What *is* the matter?"** For the life of her, Kwee couldn't explain it to Pw'eek, baffled that her sib sat there, oblivious to the disharmony, the vibrating wrongness. Mayhap Diccon hadn't had time to practice his sensitivity, but she'd obviously overcompensated, outdoing Pw'eek.

**"Doesn't it make you . . . twitchy?"** Inhaling, her jaws ajar, she let the air play across the roof of her mouth and nearly spat, gagging. Obediently Pw'eek imitated her, eyes squinted, attempting to sense what her sister sensed. **"Oh . . . never mind!"** Stalking to Diccon's side, Kwee sat with her back to her sister, staring pleadingly at her Bond. What could she say? Could she explain it any better to him than she had to Pw'eek? **"Parm, can you feel it? Feel anything . . . odd . . . about this place?"**

But Parm gave her a quizzical look and a ghatti shrug, rolling his shoulders and dipping his head. A squeal as Harrap slapped one of the ponies on the rump, encouraging it to trot deeper into the slender crevice that widened into the cave proper. The ponies fit, barely, as long as their packs were striped off first. A clatter of hooves as Daisy burst through, Mignon tight behind her, Jenneth snagging their bridles and tethering them against the opposite side. Mahafny worked at lighting a fire in an old ring of stones that had clearly served this purpose before.

Burrowing free of his wrappings, Saam shakily raised his forequarters. **"Not odd, youngling."** Ah, he sounded so old and worn that it nearly broke Kwee's heart, memories of M'wa, her old darling, her old friend, flashing before her eyes. How tired he'd been of life, especially after Bard had died! A cough, a head shake. **"Just old. Even older than I."** He relished his little joke. **"These are the very caves that Doyce and Khar, Nakum and Eadwin and I sheltered in so long ago. And of course, Felix, too. Now *that* was a long-legged dog! Oh, how he could lope!"** He methodically shook his head as if to drive away the past, fix on the present. **"Ah, so long ago. If it's not the same cave, I wouldn't be at all surprised if it's connected in some way. The mountains are honeycombed with caverns and passageways to those who know them."**

**"Could we reach the top without venturing outside again?"** Pw'eek's round, tricolored face radiated hope. **"Not get all snowy and cold?"**

But Parm had slunk to Saam's side, low on his belly, almost supplicating. **"Don't do it, old boy. Don't give anyone false hope, the wrong idea. Not if you . . ."** he left the thought unfinished, rippling his forehead, eyes widening. **"Kwee may have the right of it. There *is* something 'off' about this place. The longer I'm here, the more I sense it creeping over me. Leave well enough alone, eh?"**

**"Nothing stays the same, does it, Parm? And I'm . . . living proof of that!"** Collapsing on his blanket, Saam curled tight and lapped his tail across his nose and his eyes, his sleep so sudden and profound that Kwee was stunned. Ah, any of the ghatti could nap at a moment's notice—or less—but not descend to such depths so quickly and seamlessly. Whatever had temporarily animated Saam had fled as quickly as it had arrived. Such a thought created its own terror—what if . . . ? Was it possible that someone, some *thing* had animated him, spoken through him? Again her skin rippled and crawled, sending her into another grooming fit.

She'd turned as fanciful, as frightened of her own shadow

as Pw'eek! Thinking too hard, too much, borrowing trouble. The Elders would be shamed! Was she not Kwee—jaunty and clever, ready to face down trouble in an instant? The mountain sheep had surprised her—that was all. She'd slipped—it could have happened to any of the ghatti—claws could skid on ice. What was happening? Why did she twitch so? And this time, to compensate, overcome her own incipient terror, she *did* charge Pw'eek, sent her rolling across the width of the cave, shrieking in surprise. It felt good, utterly right, but not for long.

❧

Warmly content, Diccon squirmed and redraped his blanket, sleepily relieved they'd found shelter in time, thanks to his keen eye. As the wind whistled and howled outside, he yawned, contemplating their good fortune, and clasped his hands behind his head, staring into the dark, still not entirely sure if he were awake or asleep. Was he the dream—or the dreamer? Now *there* was a profound question, the sort Harrap might ask—and Jenneth probably answer. A smile at his twin's cleverness, the pride he took in it, just as she was proud of him for so many other things. Nice, it was. After all, *he'd* located the cave, devised the question. Besides, weren't some questions posed simply to make you strive harder, the answer always just beyond reach?

Awake, he guessed. The ponies' shift and stamp, their smells, the compact fire reduced to glowing coals, fiery orange peeping through the chinks of the rock ring, Kwee's soft breathing at his side, her restless kick, all confirmed it. Sometimes when deeply asleep, she presented her beautiful speckled-trout belly to his inspection, let him caress fur soft as down. He debated, but felt too lazy to move his hand from under his head to feel if she'd revealed it. Wasn't likely. The poor dear'd been hedgehog prickly all evening, practically springing straight up in the air if anyone looked at her the wrong way.

Odd, though. Not scary odd, but different, what he'd been dreaming. Wrinkling his brow and squinting his eyes, he struggled to focus on it. If he didn't capture it now, at least a piece of it, it would have totally vanished by morning. Funny the way the dreams did that—stole back to wherever they came from. Sort of a bobbing light in it—not big, but small and roundish, fuzzy-edged. A greenish-gold glow to it. Inviting, it had been. Had radiated the same exuberant glee a puppy or kitten did when it tried to coax you to play, entreating with mock pouncing and bouncing. And a giggle bubbling from it, fresh and airy, making you want to join in the joke. But that came only once in a while; mostly it issued a beguiling hum, like a tune he could almost—but not quite—recognize. Hearing more might help. Under his breath he tried to replicate it. Hum-hum-HUM, hum-hum-HUM, HUMMM-hmm-hm. The last three notes definitely descended, but not sadly, simply a prelude for an even more captivating call.

Sheer silliness! Him humming along like this! Did he plan to serenade the others in the morning? Not likely! Rolling onto his side, not wanting to disturb Kwee, he sought sleep again, but just as his eyes began drifting shut, the greenish-gold globe hovered at the perimeter of his vision. Damn! So he hadn't been dreaming after all! What could it possibly be?

*"Kwee, sweedling! Wake up! You have to see this!"* Bunching the blanket around his knees, he wriggled free, grabbing for his boots without taking his eyes off the globe. Fuzzy globe, he corrected himself. Soft and fuzzy as Kwee.

**"Wha? Wuzzamatter?"** Still lost in the throes of her own ghatti dreamings, Kwee made a valiant effort to wake, vigorously shaking her head. **"Doan see . . ."** an enormous yawn, big enough to engulf him, **"nuffing. Wuzzasee?"** Given the way she'd been acting, he'd anticipated instant alertness, but obviously all her nervous twitching had exhausted his sweedling.

He'd located his boots now, pulling them on, wincing at their clammy coldness, his feet all toasty warm from the blanket. *"Come on! Don't you want to see it? Find out what it is?"* Capturing the tip of her striped tail he briskly shook it, tickled her nose with it.

A restraining paw on his hand, the claws a bare warning away from puncturing him, made him back off, turn sulky. *"Fine, then, lazybones! I'll go see what it is without you!"*

**"Fine! Go!"** Unsteadily humping herself to her feet, still

half-asleep, she ambled toward Jenneth and Pw'eek.
**"Gonna slee-eep w'Sissy. Warm 'n purry-furry, no goan 'sploring, gonna cuddle."**

Lady help him, she sounded fully as grumpy as Jenneth some mornings! As grouchy-beared as Mama, even! Indulgence overcame indignation—let her sleep. By the Lady, he was absolutely reeking with sensitivity, empathy! Now where had that blasted light gone?

Listening hard, hoping to hear the humming again, Diccon tiptoed through the cave, sighting the diffuse light just often enough to reassure himself it hadn't vanished. Amazing! He'd had no idea the cave extended this far—if he eased through this cleft, he could probably catch up with the light. Yes, just a little more, lead with his shoulder, and he was through! The light seemed to bounce with joy as he caught up with it. Well, that would teach Kwee! Wait till he told her the light appreciated him and his company more than she did!

♣

Restless, mouth forming a silent mew, Saam dreamed of Nakum, of the singular world he inhabited, so like and yet so unlike their own. When he'd been with Nakum, he'd drawn strength from his presence, able to run forever, fast as the wind, the earth unscrolling beneath his flying paws. The earth's power had surged up through his paw pads, setting his fur atingle with well-being. And Nakum had freely shared the earth's bounteous endurance with him, desiring nothing more in return than his companionship, the opportunity to ask, sometimes to argue, questions he still sought the answers to, a Truth-Seeking in its own way. The young were always brimming with questions big and small.

Fleet, so fleet! A joyous freedom, and for long moments Saam had temporarily outraced the woes that still seared his soul. But in the end they remained, grateful though he'd been for the respite. Even his keen ghatti senses had become more highly attuned to the rippling chorus the wind sang, the rolling songs of the water—the tempo sometimes quick and merry, or languidly slow—and all because of

Nakum. The subtle differences of sunlight, each kind like
a different lovestroke against his shimmering blue-gray fur.
Ah, ah, ah! And with such nascent abilities already at his
fingertips, as Nakum grew, more fully absorbed his earth-
bond's powers—what need was there for Saam? One of the
ghatti, one of nature's creatures, to be sure, both less and
more than Nakum. Nakum shared his thoughts with other
powers, powers more ancient and timeless than the ghatti
Elders.

First Oriel had died, leaving him trapped within his own
mind, unable to mindspeak, turned into nothing more than
an oversize cat. Then Nakum had appeared, his presence
partially assuaging the hurt. And he'd cast Nakum aside
before the Erakwan lad had been forced to reach the same
decision. But Mahafny, prickly and prideful, had been waiting—whether or not she'd entirely realized it. Converse
with a mere animal in one's mind? Ridiculous! Unnecessary
and uncalled for! Oh, she'd had to swallow hard to choke
down the reality of it all!

Ah, when he'd traversed these caverns with Nakum before, he'd seen things the others had never noticed, that
even Nakum barely registered. The way tiny fragments of
energy followed Nakum, swarming and coalescing around
him like flies. Sometimes they glowed and hummed.
Whether this happened often, Saam wasn't sure, though
he'd later seen them swarming even more thickly and insistently around Callis, grandmother of Nakum's grandmother, Addawanna. But she controlled them, had them
brisking at her feet. Harmless they'd been, especially once
she'd thrown a stern glance at them, cowing them into a
barely visible radiance, a tremulous hum below the threshold of human hearing. If memory served, they'd been a
pleasing shade of goldish green, like fireflies, yet fluffy as
dandelion down, a mere breath able to disperse them.
Goldish green? Or greenish gold?

Opening rheumy eyes, Saam blinked in shock, voicing a
high-pitched yowl as he staggered to his feet, paws tangling
in his blanket. Damn, his legs were weak as a newborn
ghatten's! Had his eyes failed, too? No, it hung there, glowing, truly there, the sight spiking the hair along his spine.
Wake them! he ordered himself. Make them see, one of
those things is outlining Diccon's sleeping form! Kwee,

awake! Protect your Bond! "Yee-ee-OW! RAA-OOW!" His throat ached from the raw screams pouring forth, his head pounding too hard to mindspeak. No! Was he bereft of his precious mindspeech yet again?

Not his Diccon! Not his Diccon-lad, Doyce's child that he'd helped raise, had loved all these years. Let anyone harm a hair on Diccon's or Jenneth's head, and that fool-hardy soul would answer to him! Had he not promised Oriel he'd guard and guide Doyce and Khar? Did not that promise extend to encompass her offspring as well?

"YEE-ROWWL!" Ah, would no one wake? Was he going mad? Diccon lay there, asleep, yet his body floated up from the glowing outline around it, ghosting off after the green-gold light!

"**I will shred you!**" he screamed within his mind. "**Rend you into pieces so small that no one can put you together again! Leave the boy be, I say!**"

Breath rasping, eyes tearing with pain, he stumbled after the shadow-Diccon as it neatly sidestepped through a fis-sure, but to his eternal shame, his legs buckled, slamming him onto his shoulder and chest, collapsing him under his own momentum. "**Mahafny! Parm! Wake! Wake!**" Oh, please, please let them stir, awake! "**Oriel, I've failed you. I honored your wishes for so long, but I'm too weak to continue! Nakum! Where are you? Come to me, I beg you, share your endurance, your strength with me one final time!**"

❖

Diccon followed the light, a clever, twisty little thing, capa-ble of spinning in almost any direction without a second thought. Unfortunately the same couldn't be said for his body, but luckily the light usually waited, brightening and dimming, expanding and shrinking with impatience until he caught up. Once he approached close enough to touch it, starting as his hand passed clean through, his fingers mo-mentarily glowing green. Too bad Jen couldn't see it, it would've scared her silly!

Mostly he didn't notice his surroundings. Stone was stone, after all—what did he expect to see?—though he wished the "thing" had tarried at some drawings he'd noticed carved and painted into the wall. If Jen had been here, she'd have produced paper and pencil, done a rubbing of them. Mayhap Nakum could have translated them later, when they found him. If they found him in time. That made him feel guilty, left him wondering if he should return, but his good intentions vanished as the passage's constraining stone walls abruptly opened around him without warning.

No rhyme or reason to it, but he found himself standing in the midst of a primeval forest imbued with a ripe humus odor of decaying plant life, cycling its way into earth again. Trees towered so high they supported the sky on their leafy crowns, pillars upholding a vault of azure blue which ripened into midnight blue before his eyes, stars majestically wheeling across, some depending from the trees' branches to twinkle flirtatiously. White birch and silver willow whispered in his ear, supplely beckoning him to join them at the stream they lined, and he couldn't resist their rustling invitation, glad to stop and kneel, cup his hands and splash icy water on his face. The water ran crystalline along the stream's bank but cloudy white at the center, as if melting snow had deposited a residual tinge of color as it changed into liquid form.

He stood, almost giddily convinced the water had made him drunk. Over there rose giant oaks, so thick-boled and broad that they could canopy a world. A hail of acorns pelted his feet. Acorns? What season was it, anyway? But a giggle told him it was any and every season, whichever one he currently wished it to be. Playful, he scooped up a handful of acorns and shied them at the green-gold light, not really wanting to hit it but hoping to make it jiggle and dance.

No, not a wise idea! He'd nearly reached that conclusion unprompted as one of his shots inadvertently hit its target and flared into flame, a vivid, live coal dropping on dry leaves. Panicky, he rushed to stamp it out. How criminal—worse than that, sinful—if his destructive touch sullied this world! That one heedless action had almost been the undoing of it. To be responsible for such desecration would forever haunt him.

Mouth thinned tight, still appalled by what he'd done, he followed the globe at a respectful distance as it moved on slowly. Well, from now on he'd be on his best behavior, because who knew what other wonders he might be privileged to witness?

✣

Mahafny pressed gnarled fingers to Diccon's throat, gray eyes hooded and impenetrable as she sought the point she wanted, second nature after so many years of practice. Now she must empty her senses and wait, let her touch provide the answer. If she'd not caught a fleeting hint before—pure luck, not expertise—she doubted she'd have mustered the resources to wait this long. Diccon lay waxen and still, for all intents and purposes the perfect picture of a corpse. But death should not have visited a lad his age so soon. Still, it happened, and ofttimes without obvious cause.

Tenderly refolding Diccon's right arm across his chest, Harrap lifted his left wrist, probing for a pulse. "Nothing, absolutely nothing," he groaned, "and so cold!"

"Hush!" Mahafny concentrated, determined to outwait it, that faint flutter she'd felt before. Almost beyond belief a pulse could beat so slowly, yet it did, the pause between each beat longer than she could hold her breath. Yes! It came again, so swift but firm that she'd originally believed she'd conjured it from her own hopes and fears. Nice, steady, but so very long between each beat. How it kept the boy alive, she couldn't guess. But that, and the delicate misting on a pocket mirror held to his nostrils and mouth, showed that Diccon lived.

Hands clenched against her temples, her head bowed, Jenneth sat with Kwee and Pw'eek huddled tight on either side. "He's here . . . somewhere. But he's not there." She jutted her chin in the direction of Diccon's body. "I can sense him, but he won't answer, doesn't seem inclined to, or mayhap he doesn't even notice me. Makes me feel like a gnat, annoying him." Tears tracked down her cheeks. "Blessed Lady, I'd be delirious with joy if he took a swat at me right now! Anything!"

Leaving Diccon, Harrap hurried to hold her in his arms, rocking her. "We've not lost him yet," he reminded, his cheek pressed against the crown of her head.

"But what if we can't find him? And he doesn't even seem to realize he's . . . lost!" She howled the final word. "Kwee, how *could* you let him go like that?"

**"But it was a *dream*!"** Kwee's soft green eyes had gone dark and wide, almost glassy. **"I was *sure* it was a dream, and he was teasing me, so I decided to dream-cuddle next to Sissy to teach him a lesson! Show him he shouldn't play with my dreams like that, not in the middle of the night!"**

Collapsing beside Diccon, Mahafny waved a hand at his feet. "But when did he put on his boots? And why? Did anyone hear him stirring during the night?"

"Well, Saam certainly heard something!" Harrap indicated the steel-gray ghatt, scrawny and ill-groomed, intent on sitting upright, his whole body quivering with effort. "Mahafny, could you understand what he was crying? What he was trying to tell you?"

"I wish I knew." Her silvery night-braid swung as she shook her head. "I heard his cry, knew he called my name. But nothing else made sense. Nor can he make sense of it now, either. It was as if he'd been seized by a nightmare."

Giving Jenneth a final hug, Harrap began to pace aimlessly, picking up things and putting them down, fiddling with this or with that before moving on. But she'd learned to read him better than that, recognized he was struggling to reach some decision. What that was, she feared she knew, could read it plain as if it were imprinted across his brow. No, he couldn't hide much from her, not after so many years together. And if he could hide naught from her, could she conceal anything from him? Uneasily, she shifted, no comfort in the sitting—or the waiting. Hadn't been for some time.

Yes, there he went, fidgeting away, yet circling closer and closer, like a ghatt interested in something yet feigning supreme disinterest. Ho-hum, couldn't be bothered—oh, yes, why here it is under my nose! Now to steel herself to answer, except she wasn't sure, had been wrestling with herself since they'd found Diccon like this. The answer was easy—but unbearable. Not to have come so far, so close, and then be denied. . . .

She closed her eyes as he bent over her, better not to see him, his pleading, innocent face. Mayhap that would serve, not sway her in a direction she couldn't afford. But did she believe her own grandnephew deserved less chance at life than an elderly, ailing ghatt? A ghatt who wanted nothing more than to have his pain and suffering cease?

His hands on her shoulders now, rocking her back and forth, determined to force her to look at him. "I have to know, Mahafny!" He sounded so rigorously intent, so unlike himself. "Is there a chance, any chance at all, that Diccon could have gotten hold of some of your . . ." he almost spat the word in her face, "drugs?"

Eyes flying open, she stared at him in stunned amazement, trying to make her brain work, grasp this new, though unpalatable, straw. Neither would she confirm nor deny the charge, not yet. Not until she knew for sure. No snap judgments here, not until she'd assessed the facts, the evidence. And that was easily done. "If you'll kindly release my shoulders, I'll check." Kept her voice bland, not biting. No sense letting this carry to Jenneth, unduly worry her unless there was need. Unduly worry her? What did she think the child was experiencing now?

Not bothering to rise, she scrambled for her 'script case, sorting the contents onto her blanket, shielding them from prying eyes. Quickly she danced her fingers in midair over each screw of paper, counting them off. "No, I think not." Again she counted. "Absolutely not. But a good guess, Harrap. Too much of certain drugs might have sent him . . ." She shrugged helplessly.

Again he loomed over her, this time from behind, implacable in his anger. "And your waist pouch? Your private stash? Be thankful, Mahafny. Because . . . because, Lady help me, I might . . . might have killed you if your craving had harmed the lad."

Too weary to argue, she nodded her acceptance of his statement, aware that this once he'd not exaggerated. Somehow he would have made his peace with his Lady.

"Well, come on, then." He clasped her wrist, pulling her to her feet. He, above all others, always remembered her hands' condition, how a firm grasp on one would elicit exquisite pain. "We've got to get him down from here, take him back to Sidonie, if we can. Mayhap one of the Resonant-eumedicos there can diagnose what's wrong, do something about it. Roust the Bannerjees out of retirement."

Yes, now it came—what she'd been prepared to hear,

mayhap even reluctantly accept before. Give up, go back, deny Saam his final chance so that Diccon might have his chance. "Yes, I suppose you're right." She said it and meant it, though she thought her heart might break. "We can lash him to one of the ponies, even put him in a litter when the trail's clear, wide enough." A bittersweet smile, a wink at Harrap. "As you once reminded me, going down is infinitely quicker than climbing up."

"And also more painful the way—"

"We are *not* lugging him home like a corpse!" Jenneth sat at Diccon's feet, stripping off his boots. "Don't you *understand*? If we take his body away, we're leaving *him* behind!" Now she began to rub and chafe her twin's stockinged feet, as if she'd start at the bottom and work her way up, rubbing life into him. At the opposite end, Kwee stretched her chin just above Diccon's mouth, delicate sensor whiskers intent on detecting any alteration in his shallow breathing. "If we further separate the two, increase the distance between them, the less chance Diccon has of finding himself again! He'll be lost forever!"

"So what do you suggest?" Here she'd prepared to make the sacrifice, only to discover Jenneth balking her. "Hibernating in this cave with him? Hoping that come spring thaw he'll wake up, wander back into himself of his own accord?" She didn't mean to scoff, but she did mean to bring to bear every rational objection she could find. "Child, the human psyche does not simply decide to go on an excursion without its body!" Laying aside certain mental fugues and drug-induced visions, but she'd be damned if she'd catalog those possibilities. "We've no choice but to seek help. I can't be responsible. . . ." Diccon's mental state was blithely hearty, rarely prey to the sufferings and uncertainties that plagued Jenneth. If her niece's mind had fled from her body after their Sunderlies tour, she would have understood that, viewed it as a logical reaction to trauma. But even that wouldn't have meant her body couldn't be moved.

"Well, I *can* take responsibility, Aunt Mahafny. We're both of age, and I'm his closest relative, the one to decide. I do mean something like hibernating here, though I pray it won't take that long." Tossing her dark hair to veil her expression, Jenneth stared down at her twin's feet. "Pw'eek and Kwee and I plan to search on our own. We'll seek him high, we'll seek him low—in this world or in another, if we must. Won't we, darlings?''

Bordering on apoplectic anger, Mahafny sat heavily, let her hand drift along Saam's back for comfort. Who was more stubborn—Jenret or Doyce? Jenneth or Diccon? Or her? "Or me?" asked Harrap, as if he'd divined her thoughts. All in all, she'd bet on Doyce—and Jenneth—as the more stubborn, simply because they always made their choices conscientiously, painstakingly, and then followed them through, while Diccon and Jenret turned obdurate in the blink of an eye but snapped out of it as quickly. Now what should she do? Mayhap hog-tie Jenneth on one pony, Diccon on another?

**"Why argue? Not when she has the right of it—and she does. Whatever lured Diccon away from himself . . ."** Saam's head swayed as if he were palsied. **"Well, the only place Diccon knows to return to is here."**

After loosely tucking the blanket around Diccon, Jenneth crouched by their campfire, efficiently rebuilding it and preparing to brew cha. "Thought I'd see if he'd swallow a sip or two. If he doesn't want it, *I* do. I'll make enough for you both as well. And you should eat a good breakfast before you start out." Outmaneuvered, Mahafny glowered at the subtle smile playing around Jen's lips—vintage Doyce glinting through Jenret's features—the girl finally confident enough to challenge her and relishing it. So it happened with each generation, the elder yielding to the younger, though not always with good grace. But since her own wishes, her own needs were different yet complementary to Jenneth's, she'd happily obey. But she couldn't succeed alone.

"So, Harrap." How she needed him, now more than ever! "Will you stay—or will you go?" A lightning-fast stroke of Saam's paw on her wrist stung, as he'd meant it to. Where he'd mustered the strength from, she couldn't imagine.

**"Don't make him tear himself in two, wishing to stay here, wishing he were with you. That's cruel."**

*"He's a full-grown man, and it's time he had to make some unpleasant decisions, face some harsh truths."* Unfair! He had, oh, he had, before this. But she wouldn't beg, wouldn't attempt to sway him one way or the other. She

and Saam would travel alone if they must. Not a blessed
thing she could accomplish here, except wait and watch—
mayhap watch both Saam and Diccon gradually fade away.
At least she could *do* something positive, make some hard-
fought attempt to change fate!

"I think," Harrap spoke each word with heavy emphasis,
"that I will see that you and Saam reach the top of this
blasted mountain if I have to carry you piggyback—the
ponies as well. Because then I can leave you to your fool's
quest for immortality and hurry back here, where I
belong."

She liked his answer, if not his tone. But she also wondered what Parm and Saam whispered about, calico head
bent close to blue-gray one, eye-whiskers and cheek-whiskers
flexing and bristling, ears tacking through infinitesimal
shifts—the ghatti's other, utterly secret language, falanese.
Parm's ear hoop bobbed, and she wished, yet again, that
she and Saam wore those paired earring sets to let the
world know how she rejoiced in their Bond.

❣

Diccon's fingertips roamed the stubbled lichen on a stone
while he chewed a wintergreen leaf, delighted by the dense
mintiness. "Couldn't we stay a while?" he wheedled as the
green-gold globe rocked in place, gathering itself for its
next move. "It seems as if we've—well, *I've*—been walking
forever, and I'm tired." A yawn emphasized his plea, such
was the power of suggestion. "If we stayed longer in one
place, I could really look at everything. As soon as I see
something interesting, you hustle me along." Eyebrows
raised, he offered a wintergreen leaf, but receiving no response, shrugged and nibbled it himself.

Conversing with the light no longer struck him as out of
the ordinary, though it never answered back. "You make
me feel you're a magnet and I'm a rusty old nail, forever
drawn to you." The green dulled, muted to a sallow, sullen
hue. Testing it, he knelt, then swung down to rest on one
hip, stroking the emerald moss, its pile as sensuously soft
as Mama's plush robe, the one Papa'd bought her just before their haliday. But this, this was far more luxuriant,

sun-warmed and alive beneath his palm, driving any thoughts about Mama and Papa clear from his head. Could just sit here, caressing it forever. . . .

Extending his full length on the cushiony moss, his muscles relaxed, Diccon waited to see how the globe would react. Its hum graduated to a higher, quicker pitch, almost a sizzling, and he let his eyes drift closed, other senses alert, curious if it would sneak up on him. Something jerked at a lock of his hair—hard—but he pretended to ignore it. But when what felt like tiny, sharp-nailed fingers grabbed the soft flesh of his neck and pinched, he reacted, leaping to his feet, swatting at nothing. "Ow! That hurt!" he protested.

But shock canceled pain as he blinked, then stared. The surrounding landscape had altered, become each and every season at once. There stood mountain ash, its branches clustered with bright red berries, sugar maples enrobed in saffron and canary and crimson. Yet just beyond a doe and her newborn fawn, all wobbly legs and spotted coat, ambled by, halting to examine him, interested but not fearful. To his left fresh snow banked a new stream, yet at its verge, tiny blue-starred forget-me-nots beckoned, as did frothy Lady's lace and the bold orange of butterfly weed. The plash of fish competed with birds' warbles from the trees, and a cicada's drone bored through the air. A blue-winged butterfly drifted by, while a flying squirrel banked and rolled before landing in a maple crotch. A scattering of snowflakes waltzed from the azure sky to balance on the tips of blue-green spruce needles, a few bold ones kissing his flesh with a prickle of ice before vanishing.

Dazedly, he clambered over the snowbank and hunkered to touch the forget-me-nots, needing to convince himself they were real. Each tiny blossom, an impossibly brilliant blue with a darker throat, sheltered against the bleached driftwood that the stream had cast ashore. Had the stream been a river once-upon-a-time? Or would it grow up to be a river? Anything was possible. Letting his fingers roam amongst the forget-me-nots, he decided to pick one, hold it close to his eyes, but another pinch—this time on the soft, inner flesh of his forearm—made him yelp. "Fine! You think they're pick-me-nots!"

None of this made sense, but he didn't balk at it; whatever discrepancies he saw were meant to be. He was a part of it, more than a mere observer, yet less than an integral part of this world. Now, if the green-gold light would only stop pinching and poking him like that, he'd be supremely happy. Of course he made mistakes, but he was learning, wasn't he? But how to convince the "thing" of that before it turned him black and blue?

Might he have one of these rounded river pebbles—like ancient birds' eggs of all different sizes and colors—cream, pure white, green and gray-blue, a range of reds, some speckled and mottled—or was that prohibited as well? His fingers itched to touch them, tumble them, weigh each one in his palm until he found a suitable one, something that *felt* just so. "How about this?" he called without glancing behind him. "I'll hold my hand over them. If it's all right to touch them, take one for a pocket stone, hum high and happy. If it's not, hum low and slow." Body tense, anticipating another pinch or tweak somewhere on his anatomy, he studied the pebbles, their hues clarified by the water, holding his hand palm-down over them, gradually sweeping it in an arc, lowering it as nothing happened.

"I usually find that saying 'Don't!' or 'That's fine!' is far more effective, but if you prefer I hum, I suppose I can." Spinning 'round, Diccon slipped on pebbles rolling like marbles beneath his feet and landed with a crash, his hip bearing the brunt of his weight. Joy—he'd be pocked with dents all up and down his leg! "Hm, hm-hm-hmm, ha-hm-da, ha-ha-hmm. Oh dear—would you classify that as high or low, slow or fast?"

A complaining "ouch" redundant at this stage, Diccon merely mouthed the word, scrambling to right himself and determine *where* this voice emanated from, to *whom* it belonged. Had the fuzzy globe finally mastered speech—or become bored with humming? Scrubbing his eyes with a forearm, he scanned the forest, looking for some thing, someone.

"Oh, really! Behind you, lad. You've stared everywhere else, haven't you?"

Whirling on his knees, Diccon looked wildly and futilely for the voice. Finally it struck him to look not only near the bank, but to broaden his horizons and glance across the stream. There, seated on a striated rock with the stream splitting around it, moccasined feet tucked clear, sat a young Erakwan woman, dressed in a doeskin skirt and beaded tunic. The green-gold globe made darting forays at the end of her long braid, and she absentmindedly slapped at it, sending it splashing against the water, only to have it indefatigably bounce above the surface, attempt to alight on her toe. "Now stop that! You've been so fractious lately. I turn my back on you for a few hundred years, and look what happens!"

"Wha? Who . . . who are you?" Diccon's voice shot upward like a countertenor's, higher than many a young maiden's voice ever reached.

"A fair enough question," she agreed, "though I've some of my own for you. What are you doing here? How did *you* happen by here?"

"I don't really know—it just . . ." he vaguely waved his hand, "happened."

♣

Although what she most wanted was to spend every anxious moment at Diccon's side, Jenneth rough-tidied the cave, adding wood to the fire and checking on her supply, doing fussy little things like sweeping with a pine branch, organizing necessities from the saddlebags. In a less-than-pleasant way it vividly brought back how she'd passed the time when she'd lived with Pommy, when she'd had no idea who she was, had thought of herself only as the person Pommy had named Aqua. And once again she was biding her time, waiting, hoping to discover where Diccon was, when he might return.

Next she led Mignon and Daisy outside and tethered them where they could enjoy the afternoon sun while she shoveled snow from the mouth of the cave. Last night's howling storm had been more sound and fury than flakes, and now the sun seemed impossibly bright after the semidarkness of the cave with their few pitiful lanterns, the number halved since Mahafny's and Harrap's departure. If she dared leave Dic alone—oh, hardly alone with Kwee and Pw'eek on vigilant guard—mayhap she'd walk the ponies. Nothing exerting, just a little exercise, a chance to stretch

their legs—something she needed as well. While they were
tethered in the fresh air she stable-cleaned their side of the
cave, wrinkling her nose as she scooped away. At least
outside it steamed prodigiously and then froze, but inside,
it smelled richly rank. Proper little housekeeper, she was.

Virtuously scrubbing her hands in the snow after that
task, she filled a pot and kettle with clean snow to melt for
drinking water. There, she'd earned a break, the right to sit
by Diccon. Her hands were so cold! Mayhap if she touched
Diccon's neck, he'd wake with a shout. He had before,
more than once, when she'd played that trick on him. Holding her breath she planted icy fingers on his neck, but this
time he didn't stir, not even the merest flutter of an eyelid.
"Oh, Dic," she sighed, clasping her hands between her
knees.

**"I'm soo bad!"** Kwee whimpered. **"Why didn't I *see* the
truth? How could I have let him go off alone like that?"**
Racked by grief, Kwee sagged against her Bond, her chin
pillowed on his shoulder, eyes riveted on his tranquil face.

Parading across Jenneth's outstretched legs, Pw'eek
screwed her face up, tail thoughtfully hooking from side to
side. **"I wish Parm and Saam had stayed."** She paused long
enough to butt Jenneth's thigh, and then resumed her pacing, the ceaseless motion of her pert white feet almost mes-
merizing Jenneth. **"What if this *is* a Truth, Kwee? A bigger
truth than we've ever dealt with? That it's right in and of
itself, and that we're wrong to doubt it."** Faster now, preparing to pounce on her dawning idea. **"Truth doesn't
change, but sometimes it exhibits different qualities.
And . . . and here . . . in these mountains. . . . Might there
be things we've never experienced? Or forgotten, mislaid
the Elders' collective experience from long ago?"**

"Can ghatti forget?" Jenneth hadn't considered that, had
assumed both from her lessonings as a Novie Seeker and
from daily life with numerous ghatti, that they remembered
everything. After all, they had their own tales and lore,
Major and Minor Tales. Hadn't Mama been specially Chosen to relive one of the most crucial Major Tales of all,
Matty and Kharm and the First Bonding?

Laying aside, of course, those moments when ghatti
"chose" to temporarily forget—or disremember, as Khim
and P'roul had once politely phrased it. Disremembering

occurred when one of the ghatti decided he or she would do precisely the opposite of what they'd been told—such as "Please don't sleep on the new silk pillow," or "No, that crock of fresh nutter-butter is not for you."

Pw'eek spun as if stung. **"But I was *sure* you said . . . that you wouldn't mind. . . . By the Elders, must I remember everything?"**

Jenneth ruffled Pw'eek's ears. "Beloved, it was fine. Mama wasn't *that* mad. It's just that guests don't always relish finding ghatta hairs stuck to the nutter-butter. And they were merchanters, not Seekers—not exactly used to our sharing ways." But a new thought struck her now. "Do your Elders remember *everything*? Back to the earliest times? I mean, before we came to this planet?"

**"Well, of course!"** Pw'eek projected a slightly offended look, as if to say, "Who could *ever* doubt the Elders?" **"We've been a part of this land forever and ever, just like the Erakwa. It was just that they were so prickly when we tried to share our mindthoughts with them! Stung something fierce, they did."** She uttered it with such conviction that it might have personally happened to her only yesterday. Very few of the Erakwa, even today, were openly receptive to ghatti mindspeech. Addawanna and Nakum were the only two she directly knew of, and Khar and the other ghatti found themselves plagued by staticky charges when they conversed with them for any length of time. Sometimes she'd sworn that she'd witnessed sparks crackling amongst their whiskers! Touch one then and you both received a jolt! But that made her think.

*"P'week, beloved,"* and she gathered the ghatta to her, nestling the furred head beneath her chin. *"Do you suppose, well . . ."* She began again, wanting to order her thoughts before she befuddled herself even more thoroughly. *"You just suggested there might be things you've never experienced. At first I assumed you meant that you and Kwee had never experienced, but what about the ghatti as a whole."* Yes, it was beginning to come together, make a modicum of sense! Nor did she have to convince Pw'eek, merely make her see the truth.

*"Now, very few humans live in these mountains, or even visit—and those who do are mostly Erakwa—yes?"* Pw'eek's head bobbed under her chin. *"Do you think it likely that*

*ghatti once lived here? What would you hunt in the winter?
That mountain sheep would be hard to bring down, even
for a clever, brave ghatta like you."* Purring agreement. *"So,
might there not be things about these mountains, these lands,
the ghatti* don't *know? Have no reason to know since they
didn't sojourn here? Very different things—fresh, untried
ways of looking, of seeing? Even different truths worth
seeking?"*

**"But why would Diccon want to look at things differ-
ently? Not see me? Not see you?"** Almost spitting her distress, ears flat, Kwee arched threateningly at Jenneth. ***"My**
**Bondmate! Mine! Not going to share him with anyone!"***
Jenneth held herself absolutely still, heartsick and aware
that a move, even a word might be provocation enough for
Kwee to launch herself, attack. Even Pw'eek shrank at her
sister's frenetic outburst.

*"Kwee, don't torture yourself like this! Don't lash out,
drive us away because you hurt so. We all do!"*

With effort Kwee flattened her arched spine, eyes
squeezed shut to protect her dignity. Twice she extended
her tongue, but couldn't manage a grooming stroke. Instead, she lifted her head, staring down her nose at her
sibling. **"Did** *you* **like it? Were you happy when Jenneth
was Aqua? Wouldn't let you in—her mind closed to you,
locking you out? She couldn't hear you scratching at the
door in her mind, desperate to be admitted. She couldn't
hear your yowls and pleadings. Well, I can't even find the
right door! The door into Diccon's mind!"**

*"Hush, sweedling, hush! We'll find it, I promise!"* Aware
of the risk but simply not caring, Jenneth stretched across
Diccon's supine form, yearning to stroke away the ghatta's
fears, an impossible task. But she needed that contact, that
comfort as much as Kwee, for her own peace of mind. A
paw shaded in delicate gray and even paler buff slapped
her hand, the blow smarting.

**"No one, no one calls me 'sweedling' except** *him!"* She
vocalized a hiss on the word "sweedling" as she 'spoke it.
**"Oh, what have I done? I am** *so* **sorry!"** And with that,
she burrowed beneath Diccon's blanket to cloak her shame.

*"Pw'eek, keep thinking, overturn every old idea you have,
turn it inside out and shake it till it's fresh. There's a clue
here, somewhere, if we can only figure out what it is, what*

*to do with it. And don't be mad at Kwee. Didn't hurt, really."* Four thin scratches marred the back of her hand.

**"Can't be mad at someone whose heart's so sad."** A breathy sigh. **"Poor Sissy-Poo!"**

♣

Tickling his whiskers along Saam's jowl, Parm nuzzled his inner ear, as good a way as any to force the ghatt back to the here-and-now, stop his wandering in the past. Blowing on someone's ear hairs tended to cause an immediate reaction, and he exhaled gustily through his nose. Saam'd swear another storm was blustering and gusting if he weren't careful!

Ever since they'd left the cave, they'd shared Jester's back, cuddling against the cold. Except Saam insisted on riding with his head on Jester's rump, facing backward, as if it were crucial not to lose sight of the cave, though they'd left it far behind by now. *He* preferred to sight between Jester's ears, keep a watchful eye on dear old Harrap and Mahafny; infuriating as she might be at times, she was a friend. Mayhap Saam had no desire to look ahead, rejecting the possibility of a future.

Lost in sadness at the thought, Parm never registered the snatching paw that jammed his jaunty little cap over his eyes and nose, provoking a sneeze of surprise. Rattled at being so obviously caught woolgathering, he batted at his cap, irritably hooking it back into place. **"What did you do that for?"** Had Saam regressed to ghattenhood? Suddenly turned playful? Expect to rumpus next? No, his distant expression belied that interpretation. Where did Saam dwell, when he wasn't dwelling within himself? That frightened Parm, conjured up an image of Diccon, lying back there so still and pale, respirations as slow as a turtle encased in winter-chilled mud.

**"Did it 'cause you were whuffling in my ear, disturbing me. I'm trying to think deep thoughts, old boy."**

Good! that was what Parm was hoping the steel-gray ghatt might do. **"You *must* tell someone what you know!"** What if Diccon couldn't find his way back to himself, what then?

Arrogantly yawning full in his face, Saam slitted his eyes, looking as obstinate as Mahafny. **"I'm not sure what I know, Parm. It's . . . so elusive . . . like chasing a feather lofted by a breeze. You twist and jump, positive you can bat it down, but it slides right by your paw. You try to be subtle, you try to be quick—but no matter what you do, it just keeps . . . drifting away . . . from you."** A long speech for Saam these days. **"Diccon and Jenneth are as much my younglings as Khim and P'roul, but I can't seem to. . . . So feeble . . . like being hollow inside . . . and the thoughts . . . echo, mocking me. . . ."**

Greatly daring, Parm uttered a warning hiss, praying to the Elders and the Lady that neither Harrap nor Mahafny would hear. Intimidation was hardly his style, but he'd do what he must. **"What? So wrapped up in yourself and your own passing that you can't think how to help anyone else? What say the Elders?"**

**"Haven't asked. Don't plan to."** With weary dignity Saam rubbed his nose against his paw. **"Takes too much energy . . . to climb the spirals, and I can't afford it—not and do what I must here."** Again he paused, gave a worn-toothed grimace. **"Too tempting for me to . . . to stay . . . there with them. Then nothing could lure me back . . . here. Not love . . . nor loyalty . . . nor hurt . . . nor hate."**

Parm understood; no longer young himself, the passage of time had caressed him more lightly than it had Saam. Came of having light thoughts, a light heart. Took a major catastrophe to make him feel really low, yearn to fade away. After all, who knew what he and Harrap might still have in store for them? Good meals, good friends, toe-tussles beneath the covers, chances to see and do a myriad of things. Why, they'd never even visited the Sunderlies! Harrap would relish meeting that female Shepherd Theo pined over—Dannae, plucky and plump, and topped with a reverse tonsure that made her red hair stand up like a rooster's comb! Harrap could discuss fine points of theology and the Lady's path with her while he sunned himself and watched the antics of the jewel-bright bijou birds that Khar'd told him about. Silly things twittering in their dust baths!

**"So, what will you do? When will you know?"** he finally ventured.

"The time isn't right yet," Saam admitted. "When I know . . . I'll know. And I must depend on you, old friend, to aid me . . . even though it may pain . . . those we love." Without awaiting Parm's response, he went all dozy, head bobbing like a languid flower atop a fragile stem. Laying his chin across Saam's neck, Parm pressed against Saam's wavering head until it descended to rest safe atop his paws. Didn't want his old mate's ear-petals shaken off, carried away by a breeze, nor the rest of him either, he didn't.

❖

"Beloved, you have to stay, you *must*!" Standing sideways Jenneth used her slim body to barricade the fissure at the rear of the cave. Kwee had already entered, had ranged mayhap two meters along the passage, eyes incandescent in the light from Jenneth's collapsible lantern. Really old, it was, had been Mama's long ago when she'd ridden circuit. Mama, who always had something for every need tucked in her saddlebags or stuffed in her pockets. Mama the pack rat, but she only stored useful things, not like Diccon, who'd collect anything and everything—no matter how unlikely the need.

Pw'eek had plunked her rather considerable bulk on her foot, pinning it unless Jenneth chose to be rude about removing it. How could she resist the entreaty spilling from those delicately green-tinted eyes? "Going with you! Let Kwee stay with Diccon, not me! Like Diccon, truly I do, but he's not my Bond. *You* are *my* Bond!"

"And that's exactly why you must stay, why Kwee must go with me. She and I are more acutely aware of Diccon's . . ." She floundered for a word to encompass the magnitude as well as the elusive quality of what she sought—spirit, essence, being? "Of anything that truly feels like Diccon, because she's *his* Bond." She'd thought it through long and hard, anticipating Pw'eek's reaction, her determination to remain at her side. "And . . . and . . . if anything goes wrong, mayhap I'll be close enough that you can call me back—to myself, if necessary." What if she were to be struck down by the same thing that had stolen Diccon?

What she must venture into was mind-numbing in its unknowability—Diccon somehow divided, body separated from soul. Huddling beside Diccon dripping buckets of tears wasn't doing a bit of good, wasn't going to bring him back. Blast Diccon for indulging in this mad hide-and-seek, but whatever and wherever she must seek, she'd find him. Or else!

Abristle with nerves, Kwee flexed to lick her lower spine, front teeth savagely biting as if a flea had nipped her. **"Hurry, Jenneth, please! Pw'eek, Sissy-love, guard Diccon with all your heart—just as I'll guard Jenneth for you."**

Aware she'd failed, Pw'eek eased from Jenneth's foot, only to lean her full weight against her knee, desperate for reassurance, affection. *"Beloved, you are so dear unto my heart. Don't lose touch with me, or I'll believe everyone's abandoned me."* How to survive if Pw'eek could no longer touch her mind, already bereft without Diccon tickling at her, his casual presence such a constant that its absence was an amputation. Like Uncle Bard without Byrta, his sister-twin. If *this* was how it felt, Jenneth was at last beginning to comprehend the enormous void her death had created within Bard.

Pw'eek reared on her haunches, white forepaws flashing lethal claws. All except for the scallop that indicated her poor, absent toe. **"Fight anyone, *anything* that tries to harm Diccon. Shred them, rip their eyes out. Will shred Sissy-Poo if she doesn't take equal care of you. Oh, my Sissy-Poo, oh, my Jenneth-love!"**

*"We'll come back, both of us—I promise. Can you feel me lying? And with luck, we'll have Diccon with us, and we'll all be together again."* Fighting to believe it was the truth, she went to one knee, hugging the ghatta so hard that a little "ooph!" escaped her, but Pw'eek purred ecstatically. *"Dic found me when I needed him, just as you followed, found me. Now it's my turn to find him."*

**"Could hurry, hurry back home and get Maeve—Diccon'll come panting back!"** A distinctly hopeful rise to Pw'eek's 'speech, but then it wavered. **"No, I know. Go, beloved. Hurry and find him. Hurry, Kwee. I love you both."** Head high, she padded to Diccon, curling in a compact mound at the curve of his shoulder and neck, staring unblinkingly at the fissure, not wanting to miss this final sight of her Bond.

Breath tight, Jenneth raised her lantern and slipped into the crevice after Kwee, clueless as to where it might lead them.

❖

Enclosed in a bubble of yolk-colored lantern light, Jenneth wished it would expand, dispel the unknown, chase away her fears. Lantern like a talisman in front of her, she began following Kwee, concentrating on keeping her shifting form in the periphery of the light. She'd not have admitted it aloud, but each time Kwee ranged beyond the light, her stomach clenched and the hand holding the lantern quavered, made the shadows hungrily reach at her. Oh, to have Pw'eek here—at least her white would stand out—but Kwee's subtler hues merged with the dark, with the walls, her paler buff and cream highlights mingling with pewter shadows.

Trying to breathe normally instead of holding her breath, Jenneth moved cautiously, swinging the lantern from side to side, up high, then down low. Whether it was a trick of the light or her own morbid imaginings, the walls of the passage leaned inward, the fissure tapering overhead, and their intimate, yet utterly impersonal, implacable hovering gave her the uneasy sensation she'd slipped between giant jaws, poised to snap and grind her between them until naught but bone meal remained. Sparkling sand crunched underfoot, setting her to wondering if a river had once flowed through here.

*"Diccon? Diccon! Are you here? Where are you?"* She varied her calls as she went—sometimes calling aloud and sometimes in her mind. Either way her cries echoed with loneliness, sounding dreary and so puny they couldn't pierce through her sphere of light to reach Diccon. Kwee called for her Bond as well, then would dash ahead, buoyed by an unfounded conviction she'd surprise him just around the tunnel's next bend.

At regular intervals Pw'eek called, **"Beloved? 'Speak me, please!"** though Jenneth suspected that the silences between cries grew shorter the longer they were separated.

*"We're fine, love. Kwee's still Kwee, and I'm still Me, still inside me, I mean."* Anyone other than Pw'eek might have considered it a peculiar response, not exactly confidence-building, but it reassured her darling that whatever had befallen Diccon hadn't yet affected her, she remained Jenneth within and without. Mulling over a better way to phrase it, she placed a foot with less care than she should have and elicited a protesting, high-pitched squeak from the sand beneath her boot. Had she been ghatti, her hackles would have risen. Instead, she shivered.

At times the passage bent or branched, and at each fork Kwee tested the possibilities, only to return and regard her, waiting a decision. Once the ghatta vetoed her choice, and Jenneth acquiesced. One way had as much potential—or peril—as another, but maintaining a particular and consistent pattern would more likely lodge in her mind, allow them to find their way out again. Smooth walls gave way to ones with fault marks, then smooth again, followed by tight-clustered ridges that made the walls seem to undulate. Darker walls, lighter walls, some veined with brightness as though lightning had solidified within the stone, some a dull dun, some a mix, or tiered like a layer cake.

Again she dutifully responded to Pw'eek's mindcries, sorry she had nothing positive to report, nothing positive to hear. The lantern's candle wouldn't burn much longer, though she'd tucked a stub in her pocket, along with extra lucifers. Touching her pocket to reassure herself, she stopped dead, slapping at her hip, jamming her fingers deep into the pocket. Damn! Gone! Must have been that narrowing back aways—room enough once she'd turned sideways, but she'd charged it head-on and momentarily jammed. Must have forced the candle out of her pocket, though the lucifers still remained. Lady help her, how she yearned to light one, then another and another. No! Ah, how they cried out, wanting to bloom with flame between her fingers! Such solace to light one, then another, burn away her anger, extinguish her fears. But it didn't truly work that way, gave but a momentary respite. Don't let the urge consume you—concentrate on where Diccon is!

She'd finally abandoned calling aloud, the walls mockingly casting her voice back at her, lonesome and spine-chilling by turns. *"Kwee. We'd best turn back soon, candle's almost burnt down. Afraid I lost the other one along the way."*

**"Will *not* go back! Not till we find Diccon!"** Poised to whirl and race ahead, desert Jenneth if she must, Kwee held her defiant stance.

Eyeing the candle, then the ghatta, Jenneth couldn't guess how much longer they had before total darkness overwhelmed them. Not much, though at least the glass panes protected the guttering flame from any air currents that might sweep from another crevice. Mayhap it wouldn't bother Kwee, ghatti vision was far superior, even in almost total darkness, but it would shave her nerves ever thinner and finer, give her a legitimate reason to strike a lucifer. No, she would not! *"We'll walk to that next bend and peek around it. Then back we go to check on Diccon—do you understand me? We'll try again later, once I have more candles."*

Would Kwee obey? Would *she* genteelly acquiesce if the roles were reversed, someone insisting she abandon her search for Diccon when she wasn't ready to give up? Couldn't Kwee accept this temporary setback? She wasn't prepared to admit defeat either, but best to be cautious, conservative. Their lives, their very beings—hers and Diccon's, and the ghattas—were interdependent, woven into each other's. They couldn't afford to lose, misplace—whatever one should call it—another soul, let alone a body.

Not deigning to answer, pretending to ignore her very existence, Kwee crept forward, body pressed close to the wall and low to the ground. *"Did you hear me, Kwee? You can't shut out the truth, and what I said was true. We* will *come back. Again and again and again—as many times as it takes to find Diccon. And we* will *find him. But for now we have to go back."* But Kwee remained sullenly silent, not yielding to common sense. Such disagreement, discord, while Diccon lay so still and pale left Jenneth hurt and angry at Kwee's stubbornness as well as her own inability to make her see reason.

Determined to bodily haul the ghatta back if she must, Jenneth sprinted after her and suddenly found herself nearly treading on Kwee's tail. Anyone living with ghatti, whether Seekers or family members, soon learned the art of near-levitation when something under their feet felt sus-

piciously like a delicate paw or tailtip. Scraping the heel of
her hand on the wall and banging her elbow as she caught
her balance, Jenneth groaned in disbelief. No wonder Kwee
had halted! Dead end! The passage had constricted, narrowing into a cranny no more than a finger-width across.
Fighting disbelief, dismay, she brought the lantern closer,
as if willing it to widen, open, and let them pass. Nothing,
nowhere to go ahead of them. This was *not* the way she'd
planned on winning her argument!

**"Horrid, nasty wall! Hate it! Hate it, hate it, hate it!"**
and Kwee rowled at the top of her lungs, vengeful eyes
reflecting her irrational rage at an inanimate object. **"Horrid walls, hateful tunnel that swallowed up my Diccon, my
Bond! Kill you, rend you to shreds!"** True to her word,
Kwee whirled at the wall, springing as high as she could,
claws scrabbling against the stone with ear-splitting
screeches that savaged Jenneth's nerves. For a moment, the
ghatta clung in midair, her claws snagging on something,
an extruded mineral vein, mayhap, and she set her hind
feet in motion against her prey, kicking and clawing with
rising fury.

Nearly dropping the lantern in awed disbelief, Jenneth
watched as Kwee—and a segment of the wall—swept outward. Gliding in absolute silence, ghatta and door—what
else could one call it—described an arc and gradually
halted. **"Ha! There!"** Hard to miss the satisfaction in
Kwee's 'speech, as if she'd uncovered this fantastical entryway by choice instead of by chance.

Not sure she dared stand directly in front of the opaque
opening, Jenneth planted her back against the wall beside
it, praying it would remain reassuringly solid behind her,
not pitch her into nothingness. *"Kwee! Come beside me,
now! Don't even think about entering unless I give the
word!"*

Tail lashing, Kwee reluctantly obeyed, Jenneth sighing
with relief, she'd not been sure if the ghatta would behave.
As bad as Diccon sometimes, always leaping before she
looked—and this time Jenneth wasn't sure if she should
kiss her or cuff her for it. And she also realized why Kwee
had obeyed this time: the ghatta now thoughtfully sniffed
the edge of the opening, the way a connoisseur inhales a
wine's fine bouquet. Physical and mental senses fully ex-

tended, she seemed to drink in the atmosphere, sifting it through each faculty.

**"Diccon was here!"** she announced with a tremulous purr as she gazed at Jenneth. **"Can smell his mark."**

*"You mean he peed on the wall?"* Scandalized at such ill-bred behavior from her brother, she reluctantly forced herself to admit that if nature called, Diccon hadn't had much choice about where to answer it.

**"No, ninny!"** Clearly she'd dropped another notch or two in Kwee's estimation. **"Even humans deposit scent marks, though not on purpose the way we do. Hands leave good scent marks, stinky underarms draped across something, bare feet on a floor or footstool. It tells us which humans have come by recently—don't even have to mindspeak to ask who."**

Logical, she supposed, and suppressed a thought about washing her hands. *"And you're sure that's Diccon's scent?"* Not that she doubted Kwee; she just craved hearing her say it again. An awesome discovery, wondrous words—Diccon's scent, his mark, Diccon here, nearby! Apparently Diccon's essence possessed an essence as well!

But why did Kwee remain by her side? Why hadn't she gone dashing through the doorway after Diccon, leaving her behind? Still hugging the wall, she bent to stroke Kwee's head and felt her tense, startle. This close—and they'd both gotten cold feet, were hanging back! Except she felt it, felt something that evoked a queasy, tingling uncase, so imperceptible that a more self-confident person would have ignored it or not even noticed it. *"What's inside? Can you see? Can you see him?"*

**"Hold me? Hold me tight so I won't fall in?"** Kwee implored, and Jenneth set down the lantern and locked her hands around the ghatta's middle. Stretching her neck as far within as she could, Kwee strained against Jenneth's hands, practically overbalancing them both, then abruptly jerked back as if she'd received an invisible cuff. **"Can't see. Can you hold me and hold the lantern inside?"**

Disliking it but lacking a better choice, Jenneth mentally apologized as she sank her right hand deep into Kwee's scruff and hesitantly extended the lantern with her left, half-convinced something would snatch her wrist, yank her within. Instead, with mounting disbelief she watched as the lantern, her hand, and her arm were swallowed by utter blackness, all shape, all form, all light obliterated, the golden sphere of light collapsed like a soap bubble pricked by a finger. Whatever lay beyond the doorway had consumed the light, hungered for more, sucking at her, absorbing her arm as she stared dazedly into a void of swirling dark with the shimmer and sheen of black taffeta. The next thing she knew the intensity abruptly slackened, arm and lantern popping free, sending her tumbling backward to land atop Kwee, both of them scrambling away, avoiding the entrance. Kwee spat out a shred of pale green tabard trim, ripped from the tail of Jenneth's tabard as she'd jerked her clear.

Whatever this thing was, it seemed to have consumed Diccon. **"Jenneth, beloved! Don't, oh, don't go in there!"** From a great distance Pw'eek's mindvoice painfully shrilled inside her brain. **"Shut the nasty door and run! Drag Sissy-Poo clear, too!"**

Backing until she felt marginally safer, she stared at Kwee. *"What do we do? What should we do?"*

**"Don't shut the door!"** Kwee implored. **"Let's leave it open, go back to Pw'eek and Diccon. Mayhap we can coax him out, but we can't venture in, or we'll be as lost as he is."**

Rubbing her brow as she slumped against the wall, knees weak, Jenneth's mind churned. *"You mean we shouldn't drag him back—kicking and screaming—from wherever he is?"* It made a sort of sense, especially considering Diccon's personality. Things always went more smoothly when he did what he *thought* was his idea, did it voluntarily, without needing to be coaxed or cajoled or commanded. *"I'm just afraid of what might come out—besides Diccon."* An exaggeration, but she couldn't help it. As strange, as utterly alien as the doorway, the darkness was, it didn't strike her as intrinsically evil. *"Kwee? Do you think whatever it is is bad? Or is it just headstrong, like Diccon? And with far fewer manners!"*

Unwilling to take her eyes off the black blankness of the opening, Kwee swallowed. **"I know. It hurts, but doesn't mean to. Overeager? But now we're prepared, Diccon wasn't. Must be brave and resourceful for Diccon."**

Must be brave for Diccon. Fine, but she hadn't expected

to have to show courage over something so elusive and inexplicable. She'd choose a territorial ram over this any day! She'd fight, kill to save Diccon's life—but what was there to strike at here? Who—or what—was responsible for this? The candle began to sputter, and that decided her, the last thing she wanted was to be trapped in the dark beside this greater darkness. Pw'eek's frantic pleas continued, unabated. *"We're coming, beloved. We're safe, don't worry."*

♣

The candle wasn't the only thing that had nearly expired— so had her fire, Jenneth discovered as she and Kwee burst back into the cave, only to be nearly flattened by Pw'eek's ecstatic greeting, her exuberant purrs doubly loud. Once she'd checked on Diccon, Jenneth hurried to the mouth of the cave, desperate to recover a sense of time, gauge how long they'd been gone. The sun's height should tell her. Ah, well past noon—it only felt as if they'd fruitlessly searched for a whole day. She squinted at the sun again, lustrously reflecting off low clouds gravid with snow. More snow? The clammy touch to the air, her breath hanging thick and white without lifting, made her clasp her arms tight to hug warmth back into her body. If only she could hug warmth and consciousness back into Diccon's body! If it snowed again, would Aunt Mahafny and Harrap, Saam and Parm, find shelter?

Mignon and Daisy whickered a greeting as they pushed toward her, greedy for attention. As she played with their forelocks, stroked their soft noses, she chewed at her lip, the thought of another storm making her doubt her previous arrangements. Best collect more wood from the deadfall they'd raided last night, down the trail below the cave. With a final pat to the ponies, she determinedly trotted down, wishing she'd brought the hatchet but too anxious to return for it. An awkward armload tucked against her hip, she wrestled with a thick, recalcitrant branch that had snapped free from the snow's weight. Its limbs snagged as she dragged it one-handed, and she fell, her wood scattering from beneath her arm. Scrambling up, she stomped back and kicked the offending rock, kicked the branch for good measure. Other than freeing the branch, it did no good, still left her shaky and on edge—the last straw in a horrible day that wasn't yet done. Unfair! Everything was *so* unfair! Diccon trapped somewhere, somehow, outside his body, Mahafny and Harrap toiling up the mountain, her so alone! And she was too tired, too wrung out to even cry! Piece by piece she regathered the firewood, cursing under her breath, and trudged back.

Hastily piling the wood in the cave, she retrieved the ponies, briskly slapping their rumps even though they didn't hesitate at the entrance, as eager as she to escape the leaden atmosphere. Now her stomach growled its hunger, and though it was the last thing she wanted, she knew she must eat, not allow her energy to flag. Nothing appealed; she often felt thusly when traveling, too restive to really care if she ate, every choice sounding equally unpalatable and unwilling to settle in her stomach. Not that that ever bothered Diccon or Kwee, and Pw'eek always worked up an appetite, even sitting still.

Disconsolate, she slumped beside the fire, only to realize she'd never gotten around to rebuilding it. Smacking her head with the heel of her hand, she stared at it so balefully that flames should have risen to life out of sheer terror. Head propped on her shoulder, Pw'eek let her whiskers tickle Jenneth's cheek until a dimple appeared. **"Fire's not completely dead, beloved. Just needs your tender touch to prod it back to life."**

*"Fine! Now that I've permission to play with fire, I don't really feel like it!"* Still, she poked and prodded away, Pw'eek uncomplainingly absorbing her grumbling until it finally ran out. Blessing the ghatta's unblinking patience, she concentrated, adding a stick here, a stick there until it caught, then fed in a few bigger pieces. Now to put the kettle on to boil, throw in some cornmeal. Bland but nourishing.

**"Are you adding dried berries?"** Pw'eek had draped herself across Jenneth's thigh, basking in front of the fire. **"Nicer that way. And they're sweet. Don't much like them, but you do. Trail mix?"**

"Mayhap, I don't know." Too bad adding dried blueberries wasn't the only major question she had to tackle!

Could she spoon some into Diccon? Since he wasn't exactly energetic at the moment, he could undoubtedly go without food for a few days, but she wanted to ensure he took enough liquid. She'd managed to get a few sips of cha into him before, but that hadn't been enough to stave off dehydration. Unless, of course, Diccon's essence was having a jolly feast somewhere and could somehow nourish the body left behind! Should she wish for Diccon's essence to feast on all his favorite dishes, or hope he had an invisible plate full of brussels sprouts and head cheese?

Front paws kneading, Pw'eek leaned against her chest, comically rolling her eyes. **"I like head cheese—as long as I don't know whose head it was made from."** Bowing her head, Jenneth planted a kiss on the butterscotch boundary between her eyes. As if gauging the moment, Pw'eek asked, **"What was the tunnel like? And the door? Kwee won't say. I could feel that 'thing' tugging at you, wanting you almost as much as I want you. Wasn't nice, not when you're mine!"**

She didn't much want to discuss it either, her fears too deep. To think they'd retreated, been forced to abandon Diccon's essence, his essential being, so near and yet not near enough! Who knew how far that blank void extended? Candle or no candle, Diccon would never have slunk away like that if she'd been the one trapped inside! He'd probably have taken off all his clothes, ripped them into strips and improvised a rope, tied one end to an outcrop and the other to his waist! Distractedly, she scattered a handful of cornmeal on the boiling water, then tossed in another scant handful, barely noticing when some missed the kettle, scorching as it hit the fire.

"Pw'eek, we have to go back, try again, you know." She swirled the cornmeal and water with a small branch Harrap had stripped of bark.

**"Not this afternoon, not tonight,"** Pw'eek crooned. **"Got to think, think very hard. Mayhap we can sneak up on Diccon, catch him."**

It almost made her smile. "Bait a trap, you mean? If I bait it with a sausage and cheese biscuit, the only thing I'd catch would be you!"

**"I wouldn't steal Diccon's food! But someone, something else might. Mayhap the same thief who stole Diccon!"**

Out of nowhere a clap of thunder boomed, sending Pw'eek springing into the air, hind claws gouging Jenneth's lap. Wincing, rubbing at the scratches she could envision beneath the fabric, Jenneth ruefully shook her head. Thunder?

Now all the way at the rear of the cave, crouching behind Kwee, Pw'eek wailed, **"I am *not* scared, I am *not* scared! It just startled me!"**

♣

Exhilaration! Never had he soared like this within his mind, absolutely febrile with opportunity, fey with the potentiality of it all! What a portent—and he, Romain-Laurent Charpentier, had set it off, realized what it could mean, accomplish! Of course they could learn how to control the Plumbs, set them off precisely when and where they chose. Yes, oh yes, the Goddess of Change had smiled on him, literally placed the future in his hands.

Wandering the castle was difficult tonight, but he couldn't stop himself, couldn't help it, had to move, restless with anticipation, despite the fact that he was exhausted. No longer a lackey—hadn't that been what he'd been, so anxiously, conscientiously presenting his report to the joint Domain and Ministration Lords? Humbly begging their blessing, when they couldn't even look beyond tomorrow? Well, no more of that! How foolish to have hoped he could work miracles from within, move a monolithic organization to alter itself. How naïve to think he could gradually change an ossified structure, rebuild and modernize it. Simply discard the old, start new, afresh. Seize the initiative! Change, change it all!

No longer would he wear the sky-blue livery of the king, the ridiculous thigh-high hosen—what had he thought to gain from it? Even Eadwin hadn't been prepared to truly listen, discard old ideas, displace what must be displaced— whether it was the supposedly immutable landscape or the ignorant, childish Erakwa who inhabited it. The man was receptive up to a point, a very limited one, had near-seduced Romain-Laurent with his willingness to discuss new options, but when it came to *doing,* that was something else again. Hadn't Eadwin's reaction to the Plumbs told him more than mere words could ever convey? Why had he expected differently?

Tonight it was more difficult for him and his teaming horde to move unobtrusively through the corridors, especially when he wanted to dance, cavort, scream with joy. Somehow he'd managed thus far to control himself, though the horde had different ideas, did his dancing for him. So he wrote, jotted words, sentence fragments on his pad, muttered judiciously if someone recognized him, soberly clad in black trousers, black tunic, and a maroon overvest. Had stored them in the trunk, the vestiges of his collegium days, student wear, nothing fancy, just serviceable.

Sometimes the curses in his wake registered, the foul looks that went with them, though he'd humbly labored, done every dirty, demeaning task asked of him these last three days. No, he'd not meant to activate the Plumb, endanger lives, create the damage that workers were still attempting to repair. And of course, they'd repair it just as it had been before, naught changed or altered if they could help it. What a metaphor for stagnation! Couldn't they *see* what a golden opportunity he'd given them, even inadvertently? Well, this was a mere foretaste of the future once he got his hands on the rest of those Plumbs! The horde roared its approval, and he took an imaginary bow.

More than one man could accomplish alone, though it hurt to admit it. Even the horde had agreed the time was ripe to call in reinforcements. How much had he spent sending messengers to take word to Alex and Lily in Bertillon, Etienne, Padric, and Florimel and the rest? Not the best time to find messengers, but he had. And soon, soon, they'd all gather 'round him, acolytes at his feet, because he—he alone—possessed an unerring, firm grasp on Change, could make it work for him. Lily and Alex would undoubtedly be the first to arrive, Bertillon an easy journey from Sidonie; Florimel next if she could leave her precious mill. Padric would need more time, Etienne as well, not that he was far distant, but simply to wrap his mind around the grandeur of the concept, decide to cast his lot with them. But of course they'd all join him; where in the world—in this world, at least—would they ever find another opportunity of this magnitude?

Oh, they'd not always taken him as seriously as they should have at Montpéllier, but that happened to those who exhibited a greater seriousness of purpose, poised for greatness. Not always easy to see that, though he forgave them. After all, a touch of jealousy was to be expected. But melded together, with him at their head, they would be unstoppable.

Oh, why, *why* did people refuse to see? No, not everyone could be a visionary, such as he, but didn't they *ever* wonder how to better things? At least wondering was a step forward, an acknowledgment that not everything in life was rosy or perfect as it stood.

Where? What? Somehow his feet had carried him toward the castle's strong-rooms, deep into the interior and down low though, thankfully, not in the subterranean depths.

"Halt!" ordered a voice, and Romain-Laurent blinked, shook his head in surprise. Not a castle guard in the standard sky-blue livery, but a hard-eyed soldier clad in a slate-gray military jacket with red piping and a yellow sash, an astrakhan cap firm on his head, the uniform of Arras Muscadeine's elite troop.

"What do you want here? This is off-limits." How odd. Romain-Laurent backed a step to take it all in, finally aware that four soldiers had created a half-circle around him, each with his hand on his sword hilt. Nor did he like the pikes that two more soldiers had crossed in front of a pair of heavily barred doors. "Oh!" his face ablaze with sudden comprehension. "Are you guarding the Plumbs? Are the other Plumbs there?" he waved toward the door and a hand gripped his wrist like a vise. "Behind the doors?"

"Might I impress upon you, sir," said the lieutenant, "the desirability of immediately vacating this area. Now!"

"But . . . but . . ." a deep longing had overtaken him, and he wheedled, "mightn't I just see them—look at them? I helped find them, you know. I'm sure the king would approve. I certainly won't touch them!" He tried to make a small joke, an intimate sharing with the lieutenant. "Wouldn't dream of that, now that I know. But it was *such* an experience!"

"I'm sure it was, sir. Now please be so good as to leave, before we bodily remove you." The pressure on his wrist hadn't slackened, didn't appear it would ever slacken until he left. Yet still he hesitated, scanning his surroundings as much as he could without being obtrusive. Hadn't he been down this way before? Wasn't there some other entrance?

"Sir, this is your final warning. I can admit no one other than the king and Lord Muscadeine. Unless you'd like to attempt it over my dead body." A deadly composed smile, a lurking desire for him to attempt such an action, Romain-Laurent judged.

No, not here, not now, much as he yearned to see his babies again, show them off to the horde. Hardly worth pushing this man, not when there were other ways, *had* to be other ways. But seeing them, just seeing them would be bliss . . . harbingers of a new world. And such irony that a new world would be built on the rubble of this old one. Thus did civilizations rise and fall, fall and rise. . . .

"No, of course!" he managed with a humility he didn't feel. "I totally understand. Was carried away, I suppose." Backing a step, he waited for the crushing grip on his wrist to cease, for the soldier to release him. Black thoughts raged, the horde howling at the unfairness of it all, the injustice, the horde furiously whispering, suggesting how to trick or decoy the soldiers.

He didn't dismiss their suggestions out of hand, simply stored them away for later use. Better to wait until the others, his flesh-and-blood colleagues had arrived. But soon, soon. . . .

The lieutenant continued ahead, Romain-Laurent having no choice but to follow, wrist still held tight, the man literally towing him along behind him. "How did this idiot get by you?" the lieutenant snapped at a soldier stationed at intersecting corridors, and he himself wasn't sure how he'd ghosted by the man, except that he had. The soldier looked stung at the reprimand, transferring his anger by glaring at Romain-Laurent.

"Don't come back this way again, or I'll see you thrown in the dungeons. I've authority to do so." Rubbing his wrist, staring submissively at his boots, Romain-Laurent continued on his way, shoulders slumped, mind hard at work, the horde at his heels, eager to make laughingstocks of the soldiers, most especially the lieutenant.

Later, there was always later, he soothed them, soothed

himself. A promise to be kept. Besides, he must, he truly must set up his radio telegraphy machine, contact Carrick— if he could only decide what the message should be. Short and sweet, send the dots and dashes into space, then wait. Why, *why* must he always wait? Soon, very soon, the waiting would be done.

❖

Nakum had been loath to come, this role not of his choosing, but a duty that devolved from his heritage, a part of the role he prayed never to play. Now, patiently, he steadied Quaintance Mercilot on his arm as she picked her way along, spine perpetually bent, but dark eyes assessing as her cane shoved debris from her path. Behind them came the Lady Fabienne, on the arm of a groom, both women surveying the damage, stopping to listen to the people who flocked to them, eager to recite their personal tales of disaster and near-disaster, or offer words of thanksgiving that the king had been unharmed.

Fabienne had begged him to accompany them, requiring moral support in dealing with the Lord of the Sud. The poor dear, shaking her head emphatically, making croaking sounds of condolence, and not hearing one word of ten being poured into her deaf ears. "Ye don't say!" she'd bellow at intervals, and "Tsch! Horrible, it was, wannit?" Actually, that seemed to suffice, Nakum discovered, though he winced on more than one occasion, ears ringing. Where her great-granddaughter was, he didn't know, but he was coming to suspect that Fabienne had purposely set Monique another task elsewhere, determined Nakum should venture out, meet and greet some of the populace. After all, the Lady Fabienne was kind, compassionate, and highly pragmatic.

Practically every Domain and Ministration Lord had been out and about as often as their duties allowed the last three days, showing the public that Marchmont's rulers and governors cared, were concerned about rectifying the damage the Plumb had caused. The press of flesh, the compassion *did* make a difference, Nakum gradually realized, showed people they weren't alone in their tribulations, that those at higher levels hadn't abandoned them, had suffered as well. Suffering was a great equalizer, Eadwin had told him grimly on his way to yet another emergency meeting.

Although Nakum genuinely sorrowed for the human suffering around him, in truth he would rather have been wandering below the castle again, or seeking out other spots here in the city where the earth had been fractured or crushed. That was where he could do the most good, let his natural compassion shine. Nor did he feel comfortable in the violet shirt with white cuffs and collar that Fabienne'd insisted he wear—the royal colors—though she'd not forced him to become a complete popinjay, ignoring his heritage by attempting to totally dress him as an Outlander. She'd produced a clean pair of buckskin pants and a short vest, new moccasins, all more formally tailored than he liked, and all discreetly decorated with violet-and-purple beading. A reasonable compromise, though he still felt ill at ease.

"Have you noticed?" Fabienne had caught up with him, a hand on his shoulder. "Loaded carts and wagons, piled high with all sorts of household furnishings and goods? What do you think it means? I suppose some people are shifting to new quarters from damaged houses, but it seems too many for that, doesn't it?"

He looked around, studying everything, trying to see this city-world as Fabienne viewed it. From the appearance of this street, as well as the others they'd traversed, most of the houses seemed habitable, the damage not that severe; the situation had been far worse in the castle's immediate vicinity. Fabienne was right, too many people were on the move, and apparently with all their earthly possessions in tow.

A finger prodded his chest and he looked down to find Lord Mercilot peering up at him and Fabienne. "Rats!" A contemptuous curl of her lip. "Faugh!" Almost he snatched her by the waist, ready to swing her up in his arms, concerned that mayhap a rat had dashed beneath her skirt and petticoats. Indeed, Fabienne gingerly surveyed cellar openings, any place where a rodent might have taken cover, preparing to dash in their direction.

"No, your Lordship," he enunciated each word, overemphasizing his lip movements. "I see no rats. But some may be around, stirred up by the Plumb."

"Well, of course they're around—four-legged kind always is. Had to keep my wee spaniels from them, they would try to fight so, but I didn't want the sweet babies tackling rats. Nasty bites, get infected." With visible effort she drew herself back to the present. "No, human rats fleeing the city, fleeing Sidonie, like rats fleeing a sinking ship."

"Or the way people flee a plague." Fabienne's voice was distant, as if she, too, were enmeshed in memories. "Saw it once when I was a child. She's right, Nakum. People are fleeing the city, they're afraid."

His brain felt dense, dulled. "But why? Now that the explosion's over . . ." and read the answer in Fabienne's weary eyes and taut mouth, so haunted around the corners. "Because . . . six Plumbs still remain in the castle. That we don't yet know what to do with. And if all six should explode at once . . ." No point in finishing his thought aloud; it would wipe out Sidonie. As if on cue, Quaintance relieved herself of a mighty burp, making him startle as if all six Plumbs had simultaneously detonated. The poor dear had no idea how that burp had reported, resounded!

They walked onward with slow dignity, giving people a chance to leave their cleaning up, their repair work to come and talk with them. As each approached, Nakum steeled himself, never sure when someone would look at him with disdain, offer some grievous insult that he mustn't react to, school his face to serenity, indifference at the least. And sometimes the nicest, kindest people delivered the worst insults, completely unaware they did so, or somehow assuming that Nakum was different from or superior to other Erakwa, would agree with their assessment. Being solicitous, concentrating on their woes wasn't an easy task when every fiber of his being screamed at him to be wary. But to his amazement and growing delight, more people were pleasant than he'd anticipated.

As he hesitantly spoke with two little girls, his back to Fabienne, he caught the drift of the conversation she engaged in with a woman who earnestly suggested burying the Plumbs in concrete, pouring it into the strong-rooms until it became a solid block—too big to be moved, too thick to be broken into without the most intense effort.

And Fabienne gravely promised to take her suggestion back to her son, but before she could be properly thanked, another man jostled the woman aside, trying to strike a deal to have the Plumbs buried in the midst of swampland. The man owned the swampland, Nakum gathered, or hoped to soon own it. Didn't he realize that if they exploded there the earth would still be hurt? But to the man, money assuaged all hurts—and how, he'd inquire, would he be hurt by those damnably dangerous things erupting in a Lady-forsaken swamp?

At Lord Mercilot's side a zealous soul explained that the explosion was punishment for some obscure but deadly sin that Sidonie and her citizens were guilty of committing against the Lady. Only fasting, prayer, atonement, and numerous trips to the Bethels could convince the Lady to spare them, end the danger. From the little he knew of the Lady and her religion, Nakum had never judged Her the vengeful sort. Or did this evangelical soul enjoy suffering, the abnegation of body and spirit?

Finally, wearily, they turned toward the castle, Nakum gallantly carrying Quaintance the last of the way, Fabienne's groom unable to locate her litter, most streets still closed to carriages. At the first reasonably reputable tavern they passed, Quaintance vociferously insisted on halting for an ale. "Throw a bit of money 'round, lad," she'd blithely yelled. "Makes the little people feel good when we spend money, shows we've faith in them and their establishment."

Ah, well, at least the tavern had carved arborfer cornices!

♣

A knock at the door, and Urban Gamelyn gave full rein to his irritation at losing track of his calculations yet again, shouting "Enter!" in a tone approaching a snarl. With nearly every breath he took, one aide or another presented him with the latest synopsis of claims. Lest anyone think that required but a single sheet of paper each time, the rebuttal stared him in the eye, bulging files of backup materials, each one detailing claims for damage. Blue for structural damage—by the far the fattest files—yellow for loss of business, mayhap a quarter as thick as the blue but growing; and red for physical injury, by far the thinnest—thankfully. Of course some unfortunate souls had claims in each file: a butcher whose shop must be demolished due to structural damage; plus the ensuing loss of business (if temporary quarters couldn't be found); plus the fact that the unlucky butcher had been working late, had been felled by a half-carcass of beef that smashed his head against the stone floor. It might sound amusing—The Revenge of the Slaughtered Bovine—but it wasn't, because it all added up to a large amount of money.

Only Eadwin would insist that emergency funding from the treasury be disbursed to all who needed it. Except the king hadn't even considered the sums that would be involved. "Damn it, I said 'Enter!' I haven't time to send an engraved invitation—if you want in, come in!"

The door fractionally opened but swung no further. Fuming, Urban finally dropped his gaze downward to discover La'ow just inside the door, his fluffy tail asway. "Cinzia," he called, sparing a smile for La'ow, "I won't bite, I promise! Though I feel like it." Sometimes he wondered what he'd ever done to deserve two such staunch friends, and when that occurred, he did as he always did, thanked the Lady for Her grace. So few willingly took him as what he was.

Her gamine head with its blonde hair poked around the door, observing the stacks of files, relatively neat considering the influx, and Cinzia entered, a small package in her hand. A woman after his own heart—she'd found something worth buying in the middle of this catastrophe!

"That bad?" Leaving it to her to judge, he silently passed over the most recent summary sheet, and after a quick perusal, she whistled.

Beckoning La'ow, he cleared a space on his desk and the ghatt jumped up, allowing Urban to stroke him, sink his fingers in the long, soft fur. "This is the reality of the aftermath of a disaster, you know. Someone has to pay for it."

"I suppose we could dock Romain-Laurent's wages, but it might take eight hundred years for him to pay Eadwin back." Moving a stack of folders—blue, naturally—she sat, one leg casually thrown over the other, ankle on knee. "Is this coming out of emergency funding or Eadwin's own pocket."

A quick run through a column of figures to double-check himself. "At the moment, mostly Eadwin's. And even that's running thin for ready cash at hand." He tugged at his collar to resettle it, then rolled his cuffs with finicky precision. "People seldom understand that we don't sit on a mound of gold, that money—be it emergency funds or Eadwin's purse—is invested, takes time to reclaim. A goodly number of investments can't be tapped right now, not unless we want to bankrupt businesses already suffering loss or closure from the explosion."

She turned the package over in her hands, fiddling with it. "Is it me, or are prices shooting up? La'ow and I've overheard several heated arguments." La'ow gave him a little wink; the ghatt was such a gossip!

"Well, for one thing, there's a run on building supplies, repair materials—hardly unexpected." As if preparing to deliver a lecture, he rose and cleared his throat, winking back at La'ow. "The Law of Supply and Demand: Let Demand increase against a finite Supply, and the price will escalate. If you'll willingly pay more for tiles, should the tile maker sell them to you or to me, even though he and I have already agreed on a price?"

"Did you put a deposit on them?" she asked with wicked innocence. "Shake hands on the agreement?"

"That's not the point, and you know it, dear. In an emergency, prices rise because there's always someone eager to profit on another's pain." Sighing, he sat again, massaging La'ow's spine with both hands, working his fingers deep beneath the fur until La'ow trilled with delight, nose pointed ceilingward to better appreciate the sensation. "I'm going to recommend to Eadwin—if I can ever catch up with him—that we freeze pricing for a short time. At least until outlying suppliers can transport their goods into Sidonie, give us some healthy competition. Tinian and Lysenko have already sent word as far as Canderis—it may be winter, but if several merchanters caravan together, they should be able to bring in extra supplies."

They both sat in companionable silence for a few moments, Urban praying no one else would intrude, interrupt. "How's the little girl doing? And her precious Baby? Has Hru'rul gotten over the shock of becoming a papa?" La'ow wriggled beneath his fingers, his muzzle scrunched in silent ghatti laughter, eyes twinkling. "Oh! You *did* notify the child's parents, didn't you?"

"Of course!" An indignant, impudent roll of her eyes. "According to La'ow, Hru'rul still looks as if he's been poleaxed. Proud, but poleaxed. And very contrite, concerned that Khim and P'roul may think less of him for his unfortunate fling with a common barn cat." Again she played with the package, and it irritated Urban to see her so fidgety. "Telka and Baby are fine—oh, by the way, Baby's name is actually Y'ew. Afraid I've not had much time for them, so I've dumped the pair on Harry and Francie, much as I hated to. I haven't a clue as to what abilities Y'ew may or may not possess." La'ow stared even harder at the ceiling. "And La'ow won't say. Mayhap doesn't know himself, not that he'd ever admit not knowing something! That's men for you!"

Leaning forward in her chair, she let her arms dangle and then gave a prodigious stretch that made Urban fear for his stacks of folders. "You may be languishing behind a desk, but some of us have been out and about—constantly, it seems—surveying damage, resolving problems when we can. Which reminds me, that's one of the reasons I dropped by. Any cases where you require a Seeker Veritas? Where your aides are convinced the claim is being inflated, whatever? Theo and Khim, Holly and P'roul will help as well—clearing rubble, doing repairs isn't exactly part of the Seeker Veritas job description, though we've been happy to turn our hands to whatever we can."

"Ah, if you'd only continued your plumbing lessons with Master Xavier," he bantered before becoming all business again. "I think I might." Ruminating, certain cases came to mind. "Check with Suzetta and Jacquard, will you? And what's the other reason you dropped by? Not that I'm not pleased to see you. Do you want to file a damage report? Blue, yellow, or red?" Pencil poised, he grinned.

"No!" As if she'd forgotten it until now, she stared at the paper-wrapped parcel in her lap and held it out. "La'ow, if you please," and the ghatt neat-footed across his desk to take the parcel in his mouth and bring it to him. "And don't either of you drop it!" she implored. "Now go on, open it."

Crumpled paper inside, then excelsior, and nested within

that, the deep blue-green of glass, almost black at the most solid part, but translucent at each extremity. A figurine, a whorled-glass snail, all fluid curves, no bigger than an up-ended egg. With his thumb he stroked its head and neck, discovering the two tiny horns, its snout. "Cinzia, La'ow— it's lovely!" How it fit into the palm of his hand, so cool and solid, so smooth to his seeking fingers! He held it to his cheek, his eyes closed, afraid of disgracing himself with tears. Such friends! More than friends, family, almost.

"Won't make up for what you lost, but it's the nucleus of a new collection." He placed it reverently on his desk to admire it from a distance, entranced by the light's play on it and through it. "Amazing that Aubuchon had a piece left that wasn't broken, that this fellow came through intact—must have taken cover in his shell. I suppose the one good thing about glassblowing is that you can melt the damaged stock, reuse it." Pensive now, she considered. "Urban, do you think old dreams, old shapes, become locked inside the new pieces?"

La'ow delicately sniffed at the snail's horns, and for once addressed Urban directly. **"And not slimy at all, is it? Otherwise, ugh!"**

A pounding at the door, hardly a polite rap but the percussive thud of someone demanding entrance in no uncertain terms. But before Urban could invite anyone in, Jacquard and Suzetta burst through the door, struggling with polite insistence to contain a tall, barrel-chested man dressed in dusty but expensive clothes, multipocketed work overalls made of fine gabardine, a collarless linen shirt. "Ah, welcome, Kees." Urban sleeked his hair behind his ears as he came around the desk and held out his hand. "Suzetta, Jacquard, thank you, and see about stationing two soldiers outside the door after this. I'm sure Master Swinkel will be on his good behavior, especially given that there's a Seeker Veritas pair in the room." The veins in his forehead and neck bulging with effort, Swinkel let his anger simmer, abruptly silent, clearly unaware until now that Cinzia and La'ow were present.

"Now what seems to be the problem?"

"Now listen, you sissy fig!" Stalking to the desk, he hefted the glass snail, insolently bouncing it on his palm, staring at it in disgust. "Mimsy little thing, just the sort of frippery your kind relishes, I suppose." La'ow extended a paw to drag the man's wrist back over the desk, making him deposit the snail.

"I doubt if you've come to critique my taste in 'frippery,'" and Urban relived other times, other bullies, the insults, the vile comments that stung more than their blows because they'd been true, and he couldn't help being what he was, no matter how hard he'd tried, "so I assume something more pressing brought you here, Swinkel, rather than filing your case with one of my assistants."

"Not claiming a case! Business is booming, as far as I'm concerned." He stood practically chest to chest with Urban now, and he could feel the disgust radiating from Swinkel at forcing himself so close to a "fig," but fully confident of intimidating the smaller, slighter man.

Why must it always be like this? Did the posing, the masculinity contests never end? Aware of the answer, Urban sighed inwardly and gathered his resolution, leaning forward until he was pressed belly to belly, chest to chest with Swinkel. A temptation to flirt, and he rejected it out of hand. This should suffice. And it did, Swinkel hastily retreating a step, mouth working in disgust, practically spitting. Let him! And let him momentarily forget whose office he stood in—the Exchequer Lord's! Never wise to insult a Ministration Lord.

"I've heard the rumors," he snarled, full of belligerence, his hands at chest level, poised to ward off Urban should he venture too near again, invade his precious masculine space. "Rumor has it the king will freeze prices tomorrow—on your say-so! What law states an honest Sidonie businessman can't make a profit? Has to be told how much profit he's entitled to make? I pay my taxes! And the more I earn, the more taxes I pay!"

"If someone loaned you money but demanded fifty percent interest the first octant, sixty the next octant, and so on—what would you call that, Master Swinkel?"

"Usury, outright thievery!" came the prompt response, although obviously any similarities hadn't sunk in. "I'm neither borrowing nor lending, just selling lumber! Milling more as fast as we can."

Cinzia beat him to a response, shifting to perch a hip on the edge of Urban's desk, her arm around La'ow, his size making her look more childlike than usual. "Sawmill wasn't damaged, then? Nor the lumberyard? Nor the offices?"

"Luckily, no. So what's that to do with it?"

"Plenty of lumber on hand? Timber to be milled?" she persisted.

Swinkel nodded, puffed with pleasure. "More than enough. More on the way, once my regular supplier gets through. Other lumberyards weren't so lucky—their lost luck found me."

Urban hardly objected to a friend jumping to his defense, was prepared, in fact, to rather enjoy it, have time to appreciate Cinzia's technique.

"How lucky you are to be in a position to aid Sidonie's citizens with their rebuilding efforts. Why, no doubt you'll sell far more lumber than you normally would . . ." Cinzia's leg began swinging just a little more rapidly. "But at exorbitant prices? Really, Master Swinkel. You want to quote the law? No law against profits, you said? But isn't there a law against *exorbitant* prices, Lord Gamelyn? It's called profiteering, sir, when you engage in making excessive profits on necessary commodities in short supply."

❧

A second flash of lightning shattered the sky, searing Harrap's eyes, already blurred by the first bolt as well as the driving snow. "One Canderis, two—" he roared back at it, shaking his fist skyward at a boom loud enough to crack his eardrums. Not wise to have released Jester's bridle, but rather than rearing and plunging in panic, the pony plastered himself against Harrap, buffering himself against the wind that plucked and tore at them, pounding snow in their faces.

"Find shelter!" Harrap bellowed with all his might, embracing the pony's neck, its mane and forelock, even its long eyelashes crusted with icy snow that scraped at Harrap's already raw, stinging face. How close behind was she? He'd lost track, had been plodding half-bent, crooked arm shielding his face from the snow. "Mahafny! Do you hear me?" The Lady only knew where his words had been tossed—he might have been heard loud and clear atop the

mountains, his warning buffeted that far, or hurled down
to Sidonie, crashing and clashing all the way.

*"Parm, 'speak Saam! Have him tell Mahafny—"*

The mound of snow on Jester's back fractured and a red
pom-pom blossomed forth, followed by a wool-capped
head, whiskers flattened by the wind. Parm dropped his
chin against the pony's back and threw a paw over his eyes.
**"Did already."** Snow peaked on his woolen vest like stiffened meringue **"Harrap, is the snow falling down—or up?"**
Normally Harrap would have enjoyed the question,
whether nature could perform something unnatural, against
its grain, but now was not the time. **"Did I mention
sideways?"**

*"Parm, don't natter! Where did they take shelter? We have
to reach them."* What if they were separated now, him wandering lost, exposed to the elements, freezing to death so
near, yet so far from her side? Close to his dear Lady's
bosom at last, yet so distant from that infuriating yet captivating soul who made it clear to him how valuable this
ordinary, everyday life was. Would she miss him? Mourn
him? Or would he simply become another obstacle—a frozen mound—she'd surmount to reach the peaks with Saam?

**"Oh. She's digging into the snowbank. Left-hand side
back, oh, ten meters—a mere ghatt scamper. Think the
thunder and lightning have stopped? Had my eyes shut
tight, but I could see it anyway."** Despite pulling at Jester's
bridle for all he was worth, the pony refused to turn, fighting to lower his head against the wind and wait it out.
**"Want me to coax him? He's cold and feeling sorry for
himself."**

Come to think of it, he was feeling sorry for himself as
well. *"Yes, Parm, please!"* First things first: locate Mahafny,
find shelter, pray to the Lady for deliverance. Prayer had
counterpointed every step he'd taken since this morning,
not for himself and Mahafny as much as for Diccon, neither
alive nor dead, trapped like a fly in amber by some force
he didn't comprehend, it strayed so far from the Lady's
ways. Yes, he'd seen his share of humankind's follies and
vices, evils and depravities, but this fit none of the categories he'd ever witnessed. Even his Lady could and did insti-
gate inexplicable happenings that innocents and unbelievers
labeled as unfair, unjust, downright cruel because they

stood too near to view life's greater pattern, aware only of the warp and woof of their small piece of the human fabric. Each time he tested himself and his knowledge of the Lady against what had stolen Diccon, he was stymied, unsure if Diccon were held by a benign or baneful being, if being it was. How could he have climbed so high and yet find himself so out of his depth on this mountain?

Ah, reluctantly, awkwardly, Jester turned, attempting now to shelter his face behind Harrap's bulk. Stuffing a glove beneath his arm, Harrap laid his warm hand over first one of Jester's eyes, then the other, melting the frozen snow and ice. A snort of relief and now, back to the wind, the pony began willingly picking his way down the trail as Harrap tried to calculate the distance against the blank whiteness. Now Jester was so eager he'd likely gallop all the way to the mountain's base, find the closest warm stable and never venture forth for the rest of his life—especially with crazy Canderisians! Harrap sympathized—a soft bed, a warming pan, a downy comforter over flannel sheets. And Parm snuggled next to his bare feet, snoring away! The sound of Mahafny in her upstairs den, limping around, grumbling, muttering to herself, waiting for them to awake, join her and Saam.

**"Saam says not to forget the buttered toast and hot chocolate."** So, he'd broadcast his fleshly failings so far and wide they'd reached Saam, intruded on his rest. **"I'd like some smoked salmon, sliced paper-thin, so thin you can near see through it."**

*"Why not?"* Harrap agreed, counting his strides, scanning for some sort of hole in the banked snow, Mahafny digging her way in like a badger. *"A big, pinkish amber slab of salmon, that kitchen knife Mahafny makes me keep scalpel-sharp, and I'll shave it so thin it'll curl like a ribbon. Mound it high on buttered rye toast."* And he would, too, if he could. Would willingly cater to Parm's moods, silly or serious, his whims and wants, as well as coax him to lick down that oily glop that made the hairballs pass more easily . . . anything his dear Bond desired.

**"Just as Mahafny'd do anything in this world she could for Saam,"** came Parm's reminder. **"Stare death in the eye, draw a line with her toe and dare death to cross it. That part's fine—it's just that she won't let Saam cross the line**

from his side. Why does loving hurt so much, Harrap? Does loving your Lady hurt, too, sometimes?"

Had the storm snatched away his brain, his very thoughts? Tossed them far and wide to litter the land with the yearnings of an old man who'd sought, for so very many years, to find a balance for his life, the temporal and the spiritual? His mind was empty of any honest answer for Parm, always so tolerant and abiding, so seriously silly and ofttimes serious. Clearly he was freezing to death—his robe gusting and flapping like a sail around his legs, his pantaloons slapping his shins—mind playing tricks, losing answers . . . even foolishly thinking the snow was lessening, that he could almost see ahead of him. Yes! There was Willy, stocky gray body blocking the concavity Mahafny'd dug into the snow, sheltering Saam with her own body, her exposed back covered with snow.

"Just a squall." Parm sounded smug. "A real whizzer-whipper, though. Look, there's the sun again!"

To Harrap's surprise, the sun *was* breaking through, a gloriously buttercup yellow surrounded by fragments of intense blue—if there's enough blue in the sky to make a pair of britches, the weather will be fine, said the old saying—the blue patches expanding, the sun's smile chasing away the lingering clouds. A sight to make the heart and spirit sing, soar like a swallow. *"Parm, I love you, you know."* He wanted to say it aloud, shout it, not just let Parm read it in his heart and his head.

"Nonsense! You're shading the truth, Harrap. You adore me!"

Scooping him from the pony, Harrap set Parm on his feet. *"Then come, adorable creature, my crazy-quilt ghatt. Give me a hand digging out Mahafny and Saam. Can't let them hibernate yet."*

❖

The lowering grumble gained volume, and Jacobia identified it as thunder just as an ear-splitting crack and a flash of light cleaved the sky. No matter how often she'd experienced thunder and lightning, she didn't like them, plagued by the absurd feeling the sky would shatter and something dire fall earthward—not just rain. Another deep-throated rumble and crack, more distant this time, and she breathed a sigh of relief. Never had she experienced a thunderstorm in the midst of a snowstorm, as if nature had become dreadfully misaligned. Logic told her she was hardly the highest point in these mountains, not with trees and taller peaks so invitingly near, but she'd felt nakedly exposed, riding piggyback on tall Lennap, hers the highest head around.

To her consternation Addawanna had stopped dead as the sky began its clamor, shielding her eyes from the pelting snow as she stared hard at the heavens. The other Erakwa went still and equally intent, heads cocked as they listened, Mataweeta almost trancelike as she strained to decipher what the skies roared. Seizing her opportunity Jacobia had slipped from Lennap's lax grasp, sliding down his back until her feet touched the ground where they belonged.

Their rapt expressions made her feel like a child at a grown-up party, ignored by adults involved in an intimate discussion that precluded her, even her simple presence unacknowledged. Limping, she sought out Feather, whose expression flickered between the here-and-now and the deep plaint from the skies. "Feather!" Had her presence registered on Feather? Or would she have to shake her before she'd pay heed? "What's happening? What is it?"

"Hush! Listen!" A closing peal of thunder rumbled dyspeptically as it faded away. Focusing at last, she absently blocked Jacobia's hand before it could touch her shoulder. "Hard to believe, but if I'm right, we must make even more speed."

"Why? What for?" Oversized, swirling flakes of snow veiled Feather's expression. "What was that meant to be— a message from on high?"

Feather scowled, unamused by her comment, and shuffled her moccasins in the snow. "I know what I know, what I heard, though not as clearly as others may have," she lowered her eyes, mulishly stubborn, practically daring Jacobia to argue. Over what? Weren't thunder and lightning mysterious enough without Feather attempting to further mystify her? How could she argue when she didn't even know what to argue about—or was Feather goading her? If so, she'd give as good as she got—but was it worth it? A mercantiler didn't arrange an advantageous transaction by being obdurate. The stubbornness came from not giving up, continuing to bargain, all the while seeking common ground upon which they could both comfortably stand. Play it that way, and she might succeed, at least have a chance at success. Except what could she yield that Feather would accept? Absolutely nothing, truth be told. If it weren't for Feather and Addawanna, Lennap and Metaweeta and the others, she wouldn't even be here.

"Feather, I feel like an appendix, a useless appendage that's carried along whether the host body needs it or not!" she blurted before she could stop herself. That's what came of having a sister-in-law who'd trained as a eumedico, not to mention an aunt who'd been one of the finest—eumedico similes by double-eights! And Feather, too, was a eumedico.

To her surprise, Feather treated her to a succinct grin. "And when inflamed, best to excise it immediately." How literally should she take that rejoinder? If she'd interpreted it correctly, it indicated that Feather and the others could and would separate from her whenever the necessity—or the mood—struck them. Abandoned on the lower reaches of the Stratocums, without a clue how to continue on to find the twins! Damnation, couldn't she ever keep her mouth shut? Come to think on it, being a necessary burden to be lugged along didn't sound half as distasteful as it had earlier.

Snow caking her deerskin skirt and tunic, obscuring the beadwork design, Addawanna materialized out of the falling snow, switching her long braid the way a cat switches its tail. "So, Jacobia," her face so close that Jacobia could feel the heat of her breath on her cheek, "we be needin' to take 'noder way, goan 'way from yer wanderers fer now, den we all gather at same place—if I hear earth true."

"I'm not sure what you mean." And she wasn't, entirely. "Are you saying I should continue with you, or make my own way?" Please, Blessed Lady, don't let them abandon her, leave her wandering alone in this wintery landscape that even the Lady must have temporarily forgotten or overlooked! How long before her only choice was to freeze to death? "You've been unstinting in your friendship, your help thus far, and for that I'm more grateful than I can express. I know Jenret and Doyce and Damaris will be equally thankful. Can I—is there *any* way I can aid *you*—yet not compromise my search for the twins?" Give some, get some.

"I t'inking you should come 'long as witness, try an unnerstand."

Didn't the Erakwa ever offer an unambiguous answer—a nice, straightforward yes or no? Always it seemed hedged, conditional, elliptical. But Addawanna bestowed a kindly, almost pitying look on her, the sort one gave a slow child, before turning to present her back to Jacobia, crouching slightly so she could jump aboard. "We be findin' yer dear ones on Callis's and Nakum's mountain—if t'under only beat chest, if lightnen only threaten, tease dat it strike it. If so, nature is out of balance, diff'rent t'ings battlin' each oder, no knowin' allies from en'mies."

Climb aboard or remain, alone? Jacobia jumped, Addawanna's strong arms hooking her thighs in place over her hips, and Jacobia lightly rested her hands on the woman's shoulders. "But why is nature fighting with itself?"

" 'Cuz Outlanders confuse it. Whad else you t'ink Plumb do? Dat only beginnin'. Now confusion trough land. Sky wantin' more power, water dom'natin' land, earth weepin' at rip in its heart. Must be stopping dis, find Nakum soon. An finding Nakum, mayhap reachin' yer goal."

From her perch the land unscrolled beneath her, Addawanna's feet moving more swiftly than before. As the snow finally let up, she thought she glimpsed the Merebal, a broader expanse of water behind Pettibal's tail, as the mountains on her right receded. "Why are we leaving the mountains?" Where did Addawanna plan on going? They weren't going to locate Nakum in the Balaenas, but Addawanna's stride never faltered, her arms tightening as Jacobia struggled to dismount.

"Ha, eben Addawanna git sore knees, all dat up an down an down an up! Ole age not pleasant alla time—more wisdom, yes, but worn-out body." Hard to believe Addawanna the Indefatigable could tire, be weary—not the way she charged on. "Easier skirt 'round mountains on flats, den climbin' when closer. You know 'spression, 'As crow flies'?" Without waitin for Jacobia's answer, she continued. "Well, Erakwa not manage crow flying yet, but same t'ing, use yer head."

Lady bless! How stupid could she be? No sense climbing mountain after mountain, covering how many kilometers vertically, but gaining very little horizontally—true distance. No wonder the Erakwa looked upon most of her people as ignorant!

❖

Should he invite her to leave her rock, join him on the bank? Wade out to her rock? Diccon wasn't sure how to proceed, hating to broach her territory any more than he had already. And he'd best stop staring, gawking like a fool, lock his limp jaw into place. Scrubbing a self-conscious hand through his hair to tame it, he knew it had gone all unruly again—as usual. Yes, comb it into place, neaten up a tad, let his glance swing by her once more but not linger. Exhibit a polite interest, not a rude appraisal.

Her voice, at his ear now, sent him into an ungainly lurch that practically carried him into the stream. "I knew someone with hair like this . . . or I will know someone, someday," she mused, tugging at a lock of Diccon's brownish-red hair, tucking it into place. Merciful Lady, her legs and moccasins were bone-dry! How could she have left her rock to join him on the bank without wading, getting wet? Again he checked the distance to confirm it—way too far for her to have jumped.

"But I think the person with hair like yours is . . . a woman," she continued, completing her thought, and Diccon realized he'd entirely forgotten she'd been commenting on his hair, of all things.

"What?" Cautious, he touched the lock of hair she'd rearranged, wondering if it had been altered in some subtle way. "Who? Hair like mine?"

"It's hard, you know." She sat now, crossing her ankles and leaning back on her hands, merrily regarding him. "I mean, being in a time before there is . . . or was . . . time. It's difficult to recollect what I already know from what I *will* know, if you follow me. But definitely a woman, of that I'm sure." She conversed with him as if he were an old friend, and mayhap he was, for all he knew. The green-ish light hovered comfortably at her hip, dappling the pale doeskin with hues of new leaf green and autumn gold, mutable as sunlight.

"I . . . my name's Diccon. Diccon Wycherley." Extend a hand, offer to shake? Holding out his hand, palm up, he left it at that, waiting to see if she'd clasp it, or lay her palm against his. To his utter bafflement a tiny toad now sat on his palm, its gold-and-black eyes sleepy, its creamy throat sac bulging, its skin buff with bumpy, gold-edged darker splotches. Its toes looked as thick as an eyelash.

"Now stop that!" the young woman admonished, shaking a finger at the light. "Enough of your games!" As Diccon continued staring at the toad, she softly laid her hand atop his and pressed, her palm pivoting until their thumbs interlocked and she shook his hand. Gasping, he recoiled, expecting something revoltingly moist and squishy plastered in his palm, but it lay cool and dry against hers, the wee toad had vanished. "Doncallis. Most call me Callis, for short. Pleased to meet you, even unexpectedly. Although I think I understand how it happened, don't I?" Her question was directed at the fuzzy light, throbbing and thrumming with what Diccon had to label smug satisfaction.

Why did her name sound so familiar? But the more he chased it around his brain, the more his thoughts dispersed, light as cottonwood fluff in a fickle breeze. Come to think on it, he couldn't recollect what he'd told her *he* was called. How very odd! Not that it mattered; after all, she was She, and he was He. Still, names were nice, served as handy tags, labels. Green-Fuzz, for example. *That* would be a perfect name for the globular light that had led him on this merry chase.

"What is . . . ?" he pointed, the ideal name having vanished neat as a gliding garter snake, "that?" It seemed rude to point, but he wanted her to be sure what he referred to. "I've never seen anything like it, so much energy. It hums prodigiously, sometimes it sounds as if it's purring. Though it can be a bit on the mean side, cranky, when it chooses." The pinch mark on the inside of his arm had turned black and blue.

She shrugged and concentrated on fingering out the thing's fluffy edges, her eyes downcast as she groomed it. Finally she tossed her head in his direction, and he admired the sweep of her hair, almost blue-black, the color as dense

as a night without any moons. Impossible! Ah, to interweave silver stars within that hair, just like the night skies!
But since that couldn't be, he did the next best thing, chain-
ing daisies together to crown her head. In the heart of each
daisy a perfect golden sun, sunshine running round her
head. He . . . She . . . sun . . . moon . . . stars . . . to create
a universe. . . .

"Mostly it's harmless," and She tickled the globe as
proof, her fingers sinking into it as if she'd plunged them
into thick, verdant grass. "It doesn't always realize its own
power. I hadn't reckoned with it getting free just now—
should have realized sooner than I did. When I reside here,
it's easy to ignore the outside world. The cries and pleas
sound like distant birds, or the repetitive chirp of crickets
on a hot, humid night. I've been careless." A sigh, part
vexation, part amusement.

Splitting a daisy stem with His thumbnail, He asked a
question, just to hear Her speak again. "How did it get
free? Was it imprisoned?" An idea came to Him, then.
"We could bind it with daisy chains. Though why anyone
would wish to be freed from You, I'll never know!" And
He meant it—not as flirtation or flattery—but as honest
truth, plain as the nose on His face.

"Imprisoned? Oh . . . yes, and no. You really ask too
many questions, always trying to pin things down, analyze
them. But if You really must know, Your people accidentally loosed it, and then carelessly broke the cage that contained it. Oh," a wave of Her slim hand, "not exactly a
cage, but that's close enough."

Rising with the lithesome grace of a willow, She snapped
Her fingers and the green-gold globe sprang onto the palm
of Her hand. "If I let you wander for a bit, do you promise
to behave?" It darkened, sulking again, then gradually
shimmered and brightened, hovering just above her palm.
"I need to talk with this young man, and I don't want
you playing tricks on us. Understand? No tricks, no jokes!
Remember, when you're bigger, you won't be near as cute
and people will become even more angry at your pranks.
Now, scoot!"

It bounded from Her hand, floating until it touched the
grass, then bounced and sprang away, somersaulting as it
went. He could have sworn its shape altered as He watched

it recede: for a moment it appeared to be a little boy, then
a fox, next a crow, and finally a weasel. Such teases, all of
them. But She was beckoning Him, holding out Her hand,
waiting to meld Hers with His, and that was of greater
moment than puzzling over the green-gold light's shifting
forms.

♣

Ooo-oo-ee-WAH! Ha! Ho! So good to be let out, released!
It'd roamed too far from home and how good to be back!
Capering, it bobbled and bounced up the trunk of an oak,
hovering in front of a split that opened into a hollowed
space. With a hum of delight it shone brighter, brighter,
chortling as the owl within blinked and squinted, feathers
ruffling, hooting and hissing its dismay at the disturbance.
Tease and tickle, trick and play, annoy, then giggle-wiggle.

Rolling down the trunk, it landed with a splat on the
grass and transformed itself into a small, naked boy, arms
and legs outstretched, reveling in the touch of each tender
blade on his skin. Silly old oak! Silly old owl! What else
could it twit, whom else could it bait? Find a badger and
badger it? Waving one leg in the air, examining its toes—
odd little things, cute enough to nibble—it considered possibilities. People in the other world, the outside world, offered so much more scope, were so naïve when faced by
anything unknown, unforeseen. The more complex and
complicated the beings were, the easier to fool them. So
gullible even its oldest tricks took on novel aspects, de-
lighting it anew.

Whoosh! Howl, moan! Now it spun itself into a miniature
whirlwind, but there wasn't a soul near enough to cast dirt
in their eyes. Boring! So it was most of the time, Doncallis
keeping it tethered to the other world, much as it loved it.
But anything tethered yearns to break free, control its own
destiny. These words, these thoughts were larger, more profound than what it usually experienced; were they new
born? Or had it camouflaged them before, even from itself?
Not that it truly had feelings—though it suspected it was
catching some from this outside world. Rub against this
outside world as much as it had lately, and all sorts of
things stuck burrlike to its green fuzz.

Capering and prancing in fox-form, it pounced stiff-legged on a field mouse, tossing it into the air with a quick head-flip and swallowing it whole as it descended. Ah, yes, fuel. Whatever form it took, some sort of fuel was necessary. Emotions fueled the green-gold globe best, and it greedily sucked them in whenever it could. Ever since life had begun, so had it, coexisting within this outside world whenever it could, feeding off it. Sometimes it grew stronger, and sometimes weaker, until it feared it'd fade from existence.

None of this caused tears of joy or woe, happiness or pain. It simply "was." "IS!" it challenged the skies above, the streams and lakes, the very earth. "IS BE—ME!" Oooo-oo-ee-WAH! The man-boy had been fun to play with for a time, coaxing him along like that, teasing and toying with him, but a mistake to lead him to Doncallis, think it could slip in and out with impunity. Now it was bored, needed something new and fresh to bother. What next? Where next? Doncallis didn't truly believe a promise could hold something as primordial as it, did she?

Flapping glossy black wings, it rose and circled above the trees, searching. Yes, it could slip through right there! There must be other living things it could annoy in this world's mountains even in the dead of winter—it could almost feel them. A shame it'd chased away Nakum, but mayhap he'd return, and then they could resume their battle of wits. Until then, it'd just have to find someone, something else.

♣

Like a child towed on a sled trailing a sleigh or wagon, Mahafny slid along behind Willy on a litter Harrap had improvised by lashing together the thick stubs of severed fir boughs. He'd tied his best slipknot, insisting Mahafny wrap the free end of the line around one hand. Should Willy lose his footing, fall off the ledge, she could jerk the rope and her "sled" would break free—if she reacted quickly enough. A small comfort, the best he could contrive. Neither had felt comfortable astride the ponies, not worming their way along these ledges, afraid they'd overbalance the poor beasts, send them all hurtling to the bottom. More exhausted than she'd willingly admit to him, Mahafny stiffly rose as necessary from her sled to navigate whatever obstacle they'd encountered, edging by a boulder, jumping a crack.

The trail's slope had increased even as it had narrowed, marred in spots by fissures and mounds of debris that had slithered or fallen to this temporary resting place, ready to be swept lower by the next storm. Head down, picking his way, Harrap ignored things as best he could until Jester shied violently and reared on his hind legs, pawing at the green-gold sphere of light that materialized from nowhere in front of his head. Shouting at the pony, trying to distract him, Harrap fought to reach his head, grab the bridle, and soothe him. Not that the bizarre apparition made him any calmer or steadier than the pony—he, too, fought a terrible urge to bolt, kilt up his robe, and run, just as he had as a child, outracing the bullies and teases.

As Harrap hauled himself hand over hand along the reins, the light brashly shimmied and danced in his face, dazzling his eyes but filling his nose with a grassy green scent. How incongruous! As he wrestled to control Jester, Harrap's foot slid perilously close to a crack overlaid with the merest crust of snow as disguise. Only when his boot broke through and found no purchase, did he realize his danger. Even worse, his dead weight dragging at the reins made Jester falter, the pony's bulk looming like a wall prepared to fall and crush him flat. Fighting the pull, Jester finally collapsed on his knees, keeling onto his side and nearly rolling atop Harrap, wanting nothing more than to clamber clear but unable to move.

The crack gripped his thigh like a vise, his free leg crumpled beneath him, Jester thrashing and squealing, his hooves flailing, unable to find purchase. Lady help him, help them all! As if content with the mayhem it had created, the green-gold ball pirouetted in midair and floated straight toward Willy.

"Mahafny! Yank the knot, slip it free!" She'd slide backward, but that would temporarily remove her from Willy's likely panic. Not to mention the possibility that Jester might labor so hard to rise that the impetus would send him coasting downslope to crash into Willy and Mahafny. Too likely, because Harrap could just make out the shimmering light bouncing at Willy's nose, good, biddable Willy, who uncomplainingly carried Saam and Parm on his back, as well as pulling Mahafny behind him.

"Come on, Jester!' he encouraged the pony, slacking the reins so the frightened beast could lift its neck and head. As best he could, he shoved his shoulder against Jester's withers to right the beast, let him plant his feet beneath himself and rise. "Mahafny! Did you hear me? Cut loose!"

An affirmative shout floating up the trail indicated that Mahafny had obeyed with more alacrity than he'd credited her with, stubborn old woman that she was. Good, with luck and the Lady's guidance, she'd slide mayhap twenty meters before crashing into the snowdrift they'd scrambled around and over. If not, he didn't want to envision her soaring into space, except she'd kick her heels into the fir boughs and demand the best ride of her life. Or, he prayed, she'd have the sense to roll off and hug the wall, even if her dismount knocked the wind out of her.

A mighty heave as Jester brought his haunches under him and came fully upright, blowing, eyes rolling to locate the lively green light, see if it still threatened. Had it vanished as suddenly as it appeared? Willy stood stolidly a few meters behind Jester, apparently unperturbed by the light's appearance. Was it real, or had it been some trick of the sun on the ice and the snow, an ice shard acting like some sort of prism, splitting the beams, capturing the green-gold and projecting it? Mayhap, but not the scent of grass, and he'd not imagined that, because Jester was sniffing around, his expression indicating that the scent lingered.

"Parm! Keep an eye on Mahafny, would you?" Placing a hand on each side of the crack Harrap tried to lever his body upward, relieve the pressure on his leg and yank it free. "Parm?" No answer. *"Parm? Where are you? What's happened? Are you there?"*

♣

**"Now or never,"** Saam grunted as he fought clear of his swaddling and balanced atop Willy, gauging the distance to the ground. Hmph, ponies were considerably higher than he remembered them. Ah, well, everything altered—bigger or smaller, important or trivial—with old age. **"Coming, are you, Parm?"** The frosty air felt good—invigorating his tired, aging body, and he inhaled a great lungful.

Embarrassed at exposing his weakness to Parm, he clung to Willy's pack with his front claws and let his hindquarters droop off, unfurling until his hind feet dragged in the snow before releasing his grip. No sense springing, breaking a hip, smashing a jaw, not when he couldn't guarantee if his paws would support him as they had in his youth. He knew full well he resembled a mangy, starved stray—fur matted and lusterless, worn away in spots, bones protruding like the derelict remains of a ship deserted long ago. But at least—for these few moments—his mind was sharp and alert, his yellow eyes bright and all-seeing, all-knowing, for the truth had come to him.

Letting himself roll, not fighting it, he waited until he'd exhausted the momentum from his unorthodox dismount and inventoried his bones. Reassured he could account for them all and their wholeness, he shakily got to his feet. Woo! Stimulating, nothing like a roll in the snow! How it banished the scent, the stench of illness, old-age, and infirmities! Made his paw pads tingle! Funny how he'd conveniently forgotten that part. **"Parm? Coming?"** Now where had that old rascal gone? Gotten too soft for a little adventure? Shouldn't think of it like that, not when Diccon's life hung in the balance, but Diccon would enjoy calling it an adventure—Saam's Final Adventure. That cooing, mawkish woman who'd penned *Lives of the Seekers Veritas* would have some major updates to include in the next edition!

Yes, that crack right there, the one from which the green sphere had zoomed, giggling all the way. He'd felt a stirring within him and had suddenly known, remembering the tales Nakum had sometimes told, testing his memory by reciting them to his grandmother, Addawanna, who'd so painstakingly taught him. Nice, and very like the way a mother ghatta instructed her ghatten in the eight Major Tales. Must have them perfect, not falter, mislay a crucial word or concept.

**"Saam, what *are* you doing?"** Parm came puffing up behind him and Saam decided he'd had enough of that silly cap. A swipe and it flew from Parm's head, the old dear shrieking and flinching. Had Parm thought he'd meant to hurt him? Turn on him after all these years?

"Now slither out of that silly vest," he instructed. "If we should meet the Elders before our time, I don't want you dressed like some child's baby doll."

"But it's so warm! And Harrap knitted it for me!" Parm beseeched, mightily put out by the demand, but Saam glared without blinking. With a whimper Parm plopped on his bottom, hind leg kicking at the vest, ineffectually attempting to peel it over his head and drag his front legs clear, but succeeding only in tangling himself. Taking pity on him, Saam snagged the neckline in his teeth and ordered Parm to back free.

Wistfully kneading the vest one final time, Parm let himself be carried away by the exhilaration of being a complete, unhampered ghatt, his mindvoice trilling. "Can you do it? Can we do it? Bring Diccon back?"

"If we can join the two halves, we may get him whole." And if they stood nattering any longer, his paw pads would turn to ice. "Parm the Brave and Saam the Cunning are going hunting. Are you with me, old friend?"

*"Parm? Where are you? What's happened? Are you there?"* Harrap's 'voice reached him as well as Parm, the Shepherd crying his fears for all to hear—or all who comprehended mindspeech.

Parm's head went up, his calico markings forming a new, compressed pattern as his features bunched with indecision. "No, don't answer him, Parm. I'm sorry, old chap, but let's be gone. Now!" Swaying on his feet, Saam measured the crevice's width with questing whiskers, then began to wedge himself inside, scraping his shoulder on a rough spot. Tight squeeze for Parm, that was for certain. But where there was truth, there was a way. "Exhale with all your might when you start in, Parm. It widens the deeper we go."

♣

Coasting more slowly now, Mahafny dragged both feet and glided to a halt. Her hat had sailed free along the way, but she'd retrieve it later, a minor inconvenience compared to this unexpected ride. Amazing how one never forgot the basics learned as a child: she'd steered by dragging one foot or the other, though she'd belatedly remembered that maneuver only after she and the impromptu sled had spun twice, the sky and mountains pivoting around her, leaving her dizzy with delight. Too near the edge and its sheer drop, she'd thrust out a foot to correct her course, face downhill to let the branches slide sleeky over the packed snow.

Rising, dusting her knees and bottom, she assessed her body for its assorted aches and pains, curious what this wild joyride had worsened. Hmph! Nothing, so it seemed. And wild joy it had been. A hectic gaiety suffused her at the unexpectedness of it all, and her reaction to it, her spirits soaring, her body alive at her momentary closeness to death, death cheated as she'd guided her fir-bough steed clear of the edge. Mayhap she wouldn't need her next dose after all, not if she felt like this without it. A better thrill than the *thebie* gave, that was certain. Great goddess, how good to be alive, in control!

Her hair blew free and wild in a silvery-white scrim against the dark gray of her jacket, and she tossed her head, relishing the sensation. Even the climb to reach Harrap and the ponies, Saam and Parm, was a small price to pay for such enjoyment. Speaking of which—what had made Harrap cry for her to yank the line free? And what in the name of sane, scientific analysis was that greenish light that had pounced at Willy? "Harrap? Are you all right?" She cupped her hands and shouted, began trudging upward without awaiting an answer. Chunk, chunk! She drove each foot securely into the churned snow; a fall would be anticlimactic after her ride.

"Harrap?" she tried again, a shapeless sense of distress leeching the gaiety from her. *"Parm? Saam? What's going on? Why isn't Harrap answering?"* Just ahead she could spy Willy's shape, somehow less bulky, more trim than before. Yes, the saddlebags with their supplies hung in place on either side, but no ghatti rode atop them.

Now she began to trot, breath harsh and fast, her mind churning over possibilities, each more dreadful than the last. Harrap hurt, the ghatti by his side, comforting him. Had he fallen, broken a leg? Been swept over the edge? But why, then, hadn't Parm or Saam answered her? Could

the greenish light have affected their mindspeech? A
steeper segment of trail and she automatically pressed her
back against the cliff, methodically kicking the outside of
her left foot, then the inside of her right into the snow to
make them grip. Her leg muscles did not appreciate that,
but she didn't care, only wished she could move faster.
"Harrap!"

A breathless, blustering cry came in response, and as she
climbed the final stretch, she spied him, face and tonsured
scalp scarlet with exertion, his body crumpled against the
trail like a pile of dirty laundry. Even from here the bulge
and play of his shoulder and neck muscles was visible as
he thrust his hands against the snow to lift himself. "Harrap? Are you hurt? Where are the ghatti?" Now she began
to run, ignoring each throb in her joints, the way her feet
were beginning to hurt.

"Wedged tight!" he gasped in greeting, still struggling
and heaving with all his might. "Pinned in place like a bone
a dog refuses to yield!" She stroked his head, let her
twisted hand inconspicuously slide to check his pulse at
the neck. Steady but quick, nothing unexpected given his
exertions. "And no, I haven't a blessed idea where those
two have disappeared!"

Stretched on her stomach now, Mahafny hiked Harrap's
robe, grateful for the garish purple pantaloons beneath it
so he needn't die of mortification. Nothing she hadn't seen
before, but public exposure offended his sense of modesty.
Not that this mountain qualified as a public space! "Damnation! You're wedged tighter than a bottle cork!" It must
be painful, uncomfortable at the very least. Levering herself
onto her knees, she leaned on Harrap's shoulder and rose.

How to get him free? Parm's and Saam's inexplicable
disappearance would have to wait. One puzzle at a time.
"Do you think they're hurt? Frightened? My dear little
Parm!" In anguish he pounded the snow with both fists.
"If that green globe snatched them up, I'll—"

"Oh, hush, Harrap! Let me think! You think, as well, or
pray. Pray to your Lady that we can figure out how to free
you." Waspish as usual, but what did he expect—especially
when his wailing made her want to join in.

"Yes, Mahafny, think! Or I suppose you'll leave me here

till the hells freeze over. Not that I've far to go, since this whole journey has been a shortcut to the hells!"

"I am *not* going to leave you!" she snapped back, wincing internally. She'd left Diccon behind; no wonder Harrap assumed she'd show no more compunction than she had over the lad's plight. "But I swear I'll stuff my mitts in your mouth if you're going to thrash and moan and do nothing to help yourself." Circling Harrap, making sure she stepped completely over the fissure each time, she assessed the problem from all angles. "What I wouldn't give for a Plumb right about now," she said grimly and set to work.

♣

Parm gave a shivery wheeze of excitement as he scampered and scrabbled after Saam, priming his courage with such silent yet heartening comments as "Here we *go,* now!" and "*That* wasn't so bad!" It *was* bad at times—spiderwebby and noisome, close and confining—but he wasn't admitting that to himself, or to Saam. Oh, what a ghatt he was, still raring for adventure at Saam's call and, indeed, his ghatt senses seemed keener, heightened. Yessiree, together they'd find Diccon, make him whole again. A shiver rippled along his spine—a tad nippy without his lovely vest—and he hoped Harrap wouldn't be too alarmed when he found it, and his cozy cap, just cast aside like that. Oh, dear, what if Harrap thought something had caught him, stripped him before eating him!

Eyes wide in the dark, head craning so as not to miss a thing of interest—phew! . . . *that* explained the smell, bats, hundreds of wee, peach-fuzzy bats hanging in clusters like grapes—Parm saw enough sights that he had no chance to be scared. Truth was, he'd gotten soft living with dear Harrap, his Seeking days behind him, though occasionally they'd make minor forays into the secular world as real Seekers—halidays and suchlike, or filling in on a nearby circuit when a Seeker-Bond pair needed a few days' leave. Like the time young Tris had a nasty toothache. Life was comfortable, predictable, and placid with Harrap—though Parm worked assiduously to ensure that none of the moments grew *too* dull. And he *had* rather come to savor the Mystery

Chants, whether sung by the full choir at the Bethel or privately in Harrap's bedroom. Really, when he considered it—which he did oftener than most people credited him— Harrap's Lady and the ghatti Elders *did* boast certain similarities. And wouldn't the "whys" of that fill years of debate!

Hmm, downslope mostly, Saam padding along, neither fast nor slow. Trust a ghatt to conserve energy, no sense being prodigal. Unless he'd totally muddled his sense of direction, they were spiraling down into the mountain's heart, round and round and lower and lower. Ha—the reverse of the Spirals all ghatti traveled to reach the Elders and their font of all-wisdom, perplexing though it often was. That was truth for you. What had Saam remembered, figured out? Mayhap it had something to do with him having been here before, something he'd seen or heard, even secondhand. Be nice to know for sure, would let him help Saam more, but he was content to follow if it meant they'd find Diccon. Oh, don't let Harrap be *too* upset that he'd gone missing like that! Parm flicked his hooped earring, stomach hurting at the thought.

Dear Harrap! His and no others, so easy to pretend his previous Bonding had never existed and, in many ways, it hadn't—not after Georges' mind had turned. Couldn't accept hearing all the voices, he couldn't, though Parm had done his best to soothe and explain without explaining, revealing a truth that wasn't his to tell. Ghatti had known about Resonants forever, but saw no point in mentioning it to their bonds, especially when it had no bearing on their Truth-Seeking. Privacy was to be valued, after all.

Wha! Aa-choo! It came over him all sudden-like, the sneeze exploding out of him—that scent! Yes, he'd recognize it anywhere. Except . . . it was soft spring-scent and crisp autumn, frosty winter and sun-baked summer all rolled into one. Nose still scrunched from the tingling and tickling, he rammed it straight into Saam's private parts. Oh, dear, he hadn't realized Saam had halted, indeed, had sneezed into a very personal place! **"Sorry about that, old boy,"** he 'spoke with all the contrition he could summon. Better to use falanese in a secretive venture like this, all whisker and vibrissae twitches, eye-slants and ear shifts, but it didn't work very well single file.

"**Just stifle any more sneezes, Parm,**" Saam instructed, leaning hip and shoulder against the rock wall. "**Harrap's not here to pat your nose dry, and I'd appreciate it if, in the future, you wouldn't wipe it where you just did.**" Parm flinched at Saam's brusqueness, ears and whiskers wilting at the rebuke. "**Parm, I've too much on my mind. Sorry, old boy. But tell me, what can you sniff up ahead? Take it slow and easy, slide right by me and then stop about two ghatt-lengths from the opening.**"

Low on his belly, Parm sleeked ahead, saddened by how rough and unkempt Saam's fur felt against his. Not light ahead, but a lighter shade of dark, better air movement and an opening nicely sized to fit a ghatt. Compacting himself into an oblong loaf shape, paws folded directly under him, ready to spring and flee if the scent threatened, he took his time, nose high to test the air, weaving a pattern through the currents. A sample here, a sample there—test and compare. Familiar, yes. Sweetly familiar, Jenneth's youngling Bond, Pw'eek! That dainty, delectable calico, so curvaceously soft and plump! Shame on him for such lascivious thoughts—that's what came of feeling so young and lively and daring once more! And—he rationalized, only because it was truth—Harrap *did* need reminding about handing out Parm's contraceptive 'script at times. Just because his seed never caused any ghatta to bear ghatten didn't mean he lacked natural urges, and they required curbing—just like any other ghatt's. Harrap's solution—liberal applications of cold water to control similar human urges—was *not* appealing!

"**It's Pw'eek!**" he told Saam, though he suspected the ghatt sought confirmation, had already deduced the scent's identity. "**What's *she* doing here? I can't feel Jenneth or Kwee anywhere near, can you?**" A sudden itch made him yearn to scratch behind his ear, but he controlled it. "**Nor Diccon, alas.**"

But his question was answered as he heard a plaintive "Raow? Raow?" intermingled with "**Diccon? Come out, Diccon?**" Oh, how sweetly seductive she sounded! How could anyone resist, refuse those delicate, wistful come-hither cries? That darling white mustache under her two-toned nose, that lovely broad white bib, and such dainty white feet. Oh, the tortie-tiger Kwee was an absolute

charmer, too, but he couldn't resist a lovely calico, especially one decked in subtle gray and butterscotch and white,
the pastel version of his bold black and orange and white
splotches.

**"If you've finished mooning over her, you might try to
attract her attention without frightening her out of her
wits."** Saam's broad head now rested on Parm's rump, and
he could hear the tiredness in his old friend's mindvoice.

Politely edging from beneath Saam's head so his chin
didn't go thump on the ground, Parm crept closer to the
opening and *willed* her to sense their presence. The air
currents should have carried their scents to her, mingling
them with whatever other odors the passage contained. But
she might be so busy searching for Diccon that she'd discount what her nose told her, believing them far away by
now. Very unwise to ignore the truth, especially the truth
the eyes and ears, the nose and whiskers provided. That
was concrete truth, the best kind.

Ha! He could just glimpse her if he held his head just
so. She'd halted to lick her shoulder, then half-raised a hind
leg as she canted her head around—going to scratch behind
her ear, just as he'd longed to a moment before. But before
he could blink she loomed at the mouth of the opening,
skitter-toeing sideways, back arched, a daunting sight as a
white paw lashed within, nearly striping his nose. Instinctively he jerked clear, only to smash into Saam.

**"Don't you play games with me!"** she spat. **"Making
scents that I know and love, tricking me into believing what
isn't there! I am Pw'eek the Brave! You give me Diccon
back right now or I'll rip you to ribbons!"** She continued
to block the opening, rearing to slash the air with both
forepaws. Oh, rapture—that broad, lovely, lily-white belly!

**"Pw'eek, tender Pw'eek. It *is* old Saam—and Parm.
We've come to find Diccon. Your strength, your youth,
your courage can aid us."** Still attempting to put himself to
rights after his tumble, Parm admired Saam's easy way with
the ghattas. **"May we venture out? Or would you prefer to
come in and join us?"**

**"Really dear Saam? And my jester-calico Parm? Toss
out Parm's cap and prove it!"** Ho, this ghatta would accept
nothing on face value, not even sweet talk. What a wise,
canny, voluptuous creature she was!

"Can't, youngling. I made Parm take them off before we left. One shouldn't attempt such a serious task, fraught with danger, and be forced to meet the Elders sporting a knitted vest and cap! With a pom-pom, no less!" All the time Saam had been creeping nearer, until at last he gingerly stuck his head through the opening. Almost in wonder and in awe, Pw'eek greet-sniffed his cheeks, his nose, his mouth. "Didn't bring my blanket either," he noted a bit sadly, apparently missing its warmth. "Why are you exploring on your own, my intrepid ghatta?"

Sliding in beside Saam and ahead of Parm, she rotated her majestic bulk in an impossibly small space to snuggle tight against Saam. Silently blessing her acumen, Parm did the same against Saam's other side; together they'd cozy Saam between them, they would! "Jenneth and Kwee are too affected by their emotions, not thinking clearly, sorrowing over Diccon. But I am Pw'eek. I know what it's like to be afraid, and what it's like to be brave. So I must find Diccon for *both* my beloveds—and I will!"

"Would you consider joining us on the hunt, then?" Parm thrummed with joy at Saam's invitation. Relief, as well. How long Saam could continue, he didn't know. The ghatt possessed deep inner resources—and all without a taste of Mahafny's pernicious drug—but at some point that determination would waver, mayhap even flicker out completely, and Parm would have to decide what to do: continue searching for Diccon, or return aboveground and inform Harrap and Mahafny that Saam had died. Neither was a very palatable thought.

She considered, neatening her white paws with her tongue while she thought. "Only if I have first strike at that nasty, fuzzy green light! Going to shred it so badly it'll think it's hedge clippings. May I, wise Saam? And clever Parm?" The story of his life with the ghattas, forever an afterthought in their fickle minds!

He permitted himself a light doze, the others' breathing reassuring him that they did likewise, each absorbed in private musings. It was a necessary part of ghatti protocol, an opportunity to recover their presence, their inherent wholeness, each similar yet so very different. If only they could find a way to restore that gift of wholeness to Diccon!

♣

The green-gold globe gave a tentative bounce, wavering over what it might do next. Attempting a trial foray here, another there, it halfheartedly tried to coax the older woman and the man stuck in the crevice into noticing it again, but they acted oblivious to its presence, too involved in their business—and their bickering—to play. It rapidly brightened and faded, brightened and faded, but still no one paid the least attention. Spook the ponies again? No, it had already done that—and besides, ponies were so utterly predictable. Booor-ing!

Spinning up the concavity the wind had cored into a snowdrift, it slid back down, amusing itself with that. If Nakum had returned, mayhap they could play snow-snakes. That was fun! Wait until Nakum tossed his stick down the slick channel of snow and ice, and then disrupt its passage, snatch it like a dog grabbing a stick and running! It'd only played that once with Nakum before the Erakwan had given up, puzzled as to why his sticks had constantly jumped the channel or collided against its sides. But it could feel Nakum's continued absence.

Play with the arborfer since Nakum wasn't there? Their tiny needles were pricklish-nice and smelled so pleasant. It liked to swirl around them and rub itself with their scent, a harmless pastime, though on occasion it accidentally bruised a branch. What oozed forth was pure ecstasy! Caressing the arborfer would occupy some time, but it needed something more stimulating than that!

Oh, yes, yes! That was it! Why hadn't it noticed before? People were climbing toward Nakum's mountain peak from the west! A green-gold shimmer of excitement seized it, set it pulsating, expanding. Yes?. . . ah, no . . . and it deflated—Erakwa—not much fun. Generally they caught on to its tricks too quickly—Nakum had been an exception, too distracted by his duties to realize, think back on the old tales. That, and it'd been extra-cautious about exposing itself in any form. Ah—wait! Someone—very similar to the ones it had just startled—toiled up the slopes in the midst of the Erakwa. As well as another, Erakwan ways intermingled with Outlander ways, uncomfortable with both, clashing. Those two might harbor potential, rise to its bait.

Chirping encouragement to itself, the green-gold globe dampered its energy, conserving it, and began to spin, floating on occasion, for the sheer joy of it. Whee! Ee-ee-aa-WOO! Bounce and spin, trick and tease, shake up this stolid world. Better than meekly returning to the world within and having Doncallis tether it there, fading away from lack of excitement. Ee-ee-aa-WOO!

❖

Diccon walked with Doncallis through meadowland, their shoulders and, occasionally, knuckles, brushing companionably. Boldly, Diccon interwove his fingers with hers, and when she didn't withdraw, he let their joined hands swing. A rightness to it, as if he'd been joined not only to her but to the essence of the natural world, her hand a conduit to all that the grasses and the soil, the sun and the breeze, the blackberry brambles and the furzy-headed orange and yellow blossoms on impossibly long, pliant stems were thinking and feeling. No, not exactly that, what they were *being*.

Words were unnecessary, not when this new essence expanded the very core of His very being, and She graciously shared with Him something as essential, as life sustaining as water to a thirst-crazed man. He could live here forever, even longer, and remain content, His soul and spirit nourished. Thrushes warbled a chain of liquid notes amongst the bushes, and an errant swallowtail butterfly hovered beside Her shoulder, Her very presence nectar-sweet and nourishing.

Odd, though, those green-gold eyes gleaming at the meadow's edge, two pairs low, one pair higher, ensconced in a chestnut tree adorned with waxy white, candlelike blossoms. Not disturbing, precisely, a part of this unity, and yet their presence called to Him in a way that subtly unsettled His equilibrium, His sense of rightness. At first He'd assumed Her companion, the greenish-gold light had returned with its brethren, poised for some naughty action, though He sincerely hoped it didn't involve any more pinching!

Now She led Him by the hand to a plum tree, not tall but with a multitude of fanning branches, each loaded with

plums of a deep, purplish blue beneath a whitish coating
of dust. Touch one gently, rub a thumb against it, and the
blue-purple skin shone. Even without tasting one, He
judged their deep golden flesh to be honey-sweet but not
cloying. Did He dare pick one?

As if in answer, She took His hands and cupped them,
filling them with plums until no more could be piled in His
mounded hands. Raising laden hands, He sniffed the fruit,
touched them against His cheek with reverence. Retrieving
one, She buffed it against Her doeskin sleeve, admiring its
midnight skin, holding it high, then low, turning it this way
and that in supple, coppery fingers. His eyes followed its
movement, entranced, as if She presented the fruit to the
sun, the air, the very land itself. Bringing it to Her mouth,
She bit into it to reveal its golden flesh, a hint of rich red
separating skin from flesh. He swallowed hard, tasting it
through Her, savoring the sweetness on His tongue, like
a kiss.

Now She held it toward Him, and He opened his mouth,
tremulously expectant as a baby bird waiting to be fed. But
before it touched His lips, a voice intruded.

**"Callis. That isn't wise. You're forgetting yourself, for-
getting who he is."** An ancient creature with blue-gray fur,
shabby and moth-eaten, rubbed against Her shins, its muzzle wrinkled in concern. **"You're lost in the moment, as
you so often are, but Diccon mustn't be allowed to be lost
as well. His time is more finite than yours. That is the way
of things in the outside world."**

Oh, how He despised this creature, this catlike beast who
did and yet did not belong here! The plum wavered in front
of His mouth, was reluctantly withdrawn. "I want it!" he
shouted, shocked at how his petulant cry marred the world
around him, how it began to splinter and fragment. "Let
me taste it, please!" How could that creature do it?—act
more cruel and callous than the green-gold globe had ever
been with all its pinching and poking!

An incredible gift, nearly within his reach, his taste, bru-
tally ripped away, a taste that had promised consummation,
sealing him to this world—shattering, disintegrating before
his eyes! Glowering, he scattered all the plums he'd cupped
and lunged for Her hand, determined to snatch this one

tempting fruit and cram it in his mouth. But no matter how quickly he moved, Her hand and its prize eluded him.

"**Greedy**," a voice chided. "**Diccon, please! Think! Listen!**"

Think? Listen? Greedy? Let Diccon—whomever *he* was—obey, do what the creature asked, because He was not about to comply! He longed to wail like a babe pulled from its mother's breast, sated, no longer craving nourishment but fighting against such separation. How could He be denied like this when He needed it so? "**Diccon? Diccon beloved,**" this voice came soft and caring, caressing, as another of the creatures reared on hind legs and began to knead her paws against his hip—push-flex, push-flex. Ah, she knew as well what it was like. "**Diccon? What of your twinsib, your Bond? What of Jenneth? Kwee?**"

Sobbing, he threw himself full-length on the grass, pounding his fists, mourning all that was lost, rejoicing in what now remained—reality. A sister closer than his heart, a Bondmate whose blithesome spirit matched his own. "Ah, Jen, my love! Ah, Kwee!" Always a touch of hurt would remain, but his loved ones would balm it with their caring.

# PART
# FIVE

Eyes widening as he stumbled out the doorway, Diccon steadied himself against the opposite wall and watched, bewildered, as his hand sank through, minute stone particles, powder-fine and compressed by the weight of ages, glistening within a shadowy outline of skin and bones. It made his stomach heave, his head dizzy, to realize he'd turned insubstantial, worn away to nothingness, and he crumpled into a sitting position as Callis and the three ghatti followed him from the darkness.

Rubbing his eyes—a relief to discover his fingers didn't inadvertently poke through his eye sockets and prod his brain!—he struggled to peer inside the entrance, but it swallowed his vision, reflected no light, just shimmering dark. "But why? I don't under—" and choked back a shriek, because the woman who folded herself beside him on the ground, far more gracefully than he'd done, was *old*. And come to think on it, *how* could he even see her . . . or Saam . . . or Parm . . . or Pw'eek? Not when he couldn't even see his hand in front of his face! He tested again, just to be sure. It was there, but barely so.

"Don't take it so to heart." A reassuring hand on his knee. "Mayhap some of the ghatti's traits are rubbing off on you." A longish pause as he pondered a response. "That was *supposed* to be humorous," Doncallis chided. "Here, mayhap this will help." A sound of hands being briskly rubbed together and an indistinct glow illuminated the cave. Yes, arms, legs, torso, all visible, except that striations in the stone floor, pebbles, also showed through his legs, faintly distorted, like looking through shallow water to the bottom of a pond. No darting minnows, at least!

What the light revealed left him even weaker with wonder and astonishment. "I don't understand!" This time it came out unbidden. "I'm translucent as parchment, and a moment ago you were . . . and now you're . . ." he waved a feeble hand, unable to encompass the enormity of it all. Should he say it? Did she *know* that once she'd stepped over that threshold she'd turned old?

**"Gotten yourself into a pretty pickle, haven't you?"** Parm stretched across Diccon's ankles and the ghatt's solidity felt reassuringly real, though Parm appeared to float on a cushion of air. **"Fairly sure she knows, but you can check with Saam to be sure. It's camouflage of a sort, at least that's how I view it. Look deeper, look within and you'll see her as she was before. Just as there's still a young ghatt in Saam—and in me. Of course even then I played the fool, another disguise—when the world jested about my markings, I became their jester."**

Needing to touch something solid, he gathered Pw'eek and settled her on his lap, listening to the mounting intensity and volume of her purr. *"How is she? How's my sweedling, your Sissy-Poo? And my Jenneth?"* He wanted to know, badly, but before she could respond with more than an extra-loud MMMR-mmmr, Doncallis began to speak.

"Yes, I'm old, though not nearly as old as these rocks, as this mountain surrounding us. Does my name mean anything to you now, Diccon—Doncallis? Callis, for short." Limping, Saam crawled into her lap and she rubbed with exquisite tenderness along his jawline and behind each ear, over and over, until he half-swooned, replete with satisfaction.

A deep breath. "Of course. You're Addawanna's grandmother, Nakum's great-great-grandmother. Mama's told us about you." But if she were *that* old, shouldn't she look even older?

"Old and worn as the hills, you mean?" And this time he laughed with her at his naïveté, although his throat was rusty. "Not quite, but almost. We Erakwa don't age along the same time line as you do."

"But how'd I . . . how'd you . . . ?" Easier not to finish a sentence, because to voice his thoughts made them even more implausible. Instead, he stared hard at the door with a certain fascinated loathing. He couldn't remember passing through it, though he must have. Couldn't remember at all! He and Kwee had explored, but they'd returned to the cave, gone to sleep with everyone else—Jenneth and Auntie Mahafny and Harrap, the ghatti and the ponies. *That* he could recollect with surety, but beyond that, nothing. It was like suffering a blow on the head, and he gingerly touched his skull for lumps or soft, spongy spots. Nothing.

Perfectly at ease on the floor, Callis indulged Saam by dangling a strip of her doeskin fringe within striking distance. "Your Kwee was truly clever to discover the doorway, sense that you'd passed through. If I hadn't felt the draft from the open door, it would have taken me much longer to locate you." Saam gave the fringe a bat, rolled on his shoulder to employ both front paws. "And equally wise of Jenneth to hold back, not enter. If she had, I'd have been searching in different directions for each of you."

"I was lost, then?" Distinctly more daring, he pressed her. "Then where did you find me? And how come you were one person inside, and now you're another outside, out here?"

**"Not very tactfully put,"** said Saam, never taking his eyes off the enticing fringe.

A certain chagrin wrinkled her brow. "Don't you remember *anything*?" Scrutinizing his puzzled demeanor, she relented. "Once, long, long ago, long before time was time as we know it . . ." It sounded like stories Mama had told them, but they had always begun 'Once upon a time.' "Deep within the heart of the outer world is the world within—the world as it was, as it is, as it will be forever—I hope. Any season and all seasons, whatever you wish it to be. You *did* miss the walking trees, though, and quite a few other notable sights. The arborfer tend to be reticent. But you've seen far more of the world within than most of your people ever glimpse. Even dear old Constant couldn't manage more than a look or two at a time. Said it discombobulated him—isn't that a lovely word?"

Was it possible? Had Callis really befriended Constant I, Marchmont's first king, one of the original spacers? And Mama had sworn that she'd met not only Callis, but Constant, though Jen and he had always suspected Mama'd stretched the truth about Constant, the kind of stretching that tale-telling encouraged. Add an outrageous flourish

here, another there—why Uncle Arras did it with a perfectly straight face! Even the ghatti didn't mind such embel-
lishments, as long as it didn't involve one of their Major
Tales.

"Sometimes I can be as young as the world is . . . was
back then. But it's confusing to look that way out here.
Confusing and a little sad, as if I clash with it. So I remain
the same within, but outwardly different."

"But you're still an incredibly handsome woman!" he
blurted, and it was true. "You wear your experience lightly
on your face and form, not bowed beneath it like so many
old people."

She continued stroking Saam, running her hands down
his body from his ears to the base of his spine. While he
wouldn't have believed human hands could accomplish it,
her stroking had the same effect as a ghatt's grooming
tongue, Saam gradually looking sleeker, slicker, his blue-
gray coat taking on a luster too long absent. His bones still
protruded, the way he held himself still told of aches and
age, but Diccon could once more *see* the courageous,
selfless ghatt who'd given so much to his Bondmate and to
those whom he and his Bond had loved—himself included.
Parm had been right! A crackle of static sparked through
Saam's fur.

"Is your . . . fuzzy green light-thing coming back?" He'd
been watching out of the corners of his eyes, afraid it might
sneak up on him again. That still puzzled him—hadn't exactly liked it, hadn't exactly disliked it. And apparently destined to remain forever ignorant of what it was.

"Would you like me to summon it? Assuming it obeys?"
Callis's smile puckered, as if she'd tasted something sour.
"I let myself wander too long in the world within. Didn't
realize it had been accidentally loosed on your world. Mayhap wouldn't have realized at all if I hadn't finally heard
Addawanna calling me to look for it. Given Nakum's
grumpiness before, I should have put two and two together—"

"And gotten what?" he interrupted, bouncing Pw'eek in
his lap as he sat up straighter. "What *is* that little thing? It
could use some discipline and training, whatever it is. A
piddling puppy exhibits better manners! I swear it was
downright malicious at times—pinching and twisting me."

Rolling up his sleeve he stretched out his arm to show her, and now couldn't find a mark on it. "Still hurt like the blazes," he insisted.

"But it didn't really mean to." Callis fell silent, studying the top of Saam's head, licking a thumb to sleek his eye whiskers. "Oh, tosh!" she exploded. "I wish Constant were here to explain. I simply accept it for what it *is*. He could find the right words to tag it, though not tame it." Tapping her lower lip, she sat in silence a while longer, making umphing sounds to herself, sounding exactly like her grand-daughter, Addawanna, caught in the coils of a dilemma.

"I think the right word—in your people's tongue—might be Trickster. Though it isn't inherently bad or evil. Some-times this world—this world of now that your people in-habit so uneasily with nature—sends too many conflicting messages, awakens it, releases enough energy to invigorate it. It feeds on those conflicts and confusions, the disorder that threatens the earth and its brother and sister elements. And it has to release that energy—somehow.

"It likes to lure people along after it, play games and tricks on them. If there are no people near, it'll tease ani-mals or birds, tickle trout. The more it discombobulates *them,* the stronger it glows and grows. And the stronger it becomes, the more tricks it wants to play. It can shape itself any way it wants to, whatever it thinks will best serve to attract the unwary. And what this means," she gave a heartfelt sigh, "is that the land is in more trouble than I realized. This disturbance must be halted, and to do that, we must figure out what ails the earth and cure it. It may be only worry, a foreboding right now, but I've a sense far worse has already come to pass."

"Can it be stopped?" Did he mean the trouble or the "it"? A crystal-clear answer would be nice, but he sus-pected he wouldn't receive one, couldn't expect it for being so murky himself. That was the problem with being an adult, reckoning all the shades of gray. "Once I take Aunt Mahafny and Saam to the top of your mountain, find Nakum—I could help. Jen and Pw'eek and Kwee and I would be glad to." It would be nice to help this elderly Erakwan woman in return for what she'd done for him. "Jenneth! Lady bless, I've got to go find her and the others! How long was I with you, anyway?" He fingered the whisker stubble on his cheek and chin, more than he could remember upon going to bed. Mayhap he didn't need to shave *that* often, but this felt like major growth!

**"It's not long enough to braid and tie with ribbons— yet,"** Parm chimed in as he flowed off Diccon's ankles.

As Pw'eek scrambled from his lap, he rose, then bent on one knee in front of Callis. "I thank you. For many things." Hands out in supplication, he hesitated. "I should take Saam with me, you know. Auntie Mahafny'll be in a bad way with him gone." At her nod he slipped his arms under Saam and lifted, sadness sweeping over him at how light, almost insubstantial the old ghatt had become; he weighed next to nothing. A perfect match for a translucent person, more spirit than substance. "Will you come with me?"

"Afraid they won't believe you, otherwise?" At his shamefaced nod she hooked a hand in the crook of his elbow and lightly regained her feet. "I think Saam and Parm might prove evidence enough. But I'll join forces with you—for a time."

"In real time? Or in a time before time was time as we know it?" he teased, his relief clear.

"However it runs, I shall be there. One way or another."

"Good!" How could he have forgotten about Jen and Kwee? Spent so much time asking questions? They must be worried sick about him! "Jen! Jennie? I'm back! Where are you? Give me a yell, twinsis!" Even at a distance, physically and mentally, he could sense that little twisted worry mark in her mind that was, and would always be, an indelible part of Jenneth's mental signature. But his reassuring cry lacked the power to carry, drifted aimless as mist, though he'd plainly heard himself addressing Callis. Had he no real voice in this form, no way to address the outer world?

"Best go in silence, lad. Don't you remember? Part of you remains with them and part of you journeyed. Now the two pieces must be joined. You must reenter yourself before you enter their world, their minds." Holding up a forestalling hand, she began to rummage in her waist pouch. "Here. A small souvenir," and slipped a plum pit into his hand, folding his fingers around it. "Now go, but softly."

Saam safe in his arms, he hurried on, Parm and Pw'eek

gamboling and mock-fighting at his heels, and behind them—still casting a fulgent light that reached ahead, guiding him—came Doncallis. His final thought as he dashed back toward the cave was, "Why a plum pit? What's Callis hinting at?" A nice memento, in a way, though he'd still much rather have tasted one of those luscious fruits. But wasn't a plum pit the promise of rebirth, renewal, new growth? Within it was compressed the best of earth and sky and water and growth—a promise of the future. Lady bless him! If Jen heard him going all fanciful like that, she'd *never* believe it was him!

❧

Jenneth awoke with a start, groggy, balking at sorting out such crucial details as where she was and why. Stone walls, solid, not brick and mortar, the work of builders, but the work of nature. Coolish but not damp, and minimal light, merely dim brightness from behind her, along with a draft of fresh air. Ponies and their drowsy sounds. Clutching the blanket, she tried to calm her racing heart, unmuddle her thoughts.

And didn't much like what she recollected as the pieces interlocked, creating a repugnant picture that made sense, matched her surroundings. Diccon, her precious twinsib, his body so still, not dead, but not exactly alive. Auntie Mahafny and Harrap, gone—with regret, to be sure—but focused on finding Nakum, saving Saam. Pw'eek?

She sat up, too fast, groping for Pw'eek, fully expecting to touch her warm solidity. Usually the ghatta cuddled close, but sometimes during the night she'd roll on her back, all four legs akimbo, sprawled to her fullest. "Airing her lily belly," as she fondly referred to it. *"Pw'eek? Where are you, love? Time to wake up."*

Pw'eek's answer came from a distance. **"Coming, beloved! I'm awake, don't fret!"** Stretching across Diccon's legs, she grabbed her collapsible lantern and lit the candle stub within, the hand with the lucifer still shaky from her earlier confusion. She'd slept beside Diccon, spooned against him in the intimate way they'd had since childhood, her stockinged feet near his chest, his feet near hers.

Nightmares had knotted her sleep, made her feel she'd slept too heavily and yet gotten little real rest. The previous night she'd barely slept at all, alert at Diccon's side, alternating between a hawklike watch on the crevice she'd explored with Kwee and an intent scrutiny of her brother's immobile form, alert for his slightest stirring. But last night, despite her best intentions, she'd fallen asleep—when, she couldn't judge—and made a poor job of it, even her dereliction a failure. Why hadn't darling Pw'eek chased away the nightmares last night? Sleep was peaceful with Pw'eek beside her, separating the "seeming" of dreams and nightmares from reality.

Braced on one fist so as not to press her full weight on Diccon, she held the lantern high. *"Pw'eek, sweetheart. Hurry up! I'll get the trail mix!"* What could have lured Pw'eek from her side? Her fingers wanted to caress the familiar, thick plush of her fur, touch each butterscotch daub on her gray flank.

Pw'eek finally materialized—from the crevice, of all places—and Jenneth's breath caught. What had her darling been thinking of, investigating on her own like that! What if she'd stumbled through that horrible opening into nothingness? Neither she nor Kwee had quite dared return, had even avoided mentioning it, hoping the open door would allow the absent part of Diccon to return to them, drawn by their hope, their presence. But nothing had happened . . . and probably never would.

*"How dare you go looking on your own?"* she scolded as Pw'eek bounded to her side, surprisingly playful. *"And without a word to me or Kwee! What if something dreadful happened to you?"* Even the mere thought of it was too much to endure, another desertion, so soon after Diccon's.

**"Beloved, we've company. Look around you, look at Diccon."** She'd avoided doing that since she'd awakened, unable to stand the unvarying sight, so depressingly the same, time suspended, static—his stillness, the bare flutter of a shallow respiration, face as pale as chiseled marble. Touching him was much the same.

"Who? Where?" Had someone, some *thing,* slipped in during the night? More rattled than she cared to admit, she swung the lantern wide, wishing she could illuminate the entire cave and scan it for anything new. As she'd expected,

Kwee, sleepily murmurous beside Dic's neck, tucked a paw over an eye to bar the intrusive light. But, but . . . it couldn't be! How? Parm lay stretched along Diccon's left side, head on her brother's shoulder, feet lightly planted against him. And then the blanket began to hump with wormlike movements until a steel-gray head popped out—Saam!

"Mahafny? Auntie? Harrap?" Had they returned during the night? Where were they now? Outside, mayhap. A foot tickled her ribs, stockinged toes twitching and prodding. "Ged'off, Sis," Diccon grumbled, muzzy with sleep. "Pinching my leg. An' stop bellowing—some of us . . . tryin' ta sleep!" Rolling off his legs as if they burned, she stared, transfixed, as he wriggled his legs and heaved a contented sigh, one arm rising to embrace Kwee.

**"Mahafny and Harrap aren't here."** Pw'eek bestowed a morning nose-kiss on Jenneth before nestling at Diccon's knees. **"Just Saam and Parm. And someone else we think you should meet."** Her usual woebegone expression had turned sleekly smug—and anticipatory. **"You *did* mention breakfast? Even Saam's admitted he's a bit peckish after all our work."**

♣

"Well, you squalled like a baby when I suggested pouring boiling water into the fissure to melt the ice," Mahafny sounded distinctly frosty to Harrap as she handed him a tin cup, "so rather than waste it, I made cha."

So she had, and hadn't filtered it very well, either, as Harrap morosely watched the leaves floating on the surface. Dusk, thick, fleecy clouds rouged a rosy bronze, Mahafny equally rouged and ruddy, aglow with false color, false health. Patience, he counseled himself. She's upset—about me, about Saam and Parm. Well, so was he, on both counts. Mahafny's eumedico training gave no security in this predicament; frankly, he'd steeled himself for a blunt announcement that enough was enough, and she'd take up a scalpel and amputate his leg. Then she'd tidily bandage the stump, somehow boost him stomach-down on a pony, and go hunting for their two runaway rascals.

Distrustful of how she held her own too-hot cha cup near the fissure, he cast her a look of mute supplication. She wouldn't—would she? Except Mahafny expected to have her own way. "If you pour it, you'll scald my leg. And it's getting colder as night falls, so any melted ice will refreeze almost immediately, shape itself to my leg, immobilize me like a cast." Without a doubt he'd be frozen here for eternity; snow this high in the mountains never completely melted each summer. Hadn't Arras and Nakum told of finding—not just bones—but the intact bodies of long-ago creatures, frozen beasts no one recognized, could identify? Or had that been farther north in the Cumulonims? Please, Lady, let it be so!

"More cha?" Her eyebrows arched in eager inquiry, enough to turn him suspicious, raise his guard. Always a reason behind her cajolery, an ulterior motive. "What? You're planning on making my bladder balloon, and then— when I can't hold it anymore—I'll have to pee on the ice! Am I right?" How shameful!

She cocked her head, considering, then shared a sheepish smile with him. "Well, I'd not thought of that, but at least it has the true virtue of not scalding. However, I assume urine would ultimately freeze, and we'd have gained nothing. Not to mention marring the snow, staining it yellow." A crooked finger tapped against her lower lip, her eyes distant.

Slumping, he shivered in earnest despite the cha, his leg hanging heavy as a cord of wood, pain pummeling it with each throbbing heartbeat. Leave her to think, she possessed a logical, incisive mind, more so than he. What *he* did best was pray, so he did. Ask forgiveness, as always, implore Her for release. And, most urgent of all, pray that Saam and Parm were alive and well. Where had they gone? What could have made the two desert like that?

*Blessed Lady, I am not afraid to die, not with the hope of joining You for all eternity, if I am fit to sit at Your feet. If not in this life, mayhap in another, if that be Your will, instead. But do You really want a Shepherd laid out like a cold cut on a chilled platter? Dignity's never been mine to have, can't usually carry it off, but this is too much. And if You decide to lift me to Your world, please spare a thought for Mahafny and Saam and Parm. . . .*

Prayers as blundering as his feet had been, the Mystery Chants beyond him—oh, he'd made a total hash of things! A heavy-lidded child murmuring prayers against its mother's side as she turned down the bedding made better sense to the Lady than he did . . . murmuring prayers . . . murmur. . . .

When he came to himself again, acknowledging and blessing the world he still inhabited—might always physically inhabit, given that his leg was between its jaws—the sun had set and Mahafny was tucking another blanket around his shoulders. "I've an idea, Harrap," she confided as she packed warmed stones around him. Holding one between his mittened hands, he rejoiced at its warmth. "I'll try not to be away too long."

"Where are you going?" It hurt to ask, hurt to know that *he* wasn't going anywhere in the foreseeable future. Rats in traps and ghatts in caps . . . *"Oh, Parm! Where are you?"* his mind and heart wailed.

She'd stripped patient, gray Willy of his pack gear and now awkwardly mounted, mindful not to brandish her torch too near his head. It flickered on the hatchet hung from her belt, shadowed the coil of rope over her shoulder into an impossible thickness. "There's a downed tree some ways back—puny, but about all I've seen of any size. Don't know if I can pry it free of the snow and ice, but I plan to try."

"And then what?" Apprehension overrode any hope he might once have harbored. Far easier to accept his fate, be done with it.

"Going to pry you free, Harrap." She shifted impatiently, itchy to be off, abandon him to his bleak thoughts. "I don't have the strength to pull you out, and the ponies can't drag you out, not without hurting you worse. Likely to break your leg—or pop the fissure wide open, make half the mountain teeter and fall." A dry cough at her own humor. "But mayhap—if the tree's strong enough—I can pry you out."

It made sense—of a sort—except for one thing. "It'll need to be long, then," he mused. "Longer it is, the easier for you." Which meant that . . . His chin, sunken on his chest, shot up as he twisted around, groaning. "Are you daft, woman! That'll put you right at the edge! Let the lever slip, take one wrong step and you'll go over—I can't

let you do it! Not endanger yourself for me!" *Yes, Lady,
I'll be along sooner than expected—if You'll have me. Better
me than Mahafny. You'd like her—in time—but she does
take getting used to . . .*

"Wasn't planning to." Clapping her heels against Willy,
she set him to picking his way along the trail, swinging her
torch to light their way. "Planning on letting the ponies do
the work—and not near the edge," she shouted and was
gone, the wobbling torch his final sight of her.

Well, at least he'd have something to puzzle over while
he waited. "So tell me, Jester," he conversationally addressed the black pony, "how goes the world with you?"
Not Parm, but he'd talk at it, to it, as long as he could
speak, make himself stay awake, invent Jester's responses
if he must. He'd been at the brink of giving up, giving in,
but he'd hold on a while longer. It was always worth it for
one of Mahafny's surprises.

♣

Knuckles puffy, fingers blue with cold, Mahafny clenched
them and willed herself to complete her task. Nasty scrape
on the back of her hand, ought to bandage it, a part of her
nagged, but she faced another, more imperative, undertaking. Instead, she rechecked the segment of tree trunk now
supported by Willy's and Jester's backs, and soothed Jester,
stiffly bending to plant a kiss on his broad forehead. Would
kiss his nether end if it would help!

Chest slumped against the trunk, his arms loosely draped
across it, Harrap's cheek lay on the rough bark, too weary
to hold up his head without support. In the chancy light of
the fire and the makeshift torches she'd lit and stuck into
the snow, she could see the sweat streaming down his broad
face, fever compounded by fruitless exertion. What his leg
felt like—if any feeling at all existed—didn't bear thinking about.

Too damn long! Everything had taken too damn long,
and the longer things dragged, the slimmer her chance of
success. Worrying at a shred of ripped knuckle skin, she
nipped it with her teeth and spat it out. *Her* success! Nothing on this bootless quest had been a success thus far! Harrap's survival, his ultimate freedom—*that* would be success!

The tree, a paltry thing, its trunk's diameter no thicker than the breadth of her palm, had been lodged in the snow, and she'd dug and burrowed, pried at it like a madwoman. Chop its limbs, amputate them and leave them frozen in place—no need for them. It had been, in hindsight, rather like the reverse of filleting a fish—instead of removing ribs, the branches, she'd been intent on excising the backbone. Hack at the ice glazing it, now angle each stroke inward, but try—try desperately—not to sink the blade into the trunk itself. Harness Willy to the trunk and drive him forward, the beast straining as she listened for the complaining crack and pop that indicated a break in the icy grip. Halt Willy, run back and hack some more. Repeat again, and again, until she'd claimed the trunk as hers. Then up the trail, weaving with weariness, half-draped over Willy to stay upright.

Back to Harrap's side, waking him with stinging blows to his face, afraid he'd lost consciousness. More cha, impatiently waiting for the water to boil while she fed and watered the ponies, cozening them with sweet talk and sugar lumps, stroking their manes, brushing their forelocks out of their eyes. She liked horses and ponies well enough, but had never seen the need to lavish them with love, except for what these two beasts had already endured and with worse yet to come. Whether her scheme worked depended on the ponies, their docility, their obedience. Half-drag, half-lead an edgy Jester through the gap between Harrap and the cliff face and position him on the other side, praise him. Now position Willy parallel to his stablemate on Harrap's other side. Somehow convince first one pony, then the other to kneel, noses practically snubbed against the wall, her cursing, slapping at cannons and pasterns while she clung one-handed on bridles to bow their heads. Finally, the icy trunk, all gashes and gouges, its branch nubs sticky and pungent with pitch, is laid across their pack saddles, directly in front of Harrap.

"We'll try it again. Harrap—are you listening?" Damn the man for not clinging to the trunk when she ordered the ponies to rise! Of course he was tired, but that was no excuse! True, it wouldn't lift him as much as she'd like, wouldn't jerk him clear of the fissure, but it ought to raise him enough to maneuver his leg clear. "Down, Willy!

There's a boy. Jester, down!" Protesting, shaking their heads, they obeyed. Now, trunk in place?—yes. "Harrap? Are you ready? Hang on for dear life! If you let go, I swear I'll—" The "what" drifted tantalizingly beyond her reach. Sit down and cry, very possibly. His face registered mute protest, but he wedged his chest tight to the trunk, hanging on to whatever knobs and branch stubs came to hand. "Up! Up, Willy, Jester!"

"I can't do it, I can't hold on!" Harrap sobbed, slumping back, earthbound, landlocked, his hands sliding free as the trunk rose. This final failure bore a perverse similarity to observing a drowning man abandon his attempts to save himself and resignedly settle into the sea, ready—even eager—to embrace death simply to end all pain and effort. The ponies acted equally dejected and forlorn as she wrestled the pole off their backs and leaned its length against the cliff face.

Picking her way to Harrap, she straddled his hunched form and bent, gripping his shoulders. An impulse to collapse on top of him swept over her, and she fought it, both in mind and body. Damn, like it or not, it was time for another dose of *thebie,* way past time, or she couldn't continue, would yield to the futility of it all. Mayhap it would clear her mind, sharpen it enough to devise some novel approach, outlandish enough to succeed. "Harrap, old friend, easy, easy!" and rubbed the heels of her hands across his rigid shoulder and neck muscles. Much the same as gentling the ponies and—hating herself for the thought—wondering about slipping him a sugar lump. "Somehow or other, we'll unstick you, old friend! Just rest easy, now. I'll be back in a flash." A brusque pat on his back and she left, stumbling, trembling, avid for the drug now that the hunger burned at the forefront of her brain, consuming all other thoughts.

Whimpering sounds leaked from between her lips and she prayed Harrap couldn't hear, didn't fathom what she was doing. How shameful to turn, find him staring his silent reproach at such craven weakness. Well, what choice was there, dammit? Either this or keel over beside him! The wax seal incredibly brittle, the paper packet stiff, her fingers even more so, and she groaned with longing as flecks of powder scattered invisibly on the snow. Dry work to down it, but she did, snatching an ice sliver, less than fastidious about its cleanliness, just yearning for the melting moisture in her mouth. Give some *thebie* to Harrap? Do so without his knowledge, his blessing, simply to ensure his survival, regain enough strength to participate in his own rescue?

One dose for him meant one less for her, and greed near overwhelmed her at the idea of relinquishing her prop, her aid. A deep, shuddering exhale as the *thebie* trickled into her system, another shuddering breath as she considered sharing with Harrap. Lady strike her dead, no! That she could even have entertained the thought for the briefest moment showed how far gone she'd been. Harrap'd beg her to drive one of her scalpels through his heart, end it all right here, rather than risk arousing his dormant addiction! Saam or Parm would have argued that immediately, almost before the shadow of the thought had formed. No matter how good her intentions, she would *not* bear the responsibility of setting that drug loose in an innocent soul unable to fight off the craving.

As the drug seized body and brain, she thrilled at the heady rush, her mind burning brighter, burning off the dross of exhaustion, her footsteps more precise, no longer dragging, the constant ache in her joints not exactly fading, but becoming bearable, something she could ignore or work through. Should rest now, sit and take stock till the exhilaration, the rush and roar stabilized, but she ignored her own advice, pacing to check the ponies, examining her contrivance from all angles while her mind raced from plan to plan, calculating the easiest, fastest way to loose Harrap from the mountain's maw. Ha! Mayhap Harrap should wiggle his toes, tickle the mountain's tonsils—make it cough him up! Down, euphoria, down! Too bad one of the ponies wasn't named Euphoria, so she could cry, "Up, Euphoria, up!" Cramming a hand to her mouth, she blocked her giggles, wiped her streaming nose and eyes.

So, Harrap couldn't cling long enough. Think, think! If he could, did it truly stand a chance of working? Side-glance Harrap, tap the pole against the stone, tap it again, stare at the dark and beyond, at the night with its scatter-shot stars, the Lady Moon and its thin crescent companion, the first returning Disciple. Shadow-dance of flames on the snow, bow and curtsy. Think, think! Damn, if Doyce were here; she'd do better, ingenious at practical matters. Seekers tended to be resourceful, both by experience and inclination. Eumedicos, too, were equally inventive, even inspired, but at very different tasks.

The pole now in both hands, resting on her shoulder as she swung it around, Mahafny narrowly missed buffeting Willy in the head, the pony too tired to shy. "Harrap, let's try again, but differently this time." Laying the trunk-pole across the ponies' backs, she painstakingly eased first one, then the other back a few paces, gauging their alignment, the pole's position relative to Harrap. "Harrap, sit up, stiffen your blasted backbone. Good, yes!" Another minor adjustment, a eumedico finickiness for precision. But don't allow it to obscure the larger picture.

"Willy, Jester! Down, down! That's my brave boys!" As the ponies reluctantly knelt at her command, Mahafny began unwinding her coil of rope from her waist, had stashed it there after she and Willy had returned with their prize. Left on the ground, she'd have entangled herself, tripped and fallen, so she'd absentmindedly belted it around her. "Harrap, throw your arms back and over the pole, can you do that for me, Harrap? For Parm?"

Eyes squinted, he tossed first one arm, then the other back and over, his broad chest straining as the pole held him upright. It was cruel, but she had no choice, the looped rope ready. "Harrap, give me your left hand, yes, that's good." Lash his wrist with the rope, ignore the bewilderment stamped so clearly on his tormented face. "Give me your other wrist." Flapping it vaguely at pole level, he clearly couldn't figure out how to maneuver it underneath. "I said give it to me, Harrap!" she snapped, snatching it when it hesitantly peeped from beneath the pole, fingers waggling. Quickly she placed the knots, no slipknot here, he *must* remain securely trussed, no slipping. There, the pole was lodged snug beneath each armpit, his arms bent back and then snugged forward, almost like chicken wings. She admired her handiwork. Now to lash Harrap's wrists together. No way they could meet, but she wove the rope from one wrist to the other, forming a strap across his chest. His muscles strained and bulged at the excruciating position, his eyes clearing at this new and unexpected indignity—unanticipated from this source. How could she martyr him so?

Still enough rope to spare for her to take the free end, use it as a whip, urging the ponies "Up!" with a commanding shout, the rope's tail lashing their rumps—unfair when they'd already worked so hard, though to no avail. Jester caught the first blow, then Willy, turning a startled and rebuking eye at her as both struggled, laboriously planting forehooves flat on the ground, heaving upward against Harrap's considerable bulk.

A drawn-out scream, Harrap's, as his body surged upward between the ponies. "Mahafny! Shoulders! Hurts! Ripped from their sockets!" he howled.

"Up!" she commanded again as, with an effort, Jester and Willie found their footing and came completely upright, blowing and shaking at the strain. "I doubt it, Harrap," she disagreed as she threw herself on her stomach, clutching at a double-handful of his pantaloon, pulling straight up so his hip joint pivoted and the leg emerged from the fissure. "Figured you might dislocate a shoulder, but that I could deal with, snap into place." Gently, she laid his swollen, stiff leg beside the crack. "Good boys, good boys!" she crooned to the ponies, Harrap still dangling puppetlike between them. "Almost, almost done, just hang on."

Digging for her knife, she stood before Harrap, straddling the crack, left foot jammed against the inside of his leg so it couldn't loll into the trap again. No way to cushion his landing, so she slashed the rope as efficiently as she could and readied herself. He started to topple forward, bending at the waist and then just hung there, his jacket arm snagged on a branch stub. She cursed long and low, and it finally tore free. As his body limply folded toward her, she countered it, thrusting both hands against his chest to lay him full length on his back.

"Ma-haf-ny!" "Auntie Mahafny? Auntie?" The voices—voices?—chimed within her, drifting up from lower on the trail, pure and sweet, as invigorating as the night air, reviving lost hopes. "Is that you?" Jenneth?—definitely. And . . . and . . . Diccon? Yes, Diccon!

**"Oh, joy, oh, rapture! Oh, good job, jolly good job, Mahafny. Rescuing my Harrap! Plucking him out like a tur-**

nip!" Sonorous with relief, Parm's mindspeech tumbled and gamboled through her brain, curveted with delight.

*"Parm? Is that you? Where are you? Where's Saam? Is he . . . ?"*

**"Peace, Mahafny. I'm here, haven't left you for good yet. Would have 'spoken you sooner, but it took both of us to lift Harrap's spirits, give him something to listen to beside the hurts in his heart and body during that final effort."**

*"At least all* you *had to do lift was his spirits!"* she countered, waspish indignation overtaking profound relief. *"Now hurry, get up here so I can hold you. And scold you."*

**"What I did was worth it, Mahafny,"** he sounded smug but weak. **"Got Diccon back, didn't we?"**

♣

The horizon trembled with a suffused band of color, as if the heavens were loath to let the day be born, outshine the few remaining stars, overshadow the ghost moon's dignified recessional. Jacobia had ventured from camp, wanting solitude to ponder the import of the rogue Plumb, its destructive force unwittingly loosed upon the land once more. Almost impossible to encompass the idea of a Plumb existing, let alone exploding, altering perceptions of the past—and the present—reshaping the future. Here on this knoll above camp, alone but for the rising sun, she let her mind go blank and still, receptive to transcendence, trodding byways of the mind her people rarely traveled.

Almost like fragments of a tale told long ago, they'd begun to coalesce within her, only to scatter again, harder to gather than stars in the sky, grains of sand. Ah, how they sought refuge, longed for a home, but they were so wary of rejection! A major undertaking, to be sure—or perhaps she'd constructed an imposing edifice of words that went nowhere toward solving or sheltering a thing!

But first she needed a place to sit; contemplation could be painful enough without the fact her feet were still sensitive. Interesting, the way the knoll flattened on top, sweeping outward to provide an unobstructed view, rather like a patio built expressly for her pleasure. Yes, this outcrop would serve as a bench. Now to finally quell the words playing through her mind—"appendix . . . appendage." Up here, alone, she was a being, not merely a burden ungraciously hauled along because there was no place to deposit it. Oversensitive, wasn't she? Only Feather gave her that uncomfortable feeling; none of the other Erakwa did, from Addawanna to Lennap and Mataweeta to slender Glashtok, who now chattered a blue streak when he carried her, dimpling when she smiled at him. Let it go, let it float away. It was Feather's problem, not hers.

The sky continued to lighten, aureate beams gilding the peaks and snow with a luminosity that made her heart ache at such beauty. She was hardly the first, let alone the only person, to witness such transitory splendor, but the sight might have been birthed exclusively for her, so at one was she with her surroundings. A sigh, and she swallowed the lump in her throat. Now came the true sunrise, like a vision, a penetrative citrus, her eyes tearing with joy at such radiance flooding the world, intensifying the colors night had swallowed and now only reluctantly disgorged.

"Ah, 'noder dawn, and it is good," came a voice and she turned, almost unwilling to share—even with Addawanna. The elderly Erakwan stood beyond Jacobia's perch, very near the outer edge of the knoll's flattened top, bathing her spirit in the intimate touch of the sky and air. Arms raised high in salute, Addawanna basked in the expansive light, her face upturned, eyes closed, at peace. Beside her, Feather shuffled her feet, impatient yet awed and moved despite herself at the sight, not fully comfortable with acknowledging its power over her. Strange that both she and Addawanna could respond to it so completely, unreservedly, while Feather fought against experiencing such rapture.

Seemingly out of nowhere, a green-gold sphere materialized, feinting and dodging, frolicking about Feather's moccasins, abruptly changing course toward Jacobia, then bobbing at Feather from a different direction. Some inner instinct reassured Jacobia it was harmless, but she did feel puzzled, even more so as Feather emitted a piercing shriek, her nerve dissolving as she turned to flee. "You fergit legends, child?" Addawanna chided, strong arms encircling Feather to stay her flight. "T'ink, child, is—" But before Addawanna could finish, Feather broke free, frantically shoving the older woman and bolting like a panicked deer outracing a forest fire.

"No!" Jacobia exclaimed, viscerally certain of the outcome but unable to halt its progress. At Feather's shove, Addawanna staggered to regain her balance, except she lacked enough space for more than a step or two before reaching the lip of the debris-laden downslope that dropped away into nothingness. Normally light on her feet, surefooted as a mountain sheep, Addawanna landed on her back and with a supple flex worthy of one of the ghatti, somehow flipped onto her stomach, lunging upward as she started to slither over the edge, one hand clinging to a knob of rock while the other flailed for a grip.

The green globe, rapidly fading around its edges, paused, throbbing in place about a meter above the ground, curiously indecisive. Without time for thought, Jacobia launched herself at the lip, praying she could wedge her body in place if she caught Addawanna's hand in time. "Feather! Come back! I need you!" she shouted, hoping against hope that Feather would regain enough presence of mind to react in an emergency.

There! Hand locked around Addawanna's wrist, she set herself to snag her free hand, but Addawanna found hers first. Not a good, solid grip, but a start. Sore feet outflung behind her, Jacobia spread-eagled them in search of anything—a stone, an ice hump—to hook them on. "Let go of my hand, grab my wrist," she grunted, grimacing as Addawanna's iron grasp threatened to crush knuckles and fingers.

Hesitantly hovering at her shoulder, the globe hummed annoyingly in Jacobia's ear, the sound broken by an occasional interrogatory chirp. Whatever it was, she sensed no malcontent or ultimate evil within it, indeed, if it had possessed an expression, it would have registered perplexity, almost embarrassment. Except she lacked time to analyze it, wonder who or what it was. What she wanted to discover was whether it could be helpful! She couldn't continue holding Addawanna like this forever!

"You! You whatever you are," craning her neck as best she could, she fixed it with a violet-sparked glare to cow it, "you ought to be ashamed! This is all *your* fault!" Well, Feather bore some blame, but she'd deal with that later.

"How do you plan to make up for it?" Ridiculous to address such a thing—more than likely a figment of her imagination, if it hadn't been for Feather's reaction. It bobbed, as if nodding, and she snapped, "Well, then, do it! Don't just float there!" Despite the gravity of the situation, she could have sworn Addawanna chuckled.

Over the lip it floated and hung in thin air, then dove with sickening speed until it vanished from view. No doubt it had raced off and away, content with the mischief it had wrought. But to her fervent relief the strain on her arms and shoulders eased, Addawanna fractionally rising. "Steady," Addawanna instructed as, with quivering effort, she rose a bit higher. Mayhap she'd located a toehold to push against, slowly straighten her leg. Another slight gain, and Jacobia snaked backward to take up the slack, afraid if Addawanna slipped, she'd carry her over with her.

She lacked strength enough to bodily haul Addawanna to safety—had visions of them poised thus for eternity—until Addawanna's bloody, scraped hands and forearms crept over the edge. Wriggling back, back again, Jacobia gained ground, knees and feet gouging the snow, digging in. A glimpse of Addawanna's head, the crown with its center part.

A misjudgment on someone's part, and Addawanna began sliding back, Jacobia groaning at the unexpected strain, her hoisting efforts negated. Eyes leaking tears of pain, she hooked a foot into the snow to anchor herself. Where was Feather, blast her hide, the other Erakwa? Or was she meant to do this alone? "Ai-EE!" Without warning Addawanna's head unexpectedly hovered above the edge, her exclamation shouted into Jacobia's face, both of them startling. "Naughty pinch-butt!" Addawanna snapped over her shoulder, but Jacobia paid her no heed as, daring all, she abandoned her hold on Addawanna's left wrist and seized a handful of doeskin tunic at the neckline.

The Erakwan woman wasted no time, wedging her fingers in a slender crack and heaving with all her might. Another surge and rise, unanticipated from Addawanna's wide-eyed expression, and Jacobia hooked her forearm under Addawanna's arm. They lay close now, faces sweat-tracked, head nearly butting head, and Jacobia hoped Addawanna could "climb" her body to safety. Another heave

from below—was it truly that strange globe helping?—and
Addawanna lay beside her, only her feet, one moccasined,
one bare, dangling in the air.

"Ho!" Addawanna exclaimed, wiping her face with her
sleeve. Then, "Ho!" again, more thoughtfully. "Naughty
one redeem itself. You teach it manners!"

Rolling on her back, lungs starved for air, Jacobia nodded, not sure what else to say. "You no 'fraid of it?" Addawanna queried, resting on an elbow to stare into Jacobia's
scarlet face. "How so? 'Specially when it scare Feather like
dat! Dat child!" A sniff of dismay. "Fergit so much, too
much. Doan know whad I do wid her, no madder how hard
she try, she still 'needer-nor.' "

Needer-nor? It came to Jacobia—neither-nor. Poor
Feather, no longer fully Erakwan, yet certainly not fully
accepted by Jacobia's kind. But this wasn't the moment to
contemplate Feather's problems. Never had the sky exhibited such a blue, or the sun shone so radiantly! And
blessed, solid earth beneath her; she was a part of it all . . .
as was—come to think on it—the mysterious green-gold
sphere, though what niche it claimed she couldn't guess. It
had a right to be, to be here, as she did. Many things in
life gave no advance warning; that didn't make them wrong,
just revealed them as a part of life's myriad surprises and
marvels. A thoughtful smile slowly formed, broadened in
the sun's warmth, and she began to laugh, heard Addawanna bubbling over as well. Having snapped one's fingers
in death's face, laughter seemed entirely appropriate. After
all, life—for all its manifold and manifest disasters—included laughter, if only to counterweight the fears it could
never entirely chase away.

♣

Ooo-oo-ee-WAH! Ha! Ho! The women's laughter tickled
the green-gold globe to its very core, set it to chuckling
and chirping. It thrummed, considering the prudence of re-
joining Addawanna and the stranger to partake in their
laughter, but its brightness dulled as it mulled it over, remembering what its appearance had precipitated. How was
it to know the other one had totally forgotten it? That

made it want to bounce and spin after her again, reveal itself, remind her of who and what she was. But with so many other Erakwa in the vicinity, all undoubtedly now on the alert, it probably wasn't wise. The next thing it'd know it'd be packed in a lidded basket—or worse—transported back where it "belonged," as they always put it. Ha, much they knew! It belonged wherever it wanted to belong— here, there, or in between!

To occupy itself, it slipped behind a curtain of ice, flattening paper-thin until it could squeeze into a hairline crack. There, it ran through a series of progressive brightening and dimming, wishing it could see how handsome and eerie it looked from outside. When that palled, it slithered back and bounced, divoting the snow, then rolled along to connect one to another. Could even create a pattern if it wanted—so there! Nothing very tricky about that!

That was the problem: nothing remained fun for very long unless it found someone to trick and tease, taunt a bit. The mere thought made it vibrate with absorbed energy, the more intense the encounter, the more cheery it'd feel. Nobody to play with, not a soul to frolic with it. A blustery, deflating sigh, fuzz turning limp, withering like new-mown clippings fading in the sunlight. Not fair! Nobody to play with! Hadn't it helped Addawanna? Made up for setting her precious Feather in a tizzy? Wasn't *its* fault Addawanna had slipped—was it?

Their laughter still enticed, despite its best intentions to leave well enough alone, at least for a while. Ah! Zip-zoom to the peak, wait for Addawanna and the others, see if Nakum had returned, practice some tricks if he had. It hummed to itself, testing the idea, tasting it, the anticipation almost as richly satisfying, energizing as a prank. Except it could sense even from here that Nakum hadn't returned, the arborfer pining for him. Enough fun to lie in wait for Addawanna at tippy-top, bounce out and go Ooo-WAH, then dash-roll away? No, she'd be alert for it now.

Besides, it could sense Callis ascending the mountain from the opposite direction, that her group and Addawanna's would probably arrive simultaneously at the peak. If it foolishly lurked up top, it'd be caught in a pincer move, worse than a flea crushed between fingernails! Ooo! They'd bind up its powers so tightly it'd never get loose again, no matter how it pleaded and begged and promised. Naughty! No more naughty if layers of legends bound it. Enough to make it implode, it might! Ooo! Ooo!

Yes, a strategic retreat might serve best—no time to tickle the arborfer up top or join in the laughter just behind it. Sidonie—it should be distant enough to give it a clear field for its antics. Doubtful they'd ever seen its kind, its like before. A fresh audience, oohs and aahs and shrieks! Make their spines tingle, their hair stand on end! Pop from some old lady's porridge pot, roar up through the privy seat and send an old man fleeing, pantless, parading his skinny shanks for the world to view! That was just for starters! Think of the shenanigans it could wreak on younger ones with stronger hearts!

Ooo-oo-ee-WAH! Whoop! Revolving faster now, its green protectively scaled back to its most unobtrusive shading, it began its descent, scooting along the snow, sliding and catapulting itself into the air. Whee! Down we go, and down we go . . . to Sidonie! That'd teach Nakum to leave it alone and lonely, unattended on his mountaintop! Because it'd only just remembered—Nakum had gone hurrying off to Sidonie. Surprise, surprise, Nakum! Whoops! Whee!

♣

It bounced tentatively, only to dart behind a barrel when a coach drawn by four glossy bays clattered by, casting up mud that stained the green-gold globe, now tinted to its palest shading, like a distant memory of spring locked in winter's mind. Oo-oo-ee-wah! It whispered to itself, but its normally spontaneous cry to trickery wasn't especially heartening. Sidonie was *much* bigger than it had realized, far more complex, every thing, every person bustling and busy. Too busy to notice it?

Oo-oo-ee-WAH! It exploded out of hiding at a street urchin who scowled and blew a raspberry at it with wet, smeary lips. Worse yet, the urchin set off in chase after it, the green sphere rolling, unable to gain any speed as it dodged the filthy, tattered boot kicking at it, sending it spinning in all directions till it turned dizzy. More urchins joined in the game, it as their quarry, feet kicking until it absolutely hurtled down the lane, gathering mud and water as it rolled. Horrible! Thrumming with terror the green-gold globe compressed itself and dove between the grates of a storm drain, safe at last.

They poked sticks at it for a while, but rapidly lost interest, wandering off in ones and twos, leaving it panting and pulsating.

"What was that thing?" one of the boys asked as they left.

"Doan rightly know," answered another. "But it warn't rightly much fun. Mosta time me boot went half-trew it. Couldn't git a decent kick at it."

Still fluxing between fear and anger, it debated turning into a little boy, a fox, a weasel, a crow—all at once, mayhap! Show those dullards what it was made of, scare the shite out of them, it would! Hard souls they had—and no sense of imagination, clearly, blind to its potential! These city children were tough and seasoned, no-nonsensical predators happy to show the trickster new tricks at its expense! Was this what cities were all about? Did such crowds of people negate its powers?

Bedraggled, its green wisps tattered and dirt-stained, it huddled in the storm drain, reluctantly bolstering its courage to slip out, try again. Ah, how it thirsted for an injection of energy, worn out from its travels and its horrendous reception. No wonder Nakum wasn't fond of visiting Sidonie! Come to think on it, it had been a long, long time since it had last visited a city . . . well, town . . . well, hamlet. Hadn't suspected that the bigger the place, the more likely it would be treated as simply another curiosity—unusual but hardly frightening. What to do? What to do?

Avoid the young of the species—that was patently obvious! It should have known better, children in general able to see clear through it, recognize a sort of kindred spirit. With a slither it humped out of the storm drain and sought refuge beneath a horse trough, all shivery and forlorn in the damp and the fouled slush in ways it had never imagined amongst the high peaks with their pristine snow and ice.

How to redeem itself? How to regain its energy? Without

it, further trickery would be impossible, and it hungered for just a taste of shock and surprise, a frisson of fear, the panicky pounding of a heart radiating its vitality. An old person—that was just the thing. Find a nice, credulous oldster and it needn't perform very hard, just enough to snack on, then spin away to find someone more promising. The boys' boots had hurt in ways it had never before experienced. Normal kicks and cuffs simply passed straight through without doing any damage, made the person go shocky at the sight of hand or foot glowing green, adding to its enjoyment.

Courage, it told itself, and inflated as much as it could in this cramped spot, shaking fringed edges clean, fluffing and preening to make itself presentable. Ah—that sound! The shuffle of feet, the totter-tap of a cane. Easy pickings, an oldster! Then on to some pompous, self-important personage for a real feast! Yes, yes, here came the cane, here came the neat-booted little feet!

With a pop and a whoosh, it threw itself into the elderly lady's path, hovering just above knee level, atingle with delight, humming and trilling as it roiled an alarming shade of green. Backflip, rebound at the face, pulsate and into a back roll. Best to let them take a good look for a instant or two before it continued its delicately delicious mode of spookery.

Without warning the cane thumped it as it completed its back roll and flattened it onto the cobbled street. The next thing it knew, the cane stabbed, impaling it to raise it for closer inspection. Eyes huge behind thick spectacles, the old woman scrutinized it from all angles, a look of singular disgust on her face, mouth and nose scrunched as if she'd scented something revolting.

"I tell you," she complained to no one in particular, "in my day the garbage always stayed in the gutters where it belonged. Didn't come leaping at you. Absolutely disgusting what this world is coming to. Too much change, if you ask me! Spawn turned over by the 'splosion, prowbly have two-headed calves born come spring!"

Writhing and whimpering at being impaled, the green sphere deflated, energy trickling away with a horrible oozing sensation. Worse yet was its abrupt immersion in the ice-cold water of the horse trough as the woman stuck in her cane and violently stirred, then brought it up to examine the tip.

"Hope I don't poison the poor horses." Briskly shaking water off her cane, she marched on, the cane's tippity-tapping a mocking recessional.

Floating limp as green algae, it struggled against the shock to its system, shaken to the very core of its being. At length it slimed wetly over the edge of the trough and tumbled to the cobbles, just lying there inertly. Oo-oo-ee-wah . . . When had the world changed so drastically that it could no longer find a secure place for itself? Ah, how it yearned for the world within the world, ready to eschew this uncivilized place where humans lacked sense enough to be terrified! No doubt they no longer feared things that went bump in the night either! Thinking they knew everything, nothing new beneath the sun!

Anger provided just enough strength for it to overcome its dejection, and it painfully inflated, skittering erratically as it searched for some safe place where it could rest, recoup itself, decide what to do.

No! Oh, no! An orange kitten now confronted it, not backing down, her skinny tail fluffed, back arched. Drawing on its reserves, the green-gold globe weakly pulsated and ballooned a little more, mimicking—in its own way—the kitten's defensive stance. A quick paw pat and it allowed itself to roll back, then spin forward, the kitten skittering clear, wide-eyed. Now that was more like it! Feint, hum rapidly, dash at the tail and tweak it! Wonderful the way the creature bounded into the air, landing and lashing back. A worthy opponent, frightened but curious, and it sipped just a smidgeon of strength from that determination, enough for another quick lunge.

"Baby—don't! Don't hurt it!" it heard a girl call out, the thud of running feet, two pairs. Oh, dear, trouble again— more children!

"What is it, Harry?" The girl-child knelt, holding a hand near, but cautious about touching. "Whatever it is, it looks hurt. Weary and worn, at least." Emboldened, the kitten began a furious charge, only to be swept into the girl's arms, mewling its protest.

Now the boy squatted, examining it from all sides. "Huh! Never seen anything like this before. Animal, vegetable, or mineral, do you think, Telka?'' Indignant, it darted at the boy's boots, fully determined to transform into a fox, at the very least. Wouldn't be kicked again, it wouldn't—not without snapping back!

But a loosely-bunched hand reached out, and it knuckle-bumped it before it could stop itself. Found that being touched thusly was not unpleasant, not given how it felt, all wambly with exhaustion, energy depleted. Again it nudged the hand, and a finger unfolded to stroke its fuzz. It could feel the energy transfer, and it hungered for more. "Don't know what it is, haven't ever seen a thing like it before," the boy confessed. "Think mayhap it's some sort of creature all curled up on itself to protect its face and soft underbelly?"

"But why's it so green?" the girl wanted to know. "Animals aren't green—frogs and turtles, yes, but this doesn't look anything like one of those."

"Think it might be mossy. Mayhap it doesn't normally move much, and the same moss that grows on the sides of trees grows on this, too. Camouflages it, like. How it got here in Sidonie from the woods, I haven't a clue."

In shock, it discovered it was being snugly bundled in a scarf, and it glowed its indignation. "Like a firefly, the way it glows. Let's take it back to the castle, give it something to eat, a quiet place to rest. Mayhap someone'll know what it is, what it needs to make it better." A pause, as if the boy were thinking hard. "Bet if anyone knows, Nakum will!"

Nakum! It thrummed and thrilled at the words. The children were going to take him to Nakum. A trick or two on Nakum and it'd be hale and hearty! Then it could take on this city with renewed confidence, show it it had best beware!

♣

Squinching Baby with her left arm, her right hand tight on the scruff of her neck, Etelka looked at Harry for reassurance that this was the right door. The fact that he so thoroughly knew his way around the castle inspired a certain awe—he didn't even really live here and he practically had the run of the place! Common sense told her, though, that given the goings-on in the castle of late—the constant repairs and renovations, the acrimonious debate that wafted through the corridors—that two reasonably intelligent children, practically adults, could roam unimpeded, as long as they stayed clear of trouble. They might be noticed, but wouldn't be remarked upon as long as more pressing matters were at hand.

Harry rapidly bobbed his head in encouragement, arms clutched round his belly as if he had a stomach ache. "Hurry up!" he implored, grimacing and rolling his eyes. "It tickles something fierce!" Still clutching Baby, she planted her bottom against the door and shoved with all her might. Then he'd dash directly to the suite his family had been occupying of late, while her instructions involved finding a crate in the storage rooms behind the kitchens, as well as something for the strange green globe to eat. With any luck once Harry left, she could release Baby. Ever since they'd rescued the green thing, she'd carried her; if she left the kitten free, she immediately climbed Harry's leg, frantic to investigate what he'd hidden beneath his coat.

"But what do you think it likes to eat?" she'd asked. Frankly, she couldn't tell if the thing liked vegetables, or meat, or what—and she a farm girl, no less!

Outer garments shimmying, arms pressed above and below the frisking bulge, Harry had been more eager to depart than to analyze what the creature might subsist upon. Several times his eyes had popped, his cheeks, too, as he'd gasped and gulped, the thing enthusiastically tickling his ribs. "Any . . . anything green!" he finally sputtered. "Mint jelly, spinach, grass! I don't know, Telka! Your guess is as good as mine." Nice he trusted her so, but not very heartening that he had even less idea than she.

She backed inside, Harry following tight after, then sprinting away down the hallway and up the back stairs that the servants used. Now to find what she needed, then hope she could find her own way to Harry's suite. No wonder Cinzia had problems remembering how to reach different parts of the castle—it wound all over, worse than a maze! If only Cinzia and La'ow had more time to spend with her and Baby, but she understood, really she did. It was still such a shock, finding that Baby was truly half-ghatti, Hru'rul her Papa! Enough to set her dreaming, wish-

ing, but so much was happening—truly weighty things—
that she'd stored away her hopes for later.

Rummaging until she found a crate—neither too rackety
nor too good—she loaded Baby inside and scouted around.
An old saucer for water, another for food. A leaf or two
of cabbage since Harry insisted the thing needed green
food, and the kitten sniffed it, licked it. Lady bless, would
she start devouring raw cabbage? Doubtful what else to
choose, she finally filched two common crackers from their
barrel and a small, waxed cheese. Scavenging didn't set well
with her, didn't seem proper, what with everyone being so
nice, giving her practically anything she wanted, ofttimes
before she even thought of it. She put the cheese in the
crate, hoping the wax would deter Baby long enough for
her to reach the suite. Good! Baby was torn between rolling it like a ball and biting at it. As an afterthought she
loaded more common crackers into her pockets; she and
Harry could split and toast them, put cheese on them. She
was hungry again, and if she were hungry, no doubt Harry
was starving. Boys were like that once they started growing.

Up, across, around . . . or was it across, up, and around?
Crate wedged against her hip, arm uncomfortably stretched
across the top to let her hang onto a side slat, she made it
to Harry's suite, asking directions only once along the way,
ever-so-politely inquiring of the men laying down a lemony
oil on the teak floor while others in flannel booties skated
across it, buffing away. It looked rather like fun.

A cautious double knock at the door, followed by a short
sharp rap, the signal they'd agreed upon. He'd told her that
he and someone called Smir—an odd name, but he'd insisted 'twas short for Casimir—had employed a similar signal in the Sunderlies when they'd been hiding from bad
men.

To her surprise and dismay, Harry opened the door and
jerked the crate from her arm, firmly slamming the door in
her face. What was this about? Didn't he realize Baby was
inside? Perturbed, she readied herself to knock again just
as Harry backed out, the kitten under his arm. His hair
was horribly mussed and the front of his tunic all wrinkled,
a button missing. "It's acting up," he confessed, worriedly
swiping at his forehead with a sleeve. "Doing the oddest

things, popping out here, popping up there. I swear I can't keep track of it. It's really fast!"

"What do you think?" She truly wanted to see it again, take a better look, but this didn't seem to be the time. "Mayhap if we leave it alone for a while with the food and the crate, it'll settle down, not be so jumpy—mayhap go to sleep?" It seemed a reasonable idea. Creatures suddenly transported into a new environment—be it home or barn—often needed privacy, needed to become accustomed to things at their own pace.

"I hope so!" He sighed, tugging at his tunic, then brushing with both hands to neaten it. "Blast it, I swear I've got something in my ear. Can you see anything?" Flexing at the knees to lower himself, he held still while she peered inside.

She could see it, wasn't sure if she could dislodge it, wishing she had something with which to hook the shank. "I think it's your button. Why'd you put it there when it came off?"

"I didn't!" Wriggling his little finger in his ear for confirmation, Harry glumly muttered, "Told you it was fast! I think it managed to stuff the button in my— Oh, no!"

"What? Did it get out?" Whirling, she sighed with relief at discovering it was only Baby, prancing toward Hru'rul and La'ow, obviously come to visit. Except they proceeded right by Baby, Hru'rul slowing long enough to give the kitten a friendly nudge with his nose, and planted themselves in front of Harry. Even more surprising, the two tiger ghattas she'd met, Khim and P'roul, came stalking along the hall from the opposite direction, tails S-curving the air.

Two doors opened across from Harry's suite, and out stepped Seeker Veritas Theo and Seeker Veritas Holly. They'd rated a mention in *Lives of the Seekers Veritas* because of their Bonding with the great Khar'pern's offspring. A warm glow came from standing so close to all this greatness! But Etelka knew what their expressions meant, suspected Harry knew as well. Somehow they were in trouble, deep trouble. Had they been seen sneaking in the green thing?

"D–do come in, H–Harry." Beckoning, Theo swung his door open, Holly and the ghatti herding both her and Harry inside. " 'T–Telka, it m–might b–be b–better if you were to l–leave," and Theo smiled in a kindly way. "W–what w–we have to dis–cuss r–really d–doesn't con–c–cern you."

But Holly gave the smallest of headshakes. "Let Harry decide if he wants her to stay. Don't you remember ever needing moral support, Theo?"

Eyes darting from Khim to Hru'rul to La'ow to P'roul, Harry sank on Theo's bed, hands folded in his lap. "Let her stay," he told the carpet, fixedly staring at the toes of his boots. " 'Telka, sorry, but please don't go. 'Cept I warn you, I'm about to get royally reamed."

"Oh, do let's all get comfortable." Holly indicated a needlepointed footstool for Etelka as she threw herself sideways into an armchair, one leg hanging over the arm. "Theo, try not to pace. It's a generously-sized room but there are limits—too many tails to tread on."

Heeding the comment, all four ghatti jumped on the double bed, deploying themselves in a semicircle behind Harry. And wonder of wonders, Baby crawled into Etelka's lap, seemingly overcome by the seriousness of the occasion. Holding her lightly, just in case, rubbing her thumbs behind the kitten's ears until she rumble-purred, Telka wondered what Harry had done—why it required *four* ghatti to discern the truth. What could he have possibly done that was so horrible? He didn't seem like a bad sort, certainly more mannerly than most of her brothers. Clever, well brought up, though not real snobby 'bout it, and certainly not the kind to muck in things that weren't his affair unless absolutely necessary. If it came to that, she'd gladly stick up for Harry.

"W–word's reached us, H–Harry, th–that your a–aunt and uncle are on their way to M–Marchmont. P–posthaste." Elbow on the carved marble mantle above the fireplace, Theo tapped his knuckles against his lips. "I wonder why that might be—do you know, Harry? Any inkling why they're traveling fast as they can?" Goodness, she'd not realized the tall man could speak so quickly and efficiently when he really tried—not a stammer to be heard.

As she awaited Harry's response, 'Telka's brain abruptly snapped together several facts, seemingly unrelated until now. "Oh . . . !" she breathed, eyes widening behind her spectacles, but silenced herself at Holly's frown. Harry's mama was Doyce Marbon's sister! Doyce Marbon was Harry's aunt, and Jenret Wycherley his uncle! The former Seeker General and her husband—and undoubtedly Khar'pern and Rawn—were coming to Marchmont. Posthaste, as Theo put it. So much greatness gathered under one roof—and mayhap they'd know if she and Baby had any hope of being real Seekers!

Harry's eyes roamed ceilingward, then down to the carpet, one hand clutching the bedpost so hard his knuckles whitened. "I . . . might," he offered cautiously, though a touch truculently to Telka's ears. Use that tone around her house and someone might very well get a whopping.

Holly took the lead now, utterly relaxed except for one bobbing foot. "Harry, it seems P'roul and Khim received some information, oh, more than a few days back, that they neglected to share with us right away. They, however, had a better reason than you. Ghatti etiquette, if you will, a disinclination to meddle in the affairs of another ghatt unless absolutely necessary."

"Well, that's exactly how I felt, too!" Harry protested. "Blood word—Jen begged me . . . I promised . . ." A helpless shrug. "How much do you know? Have you had *any* word? I've been so scared!" Etelka watched as tears formed in his hazel eyes. "Is it bad? It has to be, if Auntie Doyce and Uncle Jenret . . ." He sat straighter, blinking back the tears, firming his mouth. "Tell me, tell me the truth. I can take it, I have to know! Is . . . is anyone dead?" His face had paled, but he still looked resolute. "In a . . . in a way . . . I almost forgot . . . tried to push it out of my mind. What with the Plumb exploding and all." Another shrug, then he hugged himself tight. "I *wanted* to tell you, Theo—came so close when we were down below the castle, but you know what happened. Then Hru'rul tried to drag it out of me afterward . . ."

Holly took pity on Etelka's perplexity. "Harry conveniently didn't mention to anyone that his cousins, Diccon and Jenneth, are escorting an elderly eumedico and a Shepherd to the top of Nakum's mountain in hopes of staving off Saam's death." Saam? The steel-gray ghatt lauded so often in her book? A legend in his own right? *Dying?* How could Nakum save him?

With an apologetic cough she removed her spectacles

and began polishing them. "But Nakum's down here, has been since the Plumb exploded—hasn't he?"

Holly rose, stood behind the chair now, leaning against it. "Very good, child. Right to the point."

"Oh, Lady bless! I never thought of that!" Harry wailed as he flopped backward on the bed, various ghatti quickly relocating themselves. "How could I be so *stupid*!"

"We know—at the moment—that they're all alive. We're hoping that the twins' Aunt Jacobia has caught up with them. But we don't know, aren't sure. Mindspeech doesn't carry all that well in the mountains, as you know. Or Parm and Kwee and Pw'eek purposely aren't responding."

♣

Water still seeped from a midpoint of the arched ceiling, brown webbings of stain marring the plaster, moisture trickling along one of the arched ribs where it collected on a boss and dripped into a bucket placed beneath it, the resulting "ting, ting" just irregular enough to make Eadwin want to hurl the bucket as far as he could. Workers hadn't yet been able to locate the source of the leak, making it impossible to repair.

The throne had toppled during the explosion, and some whispered that it was an omen, connoting his fall from power. No sense in taking such superstition seriously; he'd willingly cede the kingship to any soul with a foolproof solution for disposing of the remaining Plumbs! Would happily abdicate, set the crown on that person's head, return to tending his arborfer.

Beneath the table Hru'rul rumbled, reflecting Eadwin's churning emotional state, and he tried to concentrate, not to dismiss out of hand any remotely viable idea. A glance leftward at Fabienne, his mother, and to his right, Nakum, distinctly uncomfortable, stoically sifting through opinions and suppositions presented as hard facts. He'd invited them for moral support—and to remind everyone that the royal heir and a potential regent had a right to partake in the decision-making progress.

Taking place so soon after their first joint meeting of the new year, this emergency council had been called to weigh

ideas, suggestions, options. The first few emergency meetings had omitted Gilly Beaumarchais and Eugenie Vannevar, already returning to their respective quadrants. As
soon as word of the explosion had reached them, they'd
ridden back to Sidonie as hard as they could. Dear, doddering Quaintance Mercilot had indefatigably toured Sidonie's streets and now appeared more frail than ever, her
expression more vague, mind unable to come to grips with
any solution proposed.

Hard enough at the first meeting for people to encompass the idea that a Plumb had truly exploded—that more
Plumbs existed, rediscovered after so many years. He'd set
the problem before them as succinctly as he could: "If one
Plumb proved operative, we must assume the worst, that
the others are also capable of exploding. How easily, we
don't know. Handled properly, they might remain dormant
for another two hundred years. How do we deal with them?
What do we do with them?" A brief meeting, to say the
least. No point in stretching it out, let them go off, singly
or together, and grapple with it. Let the impossible sink in,
then decide how to deal with it. He'd unilaterally push
through a solution if he had to—as king he possessed the
power. But he hadn't any solutions, any more than the rest
of them.

Ah, Arras was speaking—still more loudly than normal,
his hearing improving but far from perfect—and the longer
the meeting ran, the more he squirmed uncomfortably.
Well, a chair cushion had certainly been in order for the
Defense Lord and Lord of the Nord.

"This situation is not unlike living on the brink of war,
with a potentially hostile army poised on our border, ten-
sions rising. In that situation, we'd have two options: Negotiate a peace or negate the danger by defeating the army,
conquering that country." He looked 'round fiercely, his
mustache bristling. "Since we can hardly make peace with
an inanimate object, we must decide how to conquer or
control it with the least possible damage to our people,
our land."

Ting! Pling! came the sound of droplets landing in the
bucket, and Urban Gamelyn looked balefully over his
shoulder, frowning.

Undeterred, Arras continued, and Eadwin suspected he

couldn't hear the water striking the bucket. Lucky man! Fabienne's fleeting smile suggested she'd reached the same conclusion. "We can continue guarding the Plumbs from now to eternity—whether here in the castle or at some other site to be determined. A new facility guaranteed to protect and store them can be built, given time. Yet time is what worries me. The longer we guard them, the more remote the whole incident will become. Even the best guards grow careless, complacent if nothing ever threatens them."

"What do you expect to threaten them?" Gilly acted especially aggressive today. "Doubt any guard can determine if or when they'll explode, so you're implying someone might attempt to steal them, use them for his own gain—hold us hostage, so to speak? Or worse?"

"Common sense suggests that possibility would always be with us," Urban reminded him. "As well as being a long-term drain on the economy for what might not prove to be a deterrent."

"Surely our lives, the lives of our people are worth any cost!" Carn Camphuysen spoke like the Public Weal Lord he was, recent events forcing him to quickly grow into his new position. "We can't endanger our people, make them live in fear, a sword perpetually dangling over their heads! Isn't there some way we can render them inoperative, be sure they're . . . what? Dead, defunct, I guess you'd say." To Carn the Plumbs had assumed the aspect of a deadly virus or bacteria that must be controlled, crushed, even, to protect the populace.

Smoothly interjecting herself into the debate, Eugenie Vannevar said with a certain distaste, "We're already attempting to find if that's feasible, Carn. Much as I dislike the necessity, word's been sent to the collegiums. They're researching information in their Verboten Rooms to see if there's anything we can do. However, let me remind you that our ancestors couldn't solve the problem, and they were more technologically advanced than we."

"Bury them, bury them deep as we can in the most isolated location we can find! Pile rocks and boulders by the ton on top of their burial site. If they explode, the damage will be minimal." Gilly blustered, glaring at them all, daring anyone to contradict or challenge him. "I refuse to have my children, my grandchildren, and future generations live in the perpetual shadow of such danger! I offer my Domain as a potential site—inter the cursed things in the Stratocums, if we must!"

Too much for Nakum, now on his feet, passionately shouting, "You wish the land to suffer such pain again? How can you? How can you leave me and my people, the land, the arborfer exposed to such potential danger? Have you no conscience, no soul?"

"Better a damn bunch of Erakwa than us!" Face purpling, Gilly pounded the table. "Your people are few and far between out there, and I'm offering *my* domain, mind you!"

"*Your* domain?" Incredulity on Nakum's face. "*Your* land? What makes it yours?"

"The king, your cousin, made it mine!" Gilly shot back. "Mine to ward as I see fit. I'm making a sacrifice, man!"

With slow, effortful moves Quaintance Mercilot gained her feet, hanging heavily on her great-granddaughter's arm. "Nakum, dear boy! Gilly, behave." Her voice quavered like a flute. "Would it be any better, any more suitable, to dump them at sea? Sail far, far out and drop them overboard, weighted down so that they'll sink to the bottom? Mightn't there be a good chance the salt water would corrode them?" Ah, one should never underestimate dear Quaintance—somehow she'd managed to follow along, even gain the lead!

Torn by indecision, Nakum finally responded, voice choked and rasping at first until he cleared it, speaking as loudly and distinctly as he could, face turned directly toward her so she could watch his lips. "Mayhap marginally better, Lord of the Sud, but the sea would suffer an equal hurt if they should explode."

"I suppose," Terrail Leclerc, Internal Affairs Lord bitterly quipped, "we could always *give* them to Romain-Laurent Charpentier. If he blows himself up, mayhap we'd all be better off."

Eadwin pounded his fist on the table, making them all reluctantly face him. "Do we have a consensus? Any at all? I'm not suggesting we've found a solution, an answer—we may never find one that makes us completely comfortable. Likely we'll have to live with the best of a bad lot. But before we go any further, I want to hear your inclinations on the matter.

"Let us assume three propositions, as follows: First, that we guard them for perpetuity as Lord Muscadeine suggested. Second, that we follow the Lord of the Ouest's advice and bury them deep in the Stratocums. Third, as per the Lord of the Sud's suggestion, we drop them into the deepest part of the Frisian Sea."

"Those in favor of the first option?" No hands were raised, not even Arras's, nor had Eadwin expected him to vote for the idea.

"In favor of land burial?" Two Domain Lords, Eugenie and Gilly, plus Ministration Lords Gabriella Falieri, Lysenko Boersma, Carn Camphuysen, and finally, reluctantly, Urban Gamelyn. So, four out of seven Ministration Lords, and half the Domain Lords.

"In favor of sea interment?" Quaintance and Eugenie, Terrail and Tinian.

Arras had abstained, voted for none of the proposals. Force him to commit himself? No, he'd never dealt with Arras thusly in the past and wouldn't start now, valued the man and his opinions too highly. "Arras, have you some other suggestion?"

"Only that we wait longer, consider every option, not embark on some hasty decision we'll all come to regret. If anyone has a right to wish the Plumbs far, far away, I'm the one, but I'm not convinced, just not convinced there isn't some other . . . way. I wish I knew what it was, but I don't." He toyed with the sling on his arm, adjusting it as an excuse to mask rising emotions. "Not yet."

"Adjourned until tomorrow, then."

♣

Time passed, yet not quickly enough to ease his mind. When, oh, when would he hear? Sometimes he paced outside the great hall, and then stood stock-still before the carved doors, literally willing them to swing wide, a voice, any voice crying out, "Romain-Laurent Charpentier? Are you here? We need you, need you desperately!"

Hated the pity reflected in Ezequiel's eyes, the chamberlain standing at ease, arms folded, waiting to see if the king should require anything. Used to it, he was, doing nothing but waiting and waiting and *waiting* for unimportant, piddling requests. "A cushion, Ezequiel," he snarled under his breath, "Poor Lord Muscadeine's arse is *so* sore!" He dug at his cuticles, peeling back the flesh, unable to stop. "The Lord of the Sud can't hear a thing. Can you come bellow in her ear, Ezequiel?"

How long, how long before they called him? How long before the responses from his former classmates made their way back to him, quickly followed by Alex and Lily and the rest, passionate, eager to implement his orders, do whatever he asked, be it sweep the floors or conceive a plan to change the world?

Plumbs! Periodic Linear Ultra-Mensuration Beamers, his, all his . . . a beginning, a chance. And that was but the start, the horde buzzing in his ears, whispering, advising, suggesting the most outrageously original schemes to build a world, a better world. And—he'd not dared think such thoughts till now—would not this new order require a new and better leader? No, no crown for him, not that, but Chief Technocrat, leading, directing a technocracy built ever higher by the robust brawn and brains of technology, fussy emotionalism and sacred tradition forever abandoned in the dust. Let the naysayers choke, literally smother in the dust of ages! Let them be nothing but dust, fit to be ground under his very heel!

Pacing, pacing, sometimes stepping neat and proper from square to square on the marble floor to propitiate the voices in his head . . . Step on a crack and you'll break technology's back . . . Strange how every society, even the newest and the best, held superstitions. To show he was his own man he began sliding as silently as possible, not making a sound, tracing each crack with his toe. Oh, to range farther, wider, as he did at night, but for now this was his self-appointed post. If brainpower alone could accomplish it, he'd will the doors open, pass through them to proclaim the beginning of the end, the commencement of the new. Did not the populace cry, "The king is dead, long live the king!" when a monarch died? But that revealed their desperate hunger for continuity, when what they truly required was a clean break with tradition.

Blood oozed around his nails—he'd dug too deeply—and he slid a hand in his pocket, not wanting Ezequiel to notice, comment on his nerves. Calm, calm. Watch at the window, not for anyone in particular, just appear at ease, casually enjoying the view. Ha, that mingy little country girl and her orange kitten with that Muscadeine lad. Now rumor had it that the kitten was part ghatti, the get of Hru'rul, no less! Much he cared one way or the other. Except . . . could . . . should . . . ghatti have a role in his new world? Depend on mere beasts? Cinzia swore that La'ow could unerringly discern truth within the human heart and soul and mind.

Perhaps not a bad idea to retain a few. Maintenance would be cheap—an occasional mouse or rat, a bowl of milk. Which reminded him, and he dug deeper into his pocket, felt it squirming, eagerly nibbling his fingertips. The explosion had stirred up things within the castle, opened new passages and entries for mice and rats, now blatantly strolling or scampering through the oddest, most public places, much to the consternation and disgust of the palace servants. New worlds for the rodents to explore and conquer, make homes. And somehow this baby wanderer of a mouse, no bigger than the tip of his littlest finger, had gotten lost. Easy enough this morning to slam a wastebasket over it and scoop it up, drop it in his pocket with a morsel of bread and cheese, a tiny mouse sandwich for it.

So amazingly tiny and delicate, each toe hardly thicker than a strand of hair, their scrabbling texture against his thumb. Entertainment, something to while away the time, calm his impatience. That silly, bare little tail like a length of thread, roll it back and forth between index finger and thumb, roll it harder and harder, twisting, sensing it warming from the friction. Ouch! The damn thing had bitten him! Pretend, pretend nothing had happened. What were those stupid children up to? It looked as if the boy had hidden something beneath his coat, both of them acting furtive and nervous. Do it boldly, he wanted to shout. If you've taken something, seized the moment, don't look guilty about it—you undoubtedly deserved it, it was waiting there for you—act proud and unconcerned. Take what you so richly deserve in both hands, make it yours!

Raised voices from within the great hall, jumbled shouts

that overlapped and collided. Yes, yes! The doors shuddered slightly, just as they did when someone put a hand on the knob, then stood talking, impatiently jiggling the hardware. Yes, Ezequiel had straightened, ready to take the door! They were coming! Coming to ask him to join them! Should he modestly demur at first, pretend he had so little to offer? Make them coax, finally implore him to share his expertise, his ideas about the Plumbs. Talk about ripe for the plucking, those Plumbs!

Squeezing, kneading the mouse in his pocket, his breath quickening, eyes moistly eager, he willed the door to swing wide. Paradise within, his for the plucking!

Digging his nails into the small creature, he sawed at a limb, slicing his nail back and forth, deathly surprised at the high, shrill shriek that suddenly emanated from his pocket. Ezequiel swung around to eye him oddly just as the door was flung back and Nakum, the king's cousin, came striding out as if fleeing the meeting.

Wanting desperately to gain Nakum's good graces since he'd not been able to see the king of late, Romain-Laurent thrust out a hand in a gesture calculated to force the Erakwan to shake hands—much as the idea revolted him. Saw Nakum's face contort in an expression of disgust, heard Ezequiel suck in his breath. That damn mouse had bled all over his hand!

Clenching his fist tight as if that would make the blood vanish, he frantically stepped in front of Nakum, mirroring his step no matter which way he tried to move, blocking him at every turn. "How goes it?" he asked. "Have they devised a solution? Do they . . . do they need me? I know precisely what—" He'd rarely paid much attention to Nakum before, had barely encountered him on his infrequent visits, but he *must* cozen the man, garner advance warning about how to play out his knowledge.

Nakum stopped short, and no matter how close Romain-Laurent tried to press himself, the Erakwan swiftly backed away, maintaining a wide space between them. "Are you truly as heedless as you act, little man?" Nakum snarled. "Ignorance is one thing, stupidity another! Almost I could forgive you for hurting the earth like that because you truly couldn't know the Plumb would work, would explode. An accident. The end result remains the same, though—destruction, defilement, rending."

Nakum's hand wrapped tight around Romain-Laurent's fist, thumb pressing between his knuckles, forcing his hand open to reveal the mousekin's remains. "You enjoy rending and destroying, don't you? Not content unless you maim and destroy—it gives you pleasure, yes?"

"I . . . no . . . you have to understand . . ." Romain-Laurent desperately wondered what to do with the mouse. "Ignore the mouse, it was an accident—I forgot I had it in my pocket. No, I didn't *know* the Plumb would explode, but I'm glad I made it happen—otherwise how would we know, how could we *plan* for the future, a future that seemed beyond—" he was gabbling now, too many of the horde shouting advice in his ears, and he couldn't straighten them out, properly present their arguments—not with the look of cool disdain on Ezequiel's face and the hot disgust burning on Nakum's.

"I can explain . . . I can prove . . . just give me a chance! Ask Eadwin for me, please! Don't throw away the country's future!"

With quivering self-control, Nakum placed both hands on Romain-Laurent's chest and eased him away. "Get out of my sight, Outlander!"

And Ezequiel was murmuring in his ear, his words colliding with the horde's importuning, grasping his elbows from behind, inexorably drawing him away as Domain and Ministration Lords began to file out of the great hall.

"Don't shout, don't call attention to yourself in any manner. Do I make myself clear?" Ezequiel's harsh, hot breath burned his ear, his words pitched to slip through the clash of continuing argument as the Lords dispersed. "One word and I'll clap my hand over your mouth, won't care if I cut off your breathing either. I will *not* have the king bothered, distracted. Go back to whatever little hole you inhabit and count beans. Squeeze them if you must—they won't shriek.

"By the way, you've a message waiting. A special rider brought it just before the meeting began. I signed for it, had it delivered to your room. Can't say it entered my head again until now."

❧

He crumpled the paper in his fist, compacting it to stifle the words that still screamed in his brain, smothering them. Would crush them to death just as he had the stupid little mousekin. His comrades were all dead to him now, he would not hear them, would not allow their small-mindedness to impinge on his potential. Hadn't he been bighearted enough to offer them a place in his technocracy? But no, they were weak, cowardly, unable to seize the moment, make Lady Change theirs.

But no matter how hard he crushed the note, the words remained embedded in his disbelieving brain. As soon as he'd seen the messenger's seal—the most expensive, quickest service in the country—his heart had soared. Yes! They were coming—the first of many! Bless Florimel for joining the cause so quickly! But three readings of the message had frozen, hardened his heart.

*Dear Romain-Laurent:*

*As soon as Alex and Lily received your letter, they hurried to confer with me, the most we could quickly gather on such short notice. I should note, however, that I strongly doubt the others will feel any differently, and they—at least—have longer to mull over your invitation. Still, the three of us stayed up all night talking over the proposal you laid out in your letter.*

*Frankly, we wish no part of your grand design to revolutionize Marchmont. At least not in the ways you propose. Romain-Laurent, I don't think you've ever completely grasped how very dissimilar you are from the rest of us. Yes, we believe in change, hope to achieve it in incremental, manageable steps. You have a monomania about it, are utterly lacking in sensitivity to the people and institutions involved. You are unfeeling—yet highly persuasive at times. However, away from the heady influence of your fervor, we've all awakened to realize that what you propose is a bad dream. Without doubt you are intelligent, talented, but you must temper yourself to the times to succeed, and we doubt you capable of that. Anything you undertake is likely to be a fiasco, a catastrophe with which we do not choose to ally ourselves.*

*We say that we wish you well, and to a certain extent that is true. However, we do not wish you well concerning anything you may choose to do with the Plumbs. Leave them be, we beg you!*

*Sincerely, Florimel, Lily, and Alex*

Monomaniacal? Unfeeling? Insensitive? He, Romain-Laurent, who'd let those ingrates crib from his examinations, lectured them time and again on what they should and shouldn't prepare for? Driving them toward the future had been worse than herding cattle to market! Meandering to graze here and there, nibble at what they pretended the future might taste like! Wasn't stagnation a slaughterhouse of sorts, killing dreams, clubbing change to death with a well-placed blow between the eyes?

Without doubt Florimel was correct; the others wouldn't join his cause either. She'd always been the outspoken one, the one who'd dared state aloud the opinions the others shared but would never utter—to him, to their professors at Montpéllier. Their counterfeit support, the camaraderie, however spurious—gone forever now.

Steadying his breathing, he worked at uncrumpling the note, flattening it against his thigh, pressing it with the edge of his hand. Not to read again—oh, no! He held it blank side up. When it was flattened to his satisfaction, he fished in his pocket for the remains of the mouse and withdrew them, centering the corpse on the sheet of paper—that wretched pale green that Florimel specially ordered—and crumpled the paper around it, harder and harder, pounding one fist against it, then the other, intent on flattening it. They were naught but mincing, cowardly mice! Opening the casement window, he threw it away as hard as he could.

So, so, so . . . mayhap a smidgeon of truth in what they said—yes, he was unyielding when it came to promoting real change. No sense having those human millstones dragging around his neck, hampering and hindering him. In mock honor of their twin failures of mind and spirit, he'd make a final assessment of himself and his goals, reassure himself he measured up to his own implacable standards. And if he planned to reevaluate himself tonight, then best to divest himself of his foolish grasping at music of the spheres, the dits and dots that he'd so zealously recorded—contact from Carrick. Ha! Carrick didn't exist—hadn't existed for more than two hundred years! Had died somewhere in space—and even if he were alive, would hardly be interested in his messages. It had been a conceit on his part, pretense, the idea of the lost, separated twin that had put it into his head when he was a child. That and being a member of a Resonant family with no one to hear him. Carrick's "voice" had been seductively real because he'd wanted so badly to hear it, commune with a past that possessed a future, a real future. Children often made up stories, created imaginary friends, but abandoned them as they grew older. Oh, the horde might discipline him by temporarily falling silent, but they'd never completely abandoned him, never would, because they were *real*.

Hadn't the horde endlessly told him *they* were the only ones he should heed? He'd assumed they were jealous at first, though he'd explained time and again that there was enough room in his head for all their voices, as long as his . . . their . . . ideas sparked and flared like a Catherine wheel, spinning ever faster and brighter. Sometimes they talked at cross-purposes, ideas clashing and colliding, and he'd have to pound at his temples to bring order, listen even harder to the whispered plans and ideas.

Why, oh, *why* hadn't they been firmer with him—made him see how duplicitous the world truly was? How duplicitous and fleeting friendship was—be it with flesh-and-blood peers or the nonexistent Carrick? Now he must prove to the horde that henceforth he would listen only to them, carry out, to the best of his considerable ability, the joint plans they'd so scrupulously constructed throughout the years. What, how to convince them of his firm resolve to seize the moment, be all that they and he were convinced he could be, deserved? They were the best part of his inner being—ignore them and he'd be wrong. If they should desert him, even temporarily, he'd be so alone he'd die, fall into the achingly empty void in his mind and disintegrate!

The trunk—yes, that was it. Undo the three locks, remove the radio telegraphy machine, so many years of arduous work. Heave it, out the window, too, jettison it! Rip the antenna from the ivy and bend it, break it if he could. All that remained was him, his brain, open to the host of ideas the horde would crowd into it. So many old familiar voices that he'd heard since adolescence. A pity others couldn't open themselves to such interior brilliance.

Now, when it grew dark, late this evening, he would walk the castle, ghost his way through it, up and down stairs, pace empty corridors and uninhabited rooms and, with luck, the voices would form a magnificent chorus in his mind, a rich harmony to his soaring solo, his ode to change. Then, who knew what would happen?

"Lady Change, I beg you. Let me hear the horde with fresh ears, a mind open to each sparkling thought."

He was hungry, hadn't eaten since breakfast, but he didn't need food as much as the harmony of the voices, a welling, magical chord of sound that would make his soul expand. Instead, he curled on the bed, fists pressed against his stomach, waiting until the castle went silent for the night.

❖

Earth—it existed in so many guises: soil, sand, clay, silt, peat, loam, friable, capable of being crumbled and sifted between one's fingers, poured from hand to hand. Such contact, communion strengthened the spirit, anchored it in the land. Organic and inorganic matter, the living and the dead, the wearing of water and wind on stone, deposits from the rivers and seas, the remains of once-living vegetative and animal matter. Earth—commonly called "dirt"—everything built upon it, everything built of it. Never had Jacobia expected it to preoccupy her every waking moment, and many of her sleeping ones as well. Dreams dusted with earth, its different scents and textures and colors, its moundings and shapes.

A slightly surreal sensation enveloped her during those moments when she pried her mind away from earth in all its guises. She relished her preoccupation; it gave wings to her feet, let her walk faster, climb higher and, when exhausted, she reluctantly resorted to riding on Lennap's back, or Mataweeta's or Glashtok's, the special bond was temporarily broken. Strange—were not these snow-covered crags and rocks and ledges and cliffs, the very mountains of earth as well? Mantled in snow, awaiting their rebirth? Yet lacking their direct touch, she became as nothing.

At intervals she crooned, hummed as one might to a small child—and why not? Was she not pregnant with being and becoming, with the potentials and possibilities of building, creating? What, she didn't know, but accepted it would come to her, though she wanted nothing more than to build now, behold herself as a mother, a maker. . . .

"I swear that if you don't stop humming and buzzing in my ear, I'll buck you over the edge!" Ever since she'd inadvertently knocked down Addawanna and not returned in time to help rescue her, Feather's very being seemed shrunken, her voice perpetually harsh and strangled. "And stop sliding your hand toward my earth-bond! It's mine, not yours! Let someone else carry you—I can't bear you near me anymore!" Now she shrieked so high that Jacobia feared for an avalanche. "I am *not* beholden to you in any way, shape, or form! What I have, what I am is mine, all mine—stop trying to wheedle it away from me, give it a home!"

Bewildered, the final notes of her private tune fleeing from her head, Jacobia rolled on her hip and rubbed her bottom. She'd been . . . what? Dumped rather unceremoniously from Feather's back, had apparently landed with a thump on her backside. What had Feather gotten so exercised about? Surely the young Erakwan woman was hardly beholden to anyone, at least not in the way that Jacobia certainly was.

"Feather!" she called at the receding back, stiff with outrage. "Please! I wasn't trying to touch your earth-bond! If you believe so, then mayhap my fingers were drawn to it without my mind realizing it. I'm sorry." At least that's what she assumed must have happened. Or that Feather had misinterpreted it as that. What was happening to her? To Feather? Somehow their roles were changing, their beings in flux, Feather becoming more and more like Kulshana . . . who was Kulshana?

Oh, Lady bless! Addawanna and the others now loosely surrounded them both, observing her and Feather with a grave intensity that this minor altercation hardly merited. Tempting to simply continue sitting here, each particle of earth channeling through her, her every sense eagerly assimilating it, but in truth, her bottom was fast becoming cold and numb. Aiming to make some wry passing comment, a small joke to ease her discomfort, she folded her legs under her and started to rise, embarrassed at being the center of attention. But what issued forth from her mouth was not of her own inventing. "I will build me a being from this earth!" something within her decreed with loving deliberation.

"Ah? Will you, now?" Addawanna inquired with wary affability, visibly straining to maintain a phlegmatic pose. "Kulshanala! You come—now! 'Side Jacobia!" With nowhere to retreat without breaking the loose circle, Feather came, feet dragging, face downcast in a scowl. Trepidation in her eyes, in her hunched stance, as if she'd been robbed of all confidence and assurance and was only beginning to comprehend the depth of her lack.

"What, Addawanna? You want a beast of burden again? That's all I'm good for, I suppose," she simmered and seethed, ready to boil over with the unfairness of the role forced on her. "I'm not Erakwan and I'm not Outlander, so I'm nothing to you! So many questions, you always complained . . . and all I wanted . . . all I wanted . . . was to . . ." tears of frustration washed down her coppery cheeks and, without thought, Jacobia reached to touch one, but Feather shied away, grimacing, teeth bared in a snarl.

"Hush, child. You hab role, oder role dan you t'ought. Have need, also. Needin' to be reborn as whole bein', but bein' born hurt fierce—ripped out of worlds you know, or t'ink you know. Not Kulshana, not bein' Shanakul, but allays Kulshanala, my precious little Feather." Addawanna wiped Feather's tears with the back of her hand, roughly caressing the damp cheek before lifting her knuckles beneath Feather's chin to raise her head, stare intently into Feather's hazel eyes. "Now, I askin' favor—fer you, fer us, fer ev'ryone. No easy favor."

Jacobia listened, heard, and a distant part of her mourned for Feather, her suffering, but her mind was gravid with being, a kindling desire to let it issue forth, regardless of the pangs of labor. Her hands clutched at thin air, emptiness, aching to touch and mold, aching to be the conduit for such potency. There, within her grasp if she but dared, but who—Glashtok? No, not him, nor Lennap, not even Addawanna.

"You let her hold earth-bond," Addawanna declared, and the younger woman screamed as if a limb were being ripped from her body. "No, child. You no take off—neber would Addawanna make you suffer so. But, but," she cajoled, "you an Jacobia, connect. Let her hold it."

With a reluctance verging on loathing, Feather opened the neck of her tunic, baring a thumb-sized pouch swirled with deep green and brown that hung from a leather thong around her throat.

With an urgent longing Jacobia sprang at Feather's throat, clutching the pouch, warm and supple from the heat of Feather's body, wanting nothing more than to snatch it away, claim it as hers alone. Selfishness, a part of her chided, because it could not belong to her alone, any more than Feather could solely possess it—not when they all were entwined by a power greater than that. Such very small beings, but all part and parcel of the world, the earth, the soil. . . . Beings. . . .

"Now you start story 'gain, Jacobia. We all lis'en, Feather lis'en, learn wisdom wears many guises."

"I will build me a being from this earth," Jacobia intoned again, some force impelling her, shaping her words, shaping the story that had been swelling within her, a world within and without.

" 'Yes, from this very earth,' the Great Spirit thought to Himself once, long, long ago, long before time was time as we know it. Already what He'd created had assumed a unity beyond anything He'd originally conceived—combing the land with His fingers to form rivers, punching a fingertip to dimple a lake here and there, raising mountains with a well-placed kick or cuff, then patiently softening some peaks while leaving others jagged as teeth. So many shapes and forms that He'd near exhausted His inexhaustible ingenuity in molding them.

"But despite such effort it appeared barren and stark to His eyes, so He set his mind to devise green, growing things so diverse that each season might boast different hues of green and other pleasing tints—the pink and white and yellow and lavender of blossoms; the reds and purples and blues of fruit; the raucous change of leaves to scarlet, orange, and gold as the air chilled and the nights grew shorter; the immutable green of needlelike leaves during bleak, short days and long, cold nights, a reminder of new greens that would venture forth again. 'Trees,' He named them, and gave each a special name: Willow, Poplar, Cherry, Birch, Elm, Apple, Hemlock, Maple, Oak, Arborfer, and more, and let them wander, gravitate to the spots most pleasing to them, by streams, in the midst of fields, even wandering up the flanks of His mountains.

"But they, too, craved company beyond their own kind. And so, from bits of matter, He set silvery fish flashing in the rivers and streams, frogs and snakes and crickets around their edges, birds to populate the very air, and animals to scamper along the ground.

"Except, much as He hated to admit it, unless He supervised every moment, all these creations grew fractious, squabbled with one another, even His trees. Much as He might like to, the Great Spirit could not linger here indefinitely to impose order—not when a whole expansive universe required tracking and organizing. SomeOne must determine if the spheres set in motion were orbiting properly; or whether certain stars required relocating to enhance their brilliance; not to mention inflating His nebulous gas clouds.

"And thus, one day, He decided to build a being. Someone both of the earth and beyond it, a guardian, an overseer. While His other creations would respect and obey this being, the being must recognize the fine line it walked, lest it destroy the symmetry of life.

"Gently the Great Spirit blew across the earth to collect a pile of dust. For dust, dirt, soil, the earth, would comprise much of this new being, allow it to remember that it had begun as dust and would end as dust, the completion of a cycle He'd set into motion for all living things. Except dust didn't cling together very well, so the Great Spirit borrowed water from the rain and the sea and the streams, and clay from their banks. All of this He blended and molded, patiently kneading it, waiting for it to rise and expand, assume its place on this earth.

"'Ah!' exclaimed the Great Spirit, chuckling at Himself over His own forgetfulness. 'I must invest it with a touch of air—let the breeze, the wind, fill its lungs, be kin to the air, just as it is kin with the water. And just a touch of fire to inspire its body, kindle its spirit.' But since He worried about His creations being careless with fire, He borrowed an animating pinch of Sun and Moon. After all, fire would venture forth soon enough—lightning's gift to this new being—once He had this being in place to supervise it.

"And so the Great Spirit created the first human, the first Erakwan. Earth-born, earth-bound, at its beginning dust, and at its end, dust. And lest it forget its origins, the

Great Spirit hung a small bag of earth on a vine around its neck. For so the earth resides within us all, a part of all of us. We guard the earth and its creatures as promised, travel softly across its surface, refusing to cause it needless pain, for we are of earth, Erakwa. And we shall never purposely harm that which we ward for the Great Spirit.

"And so it was, and so it shall ever be," Jacobia concluded, finally hearing her voice, convinced it was her own. The story had welled within her, overflowed, and now that it had come spilling out, she doubted she could repeat it if her life depended upon it. No, somehow it still lodged within her, a part of her, there to be tapped when the time came. And that time was fast approaching. . . .

Fingers stiff, she released her hold on Feather's earth-bond, a lingering sadness at letting it go. But so it was, and so it must be. Mayhap somehow, someday, she'd be gifted with one of her own, a precious pairing that must be earned. Feather had earned hers, as had the others surrounding her.

Shyly she looked around, diffident about meeting any eye but intensely curious as to their reaction to this tale that had been lofted from deep within her—unlikely vessel that she was—and that she'd breathed life into up here high in these beautiful but uncompromising mountains. At least they hadn't laughed. Hadn't shifted and squirmed with boredom.

Mataweeta, she could meet her face, Jacobia decided. Or Glashtok. But as she did so, first fleetingly, then with a more halting confidence, she was astounded to discover them still frozen in place, rapt in the skein of words she'd woven about them, even Addawanna. "Feather?" Surely Feather, with her scoffing disdain, securely anchored in the Outlander world, would not be so affected. Could, mayhap, provide a coherent reaction to what she'd heard. Or would she believe Jacobia did no more than mock them and their ways?

"Feather?" she asked again, loudly enough that it jarred her ears. To have fairly earned, gained Feather's approval, her friendship, created a bond between them beyond that of burden and bearer mattered more than Jacobia wanted to acknowledge.

In total silent submission, her head bowed, Feather removed the leather pouch from around her neck and slipped the thong over Jacobia's head. "You have earned it, become what I no longer am, but mayhap someday will be again. If I work hard to regain it."

With exquisite care, fearing she'd stepped beyond bounds, she embraced Feather, tentatively at first, then harder, a fierce longing finally assuaged as Feather dissolved into tears. "Sister," Jacobia whispered as she soothed her.

♣

"Ho!" Addawanna exulted, "blood not only t'ing dat make person one of us!"

Her feet swift and sure—and free from pain—Jacobia climbed upward with Addawanna, no longer a burden to be carried. Occasionally she surreptitiously touched the earth-bond hanging around her neck, unwilling to call attention to it or to herself. What she wanted to do was stop dead, marvel at it, admire how it nestled just above the cleft of her breasts, belonging there. Halting to stare at it might seem too much like gloating. Even though Feather had freely gifted her with it, it troubled her—Outlanders again taking what wasn't theirs to claim—yet Feather's spirits were lighter, more buoyant than ever before, even when she'd first met her in Gaernett—how many days past? Why should it concern her? Time flowed as it would, fast or slow.

"No be worryin' 'bout Feather," Addawanna instructed. "She no realizin' afore dat earth-bond wearing her down, and more she fight, the more it whittle at her soul. Once she learn stop fightin', tryin' be one or oder, she be fine. Will labor till worthy of noder one, and rejoice in it more next time. You say same way in your langwidge? 'Doan 'preciate what you got, till not having it no more'?"

Jacobia nodded. "It's true of all of us—of any age, from any place or any station. If you've never lacked or wanted for something, you don't realize how precious it can be. A simple meal is a feast if you've once been starving."

A sage nod from Addawanna, and a merrily sly side-glance, her eyes crinkling at the corners. "And so what it be that Jacobia lack afore, dat now make you 'preciate t'ings diff'rently? Oder dan being packed 'round like side of venison, eh?" Hands at the small of her back, she gave a mock groan.

Certainly that had been a part of it. Mobility had never before seemed so sweet—a seemingly simple yet complex series of movements that carried the body along, once learned in infancy. No, it hadn't been pleasant being a burden, yet because of it, she'd been obliged to *see,* experience wonders she'd never before witnessed, as well as viewing familiar scenes with fresh eyes, no longer blinded by old ways of seeing. Despite herself she reveled in a burst of speed, lightly sprinting ahead, only to discover Addawanna matching her stride for stride, not even breathing hard. "What about Feather?" Could Feather now keep pace lacking her earth-bond?

"No worry 'bout Feather. 'Bout time she draw on inner self, burn 'way dross, make her stronger, surer of what have value in life." An implacable hand on her wrist slowed Jacobia, and she nearly balked, seized with a vigor that could carry her to the top of the mountain. Never had it appeared so near, within easy reach, beckoning, hinting of secrets still unfolding! "Wantin' talk 'bout *you!*" Addawanna insisted, and with a wicked underhand flick, pitched a piece of ice at Jacobia to make her attend. Catching it as it sailed by like a comet, she cheekily tossed it back, Addawanna ducking and scolding simultaneously.

"I set out looking for the twins . . ." The twins! Aunt Mahafny and Harrap! Lady bless, all thoughts of them had been driven from her mind! Did Saam still live? Had they reached Nakum? "Addawanna?" Wildly she grabbed at her earth-bond, aching to listen, hear what the earth might tell her, just as Addawanna listened to it. But this, as yet, was beyond her skill, though murmurous noises filled her ears.

"Now we go to Nakum's. Dey reach us tomorrow at peak."

Dizzy with relief, she struggled to steady herself. Addawanna still waited, as patient and imperturbable as the mountains, expecting her not only to recite, but to explain what she'd learned. Not that she didn't wish to reveal it, yet what she'd gradually perceived was so basic, so integral that it was embarrassing to say it, a realization that any

right-minded soul should be instinctively aware of from
birth, that translocation from an inner to an outer world.
"I am earth-born, earth-bound, a part of this earth, just as
it is a part of me. Though I reside here, it is not my domain,
or my people's domain. We hold it secure for each succeeding generation, just as past generations faithfully held it
for us. Why is it so hard for people to *recognize* that fact?"

"All t'ings need harmony, not one takin' power over
oders. Earth not stay same even on its own, constant
change, shift, sometimes major, mostly minor. Trees dropping leaves in fall, giving back to the earth, making more
earth. Replenishing. Replenishing like Nakum an Eadwin
an Roland doing wid arborfer." A gusty sigh of exasperation. "Aye! I wish Nakum being dere when we 'rive. Away
too long, can feel he feelin' it, not happy."

Now Jacobia's anger, dormant for so long, began to
rouse. "You mean Nakum's not there? What about Saam,
then? How can Mahafny save Saam if he's not there? Have
they endured all this for naught?" Well, hadn't it been a
fool's errand from the very beginning? But to have reached
their goal—as Addawanna had assured her they would—
and not succeed! The twins would be distraught—and
Mahafny . . . She didn't dare contemplate how her aunt
would react to failure. Life was neither fair nor unfair, it
simply was. But would Mahafny *see,* accept that it made its
own kind of sense?

"Doan worry," Addawanna consoled. "We gettin' dere
fast as we can. Nakum not only one mayhap help Saam. I
be dere, an my grandmot'er, Doncallis, too. We work out
somet'ing till Nakum come back. 'Sides, you t'ink findin'
twins *all* you set out to do? Ha! You jes beginnin', child!
Much to do, so *much* to do!"

❧

Jenneth was thankful Doncallis had remained with them,
had half-expected her to flit off like some will-o'-the-wisp,
a figment of Diccon's imagination. She believed in her existence as long as she remained in sight. Remained near
enough to touch might be more accurate—far too easy to
believe you saw any number of things that weren't really

there, eyes playing tricks in the light or dark, the mind predisposed to "see" something. Touching something proved its existence.

No way to touch Doncallis at the moment, but Jenneth didn't doubt she was there. Unless the head of Harrap's stretcher was being toted by an invisible being. And toted was hardly the word—towed might be more like it, she and Dic stumbling at the stretcher's rear, each gripping a handle, and trotting faster than she'd like. *"Dic, what's she really like? Is she truly the same person Mama met here before—the one with the slaithe?"*

Right hand wrapped around his left wrist to ease the strain of carrying the stretcher, Diccon gave an uneven shrug. *"She just is, Jen. Incredibly old and incredibly young, old as this world, as new as tomorrow. Isn't she beautiful?"*

Her brother love-struck over an elderly woman? Forsaking Maeve and all the other young, curvaceous beauties he lusted over, though mostly to no avail? *"Well, if you don't want to answer me, just say so! Don't put me off like that!"* Both hands were blistering, she was sure, and her mittens were sticky with pitch.

Pw'eek, trotting beneath the stretcher, came to Diccon's rescue, much to Jenneth's surprise. **"He's telling the truth. I was there, I know. And she** *is* **beautiful, within and without."**

Wonderful! Pw'eek was smitten as well! Though Diccon had suffered no ill effects from his time separated from his body, he wouldn't—or couldn't—explain where he'd been to her or to Kwee, both of them feeling like women scorned. But spurned for what?

**"Not spurned!"** Pw'eek persisted. **"I swear you're as bad as Sissy-Poo, both of you sulking, acting as if he's rejected you. As if** *I've* **rejected you!"** Despite the danger of tangling in Jenneth's and Diccon's legs, the two already bumping shoulders and in such close quarters, Pw'eek eased from beneath the stretcher and reared up, front paws on the handle, head pressed close and insistent against Jenneth's hand.

*"Darling, be careful!"* The dear was sidestepping along on her hind legs, for all the world like a trained bear. Somehow she managed to brush a kiss on the butterscotch patch behind one ear. *"I'll save you the lecture—if Diccon can*

*have room in his heart to love Kwee and to love me, then
love is infinite. There's enough to share with Doncallis as
well, correct?"*

Scooting back beneath the stretcher as Harrap groaned
and tossed, Pw'eek's gray tail periscoped above the edge.
But I still don't understand, she inwardly protested. I
don't understand how Saam and Parm came back, what
they did or why they did it. How Saam knew to do it. And
what had made Pw'eek so determined to rescue Diccon
precisely when she did? Curiouser and curiouser. Yet somehow they were reunited again, resolutely climbing to the
peak of Nakum's mountain—Callis's, actually, she
supposed.

Think of something else! No, that was hardly a good
idea, either! Here it was, the dead of night and they were
transporting poor Harrap on a stretcher, the man feverish,
his leg incredibly swollen. But Callis swore she knew where
they could make camp, tend to Harrap. Behind them Mahafny trudged along, the ponies strung out behind her,
Saam and Parm on Mignon, and Kwee, sulky at Diccon
and her sib, on Daisy. Black-and-gray stone on one side of
her, and on Diccon's other side, the nothingness of the
drop. Snow, of course. White and black like an etching,
everything so terribly vertical and thin.

Harrap moaned, tried to sit up, and Jenneth automatically hushed him, the stretcher nearly ripped from her hand
as his weight shifted. "Parm's fine, Harrap. He's just being
lazy—you know him, why walk when he can ride?"

"Dear Parm!" Harrap sounded drowsy. "Came back to
me . . . you know . . . just like Mahafny. Didn't leave
me . . . after all. Just an . . . excursion."

Ahead of them, Doncallis walked on, straight-backed,
looking like a white candle with her white doeskin clothing
and the braid of white hair swaying along her spine. Did
she never tire? Jenneth had a stitch in her side and Diccon
was limping; she'd heard his muttered exclamation as he'd
tripped on a rock.

"Patience, young ones," Callis called over her shoulder,
sounding so merry that Jenneth made a face at her as soon
as the Erakwan woman had straightened her head. Shameful at her age, but it made her feel minimally better. "Just
up ahead, I believe. A halfway house."

A halfway house? Where? Worse yet, did that mean that they were still only halfway to the top? *"Still mad at me, Sis? Jenneth? Mayhap someday I can find the words to explain—"*

*"Do you really think there's a halfway house?"* The last thing she—or any of them, for that matter—needed was false hope.

*"If she says so, then it's so, honest, Jen."* Well, good for him, *he* certainly sounded utterly convinced! *"Doncallis runs deeper than truth, somehow."*

Another twenty meters and Callis eased them leftward into a spot where the trail widened, dipping inward against the mountain's flank, though not by much. Here the rock face was layered with a thick skin of ice, whether from the runoff of melt water or some outlet higher up, Jenneth didn't know. Lady help her, she was tired! Could there possibly be a stream up this high? Come to think of it, how did Nakum get water—melt snow? But then something worse struck her.

"We're not? We're not going into another cave, are we?" Heard the shrillness in her voice, verging almost on hysteria, and didn't care. "I will *not* enter another cave, Doncallis. I don't care who you are, what you know, whether this mountain is yours or not! I *won't* go in! And I won't let Diccon go in either! Or anyone else!"

"Oh, hush, child, hush!" Callis chided as she lowered her end of the stretcher and motioned for them to do likewise. "Don't upset the Shepherd. Let him rest." Hands on hips, she stood facing the sheeted ice, studying it, shifting to scrutinize it, examine it from slightly different angles. "Botheration! Leave things alone, and what do they do? They change on you, ever so slightly. Nothing remains entirely the same, immutable, I'm afraid. Stages and ages, you know."

No, she didn't know and didn't want to know! "Please, Diccon!" Clutching his tabard she pulled him close. "Promise me! Swear you won't go inside if it's a cave! I won't take a chance on losing you again!"

Wrapping his arms around her in a hug, he held her tight, tighter still, his cold cheek against hers until her shaking subsided. "Promise you, Jennie-sis. But I hope we don't have to camp on the trail—just a little too narrow for my taste, especially if I squirm in my sleep!"

"Ah! Here we are!" Callis, who'd been running the thin blade of her knife up and down the ice wall, suddenly gave her wrist a deft twist and a door swung inward. Not another door! From behind her Kwee snarled.

"Pity save us!" Callis had taken her by the hand, and Jenneth began to whimper, set her feet. "No, I shan't drag you inside, but come look. It's ice, all ice. Built block by block. The melt water's smoothed over the seams, made it hard to see, but look. Look hard." As she held up a hand, pale light glowed from it, reflecting and refracting from the ice. Within, Jenneth could glimpse furs strewn on the floor, raised sections along the walls to serve as benches or bunks. Shallow clay dishes of oil with floating wicks began to burn, one after the other.

"Amazing how warm just a few of these can make the place," Callis soothed.

It looked . . . almost cozy. "But it's very small," she demurred, somehow not wanting to sound overly critical. "Can we possibly fit five people, four ghatti, and four ponies inside?" Well, Harrap and Mahafny and Saam had first priority, that was simple enough.

Still resisting despite herself, she allowed Callis to draw her inside. Ice steps ran up one wall, leading to a square opening. "Easier to gain additional space by going straight up. Didn't want to carve into the mountain itself, after all." Jenneth nodded numbly, as if that made perfect sense. Mayhap it would to Diccon. "Two levels above this level. Ponies will be something of a problem, though, but I think we can squeeze them in, two on a side, in those storage wings. Snug as a double stall, and no bigger, I'd say."

It elicited a giggle from Jenneth. "Lucky thing we don't have horses. Their haunches would be hanging out on the trail."

"Hush, child," Callis chided again, sitting her down. "Let me get the others settled. You're more tired than I realized. I'm sorry."

♣

Unsure where he was but entirely happy to be there, Harrap massaged his temples while he vaguely stared at the ceiling. His leg hurt abominably, like a sausage in a too-tight casing, but he didn't care. No longer trapped! No longer caught between the earth's jaws! Parm's nose poked his ear, sniffing, before the ghatt began a deep, singsong purr and began scrubbing his muzzle along Harrap's jaw, whitish stubble snagging the long ghatt whiskers.

**"Scratchy Harrap,"** Parm breathily singsonged. **"Not smooth but scratchy, ooh, scratches my chin so nice . . . ly."**

*"Come closer, then, and I'll see if I can sandpaper your ears to little nubs,"* he mock-growled, gratified when Parm started. A paw patted his cheek, his mouth, the ghatt insistently touching flesh against flesh. *"Come snuggle, Parm, dearest ghatt,"* he invited, turning back the edge of his blanket, only to be hit by the sour smell of his own body. *"Phew! On second thought, stay atop the blanket."*

But Parm was worming his way beneath the blanket draping Harrap's elevated leg. **"I've always loved your toes, but right now they *do* look like five little sausage links."** As if to prove that they weren't, he gave them a considering lick, and Harrap made a hissing inhalation between clenched teeth. No doubt Mahafny would consider that a good sign: not only could he feel each excruciating heartbeat in each toe, he could discern the scrape of Parm's rough tongue.

*"Where are we?"* If Parm would just give him a hint, he might be able to gather the pieces, the fragments of memory, but he needed some way to order them, be assured he'd not fever-dreamed it. The murmurous breathing of sleepers surrounded him, the shift of tired bodies easing themselves into more comfortable positions, or at least a different position. For example, he was quite sure that Jenneth and Diccon—Diccon!—were with them again, that somehow all was well there. *"And where did you go?"* His indignation mounted. *"Why did you go off and leave me—just when I needed you the most!"* The hurt remained, a twin to the hurt in his leg, but worse somehow. Never had the ghatt deserted him like that! *"And your cap and vest—gone!"*

Slowly, sinuously, Parm eased along Harrap's good leg, ever higher, testing the waters of Harrap's anger. The large hand buffeting his head was hardly gentle or welcoming, and Parm retreated out of reach. Irritably, the hand sought him again, Harrap pleading, *"Didn't mean to whack you, my dear friend. Misjudged where your head was."*

**"Hold still and let me find your hand,"** Parm instructed, crawling higher. **"Saam and I *had* to leave. Saam remembered what he needed to, and we had to find Diccon. For no other reason in the world would I have left you, but the need was great!"**

*"Selfish of me."* Fingers danced at the back of Parm's neck. *"His need was greater than mine, but I was half out of my mind with worry and fear."* Raising his head as much as he could, he stared down his chest, attempting to make out Parm's outline. *"And believe it or not, Parm, Mahafny stayed with me, didn't leave me—except to fetch something she needed to rescue me."* A warm feeling at that, that Mahafny had cast off all other concerns to remain with him. *"Oh, but she couldn't have gone on, could she? Not since Saam was with you."* Well, that was reality, wasn't it? No sense developing misguided notions of Mahafny's loyalty or love.

Parm shifted his ears within easy reach of Harrap's fingers. **"Do you remember meeting Doncallis? Callis, that is? She came with Diccon and Jenneth and Saam and me when we rejoined you. And Pw'eek and Kwee, of course."**

Images floated by him. A cool hand on his brow, its fingers straight, not gnarled like Mahafny's icy hands. Of being lashed onto an impromptu stretcher, of being carried with a gentle sway that made him feel cradled and cared for. But what also came to mind was something decidedly odd. They were . . . they were wherever it was they were . . . in this shelter. He'd come to, come to himself for a bit, even feeling a touch cranky that the cradle had halted its rocking. And what he'd wanted most of all was a drink of water, but no one seemed to hear his whisper.

*"Parm, was there something strange about . . . Callis and Mahafny . . . just after we got here?"* How to explain? How he'd watched the two older women, both so elegant in old age, though Mahafny looked increasingly frayed, worn parchment thin. Shepherds watched people, learned to read what the body said in how it moved, how it held itself tight and close or expansive and open. Lies slid off some lips slick as butter . . . heartily repent my sins and promise that in *this* life I shall do better. But their bodies were crabbed,

tense, belying their words. And what he'd witnessed between Mahafny and Callis had struck him as being totally out of character. More than that, unwomanly, almost. No, that was unjust—unmannerly, unexpected. After all, if he harbored preconceived notions of Mahafny, he'd been disabused of them long ago, held a sharp picture in his mind of how she acted and reacted.

Making little, hooting snores against the blanket, Parm finally lifted his head and shook it, yawning. **"Mean the way they circled each other, sizing each other up? 'Round you and over you? Thought they were going to grapple with each other—or dance. Wouldn't have wanted to place any bets on who'd lead, though."**

Yes, that was it exactly! He was hardly so naïve to think that women didn't compete, didn't assess each other with very keen eyes, but it was usually more subtle, rarely was it so overt or with the overtones of aggression he'd felt clashing in the air. For two men first meeting, it wasn't unusual, especially if drink were involved, an imagined slight or slur already planted in one or both minds, an overweening desire to prove superiority, bolster masculine pride. Nor did these confrontations for dominance all degenerate into outright battle, though some inevitably did. With dawning wonder, he blurted, *"They circled each other like two roosters! Pridefully showing off! Look at my comb! See the length of my tail! The number of followers in my wake, hoping I'll gift them with a piece of melon rind, or chase away the others and let them peck at the best seed."*

**"But,"** Parm pointed out through another yawn, **"they didn't actually squabble."**

*"But was there a 'winner'?"* Harrap persisted. *"Did either back down?"*

Parm sounded sleepy but dubious. **"Well . . . Callis *is* sleeping outside."**

*"Mahafny! Yes!"* Harrap pumped a fist in the air, then was dismayed at himself, his reaction. After all, much as he revered Mahafny, he had no basis for judging this Callis person, other than the fact that she'd been involved in returning Diccon to himself.

**"Wasn't that,"** Parm argued. **"Least I'm pretty sure not. Callis is outside because she prefers to be, said she doesn't sleep much and likes to be at one with the stars and the**

sky, the mountain itself, not mewed up inside. If you knew
her at all, you'd know that's right. Even though her people
built this ice place, she'd rather not reside within it for any
length of time. Don't know how she can sit out there all
night, 'specially if it snows . . ." and Parm drifted into
sleep, leaving Harrap more curious than before, though he
couldn't pursue it any further as his eyes drifted closed. . . .
Had his Lady and his lady, but what was Callis? In the
nature of things, she must represent something . . . nature
of things . . . nature of . . . naturally. . . .

♣

Almost without volition Jenneth found herself sitting upright, listening hard, Pw'eek equally awake. On the floor
beside her Diccon and Kwee never shifted, unaware, lost
in the depths of sleep. There! There it was again, less sound
than a mouse might make around ghatti, but definitely
there—a strangled "uh-uh-uh," then a pause before it came
again, "uuh-uuh-Uuh!" Barely there and yet there, beyond
the bounds of consciousness, an unquiet body whimpering
its long-standing pain and hurt, agony finally leaking forth.
    *"Harrap?"* It made perfect sense. Of course the dear
man hurt, hadn't any idea that under the influence of Mahafny's medicaments he'd unconsciously vocalized his
body's pains. Indeed, would be distraught to discover he'd
disturbed their rest. Was there something she could do to
ease him—a mug of water, a damp cloth for his brow? No
sound of Mahafny ministering to her patient, apparently so
deeply asleep that she'd not heard. Hugging her knees, resting her cheek atop them, she waited for the sound to repeat
itself before deciding what to do.
    "Uh-um-UM!" Again it came and the poignancy of the
weak plaint in the midst of the night tore at her. **"Not
Harrap,"** Pw'eek informed her as she padded to the ice
steps. **"That's Saam!"** And with that she flowed silently
downstairs, Jenneth following as quickly as she could, stepping over Diccon, who rolled and grabbed her leg, muzzily
aware of her passing and concerned.
    *"Wazza? Jen, doan follow any green-gold lights!"* and
clung tighter for an instant until she bent to reassure him,

stroking his hair off his forehead. Gradually his grip slacked and she could move without tearing herself free. She took the stairs on her bottom, easing from one riser to the next, not trusting herself in the dark on ice steps, scary enough climbing them without slithering and slipping down them.

"Hurry!" Pw'eek's urgency made her shiver, though she was anything but cold. "He's crawled into the corner, as far from Mahafny as he can get! I can't pry any sense out of him."

Patting the floor with her hands, she navigated between her aunt's and Harrap's sleeping forms, Harrap's arms thrown wide, one hand touching Mahafny's where it lay near her head. *"Pw'eek, I can't see a thing! Guide me!"* Strange how a room so small, little more than a cubicle, could loom so large, boast so many obstacles between her and the one being she so desperately wanted to reach. Her seeking hand glanced off Pw'eek's warm flank and onto Saam's side. Oh, dear, Blessed Lady! He was shivering, absolutely aquiver with the cold, his paws blindly scrabbling against the ice wall, his claws dully striking it. And at intervals came the broken string of suffering sounds that had awakened her and Pw'eek. "Uh-uh-UM!" he'd whimper, then whine it at a higher pitch.

Almost afraid he'd shatter if she picked him up, she crouched and gathered him close in her arms, her cheek sleeking along his head and neck, her lips touching his chill ears. *"Saam! Saam, darling! What's the matter, what's wrong?"* What else did one ask at times like these—as if his answer would indicate the problem had a solution, was fixable!

"I can't wake Mahafny," Pw'eek reported. "Her breathing's regular, her heart as well—nothing wrong. I think she finally felt secure enough to deeply sleep. Even if we manage to wake her, she's not likely to have her wits about her any time soon."

*"And Harrap needs his sleep,"* she thought more to herself than to Pw'eek. *"Not that he could do much anyway."* Except comfort her, because she felt she embraced death in her arms.

Painfully leaning his head against her collarbone, Saam grimaced as he cried out, "Ah, Nakum! Let me see Nakum . . . one last time!" Shifting higher in her arms,

almost as if he climbed within his loose skin, he pressed
his forehead against her neck. **"Jen-Doyce . . . all I have . . .
give me my deliverance . . . take me . . . for Oriel's
sake. . . ."**

Pw'eek stood ready by the ice door. **"We truly aren't
that far from the top. If we don't take him now, it'll be too
late come morning."**

Too late come morning. Morning would dawn and Saam
would be dead, so close to the goal that Mahafny had
sought to save him—or at least attempt to, though she'd
known there were no guarantees. But she'd been willing to
risk all on the chance. Could Jenneth do any less? Could
she, this one time, outrun death, outpace it? Not hold herself responsible for it as she had for Bard's death? And
from that death, M'wa's decision to leave this life as he
knew it. Not an atonement, but another chance . . . to show
true courage in the face of potential loss, death . . . to try
her best, win or lose.

**"That we've *done* our best, beloved,"** the ghatta emphasized. **"Now, put Saam down and dress yourself. It's always
coldest at night."**

Hurriedly complying, Jenneth struggled into jacket and
scarf, pulled on her boots. She'd stamp her feet into them
better once she was outside. Cap, mittens?—yes. Sheepskin
tabard now and snug the sash tight. Yes, that was it! Going
to be tricky, but Saam must remain warm and she needed
her hands free. Damn! Shouldn't have tied the sash yet!
Cramming herself on the ledge bench, she untied the sash
and tossed the front of the tabard over her shoulder, unbuttoned the first few buttons of her jacket. Then, carefully,
she slid the elderly ghatt deep within her jacket, tucking
him in before bringing the tabard back into place. Really
knot the sash, couldn't take any chances on it coming loose.
Easier said than done as she worked by touch under what
was now a protruding belly.

Strangely exhilarated, Jenneth cracked open the door
and slipped outside, only to stand there in profound shock.
Snow! It was snowing, whiteness spilling over everything,
driving at her eyes, making her blink. And where was
Callis? Somehow she'd convinced herself that Callis would
be waiting, ready to offer advice and aid. Her last prop
gone, no one to lean upon.

Plowing through snow already belly-high, Pw'eek looked back at her, flakes clustering on her gray back and head. **"Come on!"**

Shifting her cap lower and bringing up her hood, Jenneth stamped her feet and followed in Pw'eek's trail, arms protectively clutching her burden to be delivered.

♣

Snow whirled and battered her, lodged on her eyelashes, no matter how often she brushed them clean. Thick flakes wedged inside her hood in the small space on each side of her scarved neck, and lodged in her nostrils before melting. *"Pw'eek! I can't see you! Where are you?"* How many steps had she taken along the trail? Not many, but already she'd lost all sense of direction, wanted more than anything to retreat, return to the ice house. Give in, give up.

**"Beloved! Listen to my 'voice, follow it. I'll lead."** Obediently Jenneth placed one foot in front of the other, kicking at the snow with her boots. Inside her jacket Saam writhed and moaned, and she wrapped her right arm beneath him to hold him still. Not the wisest thing to do, because she desperately needed both arms free to balance against the slickness underfoot. The snow reached her boot tops and gusts of wind swept at her from all directions, pelting her with both fresh and drifting snow.

*"Pw'eek, darling! This is insane. We're going to kill ourselves as well as Saam!"* Failure—could she live with failure, knowing her cowardice had hastened Saam's death? Unfair! She'd tried, hadn't she? But not hard enough, her own fears taking precedence. Always about herself, her own doubts, her own dreads—dear Lady, nothingness yawned to her right! Her foot had sensed the edge just in time! Staggering, she threw herself leftward against the cliff face, Saam groaning as she mashed his poor, thin body between her and the wall. *"Pw'eek!"* She shrieked it in her mind and voiced her plea aloud as well, heard it dully hammer the rock, slap her face as it rebounded at her.

**"Jenneth, beloved! I'm mayhap two meters ahead of you, I can just see you, even if you can't see me,"** Pw'eek entreated. **"Put your back against the cliff and stretch out your left arm, edge along! You can do it, you must!"**

Her feet followed a trail carved by Pw'eek's broad body as she plowed onward. So very dark and dim, the snow a gray swarm before her face, nothing to see. . . . And yet . . . tilting her head back as far as she could, her hood scraping the wall, how could she discern the Lady Moon up above? Its light a clean, clear distant globe of silver-white against the engulfing black of the sky, sailing on serenely, unmindful of her toil and terror while she and the crescent Disciple moon chased after her.

**"Just a little farther, beloved and we'll leave the nasty ledge. You'll swing left and find the trail winds between rocks so it's walled on either side."**

Fine for her to say! And then what? How much farther, how much longer? *"Saam, my dearest old friend, how goes it? Can you hold on?"*

Silence. Ah, she'd failed, tried and failed, the valiant old ghatt passing away before she could reach help! He soared through the Spirals to the ghatti Elders now, and she yearned to soar at his side, view this treacherous, unforgiving mountain from above, look down on it and all that had transpired—no longer a part of it. Her legs were leaden, her back ached from the drag of Saam's limp, lifeless body. What to do, where to go, bearing a corpse . . . ?

**"Nakum?"** Saam finally whispered, faint yet fierce with desire.

Relief at his 'voice. Dismay, too. Still a reason to continue striving, struggling. Step, step. Yes, Pw'eek was right, a sensation of solidity on either side, the trail slightly wider, more forgiving, although now the blizzard swept down at her, funneled into the slot she climbed, its concentrated force shoving her backward. Both hands wrapped beneath Saam now, she bent into the wind and snow, wavering forward.

And through all this, had she spared a thought for Pw'eek, nothing but her plush coat between her and the raging storm, soft paw-pads trudging through the snow? She must be half frozen to death! Could she scoop her up, let her cling to the tabard? Or would the additional weight drag her down? Somehow she'd bear it, even if she were reduced to crawling on hands and knees to reach her goal! *"Darling? Let me carry you for a ways before you're frozen solid!"*

"D–don't think I c–can jump up," came Pw'eek's chattered reply, just what Jenneth had feared. Forging ahead, she searched for Pw'eek, haltingly afraid she'd kick or step on her. Worse, overstep and completely miss her. "R–right h–here!" Pw'eek's desperate mindcry reached her.

Yes, that mound in the trail's center, snow-coated yet a hint of deeper gray in patches. Clumsily she dropped to one knee, peeling off a mitten, brushing away snow to fondle Pw'eek's head, the ears so fragile and thin—and so cold! Shifting Saam inside her jacket so he rested on the leg folded under her, she dragged Pw'eek up, the ghatta unfurling as she pulled her upward into a rough embrace. *"Can you hang on?"* And in mute answer Pw'eek's front claws sank into her tabard just below the shoulder; unable to hoist herself any higher, ride astride Jenneth's shoulders. Boosting her wouldn't work either, not unless Pw'eek could help.

Left arm supporting Saam, right arm tucked around Pw'eek's haunches, Jenneth took a deep breath and forced all her strength into her legs, rearing up with a sideways lurch. Lady bless, one more snowflake on her back and the additional weight would tip her over! I will do this! I *will* do this! If we die, we die together! The world constricted to a small length of trail directly in front of her leaden feet. Step and step. No cadence to her gait, no evenness, just plod . . . and plod, and again . . . and again . . . Saam and Pw'eek were depending on her, just as she'd relied on them in the past. Without Saam's intervention, she'd not have had Diccon returned to himself, whole. Without Pw'eek, she'd be incomplete, lacking. But worst of all, without trusting, believing in herself, she'd never be whole. Had to respect and acknowledge both her strengths and weaknesses, love what she was—and what she wasn't.

Like a drunkard Jenneth staggered on, floundering through drifts, reeling on her feet. Forward and up, up toward the peak. Coming down would prove simple, she could roll, turn herself into a giant snowball. Strange, it looked almost light and clear ahead. Was her mind playing tricks? Beckoning with an aura of light that didn't exist? Better than blackness and gloom, at any rate.

Mustering a final burst of energy from deep within her, she stumbled faster toward the brightness, clutching both ghatti, breathing in Pw'eek's scent where her icy face pressed against her shoulder. So steep, so very steep, and then she very nearly did overbalance, the ground flat as she stepped for a rise that no longer existed.

"Welcome!" Holding out her arms, Callis smiled. Whiteness against whiteness, the brilliance of sun, and to Jenneth's dazzled eyes Callis appeared to float across the snow toward them. What was that behind her? A giant's spear sunk into the ground? "You've done well, child. Now don't take my news amiss, but Nakum is away, I'm afraid."

Shoving back her hood and stripping off her knit cap, Jenneth simply stood, breathing heavily, unsure she could speak. Where was Nakum? How could she tell Saam she'd simultaneously succeeded and failed? Would he even comprehend what she was telling him?

"I do think, though," Callis lifted Pw'eek from her unresisting arm and leaned her chin against Pw'eek's head before setting her down, "That Addawanna and I might be adequate substitutes until Nakum returns. And there's someone else here who's anxious to see you." A beckoning gesture, and Jenneth's knees began to buckle as her Aunt Jacobia came running toward her.

♣

Morning, or at least he supposed it was, given the way the ice house translucently glowed. Funny how cozy it could be in a house built of ice, and he'd spent a good night, fully rested, though not especially inclined to rise. Diccon stretched a stockinged foot to give Jenneth a little kick, warn her it was time to rise, but his foot touched only a crumpled blanket. *"Blast it all!"* he complained to Kwee, determined to catch another nap while she could, foreleg over her eyes, body luxuriantly limp. *"Jen and your sib are already up, though how she crawled over me without waking me is a miracle. Lucky she didn't tread on my stomach, it's so cramped up here."*

**"Breakfast?"** Reluctant to wake, Kwee humped herself into a compact mound. **"Not . . . me,"** she grumbled, **"but Sissy . . . probably getting . . . breakfast . . . below."**

Given Pw'eek, it made perfect sense, and Diccon pulled

on his boots, wrinkling his nose at how smelly his socks had become. Not much of a chance to wash and change on this trip. Besides, who wanted to strip down in the cold and change? *"Jen? What's up? How's Harrap this morning? And Saam?"*

No answer, though he heard the rise and fall of anxious voices below as he started down the stairs, Kwee finally tagging along. She could nap below if she wasn't hungry. Jen must be outside, though his mindvoice should have carried to her. Must be engrossed by something—mayhap speaking with Callis.

Stretching and groaning dramatically; he clattered downstairs, only to feel two pairs of eyes—his aunt's and Harrap's—boring into him. At least Harrap was sitting upright, his bad leg laid along the wall bench. Parm stalked the narrow chamber, sniffing all over before returning to Harrap and sitting with his back to Mahafny. "Good morning!" Something was wrong, the day already out of kilter. Mahafny was dressed for the outdoors, had apparently already been outside, probably staring up at the peak. "Where's Jen? And Pw'eek? What're we having for breakfast? I'm hungry enough to eat one of the ponies." Hadn't realized until now just how ravenous he was.

"When did Jenneth and Pw'eek leave?" Her brusqueness wasn't unusual, but what bothered Diccon was the way her gnarled fingers twitched and flexed, as if she couldn't still them.

"Don't know," he responded, sitting beside Harrap. "How's the leg, Harrap? Had breakfast yet?" But Harrap looked distinctly unhappy and, the more he thought on it, so did Auntie. "I assume Jen and Pw'eek didn't get up that long ago. I mean, it *is* morning, isn't it? Time to make our final assault on the peak? We've practically done it, haven't we? Will have succeeded by this afternoon, I'll bet!" So why wasn't anyone looking very pleased?

With a glare as icy as the house they inhabited, Mahafny stalked out the door. "Saam's gone!" Harrap explained in a rushed undertone. "Can't find hide nor hair of him! Nor Jenneth and Pw'eek, and Mahafny can't find Callis anywhere outside!"

Parm balanced against Diccon's knee. **"Heard her stirring not too long after we went to bed. Least I thought I** did, too sleepy to check on it. Saam was groaning, the way he often does, but I 'spoke him and he quieted down." The ghatt concentrated, meditatively licking at a paw and scrubbing his face. **"Did you feel the draft, Harrap? Didn't last long, but I remember snuggling closer."**

Harrap squinted his eyes, thinking hard. "Had Mahafny's medicaments in me—I slept hard. Think I felt a draft . . . and that was . . . well, I thought something was tickling my foot, my leg. Probably just pins and needles, though. I've enough of them to open a notions shop!"

Grabbing the first coat that came to hand—Harrap's overlarge green one with the red lapels—Diccon pulled it on and darted out the door, Kwee close behind. But before long, he returned. "Auntie's still looking, yet I swear I can't see any tracks but those she's made. Called for Callis, too— Nothing!" Disconsolate he slumped on the floor, hugging the coat around him. "It doesn't make any sense! Jen wouldn't steal Saam, and neither would Callis! They have to be somewhere!"

Heads together, Kwee and Parm conferred, Kwee growing visibly more upset with every whisker twitch and ear swivel the ghatti shared. **"I think Sissy helped your Sissy reach the peak during the night. Mayhap Callis, as well. If we go there, we'll probably find them."**

"But is Saam still alive?"

**"Can't tell for sure. Can't pick up Sissy's mindpattern or his, and he's usually sending garbled 'speech without even realizing it."**

The door opened and Mahafny entered, face waxy with cold, eyes dull. Without speaking, she wrestled with the drawstring of her waist-pouch and withdrew a folded paper packet, her look defying Harrap to stop her, to even remonstrate with her. "Diccon, get yourself and Harrap something to eat, and be quick about it. We're going to find Saam if I have to search beneath every snowflake from here to the peak!"

Diccon nodded numbly as she attacked the packet with fingers and teeth, ripping at it, finally dumping white powder on her palm. Again she fixed them with defiant eyes. "This is *my* breakfast. Now get yours. I don't trust that Callis woman, don't want her anywhere near Saam."

A sick feeling swamped Diccon, made him wish he'd

never thought of breakfast, let alone been ordered to consume it. Saam . . . dying. . . . Jenneth, attempting a final desperate dash to reach Nakum in time. . . . And if she didn't succeed . . . she'd feel responsible . . . another death on her conscience . . . convinced she bore the blame. . . . And no matter what he did, she'd shrivel up and die a little more inside, not dare love or care for anyone . . . even him, or Pw'eek . . . because look how quickly life could alter. Bard and M'wa were gone because of her, one dead, one in another world. . . .

And Mahafny just sat, eyes beginning to glitter, her whole body vibrating with compressed energy. A relief of sorts when she looked away, a satisfied "ah" issuing from her mouth. "It's *thebie,* lad." Harrap pitched his voice low, but Diccon suspected Mahafny neither heard nor cared at this moment. "She's been on it for some time—practically since we started this trip. Otherwise, she . . ." he waved a hand, forced himself to continue, "couldn't have . . . wouldn't have been able to come . . . this far . . . for Saam."

Mouth in a tight line, because otherwise he was truly scared he'd start whimpering like a baby, Diccon nodded. Had a memory of that night at the inn at Bertillon, while Jenneth and Harrap were renting the ponies. Saam had taken a bad turn, and he'd helped calm him down. And Aunt Mahafny had played with a little packet identical to the one she'd just ripped into, though he'd not paid much attention at the time. *"Did you know?"* It mattered whether Kwee had known or not. That she hadn't told him if she'd known.

**"Yes. Pw'eek and Saam and Parm and I all knew. What good would it have done to tell you? Could you stop her from taking this journey? No. Could you have shamed her, stopped her from taking the drug? No. Things are as they are."**

Angry—angry at himself, at Jenneth, at the ghatti, at Harrap, and most of all, at his aunt. "I'll ready the ponies," was all he allowed himself to say, because if he said more, it would accomplish nothing—except mayhap relieve his frustration. Slamming his hand into his pocket, he discovered the plum pit Callis had given him, started to jerk it free, throw it as hard as he could. But something impelled him to hold it tight, leave it where it was. He no longer felt petulant, but he most distinctly didn't feel very happy.

♣

"Stay behind, stay here!" Mahafny urged, already astride Willy, as Harrap leaned against Jester, unable to climb on. Six standard mounting attempts had failed, and he was red in the face and gasping, as was Diccon, from struggling to boost Harrap. "We'll return as soon as we've found them." In another moment she'd jerk Willy around, more harshly than she'd intended, and start him up the trail as fast as the doughty little beast could go. Mahafny Annendahl, galloping to the rescue! A bitterness in her mouth, and not simply from the *thebie*.

How could they have snatched Saam like that, and her oblivious, drowning in sleep? To have brought him so far, so close to salvation. They'd spirited him off to Nakum—hadn't they? Or did Callis have something else in mind? It mattered more than it should that *she* be the one who lofted Saam up these final steps to the peak, to Nakum. Was she mad? Did it matter at all as long as he got there?

"I am *not* remaining behind!" Harrap still leaned against Jester, keeping his weight off his bad leg. Did he think he could bend that leg? A short time with his foot in the stirrup and he'd rue the stubbornness that drove him to continue at her side. Damnall, she *was* going to leave! Let Diccon catch up when he could, once he got Harrap back inside. She didn't need him anymore either. Just needed Saam, to be at his side, see with her own eyes how he fared.

Coursing back and forth, Diccon gave a yelp. "I think I've got it, Harrap! This may be the most unorthodox mount in history, but I think it'll work!" Letting Harrap slump against him, Diccon walked him to a spot near the house where a squarish jut of rock protruded. "If it works, you can join the circus as a trick rider," he encouraged, Jester anxiously following after them. "What you'll truly need, Harrap, is faith!"

Intrigued despite herself, Mahafny hesitated. Had forgotten how she automatically expected his presence without a second thought, took it for granted he'd be there. Companionship, the certainty of comfort and consolation. Except she didn't have *time*. What if—for some reason—Callis and Jenneth *hadn't* reached the summit, had been forced to halt along the way, Saam growing ever weaker, so close yet not near enough? How could she forgive herself for having been so laggard? Yet how could she forgive herself for deserting Harrap?

Dear, Blessed Lady! What was Diccon thinking? Somehow he'd boosted Harrap onto the rock, his back to Jester, the pony's hindquarters nudged as tight behind the Shepherd as Diccon could force the beast. "Now, lean—lean back!" Diccon encouraged. "Lay right down on his back, your head at his rump!" Buttocks now practically level with the saddle, Harrap complied, unsteadily balancing himself on one foot. "Hike your robe, hike it to your waist," Diccon demanded, and she was relieved not to glimpse Harrap's expression. Despite the purple pantaloons beneath his robe, he'd be mortified at being thus "exposed" yet again.

"Swing your good leg over Jester's head," was Diccon's next command and, with a grunt, Harrap did, Diccon elevating his injured leg so that Harrap now lay on his back, both feet in the air. "Grab my shoulder, grab for the pommel, sit up."

Circus act was right! Flailing and heaving, Harrap bucked forward, almost ended up pitching over Jester's head until Diccon eased him back. Harrap blindly stabbed for the stirrup with his good foot, and Diccon slowly raised the injured leg, Harrap wincing and swearing. But Diccon, bless his heart, had cobbled a rude sling of sorts from some leather pack straps to cradle Harrap's upper leg.

No question but that she'd take the lead—let anyone try to stop her, get in her way! Whenever Willy slowed, her drumming heels sent the gray pony fairly scampering up the steep trail. Worry consumed her at the lack of footprints. No matter how she scanned—even dismounting several times for a closer look—the snow appeared unsullied. No tracker she, but how much more obvious could it be? Moccasins, boots, left imprints in snow. So did bouncing ghatti feet, Pw'eek should have left plunge marks in the snow. Nor had it snowed during the night, a fresh layer disguising any tracks.

Behind her Harrap's low-pitched "umph-umph!" punctuated each bounce and jar. The dear fool was near as obstinate as she, just better-mannered about it! And beyond all expectation Diccon remained in the rear position on Mignon, Parm and Kwee sharing Daisy's back. A part of her would have welcomed his thoughts, speculation on the lack of tracks, but he silently hugged his concern over Jenneth close to his heart, not galloping ahead, taking any and every risk to find her. Did that mean he wasn't worried? That he was aware of something she wasn't?

And *she* was fast developing a persecution complex, assuming the whole world was against her, after her! Impossible on such a glorious day, the sky extravagantly blue with just a feathering of cloud rapidly racing away, and the sun beat against her shoulders and head, set her scarf itching around her neck. Almost, almost she could take pleasure in this expansive bowl of blue, forget the worries hammering at her and experience a rising euphoria as she absorbed the purity of this moment, this scene—the distant green of trees, the prismatic brilliance of ice and snow against the enduring peaks and crags. Raw beauty, beauty untamed. If any could see them from below, they might resemble a small convoy of ants toiling along the slopes. . . . Ant Mahafny . . . dear Lady, the *thebie* was talking through her, had temporarily wrested control from her!

Determined to regain her precious control, she slowed Willy and swung down, stumbling and clutching at the saddle, performing an intricate series of catch-up steps. Yes, better. Physical exertion would tame the drug's effects. Sky so . . . *blue*! Had she taken the *thebie* too long, the drug ultimately winning, seizing control and making her its puppet? No tracks . . . not a one. Saam so feather-light he must have *floated* to the top. . . . Ah, if only she could *float* like that . . . !

The two inward-leaning rocks with a gap between them didn't immediately catch her attention and she strode by, studying the trail, only to find a dead end just beyond, a rock wall blankly blocking her way, bare space enough for a cramped turnaround. Damn! Willy couldn't float either! Heard Diccon calling, halloing her back, and she swung Willy 'round, still craning her neck upward. One foot tripped the other and she went down. The fall shook her, and she took her time rising, shaking her head, wiping her face, dusting off the snow before she could assume even a modicum of composure. Ah . . . blue, such *blueness*!

Limping, she returned, Harrap and Diccon waiting by the inward-leaning rocks. "I can't see the top," she announced, and suddenly feared she might weep. *Oh, Saam! Where are you? Are you . . . are you . . . ?* What, she couldn't bring herself to name, even within her mind.

Kwee and Diccon bounded ahead as she finally reached Harrap. "Diccon thinks the final trail rears up this way—no more ledges!" Harrap informed her bravely, but held his hand for hers, and she accepted the intimacy while she slumped exhaustedly against him, head buried against his waist.

Springing with the wanton energy of youth, Diccon and Kwee returned, panting, Diccon's face gleaming from cold, the ghatta's fur fresh-fluffed. She'd never known Saam when he was as young and reckless, as rakish as Kwee . . . ah, what a magnificent beast he must have been in those bygone days! "It's got to be the final leg to the top," Diccon gasped. "Terrifically steep, mind you. Kinks a bit, too. Don't know," he shook his head, considering, "really don't know if we can manage the ponies. Mayhap just Jester, so Harrap can ride."

"Nonsense!" Harrap hugged her shoulders in encouragement. "Don't want the beast getting stuck, wedged in. Untruss me, lad. I'll gimp to the top, lean on you or Mahafny when I must. At least I can't topple off a ledge."

Mahafny's heart felt full, an unaccustomed sensation of unrationed love that threatened to overspill the chambers of her heart. Diccon, Harrap, Kwee, Parm . . . how she loved them all, for what they were . . . and what they weren't. Stubbornly individual, each themselves, beings she couldn't mold in her own image, expect to live up to her expectations, but then . . . she undoubtedly hadn't lived up to *their* expectations of her. Other than relentlessly driving them onward. If Saam were dead . . . she swallowed . . . *dead* . . . there still existed small reasons to live, moments of love, needing, caring. . . . Not enough, mayhap, yet a start . . . but she was too old to begin afresh, start anew. *"Saam, I love you! I'm grateful for all you've given me through the years! More than I deserved!"* she let her mindvoice soar, not expecting a response, but needing to say it crystal-clear if any could listen, hear.

"Diccon, Harrap, I love you both, very much, in case I've never gotten around to mentioning it. Parm, Kwee, you rascals—you, too."

Their faces were a study in shock, enough to make her smother a laugh. Oh, bless the *thebie* for releasing that love from within her! "Now, shall we climb? Discover what awaits us at the top?"

♣

It appeared that Mahafny had lost her mind. That was enough for Harrap to ponder, and it went a long way toward canceling the pain in his leg as he wobbled along the trail, clinging to the rock wall, bracing his forearm against it, his other arm flung across Diccon's shoulders.

**"Mayhap she hasn't lost it, but found it. And it's her heart, not her mind,"** Parm turned back to study him.

"Aren't you worried about Jenneth and Pw'eek?" he sputtered into Diccon's ear.

Gripping Harrap more firmly around the waist, Diccon eased him along, intent, concentrating on each move to avoid jarring him. "Yes . . . and no," he huffed as he shifted half Harrap's bulk around a nasty bend in the trail. "Don't know if I'm going to face disaster at the top—or what." He and Harrap now maneuvered their way up an uneven series of natural steps, if they could be thusly named out of politeness. "Scared me to death when I discovered they'd slipped off like that. But I had to tell myself that Pw'eek's with her. Callis, too, unless I miss my guess. Something's going on. I'm not necessarily meant to understand it, any more than I understood everything Callis told me when we were together in the world within—"

"World within?" Harrap echoed. "What do you mean, lad? I never really had a chance to ask you what happened before—where you were when your body was in the cave but the rest of you wandered elsewhere."

**"It's a very pleasant place,"** and Harrap stiffened, nearly stumbled, at Parm's unexpected contribution. **"Can be anything and everything you've ever wanted in nature. Un-**

**spoiled, untouched, time without time . . . wouldn't have half-minded staying there."**

The ghatt's revelation was too much for Harrap. "You mean *you* were there, too? Is that where you and Saam slipped off to?" Lady help him, but sometimes he absolutely yearned to shake the ghatt until his teeth rattled. Shake sense out of him! Oh, not truly, but the mere idea temporarily alleviated his frustrations. Too many disparate things were converging, and he couldn't begin to understand, could only provisionally accept them and pray there was some context into which they'd fit. Even that green-gold globe apparently had a part in the puzzle.

**"I know, nuisance, isn't it? Diccon said it absolutely pinched him black and blue in spots."**

Diccon had encountered that . . . that *thing*? Whatever it was. But when, how? Truly, this whole trip had seen him venturing deep into another world, with only his faith in his Lady to guide him.

**"And *another* lady," Kwee cheekily interjected. "Not sure if I like her, but if she's good enough for Saam, I suppose she's good enough for me. And speaking of which . . ."**

Mahafny toiled ahead without halting, driving her feet onward like an automaton. Her harsh breathing filtered back to them, and Harrap despaired of ever catching up with her, not like this, no matter how hard he labored. For a shameful moment that lasted longer than he liked, he yearned for a dose of her drug—anything—to give him the strength to scale these final steps. Mayhap a kilometer, possibly less, the beckoning, empty blue sky at the top, proof that the peak could be surmounted.

A cry from Mahafny—triumph or despair? The stiffening corpse of a skeletally-thin gray ghatt? Jenneth? "Go!" he begged Diccon, releasing his grip on the lad's shoulder and shoving him forward. "Go! Parm, go with them, please! Tell me! Tell me what's happening!"

They shot off without a backward glance, and Harrap climbed as best he might, alone and vulnerable. Too late even to ask the Lady to reconsider, accept him in the stead of the soul She now cherished to Her bosom. Nor did the Lady affirmatively answer all prayers, though She always responded. So it was, so it would be . . . if not in this life, mayhap another. The sun burned at his bare pate, made it itch with sweat, left him wistful for a hat with a wide, shielding brim.

**"Found Jenneth's mitt!"** Parm reported. **"At least it proves she did come this way. It's saturated with Saam's scent, a good sign as well."** Reconsidering, he amended, **"Well, a sign."** Such conservatism cost Parm, leached the sparkle from his 'speech.

He no longer cared that his leg hurt, ignored the jolting pain coursing through him at each hobbling step. Mind over matter, the body would heal, would take longer because of the abuse, but he'd catch up with them. Faster now, faster. Stare at the path ahead, check his footing, glance up at the cerulean sky, compel the pain to recede, temporarily conquer it. No drugs! None! *"Parm, I'm coming! Wait for me!"* Whatever was to be, he must behold it with his own two eyes as it unfurled. Life, death, beginnings, endings, all must be witnessed, even if their meanings could only be hazily deduced.

❧

Each gasping breath seared her lungs, her chest afire, the pain doubling her over, one hand clamped against the stitch in her side that threatened to tear her in two. Shallow mouth breaths—yes—stop her damn lungs from expanding and contracting like a bellows. Better . . . marginally. Steadying herself against the rock wall with bloody knuckles, Mahafny pressed on, feet dragging, tripping. Nearer, nearer, mere meters away now. Couldn't spare any breath to call aloud, wouldn't allow herself to 'speak Saam for fear of the emptiness awaiting her. Silence, and she'd collapse on this stony path and move no more. Neither up nor down, simply abide here for all eternity, until she, too, turned to stone.

The *thebie's* effects hadn't lasted near long enough this time, had failed her. Absently she swatted Diccon's helping hand and scrambled onward, Diccon hovering behind her, clutching Jen's mitten. Her legs wobbled and, to her dismay, folded on her, sending her toppling. Crawl? Why not? Hands and knees, drag herself ahead and up, always up.

Her hair had come unbound long ago, and she suspected she looked like a wild woman, but she didn't care. To see Saam one final time, for one final touch . . . And Jenneth, as well, if breath remained to apologize for her ill usage of her and Diccon.

"Auntie, enough!" Strong, young arms wrapped around her waist, hoisted her into the air and she struggled vaguely, flailing to be released. "Stop it! Stop fighting me and listen!" An insistent shake and she hung limp. "Auntie, on my back! Please! I'll carry you the rest of the way."

Little weight, she knew that, these past days plus the *thebie* had burned away any excess kilos she might have carried, though they'd been few to begin with. More as if Diccon uncomplainingly carried a bundle of reeds wrapped in tissue-thin, aging skin. Small but wiry, Diccon leaned into the slope and climbed, faster and faster, Kwee leading, Parm at the rear, and Harrap, somehow, not that far behind. *Oh, Saam, dear Saam, I'm coming,* and hugged the thought in her mind.

Sunshine glare in her eyes, a watery blur to her surroundings. Such a *vivid* blue, shimmering like blown silk, the sun staggering drunkenly almost at the top of the world. Everything white around her, all white now. Never melted up here, people said. Snow as old as she, older, snows of the ages . . . such purity. And she had presumed to outwit, outmaneuver nature, make it bend to her will. . . . Had been willing to do anything to accomplish it, when it was immutable, incapable of being changed by the mere wants of a puny human being. Hubris. How had she presumed that she could, that she had the right . . . ? Everything indistinct, just profoundly blue and white . . . like an aura.

And then . . . against the white . . . a gray blur . . . moving, zigzagging. . . . No doubt her heart had finally given out, her fading mind seeing Saam once more, blue-gray coat gleaming in the sun. . . .

"Saam!" she cried with all her heart, feebly beating at Diccon's shoulders. "Saam!" Let her have this last, this final vision as she died, that she held Saam in her arms, each consoling the other, going together to whatever unknown awaited them.

Somehow she was kneeling on the snow, arms outstretched in encouragement, in yearning, praying to hold him just once more, bury her face in the back of his neck. She had been *so* wrong! Death was beautiful, so transcendently alive with promise . . . "Saam!" and her arms enfolded his warm, sleek form, slightly filled out now, his whiskers scraping her cheek, so real, so alive she could almost believe, *did* believe she'd been granted this final moment, unreal as it might be.

**"Mahafny, no!"** he cried in her mind, his head beside hers. **"Don't go, don't leave me! Not another desertion!"**

*"But I'll never desert you,"* she promised. *"Always you're with me, and I with you, no matter where, no matter how— oh, my darling, bless you for sharing my life, for enriching it, making me realize . . ."* Arms slackening, falling away from him, Mahafny's gray eyes slowly closed, her body swaying until it overbalanced and laid itself full-length against the white snow, her silvery-white hair tremulous in the light breeze, the sky a saturated blue, so *blue,* as Mahafny Annendahl obtained her dearest wish, an extension of life and vitality for Saam. Not for her, but for him. All gifts had a price.

❖

Harrap wept, inconsolable. Had viewed the end from the near distance, reduced to a mere spectator as death swept across the snow-white stage with its strange pillar in the background, the white domes with their glass windows ablaze in the sun. Had been unable to reach Mahafny's side as the action commenced, another three or four laborious strides to reach the top, his head just high enough to view everything before him as if his chin rested on a tabletop. Had prayed that what transpired before his eyes was not real, that he imagined it, misinterpreted it, that all would be well. But it would not be, he knew.

Had been privileged to hear, share in the final mystery as the ghatti—one by one, first Saam, then Parm, followed by Pw'eek and Kwee—began their chant, **"May you see with eyes of light in everdark, may your mind walk free and unfettered amongst all, touching wisely and well, may you go in peace . . ."** And finally, Saam alone, **"But wait for me, beloved."**

"Ah, wait for me, beloved!" he cried in his heart. And so, at the very end, she *had* abandoned him, one lady less for the Shepherd to worship, as distant and mysterious and unbending in her own way as was his other beloved Lady. Kneeling to blot out the scene, he pillowed his face on his arms and wept, refusing to hold back his tears, letting them flow to wash away a small portion of the pain of loss.

Parm, burrowing under his arms, saying nothing, simply being, gradually reminded him of life and warmth and love, not like Mahafny's, but uniquely his own. Lady bless, was he dribbling on Parm? Nose like a faucet, eyes overflowing with tears, drenching his dear beast?

**"She did what she set out to do, succeeded,"** Parm reminded him. **"Saam lives—that part you didn't imagine. Nor any of the rest, alas."** A pause, as if he wondered whether to continue, Harrap now reduced to hiccups between sobs, eyes still leaking. **"She would have survived as well—except for the *thebie*. She reckoned the price and paid it, Harrap. She didn't begrudge it, and you mustn't begrudge her her choice. Saam doesn't, understands now what he didn't before, and what Mahafny didn't understand, though she acted on it."**

Hands, many hands, touching him, gradually lifting and cradling him as they carried him those few final steps—the ones that Mahafny had made alone. Wanted desperately to ask Parm what he meant—silly old ghatt, dear old beast—who always made sense despite seeming not to, but he was so very tired, so forlorn, bereft. . . .

Cool compresses against his swollen eyes, as scratchy as if someone had thrown sand in them, as if he'd stood wide-eyed in the midst of a dust storm. His lips puffy and strained as well, his nose redly raw. Funny how tears could do that—the salinity, mayhap? He could spend eternity like this, relishing the coolness, the blankness the cloths provided, not having to see, to think, to remember. Would have to, sooner or later, come to grips with it and so much more.

Start with something small, find the solution, answer a question. So many hands carrying him—whose? Diccon's, probably Jenneth's, Callis's? Still not enough, not the way he'd been so lightly borne across this expanse at the top of the world . . . the end of the world.

*"Parm? Who . . . how?"* And please don't let the ghatt riddle him, unroll a story that meandered like a butterfly sampling nectar from numerous blossoms before the answer came! Just one succinct, comprehensible answer was all he asked!

"Oh, dear Harrap!" He recognized the voice but couldn't place it. Clearly feminine but more mature, a pitch deeper than Jenneth's. Not Doyce's, because it was impossible for her to be here, and the thought of that made him wince with guilt. "Everything seems passing strange, I know. And I miss her, too. A brave heart, a brave, loving soul, so rigorously hidden beneath a curmudgeonly exterior. I can't decide whether to be sad or glad that at the end she was able to acknowledge it."

"Jacobia?" Lady help him, was he hallucinating? Pushing away the compresses, he struggled to sit up, focus. "How did you . . . why . . . what?" Strange, she looked older, somehow, yet more timeless. And behind her shoulder, surveying him with compassion, not just Callis, but Addawanna, as well. Other Erakwa he didn't know, had never met, all somehow jammed into this ovoid room. "The twins?" That suddenly seemed a more pressing concern than how Jacobia, Addawanna, and the rest had appeared here, arriving ahead of them. "Jenneth—is she . . . has she . . . ?" Did a whole, complete thought still reside in his head, or was everything fragmented, waiting to be pieced together?

"They're deeply saddened, but Jenneth's reconciled herself." Now Callis took up the explanation from Jacobia. "She's slowly discovering she's not responsible for everything or everyone who passes away. That her flight with Saam during the night did not precipitate Mahafny's death, but gave her aunt an unanticipated opportunity to discover different qualities within her—not just a chance to see Saam once more, partially healed, more hale than before. Neither her actions nor Mahafny's were in vain." Harrap intently studied Callis's face, gradually assimilating the gentle flow of words. Gratitude for that, her compassionate refusal to blame, though he was still adrift in loss.

"I must go to Jenneth, Diccon, console them, cry with them." With effort he sat up, unsure if he could stand unaided. No one could stand unaided, all needed love, help,

someone to lean upon at various times, just as he now
required it. "Then, I must see about the body." It washed
over him, an apprehension of what lay ahead. How, how
could he possibly remove her body for burial? Must he
leave Mahafny here, alone but for Nakum? And, come to
think on it, where was Nakum?

As if she could read the questions on his face, Callis gave
a mild frown, considering. "Nakum has pressing matters to
attend to in Sidonie. In fact, I must join him there soon.
But Addawanna and I were able to help Saam for the time
being." Rolling ungracefully onto his knees, Harrap
strained to rise, relieved when Addawanna and Jacobia
each took an arm and helped. More fitting to look at Callis
from this level, not have her looking down at him. Passing
strange to realize that Callis was far older than Mahafny,
generations older; that probably Addawanna was older as
well, though their years sat lightly on them.

Extending a fisted hand, Callis waited until he hesitantly
held his hand below hers, wondering what she hid, what
she planned to bestow on him. "Mahafny's body will be
taken care of in a seemly manner, though mayhap differently from what you're accustomed to." Her hand released
a thin circlet of braided, silver-white hair that now rested
on his palm, feather-light. "We would not let her depart
this world without leaving you a token of her love." It
looked as if it would fit around his wrist, would be with
him always—should he ever require a reminder. Not that
he thought he would, but it was comforting, nonetheless.

♣

"That's really a tree? I mean, it *was* a tree?" Conscious of
where he trod, careful to stay within the paths, Diccon circled the blasted remains of the giant arborfer trunk, viewing it from all sides. "How did it manage to grow up here?
I mean, it had to sink its roots into the soil to survive, to
grow, didn't it?" A stark, smooth white, the bark gone. Yet
within that white he could envision every hue under the
sun, reflecting off it like a long beacon when the sun was
right.

"Should think it would've been struck by lightning—

more than once. Highest point around, I'd guess—is that
what happened to it?" As he turned, he smiled apologeti-
cally at the young Erakwan woman who'd accompanied
him. "You work with Davvy, don't you? At the Hospice?
Thought you looked familiar. How'd *you* get up here?"
Now *that* was certainly witty repartee! What did he think—
that she'd flown up here?

Feather continued staring at the tree, almost worshipfully, to Diccon's mind. Lady knew, it deserved a certain
reverence merely for having survived up here in this unforgiving environment. "Do you ever stop asking questions?"
she asked, more mildly than he deserved, rubbing the base
of her throat, fingers seeking something that wasn't there
and then self-consciously dropping. "Always wanting to
know? If I answer, will you listen?"

"Of . . . of course," Diccon stammered, flustered.
Frankly, she was attractive—oh, a bit older than he, though
not by that much. Lovely black hair, a different luster to it
than Jen's or Aunt Jacobia's. Amazing how it set off her
glowing, red-brown skin—not terribly dark, yet almost metallic, and so smooth! Not very tall—all to the good—and
nicely built, a solid armful. She could wrestle him into submission any day she liked! Great goddess bright, he was
disgusting! Auntie Mahafny dead only this morning, and
here he stood, lusting after a woman! A woman less than
likely to take him and his genuine admiration sincerely,
especially given the amount of lust intermixed with it!
Come to think of it, given the way the Erakwa aged,
Feather could be his mother's age—or older! That damped
his ardor more effectively than the freshening breeze now
whipping across the snow, tossing her hair.

"If I answer a question or two for you, will you answer
one for me?" Her hazel eyes had turned opaque, unreadable, just the way Jenneth's and Mama's did sometimes.
Enough to make him take notice, beware when they looked
like that. Mama wore that expression when she strove for
studious neutrality, personal emotions held in check. Many
Seekers did it almost automatically. Jenneth did as well,
though with her it was protective, a way to shield herself
from others. Funny, he wasn't sure he'd ever consciously
analyzed it before.

"I will." He straightened, thrusting out his chest and

squaring his shoulders, assuming a more manly stance. "In fact, I'll answer your question first, if you like. Two, because I've naught to hide from you." Well, he did, but his tabard loosely covered it, especially with his hands in his jacket pockets to thrust the front outward.

Feather laughed, clapped her hands. "Ah, an honorable Outlander." Her words lacked sting. "No, I'll take your questions first, unless you want me to just generally answer some of your thoughts about the arborfer, explain its background, how it came to be here?"

As good an offer as any, since the questions he really wanted to ask might prove too personal. "Could we walk through the greenhouses, do you think? Would Nakum mind? It's hard to believe those little green sprigs could someday be giant arborfer. And someone should check, see if they need watering. Knowing Nakum, we'd best record what we do."

Seeing she made no objection, he came to her, offering her his arm to escort her there. To his intense pleasure, she took it, but when her hand touched his arm, she stopped short, her glance suddenly sharp and assessing. "Callis gave you something? Didn't she?" A finger briefly touched his lips. "No, don't answer. I'm not ready to know. But I can sense it. First Jacobia, now you, more worthy of earth's gifts than some of us Erakwa are."

Visibly controlling herself, she docilely walked with him into the greenhouse. "I'll tell you about Hatachawa, first arborfer of them all, and how he came to live up here, all from the goodness of his heart, helping other creatures of the earth when the sky pressed downward and tried to crush them."

Inside now, the air warm and moist, the setting sun washing the glass with vermilions and crimsons, flame orange, almost blinding, a spectacular display meant just for the two of them. And if he attempted to steal a kiss, most likely no one could see them, not with those colors awash on the glass. Would he dare?

At each small seedling pot with its shredded bark and moss on top, she touched the dirt with her fingertips, judging the soil composition—sandy or loamy, likely to hold water or drain quickly—assessing each miniature arborfer, whether its needles hung limp or crisp, the shade of green.

Sometimes she murmured for him to pour just a little water here or there, and he obliged, measuring the amount in a marked beaker, scribbling the figure on a slate chart.

"I've wanted to ask—what was your reaction to the Plumb? You were nearer than we when it exploded—you'd just started up the mountain, I'd guess? I take it it didn't do any severe damage to your party?"

Water overspilled a pot, flooding the tray beneath it, flowing over the side to inexorably drip on her moccasins. A faint complaining sound issued from between her parted lips, a wrinkling of her brow at the flood. "Plumb!" Diccon exclaimed, voice rising a full register, shrill with shock. "You're joking—aren't you? I . . . we . . . there was an avalanche the first night we camped on the mountain, made the ground rumble and tremble something fierce! How could it have been a Plumb? That's impossible!"

"So, you do not even recognize, acknowledge the handiwork of your own people?" Then, almost triumphantly, "So clever, yet so intensely ignorant of consequences!"

"That's not fair! I don't know *what* you're talking about!" Setting down the beaker harder than he'd intended, he flinched at hearing a sharp snap as a crack shot up its side.

She looked as shaken as he by the result, tracing a finger across the hairline fracture. "I *am* sorry. I'm still learning to censor my tongue, as Jacobia can attest. Old habits, old ways of thinking die hard—especially wrong ways of thinking."

To his surprise, he began to cry, her last sentence reminding him too much of Mahafny. How was he *ever* going to explain to Mama and Papa? "I'm not crying because I broke the beaker. It's just that I can't understand so much . . . ! Mahafny dying, Saam living . . . you and Aunt Jacobia being here. Plumbs . . . arborfer . . . Hatachawa. And Callis . . . every time I try to think about that place, that world within, the memories grow more and more hazy. And that pesky green globe! Humming and glowing, pinching me!"

Now it was she who looked shocked. "You *saw* it? You *followed* it? You're braver than I was—"

"Or more foolhardy," he giggled through his tears.

"What?" Callis stood behind them, her passage so soundless they both jumped guiltily. "No wonder no one could find you. Come, come along, Jacobia's waiting. We must leave now if we'd reach Sidonie by morning. A major undertaking awaits us."

Feather shook her head in abnegation. "You can't want me. I've nothing to contribute, no earth-bond. Glashtok or Mataweeta would be better suited to your needs than I."

Hustling them ahead like errant children, Callis laughed, though Diccon didn't think she sounded either amused or happy. "And how do you know what I need, when I barely know myself. We will all grow into our roles, Jacobia, Diccon, you, and I."

The sun had now completely set, and Diccon shivered as they stood outside, waiting for Jacobia to join them. He wasn't physically cold, but a frisson of the unknown worked its way along his spine, an alien sensation that set his whole being aquiver with the potentiality of uncharted things. "How . . . how are we going to descend the mountain? The slaithe?" Mama's stories about it had been more than vivid—how she'd nearly left her stomach in midair, or worse! He had no confidence that he'd do any better, not when boats made him sick. Most likely he'd decorate the landscape all the way down!

"No, not the slaithe, Diccon, though I think Feather might appreciate the ride." At that moment Jacobia appeared, bathed in moonlight, and Diccon belatedly registered that the only outerwear she wore was a leather vest over her tunic and trousers. Moccasins had replaced her boots, and she stepped so lightly that she seemed to float, hover just above the surface of the pristine snow. At the open neck of her tunic he glimpsed a hint of green-and-brown leather hanging from a thong when she moved just so. Feather seemed unable to wrench her eyes away from it, full of yearning sadness and resignation. "So, did you find them?" Callis asked Jacobia.

"Yes," called his aunt easily, "though Mouton has a lingering headache, still isn't in a very good mood. But Bélier and Ag'neau and Ag'nelet are enthusiastic, happy to be of service." Slipping her thumb and ring finger into the corners of her mouth, she issued a piercing whistle. Criminy! He'd forgotten she could do that!

White against white they moved, dark hooves, darker

horns standing out against the snow, the glowing brown-orange of eyes, the heavy, matted pelts. Mouton—the mountain sheep, the ram that he and Kwee had tormented! Bélier must be the ewe, his mate, and Ag'neau and Ag'-nelet their offspring. The ram lifted his massive head and sniffed, large nostrils flexing as they drank in Diccon's scent. One foot began to paw at the ground as he snorted, lowering his head.

Diccon found himself backed tight against Feather. "Are you sure we can't take the slaithe?" he implored.

Hands on hips, Callis gave him an impatient look. "Hurry, lad. We can't spare any more time. Aren't you forgetting something?"

"Wha . . . ?" She actually expected him to climb aboard one of those beasts, ride down the mountain? In the dark? Expected all four of them to do so? "Wha . . . what have I forgotten?" Hadn't a clue, could be anything, the way her mind ranged so far ahead of his.

Callis exchanged a glance with Feather and Jacobia—how he hated that glance, had seen women of all ages silently converse with a canted eyebrow, the rolling eye that indicated as clearly as words: Men! I swear they're so dense sometimes! But at last Callis took pity on his ignorance. "Aren't you forgetting Kwee?"

♣

"Nice sheep, nice Ag'neau!" Where in the Lady's name was he supposed to hang on, how was he to keep his seat without a saddle? What was he supposed to do with his legs?

Ag'neau twisted his massive neck, not yet nearly as thick as his sire's but solid, nonetheless, and gave him a skittish look. A quick, calculated frisk in place and Diccon slithered forward, nearly bumping off Kwee, afraid he'd continue right over Ag'neau's head—or become hung up on his horns.

" 'Ware! I don't want to walk down!" Kwee had grimly settled herself ahead of him, claws clinging deep in Ag'-neau's thick fleece. "Not much different than clinging to your tabard. I'd really have to work at it to pink his flesh."

Easy for Kwee to say—his fingers couldn't penetrate the way her claws did, not the way he'd grip a horse's mane when riding bareback. Well, Feather didn't look any more comfortable astride Ag'nelet, was obviously experiencing similar problems. Aunt Jacobia, on the other hand, looked at ease on Bélier, her knees drawn up high on the ewe's withers—well, he guessed that's what they were called—as if she were a jockey readying for a race. Damn uncomfortable to cling like that without any stirrup support. The thought of it set his thigh muscles to cramping. Now grab Ag'neau's horns. Nothing to compare with Mouton's, but they did curve back rather like a steering bar.

*"Ha! Try to steer me, and I'll buck you off! As if you know where to go!"* Ag'neau snorted and bobbed his head, Diccon nearly falling off of his own accord, astounded beyond belief that Ag'neau had 'spoken to him. *"And by the way, I prefer to be called Neau. Sounds more powerful for an up-and-coming young ram, don't you think?"* He danced forward, feinting with his sib, Nelet, lowering his head and mock-charging. *"And I'll butt anyone's head who thinks differently!"*

This time Diccon totally misjudged Neau's maneuvers and fell off in a heap, jaw still lowered in amazement at having conversed with the beast. A rapid roll as he sought to escape Neau's lowered head, the young ram playfully butting him along, rolling him faster, as if he were a log. "Ow! Don't!" Neau's broad head shoved first at Diccon's shoulders, then his bottom. Even worse, he could hear Feather's giggle as he struggled to escape.

**"Full of bounce, vim and vigor, isn't he? And much less taciturn than his Papa—all I wanted to do was 'speak Mouton, but things did get out of hand."** Kwee stretched along Neau's neck, the two beasts staring down at him, both with a mischievous spark in their eyes. Funny, he'd never noticed before that their eyes were rather alike, the pupils vertical slits. **"Apparently he has to keep in practice to challenge other rams his age, work his way up from there."**

*"Dare you!"* Neau tossed his head, lowered it provocatively. *"You're a poor excuse for a mountain sheep, but I can pretend. Get on your hands and knees and rush me!"*

Diccon had no intention of complying and scrambled to his feet, hoping his height might make a difference. But no,

Neau reared on his hind legs and pranced at him, front hooves striking the air, eager to tussle with him.

"Enough! I swear it doesn't matter the species—young males are *all* alike! And it's not even spring yet!" Grumbling, Callis swung aboard Mouton, hooking her feet behind her over his back. No way he'd attempt to replicate that. "We really can't waste any more time—Nakum and Eadwin need us! Now mount up!"

Warily Diccon complied, releasing his grip on Neau's pelt long enough to wave farewell to Jenneth and Pw'eek, then closed his eyes for a brief prayer. That turned out to be a mistake if there ever was one, for Neau hurtled after his parents, Nelet and Feather beside them, jockeying for position.

"Oh . . . my!" the ghatta uttered faintly and Diccon's eyes flew open, Kwee pressed tight against him as Neau plunged downward.

Down, down the mountain they hurtled, the mountain sheep springing from icy crags and landing on impossibly small spaces, barely hesitating as they launched themselves into space again, despite the distortions from shadows, the Lady Moon's fulgent light. They sprang and bounded, caromed from rock to ledge to pinnacle, Nelet and Neau constantly striving to outdo each other in creativity, their leaps alternating between acrobatic and artistic.

Apparently the mountain sheep disdained the trail that humans used to reach the peak, blithely making their own shortcuts, following their own natural passageways, a route no human would dare attempt. Legs aching, he clung with all his might, Kwee warm against him as the cold air whistled past, ruffling his hair. Neau generally landed lightly, but several times Diccon knew he'd compromised the situation, half-rising in the air—he could feel it rushing beneath his bottom—and landing hard on Neau's back, the young ram grumbling and once, taking extra steps to catch his balance.

This was horrible, a nightmare! Eyes open or closed, Diccon endured as best he might, stomach rebelling at the continual jouncing, bile rising in his throat. Once he glimpsed their shadows flying across the snow as the sheep took a particularly long downward lunge, Feather resolutely hanging on, caught somewhere between stark fear and exhilaration, thrilling to each swooping dive. Well, good for her! *"I used . . . to think . . . I was a thrill-seeker, couldn't wait . . . for the next adventure,"* Diccon gulped, nearly biting his tongue as Neau landed. *"I think . . . I can wait . . . now!"*

Kwee now streamlined herself against Neau's neck, and he wished he could, too, but feared placing his weight so far forward might make it harder on Neau. Besides, his upright posture probably created a drag, mayhap slowed the young ram just a fraction. Or so he hoped—any more speed and he'd be ricocheting down the mountain on his own!

**"Absolutely fearless, isn't he?"** Kwee exhibited a certain admiration, a connoisseur's appreciation of such vigor, spirit, and skill. **"Jumps like a flea,"** she considered before continuing. **"I suspect that's what we look like to someone down below if they spotted us descending like this—but white on white, the sheep probably don't even show up. Oh . . . in case you haven't taken a good look, we're nearly halfway down."**

Diccon opened his eyes again, a mistake, because just at that moment Neau soared into a takeoff, purposely springing high enough to overleap Nelet and Feather, as if they played leapfrog. Frightening though it was, he was relieved not to be in Feather's place, looking up to see him and Neau rocketing by overhead—probably their silhouettes showed against the Lady Moon!

More trees now, the forest growing thicker as they descended. Not that they were likely to run headlong into one since the mountain sheep still stuck to their crag-strewn path, ledges and natural slopes, occasionally engaging in an upward run, gaining momentum before casting themselves into space.

**"Callis needs to ask you something,"** Kwee announced, and Diccon struggled to turn his hunched head to see her, none too sure he could hear, sure the wind would whip her words away.

Feet still easily hooked over Mouton's broad back, Callis rested comfortably, elbows downward pointed on either side of the ram's withers, wrists crossed, fingers lightly clamping his fleece. "You kept what I gave you—didn't you?" Frowning, he tried to think what she might mean.

"What I gave you after we exited the world within," she finally amplified.

Comprehending at last, he desperately slapped at his pockets with one hand, feeling for the plum pit. A mistake, a serious one, to have let go with one hand, and he found himself sailing into space beside Neau, staring across at Kwee, as shocked as he as they swooped downward side by side.

"Oh . . . no!" he wailed, flapping his arms like a bird, but it did no good. He couldn't even glide, just kept plunging, the earth rushing to meet him. Snowbank, please let there be a nice snowbank, a cushioning snowdrift, or he'd fracture every bone in his body! How did he want to land—on his stomach? On his back? Feetfirst or headfirst? Nothing sounded very appealing, but headfirst sounded worst of all.

How far down? Yet a part of his mind slowed everything, almost as if he had forever and a day to fall . . . and fall . . . and fall. Funny, his stomach wasn't bothering him a bit now, he had other things to consider. *"Kwee, I'm truly sorry about this!"* The poor dear, his little sweedling, Bonded to a pancake, flattened beyond recognition! *"Please, tell Jenneth and Mama and Papa that . . ."* Could tell them himself that he loved them—Resonant powers in extremis could undoubtedly reach farther than he could normally 'speak. It was just that he didn't want to be joined to Jenneth's mind on this final downward death plunge, have her vicariously experience it through him. Some things were not to be shared, not if you loved someone enough. Well, might as well find out one thing during this slowing of time—did he still have that blasted plum pit? Pretty funny—considering that Feather'd told him a real Plumb had exploded!

Unbelievably, hands grasped his upper arms and he felt his speed momentarily slacken, the plum pit grasped so hard in one hand it indented his palm. Risking a wild glance he saw Callis and Mouton on his left, Jacobia and Bélier on the right. Nice of them, really, but what good would it do? The sheep could land lightly but he couldn't—he'd probably drive his legs right up to his ears. Oh, fine—just what he needed, to be shorter!

Downward they dove, Jacobia and Callis struggling to raise him high, the ground rushing at them with a swooshing finality, closer, ever closer. "Ya!" Callis yelled, and Diccon was catapulted forward and he gathered himself tight as best he could, pretending to be a ball. Felt himself plowing through snow, jouncing and tumbling, burying himself deeper and deeper. Never a feather bed around when you needed it, and wondered how to slow himself before he went sailing off another ledge or whatever before he could stop.

But stop he did, cautiously unfolding himself and staring back slack-jawed at the path he'd carved through the thick snow, discovering Callis and Jacobia, Mouton and Bélier all picking themselves up as well. Even the mountain sheep had been unable to land with their normal grace and aplomb. Skipping across the snow, Kwee still on his back, Neau sniffed him over, prodding him with his nose, his forehead. *"Stupid human! Now Nelet's two points ahead! Well, hurry up, climb back on—we've still got a chance to beat him, though it's slim."*

Clearly the fall had damaged his brain more than his body, now decorated with bumps and bruises galore. The fact that he could feel them, though, was glorious! It was his brain that worried him, must have totally addled it in the fall, because why was he climbing right back on Neau?

**"Because we have to reach the bottom, beloved. And given the vile looks Mouton's casting your way, I'd suggest you climb aboard and put some distance between you and him."**

♣

Jenneth and Pw'eek watched Diccon and the others out of sight, then approached the blasted remains of the tree. A rare splendor in such starkness, but then everything here at the mountain's very peak was starkly beautiful, pure and uncompromising. The eye found respite only within the egg-shaped domicile that Nakum called home, and that Callis had called home before him. But Nakum wasn't here, Callis and Diccon and Aunt Jacobia had left, and Auntie Mahafny was dead—hadn't failed but hadn't quite succeeded, had died in the attempt. How many other things in life became stuck at half measure?

"You t'ink she no succeed?" Addawanna stood holding

two mugs of cha, steam ghosting up from them. "Come, I been so busy wid Jacobia and Callis that we no haf time for chat. Chat go good with cha, I t'ink."

She lifted a shoulder in the direction of a sunny bank of snow neatly carved to form a bench; on it, basking in the sun, face lifted worshipfully toward the sun's rays, lay Saam. Ceremoniously taking one of the mugs from the Era-kwan woman, Jenneth draw near and sat, anticipating the sting of cold, surprised when it didn't come. Surreptitiously she brushed her hand across it, hard and sleek as glass yet neither cold nor hot.

**"Did you think Saam would lie on it if it were that cold? Trust the ghatti to find the perfect spot to catch the sun."** Pw'eek had a point.

Acknowledging them with just the barest turn of his head and a low purr, Saam continued savoring the sun, his coat glistening and silky-looking, the worn, bare patches downy with new growth. Oh, he still looked aged, a venerable ghatt, but now appeared more as she remembered him six or seven years ago. Was it possible he'd gained weight, his bones no longer so obviously jutting, in just the short time since she'd brought him here? Hesitant, she stroked him, heard his fur crackling with energy, his body elastic and firm beneath her hand. A miracle, or almost akin to one, but the miracle had exacted a heavy price. She desperately wanted to ask Saam if he missed Mahafny, but couldn't bring herself to broach the subject.

Addawanna gave a noisy slurp of enjoyment and sighed with pleasure. Jenneth stared into her own mug, as if the wisps and whorls of steam could be deciphered, reveal a message she yearned to hear. But there was no message, only mystery. Best stop wishing for answers when there were none. *"Pw'eek? Isn't an answer often the truth? I mean—an understanding, a comprehension of the solution?"*

Lily belly exposed to the sunlight, her head jammed against Saam's flank, Pw'eek wriggled.

**"But that assumes there was a problem, youngling,"** Saam answered in her stead. **"Problems can be resolved in many ways, but the resolution isn't always a cut-and-dried answer. But in answer to one question: Yes, I miss her greatly, but she resides in my heart, mine and Harrap's."**

*"And mine as well."* To hide her emotion she took a

cautious sip of cha, shocked to discover it had been sweet-
ened with honey, and she drank more eagerly, having
missed the sweetness of sugar or honey during all these
days of climbing.

"So, you wanna un'nerstan', eh?" Rummaging in a
pocket she exposed two shortbread biscuits on the palm of
her hand. "Nakum's. Inna nice, tight tin. Eadwin give, I
bet." After Jenneth claimed hers, Addawanna dunked the
remaining biscuit in her cha, suddenly hurrying her hand
to her mouth as the biscuit dissolved faster than she'd anticipated. Jenneth giggled as the bottom half broke free and
splashed back in the cha. "Phah!" Addawanna poked it
with a finger.

"I wanna un'nerstan', too. You cool, so calm, no weepin'
an wailin' like Shepherd. Not ev'ryone same, but seem
hardhearted ta me. Heart too hard ta weep? Or Maf'ny not
wort sheddin' tears ober?"

"How dare you say—" Instead, she swiveled away from
Addawanna, staring off at the snow-capped peaks edging
the horizon, concentrating on steadying her breathing,
schooling her face to impassivity. The woman had *no* right
to suggest that, to equate the number of tears with a depth
of love! So unfair, because if she started crying, she'd never
stop, would flood every ravine and gorge and valley in the
mountain range! Then they'd freeze, further encase this
world in ice. Better, safer, to lock it within her, batten it
down, just as she had Bard's death, M'wa's desertion. Finally, she stated the obvious. "I should never have stolen
away in the night like that with Saam. Not without telling
Mahafny. If I hadn't done that—" she shrugged, "mayhap
she'd still be alive."

**"And I'd be dead. Would that have made her any hap-
pier when she awoke—finding me cold and stiff beside
her?"**

With Saam on one side and Addawanna on the other,
Jenneth had been neatly trapped, not only physically but
emotionally. "What? Was it a trade-off of some sort, a tit
for tat? Saam lives and Mahafny dies? You die and Auntie
lives? Can't things ever work out right? Can't I ever get
things right?" Rising, she stepped away as far as she could
to escape them, unreasoning anger sweeping over her as

she brought back her arm and threw the mug as hard as she could, watching it plummet, disappear from her sight.

Addawanna umph-umphed disapprovingly. "Now Nakum no got set of mugs."

Rounding on her, Jenneth screamed, "So what? What does it matter if he has a full set of mugs or not? I should think it'd be the *last* thing Nakum could possibly care about, not with Saam and Mahafny to think of first! And why didn't he? Why isn't he here?"

Now standing as well, Addawanna reared back on one leg, then abruptly lunged forward, sending her own mug sailing after Jenneth's, but arching it higher and farther than her own had managed. "So now he missin' noder one, eh? Doan mind so much, 'cept we got more comp'ny comin' an a'ready short on mugs." Dusting her hands together, she returned to sit, almost demurely smoothing her doeskin skirt over her knees.

"Funny, how it doan look like storm drop any snow up here," she mentioned conversationally. Oh, wonderful—a conversation about weather! "One t'ink it no snow at all, 'cept you and Pw'eek stagger t'rough snow an wind, yes?" Jenneth managed a minimal nod, frustrated at the twists the conversation was taking. "Mebbe you make storm? Snow an ice an wind batterin' you be from wid-in you? Yet you struggle t'rough, yes? Doin' what hafta be done?"

"You mean there was no blizzard, no storm last night? Just me . . . battering through my . . . frozen emotions?" Incredulous, she took a step toward Addawanna, wanting to stare into her face for the truth, wanting—in truth—to batter at her, as if she bore responsibility for last night's terror and danger, dear Pw'eek near-freezing, Jenneth and Saam almost falling innumerable times, driving forward against all odds. "Not you—but Callis! Am I right?" Pw'eek sat up now, anxiously watching her, trying to gauge if she planned to strike Addawanna, do something else equally unforgivable. "*She* conjured up the storm out of my own fears, made me suffer through them, experience them!"

"One good t'ing," Addawanna pointed out, unperturbed. "You git angry, t'row mug preddy good distance! Even git mad poor ol' Addawanna! Good start—'cept I t'ought you wanna t'row me affer mug!"

A giggle leaked out, strengthening at the memory of the mug sailing away. Lady bless, that had felt *good*! Not holding it in, just letting it rip! **"Might try it more often, you know,"** Saam's knowing yellow eyes regarded her with a sort of sad joy.

"I know Maf'ny long time. Me an my people take her, your mot'er an father, an Harrap as pris'ners. T'ought dey doin' somet'ing bad, but wasn't dem. Maf'ny hon'rable woman, strong in spirit, hard when it count. Still hard when bein' soft count more, not easy change. She love your mot'er like daughter, but you t'ink she eber say it? Ha!" A scowl creased Addawanna's face. "Come t'ink on it, Doyce hide 'motions, too, but dif'rent. She always t'ink she failure . . . gonna fail, if not already doin' so."

"I guess Mama's not always very self-confident, but mostly she manages not to show it." A difference, though, that Addawanna had skimmed over; Aunt Mahafny was physically incapable of revealing her feelings, but Mama could and did.

"You t'ink afore that Maf'ny not fail yet not quite succeed, yes?" Jenneth nodded, puzzled, sure she'd thought that, never voiced it aloud. "An you wonner how many oder t'ings in life get stuck at half measure, needer winner nor loser?"

Now she was *sure* she'd not said that aloud. *"Pw'eek? Did you tell Addawanna what I was thinking?"*

But Pw'eek was a picture of wronged innocence, eyes large with reproach at Jenneth thinking she'd betray her beloved.

**"Jenneth, little one,"** Saam chided, **"blame me, if blame you must. If you can save me, then the least I can do is return the favor."**

"But I'm not dying—am I?"

**"Only from inside, by slow degrees, turning colder and colder, until even Pw'eek could feel it. No wonder her precious little white toes were almost frostbitten last night!"**

"Now lis'en, child." Addawanna had pressed her down, standing in front of her, a hand on each shoulder, as if Jenneth planned to bolt and run. "Most of life is half measure. Bein' born, full measure. Dyin' full measure, too. In'-tween, life is muddle, tryin' hard, doin' best—not alla time nice'n neat. Not win, not lose, jest makin' t'ings liddle better than afore, den tryin' again an tryin' again."

"You mean no one ever gets it completely right?"

**"Only the first time and the last time."**

"Doyce know dat, dat why she keep makin' effort. But Maf'ny wan t'ings *right* ev'ry time, alla time. Dat her strength, dat her flaw. Try so hard it kill her. Not you. You be good muddler if gif yourself chance—dat mean bein' able to mourn not succeeding, enjoying almost succeeding. Feelin' both, an all feelin' in'tween."

A rainbow overhead? The ice refracting colors? Strong shades and between them more delicate blendings of many hues. And mayhap, at the other end, was Aunt Mahafny's spirit, learning at last to admire such commingled beauty.

Crying now, softly at first, her head pressed just below Addawanna's breasts, contentment at the sound of another human heart. No, it wasn't fair that Bard had died; she might feel guilty over it, but it *hadn't* been her fault—he'd been searching for death in many different ways for years. She'd known that, had always sensed it within him despite his love for Lindy and Byrlie, as if he ceaselessly traveled road after road that always circled back to life, unable to find the directions to lead him where he longed to go. If anything, she and Pommy had pointed the way to what he'd sought for so long. The tears came harder now. . . .

M'wa! Had had a choice to make and had made it, had wanted above all to remain with his Bond. Whether he still lived—somewhere in the Sunderlies—or had joined the Elders, she couldn't be sure, but he'd walked his road with confidence, relief. The tears burned, made her nose raw, and the hurt was wonderful, a relief, an easing of pain so long-bottled it had become near vintage.

And Mahafny. Crotchety, persnickety perfectionist. Who'd turned to her and Diccon, to Harrap in her time of need, willing to risk all to save Saam, whether or not he wanted to be saved. Even *he* hadn't been able to read the pattern aright for some time, had balked at what she strove to accomplish. . . . Nothing had stood in her way—not a mountain, not a recalcitrant niece and nephew, a doubting Shepherd . . . ! Not funny, but it was, and now she laughed and cried, cheering on Mahafny's spirit, hoping for just a touch of that same determination and courage.

"But you already have them, beloved. Once you look within, you'll find them stored right where you left them." Pw'eek in her arms now, Saam nestling against her side as Addawanna gently disengaged herself, thrusting a handkerchief in her hands. Gratefully, Jenneth blew, honking through her swollen nose.

"Now, we got vis'tors comin'." Addawanna acted anxious, hundreds of details flittering through her mind. "No sure when, but soon nuff, since der work to do. When you ready, you come 'long, help."

"What?" Jenneth honked again, her nose clogged. "Housework? I swear that's *all* I ever do. Forever neatening camps, huts, whatever!"

"Oh, more dan dat to do. Dis be special. An Harrap need you, too. He hurt fierce, life feelin' empty right now. His Lady comfort him, but his oder lady gone."

♣

Jacobia brushed a brief kiss between Bélier's eyes, and the ewe pridefully tossed her head in the direction of her offspring. "You've every reason to be proud—Neau and Nelet are going to be marvelous beasts when they're full-grown. Of course, given Mouton as a father, not to mention you for a mother, who could expect less? Thank you!" And meant every word of it as Bélier trotted away, her hooves making a sharp clack-clack on the rocks and ice. Neau and Nelet followed, Mouton lingering for a final word with Callis. Swinging around to leave, he sideswiped Diccon with his shoulder, sending him tumbling. Massive head high, eyes rolling back to gauge Diccon's reaction, a certain self-satisfied jauntiness marred the ram's stately pace.

Holding out her hand, she levered Diccon to his feet. "I'm getting tired of brushing you off. This keeps up, you'll need a full-time valet."

"Ow!" Diccon fended off her hand. "I swear Mouton knocked me onto the one place that *didn't* hurt before!" He limped heroically, exploiting his bruises for all he was worth. "Oh, Jacobia! You should've seen Mouton charging after Jenneth, she and Pw'eek running flat out and Jen waving her tabard behind her!"

"And why was that?" she inquired with a maliciously sweet innocence. Without a doubt it was Diccon's doing, and Jen had come to the rescue yet again.

Massaging the back of his thigh, Diccon admitted, "Well, Kwee wasn't exactly polite, and Mouton got all crotchety—honest, Auntie, if we'd known . . . He nearly flattened us till Jen lured him away. And then she sprang over that rock and draped her tabard over it! Well, Mouton was seeing red at that point, and he didn't swerve, just ker-smashed right into it, headfirst! Ker-POW!"

Sinking her thumbs deep into Diccon's thigh muscle from behind, Callis's hands traveled upward. A brief, high-pitched yodel issued from Diccon, and then he relaxed. "Phew! Thank you, Callis. That feels better." He scuffed snow at Kwee. "I should have known better, and Kwee as well. I *did* try to stop her."

"Not enough." Callis now worked her thumbs along Diccon's spine, her hands disappearing farther and farther under the tabard while Jacobia watched, wondering what Callis saw in the lad, what had made her bring him along. Mostly she enjoyed his perpetual hijinks, had even encouraged him in some; now she felt considerably less indulgent. Not so much that she regarded him through different eyes, but that she saw herself differently, realized how she'd changed in ways both large and small.

"Shouldn't we be getting on to Sidonie?" What awaited them, she didn't know, but an incredible anticipatory sensation flowed through her, had been building and building the lower they'd descended. But it was still a long way to Sidonie, and she was restless with fear they'd be too late. Too late for what? Didn't know, wished Addawanna were here to ask. Callis was an unknown quantity, and she missed Addawanna and the others, had departed without time to offer real good-byes, a final sharing.

A force to Callis, that went without saying. Indeed, Feather stayed as clear of her as possible, as if afraid her mere presence might sully Callis. Clear, though, that Feather was awestruck, idolized Callis, and Jacobia half-expected her to pinch herself to prove this was no dream, that Callis existed in the flesh, not simply in stories. If she journeyed toward comprehension, Feather had been on an equally arduous trip, mayhap still had even farther to travel.

"We should reach Sidonie by first light." Callis stated it as if it were the simplest thing in the world to accomplish. Taking Feather's hand, she motioned for Jacobia to grasp Diccon's, but he sprang back, openmouthed.

"That's ridic— impossible!" he sputtered. "It should take two full days—at least! We did it faster coming here, thanks to Gaetan's barge. Are we catching another boat? Are there horses along the way?"

"Don't 'no' me what you don't know, boy! Weren't many things possible in the world within? Other things are possible in this outer world, especially when one is of the Erakwa." His mouth moved, but no sounds issued forth. "And don't grumble under your breath like that. No wonder Kwee has learned such rude manners!"

♣

A way! There *had* to be a way, there always was, though the path be rocky and fraught with peril. Just like those damn Stratocums! Show them how a road could be built, how one could blast straight through a mountain, and who *cared* if it blew to kingdom come! Eadwin's kingdom would crumble and vanish, a technocracy in its stead! He would take the Plumbs—who else possessed even an inkling of how they might be used?—and accomplish his goal. Think! he commanded the horde drifting at his heels, wheeling around him, so eager their voices gabbled like starlings around his head, ideas and plans colliding with other plans, plots and counterplots. Think, he commanded them, daring greatly to do so, but it was time they acknowledged who was really in charge, who gave them leave to roam and rummage through his brain, mine the greatness residing within.

Last night had been useless, except for wearing him out, allowing him to sleep. Mayhap just as well, because he'd had all of today and tonight to reconcile himself, open his mind to possibility and potential. Take in everything, assimilate it, store it away, check this, check that—don't assume, be sure, but within that surety, let the mind remain open, receptive. Stack fragment upon fragment of possibilities, configure them with what else he knew, what else the voices might suggest. Patience! It all required such patience.

Each circuit he'd made of the inner castle he'd scrupulously avoided the guards at the strong rooms where the Plumbs were stored. More important to watch, unobserved, discover their shifts, who rotated when. Hide and watch, count and time them. Neat and tidy, regimented little minds. It might be important to know.

The stoppered amber bottle in his pocket offered a possibility, though he wasn't yet convinced. Worrying at the sticking plaster on his finger, he meditated over how chance had fallen his way. A visit to the castle infirmary this morning. One of the mousekin's needle-sharp teeth had pierced his finger next to the nail, the flesh turning all red and puffy, the puncture leaking fluid. Anxious about infection, he'd stopped to have it checked and cleaned. Still hurt, but what did he expect, the eumedico had said without much sympathy. But while he sat, waiting, inspecting his finger, increasingly convinced they'd amputate—if only to get back at him—some assistant had bustled by with a whole tray of medicaments and supplies. Had set it down for a moment to have a word with someone else, and the stubby amber bottle had caught Romain-Laurent's eye. "Chloroform," the label read, and he'd slipped it in his pocket, determined that the next mouse he captured would be comatose. But chloroform worked on other beings, not just mice. Something to bear in mind. A possible solution to one part of the puzzle, should he need it.

To be a pioneer, building a new world! Of course it wouldn't be easy; it hadn't been for his ancestors, but the difference was that he would be the Plumbs' master, not their slave. Turned in cowardice and ran, some of them had—even Carrick, in whom he'd wanted to believe so desperately. What a naïve child he'd been—adult as well, allowing himself to once again believe like that! Must have been touched in the head!

One voice asked, "Who holds the keys to the strong rooms?" A pertinent question—probably Eadwin, very possibly a second set with Arras Muscadeine . . . or, he thought on it. Urban Gamelyn—as Exchequer Lord, mightn't he . . . ? Another voice clamored for attention. "Lady Fabienne? Surely dear Tante Fabienne also had a set of keys? Who else more trusted than the king's sainted mother?" He kissed his fingers in salute to that voice.

"But," scoffed a coolly collected, almost disdainful voice that put him in his place, as he deserved, "keys are all well and good, but do you expect to just prance in and out, lumbered by six Plumbs? Think, Romain-Laurent! What do you plan to say, man? 'Just inspecting the locks, sirs, special survey for the king—king wanted me to check, always a case of bolting the stable after the horses have been stolen. Just want to make sure none of these odd keys work.' Not bloody likely!" No, he didn't like that voice, he didn't, despite the fact the advice was sound.

Well, keys might or might not prove necessary. Oops— quick! Footsteps! Swing 'round the balustrade, spring up a half-flight of stairs, stay in the dark corner. Tread softly to the top of the second half-flight and sit and think, staring into the darkness. Cudgel his brain, exhort the horde to sweep over him in a brainstorm, expand his mind to every possibility.

"Raow? Y'ew?" Something with a small but extremely hard head butted his elbow.

"Get away, you stupid cat," he venomously muttered, swatting at it. His fingers itched, though, for the long, thin tail—must be twenty-seven or eight centimeters long. Long enough to knot? "Nice kitty?" Flipping over to kneel on the fourth step from the top, he let his finger track along the lip of the highest step, tantalizing her to chase it, pretend the finger was unattached to his hand. Damn cats were noisy as hells, though—probably wake the dead if he toyed with her.

"Oh, Romain-Laurent, you're so shortsighted sometimes," sighed a voice. "Don't you realize what you have there? Not merely a cat but a beast who's half-ghatti, offspring of Hru'rul—doesn't that suggest anything, Romain-Laurent? And let's not take too long coming up with an answer, because how often have you seen that little bespectacled girl separated from her precious kitty?"

The kitten pounced, tiny claws striking home. Not a pleasant sensation, but he refused to jerk it clear, made his finger wriggle as if it possessed a mind of its own. Possible hostage? Not much of one, but potentially useful. Something more? Hostage and lure for another—some better hostage?—human, of course. Someone attuned to the little thing's cries and rushing to investigate? Like its dear owner? If he couldn't handle a twelve-year-old girl, he might as well give in, give up.

"Yes!" urged the voice with enthusiasm, proud that Romain-Laurent had worked it out. "And mayhap, in turn, the child's cries will attract someone even more valuable."

The sound of a door opening and closing very discreetly, the way lovers do when departing a bedchamber they shouldn't be visiting in the middle of the night. The kitten looked away, mewing happily and, while it was distracted, he scooped it up and slipped it inside his shirt.

"Well, at least it's settled down, Harry," the girl-child consoled, mouth near the crack of the door. "Mayhap it'll sleep through the night—if it's half as tired as we are from cleaning up disaster after disaster. Least it didn't damage too much. Goo'night."

Turning, she headed toward the stairs, whispering "Baby, Baby," as she came closer, and the kitten struggled enthusiastically, trying to free itself, not exactly perturbed but anxious for its freedom. "Oh, good evening, sir!" Startled in mid-whisper, she acted embarrassed at being caught out like this, wandering in the middle of the night. "Have you seen my orange kitten?"

"Y'ew? Mr'row?" Baby vocalized from Romain-Laurent's midsection, claws prickling.

Romain-Laurent laughed softly, finger to his lips, as he beckoned her closer, looking around conspiratorially, inviting her to join in. Sometimes he could use his voice to gain what he wanted, but that required a declamatory mode, a decision that oratory could weave a spell. Seldom was he able to capture the elusive quality of common speech, but then, rarely had he wanted something so badly. Pretend the child was an audience of one, charm her, lull her, invite her participation in some secret enterprise.

"I've got the little rascal safe right here!" A wink as he patted the small, writhing bulge at his waist, an exaggerated, furtive glance over each shoulder. "Didn't figure she should be wandering alone at night like this. Who knows what trouble she might get into—and I hear she's already gaining a reputation for that." The girl looked abashed, and he hastened to reassure her. "Never a kitten did I know that didn't manage some mischief now and again and, of course, given her distinguished lineage, I'm sure she's far cleverer than most." Ah, that was doing it.

"May I have her back, please, sir?" She was no longer scared, just determined, hands stretching to reach, retrieve the kitten. To disguise her gesture she pushed her spectacles up her nose.

"Tell you what?" Cautious about touching her, being too familiar so soon, he bowed with outswept arm. "As long as she's comfy, busily exploring my circumference, let me escort you to your room, hand over the kitten there so she can't make any more mischief along the way." He had no idea at all in what direction her room lay, so he hesitated, waiting for her to lead, falling into step just behind her, leaning occasionally to whisper a remark at her.

Right hand in his pocket, he set about loosening the cork in the amber bottle, free it just enough to simplify things but not find himself with a pocketful of chloroform wafting up at him. At least it might stop the kitten from slithering 'round and 'round—he swore she was chasing her tail inside his shirt! Handkerchief in the other pocket. How much would it take to render her sleepy and limp, too far gone to cry out? Hadn't ever studied things of this sort. "An obvious lack!" sniffed a voice in his head, undoubtedly because he'd seized the initiative from the horde.

"Does Baby have brothers or sisters?" he asked to keep some sort of conversation flowing, mayhap even throw her off-balance a bit. "I mean, if she had littermates, is Hru'rul their father as well? A whole litter of semi-hemi-demi-ghatten. What would *you* call 'em?"

He'd thought the idea would delight her, was utterly confounded to discover tears leaking from beneath her glasses. "What, darling?" he encouraged, bending low, gripping the bottle by his side now, then casually raising his hand to his mouth, using his teeth to pull the cork. He waved the handkerchief ostentatiously, suggesting her need for it.

"Baby was the biggest, most special of . . . of the litter," she wailed, eyes screwed shut. "But Da's probably had them all drowned by now!"

"Ah! No!" A deep breath, and hold it! He held his breath as he sprinkled chloroform over the handkerchief, quickly pressing it to her face in an apparent act of kindness. Ouch! Damn that kitten—knot her tail, he would! That was pure spitefulness, the way she was clawing! Fix her as soon as he could, sooner if he had a choice!

She swooned against him, spectacles jamming her face as her head wobbled against his chest, her knees gradually buckling, collapsing. Grab her, don't let her fall, hook her over a hip, wrap an arm around her waist! Holding the sodden handkerchief as far from him as he could, he took a deep breath, then thrust it inside his shirt to sedate the kitten.

Now scoop her into both arms. Where to go, what to do with her? For a moment he nearly panicked, sure the corridor would abruptly fill with people striding back and forth as if it were broad daylight. No, she'd pointed out which door was hers, and all he had to do was make for it, get inside. One step at a time, a step accomplished.

Time enough to prepare for the next step, and he could hardly wait, thrilled by the sense of power that had swept through him when she'd slumped like that. But plans, plans were crucial. Brute power was nice, but plans, organization and preparation were better, would gain him what he wanted. What was the child's name? Did he know? What had he heard around the castle, the casual scuttlebutt of servants, listened to for the momentary sense of inclusion, the possibility of knowledge, but otherwise discarded—Teleka? No. Close, but not quite right. Telka? Yes, that must be it.

"Come, little Telka, little kitty," he gloated close to her face as he walked smoothly and purposefully, the horde applauding as if he progressed down a wide aisle of admirers. "We've such a busy night ahead of us."

❖

Tired but pleased, Romain-Laurent sat on the foot of the girl's bed, bedecked with a coverlet of pink roses and rosebuds, and surveyed his handiwork. It hadn't been easy, making do with whatever came to hand in a stranger's room—and a stranger who'd apparently arrived with little in the way of baggage—and from his own pockets, but it should suffice.

Bless the eumedico for having given him some extra sticking plaster for his finger. That went across Telka's mouth. The burlap bag, water-stained and muddy, that he'd found in the closet, hung as neatly as if it had been a fine leather valise, provided strips to bind her hands behind her. All the time he'd worked at that, using his best knots, he'd worried whether to tie her feet, worried about the kitten, fearing it would wake. Hated the sensation of the warm lump so intimately tucked inside his shirt, but figured she'd be less likely to escape.

Bind her feet, and he'd be forced to carry her—that would limit him. Finally he'd loosely braided some burlap strips to connect the loops he'd placed around each ankle, effectively hobbling her. She'd be able to walk, but had no chance of running. Boots were brown, mayhap the burlap sacking wouldn't show too badly in the dark.

The kitten presented real problems, but he rose to the occasion. Finding one of Telka's spare stockings, he snipped a bit off the toe for an airhole, then thrust the stocking over the kitten's head, wadding the extra length around its neck. A little more delicate than he liked, but he couldn't think how to reinforce his crude muzzle. The mate to the stocking he cut into strips, watching the sides curl in on themselves, creating nice, supple, narrow lengths to lash all four paws together. Perfect, he could wear the little darling on his wrist like an orange bracelet if need be! Fingers sore from wielding his penknife like a scalpel, he flexed them, still transfixed by the kitten. She was—he hated to admit it—rather cute—and he scrupulously forced himself again to ignore her long, limber tail, just crying out for a knot in it.

For a time he simply sat, tired but pleased, girding himself for the next step. A final exploration of the room to see what he might have missed. Use the flusher facilities— lucky child, having her own, not being forced to share! As his grandfather had always said, "Never miss a chance to piss, boy. Hellish holding your water, makes you a dancing fool, gets bad enough." Hardly an elegant or eloquent saying, nor something one should probably quote, but it *was* sound advice, and Romain-Laurent obeyed it, fastidiously washing his hands afterward. Then he moistened a hand towel and returned to the bedroom, sponging Telka's face, proud of himself for remembering to remove her spectacles first. The horde didn't think of practicalities of the mundane sort.

Her eyelids fluttered and, here in the bedchamber with the two oil lamps lit, her big brown eyes were luminous and deep. Again he wiped face and neck with the damp towel, brushed back the little tendrils around her hairline to create a smooth curve, and earnestly inspected his handiwork. "Come on, Telka, Telkie, wake up, there's a girl." Eyes staying open longer now, richly puzzled, her jaw wriggled, testing the sticking plaster's clinging adhesion. Politely he slipped on her spectacles, making sure each bow was securely tucked behind an ear.

Racking, choking noises, her face turning crimson, eyes bulging, Telka's body spasmed as she tested her bonds. Still, the noises frightened him, left him fearful she'd vomit, choke, and die—then what good would she be? Dragging her upright, he leaned her against him, patting her back, prepared to rip off the sticking plaster if need be. Vomiting was *so* revoltingly, disgustingly messy! Noisome! His own stomach lurched in sympathy.

But no, she wasn't throwing up; now she cast her eyes in all directions, frantic to locate that revolting kitten. Grabbing her under the arms, he sat her against the headboard. Now where had he left the kitten? Out of her line of sight, that much was clear. Oh, yes, he'd dragged the chair around, used the seat as his work space because the light was better for all those intricate knots. A cat's limbs lacked the human equivalent of wrists or ankles, no narrowing before the hand or foot extended outward. Securing the kitten had been more work than the girl had been.

The temptation was finally too great. Wrapping his hand around the kitten's tail, he briefly hoisted her in the air, dangling, paws joined together. It reminded him of how his older brothers had exhibited the trout they'd caught when they were children, standing there so prideful, arm extended at shoulder level, displaying the dangling, dead fish, a willow branch strung through the gills.

Muffled snorts and squeaks from the kitten, and he feared Telka might levitate from the bed, attack him as best she could, ram her head into his gut. Quickly scooping his free hand beneath the kitten's back, he brought her to the bed, laid her on the girl's lap. Merciful Lady, how she could glare! Could probably ignite the hobbles binding her ankles if she stared at them long enough!

"Now, I *am* sorry about this." Well, truly he wasn't—it was needful, she and the kitten were a partial payment to Lady Change. After all, he'd muttered enough mendacious apologies in the past that a few more scarcely bothered him. "I don't want to hurt you or the kitty unless I have to . . ." and stood tall and merciless, fists clenched at his sides, face stern and resolute, "and I hope that it won't be necessary. Shouldn't have picked up the little tyke by the tail like that—literally the first thing that came to hand."

Was that growl erupting from the kitten or the child? "I need your help, need you to do exactly what I say—or I'll be forced to hurt the kitty. You wouldn't want that, would you?" He waved his penknife menacingly, wishing it were larger, more imposing-looking. "If you don't do exactly what I say—when I say it—the kitty's tail will become distinctly shorter. A few centimeters at a time."

Face whiter than the sticking plaster, she hunched her knees to her chest, warding the kitten as best she could. Mayhap it was the lamplight on her spectacles that turned her glare so ferocious.

"Do as I say, when I say, and I'll let you and the kitty go. Do you understand?"

A slow nod, a questioning quirk to her head as if asking, "What do I have to do?"

"That's better, much better now." How to explain to her, give her enough to understand, ensure compliance without overburdening her? Taking out his pocket comb, he slicked back his hair, running his hands over it to make sure it was in place, give him time to think.

"You're bait, you and the kitten. Lures for something bigger. Or rather, someone," he corrected himself. "That person, in turn, will serve as the lure to let me catch what I want." Why was he still fixated on fishing, his brothers with their trout, him forever separate, unpaired, with an empty creel and a host of mosquito bites. "The kitten was the minnow that let me trap you, the little fish. Now, as little fish, you'll help me catch a medium-sized one, and so on." Fish eating fish, each complacently convinced it was the biggest, never realizing that lazily swimming behind it, mouth wide open, was another, even larger fish. That was how Change would devour everything, until he and Change would be the biggest fish in the pond—though Change would never dare consume him and his horde!

"Now, do you feel up to it? Want me to sponge your face again?" Somehow he wanted to take the time to re-braid her hair, its messiness offending him, but he contented himself with retying the braid end that was coming loose. She jerked away as best she could, hunching her legs toward the edge of the bed, stopping there, unable to stand without dumping the kitten to the floor.

"Don't worry. I'll carry her, since your hands are tied behind you. I'll tuck her back inside my shirt." Would rather have tucked the beast inside Telka's shirt, but that seemed rude. Besides, this way the kitten would be at hand if frustrations seized him. "Let's be off, then, nice and quiet. You can walk, but just don't try to take any giant steps—I haven't given you permission, have I?"

♣

*"Stop stomping me!"* Holly emerged from beneath the down comforter, shoving at P'roul, who was persistently marching back and forth across her diaphragm. *"What . . . is it?"* Usually she awoke more quickly, rallying to the call, but then, she wasn't generally on haliday, had given herself leave to sleep deeply, not remain subliminally alert for trouble. Then, if trouble lurked, either she heard it for herself or P'roul 'spoke her awake.

**"I *have* been 'speaking you. Even insults about your weight didn't work—and you know I save them as a last resort."** For emphasis she daintily planted a paw on Holly's full bladder and Holly came fully and instantly awake. **"Ah, that usually does it."**

*"Fine, then guide me to the flusher chamber, make sure I don't trip in the dark."* Hiking the unsuitably frilly night-dress that she'd bought for no reason at all—did she think a man was *ever* going to see it?—she scuttled along. *"Now what's the matter? You want me awake, that's clear, but it can't be all that serious or you'd have blurted it out by now."*

Sighing with relief she padded back, found the enameled

box of lucifers on the nightstand and struck one, settling for a candle rather than fiddling with the oil lamp. Theo had the room directly next to hers, indeed, they shared the bath facilities, and he'd likely come alert at anything beyond normal night noises. Had ears like a bat, hearing the slightest sound—except when she asked him to do something he didn't want to.

P'roul jumped beside her on the bed, pacing across her lap, unable or unwilling to settle. **"I don't know if there's something wrong . . . or not. I just had the most fleeting impression of little Y'ew's mind touching mine."**

*"But that's good news—isn't it? She may possess more ghatti abilities than we've realized."* Baby was a darling, but not a soul had had much spare time for her or Etelka, not even La'ow or Hru'rul. Whatever training she might receive—not to mention testing—would have to come later. She captured P'roul in her arms. *"You wouldn't have woken me just to mention that, not when it could have waited till breakfast. Did you have a sense of something wrong—that she was getting into mischief again—something she couldn't handle? Is that it?"*

Neatly stepping through the encircling arms, P'roul jumped down and cast a yearning glance at the door. She could open it herself, Holly knew that very well, but it took both effort and patience. **"First she was all bouncy and then she . . . well, she just dropped away, her mindspeech vanishing. I felt a residue of startlement, and then not even that. Just blankness. I've tried to 'speak her, but haven't had any luck."** A paw batted the doorknob, testing the firmness of its stem. **"I don't suppose . . ."** she left the rest of the thought suggestively dangling, as if she could lure Holly into playing with it.

Holly had already half-pulled on her trousers, deciding the filmy nightgown could be tucked inside. Just throw her tabard over it and she'd be decently dressed for a midnight ramble through the castle—just what any well-bred young woman would wear! Wondered what Cinzia slept in. *"That we could go and check on them? Tuck them into bed, give them some warm milk, whatever? P'roul, someday you'll be a superlative mama."* Bedroom slippers, not boots, there were limits. Besides, she was already so sartorially incorrect that this could hardly spoil her ensemble!

**"Think we ought to ask Khim and Theo along?"** P'roul looked torn, always happy to have Khim by her side, yet perfectly self-sufficient without her sib.

*"Let them sleep. We'll scare poor Telka and Y'ew half to death if all of us surround her. She'll be sure she's in worse trouble than Harry was."* Tightening her sash, she picked up the candle holder, reached in the drawer for a spare, as well as some lucifers. Do things automatically and you weren't caught short—even on haliday. *"Anything else?"*

P'roul's shadow-stripes swirled as she wreathed herself round and round. **"Know it sounds silly, but humor me."** Her amber eyes shimmered the color of old gold in the light. **"Take your sword. Khim and I've heard the strangest things roaming the hallways recently."**

Belting on her sword, holding the sheath to keep it from clanking, Holly shook her head at her Bond. **"With our luck someone will think we're stealing around, planning to assassinate Eadwin!"**

**"No, just say we're hunting rats—mayhap the two-legged variety. Merowmepurr heard Arras tell that to Ezequiel's grandfather, Ignacio, years ago. He was *not* amused by the idea of either variety in his castle."**

Holly bore down on the knob to muffle the sound as she turned it. *"Doubt that Ezequiel would be any happier at the suggestion of rats in his castle either."*

❧

Fuming to herself, Francie marched toward Etelka's room, her cane dragging against the carpet. Should have brought a candle, but had been too aggravated to think straight. Woken out of a sound sleep, no less! And poor Arras relaxing in the bath, trying to take his mind off things—he'd been working so hard and long, and him still not healed from his wounds or his broken collarbone. Oh, what a relief when they moved back into their own home, away from all the insanities, both large and small, that had overtaken the castle and its inhabitants!

That, that green thing! Roistering like that, bouncing and buzzing, wrecking the room, Harry standing on the bed, ineffectually fending it off by waving a towel! Admitting that he and Telka had smuggled it into their suite, even though they hadn't the slightest idea what it was—other than blithely destructive! Near scared her out of her wits, it had—and then practically glowed with triumph! Somehow Arras and Harry had captured it under the crate again, Arras sitting on it to pin it in place. Well, they'd better have found another way to securely contain it by the time she returned with Telka! She could care less that it was the middle of the night—she planned on lecturing both children, making them clean up the mess, determine how much damage had been done. Said damage, she'd already decided, would come out of Harry's pocket money.

Wisp, wisp, wisp went her cane along the carpet, more slowly now because she was so tired. As if that green thing were the only thing Harry had to answer for! Flanked by Holly and Theo, he'd diffidently entered the suite this afternoon and admitted to what had been burdening him since Bertillon. With his confession backed up and amplified by what Theo and Holly had learned from Khim and P'roul, Francie had been aghast at the news. Her niece and nephew escorting Mahafny Annendahl and the Shepherd Harrap to Nakum's mountain, no less! And Doyce and Jenret on their way, practically without pause, from their haliday on the coast!

When she'd told Arras the news, begged for help, asking that he send some of his soldiers—someone, anyone—after them to determine how they fared, fetch them back, he'd wearily said he could spare no one. Acted dismayed, but took only small interest, brain still churning with what to do about those damned Plumbs! Nor had she been able to track down Nakum, ask for his help, or at least his advice! Saam, the old dear! And Jacobia was missing, no word of her for days, not since she'd taken off after the twins, determined to track them down and retrieve them. No doubt about it, collective dementia had overtaken most of her nearest and dearest, and she was the only sane one left!

Rapping lightly but insistently on Telka's door—according to Harry the child hadn't gone off to bed all that long ago—she dredged up a touch of pity for the child, swept along by circumstance, certainly not of her choosing. Still, she had to bear some responsibility for that new "pet," that spherelike thing upholstered in what looked like lush lawn! No response, so she knocked harder, torn between simply entering without leave or awaiting a response. Even children were entitled to a certain amount of privacy, although at this stage she was beginning to wonder if she'd ever let Harry out of her sight again until he'd redeemed himself—mayhap by the time he reached his majority. "Etelka, it's Francie, Harry's mother. Open up, child, we need to have a little talk—and I mean now, not later." Good, the proper amount of sternness, the kind that a well-brought-up child like Telka should respect.

Why was it all dark hallways turned spooky at night, no matter how well you knew them? It happened in her own home, not just here. The dark made everything amorphous, large shapes looming, smaller ones either vanishing or mutating into fearsome things beyond their daylight potential to threaten. Clutching the lapels of her robe with one hand, she leaned against the door casing and raised her cane, readying herself to knock again, hoping she wouldn't waken anyone else nearby.

The door opened a crack, a vertical line of light slicing at her eyes, so accustomed had she become to the night dark on her peregrination down the hallways. Odd word, that, to pop into her mind right now. "Telka?" The door swung wider, and Francie's heart leaped, began racing as she discerned Romain-Laurent standing there, a finger to his lips.

That unadulterated idiot! What was he doing in Etelka's bedchamber at this time of night? She'd thought him many things in the time she'd casually known him—had thought far worse of him since he'd set off the Plumb—but she'd never typed him as depraved, a man who'd have his way with an undersized twelve-year-old girl! Near sickened at the thought, she prepared to slam her shoulder against the door, fully open it, her cane poised to strike. And she knew precisely where she planned the first blow to connect! But he'd swung the door open just as she threw herself at it, and he caught her, urgently whispering, "I don't think Telka's feeling too well. I found her wandering in the hallway, feverish and mumbling to herself."

Lady bless! Had she been the idiot herself? Thinking vile, unspeakable things of a man who'd only tried to aid a sick child, and she'd planned to beat him to jelly! In the wavering light she could make out Telka's form on the bed, back to the door, a blanket loosely covering her. A part of her registered that the kitten was nowhere in sight, when she'd expected to see her orange form on the bed, or at least a lump under the blanket.

Now something moist and smelly slapped across her nose and mouth and she inhaled without thinking. Then, as the wooziness hit, she held her breath, struggling to raise her cane, but somehow Romain-Laurent had wrested it . . . from her increasingly lax grip . . . couldn't hold her . . . breath . . . very much . . . longer. More she . . . fought . . . more she needed . . . to gasp . . . for air. . . .

Her weak, misshapen leg buckling under her, Francie crumpled.

❦

Tidily laying her out on the floor, Romain-Laurent left his handkerchief in place to ensure she'd remain comatose, then finally sat back on his heels, torn between delight and dismay. Oh, he'd wanted a bigger fish, someone more vitally important than the child, but he wasn't entirely convinced this crippled woman was it. Leave it to him to catch a gimp. Still, she'd literally fallen into his hands, and he'd simply have to make do. In fact, mayhap it was even better than he'd initially realized, he decided as he busied himself tearing more burlap strips to gag and bind her.

Have to think about this—and he sat back in the chair, admiring his handiwork, ignoring the child, who'd rolled over on the bed and was glaring at him again. Francie Muscadeine, wife of Arras Muscadeine, Lord of the Nord and Defense Lord. And if there was anyone in all of Sidonie, let alone all of Marchmont, whom Eadwin respected, depended upon, and deferred to, it was Arras Muscadeine. Mayhap his wife wasn't such a bad catch after all. Even the child and her kitten had risen in his estimation as possible pawns. After all, she'd helped save the king, as well as Muscadeine and his son.

Damn, damn, damn. She *was* crippled, needed assistance to walk. "Could be worse," a voice simpered and smirked. "What if you'd snagged Quaintance Mercilot? Doddering old lady who couldn't hear a threat if you shouted directly into her ear!" Grinning, Romain-Laurent had a sudden vision of himself saddled with the Lord of the Sud, piggy-backing his hostage from place to place, depositing her so he could write notes, determine how near or far to hold them so she could read and obey. Talk about being hampered!

But he didn't trust Francie Muscadeine with that cane at all—had seen a flicker in her eyes as to how and where she planned to lay about her with it. "Couldn't the child serve as a crutch?" suggested an encouraging member of the horde, one of the voices he depended upon for its common sense. More work, more time wasted, but worth it in the end.

"Telka, I've a proposition for you." He kicked the end of the bed to capture her attention, tear her worried look away from Francie and to him. "I'll need your help with the Lady Francie, because otherwise she might get hurt. You know how she has trouble walking?" The child nodded energetically, enough so that her spectacles slipped and he sighed, rose to push them back in place. "You're going to be her human crutch, because otherwise she's . . ." He paused, confident she'd imagine the worst, stew about it, before he said it. "Worthless to me. Absolutely useless, literally a drag on me, on my plans."

Edgy and exhilarated, he circled Francie, taking his time inspecting her, checking if she'd begun to stir. "Can't take the risk of leaving her, having someone discover her before I'm ready. Could shove her in the closet, I suppose." He made an ostentatious show of inspecting the closet, stepping in and partially closing the door. "Dark in there. Stuffy, too. Might be kinder to just kill her here and now—if you won't help."

"Now, I'm going to undo your hands and retie them in front of you." Was there anything left in the amber bottle? Had it all evaporated? "I can put you to sleep again while I do it, or you can give me your solemn promise not to struggle. Which will it be?"

As he'd expected, of course, so he cut her bindings with his indispensable penknife, not wanting the bother of unknotting them. Still had enough burlap strips, though they were running low. "Could use sheets . . . any number of things . . . don't worry," a voice reassured him.

Francie groaned, began stirring as he finished, so he lifted her—my, she was petite but ungainly like this!—and propped her in the chair, politely allowing her some time to come around, decipher what she'd fallen into. Again he busied away time in the flusher facilities, savoring a long drink of cool water, sorrowing that he couldn't offer any to his guests without removing their gags. Genius was thirsty work! Wash his hands with a tiny rosebud soap, thoroughly dry them. Prod the kitten as he passed by. Oh, that tail!

Back to work again. No sense hobbling the Lady Francie, she had problems enough walking as it was. Pick up the child, much easier, more compact and stand her in front of Francie's chair, her back to the older woman. Now, lift Francie's bound arms over Telka's head, lash her wrists to the child's so they were connected. Add some lashing above their elbows so their arms were joined, Francie snugged to the girl for support. Not bad, not bad at all, she could lean on the child's shoulders, walk behind her, and it made such a nice, compact package. Two hostages all tied into one. Economical, Urban would no doubt proclaim it!

"Now, ladies, it's time we were off." Blast! Had to take the kitten, too. Pop it inside his shirt again. "No! Don't do that!" He swatted the lump under his shirt. Lashing her paws together didn't stop her from extruding her claws, sticking him unmercifully. At least she couldn't rake him. Nice to nip off those toes one by one, rid himself of those nasty claws. "To the strong-rooms, if you please. Come along nicely, now."

♣

Up, down, and roundabout, Romain-Laurent led his charges. It felt decidedly odd to have living, breathing people by his side, rather than the swarming horde that usually accompanied him each night. "Certainly not much in the way of conversationalists, are you?" he hissed, knowing the horde would relish his witticism. Frankly, traveling with the horde was a great deal easier.

Imperative not to be discovered too soon. Imperative that *he* determine when to show himself, display his captives. And most of all, he mustn't let anyone sneak up, attack from the rear. Easy enough to play cat and mouse, hiding here and there at the sound of approaching footsteps, dodge into this darkened room or that, tug his charges into the deepest shadows and warn them to remain scrupulously still, not move a muscle. He either prodded them from behind—not entirely satisfactory, since it meant Telka received her instructions from Francie, in the middle—or led them by their conjoined arms, the easier way.

Going down any flights of stairs was a true trial, the woman overbalancing despite her best efforts, practically tumbling both her and the child down the flight. What he did then was to turn and face Telka, place a hand on each shoulder, ease her back if she tilted too far forward. Once they all fell in a jumble, though luckily not too far from the bottom, and he ended up at the bottom of the heap, the kitten squealing through its muzzle. Damnably awkward and effortful to get everyone righted, and he swore Telka had driven her knee into his chin as hard as she could out of sheer spite! The malicious thing needed to be taught a lesson, she did, except he didn't have time to spare to slice off a few centimeters of the kitten's tail.

A lightening in some corridors, dimness lifting as dawn approached. Too bad—darkness better suited his purpose. Darkness cloaked them anew the closer they came to the strong rooms. Fewer windows in the corridors the deeper they plunged into the castle's interior. Yes, pause here, slip his new friends behind the tapestry. The guards should be changing shortly, and he might as well wait. No sense commencing with both sets of guards there, the ones about to be relieved as well as the fresh squad. So, it *had* paid to keep track.

It'd be good to sit, but he couldn't. Didn't dare take his ease, relax overmuch. Before he knew it, he'd start daydreaming again, one of the voices recounting some plan that deserved his total concentration. No time for distraction. The woman was breathing heavily, more so than he liked, and the child looked half-wilted. He wished for some water and a towel to sponge their faces. Wouldn't do to have them worn out, incapable of responding.

And all the while he continued his rough count, thrumming one hand on his thigh to mark the passage of time, how long it would take for the retiring guard to get well clear of the strong rooms, the new squad to separate to take up their assigned positions. Yes, patience, another count of eighty plus eighty. That should do it.

He decorously eased the two from behind the tapestry, escorting them beside him. Now, step into the corridor that fronted the strong rooms, back planted against the wall, the two in front of him as a shield. My, he'd been so silent none of the guards had blinked, still stared straight ahead. The one to the left of the double door had a constant fidget.

"Ahem!" Oh, really! Couldn't he make a better start than that? "Gentlemen! It might be wise if one of you were to rouse the king and Lord Muscadeine. And make sure they bring the keys to the strong rooms."

Pikes dropping, the two door guards whirled toward him, the nearer one grimly advancing, pike at the ready. "Oh, I wouldn't come any closer, if I were you." Romain-Laurent warned, his penknife at Lady Francie's neck. A paltry weapon in their eyes, no doubt, but sharp, lethally effective since they were trussed like capons. "Either you'll skewer the child and Lord Muscadeine's wife, or I'll slice an artery. Or I could trim an ear for you to take to Muscadeine as proof."

❧

It took three soldiers and two of the liveried house guards to bring down Arras Muscadeine when the king brought the news of Francie's abduction. Eadwin leaned against the wall, out of harm's way, as one by one they grimly awaited an opening to tackle Arras, control him without inflicting any major bodily harm. He'd anticipated exactly such a reaction, had warned the men that until Arras mastered himself and his emotions, he was to be treated thusly, restrained for his own good. Much as he might want to watch Arras tear Romain-Laurent limb from limb, it wasn't advisable—not if they wished to keep Francie and Telka alive.

And Y'ew, Hru'rul's offspring, as well. The ghatt was nearly as livid as Arras, fluffed to twice his size, a monotone growl rumbling in his chest. Finally he relented, at least as far as Hru'rul was concerned. *"If you think you can control yourself, go. Scout around, send me word. But don't, don't, I beg you, do anything foolish that would endanger Baby or Francie or Etelka."*

As Hru'rul turned, the look of thanks in his tawny eyes enough, Holly and P'roul rushed in, Eadwin eyeing her attire despite himself. Hints of a filmy nightgown peeked out around her tabard, somehow calling attention to her near-nakedness beneath the tabard. The slippers—what did Mother call them, mules?—with the silk rosette on each toe were complemented by the bared sword, and he had all he could do not to examine her more openly.

"P'roul, go with Hru'rul, keep him in line," she ordered the ghatta, and the two sprang away. "Telka's missing, but I gather you already know something's amiss." A muffled roar and one of the soldiers was bucked into the air. "Who else? Harry? It would figure, wouldn't it?"

"No, not Harry—" he broke off. "I said keep him down, just hang on. Watch his collarbone! Arras—please! I need you, and you need me if we're to get through this together. You don't have to calm yourself, but you must listen to me."

Weaving amongst the writhing bodies on the floor, Holly snatched a water carafe from the nightstand, expertly kneed aside a palace guard's head, and emptied the water directly into Arras's face, aiming for maximum efficacy. Maximum efficacy was right—she'd tossed it directly up Arras's nose! Clearly not a woman for half-measures, but then that had been driven home to him on learning she'd singlehandedly dragged the trunkload of Plumbs up from the cellars.

More people crowded the doorway and, with a nice sense of propriety, the soldiers on guard outside judged precisely whom to admit. Hardly surprising, Theo and Cinzia with Khim and La'ow were in the first cluster, along with Ezequiel, who whispered, "I've servants waking your mother, as well as sending messengers to the Domain and Ministration Lords. Has anyone seen to Harry?"

Arras now sounded as if he were merely in the throes of a coughing fit, no longer gagging and snorting while Holly pounded his back, soldiers and guards still pinioning his arms and legs, wary for any untoward move. "Damnation!

I never thought!" Had the boy woken in the adjoining bed-chamber in the midst of this chaos? "Go see, would you? Get him dressed and bring him in. I won't lock him in a room with some adult to watch over him—he's too old for that, doesn't deserve it."

" 'Nuff!" growled Arras, winded by the coughing. " 'M listening, Eadwin." The water had wilted his mustache, making him appear vulnerable, his dark eyes pain-filled.

At his nod they lifted Arras and sat him in a straight-backed chair, two of his soldiers remaining, their expressions of concern countermanding the distasteful duty they'd been called on to perform. Running his fingers through his sodden hair, more gray to it than Eadwin had realized or acknowledged before, Arras tossed his head to clear it, snatched gratefully at the silver flask that Holly had un-earthed. Two gulps with no drawn breath between them, and Eadwin vicariously felt the steam seeping from his own ears as the scent of celvassy assaulted his nose.

In a strangled voice Arras announced, "I assume that *bastard*," he bit down on additional choice expletives, "wants the Plumbs in exchange for Francie and the child."

"That hasn't yet been stated in so many words." Eadwin found himself employing caution, wanting above all not to make anything worse than it already was. Could it become worse? Oh, it could, it could! "He's asked for the keys to the strong-rooms. I expect we'll find out when we talk to him. I'd like you with me, Arras, if you think you've re-gained your . . . composure." He spoke distinctly and more loudly than usual, unsure if Arras's hearing had completely returned to normal. This was not the time to be misunder-stood. As Resonants they could converse in mindspeech, but best to have witnesses, a public record of his words. "If not, I'll ask Nakum or Urban. Mayhap Holly, but I'd prefer a Marchmontian. No offense," he offered a quirked smile at Holly.

"Aye, I'll be at your side, Eadwin. No other place could better suit me." With exquisite caution he rose, favoring his bad shoulder, intent on not making any sudden moves that the soldiers might misconstrue. "As long as we under-stand one crucial thing from the onset, Eadwin." A deep, shuddering breath, his shoulders suddenly rounded with the weight of the world. "I'd kill myself rather than see Francie come to harm, but we can't save her and the little girl at the expense of our country, at the expense of letting those Plumbs get into the hands of a madman!" Another pull at the flask. "Of all the sacrifices I've thought I might be called upon to make through the years, including losing my head to Maurice, this possibility never entered my mind."

"Nothing's certain yet," Eadwin remonstrated. "It's too soon to draw a line in the sand, say we won't step across it. First let's assess the situation." Ezequiel was at his side, hand on his elbow, and he swung to face his chamberlain, noticing how Ezequiel adroitly shifted to ensure his face was concealed from Arras as he muttered, "I can't find hide nor hair of the boy. Room's an utter disaster, more than what you'd expect from a lad his age, not to mention Harry. I'd say he's dressed, but where he is, I don't know."

"I suspect I know, and so do you. He overheard enough to sneak out, try to rescue his mother. Would you expect anything different from him?"

"I'll have servants start looking as discreetly as they can, just to spot him. It may take Arras to halt him." Moving around him, Ezequiel now offered Holly a sketchy bow. "I've arranged additional clothing for you. The slippers are charming but not very suitable for fast footwork."

Eadwin consciously distracted Ezequiel, aware how he was staring at Holly—more entranced than lustful. "Has anyone seen Nakum? I want him here as well."

As usual, he'd been anticipated. "So far, nothing. I think he's gone belowground again, though I've had no time to send someone to search him out."

Nor, Eadwin reflected, would many voluntarily search the castle's substructure. "I swear he's worse than Hru'rul—always prowling somewhere!"

"Worse than a ghatt, you mean?" A fleeting wink. "You've the keys? I've brought the third set from their hiding place, just in case."

"No, I've mine, Mother has a second set, and Arras the third. Make sure she's guarded as well, Ezequiel. And guard that spare set with your life."

# PART
# SIX

Back jammed tight against the castle's outer wall, Harry slipped along the ledge that ran just beneath the windows, ivy brushing the back of his neck, snagging his hair. Wasn't any worse than when he and Smir had gone galloping along the rooftops in Samranth, he reminded himself. Heck, even wee Siri and Byrlie had navigated the roofs like veterans. But then his knees hadn't been near so jellylike, quivering like a particularly revolting aspic mold that sometimes made an appearance at luncheons. First Papa had nearly lost his life, and now this—Mama taken by that prissy, perfect Romain-Laurent! Perfect, his Aunt Fanny! No common sense at all, unpacking that Plumb when he hadn't even been asked to, playing with the buttons. Children way younger than he knew better than to do such a stupid thing!

And not just Mama, but Telka, too! Since he hadn't heard word of Baby, he hoped she ran free, wasn't in any danger. Not likely, though. Telka and Baby were pretty hard to separate. Pausing outside one of the windows to his parents' bedchamber, he listened some more, snuck a quick glance to determine if he'd be observed edging by. Most likely not. All eyes were riveted on Papa, struggling on the floor, and he wanted to jump inside, smash a chair over one of the soldiers, make them let Papa up. But Eadwin was probably right—Papa wasn't a beserker like Bard, subject to mad, bloody rages, but this was enough to make any sane soul sizzle! *Oh, Mama! Mama!*

An interrogatory chirp from within his tunic, and he patted his bulging front reassuringly. At the last moment he'd snatched up the green thing and taken it with him. Firstly, he didn't know what trouble it might initiate while he was gone, and no one needed any more trouble, even minor aggravation right now. But mainly he was lonely and

scared, wanted the comfort of its company. Besides, it kept
his stomach warm, because it was damnably cold out, especially flattened against the stonework like this. Didn't really
weigh much of anything, light as a feather, and he thought
he could convince it to mold itself against him, if he had
to. Only thing was, sometimes it glowed, absolutely pulsated with a lambent green light, and he was afraid it might
shine right through his tunic, give him away. When he held
a hand in front of him, a tinge of green reflected on his
skin.

The other thing he'd snatched up when all the commotion started was Papa's set of keys to the strong-rooms. The
darned green thing had somehow collected them when it'd
snuck into Mama's and Papa's dressing room while Papa
was bathing. Harry was mortally terrified to have them in
his possession, was surprised Papa hadn't thrown a fit when
he'd discovered them missing. Probably would have, if he
hadn't been so occupied trying to capture greenie. Rather
than leave them unguarded, Harry'd slipped the gold chain
around his neck the way Papa always wore it, the keys safe
and close to his heart till he could return them. 'Cept he
couldn't just stick his hand in the window and drop them
inside, have Eadwin learn they'd been out of Papa's
keeping.

Easy does it, shoot by the window. Pause, check at the
next window just to be sure. No sweat, no one even near,
let alone looking that way. Could probably slip back inside
whenever an open window presented itself, but he'd attract
less notice out here. Things were already happening fast
and furious, too many people charging all over—Papa's soldiers, palace guards, and anyone else who could find an
excuse to be near. Not the moment to try to be invisible.

If only he could reach Nakum! Even thinking the thought
seemed to make the green thing happy, set it humming. He
knew which bedchamber Nakum usually occupied when he
visited, so he continued sidling along the ledge, resolutely
not looking down. Mama'd have a fit if she found him—
*oh, Mama!* Have to shift down a level soon, a drainpipe
there and some ivy, he hoped. He froze, foot nudging something in its path, and he couldn't look down proper to see
what it was. Twiggy, mainly. A disgruntled coo and a flap
of wings, loud like a handclap beside his ear. Damn pigeon

nest! Stupid birds'd nest anywhere, hatch squabs any time
of the year! Still, he overstepped it, mindful not to hurt the
little'uns. Was it true what he'd heard—not that he'd been
meant to hear—about what Romain-Laurent did to little
creatures, mutilating them? If so, that was the worst kind
of ick-making! Really sickening cruel, for anyone, grown-
up or child, to torment creatures like that. The green thing
thrummed its agreement.

Drainpipe. He needed to cling to it, press tight against
it, so he pouched his tunic at the side in hopes the thing
would scuttle round, shift to his back once he hugged the
pipe. It did, but Harry quivered as it slithered up his spine,
just a fringe peeping out from his collar, right over his
shoulder. Aw, it was casting its green glow on the pipe so
he could see better. He rubbed it with his chin in thanks.

What Nakum could accomplish that Papa and the king
and everyone else couldn't, he didn't know—not for sure.
It was just that however much everyone wanted to get rid
of the Plumbs, Nakum wanted it even more. Mama'd tried
to explain that Nakum had too much empathy, felt the
hurts of others as if they were his own. And to Nakum,
the earth, the land was a being to consider, something nobody else seemed to be doing. 'Cept for the Erakwa, he
guessed. They took more stock in the feelings of things—
animals and trees, water, wind, the earth beneath their feet.
Kinda nice, come to think on it.

Good! Nakum's window was wide open, even in winter.
Softly calling Nakum's name, he climbed over the sill. Had
to watch where he put his feet, scoot them ahead in the
dark to find things—especially Nakum. He didn't always
enjoy sleeping in a bed. Shame to tramp across him. But
no, no one was here. Disconsolate, he plopped on the floor,
sitting tailor style. Now what to do? How could he save
Mama and Telka? Where could he find Nakum?

He had an idea, but it didn't much appeal. Go down
below, into the cellars and subbasements. Nakum had spent
time down there since the Plumb, exploring its farthest
reaches, places where the earth still retained its naturalness,
untainted by men. The thought of returning, even though
most of the water had drained clear, made Harry hug himself tight for courage. Could he face it again, lacking any
idea where to go? Well, he'd learned about the ceiling

markings—not that that did much good, since he couldn't reach them. Get someone to go with him? Cinzia'd been down before, looking for them—La'ow, too. Mayhap Theo, or Ezequiel? Holly? Unfolding his knees he brought them to his chest and hugged them, the blasted keys pressing hard against his breastbone. *Oh, Mama!* Why couldn't Aunt Doyce be here when he and Mama needed her so!

♣

Nakum ran with long, lithe strides toward his bechamber, anxious not to be seen. What he wanted more than anything was to rest, digest the news the earth had shared with him. Happiness that Saam had survived was tempered by the earth's whispers of Mahafny's death. He'd not always liked the woman but had respected her, as strong in her own way as one of the Erakwa. But the earth had also vibrated with—well, not exactly rumor—but tidbits of news, as it so often did, picking up a story here, a happening there. Undoubtedly Addawanna could have pieced it together with whatever she'd already heard bruited about, but to him it made no sense.

Something regarding Callis, but then the earth had grown coy, mayhap fearing it had already revealed too much. And finally, grumblings and rumblings, worries and woes, its fear of the Plumbs still at fever pitch. Just because the earth had become purposefully vague didn't mean it wasn't fearful. Mayhap it suffered some sort of nightmare, a reliving of the danger.

A furtive glance revealing that no one was nearby, he slipped into his room, only to let out a strangled yelp as he tripped over something planted in the center of the carpet. So much for his vaunted Erakwan senses, as he rolled over and rubbed a bruised elbow. "Harry, is that you?" Of course it was Harry, but the point was: what was he doing here in Nakum's room at this time of night—or just before dawn, to be precise? The boy should be sleeping now, not paying social calls!

Wedged beneath the bed, where he'd scrambled to evade Nakum's feet—though Nakum was sure he'd kicked Harry a good one in the ribs—the boy groaned and extended an arm, hand waving. Taking his wrist, he dragged him clear, struck by the green-gold light that glowed between the buttons of Harry's tunic, casting an unhealthy tint on his screwed-up face.

"Where've you been!" the boy demanded, levering himself off the floor, an arm clapped over his midsection. "We *need* you! You've got to help Mama!"

"Did I hurt you?"

"No. Yes—a little, but it doesn't matter." Wiping his nose on his sleeve, Harry peered at him in the dimness. "That . . . that *awful* Romain-Laurent has taken Mama and Telka captive—wants Eadwin to hand over the Plumbs in exchange!"

A sickening dread coursed through him at Harry's words—so *that* was what the earth had been hinting about, already sensing how chaos was about to be loosed once more. "I'm sure your father and Eadwin will figure how to save your mother and Telka," he soothed, running his hands along Harry's ribs to see if they were intact, only to scare himself almost witless when his hand encountered a squirming, shifting mass that clearly was not Harry. "What have you got, a little animal in there? Telka's Baby?" In truth, he'd barely had time to notice the child, other than that casual dinner together, but the orange-striped kitten had been irresistible. Had reminded him how lucky Eadwin was to have Hru'rul, and how much he missed Saam, the other ghatti he'd come to love, to know so well—Khar, Rawn, and others. What a joy to have one of the ghatti reside with him on his mountaintop domain!

As his hands continued prodding, a high-pitched giggle broke out, and the hair crawled on the back of Nakum's neck. It wasn't Harry, couldn't be! That giggle was unforgettable—especially since he'd heard it last at his own expense! The greenish light intensified as he undid several buttons on Harry's tunic and peered inside. Ho! Having no desire to become as intimate with it as Harry apparently was, he hunkered on his heels, moved his hands clear. Of course! So *that* was what had been teasing and tormenting him! He'd never thought . . . it had never even occurred to him . . . that it had gotten loose! So of course it had reveled in a prime opportunity to make a total fool of him, richly-ripe for its next trick! And ripely deserving for not

piecing together the clues. Should have sent it packing back
to Callis long ago. But there was no time for that now,
more important things took precedence.

"Do you know what it is?" Harry asked, resettling it.
"It's not exactly nasty, but it stirs up trouble, leaves a swath
of minor destruction in its wake, and I'm the one who has
to clean up after it. Well, Telka's helped, too. Doesn't seem
very interested in eating or drinking, but it's more chipper
than when we first found it. Nearly flat and really woebegone then."

Undoubtedly it was, Nakum thought, suppressing a smile
and wondering how Eadwin would react to discovering his
castle invaded by a resident Trickster. "Basically it's harmless, Harry. It feeds off people's emotions, mostly transitory
shock or surprise or fear that it startles people into projecting. Not very disciplined, loves practical jokes, and not
very refined ones at that." Leave it behind while he and
Harry determined what was happening with Romain-
Laurent? No, better to keep it with them, control its
actions.

Rebuttoning Harry's tunic, wishing he had some way to
seal it safely inside, Nakum put an arm across the boy's
shoulders. "What, precisely, do you think I can do to
help?" he inquired as they left the bedchamber, Harry
breaking into a jog trot and Nakum following after. He
wanted to help, was more than willing, but what did the
boy innocently expect him to accomplish?

Stopping dead to face him, Harry beseeched him, "I
don't *know*! Wish I did! But the king really needs you—
I'm not sure how much help Papa can be, since Mama's
involved. He . . . he . . ." firming his lower lip, Harry
continued as matter-of-factly as he could, "said that Romain-Laurent mustn't have the Plumbs under *any* circumstances! Better to *sacrifice* Mama and Telka than meet his
demands! Oh, Mama, Mama!"

What a thing for a thirteen-year-old boy to hear, that
someone so dearly loved was expendable! It didn't matter
that Nakum understood, agreed with Arras's hard logic, it
was still an onerous burden for anyone, let alone a child.

Motioning him closer, Harry grabbed Nakum by the
shoulders, looking around fearfully before whispering,
"And I've got Papa's keys to the strong rooms where the

Plumbs are—greenie snatched them! I'll guard 'em till I can give 'em back to papa."

Keys that could be bartered, traded for Francie's and Telka's freedom. Had the boy thought it through, realized the possibility? Would he purposely contravene his father's edict? "Come on, then!" More than anything Nakum wanted the keys in Arras's hands, but wouldn't humiliate Harry by taking them away from him. "What an unholy mess this is!" he muttered to no one in particular as they hurried toward the castle's center.

❖

"We lose nothing by talking with him," Eadwin reminded Arras in a level undertone as they approached the strong rooms. "Don't automatically assume it's hopeless." Guards and soldiers lined the route, formed a half-moon around Romain-Laurent and his hostages but well-distant, as the situation demanded. Few others had been permitted this close, at Eadwin's orders, and he and Arras had already forced a path through the knot of eumedicos he'd called for, as well as Eugenie Vannevar and Gilly Beaumarchais, his mother Fabienne, and all six of his Ministration Lords. Apparently Ezequiel hadn't had the heart to waken Quaintance.

"If you've any suggestions for solving this crisis," he'd told them without slowing, "pass them along to the Lady Fabienne. I'm eager to listen, but I must speak with Charpentier first." Hands patted Arras's back as they passed— Eugenie, Urban, Lysenko, Terrail, all sincere in their sympathy, but Gilly shoved in front of Eadwin, forcing him to a momentary halt.

"I *told* you we should have taken *immediate* steps to bury them! Done something, *anything*, with them!" A pinched look to Gilly, the skin around his nose and mouth taut and white. "Whatever you do, Eadwin, he *mustn't* be allowed to get his hands on them—I'll *never* vote for that!"

"It hasn't come to that yet, and it won't," Eadwin reassured. "But you've forgotten one thing, Gilly. I *am* king, and the matter will be decided by *me*. I'll take any suggestions under advisement, but not criticism, no recriminations—is that clear? I am *king*, and any power you possess devolves from me. Vote all you wish, but it will *not* alter what I ultimately do—or don't do." A growing anger at his old collegium friend, as well as sorrow that Gilly so misunderstood this crisis, assumed him too weak or indecisive to forcefully deal with it. The briefest motion to two of his guards, and they removed Gilly from his path, but the confrontation still rankled as they approached Romain-Laurent.

Arras's stolid, cold expression never faltered the nearer they came to Francie and Telka, his eyes never straying toward his wife, now seated on a stool, the child awkwardly perched on her lap. Apparently Charpentier had ordered a soldier to procure a seat, not out of kindness, Eadwin surmised, but from concern that Francie remain reasonably rested, ambulatory if he require a mobile shield.

Hru'rul shoved through legs to his side, and he stroked his head. **"Mine!"** the one word fraught with a grim finality. Hru'rul had already reported that Baby—Y'ew, he corrected himself—was also a hostage, bound and muzzled within Romain-Laurent's shirt. **"Kill him. Mayhap let Arras have leftovers."**

P'roul and Hru'rul had stealthed and sleuthed, reporting any and every pertinent detail they uncovered, maintaining constant contact with La'ow and Khim. Their Bonds and Ezequiel were feverishly searching out building plans, the papers already jumbled and disorganized from the earlier hunt for underground plans and prints. Eadwin doubted it would serve any purpose; the objective of having a strong room was to have it inviolable. What did he expect—that Constant had constructed secret entrances, a hidden trapdoor in the ceiling? That he could slip soldiers inside, have them burst out the doors, attack Romain-Laurent from the rear, and overpower him before he could harm his captives? Still, he'd ignore no possibility, no matter how remote. Sometimes the smallest thing could provide leverage. . . .

Romain-Laurent almost capered with glee as he sheltered behind Francie and Telka, his back against the double doors. "So, are you ready to hand over the Plumbs?"

Eadwin mentally steeled himself. "Are you sure that's

what you really want? Not when there are other things you might rather have?"

"And what can someone like you know about what I'd rather have?" A scornful twist to his mouth, though his eyes were big with longing, as if some indescribable thing had come to mind, something Eadwin would never be able to envision in a thousand years. "You know so little about me, what I live for, what I want to do! You give lip service about listening to new ideas, but Lady forbid you accept them, act on them!"

A faint groan from Arras. "I know, and I've been thinking deeply about that. Sometimes we must be forced to see things with fresh eyes. What you want, and I want—what our country thirsts for, Romain-Laurent—is Change! Surely that can be accomplished without the Plumbs. Not a one of us, yourself included, knows precisely what they'll do. Will they work as well as the first one you set off? Will they fizzle and flame and die? Or mayhap not even that, that no matter how many buttons you push, they're dead— suitable for bookends, nothing more. That's *chance,* Charpentier, not Change. Let me offer you something *real,* tangible, for being foresighted, modify your immediate plan, release your hostages. Only you can direct the changes Marchmont needs—now and for many tomorrows!"

"And what changes might those be?" Sickeningly coy, he rested his chin on Francie's thin shoulder, peering around her before jerking back. "No, I'm not giving in!" he shouted to his right, only to jerk the other way and snarl, "I'll do as I please, and if I please, I'll listen! Don't ever take that tone with me again!" And then, more desperately and directly at Eadwin, "They just *don't* understand! They think because they've contributed so much before that now they—" Sweat beaded his haggard, haunted expression, and he licked his lips before continuing.

"So what are you offering me?" he continued in a perfectly sane, reasonable voice. "I'm listening."

Eadwin involuntarily shivered as the chill sweat of fear traveled down his spine. Was the man mad?

Hru'rul edged fractionally closer. **"Remember? You sense different voices in his voice—all so nicey-nice and seductive?"**

*"He's mad, then?"* It made sense, but if Romain-Laurent

spoke with different voices, heard different voices, did he contain an array of souls, of beings within him? And if so, with whom was he supposed to negotiate? Very possibly whatever he offered would please someone, but not everyone.

"What I've been planning, Romain-Laurent," keep calling him by his name, remind him who is supposed to be in charge, "is to make you chancellor of Montpéllier—just for a start," he added hastily. "We need more young people properly trained in your methods, and the time is right."

"And. . . . ?" Fastidiously, Romain-Laurent took the tip of his penknife and cleaned under a nail, as if that niggling detail took precedence over everything else.

"While molding young minds to create a new, techno-techno-logical," he stumbled over the word, "world is important, your mind is too creative to be forced to contemplate administrative matters day in and day out. You'll require a very large fund of money for personal experiments and research, and complete access to all relevant material from the past to expand upon it, in order to enhance it with your own unique vision of our future."

A commotion behind him, and Eadwin didn't dare risk a glance over his shoulder, his eyes locked on Charpentier's to give him less of a chance to focus on whatever was happening. Running footsteps, Harry's voice calling, "Papa! Papa!" and Nakum's urgent command, "Get back! You've no right here . . ."

"As much as you—more, mayhap!" shouted Gilly as he shoved between Eadwin and Arras, Nakum clinging to his arm, trying to bodily restrain him. "You listen to me, Charpentier! Never will we let you have those Plumbs! Nev—" and Nakum's arm locked around his throat just as Arras's fist crashed into Gilly's chin.

Aware that within this melee somewhere was Harry, Eadwin held out his arm, relieved as the boy slipped into its welcoming shelter. Had to endure seeing his mother, his new friend, trussed like that, incapable of moving or speaking, totally at Charpentier's mercy. And undoubtedly all-too-aware of father's devotion to duty. Not something anyone should be forced to witness.

"No! No! No!" With each reiteration Romain-Laurent stamped his foot like a petulant child. "*Mine*! *My* Plumbs!

Give me my Plumbs! I want the keys—now!" fists beating at Francie's frail shoulders as he spoke. "They need me! No one else 'preciates them, wants 'em—think how they must feel!"

Arras finally intoned the words that Eadwin had dreaded hearing, had known they'd come, sooner or later, though he'd never expected Gilly to precipitate the final crisis. "Charpentier, the Lord of the Ouest is correct. Neither the king nor I will allow you to get your hands on those Plumbs, and I say that knowing full well that one of your hostages is my wife, the other a child who saved the king's life, not to mention my son's and my own."

Readying himself, reaching for his concealed knife, Eadwin awaited the next words, the code that would signal their attack—he and Arras and Hru'rul, the two nearest soldiers, whom Arras had instructed by mindvoice. Their sole hope lay in speed and startlement. Very possibly Romain-Laurent would kill Francie or Telka—mayhap both—before they could reach him, but once overpowered, the crisis would be over.

Oh, sweet Lady! He'd not counted on Harry pressed tight by his side, witnessing his mother's slaughter! But what happened next passed beyond the realm of anything Eadwin had ever experienced or imagined. "Mama! Telka!" Harry screamed and doubled over, vomiting on Eadwin's boots, but what set Eadwin reeling backward into Nakum was the black crow that exploded from the front of Harry's shirt, a gold chain dangling in its beak! And from the chain hung the keys he'd given Arras for the strong room's doors.

The crow swooped low at Telka's and Francie's faces, barely grazing them as his wings beat furiously. Higher, higher as he climbed, circling, trying to find a window. As Romain-Laurent lifted his arm to fend off the crow, it loosed a raucous, crackling caw of laughter, the chain slipping from his beak and onto Romain-Laurent's arm.

Too much now, everything happening both too quickly and too slowly. Gilly loose, impeding everyone else as he struggled to reach Charpentier, Arras skating in the vomit, crashing into an advancing soldier, Hru'rul overleaping bodies, jaws snapping in midair to capture the orange bundle thrown to stopper his gaping, fanged mouth. . . .

Enough time, sufficient chaos for Romain-Laurent to unlock one door, bodily drag Francie and Telka within, slam
and relock the door as bodies collided against it.

Romain-Laurent had gained entry to the Plumbs.

❧

Nakum had eyes for naught but the crow as it restlessly
looped in figure-eights as close to the ceiling as it could.
Finally it landed on a cornice, clinging with its claws, wings
aflutter as it sought a reasonable-sized horizontal surface
on which to roost. At last it uneasily settled, hunched just
below the ceiling, head drawn tight to rest on its shoulders.
Unregarded in the volleys of recrimination and counter-
recrimination that flew about, Nakum willed himself unno-
ticeable, no easy matter within a castle, and slipped after
the crow until he stood below it.

"No easy way out, you know," he informed the ceiling
in general, not directly meeting the bird's eye. "No windows for quite some ways, just more corridors to flap
through, wondering which way to fly next. And by then,
someone's sure to notice. Do more than just notice you. A
broom in the tail feathers will be the least of it. Infuriated
ghatti springing after you, faster than you might think, even
if you turn into a fox to fight, defend yourself."

Jet black feathers rustled as the crow uneasily shuffled
in its cramped position, and Nakum sidestepped the deposit, the bird's brief, inelegant response. "I know you
meant to help—in your own way," he soothed, "but you
totally misjudged the situation. I know you like the boy
and the girl—they've been kind to you—but that wasn't the
way to help." The bird uttered a miserable "Crawp" and
buried its head deeper into its chest feathers, eyes slitted
as if it planned to fall asleep, awake when things appeared
more promising.

"I might be able to help." More things than the crow
engaged his attention, things he'd rather be a part of, doing
something to help. Harry, desolate, engulfed in Arras's
arms, both of them weeping. At some point Cinzia and
Theo had arrived, were freeing Baby, massaging her little
legs, under Hru'rul's anxious eyes, his tongue swiping

across the triangular orange face every time she mewled in pain.

"Battering ram, sire?" briskly queried a captain. Finally realizing that he'd received no response from the Defense Lord, he amplified, "We can ram down the doors, capture them inside."

"Crawp? Caw?" As if having said too much, the crow began to busily pick under his wingpit, head conveniently cocked to follow the activity in front of the strong-rooms. Nakum risked a glance upward, just the proper moment to catch him, and winked at the bird, as if they shared a private joke.

Scraping his boots on a clean segment of carpet, Eadwin finally addressed the captain. "Have you thought what would happen as you cleared the doors?" His tone was deceptively mild, but Nakum could palpably register the frustration and anger emanating from his cousin.

"Why, we retrieve the hostages—if we can—and take Charpentier by any means possible," the captain responded with crisp certitude, then hesitated, almost wilting as the ramifications sank in. "Sire, Lord Muscadeine! By the Lady, I'm a fool! I'm so . . . " He saluted and managed to stand at rigid attention, thumbs aligned along his outer trouser seams. "Charpentier is in there with the Plumbs, can set them off before we can break in, as we break in! In the heat of the moment, I forgot the hunted became the hunter once behind those doors."

Nakum sympathized. So easy to believe the old rules pertained, to forget that new rules were being written with each step of this fiasco. "So, what's it going to be, my Trickster friend? You can stay perched there for eternity—till dust turns your glossy black feathers plaster-white. Come down now, and I'll hide you. Mayhap there's still something you can do to help Harry and Telka, make up for things."

An iridescent shimmer of black transmuted itself into deep green, quickly fading to the palest tint as the thing floated down from its perch and dove for the safety of Nakum's vest. "And don't glow!" he admonished, patting it to settle against the small of his back. "People find reasons enough to dislike, distrust Erakwa without one of us glowing green." Not for the first time he wondered what the Trickster was actually made of—right now it felt like a particularly nappy suede. Didn't matter, it'd undoubtedly change again.

As unobtrusively as he'd left, Nakum returned to Eadwin's side. From the corner of his mouth, his cousin asked, "Did you retrieve it?"

"What?" Best maintain innocence—Eadwin had enough on his mind. No reason to burden him with this.

"You weren't completely invisible, not to one who knows you, has learned where and how to look. It was an accident, wasn't it? Just a horrible piece of bad luck? Of course Harry wishes with all of his heart to free his mother, but he's a Muscadeine, after all. Doubt he'd have yielded it on his own. Whatever it was only wanted to help."

At times Eadwin never ceased to amaze Nakum. "What?" the king asked. "Addawanna *does* drop by on occasion, more often than some of her relatives I could mention. And I was snowbound for two glorious days up at Roland's nurseries four winters back, had time to hear all sorts of stories, legends." He sounded wistful as a child remembering a happy event that would never recur with the same perfection. For these few moments, it felt as if the two of them were alone together, not subject to the swirling events around them, but Eadwin's demeanor swiftly changed back to that of one enduring yet more abhorrent duties.

The Lady Fabienne, followed by Urban, Terrail, and Carn Camphuysen, had nearly reached Eadwin's side, and Nakum made to slip away, see if he could comfort Harry. Do something, anything!—but Eadwin held him in place. "So, my sainted Maman, and my esteemed Lords of the Exchequer, Interior Affairs, and the Public Weal. What do you think it signifies, Nakum?"

Nothing he'd relish hearing, but realized Eadwin needed him by his side, a rock to lean upon while Arras was incapacitated. "Do you think they approach as individuals or in the guise of their offices? Your mother excluded, of course." He pondered it, but could draw no conclusion. "Internal Affairs and Public Weal are relevant, given the situation, but I'm not sure about Exchequer, though personally I trust Urban's logic and good sense."

A momentary detour as Fabienne swept up to Harry and Arras, briefly embracing them in one encompassing hug,

Arras barely able to raise her hand to his lips, not in homage but in gratitude for her silent compassion. Urban halted as well, handsome face grief-stricken, and rested a hand on the back of each of their necks, and a snicker rose from someone well-hidden behind others. That Urban had heard it, Nakum had no doubt, swiftly withdrawing his comforting touch as if it had tainted Harry and Arras. "Gilly," Eadwin muttered, "once my dear friend," raw disgust clogging his voice.

But Terrail clasped Urban's suddenly stooped shoulders as they drew before Eadwin, let his arm remain for all to see, remark upon if they would.

"You nearly had him in the palm of your hand, Eadwin." A plain statement of fact. "What happened after was no one's fault, least of all yours. And I say that not as your mother, but as a judge of people. The unforeseen is always with us, waiting to trip us up."

"Thank you, Maman," and he kissed her on both cheeks. "But we've still a long, sad way to go before we resolve this." He looked and sounded numb, drained of any ideas that could break the impasse.

"Well, you know what needs to be done next, don't you?"

Now Eadwin's pent-up anger and frustration finally showed. "If I *knew,* Maman, I'd be doing it! Do you and our esteemed colleagues have any ideas?"

Swaying like a reed, Carn Camphuysen cleared his throat, cleared it again, dreading what had to be stated. "Sire, we must evacuate Sidonie. Give people the opportunity to escape far as possible, should the Plumbs explode. To not . . . to not do so . . ." he narrowly avoided strangling on his own tongue, "would be akin to murder, allowing them to innocently go about their lives, unaware, not knowing . . ." he gave up, gasping for breath as if winded.

"We must give our citizens every chance, Eadwin," Fabienne urged. "We can't have their deaths on our heads when there was another, better way! Thankfully some fled immediately after the explosion, so the city holds fewer citizens than it normally does."

"And how many will be trampled in the stampede as the rest flee? Or die of heart attacks, strokes, in the panic? How many parents and children separated? How many of the sick or the elderly abandoned?" Eadwin mused, almost as if it were an academic problem.

"Quaintance Mercilot suggested it, my lord," Terrail informed them. "Gave your mother the idea, and backed by her fund of knowledge, we're already organizing."

"At least in a land of Resonants, the word goes out swiftly," Urban interjected.

"Which reminds me, I must find a free moment to contact Jenret Wycherley—Arras said they were on their way to Marchmont. Poor Doyce—her sister hostage!" Eadwin shrugged uneasily. "Yet another unpalatable task! Proceed with your plans, under the supervision of the Lady Fabienne and the Lord of the Sud. I've no problem with my power being usurped in a good cause. Try to remove those closest to the castle first."

"Will you 'speak a message to hearten your subjects, my lord? Let them all hear directly from you, whether or not they're Resonants?"

Unable to bear it, Nakum moved away, craving the air, the outdoors, even at the risk of being trampled by half the populace of Sidonie. These, these and more, were but a sample of the sorts of bitter decisions a ruler had to constantly make! While he, Nakum, would drown in fear and indecision if ever forced to succeed Eadwin. Air, he *had* to have fresh air, the open sky above his head, the earth beneath his feet, not pavement! "I'll be back!" he called in Eadwin's direction and meant it, but for now, he must get free before this world choked him! Clutching his earth-bond like a lifeline, he pushed his way through, unable to maintain even a semblance of shadow-being. At the small of his back, the Trickster hummed and stroked, giving a worried chirp.

♣

Pitch-dark, enveloping blackness with nary a crack of light. Telka hadn't expected that as she and Francie were rudely dragged within the strong room, the door slamming behind them with a leaden thud that echoed and reechoed in her head and throughout the enclosed space. So dark, why couldn't she see? Bad enough to be gagged, but now to be blindfolded! She stumbled over something, nearly went down because of the hobble, but Francie managed to lean back, keep her from crashing face down, though Telka landed on one knee, her hands and Francie's close to her mouth, Francie's thumb nearly snagging her spectacles.

Then Francie's thumb shifted, scraping at the sticking plaster across Telka's mouth, picking at it to loosen a corner. Sometimes it peeled, sometimes her skin painfully lifted with it, but Francie persisted, and Telka stayed still, praying she'd succeed. Why, why hadn't she thought of that before? Either one of them could have removed Francie's gag or her sticking plaster, since their hands were bound in front of them. Ah! Sensing Francie had a firm grip on one end, Telka jerked her head hard, not caring if it hurt, only wanting the plaster gone.

Leaving it dangling against her cheek, Telka pushed her hands and Francie's upward, not sure which hand, or whose, would reach the gag first. Ooo—it was all spit-soggy! Despite that, she clung to it, working her fingers around it, while Francie did the same on the other side, tugging downward as Francie struggled to rear her head clear.

"Child," Francie breathed in her ear, "dear child, be brave!" She coughed, a harsh, dry sound that tickled Etelka's ear. Then, so much like her Mam that it made her want to giggle, Francie asked, "You're not afraid of the dark, are you, dear?"

"N-not really." Ow, her lips felt sticky and sore, little rips on them in some spots. "But—but why's it *so* dark?" Wouldn't have admitted for the world that this depth of darkness, the silence, the stuffiness, scared her witless. Wouldn't do that to Harry's Mama, just as Harry wouldn't do it to her Mam if their roles were reversed.

"No windows, dear. Center of the castle. Windows would offer thieves a way in, wouldn't they?"

"N–no lamps, neither?"

A tired sigh ruffled the loose hair by her ear. "Can we sit on the floor? Don't think I can stand much longer." Going down on both knees, Telka strained her arms up and over her right shoulder, felt Francie landing hard and ungraceful, not able to fold her legs proper, so Telka made herself limp, let herself be dragged wherever Francie needed so she could find some comfort. Without seeing it, Telka thought that Francie reclined on one side, her bound arms still around Telka, with her tucked against the bend of Francie's waist. A rasp, a harsh flare of light as Romain-Laurent struck a lucifer, looking at the wall with the door.

"Yes, there are lamps, but would you have left them lit beside the Plumbs, with not a soul inside to watch them?" A gulp as Etelka worked that out.

"Mam would've had a fit."

"Blast! Damn!" The light winked out as Romain-Laurent shook his hand, the dark momentarily returning, along with the sound of the man blowing on his fingers. "Don't go wandering, ladies. I'd hate for you to trip over a Plumb!" What? Did the man think he was being *funny*? Another lucifer swooped through the dark like a falling star, Etelka straining to see, but the dazzle of light hurt, revealing only the momentary shape of a hand before it again went out. But apparently the man had seen what he wanted, because at the third lucifer a lamp began to glow, followed by curse words as Romain-Laurent tardily extinguished the lucifer. He fiddled with the wick, turning the knob that fed it upward, and the room became merely gloomy.

Still basically ignoring them, other than reassuring himself that they were there, casting their shadows not far inside the door, he began lighting more and more lamps, Telka squinting, then relaxing as her eyes gradually became used to the light, twisting to stare every which way. Inside the king's treasure chamber, no less! Phew! Who'd *ever* believe that?

Apparently with all her twisting and squirming, Francie had caught a glimpse of her intent, rapt face, the increasing disillusionment. "What did you expect? Piles of pearls? Heaps of gold, trunks overspilling with diamonds and rubies and emeralds? The royal diadem resting on a velvet pillow with tassels of golden bullion?"

Miserable with embarrassment, she nodded. Credulous little country girl, 'course Lady Francie'd think that—who wouldn't?

"Can you see the shapes along the walls, long, horizontal rectangles? Built-in drawers for the jewelry, cupboards up higher. Down below, bins for gold, some in ingots, some in coin of the realm. The room behind this holds papers, deeds, and so forth." Resting uncomfortably on one shoulder, Francie pointed her head to the center of the room. "But that's what I'm more interested in."

"Looks like sandbags. All nice and neat-stacked, like a pen of some sort."

Another slow, tired breath from Francie. "I hope so, child. Arras insisted they be packed around the trunk holding the Plumbs."

She'd forgotten—on purpose, belike—for just a while, her brain needing the respite. But now it all came back, too, too vividly. And Baby! But at least she was outside, had escaped, even if Romain-Laurent hadn't meant the gesture as such. Dear, precious Baby was safe, and Hru'rul'd be so happy! But now she'd *never* know if Baby would merit a mention in the newest edition of *Lives of the Seekers Veritas*!

As if drawn to it by their looks, Romain-Laurent now flittered around the sandbags like a moth around a flame, except he carried his own lamp, swooping up and down and round, studying every detail. She couldn't guess for certain, but the sandbags had to weigh twenty kilos each, more, mayhap. 'Course Da'd say it'd depend on whether the sand was wet or dry, whether it was fine packing sand or coarse and gravelly, not settling as tight.

Must be heavy, the way Romain-Laurent was shifting them from the top, clutching each one tight and low to his belly, grunting with the effort. Then again, he didn't look as if he'd done much heaving and lifting in his life, nicely built but no real muscle or heft to him. Why, Levi'd unload the wagon, hoist a bag of grain or fresh-milled flour on his shoulder, another on his hip.

A creak as the lid of the trunk rose, bouncing off the restraining sandbags behind it before snapping back down across Romain-Laurent's wrist. Had to hurt worse than his singed fingers, couldn't precisely fault him for swearing. He tossed three more sandbags with a fury and energy he'd not previously exhibited to make room for the lid to lean back. Then the rustle of crumpled paper like autumn leaves as he tossed it out, half-disappearing as he leaned inside. Wished she had a slingshot, she did, given the target he presented!

With effort, Francie sat up, Telka helping as much as she could, though that nearly laid her across the woman's lap until she got herself squared away. "So, Romain-Laurent, what's the next step?" she asked, raising her voice over the crinkle of paper. "The Plumbs are yours. What's the next step?" Slithering over the sandbags, a Plumb cradled in his arms, Romain-Laurent sank to the floor, admiring it, a rapturous smile on his face.

"Plumb, mine!" he cooed. "Sweet, precious, little Plumb!" Then his eyes went so dagger-sharp that Telka flinched against Francie, hoping they'd pierce her first, and not Harry's mother. "Of *course* I have a plan. Wanted this for so long, thinking it out each—" His voice dropped, went low and censorious. "Oh, wonderful! *You* haven't been listening, haven't been taking notice. Forever assuming we'll pitch in, come to your aid! Well, *I* wouldn't have minded being Chancellor at Montpéllier—did you *ever* consider that?"

Faintly incredulous, slightly mocking, Francie said, "You *have* a plan? Good, let's hear it. I've nothing better to do. Neither has Telka, for that matter. Tell us all about it."

"Gonna . . . gonna . . .make'm 'splode! Gonna be . . . *biggest* boom!" Shaking his head, droplets of sweat flying from his dark hair, he visibly fought for some sort of internal control. "I plan to show them," he held his breath, waiting for something within to quiet, then calmly exhaled, "that it is perfectly feasible to build a new highway from Gavotte to Sidonie. Once I show them how easy it is to blast those mountains, I'll be overwhelmed by all the help I could possibly need." He sounded winded.

"Yes, Arras mentioned your plan, thought it might have some merit with more practicality behind it, a better appreciation for what can and can't be accomplished." Again the look he gave her was dripping with disdain, as if she could possibly have any idea what was necessary. "But how do you plan to move the Plumbs from this room to the Stratocums?"

"I . . . I'll . . ." again his eyes flickered from side to side, as if looking for help, for answers, and Telka couldn't stop watching, how he changed to different persons—if such a thing was possible. "I'll . . . I'll. . . . Help me figure it out and I'll let you go," he wheedled, a brittle smile dimpling his cheeks. "How'm I . . . how'm I *ever* . . ." he wailed, pressing his forehead to the Plumb and rocking back and forth.

Lady bless her, Lady Francie was toying with him, working under his skin! What good it might do, she couldn't judge, but wished she could help, anything to relieve some of Francie's burden. She was real frail, one arm and hand kinda twisty and smaller than the other, weaklike, just as one leg was, not real strong overall, and 'twasn't fair she should have to do everything.

"Could get a dray," she hazarded, surprised at herself. "They can carry a mote of stuff. Not that the trunk's that big, best as I can tell." She thought harder. "Mayhap a hayrack—that's what you fork mown hay into—has real high sides. Could have it packed with straw, cotton-wool, batting, I don't know what all. Make sure the trunk rides nice and smooth all the way to the Stratocums."

A secret kiss on the back of her neck told her that Francie was pleased with her contribution.

"But how they . . . gonna know I need a . . . whatayoucall it, hayrack?"

"I suppose you could slide a note under the door." And with that, Francie crumpled against Telka.

♣

Still running, desperate to find open space, a park, a square, Nakum found himself straining against a press of people, the streets filling with young and old alike, prosperous and poor, haughty and humble, all jumbled together. At length, tired of fighting, his nerve returning, he slowed, awed by the enormity of it all, bearing silent witness to this massive flow of people, some standing uneasily in line, others walking purposefully, carrying small bundles. Small children cried, others darted through the throng, sometimes pursued by frantic parents. Adults gossiped, others stoically shuffled ahead as lines gradually moved, while others disintegrated into panic, ranging from white lips and knuckles on hands clamped on children's wrists to those in full-blown hysteria.

So this, this was what a mass exodus looked like. The relative orderliness of it all, the look of purpose on most faces impressed him. Every little way a soldier, a guard, a

eumedico or Shepherd, a levelheaded citizen with a white
band tied around his or her arm, directed people, calmed
them, explained whatever they could. They gave directions,
called for aid to locate a missing child, assisted a woman
in the throes of premature labor. The cold, early morning
air shivered with Resonant vibrations, mindvoices casting a
net across Sidonie, passing word as to trouble spots, street
blockages. This he knew only as those with red armbands,
Resonants, called out the latest word or passed instructions
to those serving as wardens.

> *"So bring on those nasty Plumbs,*
> *And let's quaff down plenty of rum.*
> *'Cause what we've got here,*
> *It's nothing to fear,*
> *Just a royal pain in the rear,*
> *And I'd much rather drink some rum!"*

sang a carrying tenor voice, more and more people gradually joining in his song.

Nakum began to work his way along the line, talking
with people here and there, smiling, trying to assuage their
fears, and found in the process that his own had receded.
Every now and then his feet touched earth, real soil, and
he almost went limp with relief, hand on his earth-bond,
drawing strength from the contact, sharing it out with others in more dire need. No one commented on the fact he
was Erakwa, simply accepted him as another soul snared
by the same strange destiny that had trapped them.

A sharp snap on one of his braids from behind and he
whirled, planning to scoop up a disobedient child, only to
discover Quaintance Mercilot—swathed in furs, a violet-
and-white cockade on her high fur hat—clutching a length
of ribbon in her hand. "Got cockades, ribbons, show 'em
we represent the king." Dark, shrewd eyes glanced around,
inspecting faces. "Blast! Lost'm again. Now, you want a
ribbon or a cockade? Was tying a ribbon on your braid
when you spun 'round all nervy."

"Ribbon," he decided. "Cinch it around my upper arm."
Far taller than she, Nakum looked over her head, caught
a flash of bright auburn hair, no mistaking it, and called,
"Ezequiel—over here! She's with me!"

Plowing through the crowd, Ezequiel made his way to them. "Good! You take her 'round—I really must get back to the castle, so much to organize there! Couldn't let her out on her own, Ignacio'd rise from his grave, strike me dead for such discourtesy to the Lord of the Sud!" Respectfully kissing Quaintance on each cheek and tilting her fur hat off her forehead to let her see better, Ezequiel began worming his way back to the castle. "Cinzia's out here somewhere, some of the other Lords, too. See if you can join them." Implicit in that statement was a subtle hint to saddle some other poor soul with dear, doddering Quaintance.

Leaning heavily on Nakum's arm, her cane in the other hand, Quaintance toddled along, occasionally strategically deploying her cane to shift an unsuspecting citizen, or make one pay attention. "Ain't ye fleeing, yer Lordship?" called a man wearing a mason's smock, meaty arm supporting an elderly relative or neighbor.

"Ho!" Quaintance reared back, head high and regal, reminding him that she was not only a Domain Lord but a direct descendant of Constant the First, a scion of the blood royale. " 'Course not! Not when we got so many others to move first. 'Sides, I'm waiting for me rum!" A waggish head toss—flirtatious, even, Nakum decided—and she began to sing in a high, cracked voice, "So bring on those nasty Plumbs, and let's quaff down plenty of rum . . ." The man's laugh was deep, infectious, as he joined her on, "Just a royal pain in the rear, and I'd much rather drink some rum!" Quaintance stuck out her aging bottom and waggled it, continued limping along, the song following her as she went.

"Doing well, I'd say," she said in a conversational voice. "Our people are a stouthearted lot, if you give them reason to be so." Nakum was struck by the fact that she seemed to be hearing perfectly well, almost normally. To confirm it, he turned his face away from her as he answered. Actually, he couldn't hear all that well, given the street noise, the shouts, the shuffle of feet, the crunch of wagons and carriages in the distance.

"Testing me, are ye?" Hugging his arm tighter, she pattered along with tiny steps, the tiredness clear in the tightly clenched wrinkles on her face. "Figured you as a smart one, always did. Suitable for a king, if need be, though we both hope there's no need, doan we?" He nodded. "Nay, I'm not near as deef as I pretend, though I don't hear as well as I used to. When you've grown as old as I am, you've heard almost everything worth hearing—again and again and again!" A wheezing chuckle. "Think those joint Domain and Ministration Lords meetings cover much new ground? Trust me, Nakum, lad, there's very little new under the sun! And a good thing, too, I think sometimes."

On they went, slower and slower, halting by design or because someone reached out an imploring hand, desperate for reassurance, which Quaintance doled out unstintingly. And along the way, someone offered her a tot of rum, which she downed in one gulp, the people applauding. Impromptu camp kitchens had been set up on various street corners, people passing out hot cha, warm soup, and bread, so many having started out on an empty stomach.

At in-between moments Quaintance explained the system, the logic behind what was happening. "Moving them out in stages, best we can. Eugenie's a clever girl, thought of that. Those closest to the castle move out first, on foot if possible. Streets are too narrow for a crush of carriages and wagons. Outlying starting to flow out as well, midtowners moving into outlying areas, while close ones move into midtown."

"But where *are* the wagons and carriages?" Nakum had been constantly aware of the rumble of wheels, the creak of heavily loaded carriages for some time, but had yet to see one. If the Plumbs exploded any time soon, far too many people would still be too near, would suffer.

"Lysenko and Gabriella have commandeered every wagon and carriage, any conveyance in town, from brewery drays to donkey carts. Need a full load for each one, keep families together if we can. Staging points have been set up. That's where most of the lines you see are advancing to."

"But where will they go?" How could one evacuate thousands of people without a place to put them? It boggled his mind.

"What? What? Oh!" Quaintance was hugging a young mother with a baby in her arms, stretching up to pat away her tears. "Those closest to the LaPierre are being instructed to cross the river and go as high into the foothills as possible. Don't know, but Tinian and Terrail are worried 'bout the LaPierre changing its course if all six of those cursed devil Plumbs go off 't oncit." Water, giggling, escaping, running free, flooding the earth, trying to gain a foothold that earth would never reclaim. Nakum shivered, not at the cold, which he seldom felt, but at the thought of the balance being destroyed yet again, the elements fighting with one another, making the most of new opportunities.

"Don't worry so," she commanded, as if he too were but one of the multitude needing consolation and faith. "Eadwin won't let those nasty things hurt anyone. If there's a way, he'll find it, stop that little jackanapes in his tracks!"

"Do you truly believe so?" Ah, how he wanted to believe! A stirring at the back of his waist as the Trickster shifted. He'd forgotten his presence in the press of activity, though now he wondered if it hadn't shared its energy with Quaintance, letting her play the wag as she had. No, Quaintance was perfectly capable of that on her own.

She remained silent too long, eyes distant. "I don't know, lad. I *want* to believe, with all my heart, but it may be asking too much. Don't mind dying, myself, old enough for it. But, oh, I don't want to see our people, our land suffer!"

Nor did he—he didn't want the earth to suffer, or the innocents who walked upon it, even if they had brought it upon themselves through their own ignorance. He felt so alone here, out of his depth! How could he have ever imagined he'd find some way to heal his precious earth, ensure it suffered no more! How could a single Erakwan expect to change a world that wasn't even of his own making, a world created by Outlanders!

A small, leather-gloved hand patted his, commiserating. "Come along. Do our part best we can, let Eadwin do his. 'Less you can think of something to help, I'd best head back to the castle afore I wear out. Can always requisition another nice, strong young man to walk me."

They were about to pass an alleyway between shops, the earth muddy and churned from the many passing feet and, without thinking, he scooped up Quaintance in his arms to carry her across.

"Ouch!" someone yelped in his ear.

At first he thought he'd hurt Quaintance, but she, too, bore a puzzled look, eyes squinting into the deeper dark of the alley. And the complaining voice had been distinctly masculine, though young. Reaching around Quaintance's shoulders, he let his fingers brush his earth-bond, concentrating, piercing through shadows, darker shadings, observing things that were there yet invisible to eyes confident of the expected.

"Diccon? Is that you? Callis?" The white of her doeskin showed clearly now, almost impossible to disguise its presence. Two more figures stood partially hidden by Diccon and Callis.

"Rammed your knee right into me, you did." Rubbing a bruised thigh, Diccon grinned. "Yet another bruise! Wish you'd hung a sign halfway up the mountain saying you weren't home!"

Callis shushed him. "So, you think one Erakwan is not enough to solve the earth's problems, eh? Mayhap three will work better, Feather and myself, plus you. And someone who is now one of us, has learned more thoroughly than many of our own people. Even Diccon plays a part, though he's too busy complaining to realize, unless I keep after him."

He saw her now—Jacobia! Still as beautiful as his memory always told him, yet different, mature, with wells of knowledge she'd lacked before. Something about her wakened a kindred sensation within him, that she was a part of this all, not fully Outlander, not fully Erakwan, but an integral part of both. Only then did he notice the earth-bond around her neck.

"Well, you going to introduce me to these people?" Had Quaintance been able to see them, too, before they'd come near, those wise old eyes able to penetrate the shadow world? Mayhap so, often great age also brought great wisdom with it. "Not often I get to meet someone older than I am! Makes me feel like a youngster again!"

❧

"I suppose we could wait, starve them out." Terrail Leclerc examined his hands, both front and back, as if he'd never seen them before, then looked rueful. "Except for one small thing: he's on the wrong side of the door. When he wants dinner, we're going to know it in no uncertain terms!"

Eadwin gave a "hmph," his nose twitching, lips trembling. Arras relieved him of the necessity of strangulation by seizing his shoulder, giving him a shake. "It's funny, Eadwin. Morbid as it is, it's funny, and if we don't laugh, we're like to explode from inside. Someone has to relieve the tension. Mayhap you should appoint Terrail as court jester."

But Terrail had taken on a greenish tint, Arras realized. "I'd fetch him breakfast, lunch, and dinner if I thought it would give me a chance at freeing Francie." Still, he was relieved Harry wasn't there to hear their ghoulish humor, because it would worsen before it got better. It was what soldiers did on the eve of battle: the more outrageous, the more repulsive the humor, the greater the hope that death would pass them by. Death, however, had its own unique sense of humor. Likely Harry would hear some of it before this was over. He'd sent his son off to eat some breakfast, Theo taking him in tow, Khim doing the same with Baby. After that, he'd have to devise something else to distract the boy, and not just make-work, because Harry was too mature to be fooled by that. Hru'rul lounged, flexed in a curve by his Bond's feet.

The barest whisper of a rustle and Hru'rul sprang, nose at the crack beneath the door as a piece of paper shot through. Pinning it with a massive foot, daring anyone else to take it, Hru'rul waited until Eadwin bent and retrieved it, then sniffed beneath the door to reassure himself nothing else would shoot through and surprise him.

Eadwin motioned them over, Arras standing close behind his shoulder, Urban to his left, Terrail to his right. Carn Camphuysen had gone to do what he did best: organize soup kitchens on street corners, ensure eumedicos were everywhere they could be needed, delegate people to worry about sanitation facilities, foodstuffs, bedding. All the things that concerned the people's welfare, especially people turned into refugees. He'd departed with relief written all over him—these were problems he could handle, heavy though they might be. What to do about a madman holding Plumbs and people hostage was beyond his ken. Terrail, too, would be off in moments, the Internal Affairs Lord more valuable in the field than here.

"If you don't hold it away from your chest, you'll never

know what it says." Arras prodded, coldly controlled, prepared to hear the worst. "Can't turn bad news into good by trying to hatch it." He feared what the words would baldly state: Romain-Laurent's terms.

Narrowing his eyes, extending his arms to bring the letter into focus, Eadwin read silently, the others doing the same. Arras was shocked at the childish handwriting in pencil, the painfully polite phrasing, so like Harry's when he wrote a letter. Etelka had been assigned the role of scribe:

> *Your Royal Highness, Sir:*
>
> *If you please, Mr. Charpentier would be obliged if you would provide him with a hayrack and a team of four in the courtyard in front of the castle at your earliest convenience. If you don't have a hayrack here in the city, I think a dray would work fine, but it must have high sides. Mr. Charpentier would be obliged if you'd pack the hayrack with straw, cotton-wool, old comforters, anything of that variety to ensure that it is thick and cushiony, deep and comfy as a feather bed that you can sink out of sight in. (The final five words were more heavily penciled, the faintest of underlinings beneath them.)*
>
> *Also, we would all appreciate finding food and water in the hayrack, as it has been a very long time since dinner last. We are all holding up very well, though a touch tired.*
>
> *Sincerely, Etelka Rundgren*
>
> *P.S. Can someone help us carry the trunk? Only Mr. Charpentier says that it had better not be Lord Muscadeine or the king.*

"Oh, the dear, dear child!" Eadwin stroked the letter, passed it to Arras. "Can we get a . . . what does she call it? . . . hayrack? Lysenko's got everything on wheels under his thumb—find out, Terrail, would you?

Easing him away from the door, looking back at it as if the wood panels might have sprouted ears—and well it might have—Arras pitched his voice low, wanting as few as possible to hear. "Not just a dear child, Eadwin, but a bright, clever one, as well!" While in all honesty he might not have chosen Telka as a companion in adversity for Francie, it was a blessing that the Lady had chosen her. "Don't you see, Eadwin? She's giving us a hint, a way to get at Romain-Laurent!" Eagerly he pointed at the crucial words in heavier penciling—"sink out of sight in." "Suppose, just suppose that two or three of us are hidden in that hayrack, buried under all that straw and cotton-wool and whatever! We'll have a chance to take him—very possibly without any explosions! I'll need someone backing me, but only one other person need risk his or her life. Now, when it comes to removing the trunk, I'd like to see it carried by—"

But Eadwin was shaking his head, shaking and shaking it as if he wouldn't stop until Arras finally ran down. "What do you mean, 'No'? Why do you keep shaking your head?"

"Because it's time you used yours, Arras." Eadwin paced farther along the hall, speaking under his breath as Arras followed after him. "Air vent up there—just remembered. Romain-Laurent is going to *expect* to see both you and me when he exits that room. If he doesn't, he's going to become extremely suspicious. And for that matter, Francie will expect to see you there as well."

Arras halted, almost stumbling. If he didn't see Francie, that might well be the last opportunity he'd ever have—if things went wrong. And any number of things could easily go wrong before they even reached the courtyard. Could he take that chance, lose that chance? "I . . . I thank you, Your Majesty. I became carried away." Harry needed those few precious moments as well, and how could he let Harry stand there alone, watching, hoping, praying as his mother and Telka were led by? Not be at his side, holding his hand?

"Don't want to lose you as well, Arras." The king walked back toward the doorway, his arm loosely grasping Arras's shoulders, and Arras knew he was slumping with dejection. "Now, let's decide whom the royal trunk bearers will be—people who won't set off Romain-Laurent, obviously. And," he said in the softest murmur imaginable, "who's going to surprise Romain-Laurent in bed. Any ideas?"

♣

Aching all over, Francie frowned as she picked at a strand of fabric. After being so tightly woven, the strands crimped, caught as she gently tugged it free. Most of the time she was left with a broken piece too short to be of much use. No good would come of thinking how her leg and arm pained her, her medicaments far away now. The pain was an old, familiar friend, but it hadn't visited as much in later years, not since she'd come to Marchmont with Arras. Concentrate on how good it felt to have her hands free, so she did, trying to enlarge a small blessing into a bigger one. Poor Telka still had her feet hobbled; no doubt Romain-Laurent realized she'd do her best to run at the slightest opportunity. Not that Telka would willingly desert her. Far from it. But if she could throw herself on Romain-Laurent, hinder him when an opportunity arose, she prayed Telka would seize it.

Press the fabric flat on the table, with her bad hand, her good left winkling the needle in and out of the weave, teasing a strand free. How well they'd hold, she didn't know, but that wasn't her problem. The chair beneath her felt good, too, its navy velvet worn to bareness in spots, the mahogany scuffed and dented from years of use. Had been in Fabienne's old dining room, she remembered. Good enough now for the strong rooms, a few small tables and chairs necessary for anyone doing an inventory, or sitting and pondering a selection from the trays in the cabinets.

Twice she'd been here, not counting today, when Eadwin had insisted on honoring her. Well, make no bones about it, honoring Arras by gifting her. The first time just after they'd been married, when the king had earnestly told her to select any gem she desired, and he'd have the royal jewelers set it. She'd chosen a pear-shaped pink diamond, not large but appealing, especially in the rosy gold setting Eadwin had insisted upon. The second time had occurred after Harry's birth and, greatly daring, she'd broadened her scope, her choice a man's ring set with a piece of arborfer. Oh, nothing as spectacular as Eadwin's own ring, or Fabienne's, which would pass to Eadwin's wife, should he ever marry. But *this* ring, the one of her own choosing, would belong to Harry when he was old enough, symbolizing his father's heritage and his mother's choice.

Don't think about it. Best not to, just concentrate on the job to be done. For the moment Telka was wandering, taking mincing steps, pulling out drawers here and there to examine the contents. It was she who'd discovered the antique sewing kit, an ivory case about the size of a deck of cards, bound with silver. Inside it were a pair of silver stork scissors, a thimble (once on the finger, the wearer realized it was meant to be a chimney, the stork's nest at the tip, a clutch of eggs nestling within it), a needle-threader and several needles. Oh, how Romain-Laurent had pounced on that! Even worse, he'd pounced on her, rudely ripping off her robe, and Francie had grimly prepared for the worst, sorrowing that Etelka would be forced to witness it.

"The sleeves," Romain-Laurent had chortled, clutching the robe by the shoulders and sweeping it back and forth. "Perfect!" And forthwith he'd roughly excised the sleeves and returned the remainder of the robe to her, but not before slicing off strips from the bottom. He'd explained roughly what he required, and Francie'd set to her assigned task.

Now he lay sprawled in front of the trunk, head propped against the remaining sandbags. Always his eyes were watching, though sometimes he roughly tossed his head back and forth—not for comfort, she'd concluded, but as if he wanted to drive something out, shake it loose. More than a headache.

What continued to disconcert her was that she couldn't ever be sure "who" Romain-Laurent would be when he addressed her or Telka. There was the little boy, not unlike Harry a few years earlier, blustering with pretend adult assurance, then becoming increasingly lost and insecure. There was an autocratic voice that spoke disparagingly, not to her so much as to Romain-Laurent himself, castigating him for some minor oversight. Then a more commonsensical voice might take over, cheering him, commenting on what grand ideas he had, diffidently offering a few modifications or refinements. Twice he'd made a stuttering dit-dit-ditting sound. How to explain it? Some were long, some short, and he sputtered when he made them. Other voices she didn't recognize also came to the fore, but not often enough to recognize with any certainty.

Thinking ahead, planning responses, rejoinders, any leading questions—as she'd been lucky enough before to accomplish—was well-nigh impossible without knowing whom she'd be addressing. Fortunately, Telka had written the message for him, his little boy mode in place, taking only a cursory glance at what she'd written, reassuring himself she'd conveyed the necessary information. Telka had bumped her with her knee as she bore down harder on the words "sink out of sight in," and Francie had looked, then looked harder, before continuing to industriously ply her needle and murmuring, "Very well stated, dear. You've a way with words. Mayhap you'll be a writer when you grow up."

Swinging the whole of one side of her body, then the other as she walked, Telka came to her side. "Easier to walk if I stretch the hobble. That way I don't forget and take a step I can't manage." That, and a way to amuse herself, Francie thought. Not exactly whispering but not making her voice overloud, she added, "I don't know about you, Lady Francie, but I've got to relieve myself powerful bad."

Lady bless! Why had the child had to mention that? She'd been trying to ignore the increasing pressure on her bladder, but that decided her. Romain-Laurent must have to suffer a similar indignity several times a day, assuming he was human. Fact was, she swore men couldn't hold it as well, as long as women.

"Romain-Laurent," and whom was she addressing this time? "I hate to bring this up, but both Telka and I are acquiring a pressing need to use the flusher, or anything that can remotely be construed as a commode."

Rousing himself—but he hadn't been asleep, had he? Not with his eyes open—he gave them both a lazy, good-natured grin. "Women! Always picking the most inopportune moments to decide that! Well, let me see what I can find." Rising, stretching, he began padding around, opening cupboards that stood too high for Etelka to reach. Could it be that different personalities rested at different times? That would explain some of his inexplicable changes—or did they battle for ascendancy? Draw up a schedule and take turns?

Stretching on tiptoe, he retrieved a silver object that she finally identified as a wine cooler, rife with molded lilies in full bloom and in bud, complete with stems, leaves and seed pods. "Sorry I couldn't find you a solid gold chamber pot," he commented straight-faced. "But a wine cooler should be filled with something." He placed it in a far corner, then carried over the other small table and upended it on its short side, constructing a privacy screen of sorts. His small gesture surprised and touched her.

"Go ahead," she coaxed Telka, giving her a little push, and the child swung off. Mayhap with her bladder empty she'd plant her feet together, hop like a rolapin. Too old for it, but why not? Let her enjoy being a child for as long as she could . . . as long as she could. Unseeingly, she rammed the needle into her finger.

"So, how are we coming with our project?" Sneering, he picked at the small pile of strands, already clinging to each other in a rat's-nest tangle. "They'll catch, knot as soon as you take a stitch!" Tell her something she didn't know! "I suppose you never *thought* to moisten them, stretch them straight." With what? she was tempted to ask, tempted as well to give him an answer. Making a face, he pulled one of the strands between his lips, moistening it with his tongue, then carefully and capably wound it around the flat of his hand, took another piece and began anew. "Must I show you how to do *everything,* woman?"

It wasn't the words so much as the tone which cut her to the quick, so rarely had that tone ever been used to shame her—not by her mother or father, not by Doyce, certainly not by Arras. And the way his eyebrows jutted so contemptuously!

"I'm sorry. I didn't think ahead." She stared at the ruined fabric of her sleeves, not really seeing it but unable to meet his gaze.

Kinder now but still condescending, "So few people can think ahead, plan ahead." Then, a pleading note set his voice quavering. "Just how soon do you think you can have them ready?"

This voice she felt safer with, could afford a little maternal reminder. "It's going to take a while longer, but if you straighten the thread, it'll go much faster. Besides, we can't go until the wagon and team are ready, can we? And they can't go anywhere without us," she pointed out.

"You know, if I can find something larger to wind the moistened strands around, they'd be even straighter, dry faster. That's what I mean about . . ." and off he meandered, a strand dangling from his lips, rummaging through cabinets to find just the right object.

♣

Well, Parse's "mud-buggy" had lived up to its billing, its cleated wheels chewing across packed snow and ice, frozen earth and mud. Time spun as fast as its wheels, their ceaseless churning near-hypnotic, and Jenret laid a trembling hand across his eyes, fingers clenching his temples to crush his fatigue, compel his mind to inhabit the here-and-now, not the ever-revolving fantasy world in which he spun.

Their driver shared a sympathetic grimace with him but said nothing. Hadn't said much of anything since he'd joined them just at dawn this morning, taciturn except for an occasional harshly amused "heh!" at both frivolous and somber subjects, and a positively infectious grin. A Resonant, a horse breeder who lived just below the Canderis border—Bartolphe, that was his name. He could remember it because it was similar to "Dolf," and no doubt he'd already called the man that once or twice. Lady bless, but he was tired! Two semiretired female Seekers and their Bonds served as their outriders on this leg of the journey, the women unrelated but somehow resembling each other, interchangeable. Jenret essayed a brief smile at the one to his right. He knew them, but couldn't dredge up their names for the life of him.

Damn cold here, a nasty dampness, and to counter it, Jenret hitched his collar higher. Mayhap it would burn off later in the morning. Dampness was to be expected since Bertillon was situated on the Spray; Haarls had felt similar, just not as cold. Dolf—no, Bartolphe—had efficiently guided the mud-buggy and fresh team on the ferry at first light, Jenret wincing as the cleated wheels gouged the plank decking. Couldn't be helped, but he'd wanted to apologize for the damage. Oh, wonderful! Rain? No, not quite, more like tiny ice needles stinging the mud-buggy's collapsible canvas top, a top that lacked overhang enough to completely protect him and Bartolphe from the elements.

General dampness, general gloom—that described the weather and his mood. Ah, and don't forget the stinging frustration welling within him when he least expected it. Had all his relatives grown as impetuous as he? Diccon's impetuosity made sense of a sort; the boy mirroring him all over again, though luckily lacking the pressing sorrows that had so burdened his life at that age. But Jenneth? His little Jennie, his darling? Had the child taken leave of her senses—Doyce's sensible sense? He shook his head, the corners of his mouth curling. At the merest hint of one distressed soul within a two-hundred-kilometer radius of Gaernett, tender Jen would be on full alert. Why look for any further explanation?

Ahead of him, the horses' hides twitched and rippled, unhappy at the rain, the ice needles. Poor beasts! As if registering a mute protest at being out in such inclement weather, one of the horses cast off a frozen mud clod with a hind hoof. It hit and disintegrated right on the lip of the foot box, peppering him and Bartholphe, and he wiped his face and eye, muttering words the horses didn't deserve. Damn, that stung! And the more he rubbed his eye, the more he ground in the dirt. Bartolphe cocked an eyebrow in his direction, mutely holding the reins toward him, asking if he wanted to drive? Why not? He needed something to do, to *do* something. A final probing finger in his eye as he took the reins. Still didn't help. Leave well enough alone.

And speaking of leaving well enough alone, why hadn't Jacobia? What had possessed *her* to chase after the twins? Of course, if she hadn't, he'd have bitterly complained she'd done nothing! Couldn't have it both ways. Easier to admit nowadays how much he—and the Wycherley Mercantile—depended on her, had witnessed firsthand the business savvy that made three mercantiles—two in Canderis and one in the Sunderlies—such a rousing success, with ever-expanding profits. And he really *must* stop treating her like the annoying baby sister she'd been for so long, nearly seventeen years his junior.

Swinging the team wide around a particularly large oval of glare ice that he suspected disguised a puddle capable of swallowing both mud-buggy and team and still find room for both outriders as dessert, he huffed in exasperation and rubbed his eye again. The constant patter of freezing rain on the canvas roof was making him crackbrained! Oh, to indulge in a full-throated bellow of "Enough!"—stretching it out till it emptied his lungs. Whoever had said listening to the rain was soothing ought to be trapped beside him, the mud-buggy akin to a rolling prison. The Sunderlies had been worse, actually—torrential rain. Hadn't been nasty cold, though. Damn, if only Rawn would wake, talking with someone would distract him from the pitty-pitty-pat. Make that pity-pat-pity me, distract me! No sense subjecting Bartolphe to it.

Checking how Doyce fared in the rear seat, he smiled despite himself at her cramped position in the too-short space. Lady bless, she'd be stiff and out-of-sorts when she awoke. Might have to unfold her, weigh down her feet with stones so her knees didn't snap right back up under her chin! Rawn uncomfortably claimed the scant seat space that remained, his body jammed almost upright against Doyce, chin crooked over her neck, a hind leg and tail dangling over the edge. Lacking Doyce's embrace, he'd have landed on the floorboards with a thump. Nose-to-nose with Rawn, Khar stretched atop Doyce's right side from shoulder to hip, undoubtedly constricting Doyce's breathing.

'Speak Rawn? Wake him and inform him he was ready to be entertained? Distracted, his mood lightened? No, let the beast sleep. He'd developed a worrisome little wheeze, and Jenret sternly told himself that it was the start of a ghatti cold, nothing worse. But it might be worse—at Rawn's age even the most commonplace ailment could prove fatal.

Fine! Enough procrastinating, time to ruminate on Mahafny Annendahl, his aunt. Hardly a blood relative, but the wife of his late father's brother. A short-lived marriage, their sole progeny, Evelien, dead as well, and he'd heartily wish his cousin dead a hundred times eight for what she and Vesey Marbon had nearly inflicted on Doyce as they plotted to corrupt and control the world of Resonants and Normals alike!

Still, for all her prickliness, Mahafny had been supportive when he and Doyce needed her. Her unyielding view of life and herself had unbent ever so slightly as she'd constructed her own family around her—he and Doyce and the twins and their respective ghatti; Saam, Harrap, and Parm. Insisted one received superior value by choosing, actively selecting prospective family members than by depending on blood—and then she'd winked. But for Doyce, the unexpected resumption of their relationship had been a cause for resentment, Mahafny the reason she'd been expelled as a eumedico just before completing her grueling training. And all over giving lip service to a benign lie that Doyce couldn't countenance. Now, what had been a lie had become truth as more and more Resonants trained as eumedicos.

Mahafny's informal, late-life link with Saam had filled another void. If Saam were dying—Jenret's face turned masklike—Mahafny would be beside herself. Mayhap this death was the one thing that could dislodge her from her dispassionate pedestal, allow her full communion with humanity—but at what price? Mahafny would not—*could not*—wail or suffer in public view, would lock it inside until it eroded her heart and soul.

And Saam! When he faced his own thoughts squarely, scrupulously examined his own failings and weaknesses . . . well, Saam was one of those failings. Every so often, despite his best efforts, he'd look at Saam and see. . . . Without meaning to, he cracked the reins against the horses' rumps, wishing he could send them fleeing from his failings. When he looked at Saam . . . sometimes he saw . . . the Saam of the past . . . Saam, beloved Bond of Oriel Faltran, Doyce's lover at the time. As if . . . whenever Saam hovered near . . . Oriel's ghostly presence also hovered, silently chiding him for the numerous times he'd hurt and disappointed Doyce, advertently and inadvertently. Wasn't his own conscience sufficient without calling for a stand-in? And once Saam was dead and gone, mayhap Oriel's ghostly lingering would vanish once and for all. Lady help him, what a miserable, selfish wretch he was!

"Oh, not *that* bad." As Jenret whipped around in the seat, Rawn treated him to a giant yawn. "Only reason we accept your flaws, your failings with such equanimity is that you *do* exhibit some redeeming qualities." Reconsidering, he amended, "A few, at least . . . and if you give me time to cudgel my brain, I'm sure I'll discover one."

*"My friend,"* and that described but a portion of his relationship with Rawn, *"don't you . . . I mean, aren't you . . . ? Weren't you ever . . . jealous of Saam . . . for what he meant to Khar?"*

"For what he means to Khar? Has always meant and will always mean?" A brooding sorrow in those eyes before he delicately stroked his chin against Khar's white paw where

it draped Doyce's shoulder. **"At first, yes, and for some
time after, but it was more in the way of one ghatt measuring another, sizing him up, deciding who fit where in the
greater scheme of things. But mostly I pitied him for what
he'd lost—both his Bond and his mindspeech, back then.
But pitying someone makes you superior— Look where
you're going!"** Just in time, Jenret straightened the slewing
mud-buggy, the horses tiring at the pace, no longer picking
their way as carefully along the roadway.

*"The way you take pity on my stubbornness?"* Guiltily,
Jenret devoted his strict attention to the road, ignored Bartholphe's startled "Heh?" No other travelers. A shame they
lacked time to stop in Sidonie, but he and Doyce had
agreed that Arras and Francie, Eadwin, had sufficient woes
with the Plumb crisis without them adding theirs to it. Easier—and faster—to bypass Sidonie, mayhap halt on the way
back, once they'd herded together all their lost lambs.

Wheezing, Rawn finally answered, **"No—not pity, but acceptance. I've learned to take the measure of the being—
human or ghatti. Saam is superior to me in specific ways,
just as I'm superior to him in others. The same with our
relationship."** And with a certain tart relish, **"Or your relationship with Doyce."**

*"Speaking of which, have our sleeping beauties awak-
ened? If they have, I'll let Bartolphe take over again."* Joggling his knee against the man, Jenret 'spoke him from
his brown study. *"No more lazing on the job, my friend."*
Bartolphe responded with a sunny smile, clearly taking no
offense. Ah, Lady bless, what would he and Doyce have
done without them all these past few days, calling in whatever favors, whatever goodwill was owed them along the
way—and that was considerable—more than either of them
had wanted to use or abuse. There'd been no shortage of
volunteers, Resonants and Seekers, friends and total strangers alike gladly contributing their time and presence, then
turning around and riding slowly back to their individual
homes and lives.

"What, Jenner?" In a voice as lazy as toffee being
stretched, Doyce murmured, "Don't you think Khar and I
heard you two nattering away? I swear this rain, or sleet,
or whatever it is, drives mindspeech undercover—it lingers
under the canopy, hating the sting. Makes a terrible, low-

grade buzz. Ah, I'm so tired I've turned fanciful—or is it old age?"

"Did you get much sleep?" He swung onto his knees on his seat, facing her. "Need a hand unfolding?" Already he'd flung a leg over the back of the bench.

Still pillowed along Doyce's side, Khar lowered her head, amber eyes downcast at the ignominious effects of old age. **"Jenret, if you'd be so kind. I'm stiff, and I don't think Doyce can shift to move me. Once I have my feet under me and flex a little, I'll be fine."**

Much of it, he convinced himself as he scooped up Khar and eased her onto the floorboards, was the residual effect of last spring's wounds. One hand supporting her chest, he raised her until her front legs straightened, then cupped her hips to elevate her hindquarters, her legs quivering as he gradually let her bear her own weight. **"Ooh! Pins and needles!"** she grumped, the striped "M" on her forehead rising. **"Ah, better, better."** Finally, one hind leg, then the other, extended in a languorous, long stretch behind her, followed by a dipping forequarter bow. **"Providential we ghatti require limited space to limber up."**

Crooking an elbow at Doyce, Jenret waited until she caught hold and brought her to an upright position. "Ouch!" she complained. "Jenner, you were supposed to unfold my legs first! Needles and pins is right!"

"Well, I'm sorry, but it *is* somewhat cramped with all four of us jammed back here!" For a moment he allowed his fancy full play: all four of them would continue on like this forever, complaining a bit, teasing, jesting at minor aches and pains. And every dear relative and friend a part of a private compact to never cause undue worry or dismay or sorrow! If only life would conform to his wishes!

Raising her to her feet, he sank onto the seat she'd vacated. At least by extending her legs and leaning against the seat back, she could stand beneath the canvas top without ducking. "Think we ought to try again?" *He* wanted to, needed to, assure himself they'd done all they could.

Bracing her boot beside his thigh, Doyce tilted her head, tracing her finger along the sagging canvas. "I'm not sure it will do much good, Jenner. If they haven't responded to us before, I doubt the twins are going to now—most likely our mindspeech can't even reach them, what with the mountains interfering." It had been a point of continuing contention between them.

Hands fisted between his knees, he insisted stubbornly, "I don't care! I just want them to know we're coming, that they needn't carry the burden by themselves." It mattered to him that they try, attempt anything and everything to help.

"Just humor me, Doyce," he grated, angrier than he'd willingly admit. "I need news—fresh, stale, or in between! Mayhap 'speak Arras, someone else, see if they've heard anything further, learn if there's word of our wanderers." It gnawed at him; he craved concrete details: what they were doing, where they were at each and every instant, a way to assure himself that none of them had come to harm. Ah, Blessed Lady, watch over all those I hold dear—daughter and son, sister and aunt, a special Shepherd, and four precious ghatti. An absurd but appalling image swept over him: statues of the Lady always showed her with eight hands, just as the never-changing Lady Moon had eight disciples. Eight hands, and nine loved ones! Which soul would She be unable to cup in a succoring palm? Saam might well be dead by now! Shame welled through him at his earlier musings.

Sweat iced his brow, the sleet penning him in, his private haven crumbling, and he was awash with fear. *"Jenner?"* Could she see it, too? Tell him who would fall between the Lady's hands? Had Lindy known, suspected something? *"Jenret! Saam dozes on Her lap, never fear!"* Did Doyce truly know?

With a rasping, apologetic throat clearing, Bartolphe spoke without looking back, eyes assessing the road. "Mr. Wycherley, sir. Mindmessage seeking you out. Private-like, just for you, sir. That was emphasized."

Ignoring Doyce's panicky stare, unable to look at her face, he concentrated, letting his mind open, become receptive. How long had someone been trying to make contact? At least it partially explained the throbbing in his temples; it had been battering at him, and he'd been too tense, too preoccupied to even be aware of it!

The message was short, to the point, a steeliness to Eadwin's mindvoice that he'd never heard before. "Ah, dear,

Blessed Lady!" he breathed when Eadwin concluded. What was he to tell Doyce? *How* was he to tell Doyce?

But she was shaking him, eyes huge with fear, hazel eyes glinting with greens and blues, always so intense when she was caught in the grip of strong emotion. "Jenner! Tell me—I *have* to know! Is it the twins? Are the twins all right?"

This was *too* much, entirely too much to assimilate on top of their concern over the twins, Saam, Mahafny and Harrap, Jacobia. "Believe me, Doyce—it has nothing to do with the twins. We don't know any more or any less than we did a few moments ago. But," and he swallowed, grasping both her hands in his and drawing her down beside him. From their expressions, Rawn and Khar had received a near-identical message from Hru'rul. "Francie's in danger. That maniac, that idiot who accidentally set off the Plumb has seized Francie as a hostage. A little girl as well."

"Hostage for what?" Well, how could he expect her to know, to guess, because who would have dreamed it—except a madman?

"For the remaining Plumbs, darling. He wants the Plumbs in exchange for the little girl and Francie." Now came the truly excruciating part. "According to Eadwin, Arras will *not* compromise, allow the trade—refuses to endanger Marchmont by allowing the Plumbs into a madman's hands." Could he have remained so adamant if Doyce were held hostage? It didn't bear thinking about: duty, honor, service—versus love. Selfish versus unselfish behavior for the greater good?

Head bent, fingers ceaselessly tracing a pattern on her knee, Doyce finally murmured, "I . . . see. I . . . oh, Francie! Oh, how poor Harry and Arras must be hurting!" Gathering her in his arms, he rocked her while he wrestled with his own conscience, composing himself by degrees, firming mind and heart to what *must* be done.

"Fritha! Emma!" Ah, he'd remembered their names after all! "A change in plans, ladies. May we borrow your mounts, have you and your Bonds return with Bartolphe in the mud-buggy? We urgently need to reach Sidonie, Doyce and Khar, Rawn and I." If the twins had progressed this far without them, then they could manage a little longer. Right now the most urgent thing was to rush Doyce

to Sidonie, mayhap she'd be allowed a word with Francie,
would at least be there, know how things stood, could hold
Harry close. "Darling, can you ride? Can you and Khar
manage it?"

**"We can, we will—somehow,"** Khar responded for her.

❧

"Hush!" Nakum looked in both directions before kicking
aside some old snow to expose an iron ring in the stone
foundation of a stable. Not very likely anyone'd be in the
stable to see or hear, not with all the horses long gone,
doing their duty for Sidonie. But a few stragglers wandered
the streets, now mostly deserted in this part of town. The
few remaining souls were those who'd gotten a late start
for some reason, or served as warders, now advancing to
guide the people from another sector to their designated
staging points. A crash as a brick sailed through the window
of the wine shop across the street from the stable.

"Phah!" Quaintance spat and began stumping off with
her cane until Callis gently but firmly hooked her arm.
"Damn looters! Always happens in a crisis. Some fools
have no common sense!" Hrmphing, she thought about it,
"Fools . . . common sense. Getting old, Quaintance!
'Course they don't, that's what makes 'em fools!"

"You mean they'd stay—loot, steal what isn't theirs—
when they'll all be blown up?" Diccon sounded disapproving, and Kwee appeared ready to launch herself, apprehend
the scoundrels in the act.

"Depends, lad. If you're going to be blown up, might as
well be drunk." Diccon nodded. "And if naught happens,
might as well have stolen all the wine, all the gold you
can find."

"That's precisely why Marchmont really should have
Seekers Veritas," Diccon earnestly informed her. "Assuming they survive—the thieves, I mean—how will you ever
discover who's responsible? Who should be punished?
Why, Kwee and I would have our work cut out for us
here—I'd never thought of that before! Mayhap I can convince the Seeker General we should start a branch in
Marchmont, have more than just the one token Seeker Pair
serving as the king's liaison."

Jacobia crouched by Nakum's side as he wrestled with the iron ring, twisting it, waiting for it to catch. He'd discovered several other routes in and out of the castle's subterranean levels, but exiting had always been easier than entering. Jacobia's closeness disconcerted him, turned him all clumsy and sweaty. Worse, it made the Trickster itch against his skin, stick to his sweat. Silently she scratched his lower back, just above the waist where it was stowed away, and a shimmering green momentarily highlighted the dimness until Jacobia pressed her palm flat on it, and it reluctantly dimmed.

"How'd you know?" And why was his heart pounding in his ears, his breath coming fast?

"Never mind." Imperturbably, she removed his hand from the iron ring and gave it a half-turn, pushing in at the last moment. "I don't know how I've come to know any number of things of late. I hope I find out at some point!"

Down they went, Feather first, followed by Jacobia, then Diccon and Nakum with Quaintance, giddily enjoying herself, little cooing sounds of excitement issuing from between parted lips. "Something new at my age!" she kept chortling, "Never too late, no, it isn't!"

Callis came last, shooing Kwee ahead of her. "You can 'speak Hru'rul and the others later, sweedling, but not now. Listen all you like, report what you hear, but I'd prefer our presence be secret for a time." Kwee trotted between Diccon and Callis, apparently unsure to whom she owed first loyalty, until Diccon reminded her, "I'm obeying Callis, so I guess you can, too."

"Now where do you want to go?" Nakum drew Callis aside. "Deeper? More toward the center? Where?" Her mere presence had left him simultaneously stronger and weaker. More delicately attuned to the earth and its every whisper, his power enhanced to the core, every fiber of his being vibrating with being and becoming. Except his palms were sweaty, his heart palpitating, his tongue lodging in his throat—no, he hardly blamed Callis for that, it happened each time he so much as caught a hint of Jacobia's scent.

Callis inspected him, back, front, and sideways, and somehow he managed not to trip over his own feet as he caught a glimpse of Jacobia. "Hm. I think you've been alone on that mountaintop far too long!" Placing his hand over his earth-bond, she closed her hand over his. In moments his vision cleared, the thudding in his ears fading. "Now take hold of yourself. We've work to do, important work. If we don't succeed, whatever you're experiencing so intensely won't matter in the least." A light slap on his cheek. "Now . . ." she ruminated, "I'd like us positioned under the courtyard, but not too many levels down. Think you can manage that, or shall I see if I remember the way?"

He took the lead, Callis at his side. Could hear Feather behind him. "No, I don't mind! I'm well-broken in by now, a perfect mount! Come, Lady Quaintance, up on my back, if you please."

"What are you going to do?"

By way of an answer, Callis asked, "Do you happen to have any mud around here? Left over from the flooding? If not, some dirt and water will do, though it'll take longer."

Mud? "I think we can find some, more than enough. How much do you want?"

"Oh, quite a great deal, I think." Callis airily waved a hand. "A very great deal, though clay is fine, too. Anything of that sort."

"Of earth, you mean?" a glimmer of understanding beginning to spark in his mind, excitement racing.

"Yes. I will build me a being from this earth—Jacobia will tell it, and I will invest it with life—the Great Spirit willing. We'll build a new man for the new world your Romain-Laurent so desperately wants."

Nakum laughed with unabashed joy. The old legends spoke *true*, *lived* even in this world! All of six of them creating, building a being!

❧

Ezequiel paced the courtyard perimeter just behind two lieutenants earnestly engaged in noting where archers might be concealed on castle balconies or the rooftops of outbuildings lining the courtyard. During the castle's heyday when entertainment had been at its peak under Wilhelmina's rule, elaborate entertainments had been commonplace, twenty or more carriages or coaches lining the yard's perimeter as they'd disgorged their passengers. He'd been but a boy, though he vividly recalled the expectant, expansive glow on people's faces, the constant, high hum of voices calling hellos. Or the commencement of Eadwin's royal tour of Canderis, mounted in this very courtyard, Ezequiel frenziedly checking off arrivals, suitable transportation, baggage loading, and the myriad de rigeur details a royal visit entailed—knowing all the while that he'd be left behind after all his hard work, consigned to the castle and boredom, while his grandfather Ignacio traveled in his stead, aware of every error and oversight his grandson had made as he adroitly corrected them.

Now the courtyard appeared bleakly empty, just an occasional seam of ice between cobblestones, the giant marble planters at the entrance empty of flowers, capped with snow. At least it hadn't snowed during the evacuation—still continuing, he supposed. "Can you suggest other locations?" One of the lieutenants, the one who acted ill at ease with setting archers in secluded spots, placed a restraining hand on his shoulder, jerking him back to the here and now.

He shifted the hand away as diplomatically as he could and still appear unruffled. "I'm not a tactician—or at least not the same kind of tactician as you are." True enough, though he and the army sutler would undoubtedly have a great deal in common. "About all I can tell you is how easily your soldiers can reach various locations, the quickest route onto the roofs. That sort of thing." Didn't he have enough insolvable problems of his own?

"No, don't worry yourself. We'll take what we've got, report it to Lord Muscadeine and the king. It's a contingency plan, Dunay, that's all. We must make sure every contingency is covered. One clear shot at that shite—that's all I ask!" His hand absently stroked the short bow they'd use in such close quarters, and he'd already meticulously tested angles and distances from various positions, Ezequiel flinching as arrows smashed against the cobbles, went skittering across. Crossbows, too, with their heavy quarrels, able to down Romain-Laurent or a horse, were being stationed in at least two locations. "Any word on the conveyance?" the soldier asked—sympathy or a veiled query as to how much time remained to them?

"Soon—or that's what they said a while ago." Ezequiel's

eyes strayed to the bales of straw piled just outside the stables. Hay, as well—the distinction mattered to horses, he supposed. "Lysenko Boersma's locating the best possible dray, may even scare up a hayrack. Knowing him, he'll probably find one." He could imagine the feisty little Commerce Lord, red hair now grizzled, racking his memory for any suppliers who owned such conveyances. And where each one was now. "Can't exactly dump a load of evacuees, inform them they'll walk the rest of the way. Then wainwrights have to inspect it for soundness, give it a good going-over."

"To sabotage it?" A gleam in the lieutenant's eyes, an appreciation of how clandestine deeds were accomplished. "Good show!"

The thought left Ezequiel distinctly uncomfortable. "I don't think so." It had never occurred to him, innocent that he was. "The method of disablement would be crucial . . ." he began thinking it through aloud, groping but gathering fragments of ideas, unable to leave it alone despite the queasiness it engendered.

"Just make sure a wheel falls off, an axle breaks once they're outside Sidonie."

"You'd really want that when they're carrying six Plumbs?" Ezequiel gaped at him, incredulous. Mayhap because he'd had longer than most to grapple with the reality of what an exploding Plumb could destroy, what might set it off. And six of them exploding at once . . . ? A quick swallow to send the bile back down where it belonged.

Unperturbed, the soldier grinned. "Just double-pad it, man! Easy as that!"

Two castle servants ventured down the steps, politely hailing him in mindspeech before intruding. Eadwin had ordered the castle servants to leave, be evacuated with everyone else near the castle, but a solid core had stubbornly stayed behind. Apparently they'd reached an accord amongst themselves, most of those remaining behind were gray- or white-haired, the eldest of the staff, and to a soul they boasted moderate Resonant ability, some quite a great deal. Younger staff, those married, especially those with children, had been summarily packed off. With the castle now nearly empty and echoing, it was crucial that they could quickly and effectively communicate with each other without physically searching out the person they needed to address.

"We'll be off, then." A quick bow, a raised fist, and the two soldiers were off. "Good luck, and Lady bless us all!"

"Or those of us who deserve to be blessed," sniffed Warburg, in overall charge of Eadwin's wardrobe. "We've collected the best of the best—bedding, batting and everything in between. Feather beds, swan's-down pillows and comforters in royal velvet, satin, and silk. But at my age, I refuse to be responsible for picking up the feathers if there's an explosion!"

"Hush!" Petite and silver-haired, Joressa Alembert had charge of desserts in the kitchen. "Here, brought you a bit to eat." She handed Ezequiel two biscuits, each split in the middle by a patty of warm, crisp sausage. "Have to eat to keep going, whether or not we're hungry. Your grandfather knew the wisdom of that. Naught fancy from the kitchens now, but it's filling." Grateful, he munched, Warburg staring down his nose at him, until Joressa turned on the wardrobing man. "You had three yourself, 'fore we came out. Don't begrudge him his!"

"I don't! But I begrudge him the sticky bun you've hidden away special for him." Warburg smiled thinly, any smile a rarity for him. "I'd best be going back. The king and Lord Muscadeine must be turned out right and proper when that worm Charpentier ventures out. Nothing fancy nor formal, mind—but quietly elegant and powerful-looking. Remind him who's who!" And with that he bustled off, through Joressa stayed by Ezequiel's side.

"We've piled the bedding by the lower door, not the main entrance, just as you asked. Everything separated as to type, so we can decide what we want where. Know how much we'll need?" From a pocket she produced the sticky bun, wrapped in a scrap of waxed butcher paper.

Lady bless, he was hungrier than he'd realized and, like a little boy he licked the paper, determined not to waste a smear of sweetness. "That's what I don't know." Might as well be frank about it. "Don't know what sort of wagon we'll have, nor do I have the least notion how much straw, hay, comforters, whatever, it takes fill a wagon."

"That's why I stayed out here with you." Cold, she wrapped her apron around her arms until Ezequiel struggled clear of his overvest, sticky bun stuck in his mouth, and draped the gold-embroidered garment over her shoulders. "Grew up a on a farm, I did, back when farms lay closer to Sidonie than they do now. Helped with many a haying as a lass." Unwinding herself from the apron, she snugged the vest front closed from the inside with both hands. "Takes more than you think, sir. Seems to me that this time we'd best pack things down tighter than we did when forking hay aboard, 'cuz then you've still got to toss it in the loft. I'd say pack bales all 'round the trunk, then loose hay, comforters, more bales, loose hay, comforters, layer it like." A shiver, but not from cold. "One of the eumedico assistants showed me and Cook some of the shrapnel pieces they removed from Lord Muscadeine. Baled hay'll stop more things than loose, anything woven's a bit stronger, more resistant than the loose hay, as well."

"Give it as many layers, as many different densities as possible?" That seemed to be what she was suggesting. "I see. And thank you, Joressa." He kissed her on both cheeks, realizing as he did so that his lips were sticky. "Both for the food and for the advice."

A quick curtsy. "Not to worry, sir. I'll be here when it's time to pack them nasty things. Least I can do for the Lady Francie and that little girl. Few of the others, too, those as know what's needful." She started to run, then hesitated. "You know what that Romain-Laurent told me once? That I swirled too much icing on my sticky buns, nor was I spreading it as efficiently as I might! Me—who's been doing it nigh onto fifty years! Didn't notice it stopped him from filching as many as he could, though."

Raising a hand to momentarily hush her, Ezequiel concentrated. Didn't immediately recognize the mindvoice, but Lysenko had sent word. The wagon was now departing the wainwright's with a reasonably fresh team of four. "Go have a cup of cha, and let it cool before you try to gulp it down," was the final message. "By the time you've finished, the hayrack'll be there."

"Come, Joressa. You and Cook and I are going to have a cup of cha." He didn't want it, but he'd have it. Staring at the gates wouldn't make the hayrack materialize any more quickly.

❧

"O . . . of c–course I d–don't mind!" For once in his life Theo trailed in Holly's wake, long legs somehow not quick enough, clumsy with surprise.

"That's good—because I said you wouldn't mind!" Holly sincerely wished someone had retrieved her own boots, because this pair was a size too small and pinching like sin, the baby toe on her right foot complaining with every other step.

**"At least it's every other step."** P'roul was wasting no time, either, ranging well ahead of both her Bond and Theo, Khim a half-pace behind her. **"See, always a bright side to things. A very small bright side, to be sure, but about the only sunny one I can think of."**

Putting on a burst of speed, Theo drew parallel to her, elbows pumping in that odd-looking walk employed by people who don't feel it's decorous to run. "It's j–just that I d–don't l–like the i–idea of k–killing in c–cold blood! C–couldn't we j–just t–try to c–c–c–"

Before Holly could say "capture" for him, Khim 'spoke with a sympathetic firmness, back-glancing Theo with her amber eyes. **"Beloved, no one enjoys killing just for the sake of killing. But this is an exception—the man's quite mad. If a chance to overpower him presents itself, fine, but don't expect one."**

"Hru'rul's going to be hornet-mad if we do!" interjected her sib.

Khim ignored her. **"We aim to kill with our first blows, allow him no time to react, give him no quarter. Too many other lives are at stake—not just Francie's and Etelka's. This is hardly the time to be softhearted."**

Loosening her jacket—or whoever's jacket it was, Terrail's, possibly—Holly self-consciously tucked back the lace slithering out around the collar. Along with borrowed boots and a borrowed jacket, she still wore her flimsy nightgown beneath everything. During the early morning when they'd combed the castle corridors, the ghatti collecting emotions, worries, and fears more acutely than any Resonant could, testing for trouble, she'd heard someone snicker, then another break into an outright guffaw. Apparently the nightgown had been stealthily creeping out of her trousers, falling into a train behind her. She'd been sorely tempted to have cut it off at the waist if it hadn't been so damnably expensive!

Theo's face bore a worried twist, but his set jaw showed the grim resolution she'd expected him to muster. "If Eadwin won't agree, I don't know what Arras will do. Just keep endlessly arguing like that, and Arras is liable to lash out—even at the king. Well, they can argue forever—except the hayrack has pulled into the courtyard—saw it from the window. Ezequiel and the servants are padding it now. Eadwin has to come to a decision."

"A–and C–Cin–z–zia and Urban w–will c–carry out the t–trunk?"

Eadwin and Arras stood at the end of the corridor, in front of the doors to the strong-rooms, both still hotly arguing but as circumspectly as possible, practically nose to nose yet unable to see eye to eye. The cords on both men's necks were straining, their color high, their hands flying for emphasis. Marchmontians *did* tend to talk with their hands, she'd noticed it before. At some point both men had bathed and shaved, changed into pristine clothes, Arras with his medals and ribbons asway on the front of his slate-gray military jacket. The king wore his royal pendant around his neck, the only decoration on his somberly cut dove-gray jacket, the lavender waistcoat just visible.

"W–what? D–did he b–break Eze–" he exhaled hard, "quiel's arm so he couldn't volunteer for that, too? W–who d–does Eadwin prefer for w–wagon duty?"

Slowing, a hand on Theo's arm to reduce his speed, she continued in a hurried whisper. "Eadwin wants *anyone* except Arras's choices. Amazingly, Carn Camphuysen volunteered—humbly informed Eadwin it was part of his duty as Public Weal Lord. Poor man looked as if he was going to faint at Eadwin's feet. A brave gesture, but I *don't* think so!" Theo chuckled. "And Arras insists that it be," a slight pause to determine if Theo had guessed, "us, cousin mine. Not only have we been drafted, but we've volunteered, as well."

"D–double duty, d–double p–pay?" Theo pivoted her to face him, maximize their privacy. "B–but what a–b–bout Khim and P–P'roul? D–do we have to l–leave them b–behind?"

Breaking off a conversation in falanese with La'ow, who'd come padding along the corridor to meet them, Khim gave her Bond a fond look, eye-whiskers raising as her eyes slid to Holly. Whether in falanese or human, Holly understood the look that translated as, "He's an adorable creature, but so dense sometimes!" Whether she was referring to La'ow or Theo, she wouldn't hazard a guess, would have laid even bets on both candidates to cover herself.

**"Theo, beloved."** Ah, such long-suffering patience! *"We are part of the reason Arras insists it to be us*—as in you and me, Holly and P'roul. If we're all buried up to our eyebrows in straw, *someone*—such as my sib and me—must be able to sense Romain-Laurent's thoughts, gauge the optimum moment to attack."

Face thrust so close to Eadwin's now that the king had uncomfortably bent his neck back to gain distance, Arras waved them nearer. "Will you?" The swift, burning glance was searing, beseeching, and livid with suppressed anger and fading hope. Someday, someday, she hoped that she could evoke such depth of feeling in some man.

It wasn't a question of agreeing to Arras's request, it was a question of assuaging the king, first. And Theo stepped forward, smartly saluting, speaking without a halt. "Your Highness, request permission to track down and kill or capture—as necessary—one Romain-Laurent Charpentier, who has seized a Canderisian citizen as hostage, as well as a very junior, very provisional member of the Seekers Veritas. We've served you before, and have every intention of serving you again, sir! Now has it been determined where in the wagon we should hide? Knives and truncheons are the most reliable weapons at close quarters." Holly momentarily goggled at her cousin. Theo? Knives and truncheons? At close quarters? Hardly a part of Seeker training! Had Theo been reading too many adventure tales? Well, if so, he'd at least gotten it right.

Abandoning Eadwin's side, Hru'rul came to join P'roul and Khim; totally absent was the usual swagger to his walk, his massive head low and supplicating, his shoulders rolling as he bow-stretched before the ghattas. **"Be saving my Y'ew's human? Nice Harry's mama? Asking favor of beauteous offspring of Khar'pern of the amber eyes."**

Hru'rul had 'spoken so that Eadwin and the other Seek-

ers—Cinzia, Theo, and Holly—could understand. Only
Arras and Urban were ignorant of what had passed.

Someone had to say the obvious, and Cinzia did, Holly
relieved that it didn't have to come from her. "Sire, Eadwin. We all realize that as king, you hold the final say in
all this, but do you truly think it advisable to countermand
your own Bond's choice? A Bond who is, after all, able to
determine the truth of the matter."

♣

Mud. Mud, mud, and more mud, some runny, almost liquid,
other patches oozy, and then thick, near-viscous mud. He
was becoming a connoisseur of earth mixed with water. On
his knees, Nakum waited for Diccon to shove back the
basket containing the clay he was laboriously excavating
from a seam in the tunnel wall. Clay was good, too, Callis
had informed them, indeed, had insisted upon it. Not that
they had much in the way of suitable digging equipment;
both he and Diccon had knives, as did Callis and Feather,
even Jacobia. Quaintance, though, apparently had armed
herself with a bevy of lethal-looking hat pins. The knives
served for gouging, and they'd at least found a broken
spade, its blade intact, though its handle was very short.
The longer piece of handle, with its sharp, fracture end,
worked as a sort of makeshift pick, gave them some
leverage.

In their travels through the underground passageways
they'd collected whatever odds and ends came to hand,
including a discarded tin bucket, dented and with assorted
holes, a leather bucket, and a bushel basket containing a
wizened apple. Considering the amount of mud that needed
to be transported, Nakum feared it would take forever or—
if not forever—too long.

They'd selected a spot in a tunnel beneath the courtyard
that led onward to the old stables, and Nakum had gone
ahead, foraging, rummaging, returning with another five
buckets in various conditions—two lacking bales, one crumpled as if a horse had stepped on it, and the final two of
old, splintering wood that threatened to crumble at a touch.
However, the moist mud was doing wonders in swelling the

slats, making them marginally more sturdy. However, at some point as the heavily-loaded buckets were passed from hand to hand, the bottoms would detach—that was a given.

Slithering back on his belly, Diccon passed Nakum the shovel handle, coated with clay, as was Diccon, his hair and face slick in some spots, dusty in others. "Your turn for a spell of torment. I'll carry it for now." Both were bespeckled and spattered with mud or its near kin, as was everyone else with the exception of Callis, still in her impeccable white doeskin, as if nothing she touched could mar it. She did, however, boast a smudge of mud on her nose and cheek. Nakum had given up and stripped down to his breechcloth long ago, hating the way the mud and dampness dragged at his buckskins.

At a guess, they labored no more than three meters below the surface of the courtyard, as evinced by the heavy beams and timbers supporting the tunnel's roof. Or rather, three meters from the roof to the surface, and mayhap another six meters to the tunnel floor. Say, nine meters at the most—he hoped—and Callis seemed well-content. Not all that far distant from the surface that people might not hear, if spade clanged against a bucket or rock, or one of them yelped, feet slipping in the slick mud. He'd landed flat on his back once, had the breath knocked out of him.

At first they'd all carried or scooped mud, except for Quaintance, who tidily sat on the floor, skirts wrapped 'round her knees, offering encouragement. She was in charge of their candles and their one lantern, deciding who needed the most light, when something could be extinguished, saved for later. She'd offered her enormous fur hat without hesitation as a container to haul mud. In some spots enough suitably-textured mud existed for them to set up a primitive bucket brigade, pass the laden buckets from hand to hand, Callis dumping it in a pile.

Once they'd collected enough to begin, she'd excused Feather from mud gathering with a flurry of whispered instructions, the younger woman setting to work with hands and with feet as necessary to start shaping the mud into the semblance of a being. A sort of sense to it, that Feather should be chosen as architect, craftsperson, potter, whatever. Certainly as a eumedico, she had the best sense of human anatomy.

"Kwee, behave yourself," he heard Diccon warn as the ghatta careened past. Nakum knew what she was chasing. Once he'd stripped down to his breechcloth, the Trickster had no place to nestle. Callis had assigned it the job of providing additional light, bathing nearby things in a green-gold glow; however, neither it nor Kwee could resist prank-ing each other, a lightning tag of a paw as Kwee skimmed by on patrol duty, watching for interlopers and listening for news from above. In retaliation, it diminished to a pinprick of light, landing on the tip of Kwee's tail, then darting away in the most alluringly erratic manner, taunting her to lay a paw on it until Kwee almost turned herself inside out with the effort. And Callis was being amazingly lenient with it, even when it spattered mud at Quaintance, who'd glared and splattered it right back.

Jacobia started to slip by with a full bucket, then halted, squatting to speak with Nakum. "This is my final stint of hauling. Callis wants me to begin talking to it now, re-minding it of who and what it is, telling it stories . . . I don't know . . ." Backing out, he rolled on his side to admire the pale, indistinct sheen of her face. "Imbuing it with a sense of history, of destiny, I suppose you'd say."

"And can you?" Was what they were attempting possi-ble? In other circumstances, he'd have unhesitatingly said no, but Callis was a force of her own making. Many things were possible, things that he had no inkling could be ac-complished—force and faith, belief and love, honor and honesty were all a part of it, a reverence for all of the creatures and things the Great Spirit had created. And the Great Spirit could never believe that Callis was usurping its role, seeking to out-create the supreme power.

Cupping her earth-bond in both hands, Jacobia held it to her lips. "I'm hoping this will give me the words—there are so many building within me, seeking an outlet." Laying a hand on his knee for a moment, she levered herself off the tunnel floor. "Oh, my! If Diccon didn't ache enough before, he surely will after this!" Propping the bucket on her hip, she started off. "Nakum, you won't believe it when you see it! What Feather's accomplished so far is . . . is a work of art! More than that! An act of . . . of veneration, a sort of devotion I didn't suspect resided in her."

❖

Troweling on mud, Feather patted and pummeled it, squeezed and molded, working away with both hands, even a bare foot if some piece of the expanding anatomy became unstable till more mud arrived. Beneath their coating of mud her fingers had puckered and wrinkled from the moisture, but she continued like a woman possessed. And indeed she was, in a way she'd never before experienced. Never, *never* in her life had she undertaken something so demanding, yet so utterly satisfying. Hands and brain functioned as one, an innate knowledge of bones and muscle, ligaments and tendons, revealing themselves beneath the surface of the shape she painstakingly created.

Too detailed, too finicky, mayhap, and she agonized that she'd become too caught up in things, gone too far. After all, hadn't Callis emphasized that what was needed was a relatively accurate recreation of the human form, not a perfect match? But the size, the scale, inspired her, and at moments she was convinced she could close her eyes and continue with equal confidence. The old tales had it that bear cubs were born so small and formless in their dens in the depths of winter that their mothers literally had to lick them into shape. Not truc, she knew, but if it had been, she was experiencing the selfsame pride and love and hope that those mother bears exhibited.

Not long past Quaintance Mercilot had crept to her side, little dark eyes glistening, withered hands longingly flexing. "Don't suppose," she sounded gruff, but the words had trembled, caught in her throat. "Don't suppose I could help-like? Just dibs and dabs here or there, wherever you said, you supervising, of course!"

An overwhelming desire to scream "No!", to drive the old woman back into her place, break her fingers if she so much as breathed on her creation. A great lungful of air, a snarl pulling back her lips, and then something within Feather softened, touched by Quaintance's genuine admiration while ruefully acknowledging that she was but the tool Callis wielded. Who was she to decide whether Callis might need another tool? Mayhap, too, it had to do with the fact that elderly Outlanders were so different from older Erakwa, so few of them still having any sphere of influence, younger generations needing and relying on them, cherishing their wisdom. They aged so much more quickly!

Instead, she'd invited, "Come. Take off your shoes and stockings, roll up your sleeves. Your hands are finer, more delicate than mine. If you smooth and stroke where I indicate, you'll create the final layer of skin." Now Quaintance scooted on hands and knees, reaching, stroking, caressing, humming away, her vision turned inward, lost in tactile sensation. How many children and grandchildren and great grandchildren had she soothed the same way with those still-useful hands?

Back aching, leg muscles tired, she rose to bend and stretch, step back to gain perspective on her creation. Soon Jacobia would start her tale-telling, and Feather looked forward to listening, regaining something she'd lost or thrown away. Always there were parts of a being to be discarded, replaced by newer pieces, hard-won by knowledge, just as a butterfly splits its chrysalis, fans its wings in the sun to dry and set its new wisdom. Some of what she'd learned as a eumedico came under that category. But she'd also wasted, laid waste to integral parts of her being, only to substitute less worthwhile ideas and beliefs in their place.

Despite the fact that she'd been building it, bucket of mud by bucket of mud, Feather's mouth opened in disbelief at what she saw laid before her. The being was twelve meters long, at least! "Oh, no!" Muddy hand over mouth, she groaned. Too tall—it *must* be! It couldn't stand up in the tunnel—what had she been thinking?

How, how could she shorten it? Looked assessingly at the long, supple legs, the torso with its broad shoulders and chest and tapering waist, the strong but graceful neck designed to support the head, its features still waiting to be molded.

"Holy, Blessed Lady!" Diccon breathed in her ear. "That's incredible! Gorgeous! So big yet so balanced." Squatting near, but not too near, he examined a hand, the palm more than big enough to cup a human head, the fingers the size of baguettes that she'd eaten in Gaernett restaurants. She couldn't just remove a chunk from the legs, shorten the neck, truncate that torso—not without destroying the proportions! Must she begin anew, ever more humbled?

Callis ghosted to her side, back from doing whatever it was that she did—wandering, communing with the earth, yet always aware when they required help. "I'll have to start all over again," Feather muttered dully, wanting nothing more than to slump down and wail. "I can probably salvage some of the mud, but I'll need a fresh batch to begin it. I'm so sorry." She could do it, she would do it, but oh, the pain of knowing that she'd gone astray! Gotten too caught up in the building and molding, not enough of the plain thinking needed.

"Whatever for, child?" Callis gave her a curious look, eyebrows winging up as if expecting Feather to admit she was joking.

"Because it's too tall! It can't stand upright in the tunnel. It'll crash right through the roof!" A brief hope flamed through her. "Are we going to carry it somewhere . . . where it can?" The flame of hope withered, hissing disappointment at being extinguished—she had to have five-hundred kilos or more of mud there!

"Exactly!" Regarding the ceiling and then the figure, Callis smiled. "Right through the ceiling! Good girl!"

A swirling movement as Quaintance flung her fur coat over the being's lower torso exactly where Diccon was staring, spellbound, glaring at Diccon as she did. Hastily wiping a smile off his face, he inquired with as much innocence as he could muster, "How are you going to mold the other side, his back—I mean?"

Again Feather felt her failure, her lack. To have done so much, aimed at such symmetry and beauty, and then to leave the back unfinished, unmolded.

"Why, no doubt a strong young man such as yourself can roll it over for Feather. Mayhap even pose for her if she should need help."

"All right! I brought that on myself! I'm sorry!" Groaning, Diccon went to his knees, looking for a place to brace his hands.

"Just go!" Callis scolded. "Bring the Lady Quaintance a little more finishing mud, if you would!" As he left, Callis whispered, "Still young, but he'll be fine when he matures."

Quaintance considered the matter. "More like celvassy than wine, to my way of thinking—more fireworks than smoothness to him. But wouldn't mind being about seventy years younger! I'd flirt like the very blazes with him, lead him a merry chase!"

♣

The slithery swoosh of a piece of paper gliding beneath the door made Telka start, cry out, abruptly woken from a restless sleep, her head on Lady Francie's lap. "Hush," and a hand over her mouth effectively silenced her, "I think the wagon's ready, child. They've sent a note to let us know."

Fumbling with her spectacles, Telka watched Romain-Laurent avidly snatch at the paper, reading and rereading it. "Do we know where we're going?" She spoke as if addressing her lap, wanting—above all—not to disturb or distract Romain-Laurent.

"Other than the Stratocums, I've no idea." Francie confessed, rubbing Telka's back. "I only hope *he* knows!"

Frowning, muttering, Romain-Laurent yanked back a chair, its legs scraping across the floor, and sat at the table, scribbling at the bottom of the note. A sigh, pencil tapping against his lips, and then more writing, his glower gradually dissipating till he looked almost cheerful. Least he didn't need her to write for him this time, but it meant she couldn't try to send any messages herself. Whoever Romain-Laurent was at this moment, he appeared sure of precisely what he wanted. Back to the door he went, sliding the note outside. How wondrous to be paper-thin, able to escape like that!

"Time to ready ourselves, ladies." And Telka was already rising, forgetting her hobble, engaging in a frantic dance to avoid falling. "Anyone need to use the . . . necessity?" Seeing her struggle to help Francie to her feet, he came and caught her beneath the arms, lifting her upright, Francie's revulsion at his nearness blessedly screened since he stood behind her. After a terse "No" from them both, he left them to themselves, returning again to his precious trunk, opening the lid and lifting out a Plumb, which he laid against a cradle of sandbags.

So this was what it looked like—not much by her sights. Good-sized cylinder with oh-so-many buttons and switches, sort of a silvery color with a tarnish overlay. Mayhap fifty centimeters long, shorter than some of the logs the boys chopped for the fireplace. About the diameter of a mushmelon, a nice, late-season one, all juicy sweet with soft orange flesh. She licked her lips. Don't think about it, am *not* hungry, am *not* thirsty, am *not* scared, am *not* gonna die! And what she wanted most of all was Mam and Da, and that had to be the stupidest, most *selfish* thing to wish for— wishing them right into the castle, next to the Plumbs! Shoving at her spectacles with the backs of her hands, she fisted her eyes. Would punch herself 'fore she'd let *him* see her cry! Would punch *him*, if she could!

A second Plumb now lay beside the first; Romain-Laurent struggling to slip each one into a sleeve from Francie's robe. So that's what he'd been up to, having her sew away like that, making little pouches for them! But he only had two, and if there were six Plumbs, that didn't make a speck of sense. "Why's he doing that? Acts like he's dressing dollies!" Lady Francie'd been scrutinizing Romain-Laurent's every move, lower lip between her teeth, not worrying at it, just pinching it tighter and tighter. "Someone's going to come, help move the trunk and the Plumbs, so why'd he take them out?"

It took too long for Francie to answer, as if she truly didn't know or truly didn't want to say. "I think it's an added assurance, to make sure things go as he's planned. It's the sort of thing Arras would think of," and then she turned real quiet, totally within herself, and Telka felt alone, despite the fact that she stood right beside Francie, her bad leg and arm trembling.

Finished, Romain-Laurent dusted his hands and rose. "Ladies, sorry to impose, but I'm going to have to tie you up again. Only sensible way to do it, you know." He *did* sound almost apologetic; his commonsensical voice possessed a touch of kindness along with all its practicality. "Same positions, if you please," and Francie resignedly stretched her arms over Telka's shoulders, already leaning against her a little too much. Couldn't kick him, not with her feet hobbled, but oh, she wished she dared do something, couldn't stand the thought of that scratchy burlap scrubbing at her wrists again! But hitting him wouldn't do a mote of good, just make him mad, and how he'd retaliate—and he *would*, she didn't doubt it a bit—probably devise some worse torment than having her wrists bound, Lady Francie's arms tied to hers. What if he got back at her by hitting Francie? Might, too, 'cause he'd already know she was resilient, while the Lady was stretched paper thin, couldn't last much more, frail thing that she was in body, though not in spirit.

If not in this life, mayhap in another was what you were supposed to believe, and she clung to that hope, that in another life she'd be way bigger and more clever than Romain-Laurent, could do nasty things to *his* pets (well, mayhap not *that*), knock *him* out with that stinky stuff, tie *him* up good and proper, whatever she could think of! Her list expanded more rapidly than she'd expected as he jammed a gag into her mouth. Oh, if she'd thought the sticking plaster was horrid, this was eight hundred times worse, moisture sucked from her tongue, the nasty taste, and the *itch*!

"Yes, I know that you're able to remove the gags, that you did it before. But I doubt you'll try it with me right beside you, will you, ladies?" Clasping her bound wrists, he towed her, Francie stumbling along behind, to the doors. "Almost ready now, just one final touch! The pièce de rèsistance, if I do say so myself!" A wink at them both, and he made mock show of blowing on his fingernails and buffing them against his shirt. Oh, she'd give *him* a piece of resistance, all right, if this gag were gone and her wrists untied! Then off he went to gloat over his precious Plumbs.

A high keening issued from deep in Lady Francie's throat, and Telka watched with dawning apprehension as Romain-Laurent reverently lifted one of the Plumbs in its sleeve pouch and slung it across his shoulder so it draped across his opposite hip. Picking up the second one, he advanced on them, Francie's keening growing even louder— no, not just Francie, that was *her,* as well, backing as fast as she could, slamming Francie terrible hard against the wall. "Bend your head, child," he ordered, holding the thing before her, swaying obscenely on its straps. "It's a little heavier than you might think, but not that bad."

Whether from its actual weight or the weight of her own fear, Telka's knees began to buckle and she fought against the downward drag, heaving up, thrusting back her shoulders, the strap scraping her neck. From somewhere deep inside her she sucked up every last bit of courage and defiance she possessed, glaring at him, wanting to spit in his face. Took more'n this to make a Rundgren cry 'nuff, it did! And of all the people in the world, she'd not let this . . . this person who couldn't even decide who he was half the time . . . picky, persnickety, officious . . . and evil, nasty man get the better of her!

Now one of his other voices issued from his lips. Ominous, commanding, a being who would not be balked by anyone or anything—obedience presumed, disobedience dealt with by the harshest measures, no second chances allowed. "Now, to the right-hand door. No! Back, stay back about two meters! And stand straight and tall, no twisting!" He knocked twice on the door, then undid the locks, shifting his own Plumb from his hip to the front as he threw open the door and quickly stepped behind it, so that anyone looking in would immediately see her, Francie, and the Plumb. "First one in—hands on top of your head!" Walking through the door, hands atop her head, Cinzia gave them an insouciant smile, a wink, mouthing a "Hello" at Telka and Francie. "Go halfway to the sandbags and stay, facing that way. Next! Same drill!" He barked each directive, and Urban Gamelyn, the one Telka didn't like all that much—though mayhap she should change her mind—came forward as well. "Join your partner. Stop about a meter to her right!"

It wasn't that Telka hadn't noticed it right away, but that she simply hadn't been able to take it in, assimilate what met her eyes beyond two familiar faces. Both Cinzia and Urban were stripped down to their smallclothes! Cinzia wore a sleeveless, V-necked camisole with flat lace stitched round the neck and sleeves, and a pair of thigh-length drawers. Nothing Telka hadn't seen before, though they were finer than most, looking silky-soft and supple, and so very white! Most folk, leastwise, those who weren't terrible rich, had smallclothes of coarser material, often well-darned, and usually in a light tan or gray. As Mam said, you could scrub them clean, but no need to bleach them forever, since they weren't going to get any whiter. But Urban's smallclothes were definitely that—not just small, but downright minuscule! Oh, my! No undershirting, just drawers, cut right at the hip and the drawstring well below

his belly button. Brightest scarlet silk she'd ever seen
and . . . and . . . on the front . . . an appliqué of a bunch
of grapes! All in a nice, tasteful green, tendrils and leaves
a bit darker! A helpless snort in her ear led her to believe
that the Lady Francie probably chose more understated
smallclothes for her husband. Even Romain-Laurent's
mouth was atwitch.

"Onto the sandbags now, and lift the trunk. Then back
to me and out the door, nice and slow and easy. We'll be
right behind you. Go left as you exit the door. I'll give
directions as needed." Following instructions to the letter,
Cinzia and Urban carried the trunk between them, Urban
like white marble—man didn't have much hair on his body,
very slick and smooth—and Cinzia, again managing to turn
her head and again mouth "Hello." Kind of her, it was.

A shove, unexpected, and Telka found herself staggering
after them, Francie like the tail of a kite behind her. The
Plumb swung on its strap, slapping on one thigh and then
the other, once nearly jamming between her legs, and
Etelka began to sweat, wondering how she could possibly
manage. Don't get distracted, see if there's a rhythm, watch
the Plumb, move the right leg when it swung leftward.
Watch the floor, don't trip, almost out the door. Not
"hello," but "La'ow!"—that was what Cinzia had been saying! And her boot tip caught on the carpet edge as they
entered the corridor, Telka making a strangled sound despite herself, jerking her foot to free it, Francie's weight
pulling at her. Movement behind her, an easing, as Romain-
Laurent apparently grabbed Francie and brought her upright.

La'ow! Of course! She should have been thinking of that
from the beginning—or Hru'rul! Of course it was terribly
improper for a Bondmate to converse with another human
being, especially without being invited, but it was worth a
try. *"Mindwalk if ye will,"* she 'spoke inside her head, leaving herself open. Mayhap La'ow could tell her what was
going on, what might happen.

But a blur of orange fur shot across the carpet at her,
screeching its joy at the top of its little lungs, and Telka
heard the king shout, "Hru'rul! Stop her!" Oh, Baby, Baby!
If only she could hold Baby to her, give her one good-bye
kiss! But Hru'rul and La'ow had intercepted Baby, Hru'rul

crouching atop her, ignoring her screams and pleas as he settled his weight more firmly.

"Sorry, Charpentier. Didn't realize she'd gotten loose." Now what was she supposed to do, continue walking, what? She'd not looked up until now, not realized a farewell committee of sorts stood beyond the door to send them on their way. Two soldiers, the Lady Fabienne, the king, Lord Muscadeine, and Harry. Oh, how it must both hurt and relieve the Lady Francie to see them like this—both ever-so-handsome and brave! Lord Muscadeine stood behind his son, a hand on each shoulder, Harry's hand on one his Papa's. Best bibs and tuckers on everyone, well, mayhap not best, but credibly, elegantly turned out, though on the solemn side. She guessed that fitted the occasion.

Still walking, walking after Cinzia and Urban—no, Romain-Laurent wasn't going to stop and chat with the king, supposed she couldn't blame him, under the circumstances. A final look as she swung left, and she heard Arras and Harry cry out, "We love you." Another cry, Harry's alone, "Love you, Telka!" And finally, the Queen Mother, Lady Fabienne's parting benediction, "May the Lady Bless and keep you in Her bosom, my darlings!"

Etelka was weeping, couldn't help it, was having trouble seeing, her spectacles damming the tears, forcing them to flow outward. Francie's arms tightening around her, squeezing her as best she might. No sound of weeping came from her, though Telka could feel the telltale dampness on the back of her neck.

Then, a moment beyond compare! **"Telka, dear! Be brave, take heart! I'm listening to your thoughts. Trust us. We've a plan, but I shan't say anymore, might jinx it. Just remember, Seekers never give up, never give in—and Eadwin's an honorary Seeker. And don't forget, you're a very junior one!"**

She wanted to believe, had to, because the ghatti didn't lie, but they couldn't tell if and when a Plumb might go off. No one could. But she'd try to be brave, stop blubbing, keep track of what was going on, in case any scrap of information might be useful to La'ow and the king and the others. She was Etelka Rundgren, beloved of Baby Y'ew, and she hadn't really planned on being a Seeker, had relished pretending, but hadn't 'spected it to ever happen. Not going to let Baby down, nor Hru'rul nor La'ow nor. . . . Couldn't smile with the gag in place, but felt a small ray of sunshine within herself. Khim and P'roul . . . could it be possible? No, don't! Just keep watching your feet, left, right, left, right. And above all, don't let Romain-Laurent guess the least little bit that help might be on the way.

♣

Intent on the layering of straw bales, loose hay, and comforters in the hayrack, Ezequiel flinched as Holly laid a hand on his arm. "La'ow's alerted P'roul that they've left the strong-rooms. Theo and I'd best duck under cover now." He wasn't sure which perturbed him more, the daggers strapped on their forearms, or the fact that Holly and Theo resembled bandits, handkerchiefs shrouding noses and mouths. Even Khim and P'roul had small pieces of cloth over their muzzles, and looked none too happy about it. At least it might cut down on the tickle, the dust they'd inhale from the straw and hay once they were buried in the hayrack.

"Yes, I . . ." without forethought he hugged Holly, Theo as well. "Lady watch over you and all those whom we hold dear." They swung into the back of the wagon, wobbling across the soft, uncertain footing until they stepped onto the open rectangle of hay bales at the wagon's center, waiting for Joressa and Warburg to remove the rolled blankets molding a space for them. Both lay as close to the seat as possible, the ghattas nestled near their heads.

"Let's be quick, now," Ezequiel cautioned, then wished he'd said nothing. What did he know of loading and packing hay? All of his training as chamberlain had never prepared him for that, and Joressa and Warburg, aided by two elderly stablehands with pitchforks, and two housemaids, both farm-born, worked at layering comforters and straw. His greatest contribution had been boosting up Joressa and the others, all perfectly spry once they were aboard.

"Bit like packing eggs for transit, sir," one of the housemaids had informed him, working on hands and knees to pack an even layer of straw. "And we're being twice as careful."

He still had no idea how they'd manage to breathe crammed in like that, and the mere thought of it turned him claustrophobic, breath tight, neck itching in anticipation of the tickle of the dried blades. Levering himself up, not wanting to venture any further aboard and disturb things, he caught Joressa's attention. "They won't . . . smother, will they?"

Blades of straw stuck to her, pieces speared in her white hair, on her apron and skirt, her sleeves. "They'll be warmer than warm, that's for certain. And I'm thankful I'm busy, or I'd be colder than cold." Stepping with exaggerated care, she crossed the length of the wagonbed and turned back, saying, "More on each side now, quick, quick. Layer of straw, layer of comforter, get it as high as it is in front, that's my dears! Remember, more on top once the trunk's in place, then a loose tie-down on the sides with the canvas." Reaching out a hand, he helped her sit on the tailgate, handing her his own handkerchief to wipe her face.

"Lunwahl," she called, "you still have a piece of the transport cylinder to show Mr. Dunay?" Something white changed hands until it reached Joressa, and she slipped it on her wrist like a bracelet. "Not much to show like this, but imagine it longer, sir." Holding out her wrist, she let him examine it. It seemed to be of heavy, reinforced paper with ribbing of some sort. "Thankee, Lunny," she said over her shoulder. "Twas an inspired idea." Turning back, she continued, "doubt you know Lunny much atall, being as he's gardening staff. When he was more nimble, he used to help at the arborfer nurseries ofttimes. They use tubes like these to transport the arborfer seedlings. Near impossible to crush them. Still had some extra around in the greenhouses. We laid down two for breathing tubes, though I can't guarantee how well they'll work. Lucille worked straw and hay through pieces of net, then stuck in random pieces to disguise the openings."

"Inspired is right! Bless you, Lunny, Lucille!" And he meant it, wanting to kiss them all for their hard labor, their quiet courage and cleverness, even Warburg grumping less than usual, taking orders from lesser servants who knew more than a wardrobe master about how to pack straw. He'd refused to be denied a role, had returned once he'd seen the king and Arras suitably attired.

"Here they come!" One of the four unarmed soldiers allotted to patrol the courtyard's perimeters, as per Romain-Laurent's demands, waved both arms in the air. "Get them down from the wagon, Dunay! Then all of you back off." Two more soldiers came trotting out with a loading ramp and placed it at the wagon's rear.

"Might have thought of that afore!" Joressa snapped at them as Ezequiel swung her down, then gave Lunny a hand.

"Sorry, ma'am. Thought you'd ask if you needed such." He gave Joressa a half-salute, half-bow. " 'Sides, Lieutenant said as how we should try to keep Dunay busy, occupied as much as possible so he wouldn't have as much time to worry."

"Well, don't concern yourself, I've had sufficient time, believe me," Ezequiel snapped, then gasped as he saw Cinzia and Urban in their smallclothes, limping barefoot across the cobbles, the trunk between them. The trunk! If only he'd never discovered it, or if only he'd never bothered to search for the key! And now, here it was, coming right at him again, Urban and Cinzia walking with exaggerated caution, wincing as the cold cobbles stung their feet.

Up, up the ramp, Cinzia leading, Urban behind, having the heavier job on the slope, the trunk's weight shifting toward him. Should Cinzia slip, lose her grip, the trunk would probably take him down with it. Their bare flesh rippled with goose bumps from the cold, from nerves as well, Ezequiel had no doubt, and shivered in sympathy. A restrained hoot from Joressa as she caught sight of Urban's scarlet briefs with their appliqué, but Ezequiel didn't allow himself to react, more intent on who followed after Cinzia and Urban. "Make sure the trunk's well-covered," and despite the instructions for him to remain in place, he took several steps forward, unable to help himself.

Anger burned through him, searing enough to ignite the straw, as the helpless captives came stumbling across the courtyard, Romain-Laurent just behind them, and was literally sickened as he realized what was hanging around their necks. That sick, sorry bastard had a Plumb around Telka's neck, another around his own! Well, sick and sorry he might be, but clearly Romain-Laurent was no fool. Would

Khim and P'roul sense they carried Plumbs, warn Theo and Holly?

Calmness, he instructed himself, briefly shutting his eyes against the travesty. La'ow and Hru'rul will warn them. Now it's hopeless, and whether or not Romain-Laurent will ever know it, he's gained two more human hostages, plus two ghattas! Of course they'd known what they were about to attempt was dangerous, but not a one of them had ever considered the possibility that Romain-Laurent would booby-trap himself and his hostages with the Plumbs!

Closer now, and Telka's spectacles had steamed from the cold, gave her trouble seeing, made her scuff her feet to sense if any of the cobbles had a dangerous raised edge to catch an unwary toe. She was bent forward, the Plumb dragging at her, Francie's pale face just visible behind her head as Telka half-carried her on her back. Well behind the trio, walking with calculated slowness, maintaining their distance, came Eadwin and Arras, Harry and the lady Fabienne.

Aware he had no right, was disobeying instructions and might further jeopardize things, Ezequiel stripped off his coat, his shirt and undervest until he was bare from the waist up. Waved the shirt to attract Romain-Laurent's attention, then kept both arms up and out from his sides. "Romain-Laurent, may I help the Lady Francie and Telka mount the wagon box?" How in the hells did Charpentier think he was going to get them up there, the two of them trussed together like that, the child weighed down with both the Lady Francie and the Plumb!

"Part of your household training, Ezequiel? How to graciously assist ladies, smooth over the most awkward situations?" Romain-Laurent's hand ran up and down over the Plumb around his neck as he looked from the high seat of the wagon to his hostages and back again. "Come ahead, but stay as clear of the child as possible. I want to see where your hands are at all times."

Numbly, even humbly, he approached the front of the hayrack, the team of four standing, swaying in their harness, one checking the cobbles in the hope of locating some spilled oats. He waited, trying to emulate the horses' calm acceptance, both glad and dismayed that he stood behind Telka and Francie, unable to see their faces. "I'm going up first." Romain-Laurent swung himself up on the high front wheel. "I'll guide from up here. Move up and join them, Ezequiel."

"Francie, Telka," he struggled to keep his voice even, emotionless. "I'm to help. Telka, do you think you can get up there if I lift Francie on my shoulder while you climb?"

Telka bobbed her head. How could he have forgotten she was gagged!

"I won't let you fall," he promised as he knelt directly behind Francie, bending forward as he reached for her waist. She was a petite woman, birdlike, and he had no worry about the weight, merely how to do it, especially since she couldn't hang on, help at all. Then he realized something worse: Telka's ankles were hobbled together! There was no way she could climb properly! "Romain-Laurent! May I untie Telka's feet?" He'd gnaw through the binding if he had to!

Hanging off the seat, Romain-Laurent glared downward, "I *told* you you'd forget something! Something *so* obvious! And haven't I been proved right!" His grimace frightened Ezequiel, the condescending twist to his mouth, so supercilious! "Just when I think you can be trusted, you prove how unworthy you are!"

The Lady Francie's voice came softly, as if she were far distant in everything but body. "Just do it, Ezequiel. Don't act furtive about it, make sure he sees what you're doing. Another Romain-Laurent will approve. Now I'd best shift the gag back in place," and she rubbed against Telka's head, working it back across her lips.

The knots were sheer misery, his hands shaking with the cold, his bare skin viciously complaining of the breeze. A stifled oath as a fingernail bent, then ripped. "Haven't you got it yet?" Now Romain-Laurent sounded only mildly curious, not angry. "Oh, here! We haven't got all day!" and a penknife not much bigger than a cheese paring skittered across the cobbles. The blade, when Ezequiel finally pried it open, using his teeth, was mayhap three centimeters long, a half-centimeter wide—the good castle silver included snail picks that were more dangerous! But it was razor-sharp, and he sliced away, making progress until at last the hobble parted.

"Now toss it back," Charpentier instructed and Ezequiel

complied, wondering what in the world Romain-Laurent ever found it useful for—sharpening pencils, mayhap? Or . . . tormenting little creatures, like the mouse? It clattered as it hit the floorboards. "Come on, now."

Docilely, Telka planted a foot on a spoke, clinging to the wheel rim with both hands. Again he readied himself to lift Francie, seating her on his shoulder and rising partway, legs protesting at the position he must maintain until Telka could climb higher and he could raise Francie accordingly. At last, making a stirrup of his hands, his whole body quivering with effort, he raised Francie the final way, Romain-Laurent hauling her in atop Telka.

There was nothing more to do, to say—even if Romain-Laurent wanted to hear, would hear—so Ezequiel stood back, arms rigid at his sides, gazing at Romain-Laurent as he picked up the reins and clucked to the horses. The hayrack's wheels crunched and clattered on the cobbles as they headed for the main gates, and Ezequiel sorrowed as he never had before.

♣

Wiping her face with a forearm, Jacobia continued speaking to the clay being, regaling it with tales of its past, of its place in this new world, imbuing it with purpose. Her voice grew hoarse and time was running short—her concentration broken whenever Diccon reported what Kwee had heard, what he had gleaned with his Resonant powers. The being *had* gained some mobility, could shift as Callis instructed, had rolled over with a stolid obedience to allow Feather to fashion its back. Now Feather molded the finishing touches along its spine, creating the spaces between the vertebrae by pinching her thumbs together, for all the world like a cook crimping the edge of a pie crust.

Occasionally Nakum spelled Jacobia, reciting more old tales, some familiar to Jacobia in a strange way, and others totally new. Mostly she leaned against Diccon, then, listening to Nakum, half-hearing anything Diccon might tell her about the goings-on aboveground. Quaintance, back against the wall, sat dozily, her head bobbing, lolling, before she jerked herself back to the present.

"They're approaching the hayrack," Diccon reported. "Don't think Auntie Francie's holding up very well. The little girl's pretty tired, too." Then he jumped up, Jacobia slumping flat on the floor at the abrupt loss of support, stalking up and down the tunnel, beating his fist against the palm of his hand. "Damn! Damn, damn, damn! I *don't* believe it! He's hung a Plumb 'round his own neck, one around the little girl's!" He wheeled and stood facing the wall, thumping his head against it, face contracted with pain. "It's so *easy*! All he has to do is punch the buttons if anyone disturbs him, poses a threat!"

"And mayhap it was chance that he pushed the right buttons, created the right sequence before," Callis soothed. "Something he'll never again replicate—at least not without a great deal of time and effort."

Skirts rustling and dragging as she levered her bottom into the air, Quaintance Mercilot worked her way up the wall, dirty little hands scrabbling until she reached her full height, panting but triumphant. "He won't know, lad! Callis is right. 'Cording to the king and Arras, he didn't set off the first one intentional-like. Don't want to count my Plumbs before they're hatched," she gave a cackle, "but I don't think he can hatch'em as easy-like as he thinks."

"Mayhap he can't, but we can't count on it," Diccon retorted. "And it's a bitter, cruel thing to force someone to carry her potential death around her neck!"

Feather cleared her throat and they turned, she and the being she'd molded becoming the focus of all attention. "It's as ready as it's going to be. Now it's up to you." An edge of challenge to her words, Jacobia thought, she can't help it, it just comes out. I know how she feels, share a certain disbelief as well, and with far better reason. My heritage never prepared me for anything even remotely like this.

Her hand rested in Nakum's now, and she had no idea when he'd taken it—or if she'd reached out to him for comfort. "Believe," he murmured, drawing her to her feet. "Believe! Hold your earth-bond tight and close your eyes, will it to *be*, will it into *being*!" The Trickster hovered over his shoulder, humming, pitch rising in intensity, throbs flowing through its green-gold surface.

Callis knelt by the being now, stroking its shoulder, and

Jacobia could sense its quiescent power. "To make it whole it needs something from us—a bond, a pact of its own with us." She sawed at the hem of her doeskin skirt with her knife, hacking off a rough strip. "Diccon, it's time—you first."

"But what could I have that might help it live?" Genuine puzzlement at first, followed by a yelp of glee. "The plum pit! It even *sounds* appropriate, on top of everything else!"

But it was more than that, and Jacobia instantly saw in her mind's eye a world she'd never visited, but Diccon had—the world within—and how near Diccon had been to succumbing, accidentally tempted to remain there forever. Someday she might be privileged to visit that world as well, didn't begrudge Diccon his unique visit, but did envy him for it.

Around Callis went, collecting something from each of them: a whisker from Kwee, a broach from Quaintance, who whispered, " 'Tis arborfer, from long ago, freely given by the tree and by me in this time of need." And when she came to Feather, she paused without speaking as Feather held up cupped but empty hands.

"What I give is what I've received of late—wisdom, humility, the new knowledge that I can accomplish things beyond me before."

Without speaking, Jacobia removed her earth-bond, lifting the thong over her head and placing the pouch in Callis' waiting hand. "Are you sure, child?" Chin jutting, she nodded once, the most she could manage, hands fisted so she wouldn't be tempted to snatch it back.

Nakum reverently lifted his knife and drew the blade across the fleshy part of his palm just below the thumb, letting ten drops of blood flow into his great-great-grandmother's hand before closing his fingers over the wound.

Wordlessly Callis took each gift and wrapped them in the doeskin fragment before driving her stiffened fingers into the being's back just between its left shoulder blade and the spine. Inserting the small package, she closed over the fissure with caressing strokes, singing under her breath, Jacobia instinctively joining in, the plangent beauty of the tune winding itself around her, around and through them all. The being began to move, rolling over and sitting up, dazedly shaking its head, hands on its knees.

They heard it then, the rattle of wheels on the cobbles. "Hurry!" pleaded Diccon. "They're leaving! Oh, hurry, please!" Callis sang harder, contorted with effort, concentrating with all her might, and Jacobia struggled to ascend to that same transcending plane, the effort tearing at her until she feared she might burst. Nakum joined in, then Feather, and with each new incremental addition, the being gained strength, but still it seemed stuporous, sluggish.

"So close!" Callis groaned, rocking back and forth on her knees. "Harder! Harder!" she exhorted, the cords on her neck standing out, her hands clawing at the air. "Can't . . . can't quite . . .! Oh, Great Spirit—we beg You, please!"

Chirping, its green-gold fulgently, blindingly bright, the Trickster somersaulted from Nakum's shoulder and dove into the being's ear, its eyes suddenly alive, lambent with newfound comprehension. Gaining its knees, it rested its shoulders and head against the tunnel roof, straining upward with all its might. . . .

❖

With each turn of the wheel, with each clank of a shod hoof, Romain-Laurent dared hope a little more, his eyes flicking left and right. Had they truly been stupid enough to believe those hidden archers and crossbow-men of any use, think he'd provide a willing target? Should have painted circles on his back, invited them to shoot—let a quarrel pass through him and it'd strike the Plumb. Oh, to thumb his nose at them all, the fools!

Yes, he'd *succeeded,* Lady Change smiling on him from above! As the hayrack ponderously rolled forward, his sense of jubilation ratcheted higher and tighter. Oh, glory, joy! Hosannas in the highest to Lady Change and to Romain-Laurent Charpentier, her agent, her acolyte, her equal! How absolutely intoxicating, like being drunk, he rhapsodized, and the horde joined in. A new age dawning, exhilarating, inspiring, invigorating! How Change flowed through his veins, quickening him with desire, a galvanic vitality, setting his feet into a little jig of their own making, though he sat poised and still, hands steady on the reins. Surely his face glowed with the incandescence of a thousand suns, his body expanding with the power of the Plumbs! Crack-brained, eh? Impossible to pull off? Start small—never! He'd thrown the dice and Lady Change and her sister, Lady Chance, had both smiled on him, would continue benevolently smiling on him forever!

The left lead horse tossed its head, acting skittish, throwing its weight centerward toward its harness-mate, and Romain-Laurent fought to straighten them. A mere horse had *no* right to make him look foolish in their eyes, all pity for him erased, replaced by awe! Triumphant! Ah, to look back, gloat at those naysayers, all of them now aware, overwhelmed by his superiority, transcending their petty desire that life remain unchanged, untouched! Invisible hands pounded his back, the horde convinced, confident in him, even the supercilious and autocratic congratulating him, admitting their initial doubts had been *so* wrong. Well, he'd remember which voices had supported him, those who'd doubted and denied, carped and complained, practically wringing him dry. They might not be visiting very often now—he and his unwavering supporters would wall them out, refuse them entry!

Damn! The left wheel-horse was nervy as well, its skin rippling, its ears planted back, its gait off. Checking leftward to discover what was disturbing them so, he watched with dismay that turned to incredulity as the cobbles began to heave and buckle with a rumbling, tearing noise that gradually increased in volume. *Not* his imagination! The expression on the woman's and child's heartsick faces told him that, that they, too, were experiencing the same things. The rumbling, crunching sounds increased in volume, punctuated by the snap of wood, cobbles now flying into the air like lethal missiles, the horses going crazy, fighting the reins, rearing in place, screaming, determined to snap their lead lines. Damn it, *no*! It couldn't be a Plumb—*he* had the Plumbs, all of them! *His* Plumbs!

A mound the color of red clay rose through the loosened cobbles, the courtyard hatching like some giant, monstrous egg. It continued extruding itself until it reared nearly one-and-a-half meters high—near to his shoulder, if he'd been fool enough to be standing next to it, and certainly higher than the horses' backs! With a leisurely grace the mound began a slow rotation, and Romain-Laurent started to scream, his voice joining the horses' hysterical cries. Lady, oh, dear Lady! It was a *face,* turning to deliberately examine him and the wagon, its eyes an assessing, challenging green-gold that made his bowels all watery!

The wagon-tongue snapped, one of the horses falling and tangling with it, hampering the others, pulling another down with it, but Romain-Laurent sat bemused and bewildered on the rocking hayrack, uncaring that his passengers had tumbled beneath the seat. Transfixed, he watched, watched it grow, shoulders popping through, first one monumental arm and then the other drawn out from the earth mounding around it. It flexed shoulder and elbow joints as if to work out the stiffness. Then, palms flat against the rubble, the thing began levering itself out of the hole it had fashioned, one leg at a time, thighs thick as ancient trees, rippling with muscle beneath the reddish exterior. Again it went through a series of limbering motions, folding a leg at the knee, pulling against the foot with the opposite hand, stretching the leg to its full length, rotating the ankle, then kicking out a foot as if planning to kick Romain-Laurent and the hayrack.

What on earth was it! *Earth was it . . . earth was it?* He wanted to close his eyes, yes, just close his eyes, render it invisible—and then it would vanish, wouldn't it? Of course it would! The stress, the anxiety of the past few days, the fever pitch he'd been at since well before dawn . . . not to mention the tedium of octants past, worn down by inattention, stupidity, cupidity, suffering their jokes and insults . . . ! Yes, that was it, had to be it! *Earth was it . . . was it earth . . . it was earth . . . What on earth . . . ?*

It stood foursquare in front of the hayrack now, and had he possessed sufficient courage, plus a willing team, he could have driven beneath it, right between its colossal legs. Hands rested on the slim hips, and the being let the full majesty of its green-gold orbs burn down on him, scrutinize him as if he were worthless, so much dust. . . .

"LITTLE MAN, FOOLISH, IGNORANT LITTLE MAN, WANTONLY DESTROYING AND WOUNDING THAT WHICH GIVES YOU STRENGTH AND SUSTENANCE, THAT WHICH COMPRISES PART OF YOUR VERY BEING . . ."

❖

A horse screamed again, louder, and Holly was jolted and jarred as the wagon was bodily shoved backward, an iron wheel-rim setting up a hair-raising screech against the cobbles. She'd been paralyzed in her straw bed, disbelieving what she was hearing, what P'roul was describing, the ghatta frantically transmitting the descriptions pouring forth from La'ow and Hru'rul. As the hayrack started to lean, Holly clutched her knife and readied herself to burst clear, truly not sure what chaos would meet her eyes.

"Now!" she screamed at Theo. Why worry?—Romain-Laurent was hardly likely to notice, given what was already going on! Damnation, the wagon rested on two wheels now, tottering, ready to tip any moment, slam them all—plus the Plumbs—flat on their sides. As she and Theo groggily emerged, she stumbled, colliding with her cousin, damn near impaling herself on his knife. Somehow he shoved her clear, Khim and P'roul scrambling, clawing their way out more successfully than they had. Mimicking the ghattas, she clawed at anything within reach, dragging herself forward, prepared to fling herself at Romain-Laurent, who clung with both hands to the seat edge. Better her than Theo; she had no compunction of running him through, couldn't wait for the chance! Let Theo untangle Francie and Telka, mashed together in a heap against the hayrack's side.

Damn! No joy! The hayrack was overturning—jump or go down with it, go after Romain-Laurent once they landed if she didn't break both arms and legs. **"Or get blown up,"** P'roul mentioned with a stunning prosaicality. **"Watch your head now! He's even more solid than he looks!"**

A huge arm loomed over her, the hand clamped on the hayrack's raised side and pressing downward, righting it without effort. Now the reddish hand plucked up Romain-Laurent as if he were an insect and held him high in the air, the man's legs spasmodically jerking, his mouth wide in an unending, unearthly howl. Attempt to analyze what she saw and she'd never succeed—besides, she had other, more rational things to do. "Theo, free the Plumb from around Telka's neck and pass it back! Cut them free if you can, get them out!" Figures springing across the courtyard—Eadwin, Arras, Ezequiel, soldiers—Theo'd have help.

With unerring aim Theo tossed the Plumb to her and she caught it in both arms, holding it close. **"Very nice. Now what do you plan on doing with it?"** Khim asked for him.

"Ah . . ." This was *so* blasted unfair! Didn't want the damn thing, wanted it gone, far, far way, and here she was . . . saddled with it. On impulse, she held it up in the air, almost offering it to the ruddy clay being still curiously staring at a squalling Romain-Laurent. With surprising daintiness it took the Plumb from her—no doubt the Plumb appeared about the size of a peanut to the giant being!

Opening its mouth, it dropped it in, jaw muscles flexing as it masticated, and Holly heard a distinct pop, its green-gold eyes momentarily bulging, a wisp of smoke trailing from its mouth. Well, if it hadn't suffered any ill effects, she had a few more "peanuts" for it, and began furiously tossing straw and comforters aside, burrowing through the layers, throwing bales of hay anywhere she could, uncaring, desperate to get at the Plumbs. Somehow Ezequiel had climbed beside her, was digging away as well, until the anodized aluminum of the trunk lid came into view.

"Grab the handle and lift straight up, then to me!" He did, but refused to relinquish it, forcing his end down and flipping open the lid.

The being watched with curiosity, and when it realized what Ezequiel was hefting from the trunk, it held its hand down again, palm out. As Ezequiel passed each Plumb to her, she laid it on the being's palm until all four nested there. Shaking her head, waving her hands in front of her to reveal empty palms in the universal gesture of "all gone," she waited to see what would happen.

Lifting its hand to its mouth, it licked all four Plumbs off, then—almost greedily—eyed the one remaining Plumb, still dangling around Romain-Laurent's neck. It raised Romain-Laurent to its lips in an almost-kiss and nipped off his Plumb.

"Oh, dear Lady!" Ezequiel groaned and grabbed her around the waist, pulling Holly down into the straw and comforters, throwing himself over her, P'roul already beside him.

The explosion continued for the longest time, not the

same sharp, percussive report of the Plumb that had exploded beneath the castle, but a low, never-ending rumble that bounced the hayrack like a child's toy, bits of cobbles floating by, the distant tinkle of breaking window glass. She spared a moment of sorrow for one of the horses as it levitated in the air, knowing it wouldn't land properly, would break a leg.

A haze, a reddish hue that tinted Ezequiel's bare back, that hung cloudlike in the sky before it finally began to sift and settle. Breaking free from Ezequiel's grasp, not ungently, she slithered on her belly to peer over the side, but instead of the damage she expected, the sole thing to greet her eye was an immense heap of reddish dust, and on one side of it—in darker, near-black dust—the silhouette of a human-sized figure, tiny in comparison to the mound.

"What . . . happened?" Spying the silhouette, Ezequiel leaned over the side and was noisily sick.

"I . . . don't know." And she didn't. Didn't think she wanted to know, wondering if some things in life weren't better left unpondered, unexplained. *"P'roul, if you know, please don't enlighten me. Mayhap someday, but not right now."*

P'roul treated her to a slanticular look, then continued grooming her white front, removing every particle of red dust from it. **"Merowmepurr's here, Perowmepurr, too,"** she said to no one in particular. **"We're in for it, sibling-mine. The exploding custables were nothing compared to this!"**

❧

Oo-oo-ee-WAH! WAH-WOO! Ya, ya, ya, YA! WAH! Although it had initially gotten off to an inauspicious start in Sidonie, the Trickster had finally found friends, fertile ground for its pranks and capers. Seldom had it been allowed to indulge in so much fun, frolic like that, perplex and please people simultaneously. Even just thinking about it, gave it a heady feeling that made it swell with pride.

But right now it was halfway to the Stratocums, and letting no grass grow under its feet. Not that it had bothered with feet, had resumed its spherical shape, still slightly singed in spots, and with a tendency to erupt with gas as if suffering from indigestion. And in a way, it had. In fact, right now, it had had enough of trickery and taunts and teasing, wanted nothing more than the safe solitude of the world within. It didn't think it would need to venture forth for a very, very long time, had consumed enough human emotions, both good and evil, to last it for season upon season, and all seasons rolled into one.

Despite the fact that spinning too fast sometimes fanned the embers still glowing in its furzy surface, it couldn't help itself, spun and spun like a sparkling globe, then dove into a snowbank to cool off. Stop by and see Addawanna, say farewell? Mayhap. Best get back to the world within before Callis caught up with it. After all, it had spun off without taking leave, though it didn't think she'd mind this time.

Oo-oo-OO-ee-WAH!

♣

"I'm still not sure I understand." Sitting cross-legged on the foot of the royal bed, he leaned intimately toward Callis, unsure whether or not their conversation could be overheard. Frustrated, he combed through his beard with his fingers as if it were a live thing—soothe it and mayhap he could soothe himself. Callis, seated similarly on the bed, seemed more interested in studying the cha cup and saucer poised in the center of her lap.

The whole thing was absurd, Eadwin thought, a little desperately, and if not absurd, more than enough to boggle the mind. ("Discombobulate," Callis whispered, apropos of nothing.) Certainly he was doggedly stubborn in his own way, and determined to get to the bottom of this *thing,* this incident, this . . . this piece of . . . *legend come to life . . .*" And here he sat with what?—near twenty people crammed into his bedroom—witnesses, major and minor players alike in what had so recently transpired.

People shifted, mingling, resting, eating, and he found himself momentarily watching Quaintance Mercilot holding court, mudstained and outrageous, enjoying herself, flirting with Diccon and Urban, now at least suitably attired! His dear Maman, graciously circulating as if this were an entirely normal reception . . . Cinzia, Theo and Holly, Ezequiel. From out of nowhere Diccon Wycherley and his attractive aunt, Jacobia Wycherley, and more. Hadn't Arras mentioned Diccon and Jenneth had run away? Well, not exactly run away . . . but how had Jacobia come to be here . . . and where was Jenneth? True, the castle contained more suitable rooms for entertaining this many people, rooms far more graciously appointed and correct for informal gatherings. But this bedchamber felt utterly familiar, secure, comfortable—and still had two extra beds, now occupied by Francie and Telka, bruised and tired, but recovering despite their harrowing experience. No wonder Harry and Arras refused to leave their sides! Try again, see if Callis would answer. "What precisely happened? What was *that*? Is Romain-Laurent dead, poor soul? Did that . . . being kill him?" Not a death to be mourned, more to be celebrated, but he experienced a touch of sorrow for the poor, deluded soul, a touch of responsibility as well.

A royal guard made his way to his side, whispering, "Sire, that hillock of dust in the courtyard?" As if Eadwin wouldn't know what he was talking about! "Sire, it's gone! Vanished, a small whirlwind came spinning through, scooped it all up, and carried it away! What should we do about it?" What should he do about it? Order it chased? Tracked down and required to return the dust? And such a great deal of dust, a veritable mountain of it, as if a wagon had deposited a load of dirt in the courtyard.

"Do? Nothing, Marsteller, absolutely nothing. Just see the courtyard's swept to remove any lingering traces, make sure the sweepings are respectfully disposed of." A bow, a look of relief at having a directive, odd though it might be, and the guard retired just as Nakum and the young Erakwan woman Callis had referred to as Feather entered, hands linked, both looking very mudstained but highly pleased with themselves as they made their way through the throng of sitting and standing people, people lounging on the floor.

"All taken care of?" And Nakum and Feather nodded at Callis, just a trace of a smile on all three faces, a secret sharing amongst the three of them.

"These remained behind." Nakum deposited an antique

arborfer broach and a stained earth-bond in Callis's lap, and Eadwin briefly noted a nasty slash on his hand.

Blast it all, for every question he'd asked Callis, a convenient interruption had delayed or deflected her answer! Mayhap it was intentional—he'd not put it past her. Oh, to hide in bed, pull the covers over his head, forget about everything!

"I suppose you might say that Romain-Laurent was transformed, dispersed." If that wasn't a euphemism, Eadwin didn't know what it was! Not to mention a nonanswer! Death was certainly a transformation from one state to another—from a state of being to one of nonbeing, nonexistence—in other words, dead! But how . . . what . . . ?

Start at the beginning—except *what*, precisely, was the beginning? Or the ending, come to think on it? The longer he pondered what had occurred, the more his mind endlessly remade, remolded the facts, sweeping some entirely away (like the dust?)—too preposterous, impossible to have witnessed, let alone *believe*. Near twenty people, those sequestered in this room, had seen at least some of the events; more if he added in the bowmen stationed in secluded spots, the servants who'd loaded the hayrack. Something over thirty in total, and already a tone of denial had crept into certain voices, a self-consciousness, and in later years he didn't doubt that they'd deny or downplay what they'd witnessed with their own eyes. *That* was why he so desperately wanted *to know, to understand now,* while he could, his mind open, malleable enough to be receptive to any and every thing.

Travelstained, the lines around her mouth and eyes emphasized by a light coating of grime, Doyce Marbon and Khar made their way to his bed. Ah, the poor, dear ghatta looked her age, her numerous aches announcing themselves with each cautious step! He'd fleetingly noticed Doyce's and Jenret's arrival shortly after the worst had happened— with strangely, *blessedly* anticlimatic results as far as the explosion was concerned—but hadn't been able to properly greet them. After embracing Callis, she turned her attention on him, and he took her hand, kissing it. "Ah, you've finally decided to leave your husband, become my queen!"

"Not yet." Ah, she looked tired, though not as worried as when he'd first glimpsed her. "But I promise that should

I ever decide to abandon Jenret for greener pastures, I'll seriously consider your offer."

"But there are undoubtedly so many that mine will be lost, mislaid. Nor is it especially heartening to be compared to a verdant meadow!" It felt good to banter, pretend that nothing untoward had happened—but it had, it *had*. "At least you've found some of your missing lambs, Diccon and Jacobia. I heard about Mahafny, and I'm so sorry, Doyce. Please convey my regrets to Jenret, as well. I know how much she meant to you both."

Struggling to conquer her emotions, she gave a tight smile. "I've still two more to collect— Jenneth and Harrap, not to mention Pw'eek and Parm and Saam. Callis, can we leave in the morning? We need your help to reach the mountaintop. Old age," she confided wryly, "and entirely too much travel and worry."

How he longed to accompany them, walk those peaceful, snowy trails, feel his body ache from exertion, the good kind of physical exhaustion, the demands on the body obliterating the mind's worries! Soon, mayhap soon. Well, by late spring, at the least, he admitted more realistically. After all, refugees needed to be returned to their homes, a city needing rebuilding, a way of life to be reconstructed, though not identically reconstructed, mayhap gradually altered, expanded in new directions.

"If we may," Doyce continued, "we'll return afterward. I hate to leave Francie so soon after this, but I must. Still, when we return . . ." she drifted off, not sounding happy. "We'll talk more later, Eadwin." And that would have to suffice him as she returned to Jenret's side.

A stir as Holly and Ezequiel carried in something between them, and Eadwin fought to control himself, not visibly flinch at the sight of the anodized aluminum trunk, now more dented and battered than before. There was nothing in it, it was merely a trunk, the Plumbs gone, consumed, disabled. "A souvenir?" Holly sounded unsure. "I didn't think it wise to simply leave it lying about. A souvenir and a reminder."

She was right, though he doubted he'd ever need a reminder. But then again, mayhap he would. "Did . . . that being really . . . consume the Plumbs, somehow internalize their explosion?" No wonder all they'd found was a heap of dust!

"That's what appeared to happen," Ezequiel said stiffly, almost defensively. "At least we've not yet found any other logical explanation. Have you?"

No, he hadn't—doubted he would. "Just remember that the land, the earth, takes care of its own," and Callis smiled over the rim of her cha cup, "and that we are all its caretakers, its stewards."

Raising his own cup, he saluted her. "I'll drink to that!'

❖

"Do they realize?" An imprecise query, ambiguous enough for Callis to respond in any number of directions and still adamantly claim to have answered—he should have known better. Restive, Nakum resorted to something he'd not done since childhood: he cracked his knuckles. Parm started, ears flattening, ready to scurry to safety, then looked at him quizzically, waiting to see if he'd do it again. Come to think on it, there were many things he wondered if Outlanders realized, even the best of them, like Eadwin, or Doyce and Jenret, or Arras. Others, too, more than he'd once thought: Jacobia, Diccon, and Jenneth, Ezequiel, Harrap, and even more in Marchmont, all gradually learning, growing, changing . . . just as he was. Look at what they'd accomplished together! Hadn't it taken the joint courage and wisdom of Outlander and Erakwa to conquer the menace of the Plumbs, rescue the earth?

Harrap, standing with them, watched as Doyce and Jenret, Saam, Khar, Rawn walked by the tall, barren remains of Hatachawa. "They've an inkling. At least Parm believes they should have." Ceaselessly spinning the hair bracelet on his wrist, he subsided only when Callis overlaid it with her hand.

Wriggling on his back in the snow, Parm viewed them upside-down. **"It's been building toward it. At least a year now, since their Sunderlies visit. And before, though the signs weren't as obvious."** Righting himself, he shook his fur into place, licking a recalcitrant orange patch that insisted on sticking up. **"I sympathize, but I'm far from ready yet."**

"And the Lady bless you for that!" Harrap fervently formed the sign of the eight-pointed star, only to fidget in embarrassment, realizing where he stood. The Shepherd still wasn't entirely at ease in viewing the Great Spirit as another possible guise for his Lady, and Nakum shared a smile with Callis.

"A little wager on it?" Well, one thing had to be said for Callis: she never ceased to surprise Nakum. To his way of thinking this hardly seemed a betting matter, but she must have her reasons. For that matter, Harrap looked near as scandalized as Nakum felt.

Best call her on it; if he didn't, both Addawanna and Callis would undoubtedly make life difficult for him! Mayhap Callis had already indulged in some sort of wager with Diccon and Jenneth, and it puzzled him that they weren't here, that they'd remained within the egg-shaped domicile playing cribbage. Or attempting to, since Kwee and Pw'eek were adeptly stealing the pegs. No doubt when—or rather, if—if he ever got his home back to himself, he'd find some in the most unlikely places, including his bed.

**"The twins know, agreed they couldn't bear to watch the actual moment. They said what had to be said at first light, Pw'eek and Kwee, too. That's why they skipped breakfast, took care of the arborfer, only dared come in once Doyce and Jenret went outside. Jacobia and Addawanna have things to discuss, nor did Jacobia feel it was her place, as a non-Seeker."**

It made a certain sense; Diccon, especially, would be unable to school himself to any neutral expression. Though he felt no lighter of heart than the twins, Nakum had a stake in the happenings, because at the end the burden would become his, and he'd bear it with gladness, in full awareness of the special honor. Hadn't planned it that way—but mayhap Callis had.

"So what's the wager?" Lacking much in the way of worldly goods to wager with, Nakum debated what to bet. More likely, Callis would set the price—some task she wanted done. "Harrap? Are you in or not?" Funny to coax a Shepherd into gambling, taking a fling on Fortuna, Fate, Chance, but who knew? Mayhap his Lady found it had redeeming virtues in certain instances. After all, the Great Spirit didn't take it amiss.

"It's not going to be a lighthearted trip down the mountain," Harrap mused, rubbing at his thigh where he'd caught it in the crevice. Nakum tended to agree, relieved he'd not be of the party. "But yes, I'm in." Parm danced his excitement, paws high-stepping. "We'll not be taking the mountain sheep, will we?" A sigh of relief when Callis told him no.

"Now, as to our bet." Even Callis's gaiety sounded forced to Nakum, her sharp eyes rarely veering from the figures in the near distance, Jenret extravagantly gesturing and exclaiming. "Harrap, if you win, the wager is that you and Parm will journey to the Sunderlies this spring."

"I wouldn't mind in a way." Mulling it over further, he confided, "I'd like to meet Dannae, the female Shepherd, and that woman called Bullybess. Visit another land, some place different—and warm!" The more he elaborated, the more enthusiastic he waxed, and Nakum hoped he was slowly beginning to heal after Mahafny's loss.

"What are *you* wagering, before *I* decide what to bet?" Without a doubt Callis was up to something, his body tingling with anticipation, though he just couldn't quite sense *what* she planned, hoped her wager might offer a clue. Turning full-circle, she surveyed the mountains and peaks and clouds surrounding them with gladness and longing, as if she'd embrace them all to her if she could. "That *I* will pay more attention to the here-and-now, come visit you and Addawanna more often and with greater regularity. I've been remiss in certain ways." A twinkle in her eyes. "Not quite as onerous as it might seem!"

"Ha! With that to look forward to, I hope you lose!" Oh, what a gift! Enough to make him shout for joy, race to search out Addawanna and tell her the news. "Now, what shall I wager?" He struck a pose, resting his chin on his hand, pretending to engage in deep thought.

"If you win, then you'll visit Eadwin more often—and get to know Feather better. She's decided to continue her eumedico training in Sidonie to be closer to home, have a chance to visit more often, relearn things she'd dismissed or disregarded too long."

He fought not to groan. *More* trips away from his beloved arborfer? Once spring came, he'd be so busy with his seedlings, some youngsters ready for transplanting lower on the mountain under Roland's care. But . . . an opportunity to educate Outlanders to the role of the land, of nature and its creatures? Would Feather be willing to help—two birds with one arrow, so to speak? "Wait! This is all backward, isn't it?" Ah, Callis was clever, sly, and tricky! More devious than that impish Trickster! "What do you mean, we pay up when we win? You've gotten it all wrong—it's supposed to be if we *lose*!"

"**Not the way Callis views it!**" A commiserating wink from Parm. "**Got you both fair and square, and frankly, I'm glad for the wagers . . . it's just . . .**" and now his whole body slumped, collapsing into a calico heap from impending woe. "**Don't you see? Don't you *see* how she made you bet? If you and Harrap *win* think who must . . .**"

Lose . . . and what a loss to sustain! Harrap's arm slid around his waist, Callis doing the same on his other side, all of them seeking to derive comfort from their mutual support. Parm began whimpering low and forlorn, pressing himself tight against Harrap as they watched time rush toward the foreordained end. No, not end, he reminded himself with harsh joy—a way to make the coin balance on its edge, neither side having an advantage, the outcome of the toss forever held in abeyance!

♣

The three ghatti promenaded ahead of Doyce and Jenret, Saam at the center and slightly in the lead, and Doyce was forced to dispassionately view what she'd not dared acknowledge before, the transformation beginning so subtly yet surely once they'd arrived last evening. Of course other things had taken precedence: alternately holding and scolding Jenneth (Diccon's scolding had waited for this joint session), mourning with Harrap, 'speaking her private thanks to Saam.

The alteration in Saam was the most obvious because he'd been here longest. But already the difference in Rawn showed clear, his coat gleaming with new vitality, the underlay of rustiness vanishing to leave the glossy fur pitch-black, his gait firmed, his wheezing halted. And Khar, on Saam's left, had begun filling out, losing the angularity she'd taken on after her wounding in the Sunderlies, her amber eyes keen, no longer veiled as if she sometimes descryed another world fast impinging on this one.

"So this is Callis's mountain!" Suffused with wonder, almost awe, Jenret sounded young and eager, full of the impetuosity that evoked her love and despair, often simultaneously. "Now I'm beginning to understand what made it so special—hells, unique!—when you and Nakum and Eadwin arrived up here before, totally unprepared, and I'm doubly sorry I wasn't with you. Even having met Callis before, aware I should expect something well beyond my range of experience . . ." a hand rapidly shoved a dark lock of hair off his forehead. "I *still* can barely believe the *size* of this tree, can't begin to *imagine* how majestic it must have appeared in its prime!" Throwing his arms in the air with abandon, he struggled to take it all in, lips parting as he inhaled the crystalline air, half-drunk on it, the sunlight, the pure azure sky, even lighter, brighter than his eyes.

"Hush, darling!" A restraining hand on his arm, a look at those brilliant eyes the color of gentians, so full of innocent happiness, release, and without asking she knew that he hadn't a clue that the sky was about to fall on them both, crush them in a way he'd never before considered. His ability to ignore, be oblivious to certain things was capped only by his sensitivity and perception in so many other instances.

"Don't hush me, woman!" he teased. "This place, this view, is so spectacular it makes me want to shout its glories to the skies!" Enthusiasm marginally abating, he turned more serious. "I'm touched that Mahafny *did* experience some of this before. . . ." A harsh throat-clearing. "A tough woman, but not as insensitive as she'd have liked you to believe . . . you knew where you stood with her, and I'm glad she was a part of our lives. Eh, Saam?"

*"Darling! Hush!"* More urgently now, and her fingertips sought his lips, covering them. *"I think Saam has something . . . he wants to say . . . to us. Please . . . just listen. . . ."* If only she could block her ears, her mind, Jenret's as well! But naught would change, much as she might will it to—no, not change!—remain the same.

True enough, the three had swung to face them, Saam still in the lead.

**"As you see, I'm alive. Mahafny had the right of it,**

**though mayhap for the wrong reasons."** Embarrassed, overcome by emotion, he assiduously licked at his chest and shoulder for a moment, eyes tight-closed. **"And while I linger here in Nakum's and Callis's world, so my life will linger for a long, long time."**

*"I know, old fellow. And for Mahafny's sake and your sake—ours, as well—I'm truly glad for you. Didn't want to lose you."* Kneeling at Saam's side, Jenret stroked a finger along the ghatt's neck. *"You chose your Bonds so very wisely and well—Oriel, Nakum, Mahafny—and they were blessed to have you in their lives, just as we've been blessed by knowing you. I thank you for taking Oriel's charge so seriously for Doyce's and Khar's sakes."*

Muzzle twisting in discomfort, Saam responded more as if Jenret held a knife to his throat, Doyce thought, still willing herself to avert her eyes from Khar, just catching a hint of her bold stripes, her white front in the periphery of her vision, forcing her memory to fill in the well-loved well-remembered details. So many memories, each so vivid, so precious!

Saam visibly gulped, throat working as he forged ahead as courageously and compassionately as ever he'd done in the past. **"You see, dear ones . . . Rawn and Khar'pern would very much like . . . to stay as well, join me here."**

Doyce wept silently, couldn't halt the tears as the dreaded words were finally uttered, sundering everything they'd held so dear, Jenret's hunched body beginning to quiver—or was it the fault of her treacherous tears?—his face frozen in shock as he cast a disbelieving glance over his shoulder at her. Knew he was wordlessly begging that she argue, plead, defy Saam's utterance, reassure him he'd misheard, that it had been some vile joke whose humor had totally eluded them. . . . But it was ghatti truth and honesty and honor.

Rawn took first one, then another hesitant step toward his Bond, as if fearing that—for the first time in their long, shared lives together—he might be hit, punished. **"It's true, Jenret. You know it, too. I learned it the hard way after beseeching the Elders for Khar's life—not that I regret it. I'm old, not the ghatt I once was. And despite the fact that I adore you, I'm so tired. Have been for a very long time, just couldn't bring myself to admit it—to myself or to you."**

*"But I never saw . . . you never showed. . . !"* Crushing
Rawn in his arms, Jenret rocked to and fro. *"We simply
need to plan things differently, take advantage of our brains
instead of our bodies! Hells, don't you think I'm saddle-
sore? And that's the least of my aches . . . Oh, Rawn,
don't . . ."*

Steeling herself, Doyce finally looked downward, sensing
that Khar now sat at her feet, patiently waiting for her
notice. **"Oh, beloved!"** she cried, twining herself around
Doyce's legs. **"Ah, what a life we've shared. So many long
years together—and I *know*, they're never enough!"** Her
stance abashed, but her resolve strong, Khar raised her
head, amber eyes pleading for understanding. **"Do you
wish to wake some morning, beloved, discover I've died in
my sleep beside you on the bed? Isn't that a far worse,
more final end to our love than this parting?"**

*"Never! Never that, beloved!"* And that was a truth, no
matter how harsh the hurt, the momentary sense of be-
trayal, abandonment—selfishness, all selfishness! *"Whatever
time we were allotted together could never be enough, but
it's all we have, and there's so much to be grateful for. I've
known, since the Sunderlies, that you lived on borrowed
time, blessed each extra moment we'd been given. . . ."* Her
tears had halted, refusing to come, trying to taste a little
joy, discovering it was so bitter as well as sweet. And now,
Khar, in her arms for the last time—when had she scooped
her up?—the sweet, talclike scent of her, and she inhaled
deeply, savoring it. Could she ever forget it?

The petal-pink nose kissed her eyelid, ventured down to
blot a final tear. **"We will not be dead, not up here. Can
continue *being*, forever loving you in our hearts, if not our
minds. Is that not worth something, worth more celebration
than tears—joy, not mourning? Oh, my beloved! I've always waited for you, almost tarried too long! But never,
never will I cease loving you!"**

A final kiss to the striped head, a final caress along fur
that always flowed beneath her fingers like sleek satin, before she tenderly set her down. A stealthy caress to Rawn,
to Saam, and she gathered Jenret to her, his arms reluctantly parting to release Rawn. "Now, darling! Just keep
walking, tell yourself we leave them behind but alive and
well, hold that tight in your heart and grieve no more."

Stumbling, Jenret nodded, blue eyes misty with unseeing, mouth screwed in a silent scream of loss and pain.

Like an honor guard Jenneth and Pw'eek, Diccon and Kwee, Harrap and Parm, Jacobia, and Addawanna had lined the trail head in double-file, closing behind them as they passed between them. Compassion, comprehension, pity, sorrow, and more animated each dear face, made Doyce lift her chin, hold her head high. No mourning, no grieving—they *lived,* would live, reside in their hearts forever more! *"Oh, Khar, darling, my beloved! Never will you be forgotten! Not by me or by anyone whose life you've touched!"*

One final backward glance as they stumbled down the trail, and Doyce clutched Jenret's ice-cold hand, making him turn as well. Detail was indistinct, merged in shadow, but three ghatti shapes stood darkly silhouetted against the limpid blue of the sky, the sun behind them, an aura of golden light surrounding each one, tails sinuously waving, before they turned as one and strode out of sight.

**"Never, never will I cease loving you, beloved! And in some other life we'll meet and love again!"**

# EPILOGUE

"You mean they, just. . . ." He coughed, harder and harder until tears started to form, and Jenneth discreetly handed over a napkin, tucking it into his hand when he apparently didn't notice, eyes still shut while he panted, finally drew a breath without choking. Recovering sufficiently to pull Gr'eux onto his lap, he hugged him close and, not for the first time, Jenneth privately marveled over the contrast between the two. Indeed, she appreciated this unexpected opportunity to study both them without realizing it, feasting her eyes on Raphael Aartsen and his Bond while they were oblivious, still in the throes of strong emotion. Ah, she knew how that vulnerability felt, and loved how Rafe could genuinely partake of such emotions without embarrassment. By summer he'd be a full Seeker, finished with training, exchanging the pale green trim on his tabard for the silver that denoted a Junior Seeker, one with less than an octad of experience, but still fully qualified to ride circuit, hear cases and—in partnership with Gr'eux—determine the truth. When he left to ride circuit, she suspected she was going to be very lonely.

This picnic in the outskirts of the Seeker cemetery, just the two of them—well, just the four of them, because the ghatti had to be with them, neither she nor Rafe'd have it any other way—was something she'd trusted herself to do only recently, and only with Rafe. To be alone with a young man, dare consider she might be in love, yield to his kisses without panicking or freezing tight inside herself was a new and novel feeling. Oh, the cemetery was a funny place for a romantic picnic, but it was so beautiful in spring, so many trees in bloom, petals drifting around them, almost vanishing against Gr'eux's fur. The pink blossoms had reminded her of Khar's petal-pink nose and, without thinking, she'd voiced the thought. Diffidently, he'd asked what had really, *truly* happened just after the turn of the year high up there on Nakum's mountain in Marchmont. Trusting him, confident he'd not spread it round, dine out on it, or whisper it over drinks, she'd begun to explain exactly what had transpired up there.

The broad outlines were known—had to be. Mama and Papa had returned without Khar and Rawn, nor had Saam returned either. Auntie Mahafny was dead, and dear Harrap and Parm were scurrying around of late, deciding exactly what they should purchase and pack for their forthcoming trip to the Sunderlies. Everyone had been reticent about asking for details, and few had been volunteered. Without doubt the ghatti understood far better than their Bonds did, but the ghatti hadn't seen fit to enlighten their human companions. Mayhap Rafe's reaction explained why, and while he recovered himself, she continued to admire him, determined not to stare but unable to help herself whenever he glanced away.

Rafe was easily a head taller than Diccon, and strangers initially judged him stolid and slow because of his broad, heavy build. Like a solid tree, she'd decided, able to withstand the storms. His chest didn't taper into a neat waist and slim hips, like most men, and his hands were big but deft, gentle. Nor was his big, wide face especially handsome, though it had become so to her of late—brown hair that bleached almost white on the surface from the summer's sun, only to reveal its deeper brown during winter as the last of the gold-white was trimmed. Mobile lips lurked beneath those broad cheekbones, and above them, tawnybrown eyes with the slightest hint of green. With him she felt safe, secure in a way she'd never before experienced, and the sensation was still a delicious revelation.

Physically dissimilar to his Bond, Gr'eux was one of the longest, leanest ghatts she'd ever encountered, so long and flexible that he could near tie himself into knots, and would gladly do so to please Rafe. Even his toes looked longer than average, and Pw'eek nudged her elbow, not taking her eyes off Gr'eux. **"I . . . I think his toes are . . . adorable."**

*"As adorable as the rest of him?"* she teased, though not unkindly.

**"It's . . . well . . . when I'm beside him . . ."** Pw'eek quick-glanced down at herself, then away, **"I . . . I'm twice as large as he is! Twice as fat, at least!"** she wailed.

A blue eye peered over Rafe's arm. **"Because it takes a body that generous to encompass your big, brave heart."** The compliment was flirtatious but heartfelt, and Jenneth wished she could purr her appreciation at him. It was true: he did make quite a contrast with Pwe'ek. Her girth was almost twice his, but he was almost twice as her length. Gr'eux was pale-furred, not quite a pure white, but with a rich yellow underlay like heavy cream, yet his flanks and his legs showed a subtle mackerel marking, as if he'd been cinnamon-dusted.

At last Rafe pulled himself together, gently freeing Gr'eux from his embrace and employing the napkin as a handkerchief. "Oh, dear!" he murmured on realizing what he'd done. "Can't take me anywhere, can you? No manners!" Somehow his mistake caused him greater embarrassment than his show of emotion, and it touched her that he accepted such emotion as natural. Voice still a touch tremulous, he took up where he'd left off, in the single-minded way he always did. "And they . . . just turned around and *left*? Left them there? Without a backward glance?"

Despite his efforts, a hint of reproach tinged each question, an almost audible yet unspoken "How could they possibly have deserted their Bondmates, left them there after so many years?" And implicit it that was *"I* could *never* do such a thing, even contemplate it!" Mayhap that was why Mama and Papa didn't speak of it overmuch—except between themselves, she guessed—because so many, even Seekers, couldn't encompass the enormity of their act.

"They looked back once in farewell. They're only human." Patiently, she continued to explain as best she could, anxious to get it right, make him understand. It was important that he did—not only for his sake, but for hers. "The alternative was that they'd die, Rafe. Would you want that? Want them totally bereft?" At times Papa was utterly forlorn without Rawn, while Mama took Khar's absence more stoically, didn't dwell on it as much—or at least not obviously so. "They were so *very* old, Rafe. Old and frail and well-aware their time had come. What they chose, instead, was to *prolong,* stretch time, to be *of,* yet not entirely within our world. They *live,* Rafe! Don't forget it that. Could you do it—give up something, *someone* you loved so deeply—to prolong that love, even though that soul would no longer be by your side? Auntie Mahafny did it without a second thought, gave her life for Saam's. Mama and Papa made the choice, too."

Fingers working along Gr'eux's tail, flexing it, weaving it between his fingers, Rafe had the grace to look shamefaced. "I . . . guess I'm more selfish . . . than I realized. Mayhap it's best to learn that now."

**"While I've time to work on your flaws, remold your character?"** Gr'eux rolled onto his back, digging his shoulders into the fresh, new grass, releasing the scent of spring. In the near distance the white marble, the gray and black of granite tombstones resembled peaceful, grazing sheep. **"Ah, what a task I have cut out for me!"**

**"As do all Bondmates,"** Pw'eek interjected. **"If the world truly realized how *hard* we labor, what we must suffer day-in and day-out—"**

"There might not be any more smoked salmon or other treats," Jenneth warned.

Rafe had slid next to her, slipping an arm around her waist and leaning them both back against a tree trunk, her back bolstered against his chest. "So, tell me what else has happened? How's that little girl making out with her baby Y'ew? I see them madly dashing across the grounds sometimes, as if they're perpetually late to some lesson. Will they become Seekers? And what's been happening in Marchmont with King Eadwin and all the rest? I've heard a vague rumor that Cinzia Treblicote is getting married. I met her a few years ago, before I was Chosen, when we were visiting Mother's relatives." Rafe, she'd learned, had a Marchmontian mother and a Canderisian father.

How comfortably her cheek fitted against Rafe's shoulder! "As to Telka and Y'ew, Mama swears she can't begin to guess what will happen, if things will work out. She says age may help them both—but then, what parent isn't convinced of that? Telka's prenticed to the Seekers, the first such. Makes her even lowlier than a Novie!" Rafe chuckled, both of them secretly delighted at discovering that someone even lowlier than they existed.

"Do you *really* want to hear all the rest? I mean, don't

you at least read the news-sheets each Achtdag? Or listen to *any* gossip?" An elbow prod in his ribs. "Besides, I didn't think men cared all that much about who's marrying whom, that sort of thing." Did they? She wasn't sure, might have to ask Diccon.

"I've no need to listen to gossip." Oh, he sounded lofty, and she didn't like it, gave him another prod for good measure. "All I have to do is read my mother's letters! A synopsis of the latest goings-on on both sides of the border, no less! In fact, often a great deal farther afield." Arm around her waist, he snugged her closer. "Let's see . . . of course I've been keenly interested in the forthcoming nuptials of King Eadwin and Jacobia Wycherley, your dear aunt. I think you'll make a lovely bridesmaid—especially if the Seeker General will order you to dispense with the dress tabard for the occasion. It tends to obscure your lovely figure, you know.

"And," he continued without pause, "it's been bruted about that Nakum has been seen far more often in Sidonie, usually in the company of the fair Feather. But whether *that* develops is anyone's guess—probably'll take as long as it does for an arborfer to grow! Of course Holly's marrying Ezequiel, but only after the king's wedded. Mother says that he's absolutely crazed with the plans for the royal wedding and reception, can't concentrate on his own wedding until that's out of the way! Poor man's going to need a rest home, not a honeymoon! As to the rumor about Cinzia, Mother swears its only that—rumor, speculation. She's not convinced Cinzia'll marry Theo, though Mother thinks it would be a highly suitable match."

"I'm not certain, either," she confessed. "Theo still admires Dannae, the Sunderlies Shepherd. I don't know which he'll choose. . . ."

"Or if the woman will do the choosing for him," he teased, fingers tickling the underside of her chin. "We men are usually putty in your hands." He turned more serious. "I *do* think the rumor's true that Theo wants to stay longer in Marchmont, if Berne Terborgh will give him and Khim permission. Something about the possibility of setting up a Seeker branch there."

"I know." And a wave of sadness swept over her. "Diccon's been constantly talking about joining when we finish our training next year." Should she follow her twin—or remain in Canderis? What should she do? And where would Rafe be a year from now? As if to assuage her fears, Rafe leaned over, his lips approaching hers.

"Ye-Rowl!" came a high-pitched screech from above them in the tree, not to mention a barrage of clanging pans and a veritable deluge of petals. With an ungentlemanly shove that shocked her to the core, Rafe pushed her away, hard, and she rolled across the grass, Rafe rolling in the opposite direction, barely in time to miss the bucket of water being emptied on them from above by a brotherly hand.

**"Sissy-Poo! I'm going to get you!"** Pw'eek shrieked her fury, already halfway up the delicate plum tree that had been drifting petals on them.

"Diccon! You vile beast, you!" Jenneth was scrambling to her feet when Harry and Telka tackled her around the waist and knees, bringing her down. "Get him, Rafe!" she shouted, unsure if she should laugh or die of embarrassment. Pw'eek appeared equally conflicted, torn between ineffectually swiping first at Y'ew, the ghatten clinging to her hindquarters like a burr, then lashing at her taunting sib above her in the branches.

"No, I'm not going to do a thing to your beloved twin," was Rafe's judicious comment as he brushed grass off his tabard, "and I say that with a certain air of *gravity,* I trust you note, because about now—" a sharp crack interrupted him, "that branch is going to break. After all, nature always has a way of taking a hand in things. Always remember that, Jenneth, my Jennie-love."

# Eluki bes Shahar

## THE HELLFLOWER SERIES

☐ **HELLFLOWER (Book 1)**          UE2475—$3.99

Butterfly St. Cyr had a well-deserved reputation as an honest and dependable smuggler. But when she and her partner, a highly illegal artificial intelligence, rescued Tiggy, the son and heir to one of the most powerful of the hellflower mercenary leaders, it looked like they'd finally taken on more than they could handle. For his father's enemies had sworn to see that Tiggy and Butterfly never reached his home planet alive. . . .

☐ **DARKTRADERS (Book 2)**          UE2507—$4.50

With her former partner Paladin—the death-to-possess Old Federation artificial intelligence—gone off on a private mission, Butterfly didn't have anybody to back her up when Tiggy's enemies decided to give the word "ambush" a whole new and all-too-final meaning.

☐ **ARCHANGEL BLUES (Book 3)**          UE2543—$4.50

Darktrader Butterfly St. Cyr and her partner Tiggy seek to complete the mission they started in DARKTRADERS, to find and destroy the real Archangel, Governor-General of the Empire, the being who is determined to wield A.I. powers to become the master of the entire universe.

# Tanya Huff